# DEFIANCE
## OF THE
# FALL

### BOOK ELEVEN

aethonbooks.com

## DEFIANCE OF THE FALL 11
### ©2023 JF BRINK/THEFIRSTDEFIER

Aethon Books
www.aethonbooks.com

Print and eBook formatting and design by Josh Hayes. Artwork provided by Fernando Granea.

Published by Aethon Books LLC.

Aethon Books is not responsible for websites (or their content) that are not owned by the publisher.

# ALSO IN SERIES

**DEFIANCE OF THE FALL**

BOOK ONE

BOOK TWO

BOOK THREE

BOOK FOUR

BOOK FIVE

BOOK SIX

BOOK SEVEN

BOOK EIGHT

BOOK NINE

BOOK TEN

BOOK ELEVEN

BOOK TWELVE

*Check out the series here! (tap or scan)*

1

# CATCHING UP

The purple pillar of tainted truth stretched toward the sky, its stream of profundity sealed by the ancient sigils of the Left Imperial Palace's Outer Courts. Its knowledge was locked in, but it still covered the Mystic Realm's mountain range in its light. It gave the shadows a sinister air, but also one of fatal attraction. Zac had experienced his second burst of Ultom's enlightenment just hours ago and was painfully aware of the miraculous gift that hid behind the corruption.

Yet the memories of the ancient temple, the yetis, and the pillar itself were relegated to the back of his head as Zac mutely stared at the familiar face that emerged from the shadows. If not for his honed senses and recent inroads into Heart Cultivation, he would doubt whether he had been caught in an illusion array. But his instincts told him, in no uncertain terms, he wasn't caught in a mirage, and his heart told him this was all true.

It was truly Ogras who stood before him. The treacherous goblin ghost who'd appeared from the demon's sleeves was unfamiliar, but a decade had passed since Ogras was swallowed by the spatial vortex. It was likely something his old companion had encountered in the years since. After all, the presence of temples related to Ultom proved this Mystic Realm was anything but simple.

"Sorry about that." Zac smiled wryly as he walked over. "I didn't know the ghost was with you. Didn't sound like it."

"Don't worry about it. Believe me, if that little wretch could be dealt with so easily, I would have done so years ago. I seem destined to pick up annoying hitchhikers." Ogras sighed, his otherwise ashy complexion accented by red-rimmed eyes. "You're as ugly as ever, but damn is it good to see you."

Zac dragged the demon into a bear hug, a confusing mix of emotions washing over him.

One by one, his closest people had been lost over the past years. And while he'd gained new allies and friends, they couldn't replace those who were gone. But Ogras had come back. It wasn't just a huge victory on its own. It somehow bolstered Zac's conviction that he could do the same with the others. He would get Kenzie back, and he would return Alea to her proper form.

It was all possible.

"Alright, enough of that," Ogras said as he dissipated into a mist and reformed a few steps away. "That little lass, she's with you?"

"How'd you do that? No, wait, Vai!" Zac exclaimed. "She's my guide. You didn't hurt her, right?"

"Well, she's fine except for a bump on the back of her head and a belly full of grievances." Ogras snickered. "She's around ten minutes from here."

"Let's go," Zac urged, and Ogras nodded in acquiescence as a shroud spread around them.

"Most of those annoying mongrels have fled already, after what I can only assume was your doing?" Ogras said, indicating the still-beaming pillar.

Zac helplessly shrugged in response, prompting the demon to scoff. "Figures. If anything, I should have realized it was you who had descended on this place the moment I saw that thing. Anyway, if we run into some stragglers, these clouds will make them ignore us. It will also allow us to talk in peace."

Zac nodded in understanding, curiously looking to the churning clouds around him and the energies they contained.

"Two branches?" Zac whistled.

"Not bad, huh?" Ogras said with a smug grin, which drastically soured when Zac released three Dao Fields. "What? A brute like you has somehow managed to form three of them? Whatever. Comparing oneself with a Heaven-kissed scoundrel is bound to cause one's teeth to itch."

Zac laughed. "If it's any consolation, I generally only use two branches per form."

"That's somewhat better," Ogras muttered, looking to Zac with perplexity. "In any case, how in the Heavens did you find me? I figured I would have to make my way back myself."

"Find you?" Zac said with a blank look. "Isn't that *my* cue? How the hell did you appear here? Did you enter the Stellar Ladder?"

"The stellar what-now?" Ogras blurted, turning suspicious. "Wait, you didn't come here because you were looking for me? We just, *stumbled* upon each other in this godforsaken place by accident?"

"Well…" Zac coughed.

"I see your Luck is as strong as ever. Suppose I shouldn't complain as long as I'm benefiting," Ogras said with a roll of his eyes. "Let me guess, you were out adventuring and just so happened to fall into the Dimensional Seed? Right into the opportunity in the temple?"

"This is actually the Mystic Realm of the Dimensional Seed!" Zac exclaimed, things finally clicking into place. He should have realized the moment he saw Ogras, he'd just been too preoccupied to make the connection. "No wonder this place felt so familiar."

"Where else would we be?" Ogras said as he looked at Zac like he was a fool. "And you bastard, you didn't actually look for me after I saved the day so heroically back then?"

"I did," Zac sighed. "We had a supreme powerhouse divine your fate seven years ago. She said this Mystic Realm would pop up inside the Million Gates Territory around now, so I've been collecting the items needed for the Creators to build me a Cosmic Vessel. I came to a weird place called the Void Star to get the final item of the quest, and it turns out this realm entered it."

"Void Star? Sounds vaguely familiar," Ogras hummed. "What's going on?"

Zac recounted the situation of the Void Star, its interlayered realms, and the Stellar Ladder that formed leading into the Mystic Realm.

"No wonder the lass kept calling me an infiltrator even if she was the one who infringed on my Mystic Realm. So that little bastard got caught inside," Ogras said. "More importantly, a supreme powerhouse? We have a proper backing now?"

"Not quite," Zac said with a grimace. "That powerhouse happened to be my mother."

"She returned?" Ogras frowned. "Is that good news or bad news? How powerful is she?"

"It's bad. Leandra is crazy powerful, way more than anyone in Zecia, even when she's wounded. She appeared on Earth, killed Thea, and took Kenzie away. I've essentially been disowned. Kenzie was the one who had Leandra investigate your situation in return for leaving willingly."

"That lass…" Ogras sighed. "And I'm sorry about your woman. I guess you were right to be wary of that side of the family. So, how do we get your sister back?"

"We?" Zac asked with a raised brow.

"I've done one selfless thing in my life—sacrificing myself to save your sister. Now your sister has not only returned the favor, but completely nullified my deed by getting captured. Can't have that, can we?" Ogras winked.

"I could use the help." Zac smiled. "They were headed toward a place called the Six Profundity Empire, which is apparently a top faction closer to the center of the Multiverse. We're currently too weak to even reach that place, let alone save her."

"Your mother can just waltz into the Multiverse Heartlands like that?" Ogras frowned. "Wouldn't she be discovered and hunted down? Or is this empire full of traitors?"

"I've learned a few things about my Technocrat heritage since you got stuck here," Zac said. "I think they possess unique technology that allows them to perfectly masquerade as cultivators. Or perhaps form separate bodies that can cultivate within the System's purview."

Zac recalled the scene back on Earth, where a human Leandra walked out from the portal her avatar had created. One form was unmistakably Technocrat in origin, while the other was unmistakably a cultivator. It was even possible that **[Quantum Gate]** wasn't unique to him but something all Kayar-Elu possessed.

The experiments done on him were probably the next step of that technology, where they fused their Technocrat heritage with Emperor Limitless' bloodline in an attempt to gain control over the System itself. Even if it failed, they would have a half-Technocrat half-Void Emperor scion who could take the best from both worlds.

"Makes sense they would look into ways to hide from the Heavens and the eyes of other cultivators," Ogras said. "Otherwise, how is the situation outside? Have you stirred up any more trouble?"

Zac grimaced. "It's a bit complicated, but Port Atwood and Azh'Rhodum are still standing."

"Complicated? I suppose that's usually how it goes with you," Ogras snorted. "What's going on?"

"A Sector-wide war is on the cusp of breaking out. No one in Zecia will be spared."

"What!" Ogras exclaimed, his suspicion returning. "What did you do?"

"Me? Nothing! Some people think it's my fault because I summoned the Stele of Conflict, but how is it my fault a Space Gate appeared in the depths of the Million Gates Territory?"

"Maybe the Ruthless Heavens realized too few of the factions in Zecia would mess with you after the display of the Eveningtide Asura a million years ago. It couldn't take the tranquility, so it brought in reinforcements?" Ogras offered and got a glare in return.

"Anyway, war is coming, so it's great timing you're back. We need elites to lead our armies. What about Billy? Is he okay? Is he in these mountains as well?" Zac asked.

"He's fine. That simpleton is essentially unkillable in this realm. He's not here, though. He should be in the heart of the Mystic Realm."

"Unkillable?" Zac exclaimed. "He's gained that much from this place?"

"An empty mind leaves a lot of room for the Dao to grow. Although, that's not what I was referring to. The Dimensional Seed has gained sapience, and it's become attached to the brute. I saw that crazy little gem crush space across over a hundred meters, killing thousands of beasts instantly."

"Sapience?" Zac said with surprise. It sounded very familiar to Qi'Sar, the Realm Spirit of the Twilight Ascent, who formed from the consciousness of two Autarchs through a freak accident. How had a recently born spirit gained sapience in a few short years? It might simply have been unusually talented, but there was a more likely explanation.

"I think it was experimented on," Ogras said, echoing Zac's thoughts.

"I suppose it doesn't matter much," Zac said. "Have you encountered anyone else in this place apart from Vai and me?"

"Nope, that little lass was the first. But I've sensed fluctuations over the past months, like people were trying to break in. None have come to these mountains, except for you." Ogras pointedly looked at Zac. "I guess they didn't sense the call from the temple."

"You too?" Zac said, his brows scrunched together.

What did this mean? Had he stolen Ogras' opportunity, or were they both competing for the Flamebearer title? He suspected such a possibility since the sudden pulse a few weeks back, but he hadn't worried too much about it. If some infiltrator or other outsider had seized his opportunity, he'd simply snatch it back.

Thing is, what if it were an ally of his?

"Don't look at me like a starving Gwyllgi, you lunatic," Ogras said with an annoyed wave of his hand. "I don't think we are in contention. Did you know there are at least four temples in this mountain range?"

"There are?" Zac said, his eyes gleaming.

"I can see the gears in your head turning, don't bother. You only felt drawn to *one* of the temples, right?"

Zac nodded in affirmation, realizing what Ogras was getting at.

"It was the same for me," Ogras confirmed. "I was drawn to a smaller temple in another region of this mountain. I got the opportunity inside and made some great breakthroughs. And even months later, I've never felt another calling."

"Why did you stick around?" Zac asked curiously.

"After getting a glimpse of those truths, I couldn't just give up when I knew there were probably similar opportunities hiding in the other temples." Ogras smiled wryly. "I've been trying to get inside those places for a while now without any luck. Then one day, I felt an odd ripple and rushed over, and I found your little companion by chance. You two actually used one of my old haunts, so I knew something was up when a cave entrance was suddenly a solid wall."

"Poor girl," Zac snorted. He took out the rags he'd looted from the infiltrators. "Do you recognize anyone of these sigils?"

Ogras curiously looked them over until he tapped on one—a different seal from the one Zac collected, and one of the sigils that appeared to seal the pillar of stars that still stretched toward the sky behind them.

"That one, but it's kind of ruined," Ogras muttered as he rolled up one of his sleeves. "This is the real one."

Zac was surprised to see the demon had a tattoo of the seal, though it was incomplete in comparison to the one he'd seen just an hour ago.

"It's not the same as mine." Zac pointed at the seal he was forming. "This one is mine."

"As I expected. It should mean we're not competing for the same inheritance if it works similarly to your repository back home. But I'm a bit confused. Why did your visit create a netherblasted pillar that seems intent on burning a hole in the sky? When I took my piece, I only opened a small spatial tear and let loose a beast tide."

"I'm not sure what happened either," Zac helplessly said as he looked back at the pillar. "The first time, I didn't create anything like this. It was like your encounter. It should be fine, though. Seems stable enough."

"Dragging a piece of the Lost Plane to the surface, *how* can it be fine? That madness is no joke. We've only been back together for a few minutes, and you're already—" Ogras stopped in his tracks. "Wait, this is already your *second piece*? Do you know where we can get more? I still need two to complete my quest."

"Two more?" Zac said with surprise. "Do you have a quest to become a Flamebearer of… that place?"

"That place?" Ogras said with confusion. "Why not just say Ult—"

He didn't get any further, as Zac urgently waved him to stop as he felt fate congregate.

"There are Karmic ramifications of uttering that name aloud," Zac said. "We might want to be careful just in case."

"Just the name holds that kind of power?" Ogras whistled. "I can't wait to get my hands on the real thing. What's this about a Flamebearer?"

Zac shared his Quest Screen.

"Flamebearer indeed. There are some other differences as well," Ogras muttered.

A moment later, another screen appeared between them.

**[Seal of the Hollow Court (Unique, Inheritance): Form a seal of the Hollow Court. Reward: Become a Skybreaker of Ultom. (1/3)]**

"The Hollow Court?" Zac said with a slight frown, the names foreign to him. "Never heard of it. Do you recognize it?"

"Nope." Ogras shrugged. "Think I saw a piece of it in a vision, but that's about it. I thought the thing on my arm was just a key to unlock another quest until I stepped foot into the temple. I figured it was related to the Lost Plane."

Zac turned away from Ogras' quest and focused on the unfamiliar term. "That's the second time you've mentioned the Lost Plane. What is that? How is it related to these seals and the inheritance?"

"Let me tell you about a bunch of lunatics called the Ra'Lashar," Ogras laughed.

Zac listened with interest as Ogras told him about how the Dimensional Seed had swallowed a bunch of hidden Mystic Realms, including one full of corrupted goblins. How they'd accidentally found some mysterious dimension they named the Lost Plane, and managed to become a Peak C-grade force in a scant few millennia by deciphering some of the lesser secrets of that place.

"Is that ghost of yours trustworthy?" Zac asked hesitantly.

"Not in the slightest," Ogras snickered. "I do think he's right on this one. I can feel their weird, contracted spirits have a similar energy signature as that pillar of yours."

"And you believe those temples came from the Lost Plane," Zac concluded.

"It makes sense, doesn't it? If those little goblins could get even a corner of the insights contained in those temples, they were bound to make drastic improvements."

"Flamebearers, Skybreakers, Palaces and Courts, and now the Lost Plane," Zac mused, feeling a headache coming on. "How the hell does all this connect?"

"Who cares?" Ogras said lazily. "We just need to figure out where the next pieces are and empower ourselves."

"I guess you're right," Zac said, releasing a pent-up sigh. "We can worry about the other stuff after we get powerful."

Even if they spent the next week trying to figure things out, it would just be guesswork. The most important thing in the short run was that it didn't look like they were contending for opportunities since they were collecting different seals.

"That's right. I'm more curious how you caught hold of this opportunity. Did you find another connection to the Lost Plane?" Ogras asked.

"Well, I kind of just got a vision out of the blue?" Zac said as a smile spread across his face.

"That's just swell," Ogras complained, his face scrunched up like a raisin. "Some people have to fight shapeshifting nightmares and contend with crazy ghosts for a chance, while others just fall face-down into a pile of treasures. And you even get four opportunities to my three."

Zac only laughed in response. He'd missed this, teasing Ogras with his monstrous Luck.

"I had forgotten how infuriating it could be traveling with you," Ogras muttered. "Let's go find your little guide before I drop dead out of envy."

## 2

# SHAMELESS

There were a million things Zac needed to catch the demon up on, but Ogras was right. They had let Vai wait long enough. With the pillar still acting like a beacon, Zac didn't want to stick around, especially now that there were two of them who were connected to Ultom and its related structures.

"We're about to reach the little guide of yours," Ogras said. "She's currently pretending to be unconscious. What does she know?"

"Nothing about our opportunities. I only mentioned I had a quest and needed to find something," Zac said. "We have been tracking the signal of the temple across over ten Mystic Realms until now, though, so she probably knows it's something big."

"Like the netherblasted pillar behind us isn't clue enough," Ogras muttered. "What about your identity?"

Zac coughed with some embarrassment before his face started to transform again. "I told her who I am once, but she didn't recognize my name. For now, I'm Gaun Sorom, a Wandering Cultivator."

Ogras snickered as he looked at Zac with a raised brow. "Didn't know you, eh? Must have been a blow to the second coming of the Eveningtide Asura."

"Whatever." Zac smiled, somewhat happy Ogras still didn't know about his unfortunate nickname in the Sector. "We need her help if we're to get out of here. We're deep in the restricted territory of the Void Star in the middle of an invasion, and I have… borrowed some strategic resources of the Void Gate."

"Figures." Ogras wasn't even phased. "How can that lass help us with that, though? No offense, but she didn't put up much of a fight."

"She's a researcher rather than a fighter," Zac explained. "More importantly, she's the great aunt of Leyara Lioress."

"That girl from the Base Town? The nun with the cleavage?" Ogras said, his eyes almost burning. "She's here?"

"It's that bad?" Zac laughed.

"You try being locked in this place with only a mountain of muscles and a ghost goblin for companions for ten years. If you arrived any later, I might have shaved one of those black-furred humanoids and made it my woman," Ogras grunted.

"Well, I'm not sure if Leyara's here, but we managed to enter this Mystic Realm by using a gate left by other Void Gate members. I think it might be a special unit with how deep they've pushed into the Void Star. My best idea is to find them and have them take us out. Depending on how things pan out, I might have to expose my true identity."

Ogras frowned. "That's pretty risky. Even if they don't make any connection between us and that place, we're bound to raise suspicion."

"That's why I'm hoping we can use Vai to get in contact with her niece to help us out," Zac said with some helplessness. "We don't have a lot of options."

"Why not just return the way you came from?"

"For one, the gate that took us into this particular Mystic Realm was one-directional. And even if we get out, I'm not sure it's possible to return that way," Zac said, then briefly explained the situation with the Kan'Tanu infiltrators and how the cortex broke the connections in the Void Star.

"So, we're surrounded by heart-curse-infested lunatics and stuck deep in some unstable Mystic Realm Potpourri," Ogras groaned. "Never a good, clean adventure with you, is there?"

"This is nothing." Zac laughed. "You should have seen when I ran into the real Eveningtide Asura a few years back, and a C-grade capital exploded. Now, *that* was hectic."

"You WHAT!" Ogras screamed.

Zac had already continued forward to where Vai was being kept.

This close by, Zac could already sense Vai's aura. He flashed over, only to stop in confusion when he saw six specters standing guard over Vai's unmoving body. Her eyes were closed, but Zac could somewhat tell she was awake from how her energy circulated. Apart from her captivity, she appeared unscathed apart from a big bump on her head. Zac almost laughed at how familiar the scene was to his encounter with Zakarith, the little Mercantile demoness back in Port Atwood.

The ghosts guarding Vai turned into black streams that poured out from the cave when Zac appeared, leaving them alone. Zac curiously glanced at the energy streams, wondering just what these things were. Judging by their strange aura, they shouldn't be one of Ogras' skills. Neither were they proper ghosts, like Triv or the Raun Spectrals.

Instead, their aura seemed to stem from the Lost Plane Ogras briefly mentioned, which probably meant Ogras had found some method to control the denizens brought to this dimension. Cultivators who controlled beings from other planes were generally called Warlocks, and they were extremely rare. Perhaps even rarer than Karmic cultivators.

Not only did you need a powerful soul to control a being like that, you also needed to find the creatures to bind and the Dao affinity to commune with the mysterious realities beyond the prime dimensions. It was a lot easier for Beast Tamers; the Multiverse was literally crawling with beasts to tame. But to find a weakness in the dimensional layers and form a bridge required luck, skill, and resources.

The difficulty of becoming a Warlock was only one aspect of the archetype's rarity—the other was the danger. There was a high risk of getting your mind invaded, or at least influenced, by the alien entities. It also bordered on the unorthodox since many of the methods of forming contracts involved sacrifice.

He would have to keep an eye on Ogras, just in case, to confirm he was still in control of the situation. Thankfully, Zac managed to infer some positive signs. Those talismans Ogras used to seal that sinister flag of his were freshly made with yeti hide and blood. If Zac had to guess, Ogras might have used Ultom's state of clarity to devise techniques to deal with the danger.

A second after the ghosts dissipated, Vai hesitantly opened her eyes to find Zac standing in front of her.

"You're here," Vai cried with tears pooling in her eyes, and she ran over to Zac.

"I'm here." Zac hugged the little researcher. "Everything's okay. Are you hurt?"

"I'm fine. I was worr—" Vai's eyes widened in alarm. "Behind you!"

It was obviously Ogras who had walked into view with a crooked smile.

"Oh, don't worry about him. He's not an infiltrator," Zac said. "This is all a big misunderstanding. We actually know each other from before."

"I'm sorry, little lass," Ogras grinned. "I didn't know you were this guy's wife. I guess that's my luck. Stuck here for ten years, and when a little cutie finally shows up, she's already taken by an old buddy."

"I'm-I'm not his wife," Vai stuttered as she embarrassedly took a step away from Zac.

"Does that mean you're single?" Ogras asked with a grin that made him look like a starving ghost.

"Rein it in, man," Zac sighed as Vai took another step back with a mix of disgust and fear.

"Are you really friends with this bad guy?" Vai whispered.

"We've known each other for a long time. He's not as bad as he looks. Long ago, he got swallowed by a spatial tear when saving someone's life, and it turns out he ended up in this Mystic Realm long before it entered the Void Star."

"You're the first person I've seen in ten years," Ogras added, and Zac's eyes widened when he saw the demon take out Vai's protective treasure. "I was hoping to find out where you came from and how to get out of this place. I didn't even know the Sector was at war, let alone anything about the infiltrators. I'm a righteous and upstanding citizen of Zecia."

Vai snatched back the ball and once more took a few steps back. "W-What righteous person would appear in my shadows, almost knock me out, and then rob me before asking any questions?"

"A righteous person who wants to live a long life," Ogras offered.

"Shameless," Vai muttered, looking at Zac askance. "He really is your friend. Two peas in a pod."

"That's rude. To both of us, I think." Ogras laughed.

"Anyway, we're sorry you got hurt because of this," Zac said as he handed her a bottle of Pseudo D-grade healing salve. "For your head."

"Rich guy," Ogras said, staring at the shimmering liquid inside. "Got any more?"

Zac threw over one of his spare Spatial Rings that had a kit of crystals, pills, talismans, and other necessities in case something happened with his main ring.

"Rich indeed," Ogras hollered with an excited grin.

"A-Are you okay?" Vai hesitantly asked in a low volume. "I saw the pillar while the bad guy carried me away. What was that? Are you really planning to destroy this Mystic Realm?"

"You're blowing up this place?" Ogras asked. "As much as I'd love to see this realm get blasted to the Underworld, I think King Billy would object."

"I'm not planning on blowing anything up. I don't know why that pillar appeared. I thought only a breach would open," Zac explained. Then he cast a raised brow at Ogras. "*King* Billy? What's going on?"

"Apart from befriending that annoying crystal, he also subjugated a tribe of aboriginals and formed the Kingdom of Bonk Mountain." Ogras said with a face that carried years of pent-up exasperation.

"W-What's going on?" Vai asked.

"More people have been stuck in this realm," Zac explained. "I know one of them. We need to pick him up as well before we leave. Do you have any way to contact your people? This realm is even bigger than we expected. It would be almost impossible to find them if we just searched by foot."

"I—" Vai hesitated as she glanced at Ogras, who rolled his eyes and walked farther away. She spoke low, and actually looked a bit shame-faced. "I have a distress beacon, but it's designed for the normal Mystic Realms in the Void Star. It only stretches for two weeks' travel, I think. I... activated it in the forest a few times... I'm sorry."

"Well, that's fine," Zac shrugged. "But that probably means your people have moved either toward the heart of the realm or the other side. I'm sure we'll find them eventually if we send out a signal now and then."

"We don't need to bother with any of that," Ogras said from a distance, clearly listening in on the conversation. "We can just ask

Billy's pet when we get there. In fact, that brute might already have captured or thwonked those people. You never know with that guy."

"Pet?" Vai said with confusion.

"Billy has befriended the Realm Spirit of this Mystic Realm," Zac explained, remembering how Qi'Sar had spied on him as he traveled through the Twilight Ocean. "It should be able to easily locate any other people in this place, including your fellow Templars."

"A sapient Realm Spirit!" Vai exclaimed, the uniqueness of a Realm Spirit overcoming her wariness of Ogras. "That is extremely rare! I've only read about it in ancient texts. There's so much we can learn from such a being."

"You are bound to be disappointed if you go in expecting any wisdom from that thing," Ogras muttered, prompting Zac to look over with confusion. "Let's just say Billy is the brains of that duo, and he's taught the thing everything he knows."

Zac tried to imagine a Realm Spirit raised by Billy before firmly putting the matter aside. As long as it could help them out, it didn't matter. "We have no time to waste. I want to get away from the pillar anyway."

The traveling duo became a trio, though Vai wasn't exactly enthused by the arrangement. Zac could understand her sentiment after being kidnapped himself. It wasn't something you just moved past. She occasionally shot the demon aggrieved looks, which gave Zac a bit of a headache.

Even if Vai didn't know any of his biggest secrets, he still considered her a friend and an ally and hoped things wouldn't go south. Thankfully, Ogras understood the problem as well, so he started a relentless campaign against the poor girl. He swapped between peppering her with various questions, telling jokes, and sharing some of his exploits in this Mystic Realm, most of them clearly made-up.

Like this, a few days passed until they could see the edge of the Mountain Range. Most of the yeti had gone into hiding below-ground, and with Ogras' illusory domain, they could walk right by the stragglers who remained on the mountain paths.

They exited in another direction than the one they came from, and instead of an endless forest, they spotted huge glistening lakes stretching out across a mostly flat landscape. There was no lack of vegetation either, but it looked more like the Twilight Chasm's Coral Forest than a normal one.

"Welcome to the Badlands," Ogras said with an expansive wave. "Some of the lakes are saltwater. Others are pure acid. They all have nasty bastards hiding in the depths, and there are even more nasty critters above ground. This place has been the cause of many headaches over the years."

"Are the beasts aggressive?" Zac asked.

"It's not too bad," Ogras said. "The real problem is the furry humanoids in the mountains. Since they arrived, the Badlands have been their main hunting ground. Sometimes, thousands of those black-furred bastards descend the mountains like locusts. Their actions have kicked up tides of beasts that fled straight toward the Kingdom of Bonk. It's become Billy's new Ratlight, one that has lasted for years."

"Let's head inside then," Zac said as he looked back at the pillar behind them.

Since yesterday, it had finally started to shrink. Going by the rate it was thinning, it would probably be gone within the week. The thing hadn't caused any problems, but it was still a huge relief to see it go. No matter if you considered the tremendous amounts of power it contained, or the madness instilled into the energy, it wasn't even a two-edged sword—it would be an uncontrollable calamity if it were unleashed on this realm.

"Wait, people are coming! Almost two hundred cultivators!" Vai exclaimed, staring into her sonar-like bowl. "Six, no—seven Hegemons! We need to hide, quickly."

"Where?" Ogras said.

"They're still an hour's travel away," Vai explained.

"Pretty nifty, that thing," Ogras said as he looked at the bowl with interest.

"I-It's not for sale. It's mine," Vai said with determination in her eyes.

"I was just looking," Ogras said with helplessness, holding up his hands in defeat.

"Two hundred," Zac muttered. "The Void Gate encampment we saw couldn't hold that many people. Should be invaders."

"What do you think?" Ogras asked as the illusive domain around them condensed even further.

"Keep one or two alive for questioning?" Zac asked after some consideration.

"Good." Ogras grinned, the air around them starting to shimmer. "Finally, some change after years of fighting those beasts."

"Y-You two!" Vai exclaimed. "Going by the strength of the lights, one of the Hegemons is either an elite or approaching Middle D-grade."

"Compared to Captain Teo, who's stronger?" Zac asked.

"Teo, definitely," Vai said without hesitation.

"Then we'll be fine. Can you see where they will enter the mountains?" Zac asked.

Twenty minutes later, the group arrived at a spot Ogras knew. It was a small basin no more than two hundred meters across—small enough to restrict such a big group, while Zac's skills could still cover the whole thing. It was the perfect spot for an ambush.

Vai had retreated even farther, safely hidden in a nearby cave, while Zac and Ogras hung from a sheer mountain wall inside an illusion array further augmented by Ogras' skills. After sensing just how hard to spot Ogras had become, Zac wasn't worried they'd be exposed unless the enemies had a Hegemon scout.

They'd essentially become flies on the wall, silently waiting until they spotted movement. Two scouts moved with impressive speed, one on the ground and one jumping between mountain peaks using a blood-based movement skill as they headed deeper into the mountain range. Their auras were almost as indistinct as Ogras', but Zac would definitely have spotted them even if he wasn't prepared.

"The others shouldn't be far off," Ogras whispered when the two had passed.

"Can you drop me off in the middle of the army?" Zac asked. "As close to the Hegemons as possible? Or will that mess with your skills?"

Ogras flashed a smile. "No worries. Just do your thing and soak up their attention—I will support you from the outside. Like the good old days."

"Like the good old days." Zac handed the demon the curse-warding talisman he'd picked up before. "Remember, don't stay close to those guys when they die, or you'll get infected. Take this thing just in case."

"What about you?" Ogras said as he put the talisman on his robes.

"I'm immune," Zac shrugged.

"Braggart," Ogras said with a roll of his eyes.

Another thirty minutes later, the whole mountain path lit up with [Cosmic Gaze] from the powerful auras in the army. They were moving fast and would enter the basin in just a few seconds. Zac activated [Arcadian Crusade]. With seven Hegemons holding the fort, including a powerful one, he would need to thin out the numbers quickly.

"Alright," Ogras whispered as he placed his hand on Zac's shoulder, prompting the world to turn grey. "I can't wait to see what kind of monster you've become over the past decade."

Zac only scoffed, but he *was* a bit excited himself. Most of his skills had seen upgrades in the temple, and an opportunity to try them out had already presented itself.

# 3

# CHOOSING DEATH

The world twisted, and Zac sensed hundreds of powerful auras all around him. Ogras had done exactly what he'd asked—teleported him into the middle of the infiltrator squad. The demon even left behind a hazy shroud to give him a slight edge in the ambush. Zac swung his axe, wasting no time.

The grey world lit up with sanguine luster as he activated not only the skills of [Verun's Bite], but also a few of his own. The Dao-infused axe slammed into the head of one of the nearby Hegemons before he had a chance to respond. To add insult to injury, the body was cut apart by a storm of fractal leaves as Zac unleashed his area attack of [Nature's Edge] that covered a good portion of the basin.

Zac was disappointed that he didn't feel any stronger with the upgraded version of [Arcadian Crusade], still providing him a 35% boost. Instead, the golden runes on his body had grown denser, and he could feel how his energy circulation had been improved by another level. That was pretty decent.

Mastering his techniques had taught him the importance of small advantages. Being able to activate skills 50% faster was huge since it meant you didn't need to create as large an opening to strike. Now it allowed Zac to launch a surprise strike before the Kan'Tanu cultivators had even figured out where he stood. Over fifty streams of energy entered his body from the fallen E-grade cultivators.

Zac didn't stop there. The trees of [Ancestral Woods] had already appeared, and he leaped into a tree next to him just as dozens of terrifying attacks landed on his position. Ten of his trees were disintegrated, and the attacks also destroyed most of the ownerless blood curses around him.

These soldiers weren't fools. Even if they didn't know the exact effect of the primordial forest, they understood enough to destroy it. Though most of his skill had been dismantled instantly, the sudden appearance of a forest provided an excellent opportunity for the dagger in the dark to make his move. As Zac appeared from another tree, a whole flank of the army descended into madness.

Some warriors struck their allies like they were trying to cut down the trees of [Ancestral Woods]. Others were gored by shadowy spears. Some were even killed by those spectral creatures Zac had seen before. Another 50 warriors were taken out in an instant, showcasing just how powerful Ogras had become.

These people were not just random F-grade fodder. The warriors were all High E-grade at the least, with most of them being Peak E-grade. There had to be a significant power discrepancy to effortlessly cull their numbers like this. And not even the Hegemons were safe from Ogras' all-out assault.

A highly condensed shadow lance struck a Hegemon from behind. The man had just received a bloody gash from one of Zac's fractal leaves, and Ogras' strike was launched with perfect timing. The warrior barely managed to block it in time with a defensive skill, creating a huge opening. This was exactly what Zac needed. Most of the Hegemons were still standing, and it was they who were the real threat. Less than a second had passed since the two descended on the infiltrators, and Zac wanted to take out at least two more leaders before they organized a response.

One of the blood curses had already found his trail, but he ignored the stabbing pain on his back as he activated [Earthstrider]. A step took him right next to his target, and Zac was elated to sense how sturdy his movement skill had become. Not that it was quicker than before. It was able to forcibly contract space to a higher degree.

That was especially important in battlefields where chaotic energies and Dao Fields were always present. Typically, it felt like pushing through quicksand, but the effect was greatly subdued as he plowed right into the condensed Dao Field of the scimitar-wielding Hegemon. The warrior emitted a dense murderous aura, but something like that couldn't possibly deter Zac, so he slammed into the Hegemon like a ferocious bear.

The push was the straw that broke the camel's back, and the interlocked layer of rocky scales the warrior had summoned crumbled. [Verun's Bite] followed right in tow as it bit into the forehead of the man, ending him in an instant. It was quick and clean, and showcased the indomitability of an apex predator.

A scream in his mind alerted him of imminent danger. He narrowly dodged a colossal beam of shrieking madness that destroyed everything in its path, including at least a dozen E-grade infiltrators. It had been released by the leader, a weird, hunched-over human whose mouth was bereft of both lips and teeth. His face was locked in a grotesque mask of pain as he stared right at Zac, somehow seeing straight through Ogras' shadowy domain.

Zac barely managed to move out of harm's way, and it looked like he left an opening just like the scimitar-wielding Hegemon. In reality, Vivi's vines were acting as a counterweight, and his situation was nowhere near as precarious as it seemed. Since he'd reached the Integration Stage of his Evolutionary Stance, it required a lot more effort to push him off-balance than a surprise attack.

Still, the ruse had accomplished its goal as another of the Hegemons appeared right behind him with a brutal cudgel in hand. It emitted smoldering heat like a falling meteor as the Hegemon swung it toward his head. Zac was about to strike, but a spear appeared out of nowhere and pierced the head of the bulky warrior.

It was Ogras, appearing out of nowhere to strike like lightning, using some means Zac couldn't decipher in the heat of the battle. The scene was almost incomprehensible, as Zac could clearly see the demon fighting against a group of cultivators within his and the cudgel-wielding Hegemon's sight.

The demon was gone as quickly as he appeared, and three of the E-grade warriors fell to the supposed illusion at the same time. Since his own target was dead, Zac furiously circulated his Dao and Cosmic Energy, and two clouds shot toward a fourth Hegemon. Simultaneously, a feral snarl echoed through the area as Verun appeared from his axe, and the Tool Spirit pounced on another Hegemon who was charging up a powerful skill, judging by the energy undulations.

Space was parted into an unbridgeable chasm as the hymns of Arcadia and the deafening silence of the Abyss drowned out the pained cries of the warriors. A ferocious swing of the Hegemon parried the manufactured spatial tear, but it was clear this warrior wasn't up to the task. He couldn't withstand a Peak Mastery skill like **[Rapturous Divide]** empowered by **[Spiritual Void]**, **[Adamance of Eoz]**, two Dao Branches, and his berserking skill.

His attack was broken apart, and the spatial divide carved a huge gash into his chest. Unfortunately, he barely managed to expend the final energy of Zac's skill before being cut apart. Zac had appeared in the wake of his skill, and a swift swing of his axe finished the job.

Then an extreme danger gripped him.

An enormous face appeared in the sky that radiated an intensely evil aura. Like the one who summoned the skill, the face had no lips or teeth. Neither did the avatar have eyes, or perhaps it's more apt to say it had lost them since two huge, engraved spikes pushed into its eye sockets.

Zac urgently activated **[Empyrean Aegis]**, and two golden bubbles appeared, one around himself and one around what Zac hoped was the real Ogras. At the same time, three pillars rose behind him, indicating the durability of the skill had gone up another tier. It was just in time, as the grotesque avatar unleashed a tremendous wail that tore apart space itself.

The scream was deafening, and not even his recently upgraded defensive skill could completely block out its effects. The huge avatar's wail threw Zac's mind into chaos as bleeding gashes appeared all over his body. Ogras wasn't much better off. He tried to disappear into the shadows, except space had become too fractured for movement skills, and he was immediately thrown out.

Grisly gashes marred the demon's body, and bad soon turned to worse. One of the surviving Hegemons took advantage of the overtaxed golden bubble and punched a nasty hole in Ogras' side with a mighty javelin throw. The last vestiges of **[Ancestral Forest]** crumbled, and Zac saw how one of the Hegemons was rushing toward him with murder in his eyes.

The only good news was that Zac and his companion weren't the only ones in trouble. The evil god's wail didn't discern friend from foe, and its skill covered the whole basin. It even bounced off the wall to create a dangerous superimposed effect. The surviving Hegemons barely withstood the attack by activating defensive talismans, but the E-grade warriors didn't have that kind of luxury.

Whether it was defensive skills or E-grade talismans, it all broke apart in front of the grotesque avatar. Only Zac, Ogras, and the Hegemons remained standing a second later, along with Verun who didn't seem affected by the sound wave. The problem was that the wail was unrelenting, and one of the pillars had already crumbled.

Cosmic Energy surged into Zac's right arm as four thick vines, empowered with the Branch of the Kalpataru, shot out. They unleashed an all-out offense at the incoming Hegemon, continuously breaking apart and regrowing under the seemingly tireless screech from above.

A shimmering swirl rose around the warrior, and Zac was elated to see the Hegemon run in the wrong direction.

He quickly broke Ogras' illusion, and the brief pause was enough for Zac to finish charging the Skill Fractal on his arm. Space broke apart as the enormous hand of [Arcadia's Judgement] emerged. The hand and its axe had grown even larger since the upgrade, gaining roughly five meters in length.

That wasn't the only change—a familiar feature had returned. A massive sigil formed in the sky, towering over the enormous avatar. It covered the whole basin, and Zac was amazed when the avatar was pushed toward the ground from the pressure. The weaker Hegemons weren't much better off as Zac's domain overloaded their already strained defensive talismans, and they suddenly found themselves under attack from not one but two skills.

Only two people were left unscathed—the powerful Hegemon who withstood the pressure with the help of an odd, shuddering domain, and Ogras who didn't appear affected at all. It wasn't thanks to the demon's own skill, though. An unmistakable resonance in the golden barrier around him indicated a synergy between his two skills—those shielded by [Empyrean Aegis] were exempt from [Arcadia's Judgement].

The final pillar of [Empyrean Aegis] was already showing cracks, but it was barely enough. The axe descended with unprecedented force, and the whole mountain range shook. The leader clearly knew his skill was in trouble, and four clattering skulls appeared to intercept the axe.

However, before they could soak up some of the momentum, a tremendous lance of shadow swallowed them whole.

A bloodied Ogras, now sporting four sets of shadowy wings, had released the skill, paving the way for Zac to do maximum damage. The other Hegemons could barely withstand the two skills, so they couldn't help either. The axe bit into the head of the evil god, and it was pushed the final distance to the ground.

The first half of the strike destroyed the avatar in one go, and even one of the Hegemons was turned into mincemeat. A moment later, it was like the world itself unleashed its anger on them as thousands of spikes shot up through the ground. In the chaos, yet another Hegemon fell under the combined onslaught of Verun and Ogras.

That left only one enemy standing—the lipless leader of the army. He'd withstood both the first and second half of the skill, albeit not without paying a price. One of his arms hung limply at his side, and he was covered in cuts and bruises. Zac frowned when he felt the man's aura was still rock solid.

It was risky leaving the leader for last, but it was the strategy he and Ogras had settled on. They only knew this person was powerful before the army appeared, and there was no way to tell if Ogras could even get close enough to him for Zac to launch a surprise strike. Instead, they'd opted to take out as many Hegemons as possible in a blitz and only then focus on the leader.

Even if things had gone mostly according to plan, Zac had hoped he'd reach this point without having to expend both [Rapturous Divide] and [Arcadia's Judgement]. His berserking skill had run its course, indicating the time it lasted hadn't changed. Instead, the backlash had been drastically lessened, and Zac only felt a wave of exhaustion instead of losing half his combat strength.

It wasn't a coincidence, but rather design. Zac had aimed for this when he reforged the skill. More power instead of more time, and a smaller backlash upon upgrade instead of an increased time frame. Right now, he somewhat regretted that direction as another 10 seconds on the clock would have been nice, especially when the leader's flesh twisted and turned until he was made anew like a fleshy puppet.

It definitely wasn't the unfettered possibility of Creation who made it possible, nor was it a healing skill. It was the blood curse in his body.

Zac had seen those tendrils twist and pulse in the wounds. Not only that, but he could feel a sense of danger from the curse, even at this distance.

There were no two ways about it—this guy was more powerful than Zac expected.

Since the Hegemon wasn't circulating any energy, Zac didn't immediately make his move. Zac needed the break more than the infiltrator, so he swallowed a Healing Pill to alleviate some of the exhaustion. Ogras had already disappeared again, probably waiting for the right time to strike. For a few seconds, no one said anything, until the Hegemon released a wheezing laugh.

"So, this untested Sector has some warriors with mettle, after all," the leader said, his voice a ghastly lisp. "I'm guessing you're the candidate who created the pillar?"

Zac narrowed his gaze. This warrior didn't seem ruffled at all upon seeing his army collapsing. Was the infiltrator that confident in his own strength? And was it just a guess that the Hegemon had pegged him as a candidate of Ultom, or did he have some way to confirm it?

"You have proven yourself, so I will give you an option besides death," the toothless man continued. "Return with me to the Kan'Tanu Sector and loyally assist whatever faction we sell you to."

"Sell me? What are you talking about?"

Zac obviously wasn't about to take this man up on his offer, but anything he could glean from him was valuable information.

"This is a greater opportunity than you can imagine. The exalted forces are looking for candidates. If you don't sell yourself, you will be hunted down without fail. In return, you will become a member of some of the mightiest forces in existence, something frontier cultivators like us can only dream of."

"Not interested, sorry," Zac grunted as the medicinal efficacy of the Healing Pill was exhausted.

"Then you choose death," the Hegemon said. "You leave me no choice."

"You're talking like your whole army isn't lying dead around you," Zac snorted.

"Army? These war-slaves?" The man laughed. "They are not my companions. They are my nourishment."

Hundreds of bodies exploded, and a red haze covered the entire basin. Simultaneously, the Hegemon's aura erupted to an unprecedented degree, clearly entering the levels of a Middle Hegemon. Zac felt an enormous evil coming from within the leader that was rapidly being covered in pulsating tendrils.

This was far beyond what he'd seen from any other infiltrators. There was only one answer—this man carried a curse far more potent than the others, and this was his true state. Space itself shuddered around him like it was finding it hard to contain his aura, and Zac almost felt like he was facing the insanely powerful cyborg again.

A barrage of fractal leaves shot toward the man, but the shallow cuts they left on the fleshy armor healed almost instantly. Seeing such a display proved this wasn't something Zac could deal with in his current state. There was no other option—he needed to activate the backup plan.

"Shroud!" Zac shouted, and it was like a dozen smoke bombs detonated at once, covering the basin and the surrounding mountains in thick, isolating shadows.

Death filled his being as his surroundings changed hue. Chains rattled as a coffin appeared on its back, the swirl on its lid like a gateway to the Underworld itself. In his hand, [Black Death] appeared as his other Tool Spirit returned into [Verun's Bite] before being stowed away. This was the ultimate card in his repertoire, finally made possible by Ogras' illusory skills.

"I choose death?" Zac said as his body started to grow. "You have no idea."

# 4

# ARBITER

The fleshy armor around the lipless infiltrator writhed and pulsated like a stygian horror. Even then, he looked at Zac as though he were the monstrosity when Zac completed a transformation of his own. Muscles and bones creaked and groaned until Zac was almost four meters tall. This feature didn't strengthen him, but he kept it since it'd proven useful when he fought Uona.

However, no one who had seen [Vanguard of Undeath] would recognize the skill even if he had become supersized. The thick plating that radiated a cold aquamarine of death from within was mostly gone. Instead, Zac found himself donning a mantle of utter darkness that covered most of his features.

He still gained a dark-scaled breastplate with dense inscriptions, but his helmet was replaced by a hood. The rest of his plating was also gone, and Zac was now draped in dark robes that continuously released black tendrils of the Abyss. To an earthling, he probably resembled a grim reaper, equipped with a coffin and axe instead of a scythe.

[Love's Bond] and [Black Death] looked mostly the same, except the links had grown a shade darker as they'd been imbued with the abyssal aura of his Draugr heritage. Of course, they'd also grown in size to match Zac's own, but the axe retained its shape instead of being reformed into a bardiche.

This was intentional. Even if Zac could fight mostly unencumbered with almost any type of axe thanks to his mastery, there would be a sense of imbalance when he used his Inexorable Stance. The bardiche had been pretty good previously, since he neither had any proper technique nor an axe for his undead side. Now that he had the perfect weapon, it would weaken the skill if the weapon were transformed.

There were two more additions to his new look—the first was a swirling darkness that formed a terrifying backdrop behind him thanks to the vortex on Alea's coffin lid growing in size. It probably looked like an entrance to the Abyss, one even more palpable than the darkness of **[Rapturous Divide]**. The swirl was now roughly the size of his torso, and it created a profane halo effect.

And from its depths, the final part of the ensemble emerged. A thick, scarred chain wound itself around his left forearm, essentially forming an impregnable bracer. Just looking at the scars caused his soul to shudder, as if they'd been left by some monstrous devil whose aura still lingered.

The chain didn't come from inside **[Love's Bond]** but rather from the skill itself, though there was some relation. The stronger Alea grew, the stronger this chain would become, just like how the power of his shield had partly determined the protective qualities of **[Immutable Bulwark]**.

"You!" the Hegemon exclaimed. "What manner of monstrosity are you!"

"That's coming from you?" Zac countered, his now raspy voice sounding like it was summoned from the depths of hell.

The lipless Hegemon's transformation was complete, and it looked extremely disgusting. In his chest was a huge hole from which the tendrils of his Heart Curse had emerged. In its center was a beating mass that emitted an exceedingly evil aura. Bloody veins wound themselves around almost every part of his body to form a living armor. They still rippled a bit, having mostly thinned down to a manageable size that shouldn't restrict his movements.

Zac sensed dozens of familiar auras from within those tendrils—the auras of those he and Ogras had just killed. It created an extremely discordant appearance, which was furthered by the fact the Hegemon now exuded two auras of his own.

The Hegemon and his Heart Curse were one, yet they weren't. Their auras were entwined, empowering each other like a Dao Braid. Zac knew it wasn't so simple, though. Unless this curse was utterly different from how the other curses functioned, it shouldn't have any energy of its own. It was ultimately a parasite that acted similarly to a Specialty Core, where it provided power at the expense of life force or energy expenditure.

Even if the Hegemon absorbed a massive amount of blood and energy from the corpses of his so-called war-slaves, there had to be a cost to gaining power in such a way. No matter how the transformation worked, the leader was stronger than they anticipated, and most likely a different tier of warrior than any invader he'd run into.

From Vai's analysis, this man was supposed to be just above Uzu's true strength, and with the activation of the Heart Curse, he was inching in on the strength of a proper Middle-stage Hegemon. There was nothing to be done about such a tough fight out of nowhere. This man couldn't be allowed to leave alive, whether it was because of his secrets or his connection to Ultom.

"Get away," Zac whispered into the shadows, hoping Ogras could hear him.

One thing hadn't changed since he and Ogras met last. He still couldn't completely shield the living from the effect of his skills. The next moment, a shroud descended on the basin, forming a core of unrelenting darkness in the shadow realm Ogras had erected. [Deathmark], [Fields of Despair], and [Blighted Cut] were activated at once. Zac even considered using [Pillar of Desolation] from the get-go, but ultimately decided against it.

The infiltrator had immediately recovered from getting hit by the second blast of [Arcadia's Judgement] empowered by [Arcadian Crusade], and that was before he absorbed the bodies of over two hundred warriors, including a half-dozen Hegemons. Zac couldn't waste his Supreme Pathbound skill right away until he better understood what he was dealing with and the limits of his recovery.

Hopefully, he wouldn't have to use it at all.

"I don't know how you suddenly turned into an unliving miscreation, but it doesn't matter," the Hegemon growled. "I'll rip you apart just the same."

Another grotesque avatar appeared behind the lipless warrior's back. Three faces were fused into one, locked in a silent scream with lumps of tumors and writhing flesh creating a nightmarish scene. In a perfect world, Zac wouldn't have allowed the Hegemon to activate any skills, but it was impossible to avoid.

Even after his race-transforming skill was upgraded, his swap took a bit to finish. And since they'd left the Kan'Tanu Aural Cultivator for last, he'd been given a window to complete his own preparations.

"I've never met an undead before. I heard they existed in this Sector," the Hegemon said, his voice amplified and repeated by the enormous heads behind him. Zac's soul shuddered from the effect—just speaking had become an attack in the Hegemon's current form. "I will offer your cursed eyes as a gift to the general. I know he would be interested in such a unique specimen."

Zac briefly wondered if the man didn't know about Draugr, but he guessed it didn't really matter, opting to wait and observe. This man was far too powerful just to throw out his whole repertoire at once and possibly waste the effect of his skills.

Luckily, Zac had minions who could test the waters for him. An axe-wielding wraith of [Deathmark] appeared out of nowhere behind the Hegemon, swinging its axe in a ruthless arc aimed at his neck. With its latest upgrade, the specter had become even more congealed, and its weapon no longer looked like it had been picked up from an ancient battlefield.

Its speed and intelligence had both improved, and Zac inwardly sighed when it was all for naught. The phantom only managed to start up its swing before it crumbled. Some sort of domain surrounded the Hegemon. Not only that, ten spikes shot out from the fleshy armor covering him and ripped the already collapsing specter apart. It looked like an autonomous action, which wasn't surprising considering even the lower Heart Curses had some basic instincts.

Just after the wraith crumbled, Zac was beset by a sharp pang of danger. Not wanting to take any risks, he turned into a stream of Miasma that flew toward his target. In his previous position, space tore apart as a sound wave so powerful it could be seen with the naked eye spread out in every direction.

It was the enormous avatar in the air that was responsible. One of its mouths open in a wordless scream, transferring its wail into a singular spot. By the time the attack caught up with Zac, it'd been somewhat diminished. But Zac's vision was still distorted, and sharp spikes may as well have been stabbing into his ears.

The shockwave forcibly deactivated [Abyssal Phase], and a dozen flesh spikes shot out from the Hegemon to take advantage of the opening. They narrowly missed, piercing the empty air around Zac, allowing him to regain his footing. It wasn't a clumsy mistake but rather an effect of [Arbiter of the Abyss]. Even if he'd been affected by the soundwave, his new skill was still running.

And its domain was incredibly powerful.

When Zac formed the skill, reconfiguring the taunting function of [Vanguard of Undeath] had taken up most of his efforts. It was now responsible not only for control but part of the defenses. The strength of his taunt had been greatly improved, and he could now rebuff just like he could attract.

A narrowly inflicted attack would now miss, and a lethal strike would get demoted to a flesh wound as it was rebuffed, drastically lessening the pressure on himself and [Profane Exponents]. Any skilled enemy would eventually be able to correct for the control domain, but he could just switch the direction when that happened, forcing the enemy to continuously readjust.

In other words, not only did it help with defenses while retaining its ability to drag unwilling enemies toward him, it was an effective way to ruin someone's momentum and rhythm. Being able to push his enemies and their attacks into any direction would have been even better, but that was beyond him and his skill. Such would require absolute control within your sphere of influence, rather than the more straightforward push away and drag over functionality.

Using the domain was as natural as breathing, so Zac launched a real offensive of his own, since waiting around was fruitless. The corrosive atmosphere of [Deathmark], even in its upgraded state, wasn't able to leave any lasting damage on the fleshy armor, and it looked like the specters would have to stack corrosive marks to have any effect.

The lipless Aural Cultivator was still full of certainty and overconfidence after triggering his Heart Curse, and Zac wanted to seize the momentum before he realized he wasn't as infallible as he believed. Chains oozing with corrosive death rattled as they shot toward the Hegemon while Zac himself followed in their wake.

He could sense the chains being assaulted by invisible ripples, but it wasn't enough to damage them. Alea's chains were already nigh-unbreakable for an Early Hegemon while still an F-grade Spirit Tool, and her recent breakthrough pushed her three full tiers into Late E-grade. Zac doubted even an all-out strike was enough to cause cracks in the fetters by this point.

Another pang of danger made Zac control one of the chains to push him out of the way, just in time to avoid a second smaller explosion of sound. It felt like a concussion grenade had been thrown next to him. Luckily, he'd already plugged up his ears with Miasma and the Branch of the Pale Seal. It wasn't enough to completely block out the noise, but it helped deal with the worst of it.

Another lash of a chain propelled Zac toward the Hegemon, and the colossal axe of [Arbiter of the Abyss] fell toward the Hegemon's head. There was no worry in the man's murky eyes as he took out an odd-looking staff. It was made of metal and had dozens of trinkets hanging from links embedded along its length, from mottled bones to exquisitely crafted bells.

He swept the staff upward, and the Miasmic clouds around them churned as the two weapons collided. Zac wasn't holding back, and his force was enough to crumble mountains. And yet, the Hegemon was only pushed half a step back as he blocked the strike. The chains of [Love's Bond] were already aiming for vitals to restrict the cultist's options and begin Zac's inexorable dance of death, except a confusing cacophony of discordant sounds slammed into Zac's head with just as tangible an effect as a punch.

Sharp pain bloomed in his side as flesh and ichor flew in every direction. It wasn't a projectile that ripped out a piece of his gut, but rather a Dao-infused whistle from the Hegemon himself. How the hell someone could whistle without lips was the least of Zac's concerns—the fact he could feel a surprisingly powerful Dao in his wound was a much greater cause for concern.

It would probably have been game over for an average person by getting such a wound, but his Hidden Nodes were like startled beasts whose domains had been infringed upon by an interloper. They went on a ferocious offensive, allowing Zac to contain the damage as he continued to fight.

It had been some time since he used his Inexorable Stance. Still, he seamlessly slid into the familiar patterns as his axe and chains formed an inescapable net that would only inevitably lead to death. Knowing what to look for, Zac focused on the Hegemon's mouth, lungs, and throat to interrupt his Aural skills, and he activated [Profane Exponents] to protect against further surprise whistles.

Three silhouettes appeared behind him, and a spectral coffin appeared and blocked a jab in the nick of time. The three pygmies hadn't grown any taller since the upgrade, and neither had a fourth one joined them. But their auras were deeper, and their equipment a lot more powerful, indicating the skill had been given an all-around boost instead of new features.

Even if he'd been taught some decent staff technique, the Hegemon was clearly not an adroit infighter. Between a Dao and attribute advantage, autonomously attacking armor, and the avatar in the sky, which kept unleashing localized bursts of utter destruction, he somewhat kept up. Even then, Zac was steadily dragging the fight into his favor.

Huge festering gashes kept appearing across the grotesque armor, and whole chunks of flesh sloughed off the Hegemon's body. The lipless cultivator managed to release a few barbs of his own, or rather his armor did. More than ten shallow wounds had been punched into Zac's body by the flesh tendrils, but most of the wounds were intentional blunders on Zac's part.

Zac didn't know exactly what the Hegemon was planning, but it almost felt like the cultivator was leaving behind small bombs in Zac's body. They were parts of a Heart Curse that looked incomplete on the surface, but they still filled Zac with a vague sense of danger. He guessed they just needed a trigger to start causing havoc.

Unfortunately for the Hegemon, the seeds were destroyed and swallowed by [Void Heart] and [Purity of the Void] as quickly as they appeared. The two Hidden Nodes weren't able to deal with the puncture wound in his gut, so they turned their attention to the seeds. The Dao from the whistle was a lot more troublesome, despite not being able to cause any real damage in the short run.

Zac had already realized that whittling down this man wouldn't work. Between being an Elite Hegemon and having the stolen vitality of 200 warriors, he just had too much ability to regenerate. No matter how much flesh Zac destroyed, new veins regrew with a pace that put even Vivi to shame.

He would have to finish it in one go, and Zac sensed the opportunity was about to present itself.

Suddenly, a deafening crash of jumbled sounds made Zac's head spin as most of the trinkets on the Hegemon's staff exploded. Each one released a sharp burst of sound, and together they formed a tremendous Aural attack. Even if Zac was prepared and had already turned on the active state of [Indomitable], he still found his mind a mess.

"Join us," the Hegemon sneered, his voice turning into a confusing rattle in Zac's head.

At the same time, an incredibly thick, fleshy spike shot out from the hole in his chest, like an arm had grown and shot toward Zac's gut wound. Zac's mind was still a confusing jumble from the audible overload, but the coffin-wielding pygmy skeleton came to the rescue. The shield held against the Heart Curse's empowered strike, but Zac blanched when he saw why.

It almost looked like a water cannon had hit his barrier when the bloody arm slammed into it. The curse split up into dozens of thinner tendrils that wound around the coffin before reforming on the other side. There was still a chance he could avoid the incoming attack by pushing the domain of [Arbiter of the Abyss] to its limit, but Zac did the opposite.

An enormous amount of energy was hidden inside the tendril, but he would still let it hit him. He was sure this was the catalyst for the supposed triggers left all over his body, and he wanted to give the Hegemon a false sense of victory. However, Zac didn't want the tendril to mix with the powerful Dao left behind by the whistle. The taunting domain of [Arbiter of the Abyss] once more came in clutch as it pulled the tendril toward his other side while Zac pretended to stumble.

Meanwhile, he prepared a move of his own. The chains of [Love's Bond] were already striking at the Hegemon, and the cultivator was forced to divert some of his attention to avoid getting blinded. Seeing his opportunity, Zac said a silent prayer as his left arm rose, and the abyssal chain around his forearm uncoiled.

It was even slower than his other chains, and it didn't even try to intercept the bloody tendril that was almost upon him. Instead, it flew toward the Hegemon. Zac felt a gut-wrenching pain in his side a moment later as the bloody arm punched straight through his breastplate and dug into his body.

The Hegemon's eyes lit up as Zac's body was filled with the evil energy of the evolved Heart Curse. But nothing happened due to the seeds being long gone. Zac grinned at the confused and alarmed Hegemon. A moment later, his chain lightly tapped against the Hegemon's chest, and Zac knew it was over.

"Caught you."

# 5
# PRESSURE

"You're immune!" the lipless cultivator screamed, shock and confusion written all over his face.

Zac didn't bother answering, his attention focused on a surprising shift in one of his skills. The next moment, three sharp twangs echoed out as deep wounds were carved into the Hegemon due to the finishing blow of [Blighted Cut] becoming available thanks to [Arbiter of the Abyss]. It allowed for instant judgement, and the Hegemon was almost dismembered into four chunks.

Unfortunately, the durability of the fleshy armor was too great. Even with its upgraded lethality from reaching Late Proficiency, [Blighted Cut] didn't manage to cut him all the way through. Its force was expended after digging half of the way, and thick tendrils shot out from within his innards to keep his body together.

Not even the corrosive cascade of [Blighted Cut] failing was enough to finish the job. The tendrils of the Heart Curse broke apart, and new ones replaced the old in an endless cycle until the attack was expended. A tremendous shockwave threw Zac back as the colossal Avatar in the sky exploded. The Hegemon had sacrificed his supportive attack skill to gain some breathing room, and his reaction was immediate.

He fled.

Between Zac's apparent immunity to the Heart Curse and almost getting killed, it was clear the previous confidence of the Hegemon was long gone. But it was already too late. Being able to suddenly activate

[Blighted Cut] was just a happy surprise, and not what Zac planned to rely on.

The moment the sound wave threw him back, the one chain emerging from the abyssal halo had turned into two. The first was the original one that returned to his arm after being rebuffed. The second was a spectral chain that was still very much attached to the Hegemon's chest. It wasn't the usual cold turquoise of Miasma, but instead a matte black that reeked of Pure Death.

The Kan'Tanu tried to destroy the ethereal chain with another weaponized whistle. The only result was the Hegemon stumbling to the ground when he reared to fly away. It wasn't so easy to deal with this chain. The infiltrator had been fettered by [Arbiter of the Abyss], and he would only be released after receiving judgement. Trying to break free would merely result in a spiritual backlash.

The Hegemon gave up attacking the chain and opted to fly into the sky. That wouldn't save him either. Zac didn't even bother locking up the area with [Pillar of Desolation]. Instead, a storm of energy entered the Skill Fractal of [Desperation's End], just as the Hegemon turned a rapid 180 degrees and flew straight for Zac.

His face was filled with confusion, and it was too late for regrets. Zac wasn't taking any chances, and his activation time had been cut down to a third with the help of Void Energy. Two massive wings appeared behind Zac's back when [Arbiter of the Abyss] turned the Hegemon around, and a scarred skull was now flying toward the man.

The lipless cultivator readied his staff as a last-ditch effort, but he urgently swung it to his side as another [Deathmark]-wraith appeared to strike him down. A second flourish rebuffed one of the chains of [Love's Bond] that followed him into the sky, before he finally swung his staff down toward the blade the skull of [Desperation's End] unleashed.

The swing turned crooked by a tug from the spectral chain. A swirl of darkness from the third pygmy of [Profane Exponents] moved the Hegemon even farther off-kilter at the last moment, pushing both arms and staff entirely out of the way.

The lipless leader roared in defiance and his armor rippled as his energy churned. It wasn't enough. Two balls had appeared next to him, and space sealed as the aspects of [Desperation's End] converged. It managed to restrain even a thrashing Hegemon long enough to complete the strike, and he could only look on with despair as he met his end.

A silent swish of a solitary blade, followed by a muted thud as the Hegemon's head fell on the ground. One of Alea's chains drilled into the severed head, and a surge of energy confirmed that not even the evolved Heart Curse would be able to drag him back from death's door any longer.

The body crumpled to the ground a moment later when Zac deactivated [Arbiter of the Abyss], and Zac backed away when he saw the curse emerge from the chest. Its aura was extremely sinister, and even Zac wasn't willing to take that thing on unless he had to, especially now that it gave off a sense of terminal hunger.

The curse withered away a few seconds later, and Zac believed he could even sense a wave of intense reluctance as it died out. There wasn't any second burst of energy though, which probably meant the System still didn't consider that thing a proper entity. But it was definitely more alive than the weaker curses. Zac briefly wondered if there were curses that had actually gained a semblance of life.

There were Tool Spirits, World Spirits, and even Array Spirits, so why not Curse Spirits?

Stabbing pains in his side reminded Zac of the trouble at hand, and he expended all his [Undying Mark] charges to restore most of the physical wounds. The healing skill's efficacy was better than before, but was ultimately only a Middle-quality skill he'd bought from the Sharva'Zi Dao Repository in Twilight Harbor. It didn't help with the Dao inside his body.

Still, Zac was satisfied as he deactivated his various skills and turned back to his human form. The process was swift, and Zac threw out dozens of Attuned Crystals and offensive talismans, which created a storm of rampant energy throughout the basin. It didn't completely disperse the lingering deathly atmosphere, but it was now just one among many. And some death was expected on a battlefield.

Zac was elated to see that [Arbiter of the Abyss] worked just as planned. The taunting domain was helpful in all kinds of ways, though he wanted to test its rhythm-breaking capabilities against a more technically skilled opponent. More importantly, the spectral chain was extremely useful.

His original idea was to create two stages of the taunt. The first was the domain that would work against a large number of enemies. The ghost chain could only be used once, but it would strengthen the pulling component of the domain significantly. Escaping after being tagged was both difficult and dangerous.

First of all, it should be able to block and deactivate most types of movement skills, including teleportation and various phase shifts. And no matter if the marked target destroyed the links with a powerful attack or stretched them until they broke, they'd receive an intense backlash. Just damaging the links with a whistle had been enough to make the Hegemon stumble. Completely destroying it might have even made him black out for a moment.

The only downside of the spectral chain was its short 10 second span, though the other parts of the skill wouldn't deactivate even after using it. As long as the target could avoid judgement for that long, the chain would disperse. That was easier said than done when Zac could almost control those he caught like puppets for that duration, and it turned out he could even activate the finisher of [Blighted Cut] through the link.

Zac looked at the headless corpse in the distance, feeling the fight went well, all things considered. These Kan'Tanu infiltrators were too confident in their Heart Curses, and when they turned out to be useless against him, their whole combat style came apart. Still, the Aural skills were undeniably hard to deal with. The battle would have looked very different if the Hegemon had focused on creating opportunities to use his skills rather than infecting him with the curse.

The two dreadful avatars the lipless cultivator released were a good reminder that Zac was still at a disadvantage in that regard. Sure, neither of the skills could compare with the destructive power of his finishing blows, but even Zac didn't dare take those space-rending wails head-on. And they could be continuously launched as though the avatars were mobile turrets, probably for tens of minutes if need be.

He'd have to be careful if he encountered a proper elite like the 'general' the lipless cultivator mentioned. Especially if he was supported by an actual army and was allowed to release all his skills from the back lines.

Then again, it wasn't a big problem against most Hegemons he'd encounter. You got even fewer freebies from the System at the D-grade, and most weaker Hegemons were stuck with one or two D-grade skills for a long time. Eventually, they'd scrounge up enough money for new ones, but they also needed the money to buy D-grade equipment or the higher-quality War Regalia.

You could upgrade your old skills, but that was easier said than done. It required comprehensive skill and understanding to upgrade old skills to the vastly more complex D-grade versions capable of taking advantage of a Cultivator's Core. Perhaps these things weren't an issue in the more developed sectors of the Multiverse. But on the frontier, the lack of resources acted as a safeguard for Zac.

Of course, even Frontier Factions would have adequately decked out talents, and Zac would sooner or later run into someone with a War Regalia and proper sets of skills. Those were the ones to look out for—the regalia would protect them while they activated the energy-hungry D-grade skills with extreme power.

The wound in his side still felt like it was on fire, and Zac slumped to the ground with a grunt as he ate a Healing Pill. Most of the Hegemon's Dao remained, as was the stubborn will of the evolved curse. His **[Purity of the Void]** and **[Void Heart]** were still trying to deal with it, but progress was slow and arduous.

It looked like his E-grade Nodes weren't without limits, even if the Dao wasn't completely out of Zac's scope. He suspected it was a Middle Dao Branch that had been amplified through some method, yet it was so difficult to deal with. Even with its owner dead, it refused to simply be gobbled up.

If anything, it almost felt like it'd grown more stubborn, like an actual curse from the beyond. It would possibly take a week even for his Hidden Node to deal with such powerful foreign energies, and Zac didn't have time for that. But that didn't mean he didn't have options.

If the damage couldn't be healed, it could still be corrupted.

Zac steadied his breath before taking out a Longevity Pearl. After that, he roused some Creation Energy. An endless stream of unfettered possibilities poured into the wound, and Zac grunted with pain as he felt his flesh twist and reform. The same was happening to the imbued intent. Gradually, their meaning shifted under the influence until they completely lost their cohesiveness.

They'd become unclaimed energies at that moment, and his Hidden

Nodes pounced with redoubled ferocity. When Zac took charge of the Creation Energy, his flesh turned back to normal. After another minute, the wounds were gone entirely, along with the lingering intents. The shadowy haze was dispersing by that point, leaving Zac panting in a broken valley.

"Monster," a disbelieving voice said from behind. "Are you even killable any longer?"

"You're okay?" Zac asked, turning around to see Ogras standing some distance away from him. "I saw you get gored."

"Unlike a monster like you, I can't just get stabbed left and right and walk it off," Ogras snorted. "Me getting stabbed was an illusion so they'd turn their attention back to you. So, you're still playing around with that cursed energy in your body? How are your murdery impulses nowadays?"

"I've been cultivating my soul over the past decade, and I don't get murdery any longer. And like you're one to talk," Zac scoffed as he waved at the flag in Ogras' hand.

The demon shrugged. "Well, I guess people like us have to take whatever benefits we can get our hands on, even if they have annoying side effects."

"It's amazing how much you've improved in this place," Zac said.

"Not much else to do here except cultivate," Ogras said with a grimace. "My grandpa would have bound me up and thrown me into that black hole himself if he knew I'd train so hard here. And it's not as impressive as it looked. Most of what I did would have been impossible without a bellowing Barghest soaking up all the attention."

"You're welcome." Zac rolled his eyes.

What the demon said was true, though. His kills had been ambushes that struck fast and hard with the help of his elusive Daos. However, there were limits to such a method. For example, Zac had sensed the danger and blocked it when Ogras tried to ambush him. Most real elites would probably be able to discern such a strike and deal with it, or at least have treasures to protect them.

After that, the element of surprise would be gone, and hiding from an enemy who was aware of you was a lot harder.

"Well, all things considered, things turned out pretty swell. That toothless lad must have been an elite of theirs, and you still took him down." Ogras grinned as he took a swig of the liquor he'd pilfered from Zac one minute into their journey. "By the way, I dealt with the loose ends while you fought the leader."

"Loose ends?" Zac asked with confusion.

"The two scouts. They were hiding just a few mountains over. I think they didn't dare flee without their boss. I tried to capture them, but their chests erupted when they were caught in my shadows. I didn't get anything useful, I'm afraid."

"Should've guessed they had some safeguards against capture." Zac sighed. "What about Vai?"

"I had a ghost monitor her. She never left the cave," the demon reported. "She kept looking at the bowl, though. I'm not sure if she can see affinities in that thing?"

"Shouldn't be," Zac said. "I've used it a few times. It only shows the location and approximate strength."

"Then we should be fine," Ogras muttered as he walked over to him. "A whole Sector full of unorthodox cultivators. This is going to spell trouble."

"We already gained some things from that guy blabbering."

"Wasn't good news, was it? If those ancient factions with their noses in the air come looking for our opportunity, how will we survive? Let alone *meat*, we won't even get *soup*."

"We need some answers," Zac said. "I'll see if there's anything on his body."

"Be careful to not get ambushed by a Heart Curse," Ogras grunted. "How are you immune to them, by the way? Care to share the method?"

"That'd be pretty hard," Zac laughed as he walked toward the headless body. "It's my bloodline that turns them into nourishment."

"*Of course* it does," Ogras muttered. "Why wouldn't it?"

Zac found a Spatial Ring on the leader's body while Ogras fished out some more from the ground where the other Hegemons had fallen. Zac felt something was off when he looked at it, and he didn't dare activate it for the time being.

"Trapped?" Ogras ventured when he saw Zac's frown.

"It might be... Let's pick up Vai and move away. Who knows if there are more squads en route."

The two spread a generous serving of Karma-breaking powder across the basin before leaving, and found Vai standing at the mouth of her cave with worry in her eyes.

"You're fine!" Vai said with relief upon seeing them, then she froze in shock. "Eh? You're *fine*? How is that possible?"

"It's the power of friendship." Ogras winked.

Vai ignored the demon and turned to Zac inquisitively.

"They weren't as strong as we feared," Zac said. "The infiltrators are dealt with, but we should still leave this area."

Neither he nor Ogras needed to rest. The battle lasted less than three minutes, and Zac had more than half his energy remaining, so the group set out into the vast plains as quickly as possible. However, they only ran for half an hour before Ogras slowed down.

"Well, that can't be good," Ogras muttered with a slight frown as he looked up at the sky.

"What's that?" Zac asked, failing to see anything amiss. "Did you sense something? More invaders?"

"No, it's the energy. I've lived here for ten years, and I'm rather familiar with it now. Something is changing. It's weak, but the air feels... stale. Sick, even." Ogras glanced at Zac askance. "I think you might actually have killed Billy's pet."

# 6
# COLLAPSE

"Killed Billy's pet?" Zac said with confusion. "What the hell are you talking about?"

"The pillar, genius," Ogras snorted. "What else would cause a whole world to suddenly get sick?"

Zac glanced toward the mountain range in the distance. The pillar was almost gone, but he still remembered the madness barely held in check by the nine sigils. And also how the pillar not only pierced the sky, but had also dug into the depths of the earth.

Where a World Core would typically be.

Had his actions really damaged the Dimensional Seed? Zac blanched at the thought. Even if he disregarded that he was standing inside the Mystic Realm, it was a horrible thought. The Dimensional Seed helped him open his [Purity of the Void] node. Not only that, if it hadn't been there to draw the attention and avarice of the Collector, the Great Redeemer, and the Administrator, Zac wasn't so sure he would have survived the Mystic Realm back then.

Zac turned to Vai hopefully, praying the researcher could disprove the demon's theory. "What do you think? Is it possible?"

"I can somewhat understand what the bad guy is getting at." Vai took out a few measuring tools. "But the Realm Spirit is unlikely to have died already. If that were the case, we wouldn't just have sensed a small corruption of the ambient energy. Space itself would start to collapse."

Zac nodded in thanks, but he was still worried. Just because the

Dimensional Seed hadn't died, didn't mean it was fine. He couldn't sense anything off in the atmosphere, but Zac wasn't too sensitive to small shifts in energy. If his [Cosmic Gaze] couldn't see it, it might as well not exist to him.

"The World Core might be damaged," Zac ventured. "Or do these places even have proper cores?"

"Mystic Realms need to have cores if they pass a certain size. Smaller realms only need a strong enough energy density to form a spatial field. Even a powerful lingering intent can suffice as a core for a Mystic Realm, but those are extremely rare Inheritance Realms," Vai explained. "All realms above Mystic need to have cores. At least, that's what I've read."

"What would happen if this place's core was being corrupted?"

Vai hesitated. "Well, World Cores are resilient. They can slowly refine energy, which hopefully means things will gradually return to normal after the pillar is gone."

"And if it doesn't?" Ogras asked.

"Then… we'd probably want to leave." Vai fearfully looked at the sky. "A World Core breaking on a normal planet just means it will become a dead world. Mystic Realms are different. They're hidden in pockets within the Void, and the realm will lose its ability to hold the Void back if the core breaks. Its ambient energy will gradually be drained to rebuff the collapse until it reaches a tipping point. And even if we survive the collapse, we could be thrown deep into the Void."

"That's just great," Ogras grunted, looking to Zac. "Maybe I should just tie myself to your back right now to secure my little life."

Vai looked at the demon with confusion while Zac rolled his eyes. "If you can barely sense something amiss, it can't be too bad. The ambient energy is as strong as ever, so we aren't at that point yet. Let's just hurry to Billy, he could have more answers. The real problem is that the invaders might look for him and the Realm Spirit as well. Can he withstand an attack?"

"No idea. Haven't been back to the Kingdom of Billy since I left," Ogras said. "It wasn't too impressive back then, but he's had a lot of time to fortify. And honestly, he improved quicker than me in this place. I've never seen something so disgusting as forming a Dao Branch while sleeping. He should be fine."

"How long have you been out of contact?" Zac asked.

"Who knows." Ogras shrugged. "I haven't kept track of the days in this prison. Perhaps, five or six years?"

"That long?" Zac exclaimed, his eyes thinning with suspicion. "Did you have a falling-out? What did you do?"

"I'm innocent here, alright?" Ogras smiled. "Living in such close proximity can strain any relationship. But I was mostly curious about all the pocket realms the Dimensional Seed swallowed. I was planning on returning around this time, but got derailed by all the excitement in the mountain range."

"Bad guy, I bet you just wanted to steal all the treasures in here," Vai huffed, getting a nod of agreement from Zac. "What a waste... This might be the first Dimensional Seed to appear in the Zecia Sector in millions of years, and its spirit is even sapient. It would be a huge loss if it collapsed before we got a chance to learn from it."

"Well, it's not over just yet. We might be overthinking things," Zac said, then curiously looked over at the demon. "Found anything good?"

Zac had already heard some of it from what the demon shared about the Ra'Lashar Kingdom and the Lost Plane, but he wouldn't be surprised if that were just the tip of the iceberg. Some exciting things were bound to have cropped up with the Dimensional Seed gobbling up a bunch of smaller Mystic Realms and drowning the area with Origin Dao and Cosmic Energy.

"A few interesting knick-knacks," Ogras lazily said. "Nothing that a vaunted force like the exalted Void Gate would be interested in, right? And I did loot them *before* this place got swallowed up in your ladder or whatever."

"Do you think we're scoundrels like you?" Vai muttered, but her lips curved up a bit.

"How about we just push straight through," Zac said as he looked out across the alien landscape. "I don't feel good about Billy being all alone when the invaders have already made their way in."

"And let's pray those two fools haven't done something stupid already," Ogras added with a shudder. "Knowing them, our chances aren't great."

Billy walked in circles around Gemmy, worry in his eyes. He didn't know what to do. Gemmy was sick, and nothing Billy tried worked. And it had gotten a lot worse over the past week.

"Owie, owie, owie!" Gemmy cried from within the fire.

"Ah, ah," Billy muttered, searching for solutions. Finally, he spotted a pile of Dao Stones. They always made Billy feel better, so perhaps they were medicine?

Into the fire they went.

"Oooh, pretty," Gemmy hummed as her colors sparkled inside the blazing furnace. "Nope. Owie, owie, owie! Perhaps burn another blanket?"

"Billy is out of blankets," Billy sighed. "Out of beds too. They're already in the fire."

Why didn't it work? Mama always said that good rest and heat would make you feel better. Billy had first put Gemmy in his bed to heat her up, but it didn't work, not even with *three* blankets. Not even putting Gemmy inside the fire was enough, even after the fire became so big it almost reached the clouds.

For once, Billy missed Horny Guy. He was a liar and a cheat, but he knew many things. Perhaps he knew how to make Gemmy better… Except Gemmy couldn't see him any longer. Not since he went to the nasty place.

"Maybe Billy should go?" Gemmy hesitantly said from within the fire. "If Gemmy can't help Billy, the bad guys—"

"Stop," Billy said with a scrunched-up face. "Billy is not leaving Gemmy. Billy will take a nap and figure it out. Billy always has ideas after sleeping."

With that, Billy lay down on the ground, and the warm fire helped him quickly sleep even without a blanket.

"Ah! Billy remembers!" Billy exclaimed when he woke up in the familiar world. The hidden world that only Billy could see.

Well, Billy and Statue-man.

"Statue-man, Gemmy is still sick. If you don't help Gemmy, then Billy will not come back here again, no matter how much you teach Billy!"

"Troublesome child," Statue-man sighed. "As I said, it's no longer up to you. For years now, you have resisted reality. But it is coming to an end today. The link of blood between us is all-but-expended. Any more, and my forceful connection will destroy you. This is the last time you will enter this realm."

"Another lie?" Billy tried not to squirm.

"Believe what you will," Statue-man snorted. "I have a final proposal for you."

"Billy won't create that array," Billy staunchly said. "There are already a lot of Bad Guys in Gemmy's world. Billy can't risk more things going wrong now."

"Do you remember what Gemmy is?" Statue-man asked.

"Of course!" Billy said with a roll of his eyes. "Gemmy is the Land Ghost."

"Right. Gemmy's problem is she swallowed something she shouldn't have. Something dangerous. Nothing you do to Gemmy herself will save her as long as the links to that cursed plane remain. But I have a solution."

"A better solution than fire?" Billy hesitated.

Statue-man groaned. "Yes, a better solution than fire."

Billy was hesitant. Statue-man was a trickster and a bit stupid, but he'd helped Billy more than once over the past years. Statue-man might really have a cure for Gemmy if he said he did.

"A simple trade. I will give you a solution that will allow Gemmy to reform her world into a Pocket Realm—reform it *without* the pieces that make Gemmy sick. It will hurt and weaken her, but she will survive. And as long as she survives, she can recover her strength."

"What price?" Billy knew Statue-man wouldn't give him something so good for free. Normally, he forced Billy to do silly dances until he was dead-tired, but this was different.

"If you accept my help, you have to create the portal when you leave this Mystic Realm. You have to step through it and enter our subsidiary mountain. Work hard and get stronger until you reach the Eastern Mountain where my true body resides. And you can absolutely not get involved with Ultom."

Billy didn't care about the latter part. Billy didn't even know what Ultom was, so why would he want to get involved with it? Statue-man was stupid, *as usual*. But the real price was very expensive.

"If Statue-man helps Billy now, then Billy has to go help Statue-man later? I don't want to leave Gemmy."

"If you follow my solution, you will not only save Gemmy, but she will be able to follow you wherever you go. Without it, she will be stuck in the little Mystic Realm forever. This is actually a solution I've been preparing for years since I knew you would want to take her with you. I just had to modify it a bit now that she was sick."

"...Alright," Billy said with a determined expression. "If Statue-man's idea works, Billy will make the array and step through. But *only* if it works. If it fails, Billy will find Eastern Mountain and thwonk it until it becomes Eastern Pit."

"Finally," Statue-man said with a sigh. "Ancestors have mercy on us both."

"Ah... but... Billy *is* smart, he is just not good with complicated things... Can Billy really complete this alone?"

"I've simplified it as much as possible, but the plan is a bit involved," Statue-man said. "As luck would have it, you have some competent helpers in your dungeons. I'm sure they'll help you in return for being freed. Especially if you say you're from Eastern Mountain."

"Billy isn't from Eastern Mountain. Billy is from Billyville."

"Whatever you say. This is the last time we speak here. I hope to see you again, even if you are the most stubborn titan I've ever seen. I will imprint the plan into your head, so you never forget it. Good luck."

A moment later, a storm of ideas entered Billy's mind, and it felt like he was being thwonked over and over. When it stopped, he found himself lying next to Gemmy's fire. But this time, Billy remembered. He remembered it all, and he would save Gemmy.

Now he just had to make those sneaky-sneaks work for him. Easy.

―――――

"Report," Lozo Ul said the moment the two Untested shuffled into the command center.

"That's... Ah," the Spacemelder stuttered, his face pale as his eyes were glued to the ground.

"What have you done?" Lozo asked with a calm voice.

"N-Nothing! We have done nothing," the old woman next to him urgently said. "But... The accumulation is lost. We were unable to reverse it."

"Months of efforts undone, just like that, and you have done nothing?" Lozo calmly said, but a storm was raging beneath.

*KILL. THEM. EAT. THEM.*

Lozo took a shuddering breath as he pushed down the madness. There were no two ways around it. He was losing control.

He remembered the relief when he stepped out of the forest where the souls of his 999 brothers and sisters would forever stay. His hands were dripping with blood, and his body was covered in wounds. But something remarkable was brewing within. Something powerful. He'd gone from an Untested to a Remoulded of Kan'Tanu, a rebirth of both fate and potential.

Why couldn't he have been content with his lot?

Three wives and an enviable placement after he served his term. If he'd played his cards right, he could have used his uncle's connections to be stationed at Darasko V as a lord. But no, he had seen the palaces of the Reincarnators and the power they wielded—both political and actual power. He wanted that for himself, for his family who'd never nurtured a twice-reborn cultivator.

He struggled and fought. Desperately. *Endlessly.* Until one day, he entered that cursed mountain range that reeked of death. And he emerged, once more, with blood dripping from his hands and his body covered in wounds. But this time, it wasn't greatness and glory brewing within.

It was horror and madness.

That day, Lozo's nightmare had begun. How could a sprawling palace and a harem provide any solace when you spent every single moment fighting for your very soul? Only after reaching the limits of the Kan'Tanu lower hierarchy did he understand that those twice-reborn weren't reborn equal. Those like him, without any backing, found themselves in an endless cycle of dangerous missions for the Sect's glory.

They had no choice. It was the only way for them to get their hands on the nutrients they needed to stave off the hunger of their dark passengers, lest their sanity became the nutrients. The Reincarnators the general populace saw, those who lived blessed lives in the capitals, had generations of wealth and connections to rely on. They had underlings to sacrifice and send into war to exchange for the nutrients.

Some had even been elevated in the Gate of Rebirth and firmly seized control of their Heart Patterns.

For decades, Lozo thought such would be his life. To endlessly struggle just to keep himself above water and the madness at bay. But finally, the Heavens took pity on his lot, and an opportunity presented itself. An opportunity to not only get the contribution he needed to never worry about the madness again…

An opportunity to become an Elevated Reincarnator.

He'd been at the right place at the right time. As one of the few Reincarnators they'd managed to force into this Zecia Sector to oversee the advance forces, Lozo was already gaining ample contribution. And as luck would have it, this Mystic Realm and its contents were exposed. At first, this had nothing to do with him, but fate is a fickle mistress.

The realm was sucked into this Stellar Ladder, and space collapsed on the base where the connected Reincarnators were staying. Suddenly, *he* was the Reincarnator closest to the breach, and he was urgently ordered to follow in its wake.

A year later, their plans were at the cusp of fruition. If they succeeded, Lozo wouldn't need to lift a single finger for the rest of the war. He and his family would be excluded from the draft, and he would even get a chance to pass through the gates that every Remoulded and Reincarnator dreamt of. He could fully focus on shoring up his foundations and continuing his cultivation.

But just as he could almost taste victory, everything went wrong. These Spacemelders better have an answer.

"Give me a proper explanation, Untested," Lozo said hoarsely. "Or I will find new Spacemelders who can."

"N-Nothing went wrong on our end," the male Untested said. "The arrays the Exalted Halls prepared for us were working as planned, gradually rekindling the withered pathway. But a sudden outside shock to the system caused the pathway to splinter, and a lot of the accumulated energy was wasted."

"Outside shock?" Lozo growled. "The Void Gate? Or are there saboteurs in our midst?"

"We have yet to pinpoint the exact location of the interference, but it's not from here," the other Spacemelder said. "The energy streamed to the west."

"The west?" Lozo muttered, his seething rage subsiding. "Have someone make a jump and contact Quol for an update."

"That's…" the Untested said, sweat streaming down his face. "We had that idea as well… But we just got word his plaque has withered."

Lozo swore in annoyance. Quol was one of the strongest warriors he'd managed to take through the Stellar Ladder. That was why he was sent to inspect that signal months ago. Now he was dead, just a few days after things went wrong? Someone was moving against them.

"Send another unit, one focused on speed and stealth. We need to know what we're dealing with. Have them warped as close as possible to save time," Lozo said to the Remoulder Captain standing at the side.

"There is a 60% Mortality Rate at such a jump," one of the Spacemelders said.

"Then send more to make up the numbers," Lozo said. "How do we get back on track?"

"Ah, well," the female Spacemelder said. "The outburst set us back, but we have been slowly closing the leak over the past days. Even then, I am afraid… with the resistance, completing on time will be impossible."

"The resistance?" Lozo mused as he looked at a large map in the middle of the room. "Relay my order. Activate the second, third, and fourth armies and strike at the native stronghold immediately. Find out how they are influencing this Mystic Realm and put an end to it. We must complete this mission before the pathways reopen."

# 7

# UNSEALING

The trio didn't waste any time as they pushed deeper into the Badlands, and Zac couldn't help but marvel at the environment even if there were a lot of misgivings in his heart. Enormous, calcified trees in pink and blue towered toward the sky, their branches homes to scaled beasts with four wings.

The occasional rumble heralded golemoid beasts that migrated between lakes to extract minerals. The lakes themselves were kettles of puttering death which hid gorgeous green and purple flowers. Whole fields were made of glass and mirrors, creating a mystifying spectacle as they ran.

Their frantic pace drew some ire from the locals, but Zac and Ogras made short work of the beasts who thought they were in for an easy snack. Vai was once more sitting in a chair made from Vivi's vines. Ogras had also tried to commission a seat for himself, only to be rebuffed. Vai got to sit because she was investigating the infiltrators' Spatial Rings while keeping track of powerful auras in her bowl.

As expected, the lipless cultivator's ring was booby-trapped, while the others had simple seals that the little researcher undid. There wasn't anything new or exciting in those rings, just a bunch of cultivation materials far worse than what Zac carried. The rings primarily served as a reminder they weren't alone in this vast Mystic Realm.

Yet, even after three days, Vai hadn't spotted a single additional cultivator. It looked like there weren't any larger encampments nearby, or someone would have come to investigate by now. However, the lack of pursuit had another meaning—the squad of infiltrators weren't originally there for him.

Did they know about the temples and were sent to investigate? Or did that leader have a quest for Ultom as well?

After running for another week, they were forced to stop and rest inside a hollowed-out and crystallized trunk that shimmered like a million sapphires. Running for over ten days straight while occasionally fighting had drained them, especially Ogras, who often kept up his illusive domain.

There was another reason. Zac had gotten close to opening another node from the battle against the infiltrators, and a recent fight against three crystal Beast Kings provided the final energy he needed. When Zac informed them of his plan inside the trunk, the demon looked at Zac like he was a fool.

"You're not at the peak yet?" Ogras exclaimed. "It's been ten years! What are you waiting for?"

"There were some speed bumps along the way," Zac grunted.

"So what level are you at?" the demon asked, and even Vai looked over with interest.

"Three nodes to go. Two with this one," Zac said.

"Don't you have any pills to push you to the final step?" Ogras said.

"I have, but I've been wanting to keep impurities at a minimum for my breakthrough."

"Fair, but we need every advantage in case we have to fight our way out of here," the demon said.

"You might be right," Zac slowly nodded, turning to Vai. "How is your work on the ring coming along?"

"Slow. It's not overly complex, but there are too many patterns I don't recognize. It's interesting, the Kan'Tanu base their arrays on an entirely different set of princ—"

"So that's a no?" Zac coughed, seeing how Vai was gearing up for another lesson. He usually enjoyed listening to Vai expounding on various esoteric pieces of knowledge, but now was not the time.

"I can make an attempt, but I'm not very confident," Vai said.

"I might have an idea," Ogras said. "My little buddy is pretty knowledgeable with arrays. Problem is, he's a pathological liar and a general asshole, so you might need to bribe him."

"The goblin?" Zac said with surprise.

"K'Rav, a vaunted councilor of the Lunatic Kingdom of Ra'Shallar." Ogras removed the talismans from the sinister flag he always kept in his sleeves.

"Bring him out," Zac said.

A moment later, the pocked goblin appeared within the trunk, where he suspiciously looked back and forth between Ogras, Zac, and Vai.

"Let me guess, you ignorant children have run into a problem, and you want me to solve it after trapping me for weeks?" K'rav said, giving Ogras a blithering stare. "Your trick is clever, but we'll see how long you can laugh. Sealing me means removing the barrier between you and the flag. How long can you retain yourself?"

"What's he talking about?" Zac frowned.

"Cursed artifact or cursed company, I had to pick my poison," Ogras shrugged. "Let's get on with it."

"You're right," Zac said as he looked at the Tool Spirit. "We have a sealed ring that needs to be opened. Ogras thinks you have the knowledge to show us the way."

"I might, I might not," the goblin snickered. "More importantly, why should I help you? I know who you are, but your status and fame mean nothing to me."

"What do you want?" This was like dealing with Brazla.

"Well, this gentleman is quite content for the moment," the goblin grinned. "Let's just say you'll owe me for now."

"I won't do anything against my conscience just to return a favor in the future," Zac said.

"That's fine, that's fine. I'm sure we'll be able to reach an accord." K'Rav said as he floated over toward the ring in Vai's hands.

Vai was visibly uncomfortable with the spectral goblin in such close proximity. Zac wasn't surprised. It wasn't just a matter of appearance, though the goblin looked quite wretched. He emitted a strong corrupting aura, just like that of the purple pillar—the aura of the Lost Plane.

"Those two meatheads, I understand—they only know how to swing their weapons like base animals. But what is your excuse, girl? How do these simple traps elude you? Is this the limits of the modern researcher?"

the goblin said with a scathing look. "Even a Ra'Lashar acolyte would be able to open this ring, many of them without losing a limb."

"I—Ah," Vai stuttered, utterly unprepared for the sudden dressing down.

"Less talk, just open it," Zac grunted.

"I cannot directly interfere with items in my form," the goblin said with a roll of his eyes. "But here."

Dozens of patterns appeared in the air. Most were grey, with a single blue line moving through them like a river. As the blue line passed the various fractals, they transformed, and the whole constellation was reformed after a minute.

"This stumped you for weeks? I had more intricate traps to protect my stash of candies back home," K'Rav snorted with disdain after he'd shown the solution twice. "Well, I guess I shouldn't expect too much from some lunatic who goes around erecting corpse trees. Not even we were so bloodth—"

The goblin didn't get any further, as he was suddenly sucked into the flag, and Ogras hurriedly placed a talisman on it. Vai looked down at the ring, mortified, like she couldn't believe she'd missed such a simple solution. Though Zac could tell the goblin's method was based on an incredibly deep foundation of understanding.

"Don't let that little bastard get to you, lass," Ogras muttered from the side. "Their civilization didn't even last the lifespan of a single Hegemon. Their way of research drew them straight into the abyss."

"There's no need to feel bad," Zac agreed. "You have other fields of expertise. Not knowing some unorthodox methods isn't a blemish."

"Thank you," Vai said before her eyes glazed over. "Wait, corpse trees? Why does that sound so familiar?"

"You just had to run your mouth to that guy?" Zac whispered to the demon with exasperation.

"Hey, I've been stuck here for years with only that bastard to talk to. And you told me you both showed your face and introduced yourself to the lass. How is this girl's brain wired if she can't realize the truth from those things, but a random mention of a corpse tree sparks some recognition?" Ogras said.

"Still," Zac snorted.

"Well, this is my bad, okay? I haven't needed to filter my words for over a decade, and I guess I slipped up. I'll fix it."

The next moment, the demon appeared in front of Vai in a puff of smoke.

"Lass, don't space out," Ogras said to the startled researcher as he took out something Zac had never seen before. "I found this thing inside one of the Spatial Rings as well. I've never seen it before. Can you identify it?"

"That... That's..." Vai stuttered until her eyes finally focused on the shimmering crystal in Ogras' hand.

Zac looked at it with marvel. It resembled an opalescent Cosmic Crystal but didn't seem to hold any energy. Even then, Zac found his cells greedily screaming for the gem. It was chock-full of Dao, and by the looks of it, something Zac had never seen before.

Certainly, he had all kinds of Attuned Crystals in his possession, but this was the first time he'd seen a crystal filled with only the Dao. It wasn't just one Dao either. Zac could feel all three of his Dao Branches resonate with what was within.

"Is it a Dao Treasure?" Zac hesitated.

"Doubt it," Ogras said as he took out two more. "This looks like an actual crystal that has been mined or fished out from these ponds."

"How interesting," Vai said with excitement as she took out a couple of instruments. "Let me run some readings on it."

"Could you please unlock the ring first?" Zac smiled.

"Ah?" Vai said before her eyes widened in remembrance. "Ah, right!"

"We'll stand guard outside to not disturb you," Zac nodded as he dragged Ogras onto one of the branches outside.

"Did you really find those things in the invader's Cosmos Sack?" Zac asked when they were once more isolated.

"Hardly," Ogras snorted. "We found them shortly after arriving in this place. We call them Dao Stones, and I think they were created along with the world. They were key in speeding up my comprehension, but they aren't as useful for me now that I have Dao Branches."

"How many do you have?" Zac asked.

"Why do you ask?" Ogras asked suspiciously.

"Just give me a couple of them later." Zac rolled his eyes. "I want to see if they're useful for me."

Pushing his Branches of Kalpataru and Pale Seal to Middle Proficiency was some ways off, but Zac could feel he wasn't too far from taking that step with his Branch of the War Axe. His last breakthrough was over five years ago back in the Twilight Ocean, and he'd not only massively improved his understanding of Axes since then, but even entered the Integration Stage with his techniques.

He just needed a final push to break through, and these Dao Stones seemed like a good, clean way to fuel the process. Dao Treasures always held some truths of their own, which could influence the direction of the breakthrough if one wasn't careful. Meanwhile, these things appeared untainted.

"They should work even for a brute like you," Ogras said. "I think it's trapped Origin Dao inside. Can't give out too many, though. They're my golden egg for when I get out of here."

"So stingy," Zac sighed. "I guess I'll keep my treasury to myself then."

"Treasury? What treasury?" Ogras said with a mix of anticipation and suspicion.

"This is the current Merit Exchange back home," Zac smiled as he threw over a crystal.

Ogras stared at Zac for a second before turning his attention to the contents of the Information Crystal.

"Th-This," Ogras stuttered, eyes as wide as saucers.

"Naturally, the really good things aren't put there. These are just the random baubles I picked up along the way."

"Along the way?" Ogras swore as he threw back the Information Crystal with disgust. "Did you stroll through the treasuries of an ancient faction? Fine, take as many stones as you want. I can't even look at you right now. I have to go meditate."

With that, he flashed away and pointedly sat down with his back toward Zac as he gazed out across the salt lakes from the edge of a branch. Zac laughed and sat down. But instead of brooding, Zac pushed the trapped Kill Energy into his 148th node until it cracked open with a snap.

Zac took a deep breath then ate a Soul Nurturing pill, which helped with the headache. Vai was still fast at work with the lipless Hegemon's ring, so Zac spent the next couple of hours redrawing the pathways in his head.

"I'm done!" Vai said from within the tree hollow a couple of hours later, at which point Zac was mostly recovered.

"What's wrong?" Vai asked with worry as she looked back and forth between Zac and Ogras as they entered the hollow.

"Nothing," Ogras grunted, taking an angry swig from his wine. "Sometimes, you just wonder if the Heavens have eyes."

Zac smiled as he sat down next to Vai. "Don't mind him. How did it go?"

"It's done!" Vai confirmed. "I have never seen a method like the one the… ah… gentleman, showed. It's worthy of further study. I think it might even be useful against some of the other methods of the Kan'Tanu."

"That's great." Zac took the Spatial Treasure. "You'll save a lot of lives if you manage to build some array breakers for the upcoming war."

Vai eagerly nodded while Zac turned his attention to the contents of the unlocked ring. As expected, there was a lot more stuff inside this one compared to the Spatial Tools of the previous Kan'Tanu infiltrators he'd taken out. For example, there were ten Low-grade Cosmic Crystals, which translated to 1,000 D-grade Nexus Coins.

Even for Zac, that was a pretty good haul, especially considering Cosmic Crystals were almost impossible to get in Zecia outside the C-grade continents. Apart from that, there were multiple sets of arrays, Natural Treasures, and other materials Zac suspected were for practicing sound-based skills.

There were also a few vials of a dark-red liquid that gave Zac an awful feeling. At first, he thought the bottles contained Heart Curses because of the similar energy they gave off, but Vai said that wasn't it. There was no actual array hidden in the liquid, and Vai guessed it was a unique concoction meant to nurture the Heart Curses.

Zac shuddered at the thought of having such a creepy parasite inside his body and being forced to feed it to make it even stronger. He kept a few of those bottles to himself while handing the rest to Vai as a gift to the Void Gate. Neither he nor the people back at Port Atwood could gain anything from those things, but the researchers at the Void Gate might be able to use them to manufacture weapons or antidotes against the curses.

The various items weren't that interesting to Zac. More important was a set of maps, notes, and Information Crystals. After confirming there wasn't a second layer of traps, Zac scanned the items one by one, and his brows furrowed into consternation. The maps weren't very detailed apart from a couple of sectors, but together with the notes, they told a troubling story.

"Looks like I have to eat some pills after all," Zac sighed.

"What's going on?" Vai asked, and Ogras looked over.

"The infiltrators found this realm before it even entered the Stellar Ladder, and they broke inside long before the Void Gate did," Zac said as he handed the other two the notes. "Judging by these, there might be over ten thousand infiltrators stationed in this realm alone. They're led by someone called Reincarnator Ul and have some important mission."

"Mission?" Ogras said with a frown as he started scanning the documents.

"The lipless cultivator was sent toward the mountain range over two months ago to investigate some energy signatures," Zac said.

"Your opportunity, they were looking for it as well?" Vai asked with surprise.

"Looks like it."

"Well, shit," Ogras muttered.

"Th-Then it's at least good news we came here, even if it's dangerous," Vai said, though she looked rattled. "Seeing that pillar, I bet they are up to no good."

"Are the rest of them in the area?" Ogras asked as he turned to the map.

"Doesn't look like it. This side of the Mystic Realm is mostly unexplored." Zac pointed at the east side of the map. "I can't find any mention of what their mission is, but their main base is over here."

"Over there?" Ogras said with surprise. "That's not good. Not good at all."

"Why? What's over there?" Zac frowned. "The Kingdom of Billy?"

"No," the demon sighed as he looked at the pitch-black section on the map with a complex expression. "That's the ruins of the Kingdom of Ra'Lashar."

# 8

# PREPARING FOR THE WORST

"The Kingdom of Ra'Lashar? What the hell are they doing over there?" Zac asked.

"Nothing good, I assume," Ogras said.

"Are you sure there's nothing left there?"

"Shouldn't be," Ogras said, but he didn't look too confident. "After my quest there finished, the whole thing collapsed. A Spatial Rift swallowed the central tower. I searched the area for months for anything of value before moving on to other parts of the realm. If they found something powerful left behind by those lunatics, we're in trouble. Everything they made was extremely dangerous."

"Can you ask your guy?" Zac ventured.

The demon nodded, but Zac knew it wasn't good as his face gradually turned into a scowl.

"He says he has no idea, but I wouldn't trust him as far as I could throw him."

Zac looked to the black spot on the map. He wasn't convinced the Kan'Tanu's mission was related to the Ra'Lashar themselves, and neither was Ogras, judging by his expression. Between their search for the sigils of the Left Imperial Palace, their interest in the mountain range, and now the Ra'Lashar, it felt like it was connected to this Lost Plane.

Were there more seals hidden in the ruins of the goblin empire? And if there were, should they do something about it?

The trio studied the map for a few seconds until Ogras sighed and pointed at a much closer spot on the map. "The Kingdom of Billy is around here. No matter what these invaders are up to, our first destination hasn't changed. Let's just continue on our way while we keep our eyes open."

"Give me an hour or two. I'm pushing to Peak E-grade right now," Zac said.

Zac had hoped to avoid this step and gain his levels through battle instead. The consecutive blasts of Tribulation Lightning had cleansed his body, including impurities that had gone unnoticed by his Purity of the Void. It was a shame to ruin that now, but reading the reports put Zac under a lot of pressure. He couldn't just give up a power-up that was so near at hand.

Thankfully, his pills were extremely High-quality, and there were only two nodes he needed to open. What little impurities he gained shouldn't cause any real problems when forming his Cultivator's Core. One by one, his prepared treasures were brought out, from the [Stone of Hope] to the mysterious ice that froze his soul to harden it.

The only thing he skipped was the [Chainbreaking Pills], as they weren't needed any longer since his latest Soul Reincarnation. Zac wasted no time as he chugged down four Pseudo D-grade pills in one go, eliciting a shocked gasp from Vai and a disgusted snort from Ogras. He ignored the clamor and focused his frozen mind on channeling everything into the 149th node in his head.

Half an hour later, Zac grunted as the node on the back of his head broke wide open. Zac drew a ragged breath and applied more ice. He was halfway there, and planned on riding this wave to the end. The final node of the E-grade was located right by his glabella—the last blockage in his pathways.

Waves of Radiant energies poured into the node, but it was like the mysterious swirl was a bottomless hole that couldn't be satiated. Eventually, the efficacy of his Node-breaking Pills ran out, but he stubbornly ate another mouthful. Finally, after what felt like an eternity, Zac knew he was right there.

His danger sense had cut through his turbid thoughts, and he reinforced his Mental Barriers as best as he could while [Stone of Hope] lit up and illuminated the space. Zac felt like his soul was split in two as a powerful ripple burst out from his forehead. He heard surprised exclamations from the other two, but they were distant and indistinct.

Zac was completely focused on the state of his body. Blood ran down his nose from a deep cut, and it must have looked like a third eye had formed on his forehead. Thankfully, it was just a wound rather than a mysterious mutation. An outlet Zac opened to avoid damaging his frontal lobe. Opening the node was painful as usual, but it couldn't compare to the sense of completeness that filled him.

A surge of energy coursed through his body as Zac took a deep breath. It felt vibrant and powerful, and it wasn't just the attributes he'd just gained. With his 75 nodes all being open, his pathways were finally completely unclogged. The energy gently circulating through his body was natural and unconstrained. It wouldn't do much for his actual combat strength, but anything that allowed him to handle and communicate with his Cosmic Energy was a welcome thing.

The Peak of the E-grade.

Less than a fraction of a fraction of all cultivators reached this step, yet he'd done it as a mortal. Of course, this was just the start. He was merely an ant in the grand scheme of things, but that didn't douse his excitement as he opened his eyes. Ogras and Vai were both looking at him expectantly, and Zac nodded slightly with a smile.

"You done?" Ogras asked.

"Just need to fill the nodes up with energy, but we can do that on the way."

"What was that before?" Ogras asked curiously. "Why does it look like you split in two every time you open a node?"

"It's a treasure I got my hands on," Zac explained. "I don't know exactly how it works, but it's like the treasure pushes some of the damage to an alternate reality while lessening the damage to me. Why? Do you need to borrow it?"

"No, I've long since reached level 150," Ogras said with a shake of his head. "It was just interesting. I felt the phenomenon somewhat resonate with my path. Making real damage fake, huh?"

"W-wait," Vai interjected. "You're not a Hegemon either?"

"If I were a Hegemon, I would have flown myself and the two of you over this place, no?" Ogras said with a grin as the shadows started to flicker around him.

"But you're so powerful," Vai said with wide eyes.

"Well, at least *someone* has an eye for talent," Ogras grinned, obviously satisfied with the reaction.

"Don't stroke his ego," Zac snorted. "Give me another hour before we set out, I just have to recover a bit more from opening the nodes."

"Do you have more Soul Crystals?" Ogras asked. "I used up the two in the ring you gave me."

"Be careful with those," Zac said as he threw over another one. "They're almost impossible to restock."

"You're the one who wants me to use my domain every time the lass sees a bright light in the bowl," Ogras grinned as the crystal disappeared into the sleeves of his robes.

Zac spent the next hour redrawing his pathways until they were in workable order. He would still be a bit weakened for another week, but Ogras had already said it would take them at least three to reach the Kingdom of Billy at their pace. It should be enough time not only to recover, but to push his level to 150.

The moment Zac felt able to fight without accidentally damaging his pathways, the group set out, heading deeper and deeper into the Badlands. Ogras became the primary combatant over the following days while Zac let his nodes stabilize. Zac simply became bait and a meat shield while the demon did the killing.

To expedite his level, Zac constantly held onto Peak-quality Nexus Crystals as they ran, and torrents of energy poured into his nodes. Not only that, Zac also absorbed energy from Beast Crystals he'd hidden within his robes. The messy energy was swallowed by [Void Heart] and spat out as malleable energy that became a second river to speed up his progress.

After a week passed, Zac resumed fighting, and Ogras helped organize things so Zac delivered all the killing blows on beasts above Late E-grade. It turned to a third source of energy, yet it still took two weeks before Zac managed to fill all three nodes. The group took the opportunity for a brief stop to rest up before reaching Billy's place, and Zac opened his Status Screen to check what his level brought.

**Name:** Zachary Atwood
**Level:** 150

**Class:** [E-Epic] Edge of Arcadia
**Race:** [D] Human - Void Emperor (Corrupted)
**Alignment:** [Zecia] Atwood Empire – Baron of Conquest

**Titles:** […] Grand Fate, Blooddrenched Baron, Connate
Conqueror, The Second Step, Singular Specialist
**Limited Titles:** Tower of Eternity Sector All-Star – 14th, The
Final Twilight, Equanimity, Heart of Fire, Big Axe Gladiator
**Dao:** Branch of the War Axe – Early, Branch of the Kalpataru –
Early, Branch of the Pale Seal – Early
**Core:** [E] Duplicity

**Strength:** 20,876 [Increase: 143%. Efficiency: 287%]
**Dexterity:** 8,674 [Increase: 103%. Efficiency: 206%]
**Endurance:** 15,727 [Increase: 134%. Efficiency: 287%]
**Vitality:** 14,192 [Increase: 127%. Efficiency: 273%]
**Intelligence:** 3,763 [Increase: 97%. Efficiency: 206%]
**Wisdom:** 6,940 [Increase: 104%. Efficiency: 216%]
**Luck:** 712 [Increase: 121%. Efficiency: 229%]

**Free Points:** 250
**Nexus Coins:** [D] 933,647

A single glance at his Status Screen confirmed what he'd already learned: a full 250 Free attribute points were waiting for him rather than just the ten. It was an even greater boon than the 20 attribute points he got when reaching level 75. And that was just the start. Not only did Peak E-grade provide a full 250 free points, but also a new title called The Second Step. There was even a second title waiting for him, one Zac hadn't been able to confirm but certainly hoped for.

**[The Second Step: Reach the Peak of E-grade. Reward:** All Stats
+10, Base Stats +90]
**[Singular Specialist:** Reach 20,000 points in a single attribute before
reaching D-grade. **Reward:** All Stats +10, Strength +5%, All attributes
+5%.]

As expected, it was related to the old Promising Specialist title Zac got when reaching 1,000 Endurance in F-grade. He hadn't gotten anything when reaching 10,000 Strength, but he'd learned Ogras got one during his stay in this Mystic Realm. The mention had made him wonder if it was a tiered title, and his Status Screen proved it was.

The combination of hitting level 150 and the title that came with it had narrowly pushed him over 20,000 attribute points, double the level of the first checkpoint of the skill. A quick check also confirmed Promising Specialist was gone, replaced with the new title rather than him having both. It was a bit of a disappointment, but the old title had only provided +5 all attributes and +5% Endurance. The new one was a pure upgrade, especially for his Strength.

Still, it made Zac wonder if there were an Apex title, one that would provide Attribute Efficiency. Perhaps if you reached your attribute limit?

Since he'd already passed 20,000 Strength and gotten the title to match, Zac poured all of his free points into Dexterity. Altogether, the three levels had given him almost a 5% increase in his attribute pool, and they were mainly targeted at Strength and Dexterity. That was exactly what Zac wanted. Anything that would allow him to hit a bit harder and faster at this stage was a welcome addition.

It was a shame he didn't have a quick way to gain the last five levels to his undead side as well, but the boost still gave Zac some confidence when the trio set out again six hours later. He still hoped he wouldn't find himself face-to-face with a whole army of infiltrators, possibly led by hundreds of Hegemons. A few levels and titles wouldn't help against *that*.

But some things were simply unavoidable.

Four days after his breakthrough, Ogras proclaimed they were within the official borders of the Kingdom of Billy. They'd already left the Badlands behind and had entered a much more familiar type of environment—large tree groves with grassy plains between them.

There were also signs of human intervention—enormous yet simple trenches and traps designed to deal with beast tides. However, just as the group was about to pass the battlements, Vai stilled.

"Enemies!" Vai whispered, and the air around them started to glimmer as Ogras powered up his domain before they jumped into the trench and dug a temporary hideout.

"How many?" Zac asked after they'd erected an isolation array.

"Thirty, they're moving fast," Vai said. "Looks like a scouting party."

"Do you think it's Billy's people? Those Gnivelings you mentioned?" Zac asked.

"Doubtful," Ogras said with a shake of his head. "Billy doesn't need any scouts. The Realm Spirit is more effective than any scouting unit."

"If there are scouting parties this close…" Vai hesitated.

"Then they definitely know about the Kingdom of Billy," Zac sighed. "We might be in for a fight. Do you want to stay here?"

"N-No," Vai said with a shake of her head, gripping her bowl tighter. "I'm coming with. I can still help. We are days away from the settlement, and you need a scout."

Ogras shrugged. "She's right. I can't guarantee my methods will work against all types of scouts, and it just takes one set of sharp eyes to expose us."

"Let's keep going like this, then," Zac agreed. "We avoid enemy squads as long as possible until we figure out Billy's situation. He might have relocated already."

The three waited an hour for the scouting party to leave the area before they set out, but they met another group just three hours later and a third scouting party after another five. Even Ogras had a somber expression by that point. There was still a chance for it to be a coincidence with one group. With three, it was all but certain the infiltrators were carrying out some big operation in the area.

And that operation was definitely related to the Kingdom of Billy.

Not only that, the infiltrators seemed to be expecting trouble judging by the parties.

They managed to creep closer and closer to their destination over the next three days. Until Vai's bowl almost lit up like a bonfire, prompting both Zac and Ogras to look over with confusion.

"S-Signals," Vai stuttered. "So many. Thousands."

"Shit," Ogras said. "Billy's castle isn't far from here."

"Let's go," Zac said, and they kept moving until a powerful energy wave swept past them.

"There's a battle," Zac said with relief.

"The brute is actually holding out against an army?" Ogras said, confusion written all over his face. "How is that possible?"

"The Void Gate," Vai said, her eyes glimmering. "I bet they are here fighting against the bad guys. Where else would they have gone but here?"

Zac finally understood why Vai was so adamant about joining them for this final stretch. She believed there was a good chance the elite Void Gate warriors would be found with Billy. And perhaps she was right. Twenty minutes later, they managed to sneak a peek at the battlefield.

A lonesome mountain peak stood within a barricaded crater. The whole cavity was protected by a bubble that reeked of powerful Spatial Energies, and outside, a mighty army was laying siege. Over thirty enormous towers had been erected, and Zac could sense how they were accumulating power. If he had to guess, the earlier outburst came from these things firing simultaneously.

"What are we supposed to do now ?" Ogras said. "Fight our way inside? The castle is sealed shut. They're not fighting back at all. I don't know if we'd even manage to get through the barrier. And if we do, then what? We'd be stuck inside just like Billy."

Zac wasn't sure what to do either. Eventually, he turned to Vai, who looked at the scene wide-eyed. "How many Hegemons are there?"

By this point, normal E-grade cultivators didn't really matter to him. The only difference between fighting ten and a thousand was how long it would take to win and making sure he didn't run out of steam first. The problem was the Hegemons hidden within their ranks. A defensive Hegemon could almost completely nullify his attacks, while offensive ones could unleash powerful barrages at him.

If there were too many, there was simply no chance he could take on all these people himself.

"Over eighty," Vai grimaced. "Eighty Hegemons."

"Impossible," Ogras resolutely said with a shake of his head. "There is *no way* I'm fighting that. I'm not dying like this after I finally have a shot at getting out of here."

"How about we send a distress beacon to the Void Gate to confirm if they're inside?" Zac asked, then there was a sudden change that made him freeze.

A substantial spatial bubble had started to grow on the barrier in the distance. In just a moment, it was half as big as the barrier itself, while the shield seemed to have lost some of its luster. The new bubble bulged out ominously toward a flank of the infiltrator army, who started running for their lives. The bubble popped, and over a hundred cultivators were torn apart as a beam of spatial chaos shot out.

Right toward them.

"Hurry, Gemmy is making a path!" a childish voice echoed in their ears just as Zac was about to turn tail and run for his life.

Zac glanced at Ogras, who looked positively nauseated. It was clear he recognized the voice, so it was obvious to Zac who it belonged to. There was no hesitation as he grabbed Ogras with his left hand and Vai with a vine as he rushed straight for the incoming chaos.

"I knew it," the demon groaned. "I knew there'd be trouble when I heard that voice."

# 9

# BREAKING THROUGH

The explosion released from the spatial barrier surrounding Billy's place expanded in a straight line. Every second, it grew a mile longer, already having left the army behind as it made its way toward Zac and his two companions.

"This is a bad idea," Ogras muttered as he slunk out of Zac's grip, keeping pace. "You can't trust that fool of a Realm Spirit to know what it's doing."

An ominous ripple spread through the spatial beam, as if cursed by the demon's unlucky words. Zac's eyes widened in alarm, and he activated his movement skill, but then frantically canceled it when his mind screamed of mortal danger. It was just in time as well. His contraction of space had created small fissures in front of him.

"What the—" Ogras groaned as he emerged bloody from a puff of shadows, clearly having encountered a similar phenomenon.

There was no time to answer as Zac desperately scrambled out of the way. He narrowly avoided getting split in two thanks to Vivi's vines, but he still felt a cold sensation as the spatial tear nicked him. From there, the errant burst of energy continued past as it carved an enormous crevasse into the ground.

Another one had streaked through the enemy lines, instantly killing a set of unlucky souls while cutting apart one of the siege towers.

"How can space be this brittle?" Vai exclaimed, turning visibly pale.

"Can't you feel it?" Ogras grunted as he pointed at the dissipating tear. "It's not pure."

Zac's brows furrowed as he sensed what the demon was getting at. There really was a hint of the Lost Plane's madness inside that spatial tear, though it was still barely discernible.

"This realm might really be crumbling!" Vai cried.

No matter how weak the sign was, it wasn't good news. They hadn't seen the situation improve over the past week, but neither had it deteriorated. To see hints of the Lost Plane this far from his pillar, especially in conjunction with how brittle space was, proved the situation might be even worse than they'd feared.

"We'll worry about that later," Zac said, speaking to himself as much as the others. "We need to move—they've spotted us."

"Into that *deathtrap*?" Ogras said with a raised brow.

"It'll be fine." Zac kept running toward the incoming chaos, even if he wasn't without misgivings.

It wasn't only foolhardiness and blind faith that propelled him forward, though the madness inside the tears had been an unwelcome surprise. Thanks to [Rapturous Divide] and his study of the theories in the Book of Duality, Zac had a good idea of what Billy or the Realm Spirit were planning. He'd noticed it right away. The core of the incoming shockwave was hollow and expanding.

As expected, the corridor of destruction soon collapsed, creating two spatial storms that blocked out the invaders while a third covered the sky. Between the storms, a 100-meter-wide pathway mostly free of spatial turbulence appeared, leading all the way to the walled fort in the distance. It was a solid idea, and would have been almost perfect if not for space turning so brittle.

There was no way he'd dare use his movement skill in this kind of environment after his previous close encounter. He might accidentally step into the Void if he did that. Perhaps even the Lost Plane. Even using too-powerful attacks was risky, though that was as much a strength as a weakness since it restrained the enemies as well. Most importantly, the spatial beam opened a path for them while keeping the invaders at bay.

Most of them, at least.

Zac knew first-hand how dangerous those kinds of spatial storms were to traverse, but it wasn't impossible. A few of the invaders were already making their way through under the urgings of their superiors. Some were even thrown inside when they refused to move. However, most were led by Hegemons, who used brute force to carve a path.

Dozens learned the same lesson they had, and Zac spotted a Hegemon get swallowed by a spatial tear when he tried to teleport through the storm. Meanwhile, hundreds of warriors were rushing toward Zac, wanting to intercept their approach or use their entrance.

"I'll take the left," the demon said as dark clouds made from shadows started to spread, while Zac tried conjuring a fractal blade.

Space held together even under the pressure of [Nature's Edge] empowered by two of his Dao Branches, but Zac could feel it wouldn't be able to endure much more punishment than that. Still, that was all Zac needed as he unleashed a constant stream of fractal leaves toward the right.

The closest warriors, who previously made up the army's rear, initially tried to block Zac's attacks with various defensive skills. That only resulted in a scene of utter carnage as blades empowered by two Dao Branches and a monstrous amount of strength cut through everything in their path.

The situation wasn't as lopsided on the other side, with Ogras using all kinds of tools to impede the incoming tide of warriors. Hidden spears rose from the shadows, illusions made warriors turn on their allies, and an obscuring haze led people straight into the spatial storms. It formed a dangerous web that delayed their enemies long enough for Zac and his companions to enter the pathway. In their wake, Ogras released his illusory shroud, which would give them a head start for the final stretch.

"Can you destabilize the storms even further?" Zac asked of Vai, who nodded after some hesitation.

The researcher started releasing spatial ripples from her vine seat, which entered the churning storms at their sides. The swells were instilled with Vai's Spatial Dao Branch, and the storms picked up ferocity everywhere they passed. Warriors who were narrowly hanging on suddenly found themselves overwhelmed by a barrage of spatial tears and were ripped to shreds.

She also sent ripples to their rear, opening up large, jagged scars in their wake. She managed to connect the two storms, though the barrier was nowhere near as thick as the ones to their sides. Still, having a

Spatial Cultivator proved extremely useful, and she singlehandedly averted more than five ambushes as they ran toward the fort.

Soon enough, a whole squad of warriors emerged from the storm, led by a defensive Hegemon who'd simply blocked out the innumerable spatial tears. The group was a bit bloodied and battered, but their auras were solid as they formed an iron wall between Zac's group and the wall in the distance.

Just as they formed their defensive perimeter, a deep rumble echoed through the area, and a golden mountain rose from the ground right at their feet. The Hegemon slammed down on it with an enormous, engraved pillar he carried, and it formed some sort of seal on the ground.

The seal groaned in protest upon colliding with the golden mountain peak, narrowly withstanding the unrelenting push. However, the energy the Hegemon unleashed was just too powerful, and spatial tears sprung up all around the invaders. One struck the Hegemon on his left arm, and Ogras used the opportunity to activate a familiar strike.

Two lances of condensed shadows appeared, one behind and one in front of the Hegemon, who suddenly found himself under attack from every direction. He wasn't the only one in trouble, as the activation created a series of spatial tears all around Zac and the others. Zac knew this would happen, and already had ample experience dodging them since his time in the research base.

Zac pushed through the spatial turbulence just in time to see one of the shadow lances strike the Hegemon right in his heart. It wasn't enough to kill the man—some sort of plate hidden beneath his robes blocked the strike—but the force pushed him right into a spatial tear that tore up his back.

Together, it was enough to destabilize the defensive seal, and the golden mountain below pushed through with redoubled ferocity. It contained an immense weight, and some of the E-grade warriors were crushed from the pressure alone. Others managed to avoid the mayhem but were forced back into the spatial storm.

By that point, Zac and Ogras were already upon the stragglers, and they finished off the Hegemon with a blitz assault of ferocious swings before they rounded the mountain. Even then, the three were covered in wounds due to the mountain conjuring too many tears to perfectly avoid them all.

After passing the mountain, they'd already crossed two-thirds of the corridor, and Zac smiled as he saw a familiar form standing at the mouth of the barrier like a stalwart tower. Billy looked almost exactly like before, except his hair had turned golden just like it did in his transformed state. If Zac had to guess, it meant Billy had properly awakened his bloodline.

There was also a powerful sense of oppression emanating from his fleshy body, and it felt like a mountain was blocking the gated entrance rather than a person. Just a bloodline wasn't enough to give off such a brutal aura, and neither was stacking strength. The titan must have not only awakened his Titanic heritage, but also cultivated some sort of Body Tempering Method to the limits of the E-grade.

Zac didn't want the giant to accidentally thwonk him or Vai, so his face started to morph back into its original form as they closed in on the opening in the spatial barrier. A wide smile immediately spread across Billy's face when he saw Zac's appearance.

"Haha! Super Brother Man has finally found Billy! And you even found stupid Horny Guy!" A booming laugh echoed through the area.

Zac was about to answer, but two more Hegemons appeared to bar their path. They didn't look too happy about the situation, knowing which way the wind blew. They were pincered between an unmovable Billy and Zac, who was already bearing down on them like a runaway train.

The first of the two grit his teeth and pointed at Zac, prompting a hundred bloody suns to appear above his head. Zac felt a sense of danger from them, but one didn't need his level of Luck to realize they spelled trouble. Space crackled around the glowing orbs, and the whole pathway started rapidly deteriorating.

"Be prepared in case my barrier fails," Zac said as a golden laurel appeared on his head.

Three pillars rose from the ground behind him, enclosing Ogras, Vai, and Zac in a barrier. It was one of the features of the skill reaching Middle Proficiency. With three pillars rather than two, his defensive skill would either turn more durable, or he could protect a third person.

The activation was just in time, as a rain of deadly rays descended on their position. Each sanguine sun was like a turret that released one beam after another, but the suns were also falling toward them like a manufactured meteor shower, each orb creating trailing spatial tears in their wake.

Zac frowned at the incoming mayhem, hesitant whether he would have to unleash one of his more powerful attacks. But space was already at a breaking point from those orbs. What would happen if he added |Arcadia's Judgement| to the mix? At the same time, he wasn't confident his skill could block both the spatial tears and the Hegemon's skill.

An angry roar broke the status quo as Billy swung his club. Weirdly enough, it crashed into empty space like it was a solid, and huge cracks spread toward the Hegemons. Amazingly, not a single spatial tear moved in Billy's direction—they were all heading outward. Had Billy gained insights into the Dao of Space, or was the Dimensional Seed helping him?

Either way, it forced the second Hegemon's hand. He stood guard against Billy, then made a different choice from his companion—he fled instead of taking on the giant's attack. He turned into a stream of blood that cut through the spatial chaos, the skill looking a lot like the ones the scouts in the mountain range used.

Something like that was a risky gambit, but he made it to the outer edges of the spatial storm before the skill collapsed, and he emerged as a bloody mess. He was covered in scars and lost one leg, but he was alive. That left a shocked and enraged Hegemon behind, who suddenly faced the incoming spatial tears from behind.

The Hegemon turned and unleashed a bloody storm, and the brief bout of inattention cost him dearly. Ogras appeared out of nowhere from the man's shadow, and his spear pierced straight into the man's bicep. It was far from a lethal wound, but that didn't mean Ogras had missed.

Instead of targeting a lethal point that might be protected like before, Ogras targeted the Skill Fractal for the skill in the sky. The suns shuddered, then started to lose their cohesiveness, with only the Hegemon's Dao keeping the skill together. With the skill broken, Zac no longer felt any need to activate one of his finishers.

The remaining efficacy of |Empyrean Aegis| would be enough to deal with the fallout, so Zac threw Vai to Ogras, who'd appeared back by their side with a new set of wounds. As expected, flashing over like that was dangerous, but sometimes you had to take a risk. The ground beneath Zac's feet cracked as he pushed forward with all his might, propelling himself straight through the storm of spatial tears and collapsing suns.

A fractal leaf no larger than a meter and a half swung down, its form shrouded by two extremely condensed clouds in black and gold. The Hegemon condensed another barrier, but it was futile in front of a condensed [Rapturous Divide] empowered by Zac's Dao and a collapsing spacetime.

A colossal scar in space cut straight through the man and continued into the spatial storms, swallowing the two apparitions of the Abyss and Arcadia. It even reached the army outside, and Zac watched the chaotic scene with wide eyes as dozens of energy streams entered his body. Thank god he'd angled the strike away from the fort.

With the Hegemon dead, the final obstacle between himself and Billy was gone. The giant was excitedly waving his club like he hadn't just brutalized two Hegemons and scared off another. Space was actively collapsing, but they were right at the home stretch.

Ogras caught up with Vai slung over his shoulder, and the three passed through the barrier. The spatial bubble closed behind them, cutting off the spatial tears that looked ready to swallow everything around them. The grating sound of the tearing space and pained cries of the warriors caught in the storm were cut off as well, leaving only their panting breaths and Billy's booming laugh.

"Haha, did you like Billy's mountain?" The giant grinned as he excitedly swung his nasty club like it was made out of foam.

"It was very cool." Zac grinned, relieved to see space was perfectly stable inside the barrier. "It's nice to finally see you again."

"Gemmy helped too!" the childish voice from before exclaimed as a shimmering crystal flew out from one of Billy's pockets. "Billy says you can help bash the bad guys and cure Gemmy?"

"Are… you the Dimensional Seed?" Zac asked, staring at the floating gem curiously.

"Gemmy is Gemmy," the gem hummed. "You are stupid. But why do you smell familiar?"

"Uh," Zac hesitated. "We met once when you were younger. We helped each other out to escape from some bad guys."

"Ah! Gemmy remembers! Gemmy was inside you!" The floating

gem giggled, which drew odd looks from Ogras and Vai. "Your body is weird. Hungry. Hungry Guy."

"Well, uh…" Zac coughed.

"Ah, Gemmy is tired. Going to take a nap in the fire." The gem flew off toward the innards of the fort, and Zac saw that Vai was just as confused as he felt.

"Like I never left," Ogras sighed.

"Finally, friends have come to help. Welcome to Kingdom of Billy!" Billy excitedly exclaimed as he followed the Dimensional Seed.

"So, are we just going to pretend the army outside isn't there? Or that space isn't apparently on the verge of collapse?" Ogras said as they walked through the thick wall.

"Billy hasn't forgotten how you tricked the Smallboys and stole Dao Stones, Horny Guy," Billy snorted. "And Billy has a plan to fix everything."

"You have a plan?" Ogras asked as they emerged on the other side. "I'd had hoped to die between the bosoms of two succubae, but I guess this place will have to do."

"Let's just list—" Zac said, but he was interrupted by a series of hurried steps and a loud exclamation.

"Vai! *Is that you*?"

Zac looked over with confusion, vaguely recognizing the voice, and his brows rose when he saw not one, but two familiar faces run toward them.

# 10

# ALWAYS SOMETHING

Each step Leyara Lioress took rippled with space as she was propelled forward across the fort. She looked the same as the last time they met—apart from the revealing garments she wore in the Base Town. They'd been replaced by a dress more in line with the long white robes most of the Void Gate nuns wore.

Leyara's aura was surprisingly condensed, and Zac realized Vai might have been generous when she placed Ogras at the same power level. Her aura even eclipsed most of the elites Zac had seen in the Twilight Ascent, including those from outside factions. Not only that, but she wore a set of glove-like Spirit Tools with huge gemstones on the back of her hands.

Knowing who Leyara's master was, they were probably Peak-quality Spirit tools. Who knew what other items she carried around.

Seeing Leyara here in the depths of the Dimensional Seed was shocking, but it was even more unexpected to see Pretty Peak by her side. Rather than a dress, she had opted to wear an engraved set of leather armor that emitted a powerful aura of carnage. If Zac had to guess, the leather had been tanned with High-grade beast blood to give it such a ferocious feeling, and Pretty's martial air only further amplified it.

Even then, Pretty's aura wasn't quite as condensed as Leyara's, though it wasn't that far off. It felt a bit backward after learning about the crazy Peak family. Then again, Leyara wasn't some nobody. She was a handpicked Terminal Disciple of one of the most powerful cultivators in the Sector, while Pretty Peak came from a powerful clan in the Allbright Empire.

"Ah, the slow girl is here," Billy muttered as he looked at Leyara with some trepidation. "Always asking Billy about the design, never understanding."

"Design?" Zac said, giving Billy a curious look.

Billy turned excited again, but he was interrupted before he could explain.

"You! What are *you* doing here?" Leyara exclaimed when she saw Zac standing between Billy and Vai, her pristine face scrunching into a scowl. "And why have you brought my aunt! Are you crazy?"

Only then did Zac remember he'd reverted to his original face to avoid getting accidentally thwonked. His mind momentarily froze with panic, then he regained his calm, because it didn't matter. The whole point of going undercover was to hide his identity until he could contact Leyara, which was moot now that she was standing right in front of him.

"Little Lara!" Vai cried, running over to her niece, tears pooling in her eyes as she threw herself into Leyara's arms. "I'm so happy to see you. The Void Star is a lot scarier than you said."

"I'm glad you're okay." Leyara smiled, patting Vai's head, though her eyes never left Zac. "What are you doing here? Has that guy done anything to you?"

"Ah, Lara, this is, ehm, Gaun Sorom," Vai hurriedly said when she saw her niece's guarded expression. "He's... He's not a bad guy! W-Well, he is a bit greedy, but he helped me a lot! We were on the same mission to stabilize a Spatial Nexus, but things took a turn."

"Gaun Sorom?" Leyara blankly said, glancing between Zac and Vai. "Why do you call him that? That's not his name."

"Eh, you two know each other?" Vai said.

"Why wouldn't I know him?" Leyara sighed. "Aunty, I was the one who told you about him, remember? How we met in the Tower of Eternity?"

"You have been traveling with the Deviant Asura without knowing?" Pretty smiled at Vai then looked Zac up and down. "I almost thought you had died after not hearing from you for so long, but I'm happy to be proven wrong. We need people like you for the upcoming war."

Vai looked like she'd been struck by lightning, her mouth slowly opening and closing without speaking. Zac simply let her process her thoughts for the time being while he dealt with the niece.

"Nice to see the two of you again," Zac said with a wry smile as he turned to Leyara. "I'm sorry about dropping in like this. I had planned on contacting you, but I didn't know how. And with the rumors and the bounties…"

"You think too little of the Void Gate if you thought we cared for those rumors or the Tsarun Bounty," Leyara said with a cute pout. "The Space Gate has probably been brewing in the Million Gates Territory for hundreds of thousands of years. Even if you somehow nudged the events, you could at most have sped things up by a few centuries."

Zac was inwardly relieved. He didn't really think he was responsible for the Space Gate opening either, but it was nice to hear the strongest Spatial Faction in the Zecia sector backed him up on that front. Still, it was an odd coincidence that Leyara and Pretty were in this specific Mystic Realm, considering it might have been the Dimensional Seed that triggered the Space Gate to start opening early.

Was that why they were here, to investigate the source of the turbulence? Or was it related to the Left Imperial Palace and the Lost Plane? Zac was about to ask, but Vai preempted him.

"C-Corpse Trees! Atwood… Piker," Vai stammered, her eyes wide as saucers. "P-Pervert!"

"This is why I said you need to keep up with current events, Aunty," Leyara said with a shake of her head. "You never know when you run into scary people on the outside."

"Y-You're really the Deviant Asura?" Vai asked, her face full of confusion and loss.

"Well, yeah, I guess. Sorry I didn't explain things properly before. I figured it was for the best when you didn't realize who I was. My identity is a bit complicated, and I have a lot of enemies," Zac said. "Still, you shouldn't believe those rumors you might have heard about me."

"So you didn't fight all the Sector elites and then hung them up in your corpse tree?" Vai said, blushing slightly. "B-Before disappearing for hours with a Draugr lady."

"Uh, no. Well, that did happen," Zac coughed, then glared at the demon, who'd been laughing for a while now. "What's so funny?"

"The Deviant Asura?" Ogras snickered, his grin almost splitting his face apart.

"I didn't pick the name," Zac sighed.

"You did when you broadcasted your desire for young women across the whole Sector," Pretty Peak snorted.

"I'm impressed," Ogras whistled. "Here I thought you remained the same bore as before, but it looks you've been living it up on the outside."

"Can we just focus on the matter at hand?" Zac groaned.

"First, explain why you're here," Pretty said. "It's a bit suspicious you've been missing for almost ten years, only to suddenly appear here when the place is crawling with invaders. And you've even been traveling undercover?"

"I needed some stuff inside the Void Star, so I came here to get it. Like I said earlier, I chose to sneak in because I was afraid using my real identity would get me in trouble. Things took a bit of a turn from there as a bunch of infiltrators blew up one of the Spatial Nexuses. Eventually, Vai and I wound up here."

"Fate brought you here?" Leyara asked without much surprise, which prompted both him and Ogras to look at the woman suspiciously.

"I guess you could say that," Zac said. "What about you two?"

"I have been fighting the infiltrators in the Million Gates Territory with the Empire," Pretty Peak said. "But that place is chaotic and hard to traverse, and we simply can't find the Space Gate. So I came to the Void Gate in search of solutions. Then I learned these Kan'Tanu had managed to infiltrate the Void Star, and that there might even be a path to the Space Gate from here."

"You're mounting a counter-attack through the Stellar Ladder?" Zac asked curiously.

"Well, that was the plan, anyway, but things have taken a turn," Pretty grimaced, then glared at Billy. "*Some* people are making things difficult."

"Billy can throw you back in the dungeon if you don't like it, Angry Girl," Billy laughed. "You are no good at drawing the array anyway."

"Is that about the design you mentioned earlier, Billy?" Zac asked.

"You two know each other since before?" Leyara asked when she saw how familiar they were. "How is that possible?"

"Well, Billy is from the same planet as me," Zac shrugged. "We dealt with the incursions together."

"Ah, Billy misses the Ratlight," Billy sighed. "The Ratlight was simpler than this. Thwonk things, and they give you money and make you stronger."

"Why didn't you tell us you were from the outside?" Pretty scowled at Billy. "Or that you knew Zac Atwood? We could have avoided the misunderstandings."

"You didn't ask Billy, so Billy didn't say." Billy shrugged.

"I'm sure this will all make for a good conversation later. Now, I heard there was a plan to get out of this mess alive?" Ogras interjected.

"Ah, right!" the giant exclaimed. "Gemmy is sick, so Billy is healing Gemmy. As long as Gemmy gets better, she can help us."

Zac frowned at hearing such news. This was exactly what he'd been afraid of, that him conjuring the pillar would have harmed the Realm Spirit and this world.

"What do you know about healing Realm Spirits?" Ogras asked with a raised brow. "Did you dream up a solution?"

"Yes! Billy learned it while sleeping!" Billy laughed. "Billy always has the best ideas when asleep."

"Uh," Zac hesitated.

"We were also skeptical at first, but it might actually work," Leyara offered. "Come, look."

"Are you okay?" Zac asked Vai.

"I-It's a lot. I knew you were not just someone from Salosar Seven, but I didn't imagine you were, well," Vai said as she furtively looked at Zac. However, her gaze soon steadied when she looked into his eyes. "I still think you're a good person, even if you are a deviant."

"That's not—" Zac grimaced, but the researcher was dragged off by Leyara and Pretty before he could try to explain himself.

It was very reminiscent of how Galau had been whisked off back then, and the space around the three was soon sealed. Zac could only shake his head and move toward the edge of the crater with the others. The researcher was no doubt recapping her experiences over the past months. Hopefully, Vai wasn't to put off by him being vague about his identity.

Still, the situation was even better than he'd expected. They stumbled onto Leyara, the key to getting out of this place, and plans were already well underway. Of course, this all hinged on this plan Billy had somehow dreamt up, so they weren't entirely out of the woods just yet.

Soon, they reached the crater's edge, and Zac could finally see what was hidden inside—a massive array. It had to be just over a mile in diameter, and it almost completely covered the crater. In its center, the lone peak remained—the mountain that was once an insectoid hive.

There were also some remnants of structures around the peak, but most were being dismantled to give way to the innumerable pathways. The work was still underway, with both humans and some small gnome-like beings working hand in hand, with a few floating Hegemons directing from above.

The array was terrifyingly complex, comprised of hundreds of different sections, most of which Zac couldn't even begin to comprehend. His [Primal Polyglot] wasn't up to deciphering any clues either. Judging by Ogras' surprised and befuddled look, he wasn't expecting this scene either.

"What… is this?" Zac said.

"This array will let Gemmy come with Billy when we leave," Billy said with excitement. "It will make Gemmy into a Pocket Realm."

"A what?" Zac said.

"It's a High-grade technique that doesn't exist on the frontier," a foreign voice said, coming from a Hegemon that floated over. "Hopefully, we will still have time to finish it after your little stunt."

"Bah, stupid guy," Billy glared. "Less complaining and more drawing, or Billy will throw you back into the dungeon."

The Hegemon snorted, giving Zac a second glance, and flew away.

"What's going on? Is the shield failing?" Zac asked.

"Gemmy is sick," Billy said again with a sad expression. "She can't gather much energy any longer, and bad guys outside are wasting it."

"And letting us inside drained her," Zac sighed, getting an affirmative nod from Billy. "I'm sorry."

"It's not Super Brother Man's fault," Billy smiled. "Friends help friends. Besides, Billy thinks you can help. Billy's plan is good, but it can get better."

"I'll do my best. What did you mean by throwing that guy into the dungeon?"

"One day, Gemmy said more bad guys were breaking into Gemmy's world," Billy said. "The first people were already harming Gemmy, so Billy decided to catch these ones. Gemmy did space magic and made bad guys appear inside Billy's dungeon instead of the edge of the world."

"No wonder," Zac laughed as he remembered the empty forest they appeared inside.

"What is making the world sick?" Ogras asked. "How long do we have until this all goes tits up?"

"Ah, that's…" Billy became confused.

"A dangerous energy is invading the Mystic Realm," Leyara said as she walked over with Pretty and Vai. "Vai retold your experiences. I'm sorry about how I acted. I owe you a favor for keeping my aunt safe all this time."

"She helped me just as much," Zac smiled. "What dangerous energy? When did this happen?"

"Since the start," Leyara said. "It has been a bit hard to piece together the events, but it looks like the Realm Spirit swallowed up a dimensional fragment holding something dangerous. That realm started releasing its energy, spreading like poison through Gemmy's world. By the time Gemmy realized there was a problem, it had already lost control over that region of its body."

"And let me guess, it's to the east?" Ogras sighed.

"The nasty place," Billy said as he looked at Ogras. "It got worse after *you* went there, stupid guy."

"How is that possible? I got a quest to cleanse that place. I spent a year killing the monsters. I even blew the whole thing up to kill the last of the—ah?" Ogras froze, his brows furrowing together. "*Now* you're telling me, bastard?"

Ogras' behavior looked odd, but Zac understood he was speaking with the goblin Tool Spirit.

"What's going on?" Leyara asked curiously. "By the way, what's happened to you? You didn't look like this in the Tower of Eternity. Have you become a ghost? Did the spirits speak with you?"

"Yes, to speaking with ghosts, but I am still very much alive," Ogras said with a grin. "If you're interested, you are most welcome to perform a thorough—"

"Ahem," Zac coughed. "What did the ghost say?"

"Ah?" Ogras blanked out until he remembered what they were dealing with. "Oh, yeah. Remember how the Kingdom of Ra'Lashar rose? How they gained their insights?"

"They found a weakness in—" Zac's eyes widened.

Zac had read some of Ogras' notes on the insane goblin society over the past month, and it was clear what the demon was referring to. The Ra'Lashar were once a simple species on a low E-grade world. But one day, they stumbled onto a weak spot leading to the Lost Plane. Not only did that result in their planet being flooded with enough tainted ambient energy to nurture Monarchs, but they also managed to extract all kinds of knowledge.

"The ghost figured the pathway would be gone since the whole planet disappeared, with but a small fragment being dragged into this traveling Mystic Realm," Ogras said. "But what if it's still there? What if the connection remains?"

"Bad guys are at the nasty place making things worse," Billy said, confirming the reports they lifted from the lipless Hegemon.

"The invaders are opening a path, looking for things they shouldn't," Ogras muttered.

"We're lucky," Leyara said. "Vai told me how you conjured a huge pillar a month ago? It drained a lot of the buildup in this world. The plan was a bit iffy before, but we have a shot of getting out of here alive now. There's only one problem…"

"There always is," Ogras sighed, and Zac could only agree.

There was always something.

# 11

# CROOKED SCHEMES

Nothing was ever easy in the Multiverse, at least not for those without strength or backing. And in a chaotic scene like the one they found themselves in, Zac wasn't surprised to hear there were roadblocks to Billy's ambitious plan.

"What will happen when this array is turned on?" Zac asked Billy, who clearly wasn't keeping up with the conversation.

"Ah," Billy hesitated. "Gemmy will come with Billy and leave?"

"It's not quite that easy," Leyara added from the side. "This array will break off most of the mass of this Mystic Realm before forming a true subspace that will be stored inside the Realm Spirit's avatar. We would stay inside, but the controller could simply take us out like it was a Spatial Treasure."

"What!" Vai exclaimed as she looked down at the array. "How is that possible? The energy consumption alone…"

"It normally wouldn't be possible without an extremely powerful energy source, but we have a unique advantage A sapient World Spirit who is willing to fuel the process. I doubt even my master could accomplish this without Gemmy's aid," Leyara said. "I can neither confirm nor deny any of this. Such an array is far beyond my understanding. We are only drawing it according to King Billy's specifications."

"So, what's the problem?"

"First of all, we're cutting it extremely close," Pretty said. "Those people outside have figured out we can't replenish our energy, so they're content with gradually whittling us down. Now, it looks even worse, unless the two of you are skilled at formations and energy control?"

"Uh," Zac said while Ogras studiously looked away.

"Thought as much," Pretty snorted.

"Can't we just go out and slow them down?" Zac asked.

"That was our plan in case things started to go south," Pretty said. "We have simply waited since the Templar Hegemons are needed to draw the most complicated pathways. Apart from them, only Leyara can do it. But with Senior Lioress and you two here, we finally have the opportunity to strike back."

Zac blanked out for a second, wondering if the Void Priestess had appeared as well. A second later, Zac realized Pretty was talking about Vai when she said Senior Lioress. It was easy to forget she was over a thousand years old when she almost looked like a teenager. The little researcher was studying the vast array with almost burning eyes, muttering to herself and scribbling notes.

Seemed she only needed an exciting topic of study to forget all about the matter of the Deviant Asura.

"A few successful raids will give us more time to draw the array," Leyara agreed. "But that doesn't solve the real issue."

"What's that?" Zac asked with a sinking feeling that trouble was about to come knocking at his door.

"The Kan'Tanu infiltrators are extracting too much energy from these ruins you mentioned," Leyara said. "When this array is activated, it will turn into a black hole as it swallows all the energy in this world."

"Including all that tainted energy," Ogras grimaced.

"Exactly." Leyara nodded. "We fear that activating while the source of corruption remains will not only drag all that corruption into the core of this world, it might even swallow the origin of all that tainted energy, which will be disastrous. This whole realm would likely explode, killing the Realm Spirit and us alike."

Zac took a deep breath before calmly looking at Leyara. "Let me guess. Someone has to go there and turn off the faucet, so to speak?"

"Preferably while conjuring another pillar, if possible," Leyara agreed. "The more tainted energy we excise, the more likely it is for Gemmy to survive this transformation."

"What's your plan?" Ogras asked with a raised brow. "That place is months away."

"To kill enough enemies for Gemmy to hurl a few people in the right direction," Leyara said with a weak smile. "And hope they survive the journey."

"That's it? Hurl them across half the domain? *That's* the plan?" Ogras asked incredulously. "Billy and that fool of a gem, I understand, but how can you just go along with it?"

"Well, we didn't have much of a choice," Pretty said with a roll of her eyes. "We are essentially prison labor stuck inside this place. It was either this or stay in the dungeons while that brute and his pet realm tried to solve this mess themselves. Besides, what are we supposed to do? Let these invaders run about unchecked? Better we blow up this whole place and us along with it than let them succeed in taking this place over."

"Well, let's avoid blowing ourselves up if we can avoid it," Zac grimaced. "Why are there no powerhouses here? They'd be able to solve this issue with a wave of their sleeve. Why have you guys only brought Early D-grade Hegemons?"

"We had to send back a few of our powerhouses on the way. The inner reaches have become too fragile after the sabotage," Leyara sighed. "If anything, the infiltrators want us to send Monarchs into the Void Star. Their mere presence would most likely cause a chain reaction that would splinter the Void Star, sending the realms to all corners of Zecia. If we're unlucky, the Stellar Ladder will remain intact, giving the invaders free rein. We have already been forced to detach our most valuable realms to avoid that kind of energy overload."

"Weaker Middle Hegemons can technically enter these depths, but it's not worth it. An elite Early Hegemon will give off roughly the same energy, but their effective combat strength is higher. You're a prime example of that. You're an E-grade cultivator with an aura of an Early Hegemon, yet I bet few early Hegemons are your match," Pretty Peak added. "I would really have loved to spar with you a bit if the world wasn't ending."

"Another time." Zac smiled.

Zac had expected as much from the lack of Monarchs, but it was still a kick to the groin that the Void Priestess or someone like the Starfall Monarch simply couldn't swing by and solve this mess. At least that explained why he and Vai hadn't encountered any too dangerous realms until now. Even the most savage places they crossed had Late Beast Kings at worst, with not a single one sporting the Beast Emperors who supposedly lived in the depths of the Void Star.

"Still, you were just going to let Gemmy throw you into a spatial tear and hope for the best?" Zac asked.

"We don't have any other means to reach the eastern reaches in time, and Gemmy can only do so much in her current state," Leyara explained. "And if we sent a squad earlier, we would never be able to finish the array on time."

"Let's say the plan worked out. What would happen next?" Zac asked.

"Most of this realm would collapse while the core region is reforged," Leyara said. "I have a few anchor treasures that should be able to drag people out of the Void Star even if the Spatial Nexuses are in flux."

"Why not just use those things and get the hell out of here?" Ogras urged.

"Well, for one, Gemmy is blocking us," Leyara said. "Even if she allowed us to leave, they need to be used outside a localized space."

"In the Void?" Zac frowned.

Leyara nodded. "Exactly. We need to let the world collapse and dispel its spatial field. That will place us in a localized Void of the Void Star, and we'll teleport out from there."

"What a shitty escape treasure," Ogras muttered. "Need to survive the apocalypse to use it."

"They're not meant to be used this deep inside the Void Star, and not when the whole system is collapsing. Its standard function utilizes the Spatial Nexuses that have been destroyed," Leyara sighed.

"Aren't you supposed to be a big shot with a wealthy master? Surely you have something better?" Ogras asked.

"Even if my master had better items, what good does it do me?" Leyara said with a roll of her eyes. "I'm just Peak E-grade. How am I supposed to activate a treasure that can blast us straight through dozens of spatial layers? These anchors are as good as they get for an E-grade cultivator."

Zac nodded in agreement. Even his **[Flashfire Flourish]** wouldn't manage to cross such a vast distance. But thinking of his escape item, a plan started to form in Zac's mind.

"One of the anchors would go to the assault group who dealt with the tainted energy," Leyara continued. "The moment this realm collapses, they would use the anchor to get dragged back outside. The other would go to Billy."

"To Billy?" Zac said curiously.

"If everything worked out, Gemmy should be able to send Billy outside into the Void as well, where he could activate the treasure and take Gemmy with him. Once outside the Void Star, he could extract us and send in our armies to deal with any remnant infiltrators."

"This is not just about us either," Pretty added with determination. "We cannot just flee and leave these people to their own devices. Even if we fail, we must drag them with us down to the Underworld. We cannot let them seize the Stellar Ladder."

"Are you crazy?" Ogras said with raised brows.

"War will always have sacrifices," Pretty shrugged. "If they seize this springboard into Zecia, we're done for when the real powerhouses arrive. Trading a few juniors, even talented ones, for the safety of the whole Sector is a no-brainer. We cannot let them get their hands on this realm."

"That's not the only thing we can't let them get their hands on," Ogras added with a low voice to Zac.

Zac slowly nodded in agreement as he looked down at the huge array. After reading the lipless Hegemon's reports, they'd initially thought there were more pieces of rubble hidden in the ruins of the Ra'Lashar Kingdom. But what if that wasn't it? What if the Kan'Tanu were actually aiming for the source—the Lost Plane?

The lipless cultivator had mentioned selling him off to some powerful faction. Was this their plan? To mine and extract opportunities and sell to powerful bidders. And with a prize like Ultom and the Left Imperial Palace, there would be no shortage of powerful factions willing to buy in. The whole Sector might be crawling with powerful forces from the Multiverse Heartlands if the pathway to the Lost Plane wasn't closed.

The demon had evidently arrived at the same conclusion, and there was genuine fear on his face.

"We cannot let them continue," Zac agreed. "Otherwise, the invasion will become the least of our worries."

"Fate is gathering," Leyara said.

"I hate this." Pretty spat to the side. "You two clearly know something, and so does the Void Gate. Even the invaders know, while Zecia fumbles in the dark. What the hell is going on? It's related to these, isn't it?"

Zac looked on as Pretty took out a familiar piece of cloth—the ones all the infiltrators carried around. Zac glanced at Leyara, who appeared conflicted. The scene was a bit odd. Leyara knew, but Pretty didn't? Ogras looked inquisitively at Zac, who didn't know what to say either.

He didn't have any reason to distrust Pretty Peak, but he adamantly believed the fewer people who knew the truth, the better. What if she reported back to her elders, who then forwarded it to the leaders of the Allbright Empire?

Only one person with loose lips was needed to create a disaster. The Kan'Tanu seemed to be the same. The lowest members only knew to look for the sigils, while a few others, like the lipless Hegemon, knew a few more details. Zac doubted that Aural Cultivator knew anything concrete except that his mission was related to an opportunity the Kan'-Tanu were planning to sell.

Even then, they were playing a dangerous game, to the point Zac suspected they had something to rely on. Otherwise, why wouldn't the powerful factions just annihilate the Kan'Tanu instead of bartering with them?

"I don't know all the details either," Zac said, which got him an exaggerated eye-roll from Pretty Peak. "Suffice to say, the Kan'Tanu are looking for something, and it'll be bad if they find it."

"Whatever." Pretty shrugged. "Keep it to yourselves. The truth will come out sooner or later with so many people involved. And you better pray that your secrecy won't harm the war efforts."

"Since when were cultivators required to share their secrets? Hoarding resources and intelligence is Heaven's Path," Ogras grinned. "I doubt your esteemed factions are handing out cultivation resources and manuals left and right even when barbarians are knocking at the gate."

"That's enough," Zac sighed. "I have an escape treasure that can probably send me all the way to the Ra'Lashar Kingdom in one go, but

I'm not sure how well I can steer it. I should manage to land within a few days' travel, though, and it won't waste any of Gemmy's energy."

This was the idea Zac had come up with when discussing the escape anchors. He didn't relish the thought of storming an infiltrator base to blow up a dimensional portal, but it definitely beat their original scheme. The less energy Gemmy was forced to use, the longer they would be able to maintain the shields and work on the array. And while it was dangerous, it was better than sitting around in this failing barrier, hoping for the best.

"Really?" Leyara said, her eyes lighting up. "It should work. You'd have to teleport from outside the barrier, though. Maybe use it during a raid?"

"The Kan'Tanu have locked down space as well," Pretty said. "You would have to properly break out of the encirclement to avoid any mishaps."

"We'll figure something out." Zac glanced to Ogras.

"Good luck," the demon said while giving a thumbs up. "I'll be rooting for you."

"What are you talking about?" Zac smiled. "Obviously, you're coming with me."

Ogras only scoffed in return, but his eyes thinned when he realized Zac was serious. "You're joking."

"Like you said, you've been there for almost a year. And you even have a ghost guide to help us out," Zac shrugged. "You obviously have to come."

"That was why Billy opened the path for Horny Guy," Billy nodded as he glared at Ogras. "If Horny Guy doesn't go, Gemmy will throw him out again."

"Bah, *fine*," Ogras swore. "I guess the safest place is by your side anyway. If we fall into the Void, perhaps some beauties in a Cosmic Vessel will come to pick us up."

"Perhaps," Zac laughed.

Truthfully, it wasn't only because of his need for a guide that he wanted Ogras to come with. Another reason was the ruins. Perhaps the Kan'Tanu had already unearthed another set if they were digging into the Lost Plane. And if either of them managed to get another piece, it might trigger a second pillar and drain this world of more tainted energy.

Secondly, it would be good to have the demon by his side if everything fell apart and they needed to escape. Billy would be safe since the plan required him to have one of the escape anchors, while Leyara would no doubt sort out Vai. That left him and Ogras, who would be taken care of as part of the strike group.

This way, they wouldn't be as reliant on Leyara's generosity when disaster struck. She clearly didn't have enough anchors for everyone since the plan was to leave most people inside Gemmy. And it was unreasonable to expect Leyara to save him and Ogras over her own people. After all, they'd only met for two short encounters before.

"How many can your escape treasure take?" Pretty asked.

"Not sure," Zac said. "One or two maximum. It's also a bit dangerous to use for non-Fire cultivators. It will damage your foundations."

"Are you trying to get me killed!" Ogras scowled.

"You're part shadows, so you should be fine," Zac said.

"One or two?" Pretty frowned. "Is that enough? There should be some powerful enemies guarding that place."

"Our goal isn't to take them all out but to sabotage," Zac said. "A smaller group might work even better."

"What do you think?" Pretty asked Leyara.

"Well, it's a better plan than we have," Leyara said. "Besides, we have a few weeks to refine the plan."

"Alright, I need to rest up a bit after that dash," Zac said. "We'll talk later."

With that, everyone went their own way. Leyara and Pretty once more guided Vai away, while Zac headed off with Ogras and Billy. Apparently, they didn't need to do anything with Gemmy maintaining the barrier. They couldn't even counter-attack because the barrier was a true spatial divide. Just as the invaders couldn't attack from the outside, they couldn't attack from within like you could with a conventional City Defense Array.

Billy was over the moon from hearing that his actions in the Mystic Realm had helped save Earth. However, he was surprisingly ambivalent about there being quite a few statues of him erected across the planet, including one in Port Atwood.

Billy also told him about what happened since Ogras left, which wasn't much, really. He'd spent most of his time fighting the beast tides or cultivating. Weirdly enough, Billy had occasionally fallen asleep for months at a time while Gemmy guarded his body. Seeing how he cultivated and made breakthroughs in his sleep, Zac guessed his bloodline was related to dreams or dreamworlds.

It wasn't exactly what Zac expected from a Titanic bloodline. Then again, he knew nothing about real Titans.

With only earthlings around, and Gemmy who was floating inside a brazier, Zac also told them what happened to Earth since they were swallowed by the Dimensional Seed. Billy was a great audience, audibly gasping or boisterously laughing as Zac narrated his exploits from the Big Axe Coliseum to the Twilight Ascent.

The three spent a few hours catching up, with Zac providing some of the delicacies he kept inside his Spatial Ring. Unfortunately, the evening was only a brief respite, with Pretty Peak coming to discuss a surprise raid a few hours later. She wanted to strike while the iron was hot, and the outsiders were still a bit disorganized from the spatial mayhem.

"Let's get to work," Zac grunted as **|Verun's Bite|** appeared in his hand.

# RAID

A knock echoed from the half-open door to Zac's study, prompting him to look up from the Book of Duality.

"Already?" Zac sighed as Pretty Peak walked inside.

"Apparently, we only have around five days. If you want enough time to figure out a solution over there, we have to make our move soon. And the sooner we get going, the more energy will be left for Gemmy."

"Thought we had just over a week," Zac grunted.

"Sorry, but we don't have a lot of options. Senior Salas' estimates aren't looking too promising. Everyone is working overtime, including the Gnivelings. If we want a shot at this crooked scheme, we can't wait much longer," Pretty said with some helplessness.

Zac sighed with a nod. The past two weeks had quickly turned into a struggle against time after Vai discovered some errors in Leyara's calculations. They'd believed themselves to have over four weeks before they needed to finish and activate the array, but it turned out they only had three. If they waited any longer, Gemmy wouldn't have enough energy to form a stable spatial field.

"Well, I guess it doesn't make much of a difference," Zac said. "I'm going to miss our sparring sessions, though."

"Likewise," Pretty smiled. "But who knows? We might just survive this and get more opportunities in the future."

They'd sparred almost daily since Zac arrived at the Kingdom of Billy, barring the days they had to recover from their wounds. Pretty had proven nearly as useless as he was for drawing the arrays, so they had been left to their own devices. Ogras, on the other hand, had been employed to help out a bit, though he still made some time to train and spar.

Upon learning about his chance to train under the tutelage of multiple Monarchs, the demon had been green with envy, and he was trying to glean something through Zac's stances. Of course, the Evolutionary and Inexorable Stances were useless to Ogras. Still, the theories and concepts that went into their formation were handy for anyone who wanted to improve their own techniques.

Right now, Ogras was relying on a mix of his clan's techniques and some strikes he'd invented himself, and was making rapid improvements. The demon reminded Zac a bit of himself when he fought in the Big Axe Coliseum. Ogras had found a direction that was working for him, but was somewhat lacking the foundations to move forward without falling into the same pitfalls as he had.

Ogras did have a fantastic battle sense and a feel for timing, something Zac had already seen when they fought together. Improving his techniques was probably a worthwhile direction for Ogras. However, he would be better off developing a style that struck fast and hard, rather than Zac's stances, which centered on seizing the momentum before whittling down the opposition.

Pretty Peak was also shocked at his skill since he hadn't shown any of that during his battle in the Tower of Eternity. Her own methods weren't anything to scoff at, though. This was the first time Zac had seen her fight, and her fighting style was far more in line with her bloody leather armor than her beautiful and almost dainty appearance. She was relying on her clan's battle technique when they sparred, but Zac often felt like he was fighting a beast rather than a cultivator.

She was an instinctual fighter, just like he was to a certain degree, and she refused to follow her enemy's tempo. She was full of unexpected moves, incorporating both grappling and various weapons into her repertoire. At any moment, her claws could have been replaced by two daggers or a brutal scythe, making it nigh-impossible to know what to expect.

Apparently, it was a technique developed on the battlefields, though Zac hadn't had the chance to see the real thing in action. It was devised by Pretty's ancestor, a talented captain of the Allbright Empire. He'd been strong but dirt-poor, and his weapons often broke while fighting on the frontlines. As a result, he learned to use everything on a battlefield to his advantage in some sort of loot-and-fight-approach, where he used the weapons and treasures of fallen allies and foes.

The Peak family was no longer wanting for treasures, but they still maintained the mindset to not rely on their items. In Average's and Greatest's cases, they chose the path of pure pugilism, using their bodies as their weapon. Pretty Peak had chosen a different approach, where she'd mastered multiple weapons, though her primary weapons were claws and the sword.

The claws were self-explanatory. It was close to pugilism, and the Peak family had a lot of skills and techniques for that fighting style. Mastering swords was a choice of her own, but it wasn't due to some particular affinity.

Pretty had instead explained it with the high prevalence of sword-fighters in Zecia. If she lost her weapons in battle, a sword would probably be the easiest to steal from her enemies. And there was always a good chance of finding better blades in places like Mystic Realms and Inheritance trials.

It was a stark difference from Zac's path where he planned on upgrading and using his treasures to the very end. There was ultimately no right or wrong in cultivation.

"Five days, huh?" Zac sighed. "Will the array be done in time?"

"Honestly? It doesn't look too good," Pretty said as she hesitantly looked at Zac. "I hate to ask, but do you think you can help take down another tower on your way out? It would buy us another half day at least."

Zac considered it before he hesitantly nodded. "We could take one down, but the original plan has to change."

This would be the seventh and final raid in which Gemmy opened small breaches to let them out for a blitz attack. The first outing had been a rousing success, where they had formed three parties that targeted sections with fewer or weaker Hegemons. One group was Zac and Ogras, with another being Billy, Leyara, Pretty, and a Defensive Templar Hegemon. The last group consisted of four more Templar Hegemons and twenty support staff.

The sudden attack had left 12 enemy Hegemons dead or crippled and destroyed a siege tower, drastically weakening their capabilities. The most significant contributors had been the Templars, who took down seven of the enemies by using a series of expensive talismans provided for Leyara's safety. Ogras and he had taken out another three before they were forced to retreat, while Billy's team had taken care of the last two.

The second attempt worked out quite nicely as well, as they infiltrated a series of tunnels the invaders had dug in an effort to enter the fort from below. The third raid was a sobering experience, with three of their own Hegemons falling while Billy's party was almost wiped out. If not for the defensive Templar sacrificing himself, Billy and Pretty wouldn't have gotten out with only nasty wounds.

Those losses and the new deadline were the beginning of the vicious circle that forced them to fight the Kan'Tanu army another three times. Six out of their eleven Hegemons had already lost their lives. Another deserted them by using a raid to escape. How he was planning to survive was beyond Zac, but judging by the seething anger in Leyara's and the other Templars' eyes, he would probably have to join the invaders if he wanted a shot at survival.

Even Ogras had been forced to sit out the two last raids because of wounds, and three raid parties had been reduced to two as Zac joined the Templars instead of going at it alone. It had lessened the damage they did each battle, but they had no better options. After all, the demon needed to be in tip-top shape for this one.

"You're right, we're abandoning the diversion. We'll all join you for this final battle instead," Pretty agreed. "I'm actually a bit excited to finally see your exploits up close. Some of the Templars swear that you must be a Hegemon in hiding."

"I wish." Zac wryly smiled as he got to his feet. "Give me three hours. I need to enter seclusion."

"Alright," Pretty nodded as she turned toward the door. "I'll get everything sorted."

Just as she was about to leave, she turned around again.

"You know, the real Deviant Asura is a lot better than the rumors," she said, a smile spreading across her face. "But perhaps not as interesting."

"I'm fine with being called boring if those rumors just die down," Zac muttered.

"Doubtful. The Tsarun Clan is working much too hard to ruin your image and alienate you," Pretty laughed. "Although, it can all be swept away by deeds. My grandpa says there will probably be rankings and contributions stores for this war. As long as you prove yourself, no one will care about those rumors. Those who spread them might even face a backlash."

"Looking forward to it," Zac smiled. "Is there anything else?"

Pretty hesitated before she spoke up. "Is… there really nothing you can tell me that can help me with Average and our soldiers?" Pretty asked. "I can feel it—how it's all related to the events here."

It had been a shock to hear that both Average and his old acquaintance, Galau, had gone missing under mysterious circumstances. An enormous planet in the depths of the Million Gates Territory had just up and disappeared with them on it, and the event had released enough energy to be sensed all the way to the Allbright Empire.

The Peak family didn't believe anyone in their Sector had the strength to do something like that, and thought it was related to the Limitless Empire. That was the original reason Pretty had been sent to the Void Gate, though the infiltration of the Void Star had taken precedence.

"What you've described is completely different from what I know," Zac said with a shake of his head. "From what I've seen, there are only two outcomes from encountering… that. You either gain the opportunity, or you die. There are no disappearances, especially not whole planets. It might be related, but I'm just guessing here as well."

Zac wasn't lying. If the scarred planet disappearing was related to the Limitless Empire, then it was probably associated with the Left Imperial Palace. As for how and why, Zac didn't have the faintest idea.

Pretty sighed. "Well, keep your eyes open, will you?"

Zac nodded. "I'll see you soon."

Zac led Pretty out of his quarters before he sealed it shut. From there, Zac didn't head for his cultivation chamber but rather his closet. He pushed against a wall, and a hidden chute opened up. Zac jumped inside, falling hundreds of meters until he landed in a pitch-black room.

These sections were once part of the hive's incubator, and only a few hidden pathways connected it with the rest of the hive. Here, the queen would store and slowly nurture the eggs until warriors came crawling out from the chutes. These sections were long since discovered and cleansed by Billy and Ogras and had been refitted into secret cultivation chambers or secret shelters.

A perfect spot for Zac to accomplish some things far from prying eyes.

There was only so much he could do to improve his strength in the short run. The best would have been to upgrade his Branch of the War Axe, but he was still somewhat lacking. The raids hadn't provided enough inspiration either, even if the fighting had been hard.

That left him with his second option—his undead side.

Having traveled with Vai for half a year, there hadn't been any good opportunities to fill his already opened nodes with Miasma. Thankfully, the downtime between raids had helped him out a lot. After every battle, he'd hurried down to these catacombs to use the Kill Energy to gain levels. Just filling them up required a lot less energy than breaking nodes open, and he had made a lot of progress in the past two weeks.

Even then, he wasn't quite there. His Draugr form was still level 148, just two levels shy of the noticeable attribute boost at 150. With time running out, Zac decided to finish the process with Leveling Pills. Typically, he wouldn't have eaten pills when absorbing energy from Miasma Crystals would do the trick, but he was under a lot of pressure from the upcoming mission.

This time, there wasn't only his own life to worry about. If he failed to close the pathway to the Lost Plane, then Gemmy would fail her transition to a Portable Realm, and most people here would probably perish. He needed every advantage he could get, even if that meant taking on a bit more pill toxins.

Zac sat down at his usual spot, and a bottle of Leveling Pills he'd bought inside the Orom World appeared in his hand. The [Aethergate Pills] he bought back in the Twilight Harbor were used up already, but these weren't that much worse. More than enough for his purposes. Deathly waves of Miasma coursed through his body, and the transition was complete less than a second later thanks to his upgraded transformation skill.

Two pills were swallowed without preamble, and it felt like a frigid star had appeared in his stomach. Zac directed the energy toward the empty nodes in his mind, and it poured into the first one like a surging river. The process went without any issues or surprises, and two hours later, it was done.

Now, all 75 of his nodes formed deathly swirls in a perfect system, each feeling like a gateway into the Abyss. He opened his Status Screen, and a smile spread across his face upon seeing another 260 free points added to his pool. With five levels worth of attribute boosts, he'd gained a couple thousand attribute points these last five levels of his Fetters of Desolation class.

As usual, he put the free points into Dexterity, pushing the attribute to 9,770 points. It still felt odd pouring all his free points into the same attribute. But with two classes and three Dao Branches that mainly provided Strength, Endurance, and Vitality, he didn't have much choice. Even his Wisdom would eventually pass his Dexterity if he didn't manually remedy the situation.

Zac didn't gain a new quest this time either, and neither did he gain another title. He was mostly tapped out in that regard, unless he managed to create a skill from scratch before breaking through. Still, the basic prerequisites for his attempt at Hegemony were finally complete, and in just a decade at that.

Reaching this point thwarted all but a select few mortals, and his journey was entirely different from Galvarion's struggles. The maritime Monarch had spent centuries in the E-grade, each step, and every node a perilous journey. Of course, the most challenging part remained. Figuring out a blueprint for his Cultivator's Core. This step couldn't compare with Galvarion's, considering he had shallow foundations and an Uncommon E-grade class.

There was also the matter of shoring up his foundations, which was mostly just a matter of time. For now, Zac was happy with the results, and he climbed out of the chute. There was still some time left before he needed to meet up with Pretty and the others, which was perfect. There was one more thing he needed to do before he set off for the Ra'Lashar Kingdom.

"Gemmy, are you there?" Zac asked into thin air.

"You smell bad again," Gemmy's voice echoed through his empty chamber.

"Remember, our little secret." Zac smiled and got a giggle in response.

Hopefully, that meant she agreed. Billy was already aware of the situation from the first time Zac transformed, though Zac wasn't sure he actually understood he had two races. Rather, it seemed like Billy considered it like his own Titanic transformation. Still, he'd promised he wouldn't tell anyone, and Zac trusted him to stay true to his word.

"Okay, Hungry Guy, Gemmy promises," the Dimensional Seed said.

"Where is Slow Girl right now?" Zac asked.

"She is in her room, looking at the pattern."

"Is she alone?"

"Yep!"

"Perfect, thank you," Zac said, leaving his room and flashing over to another section of the hive.

Zac knocked on the door, which swung open by itself.

"I thought you would come over," Leyara smiled as Zac closed the door behind him.

"It's time you and I have a little chat," Zac said. "About the Limitless Empire and the Left Imperial Palace."

# 13
# VIGIL

"The Left Imperial Palace?" Leyara said with large, sorrowful eyes. "And here I thought you had finally come to profess your love before riding off into battle. What a disappointment."

"Be serious," Zac said.

This was a long-overdue discussion. They'd danced around the subject for weeks, but Zac needed some clarity before setting off for the Ra'Lashar Kingdom.

"Who said I wasn't?" Leyara winked, her expression soon returning to normal. "I know you have a lot of questions, but I don't have a lot of answers to give you."

"You clearly know at least some of it, and you would have me use your escape treasure to get sent right into the hands of the Void Gate," Zac said. "You should understand the risk that would place us in."

This was Zac's primary concern. Using Leyara's Spatial Anchor would supposedly drag them right back to the Void Gate. If they wanted the opportunity for themselves, then he and Ogras would be delivering themselves to the slaughter. He and Ogras had even discussed fleeing in the opposite direction instead—into the Stellar Ladder and the Million Gates Territory.

Obviously, Zac wanted to avoid that solution. They didn't even have a Cosmic Vessel, and his escape bangle was still on its cooldown for another nine years. He would be able to set up a teleportation array, but those didn't work in the Million Gates Territory, meaning they would have to make their way out themselves.

No matter how arduous such a journey was, it was the preferable option to being blasted into nothingness by a Monarch the second they emerged. The two had made some preparations with the help of Billy and Gemmy, but Zac hoped this conversation would alleviate any need for using them.

"Well, I guess I owe you that much," Leyara said. "And seeing as you're a candidate, you will get to know the truth sooner or later. But you cannot tell anyone else about this. Fate is already fraught with uncertainties, and even the smallest of ripples can bring about a storm."

"Of course."

"You have nothing to fear from the Void Gate. We will not interfere with you or the events that are about to unfold. Neither will anyone from our side try to gain access to the Left Imperial Palace or its nine Outer Courts," Leyara said with certainty. "Nor meddle with the thing residing within."

The allusion to Ultom and the mention of the nine sigils pretty much confirmed that Leyara was the real deal and not just pretending to know things to extract information from him. Still, that felt as much a threat as an opportunity when she held the key to their freedom.

"Why should I believe you?" Zac asked. "Your faction is clearly interested in this stuff and has probably been looking for them for a long time."

"I think you have figured a few things out already," Leyara said. "First of all, the Void Gate is not our real name. Our faction is older than the System itself, and we call ourselves the Vigil."

"The Vigil?" Zac frowned. "Never heard of it."

"You wouldn't have," Leyara said. "Honestly, most of us don't know about it either. The Void Gate is just a small subsidiary force looking for clues at the frontier, and only a select few know the truth. Master only told me just before I entered the Void Star, so this is mostly uncharted territory for me as well."

"Then why wouldn't you get involved? If you've searched for so long?" Zac asked suspiciously.

"If you want to know, then tell me how you became a candidate. What was the criterion?" Leyara countered.

Zac hesitated for a few seconds before he chose to tell her the truth.

"It happened the moment I passed through the Void Star's outer film. I got a terrifying vision that almost killed me. My whole compartment was covered in blood afterward," Zac said. "After that, I could sense the pieces from a distance."

"As I suspected," Leyara said, looking at Zac with a complex gaze. "The Vigil has a mission. To watch as the river flows and to make sure fate isn't usurped or altered."

"Fate usurped?" Zac said with a raised brow. "Like a nobody becoming a candidate?"

"No, not like that." Leyara smiled. "This is a matter of those at the very peak. Small beings like us are just part of the river. How could we truly affect it as we are? I don't know what it means, but the result is that we will not interfere with you, nor will we interfere with any infiltrator who becomes a candidate."

"But you're not just observers," Zac countered. "You directly got involved when you started hoovering up ruins and realms with the Void Star. And now the outsiders are involved."

"That was an unfortunate side effect of our mission," Leyara grimaced. "My master could feel that the pillar was stirring, and she had to pave the path to let fate flow unobstructed. That presented an opportunity to these infiltrators. Now, she can't just close the connection and seal off the Kan'Tanu, since that would affect her true mission."

"So Zecia will suffer because of a technicality?"

"That's…" Leyara sighed. "You could see it that way. But that's why we're here. To try and right a wrong without breaking the precepts. Luckily, your friend has provided us with a solution by forcing us to labor for his undertaking. If this realm is removed from the Stellar Ladder, then the whole ladder should destabilize. Even if it doesn't, we should be able to do it ourselves since this realm is the origin of fate.

"Furthermore, most of the Void Gate will join the upcoming war, even if the Vigil doesn't get involved with mundane struggles. After all, this is also our home. Almost everyone was born in Zecia."

"That's the least of our problems," Zac said. "You should know what will happen if powerful factions turn their gazes toward Zecia. Will the Vigil spread the appearance of the Left Imperial Palace?"

"I don't know," Leyara said. "I'm still coming to terms with all this. I really have no idea if my faction has allies they'd bring over or if they will keep it to themselves. But you should know, even if the Vigil doesn't say anything, this cannot remain a secret for long. The ancient factions have their means to discover something of this magnitude."

Zac nodded, exhaustion in his eyes. He'd already started to fear as much, that an Eternal Heritage appearing unnoticed would be too much to hope for. Even if the Kan'Tanu didn't expose the truth to the Multiverse, it was just a matter of time before some Supremacy figured it out.

Dealing with that mess was for later, though. If worse comes to worst, he'd just have to camp on Earth or Ensolus under the System's protection until someone claimed Ultom and left Zecia alone.

"Then what can you tell me?" Zac sighed. "What did you mean when you said a pillar was stirring? Is the Left Imperial Palace one of the pillars?"

Leyara looked out from her window, down at the army camped outside.

"When the Limitless Empire crafted the System, their power alone wasn't enough. The Heavens are not so easily subdued, and they had to lend the power of others. Eight pillars were erected at the corners of reality, each one powered by something called an Eternal Heritage. Places of ultimate power, of ultimate truth. Concepts beyond the Dao itself, which was needed to contain the Heavens."

Zac shuddered when he heard the description, and the words from his vision once more floated to the surface.

*Eight Pillars. Nine Seals. One Destiny.*

"The undertaking was a success, and the pillars provided the strength the System needed to stabilize and grow during its infancy. Many tried to stop Emperor Limitless' experiment, and the Left Imperial Palace became one of the battlegrounds where even the Heavens joined the fray. But the eight pillars withstood the assault and disappeared."

"And now the Left Imperial Palace is coming back?" Zac frowned. "How will this affect the System?"

"According to master, the System is no longer dependent on the pillars. They were let loose long ago. In fact, them returning unattached is by design."

"By design? Whose design is that?"

"Who knows?" Leyara smiled. "Perhaps Emperor Limitless. Perhaps the ancient beings who crafted the places of power. I only know that the pillars were destined to return, and Vigil would be there to observe and aid the ascent."

Zac slowly digested Leyara's claims, and he believed her on most points. She knew way too much information just to be some frontier scion. As for the Left Imperial Palace and Ultom being used in the construction of the System, Zac could definitely believe it. He'd had the same thoughts over the past months, and the scarred exterior he saw in his vision lined up with Leyara's mention of battles.

It was fairly shocking that Emperor Limitless managed to gather eight Eternal Heritages. However, it wasn't without reason since many still believed him to be the strongest person to have existed. Besides, this all happened at the beginning of the era, before cultivation reached its current height.

The only question that remained was whether he could trust Leyara on the most crucial part—if her faction were really only there to observe or if they were aiming for the Eternal Heritages.

"Why *are* you only observing? What's your end goal?" Zac asked.

"No idea," Leyara said. "Master wouldn't tell me that part. If you want to know, you'd have to ask her. This is pretty much all I know. You might even know more than me. For instance, my master never mentioned anything about this Lost Plane you told us about."

"Alright," Zac sighed, though he wasn't completely satisfied.

Zac asked a few more clarifying questions over the following minutes, and he managed to get a few valuable pieces of information. She didn't know how the trial would look, or how the nine subsidiary courts played into everything. But she was somewhat confident that no Kan'Tanu infiltrator had managed to become a candidate, which was good news.

Most importantly, she believed the Void Star had swallowed no more than five pieces of various seals, while most remained in the chaotic space of the Million Gates Territory. Staying in this place was unlikely to bear fruit, especially if they managed to break the Stellar Ladder with their plan.

Their conversation concluded just in time, since Gemmy's voice appeared and told them the others were waiting at the viewing deck.

"By the way, do you know which one of the Nine Imperial Bloodlines you have?" Leyara asked as they walked out of her quarters, her voice so casual one might have thought she was discussing the weather.

Zac's heart lurched, but he managed to keep his face impassive. "Nine Imperial Bloodlines? What's that, and why would you think I have one?"

"Because I'm not blind?" Leyara laughed. "I've felt it a few times over the past weeks. Short bursts that felt like an emperor had descended onto the battlefield. An ancient heritage that doesn't belong on the frontier."

Zac was shocked at how incisive Leyara was. He had indeed been forced to use his **[Force of the Void]** a few times. It was only to slightly speed up his skill activations to push a couple of rough situations in his favor, and he hadn't thought anyone would notice. His enemies never seemed to realize, but it looked like Leyara had some means of her own.

"Why do you ask?" Zac said.

"Just curious. And to be clear, we will not provide you with any resources or manuals even if you do."

"Then I don't have one." Zac shrugged.

"Stingy," Leyara said with a laugh.

Zac rolled his eyes, but he was inwardly thankful. Leyara had probably not expected him to answer, but this was a good reminder that some could sense the Void Energy. Or if not the Void Energy itself, then the ancient aura that came with it. How much it mattered, Zac wasn't sure. But from what he could tell, both his Bloodline Talents were things that broke convention, and the fewer that knew, the better.

They soon joined the others at the viewing deck at the upper part of the mountain, the high vantage giving them a perfect view of both the soldiers outside and the work on the pathways below. By now, it was almost complete, but some of the most complex patterns remained to be engraved. The Gnivelings couldn't help with those sections, even if they'd proven surprisingly attuned to the Dao and inscriptions.

He could even spot Vai working far below, just like she had since they arrived. As far as Zac knew, she hadn't stopped working over the past ten days. The remaining Hegemons were also helping, but only two Array Masters were skilled enough to direct work rather than taking on the role of assistant.

Those three wouldn't be sent out for the raid, but the other Hegemons were slated to join them in this final push. Zac's eyes turned to Ogras, who was standing to the side. He looked a bit pale, but his aura was stable.

"How are you doing?" Zac asked.

"If I say I'm mortally wounded, can I stay behind?" the demon muttered.

Zac only laughed as he looked out at the army waiting outside, seeing that they hadn't changed their formation much since before.

"Still clumped together," Zac sighed.

Pretty nodded. "Looks that way."

Six enormous siege towers remained, each one guarded by roughly ten Hegemons and a horde of E-grade cultivators protected by a barrier. Work was underway to rebuild the ones that had been destroyed, but they wouldn't be finished in time for it to matter. Pretty even believed the work was just a ruse to divert their attention.

There were no safeguards or warriors between the six armies, almost like they were inviting you to escape like that previous Hegemon had. This arrangement was far harder to deal with compared to the previous encirclement, where they were uniformly spread out. With how they were clumped together, it was almost impossible to take out any Hegemons now, at least not without taking on some losses of their own.

For the original plan, this wouldn't have mattered. The idea was for Zac and Ogras to flee the encirclement through one of those open pathways while a diversionary squad struck one of the nearby towers. If everything worked out, they'd leave the lockdown without issue and he'd activate [Flashfire Flourish].

But Pretty's proposal meant taking on one of the six armies before leaving.

"And we really have to take down another tower?" Zac grimaced.

"It's asking a lot from you, but we simply don't have a lot of options," Leyara said. "This is a gambit—we're all joining you in striking that spot. If we can take out the Hegemons and the tower, the pressure on us will be much lower."

"The problem is that barrier," Pretty said. "By the time we break it down, the other armies will have had time to send reinforcements, flanking us."

"Don't the two of you have something left up your sleeves?" Ogras asked. "You're supposed to be proud daughters of Heaven."

"We were just a small advance party meant for reconnaissance and, if possible, sabotage," Pretty said. "If I had any siege treasures, I would have taken them out by now."

"I have a few more D-grade Talismans, but they would weaken the barrier at most," Leyara added.

"Billy can thwonk it," Billy offered.

The man looked more like a mummy than a titan at this point, with bandages covering most of his body. Zac didn't know why he insisted on using bandages when Zac had given him top-tier pills, but both he and Gemmy were adamant they were needed to recover.

Zac looked to Ogras, who curiously looked back at him. "Remember when we got trapped by the cultists?"

"Right here?" Ogras asked, as he pointedly glanced at Pretty and Leyara.

"No point in holding back if it will get us all killed. Can you cover me?" Zac asked, receiving a reluctant nod in return.

"What are the two of you talking about?" Pretty asked.

Zac didn't immediately answer, instead turning to Leyara. "Are you able to tell who or what maintains the shield?"

"Not from here, but I will when we get closer," Leyara said as she curiously looked at Zac.

"Alright, I'll deal with the shield. You guys just need to be ready to blast the Hegemons when it crumbles."

"You'll deal with it? Alone?" Pretty frowned. "How long do you need?"

"It'll be over in an instant."

# 14

# BLITZ

Zac looked up at the viewing deck far above. It was odd to see himself and the others up there, even though everyone was already gathered behind the gates. Their counterparts were illusions made by a few of the Gnivelings, which would hopefully give them a slight edge for the upcoming battle. The closer they could get to the invaders without notice, the greater the element of surprise.

"Everyone ready?" Leyara asked, getting nods of affirmation all around.

Altogether, fifteen of them would set out: himself, Ogras, Billy, Pretty, Leyara, two Hegemons, and eight E-grade Templars trained in a defensive War Array. The remaining two Hegemons couldn't be spared since their expertise was needed on the array.

"Are you sure you can do this?" Pretty asked Zac, nerves betraying her hesitation. "I'm not doubting your strength, but we've seen how sturdy those barriers are. And we don't even know if these people have used the arrays to their fullest. Keeping some strength back until a critical moment is a common strategy."

"I promise," Zac said. "As long as I can get next to it and know what powers it, I'll get the job done. At worst, I will severely weaken it."

Pretty nodded, expression turning more determined.

Zac grinned as he cracked his neck.

With nothing else to say, the group set out with Zac and the Hegemons in the front, while the E-grade cultivators made up the rear. They didn't pass through the gate but instead entered a tunnel leading beneath it. Just 30 meters in, the impenetrable barrier blocked their passage, with two Peak Gniveling scouts standing to the sides of the path.

"It's clear, no activity for half a day," the long-eared humanoid confirmed.

Zac nodded in thanks, and a shroud of shadows superimposed by a soothing spatial ripple enclosed them. A small hole opened in the barrier, and the group shot forward like a bullet. The walls turned to a blur as they rushed out from the fort, heading straight in the direction of the siege tower in the distance.

Soon enough, a soft hum spread through the tunnel, and Zac felt like an ethereal wind had passed by him.

"We're spotted," Leyara sighed, to no one's surprise.

The Kan'Tanu infiltrators had never stopped scanning these abandoned tunnels since the second raid. Zac and the others never believed they would be able to reach the enemy lines unnoticed. However, they managed to cover almost half the distance to the army before being exposed, which was more than enough according to their calculations.

One of the two Hegemons slashed out with his sword, and four beams shot upward at an angle, carving a path to the surface. The group rushed out, and were met with a sky already shuddering from burgeoning power. Just as Zac managed to orient himself, reality shifted, and he was suddenly much closer to the 100-meter-tall siege tower.

It was Leyara who'd shifted space around the whole group in what essentially was true teleportation. Space flickered around them like the skill had conjured thousands of purple fireflies, but otherwise it held. For better or worse, space wasn't as fragile as during their mad dash toward Billy's fort. Gemmy's outburst had drastically weakened the fabric of space, but it proved a temporary effect.

Still, there was clear evidence that the whole realm was declining. Even if normal attacks didn't create large spatial tears, you could still feel that space was more brittle than it should be. And that was something the Kan'Tanu invaders were making use of. Within their protective bubble, space was solidified with arrays, but the rest of the battlefield didn't enjoy those protections.

A dark sanguine light burst into life at the top of the siege tower, making it look like a lighthouse of the Underworld. The pulsating glowing sphere contained enormous amounts of energy, releasing hundreds of rays in their direction. Wherever they passed, space was roasted, creating a deadly maze of corrupted energy and spatial tears.

Zac, Ogras, Pretty, and Leyara were forced to counter the array tower's deadly blast as they rushed forward. Leyara was the one most effective at dealing with those beams, being a control mage. Those crystals on her hands lit up her surroundings, and it almost looked like she stood in the middle of a miniature galaxy as she manipulated space around them.

Meanwhile, the Hegemons infused and threw out one shimmering orb after another to their left and right, forming a 1000-meter-wide corridor. Nothing happened when the orbs landed in the grass, but they weren't supposed to do anything. At least not yet, as they were a contingency in case things got heated later.

"Going," Ogras grunted when the orbs had been thrown out, and they reached an open stretch of land free of broken space. The shadows around them condensed.

Zac felt four rapid shifts, and they once more moved closer to the barrier in an instant, though Ogras was forced to zig-zag between the bloody lasers. A thick shield rose above their heads just in time to block one of the beams. Still, they were right in the crosshairs now, with hundreds of more attacks already on their way.

A powerful fluctuation of energy had been building next to Zac for a while now, and it almost looked like a gargantuan beast swiped at the barrier as two claws tore through space and slammed into the Kan'-Tanu's barrier. The strike was quick and ruthless, but Pretty's attack only created a small ripple in the shield.

No one expected the attack to work. They just needed a fast attack powerful enough to create some energy ripples.

'*Slightly left to the tower, four masked cultivators. The Array Core is the black pedestal between them,*' Leyara's voice echoed in Zac's head, and a series of protective barriers sprung up around him, courtesy of a Hegemon and the E-grade Templars.

Zac nodded, and space shrunk as he activated **[Earthstrider]**, forcing his way through the turbulent domain toward the barrier. A tsunami of shadows rushed forward in his wake, shrouding the battlefield in darkness. A moment later, Zac was right at the edge of the barrier, and a frenzied barrage of attacks rapidly wore down his imparted shields. Still, Zac didn't care as he drew power from his bloodline.

An ancient aura permeated the area just as a tremendous lance of darkness slammed into the barrier right next to him. Hairline cracks spread across its surface, and there was even a tiny hole in front of him. A small smile spread across Zac's face as an ancient forest appeared out of nowhere, instantly summoned by [Force of the Void].

Before anyone could react, Zac had already jumped into one of the trees and appeared right next to the Array Masters within the barrier. Behind him, the cracks in the barrier rapidly closed. In fact, they had never even been there. Ogras' attack had been powerful, but not powerful enough to pierce the shield like that. The damage was merely an illusion the demon attached to his attack, giving Zac an excuse for his bloodline's ability to circumvent barriers like this.

A torrential burst of Dao-empowered fractal leaves drenched the area in blood, except for the four masked warriors. A secondary barrier had sprung up to protect them, though it was severely battered by the dozens of strikes coming from the ultimate form of [Nature's Edge]. Zac expected as much, and before the Kan'Tanu Array Masters had a chance to bolster their defenses, the next strike already reached them.

The hymns of Arcadia joined the pained screams around him as space split apart, and the ancient aura of the Void Emperor bloodline became more palpable in the surroundings. In a perfect world, Zac wouldn't use his bloodline this freely, especially not when he'd just been warned by Leyara. Except they didn't have a lot of options. More than twenty Hegemons from the neighboring armies were already closing in on them, and their window was less than ten seconds.

If they delayed any longer, they would be boxed in and over-whelmed.

The Spatial Stabilizators prevented space from completely crumbling, but it wasn't enough to block his skill. [Rapturous Divide] swept through the Array Masters' battered barrier and then through the cultivators themselves. Zac felt four surges of energy, confirming the targets were down, and the skill wasn't exhausted with just that. It ripped through the Array Core and carved a bloody path through the Kan'Tanu army.

The area rumbled as the shield fell apart. The sound was soon overshadowed by a deep groan like two tectonic plates grinding against each other. The sky had darkened beyond what the wall of shadows had elicited, but it wasn't because of some storm clouds. The head of an enormous club ripped through the shadowy haze, its size almost a match to the siege tower.

"Group 1, sto—" a Hegemon roared, only to be forced to swallow her words and dodge as a fractal leaf nearly beheaded her.

The same circumstance occurred for two more Hegemons as Zac unleashed a barrage of fractal leaves. Simultaneously, a golden laurel appeared on his head, and a good chunk of the Kan'Tanu army was showered in golden splendor. It was the restrictive domain of [Empyrean Aegis] pushed to its limits, which interrupted hundreds of cultivators from unleashing their skills.

Zac sensed how the intensity of his domain was weakened when used against so many enemies and that it wouldn't be able to prevent anyone from circulating their Cosmic Energy when prepared for the resistance. But the sudden interruption gave Zac's group a vital window of opportunity. Some of the Hegemons were occupied by Zac, and the rest soon had their hands full.

Shimmering waves of Sword Dao carved deadly paths straight through the E-grade warriors as one of the Templars unleashed a herculean strike. The other unleashed what looked like a falling sun right on top of a Kan'Tanu captain. Still, there were twelve Hegemons in this army, and they were rapidly moving to deal with the sudden turn of events.

Three of them conjured walls to block off Billy's descending strike, but they froze in place as a celestial maiden appeared above their heads. Her hair was cosmic dust, and her eyes were made from stars, and she held her arms in what looked like an open invitation. She could have been a benign deity, but even Zac felt his hair stand on end when he sensed how space around the Hegemons rapidly eroded.

The D-grade cultivators were immediately covered in shallow cuts as space fractured, and when one of them tried to respond, it backfired spectacularly. Space completely shattered around him, and Zac's eyes widened when a black claw emerged from the darkness and simply dragged the man into nothingness.

The scene was all-too-familiar. Zac had almost encountered the same thing in the Mystic Realm, except his high Luck saved him from getting captured. A Void Beast was lurking in the dark, one powerful enough to snatch a Hegemon like it was a toy. Had Leyara summoned it with her avatar? Or was it just a lucky coincidence that the Void on the other side of the spatial tear was occupied by a waiting monstrosity?

This was no time to worry about that though. The Kan'Tanu had already recovered from his interruption with [Empyrean Aegis], and was caught right in the crosshairs between his allies and enemies. Zac narrowly avoided four bloody rakes of Pretty's that ripped through the enemy lines as they shot toward Hegemons, one of them leaving a crippling wound.

Zac finished the job with a quick jab, while Ogras did the same with another Hegemon, using his shadow lance. Altogether, five Hegemons died instantly, while a few more were restrained, drastically lessening the pressure. However, the area was teeming with unfettered Heart Curses by that point, and it almost looked like a living tangle was about to be born.

The others couldn't get any closer, and Zac couldn't stay on much longer either. Even if those things couldn't kill or possess him, they could still maim his body and create a diversion.

A second rumble in the sky made Zac glance up just in time to see a large golden rune appear behind Billy's club. It emitted an aura of primordial fury, and the weapon gained a huge boost in weight and momentum. The hastily made barriers that had tried to impede it broke down, and the club descended toward the siege tower like a collapsing mountain.

The ground buckled, and a chaotic explosion swallowed hundreds of cultists as the gathered energies in the tower were unleashed on their surroundings. Zac stepped into one of the few remaining trees of [Ancestral Woods] before the wave of destruction reached him, and he appeared at the edge of the Kan'Tanu army, where he unleashed another series of Dao-empowered fractal leaves to take out another Hegemon.

The tower was destroyed and most of the Kan'Tanu Hegemons were dead or grievously wounded, which meant they'd accomplished their goal. However, they were running out of time—the neighboring armies were already moving to cut off their escape. If Leyara and the others stayed behind to deal with the rest of the army, they wouldn't be able to return.

"Go," Zac nodded upon seeing Leyara's look, and she nodded in thanks.

"Good luck," Pretty said, and they were gone the next moment, once more phased away by Leyara's skill as they desperately ran toward the fort.

"Let's go," Zac grunted when Ogras appeared next to him, sporting a few shallow cuts on his face.

The demon simply nodded, and the shadows congealed around the two. But they didn't have a chance to flash away as a second, opaque barrier suddenly sprung up to trap them. Zac found the source using [Cosmic Gaze]—a crippled Hegemon lying in a pool of blood with a cracked black sphere in his hand.

"You two stay behind," the crippled Hegemon cackled, his voice wet from the blood pouring out of his mouth.

Those were his last words as a fractal blade cut his head clean off. However, Zac didn't feel any relief even if he got a surge of energy to confirm the kill. Not only did the barrier remain even after the Hegemon's death, something was happening with the dying man's body. His hand appeared to be covered in black ink, and it rapidly spread to cover the man's arm.

The whole decapitated corpse was swallowed a moment later, yet that wasn't the end. Like a black hole, the pitch-black tendril absorbed the Heart Curses around them, even those that had already withered. The survivors weren't spared either, except for a Hegemon who used a protective talisman before digging into the ground with horror on his face.

"Another sacrifice skill!" Ogras swore. "These people are lunatics!"

Zac wholeheartedly agreed as the Cosmic Energy churned in his body. This was why he'd held back on using [Arcadia's Judgement] until now, even during the past six raids. There was no telling what hidden cards the enemy was carrying, so you needed a few of your own.

Space cracked as the enormous wooden hand emerged, just as a 20-meter-tall monstrosity of twisting tendrils and cursed energy had been fully formed. As far as Zac could tell, the fused Heart Curse didn't actually have a living controller, but it still seemed to understand the incoming axe was threatening.

With a piercing shriek, hundreds of slimy tendrils pierced into the descending hand, and Zac groaned in pain. The damage to his skill was transferred to his own body, and Zac felt like thousands of maggots had burrowed into his flesh. Still, the hand was filled with almost boundless life force, and the damaged sections regrew as soon as they appeared.

The tendrils didn't contain enough raw strength to impede the axe's descent, and it only had time to release a second mournful wail before being cut in two. The whole area shook as the world's punishment came surging from below. Zac still didn't know what powered the secondary barrier that kept them trapped, but it didn't matter in front of the wide-scale destruction.

It shattered like brittle glass, exposing them to the outside.

"Let's go," Zac smiled, but his smile froze upon seeing what was going on.

Over ten Hegemons were bearing down on them with furious momentum, with their armies not much farther behind. Even worse, the Kan'Tanu had already figured out they would probably want to escape somehow, and had unleashed a hailstorm of attacks around them, utterly fraying space.

Thankfully, the others in his group hadn't stayed behind, and they were already halfway to the fort. One of the Kan'Tanu armies was trying to catch them, but the spatial mines the Templars had thrown out worked wonders to delay their advance. That was one less thing to worry about, but it didn't help with their current predicament.

There was no way to tell what would happen if he activated [Flash-fire Flourish] in this situation. Then things changed again before he and Ogras had a chance to run or fight back. A tremendous pressure bore down on them as though an angry god had turned their attention to this battle.

Even the Kan'Tanu stopped in their tracks and fearfully looked around as the surroundings grew almost blindingly bright.

"What *now*?" Ogras groaned with exasperation.

Zac barely heard him as he mutely stared at the sky.

The clouds were on fire.

# 15

# A FATE ENCOUNTER

The sky, which had previously been overcast and dull, was now illuminated by a radiant golden-orange. However, the scene was localized to Zac's surroundings, as though an empyrean sun were trying to peek through the clouds. Of course, with the immense aura coming from above, no one would think this was a natural phenomenon.

Ogras and the Kan'Tanu looked equally confused by the sudden change, but Zac knew all too well what they were dealing with. After all, he'd seen a similar scene less than a year ago. Certainly, the flames lacked the all-consuming intensity of the burning sky in the Orom World, and it only covered a small spot. If that wasn't enough proof, there was also a familiar fiery attunement that started to appear in the Cosmic Energy surrounding them, sharing the same origin as that of the terrifying golem.

Just how was this possible? How had Iz Tayn managed to track him to the depths of the Void Star? He'd even circulated motes of chaos through his body last time, partly in hopes it would destroy any tracking measures she or others might have placed in his body.

But not even that was enough to throw this crazy firebug off his scent. Zac couldn't believe his bad luck. What in God's name was wrong with this lunatic, to make her follow him this insistently? Had he become a heart demon for Iz Tayn when he escaped from her in the Tower of Eternity?

"We need to get out of here. *Now*," Zac swore as he sought a way out.

Even if the Kan'Tanu had momentarily paused their attacks designed at destabilizing space and trapping them, they were still smack-dab in the middle of a spatial storm. Only the area where the opaque dome had previously been was still intact, and spatial tears were already closing in on them.

"Enemy reinforcements?" Ogras frowned, eyes locked on the fiery sky.

"Worse," Zac grimaced.

The rapid change to the battlefield had increased the uncertainty, except for Leyara's group. Zac had mentioned his escape measure was fire-based already, so they probably thought the powerful fiery energies were him activating his treasure. Thus, they made it through the gates of Billy's fort without even having to clash with the intercepting army with the help of Leyara's spatial shifts.

The stalemate back on the battlefield didn't last for long. Ogras, having seen the fear on Zac's face as he started making his way through the spatial storm, opted to run first and ask questions later. This time, the roles were reversed, where they were the ones who had to make their way through frayed space rather than the Kan'Tanu. Even worse, many of the Hegemons' skills were still active as they blasted the area, making the journey even more dangerous.

Meanwhile, the burning clouds in the sky slowly started to spin, forming a vortex of divine flames. All the while, the attunement in the air kept skewing further toward fire. It almost felt like someone was continuously crushing Fire-attuned Nexus Crystals around them, letting their energies spread through the area.

Zac was surprised to see that worked in their favor. The chaotic Spatial Energies were being pushed away, and some of the spatial tears were literally burned away as space mended. The Kan'Tanu's lingering attacks were also being suppressed. It was like the Dao of Fire was claiming the whole area, pushing away and suppressing everything else.

The Kan'Tanu also made their moves upon seeing that they'd made it halfway through the encirclement. Unfortunately, the invaders chose to attack with redoubled effort rather than back down, even if they didn't know what was happening in the sky. Zac once more lamented that their enemies were lunatics implanted with Heart Curses, which essentially turned them all into deathsworn who had to finish their missions no matter what.

Trying to intimidate them was useless since most weren't able to retreat.

The Templar Hegemons had crafted a set of space-stabilizing talismans as a precaution, and Zac and Ogras threw them out left and right as they made their way out of the bombardment. Ogras was somewhat better off thanks to his elusive abilities, while Zac had to continuously use Vivi's vines to intercept attacks.

A trail of broken-off vines was left in his wake, but that wasn't enough to prevent his body from being covered in wounds. Zac even briefly considered activating [Void Zone], but he didn't know how that Bloodline Talent would work in this situation. The spatial tears could technically be seen as the Void of Space leaking through due to a lack of spatial integrity.

Would his nullification sphere remove the last vestiges of protections against collapse, throwing him into the Void? There were also some witnesses he didn't want to expose his bloodline in front of, though he wasn't ready to die to keep that secret.

"This isn't working. We'll either get incinerated or cut apart by spatial tears before we get out of here," Ogras swore as he narrowly dodged a Hegemon's swing that cut off their escape path.

Zac nodded in agreement. Should he just do it? Activate [Flashfire Flourish] and hope the dense, fiery energies in the atmosphere would bolster the escape treasure enough to blast through this spatial turbulence. Or should he hold out a bit longer in hopes that Iz Tayn would inadvertently create an opening?

Suddenly, five pillars of blindingly hot flames crashed down around them, each one containing an unbelievable amount of energy. Space was singed wherever they passed, the spatial tears burnt and cauterized the moment they appeared. Luckily, none of the pillars were aimed at them, but Zac was still aghast upon sensing the extremely powerful Dao within.

Was Iz Tayn really this powerful?

The pillars were rather targeted at the groups of infiltrators who were boxing them in, and seven Hegemons were instantly reduced to cinders. They'd been prepared for an attack, but their defensive talismans and skills had proven utterly useless in the face of those flames. It drastically lessened the pressure the two were under, though Zac wasn't relieved as he looked to the sky with trepidation.

And there she was.

Descending from the sky like a demonic angel, her orange hair dancing like empyrean flames. Six burning wings gently moved behind her back, buffeted by the Dao itself. She wasn't actually flying, but rather standing on the back of a three-meter-wide hand wrought from rock.

It was from this hand those fiery pillars had emerged, and terrifying flames were still burning at its fingertips. And by the looks of it, the hand was a being of its own rather than a skill conjured by Iz. It radiated an immensely powerful aura that easily eclipsed that of the lipless Hegemon, let alone the Kan'Tanu cultivators.

Zac suddenly felt a gaze upon him, and his eyes locked with Iz Tayn's. He also heard a commotion far to the west, but he couldn't look away as Iz stepped off the golemoid hand and started to descend toward him. A Kan'Tanu Hegemon unleashed a skill toward her, but she didn't even so much as glance at the incoming bloody ray.

As expected, the attack and the Hegemon himself were annihilated by the burning hand long before the ray reached Iz, and no one else dared to so much as breathe loudly in front of that oppressive display. They could only watch on helplessly, like mortals in front of a goddess.

"You thought you could subvert the unyielding river of fate? Chaos might be able to hide you from the Heavens, but not from me," Iz said, her calm voice empowered and elevated by the Dao. "Twice now, you have fled from my grasp. There will not be a third."

"Always something with you," Ogras whispered as he glared at Zac.

"Hide us," Zac whispered, infusing Cosmic Energy into the [Flashfire Flourish].

They could no longer wait, and the surroundings were mostly stabilized thanks to the trigger-happy golem. Ogras nodded, and a huge burst of shadows engulfed the whole area. But just as they were summoned, they were dispersed, like clouds unable to withstand the sun's cleansing rays.

"What the—" Ogras swore as he looked up at Iz Tayn through the remnants of his destroyed domain.

Zac inwardly sighed before again regarding Iz Tayn. "Alright, you've found me. But we need to deal with these unorthodox cultivators before anything else. The leader is over there."

Iz Tayn frowned with annoyance as she glanced at the random Hegemon Zac pointed at. "The Black Heart Sect is irrel—"

Zac didn't hear the rest as his body was consumed by flames, and a groan next to him confirmed Ogras had been brought along for the ride. Zac's whole world was suddenly seen through the lens of fire, and his heart clenched upon seeing Iz this way.

He'd already seen that his stalker seemed more attuned with flames than even Fire Crystals when looking at her with [Cosmic Gaze], but that was nothing compared to what was displayed right now. The golem's Dao of Fire was stronger than Iz's, yet it seemed subordinate to Iz's very being.

It was almost as though she was the origin of all flames when he looked at her. Like she carried the fires of the era's birth within her body. It was mesmerizing, and Zac almost felt like he could better understand the underpinnings of the universe if he just got to study those flames a little longer.

Luckily, the overwhelming pain of being forcibly turned into a streak of fire snapped him out of it, and Zac staunchly held onto his senses over the roaring flames as he steered the treasure as best as he could. Activating the [Flashfire Flourish] was like setting yourself on fire and taping yourself to a rocket, and the enormous momentum in the treasure ripped him out of Iz Tayn's grasp.

The burning pillars were gone in an instant, as was Billy's fortress. They were moving at speeds approaching teleportation, yet he somehow managed to have a vague sense of his surroundings. Two seconds later, Zac felt they'd moved the required distance, and he willed [Flashfire Flourish] to deactivate.

Zac appeared in a foreign hillside region in a flash of scorching flames. The withered stalks of grass within five meters were incinerated, but there was thankfully no obnoxious avatar announcing their arrival. Yrial had enough presence of mind not to ruin the escape treasure that way, at least.

Tearing pain throughout his body derailed Zac's train of thought. His whole body was a scorched wasteland, and ethereal flames were still eating at his pathways and organs. Zac groaned with pain as he took out a pill bottle with shaky hands. A gust of ashy smoke escaped his lips from the exclamation, a poignant reminder his body was still literally on fire.

Yrial's prediction proved more correct than he could have known. He had said that damaging one's foundations was an unavoidable price of using such a powerful escape treasure, that it was the Law of Balance. Yet Zac felt the damage to his body wasn't that bad. The flames were stubborn, but his Hidden Nodes had already started swallowing them. As for the damage to his foundations, they weren't any worse than breaking open a node or two. With Leyara's pill and a few of his own, he should be good to go before the next battle.

As expected of a Terminal Disciple of a powerful Monarch, Leyara had all kinds of valuables in her Spatial Ring. She had given him and Ogras one pill each that looked like a golden nebula trapped in a black bubble of night sky. It was called [Resurging Star Pill], a special type of recovery pill that helped after over drafting your body.

The pill was normally meant to be used after using powerful Berserking Treasures or Taboo skills that damaged your foundations, but it should work just as well in their current situation. A weak groan echoed next to him, and Zac looked over to see Ogras kneeling. His body was covered in scorch marks, looking utterly wretched.

"You okay, buddy?" Zac asked.

"Heaven-cursed heart-eating lunatics, netherblasted spatial tears, and now crazed fire witches?" Ogras complained as he swallowed his prepared set of pills. "You'll be the death of me."

Zac laughed in response, but his smile became strained as he felt a tremendous burst of energy behind them.

"I told you there wouldn't be a third."

---

Vai blankly looked at the scene from her spot atop the wall, not knowing what to believe. At first, everything had gone according to plan. The tower collapsed, and her niece safely returned to her side without any further casualties. The infiltrators had sprung a nasty trap to catch Gaun —no, Zac Atwood, but it failed.

Then everything changed when the terrifying flame cultivator descended from the sky. Vai had never seen anything like it. Just looking at her was like staring at the true face of fire, more true than any fiery Dao Vai had ever seen. A glance at Lara, who joined her atop the wall, indicated her niece had no idea who she was either.

It was a hidden master, and someone who was clearly here for her friend—the mysterious woman's words carrying through the whole battlefield. Vai wasn't surprised. Someone like the Deviant Asura wouldn't attract common cultivators. She'd already seen as much from his two other inordinately powerful friends.

She still couldn't believe that her bodyguard and traveling companion was the man whose actions had shaken the whole Zecia Sector a decade ago, a talent who only appeared once in a million years. Looking back at it, she felt incredibly foolish.

Who else but the Deviant Asura could fight Hegemons and Beast Kings as though they were common fodder? Who else would carry a mysterious bloodline that made her very being want to kneel in obeisance? Who else would be embroiled in mysterious heritages that carried the aura of antiquity?

Still, it was difficult to combine those scattered rumors she'd heard in the monastery with the man who stayed by her side for months. From the rumors, Zac was a powerful lunatic who was an amalgamation of lust and violence, but the reality couldn't be any further from the truth.

His eyes had never carried that glimmer when he looked at her, the glimmer that was painfully obvious in his demonic friend. Neither had he taken up the invitations from the other Wandering Cultivators during their month of travel. And there had been more than one, especially after he showcased more of his power.

In reality, he was almost obsessively focused on his cultivation, where violence was just a means to an end. Over the past two weeks, she felt he'd managed to get a bit closer to the real him as well, now that he no longer carried his disguise. As far as she was concerned, Deviant Asura didn't exist, except in the mouths of others.

But as she looked at the following scene, she couldn't help but wonder if there really was some truth to the rumors.

Amid the new arrival's primordial flames, a new source of fire had erupted—right where her two companions stood. It didn't contain nearly the purity of meaning of the surrounding flames, but the fire was extraordinary in its own right. It exploded like a firework, sending hundreds of fiery streams in every direction.

Zac and Ogras had disappeared in one of those streams, and the remaining flames formed a type of imagery Vai had never seen before, depicting Zac Atwood in the middle of a swirl of roses. His features were different, worse in Vai's opinion, and his eyes contained frailty that didn't exist. The avatar showcased a sorrowful smile before turning around, and his departing back was the last thing you saw before the scene was replaced by four lines of text.

*A fate encounter, two hearts collide*
*But Heaven's Path won't be denied*
*A lonely road, the pursuit of power*
*Please forgive this lonesome flower*

Vai's mind short-circuited as she read the short poem. What? Why? Why had he added such a weird contraption to the escape treasure? And what did he mean by it? Was there some sort of sordid history between himself and the mysterious woman floating in the sky? Vai had to admit she was incredibly beautiful, even eclipsing her niece.

The mysterious woman seemed surprised by the turn of events, staring at the flickering poem for a few seconds. Then she lifted her arm, and a storm of primordial flames incinerated the illusion. The next moment, an incredibly complex array appeared where the poem hovered, its patterns far beyond anything Vai had ever seen.

The sigil turned into a thin strand of pure flames that shot toward the east, and Vai looked on with wide eyes as the woman turned into flames and entered the stream. She was gone, leaving a wide circle of scorched earth and incinerated corpses.

"No!" a panicked roar echoed across the battlefield as her powerful companion burst into flames.

It no longer cared about restraining the invaders as it rushed toward the stream. In the direction of Zac. The shocking scene created a suspended lull on the battlefield, but reality came crashing back soon enough as the battle between the invaders and the newly arrived squad of Templars to the west resumed.

"What in the Heavens!" Pretty Peak exclaimed from the side. "Deviant, a pureblooded deviant!"

"I liked it," Leyara laughed. "Both form and function."

"What should we do?" Vai fretfully asked. "It looked like that woman managed to enter the slipstream with the help of her flames. They might be in trouble."

"Well, nothing we can do," Pretty Peak grunted. "If that thing worked as that madman advertised, then he's already a month's travel away from this place. He's on his own now. We can only pray that guy can handle it."

"Don't worry, aunty. I don't think they're enemies." Leyara smiled as she ate a Soldier Pill.

"How do you know?" Vai asked curiously.

"Woman's intuition." Leyara winked. "I felt a sense of threat from her, for my long-term prospects."

"Y-you can't marry that man," Vai stuttered.

"Oh? You want him for yourself?" Leyara asked with surprise, and Pretty looked over curiously.

"N-No. I-I just feel his fate is too powerful. It's dangerous to be around him," Vai said with rosy cheeks. "I don't wish for you to be hurt."

"Don't you worry about me." Leyara pinched Vai's cheeks.

"More importantly, what should we do about your people over there?" Pretty pointed at the group of unfamiliar Templars who'd popped up out of nowhere. "They're putting up a good fight, but that crazy golem is gone now. They will be overrun unless something changes."

"Let's go," Leyara said, giving the scorched area one last look before jumping down the wall. "Lonesome flower, huh?"

# 16

# SUBVERTED FATE

The familiar voice felt like a cold shower, if that cold shower were made from scorching flames. Zac prayed he'd gone mad and it was an auditory hallucination, but the excitement from the flames still burning within his body wasn't a great sign. The next moment, the embers poured out from his cells, while the same thing happened to Ogras.

They all flew toward the same destination—the woman who calmly stood just ten meters away, in front of a backdrop of primordial flames. Iz Tayn. The embers danced around her before rushing into the fiery curtain like moths drawn to the flame. Iz looked at the embers' final journey before the curtain closed, and her attention returned to them.

Standing in front of Iz Tayn was a sobering reminder that while he'd made enormous strides over this past year, he had in no shape or form reached the very limits of the E-grade. Iz's aura clearly eclipsed his own, and possibly even that of the lipless Hegemon. Even then, Zac was certain she was still in the E-grade like him because her aura was almost impossibly condensed.

And impossibly rife with meaning.

Part of it was undoubtedly the lingering Dao of the powerful flames that just winked out, but standing in front of her reminded Zac of standing in the Dao Chamber when they cracked open the Dao Funnel all those years ago. Except that the only Dao he could sense right now was the Dao of Fire. Her very being exuded the truth of flames, to a degree Zac didn't think possible in the E-grade.

It almost seemed like her flames encompassed all Daos, though Zac knew that was impossible at her level. In a sense, he was almost looking at the opposite of himself. Her flames encompassed all while he embodied the Void.

Zac's instincts told him someone like this was rare even among the peak factions of the Multiverse. Uona Noz'Valadir was the strongest E-grade cultivator he'd fought thus far, but she couldn't hold a candle to Iz. Certainly, Uona did by no means represent the peak of the Undead Empire. Zac simply doubted they had anyone who could match Iz Tayn level for level. Unless the Primo had direct descendants running around, perhaps.

Taking in Iz's unparalleled appearance and unfathomable aura was an experience on its own. Zac's belly was still full of grievances as he looked for solutions to their predicament. Why did his escape treasure have to be Fire-attributed? Couldn't Yrial have found one based on *ice*? He didn't know if Iz somehow caught a ride through the stream of flames, or if she had methods to follow it with a treasure of her own.

What was clear, though, was that she hadn't been harmed at all by the journey, while neither Zac nor Ogras were in the best of conditions. And he was out of tricks. [Flashfire Flourish] needed time to recharge, and he wasn't sure his body would be able to take another jump anyway. His escape bangle was out of commission, and there were no motes of Chaos to make the impossible possible.

The good news was that Zac couldn't sense any killing intent coming from Iz Tayn, nor was she circulating Cosmic Energy. She just stood there on a patch of ground singed clean by her flames. Neither had that weird junior golem managed to follow her by the looks of it, leaving her alone.

That didn't help skew things in their favor if it came to blows. Based on her aura, Zac's instincts told him that Iz alone was enough to deal with both of them, even if they were in perfect condition. If you included whatever protective and offensive treasures a supreme genius from a peak faction carried, it was pretty much hopeless.

His only hope for victory was to hit her with an Annihilation Sphere or Origin Mark. Would he even get the opportunity to conjure them if they fought? Besides, killing her was out of the question. He wouldn't dare, even if he somehow found a chance to take her out. Iz's faction knew of him, and they knew how to find him seemingly anywhere.

It was game over for him and Earth if she came to harm. Perhaps for all of the Zecia Sector.

These remote places weren't valuable enough for even B-grade factions like the Radiant Temple to bother with. They just snatched up the occasional talent that emerged and extracted some resources on the cheap. A faction with Peak Autarchs as Dao Guardians for their young might simply eradicate the whole Sector in retaliation.

And while the System's shroud protected Earth from people like the Great Redeemer, he didn't hold much hope it would do the same against a determined Supremacy.

This left him in an extremely awkward situation where he didn't know what to do. Since Iz wasn't saying anything, he'd have to be the one to speak up.

"You've hunted me down halfway across the Multiverse," Zac said with some helplessness. "You caught me. Is all of this because of what I said over ten years ago?"

"Over ten years?" Ogras blurted with a raspy voice, then quickly shrunk back when Iz turned her gaze to him.

"Your fate has been swept up in his, and something mundane has become unordinary," Iz said to Ogras, primordial flames flickering in her eyes. "But can you withstand the river on your own? If not, you will be dragged under, like so many before you."

Zac's eyes widened in alarm when he felt the scorching heat in Iz's gaze, and he remembered all too well the unlucky few who'd been placed too close to this firebug in the Battle of Fates. Ogras was clearly worse off than he from the teleportation, and his skills had proven ineffective against Iz's flames.

The original idea was to lay low for a day or two and let the pills nurture them back to the point they could fight unencumbered. A battle now might worsen the damage even further, especially for Ogras, who didn't have an unnaturally sturdy constitution to fall back on.

"You came here for me, right?" Zac frowned as he stepped in front of Ogras.

"I'll... uh... let the two of you talk," Ogras whispered before retreating a few hundred meters away, though Zac noticed one of the shadows by the hills released a small flicker. He was ready to fight in case they were left with no choice.

That left a frazzled Zac standing nervously in front of Iz Tayn. He didn't dare take out [Verun's Bite], afraid she'd take that as a threat or insult. At the same time, he didn't know what to say. How do you lose someone who had already followed you across half the Multiverse?

He needed to make this lunatic leave on her own somehow, but Zac didn't even know what she wanted. Neither could he glean any hints from her expressionless face, and Zac found himself coming up short when trying to figure out what to say.

"Do you believe those words?" Iz said after a pregnant pause.

Zac grimaced. There it was. He'd called her a goddamned lunatic right before escaping, and now she'd come to collect. Could he simply apologize and pray she'd drop the matter without trying to incinerate him and Ogras? However, the next words out of Iz Tayn threw him for a loop.

"The words in the poem you left behind?"

"Poem?" Zac said with a sinking feeling. "What poem?"

Flames appeared out of nowhere between them, and Zac looked on with growing unease as they formed a field of roses. It was one thing getting himself in trouble because of his big mouth—he only had himself to blame. But if Yrial's warped desire to fuse beauty and function had caused even more trouble for him, he didn't know what he would do.

Sure enough, there was the same bastardized version of himself, though the following scene differed slightly from the first. Zac saw himself turn away, and the rose field was replaced by a short poem. The more Zac read, the bigger the pit in his stomach grew. This wasn't just a problem of taunting Iz Tayn. It certainly wouldn't help with his already tarnished reputation.

After all, that golem guardian must have seen the text as well, as had those in the fort. He'd warned about the odd feature of [Flashfire Flourish], but he wasn't sure how much that would help in front of such a scene. The flames dispersed, and Zac found himself lacking for words.

"Do you believe the road toward the Terminus is a solitary one? That Karmic Threads tie one down on the road to power?"

Zac looked at Iz suspiciously, but it didn't seem like she was joking or messing around. Her face was completely earnest as she waited for an answer. She'd hunted him possibly for ten years, and this was what she wanted to discuss?

"Uh… It wasn't me who wrote that poem. I don't have any backing, and this is the frontier," Zac slowly said. "I have to make do with whatever treasures I get my hands on, even if they have weird side effects."

Iz's lips curved upward at that, and her smiling visage almost made Zac's mind blank out. Living, breathing beings had no business being this good-looking. How were others to compete?

"That doesn't answer my question."

Zac became exasperated, not knowing what she wanted from him. It almost felt like she didn't know herself, but he supposed having a chat beat getting blasted by a fireball.

"Some aspects of cultivation are ultimately up to yourself, but I don't think it's a solitary road. I wouldn't be here without the help from a lot of people, and I'm pretty sure the same is true for you. And even if I somehow reached the peak all on my own, what would be the point of such an empty existence? Where I just sit alone on some mountain peak, churning with power? It's the Karmic Links you mention that give me purpose, that allow me to keep pushing myself."

Iz considered his words a few seconds before nodding. "Thank you. Still, I have come all this way, so I will have to test your fate with my fire. It is not just a matter of your insult anymore. You will have to prove fate strong enough to carry the title of a Flamebearer. Otherwise, the other contenders will consume you, and I will have to fight an uphill battle for the inheritance for nothing."

"That's…!" Zac exclaimed with wide eyes.

Zac's heart shuddered when his fears were realized. Iz Tayn was really a Flamebearer. He should have guessed it the moment she appeared inside the Void Star. Going by the name alone, she might be the most suitable person in the younger generation.

The fact he would be pitted against someone like her for the inheritance felt like an almost insurmountable wall, but that wasn't his real worry. Ultimately, Zac didn't hold much hope of seizing Ultom for himself after learning that the knowledge of the Left Imperial Palace was already widespread. As long as he got a few more pieces of the sigils and their epiphanies, he'd be happy. If he managed to get a small portion of the real inheritance, it'd be a huge windfall.

He was more worried about the implications of Iz's mention of other contenders. She essentially confirmed others would be fighting for the same slot. And if one scion from the Heartlands had already joined the fray just months after he got the quest, did that mean others were already here? Or was she just lucky to stumble onto this opportunity while looking for him? Had he accidentally brought trouble on their head by leading Iz here?

"You are free to use either your human or Draugr form. But if you use those Remnants you keep locked away in your mind, I will use means of similar potency," Iz Tayn continued.

Zac was already reeling from her first proclamation, but that was nothing compared to having two of his biggest secrets exposed like it was common knowledge. It felt like his world had been upended, and he looked at Iz with incomprehension. How did she know all that? And *what else* did she know?

"Did you not think I saw you back then? How the descendant of the Ignus Clan nearly destroyed your soul, yet you turned calamity into opportunity to force a breakthrough? How you transformed into a Draugr and fought the Red Hand Society assassin?" Iz said upon seeing Zac's confusion. "Why did you think I called for you?"

"I, uh," Zac stuttered, his mind still a mess as he found himself in the very situation he had so desperately tried to prevent for so long.

"And did you think my uncle would not recognize the Remnants from the Heart of Oblivion and the Spark of Creation? He was quite impressed how you managed to fuse their energies into a rudimentary expression of Chaos. He said he'd never heard of anyone doing that before," Iz continued with equanimity. "Now, pick your form."

"Ah, young mistress," a hesitant voice drifted over from a distance, where Ogras' head was sticking out from behind a boulder. "I don't think you want to fight right now."

"As I said, fate will not be subverted," Iz said without even looking over.

"Of course, of course," Ogras eagerly nodded. "Nor should it. But I'm sure that young mistress hasn't waited for years to right this wrong, only for your target to be unable to battle in his optimal state? Look at how wretched he is, how half his hair is gone and burn marks cover his hands and face. I can assure you, the situation within our bodies is even worse, even with you so graciously removing the lingering flames."

Iz frowned as she thoughtfully looked between Ogras and Zac, who could only push down his embarrassment and look as pathetic as possible to sell Ogras' lie. Well, it *wasn't* a lie, really. Between him using up most of his skills just moments ago, and the damage from [Flashfire Flourish], he certainly wasn't in the best shape.

"And that's not the only thing, young mistress! And you would want to hear this!" Ogras continued, prompting her to look over curiously. "We are actually on an important mission! To fight evil, unorthodox cultivators, destroy a pathway to a cursed universe, and save the day. If we don't accomplish our task in a few days, then our lives are all forfeit."

Zac once more wondered if something was wrong with Iz's brain, since her eyes lit up at Ogras' proclamation. It looked like she couldn't be happier at the prospect of their lives hanging by a thread. She even looked over to Zac, obviously hoping for confirmation.

"It's true," Zac reluctantly said. "If we don't blow up that pathway, this whole realm will be flooded with tainted energy. The realm will collapse, and we shall all die."

Iz Tayn looked like she'd hit the jackpot, and a slight flush appeared on her cheeks. However, she soon realized Zac was looking at her weirdly, and she regained her impassive expression. She nodded slightly, like the news was nothing unexpected.

There were no two ways about it. There was something off with this girl.

"We shall postpone our battle," Iz agreed.

"I can see this young mistress has a righteous heart," Ogras continued. "We would be doubly blessed if you joined us in this endeavor. To thwart evil and protect our world."

Iz glanced at Zac, who tried to look enthused by the idea. He had to admit that Ogras' plan was solid. Not only would this net them an extremely powerful helper, but it would give them a breather to figure out a long-term solution to this Iz problem. "You're welcome to join us."

"Then I shall accompany you," Iz said.

"It would be our pleasure," Ogras readily agreed as he bounded over. "This lowly one is Ogras Azh'Rezak, at your service."

"Iz Tayn," she said, once more looking at Zac.

"Zac Atwood," he said, wholly uncomfortable under her stares.

"Great, great!" Ogras nodded. "Now that we're all friends, can we expect your... uh... *hand*, to join us? Its strength could definitely be helpful."

"Kvalk has no interest in fighting against the Black Heart Sect," Iz said. "He is more likely to test the fate of you two. It should take him around three or four days to reach this area if you are interested in battling him as well."

"The ruins of the Ra'Lashar Kingdom are right this way," Ogras immediately said as he started walking. "Treasures and mystery await!"

Zac didn't know what else to do, so he simply followed in tow.

"As I said, our battle is only delayed. I will find you after this is dealt with," Iz added as she floated over to his side. "But I can see you are not enthused at the idea, so I am willing to offer this treasure as long as you don't disappoint."

The word 'treasure' could deal with most problems, and Zac looked over at the thing that appeared in Iz's hand. Ogras' eyes were gleaming, and Zac could understand the sentiment.

Who wouldn't be curious about what kind of treasures someone like Iz Tayn could take out?

17

# ALAVA'HAR

Bastard.

Ogras watched the two social outcasts walk in pace, and it was hard to tell who was more uncomfortable. Zac wore it plainly on his face, though Ogras could almost hear the gears turning in the head of that sheltered lass. They looked like a teenage couple full of hormones and awkward love. *Double-bastard.*

He'd spent ten years in this godforsaken realm with not a woman as far as the eye could see. All the while, this guy was living it up while pretending otherwise. The more he heard, the more Ogras' teeth itched. The Peak lass, Leyara, even that little doe-eyed researcher, kept throwing him long looks. Ibtep, that lunatic, had even created a wildly inaccurate rumor, only for millions of maidens to take him seriously. According to Pretty Peak, there were massive bounties from lonely singles for the contact details of the Deviant Asura.

And now, this celestial fairy had fallen right into this useless guy's lap? A woman who had broken Ogras' understanding of the limits of beauty. And who was apparently carrying around supreme treasures tailored for that dullard. Ogras had no idea what that ominous-looking stone was, but Zac was almost drooling, so it had to be something good.

*Triple-bastard*!

Iz Tayn reminded Ogras of Alava'Har from the stories he'd read growing up. A princess of the divine realm descended to the mortal plains in search of love and purpose. Rich, naïve, and bored. It only took

Ogras a single glance to figure out this Iz Tayn was the same—a sheltered rose of a terrifyingly powerful origin.

Who knew? This might be the first time she left the safety of her family's domains. No doubt surrounded by servants since birth, but lacking proper connections, to the point that a simple curse thrown her way had become an obsession.

Luckily, Iz Tayn had been easy enough to wrangle, even if he'd been forced to throw his face a bit. But what was face worth in front of life? Those flames were just too terrifying. It almost felt like the shadows that made up his body would collapse when she looked in his direction. So he would sing his song and dance a little dance until the young empress was satisfied.

She would join in on their 'adventure' and then return to the divine realm with her elders. Iz had clearly relegated him to a servant-type shortly after they set off, but that was fine with him. It was just like the lass said, too much excitement and he'd get himself killed. Someone like Iz Tayn undoubtedly had enough suitors to drown him in spit if they thought him getting too close to their target.

But this useless guy was blowing it. They needed to entertain, damn it! And in return, they would feed on her scraps, be they information, treasures, or knowledge. He desperately tried to send the message with his glances, but that idiot was walking along looking like a martyr about to sacrifice himself against a beast tide.

Perhaps these two were too socially inept to walk and talk simultaneously?

---

Iz glanced at the unusually mutated demon, who smiled and nodded obsequiously in return. The scene was off-putting. It reminded her of those empty smiles that followed wherever she traveled with her uncle. The smile of those who tried to benefit from the vast wealth or influence of the Tayn family. Part of her wanted to just release her flames and test his fate then and there.

But she couldn't. Mr. Bug was still unhappy about the arrangement, even after she'd shown the [Stone of Celestial Void] like her uncle suggested. Was it because their sparring session had been delayed? Uncle explained that real friendships were forged through battle.

Only when you had withstood your opponent's Dao could you truly understand who they were. The Dao was the road to the heart. But now, everything was left on an uncertain note.

She didn't know what to make of this silent yet palpable sense of rejection. She'd always been welcomed with open arms no matter where she went. Even ancestors emerged from their sealed chambers to greet her and provide small gifts of goodwill. To have someone be so overtly annoyed by her presence was a first.

It was almost liberating in a twisted sort of way. Because his opinions of her were based on their encounters rather than on her surname. Certainly, Mr. Bug knew some of it. Though to someone like him, any established family must seem like an unfathomable mountain. He didn't know what a throne represented or who her grandparents were.

Still, while Iz felt this atmosphere was novel, it wasn't what she envisioned. She remembered those scenes from the graded trial Mr. Bug joined. Of how he'd joked around with that other Draugr or the excitement they felt upon exploring their first shared trove. The camaraderie created by a shared adversary when they found themselves beneath that stream.

How was she supposed to break the tension in this situation? Iz had no idea. She was increasingly realizing that she wasn't very equipped or prepared to set out on her own. There were many types of strengths she lacked, strengths that couldn't be gained through her grandpa's meticulous preparations for her cultivation.

She couldn't bring up Mr. Bug's adventures either, even though she really wanted to know what happened between a few of her viewing sessions. Or when he'd consumed the previous set of Remnants. She only knew he had been headed toward a place called the City of Ancients, followed by a long bout of aggravating static.

Grandpa had told her that she absolutely couldn't tell any outsider about the existence of the Divine Mirror. It was a supreme treasure from a previous era. Her Grandma had found it long ago in some ruins of the Limitless Empire, and it was a treasure that would drive certain clans mad with desire. Not only that, but her uncle had told her that it would ruin her chance at friendship if she told Mr. Bug, even if Iz didn't understand why.

Thousands of her family's servants had observed her every breath since she was born, which had no impact on her daily life. But she trusted Uncle Valderak knew what he was talking about. Even if she hadn't found much use for his two weeks of friendship-tutoring so far.

Should she just give him the stone and see if that helped?

---

Zac surreptitiously glanced at the woman who walked in pace with them, her calm face giving no clues as to what she was thinking. Everything about her was confusing. She'd employed god-knows-what kind of High-grade methods to find him, and even used a Peak Autarch to ferry her over to the frontier.

But when she had finally caught up with him, she readily agreed to postpone her duel. Since then, she'd barely spoken a word. Iz appeared mostly content with walking in silence. Zac certainly had a lot on his mind. Ogras had occasionally tried making some small talk with Iz, but she either answered in single syllables or not at all. By now, the silence had almost grown oppressive.

Zac felt Iz's gaze upon him once more. Before he had a chance to see if something was wrong, Ogras had stopped in his tracks just ahead of them.

"There is a hidden cave not far from here," Ogras said. "Our original plan was to hide for a day and recover. How about we check out that place? During that time, we can also discuss the upcoming battle."

Zac glanced at Iz, who nodded slightly in agreement.

"Let's go," Zac said, and Ogras gave him another pointed look before turning away.

Zac knew what the demon wanted. He wasn't so dense that he couldn't understand the opportunistic gleam in Ogras' eyes. The demon wanted him to befriend Iz and possibly extract advantages from her. But things were not that simple, and he was still digesting the whole situation. Having gone over the events from the past half-hour, Zac had come to a few conclusions.

He should already have realized that Iz was aware of his two secrets.

Even if he hadn't expected Iz to witness the whole chain of events in the Battle of Fates, he had spoken with her in his Draugr form. The next time they met, he was a human, yet she recognized him plain as day. The Remnants were even less of a mystery. He'd used what he called a Bronze Flash in the Tower of Eternity, and the next time he'd *just* swallowed the Remnants and was teeming with their energy.

None of that explained how Iz had the **[Stone of Celestial Void]**.

He hadn't actually seen that item before, but it perfectly matched the description in the listing back in the Orom World. More importantly, only two people knew about it: he and a store clerk. The only time he ever said its name aloud was when he asked the clerk if the treasure could be brought out for inspection. After having been rejected, Zac never mentioned the item again.

So how did Iz know he wanted it? Even the Orom wouldn't know, considering how little it cared about the day-to-day inside its body. Just what happened after he fled the Orom? Or did she have some way to spy on him? The thoughts kept gnawing at him, making him unable to focus on anything else. Eventually, it reached a tipping point, and Zac turned to Iz with a determined expression.

"How did you know I need that item?"

Iz didn't seem surprised by the question, but she still looked at Zac thoughtfully for a few seconds until her eyes lit up. "My family set up some rules for me when visiting the frontier. All actions have consequences, and forming Karmic debts should be avoided when possible. If you want me to divulge secrets that would normally be out of your reach, then you must prove you are fated with that knowledge."

"How would I prove something like that?" Zac asked with confusion.

"Withstand my flames."

"Are you just making up an excuse to beat me up?" Zac asked, his eyes thinning with suspicion.

Iz's mouth curved up a bit at that, but she quickly regained her poise. "If you want to know, you would have to take a strike from me."

Ogras was looking at the proceedings with interest. "Just go with it. If there's one thing you're good at, it's taking a beating. So what's the harm?"

"Easy for you to say." Zac glared, but he still readied himself.

There was no way she was planning on going all out at this point, and Zac felt confident he should at least be able to deal with a normal attack without too much issue. A creaking sound echoed out as Vivi's vines formed a thick barrier, and **[Verun's Bite]** appeared in his hands.

"Go ahead," Zac said, and he jumped back fifty meters to give himself some berth.

Iz nodded and held up her hand. A small fireball appeared in her palm, exuberantly releasing small bursts of golden embers. Zac relaxed a bit since it just looked like a fancy version of a common **[Fireball]** attack. However, Zac's eyes widened in alarm when it shot out from Iz's hand.

Suddenly, it felt like a whole sun was bearing down on him. The little ball contained an immense amount of truths, to the point it created illusions all around him. At least Zac hoped it was an illusion since the whole area had been set ablaze, even the air. Zac felt a weak exclamation of pain from Vivi, and he realized her vines were rapidly drying out, their powerful life force unable to compete with the scorching heat.

Zac could only cut off the dried-out vines with a swing of his axe, and the symbiotic plant almost fully retreated back into its pocket domain. That left him with one less layer of defense, just as the deceptive little fireball doubled its momentum while gaining an intense golden hue. Space was being incinerated in its wake, and Zac felt like hot pokers were being stabbed into the still-tender burns across his body.

"Holy—!" Zac swore as he urgently activated **[Empyrean Aegis]**.

Two different hues of gold clashed for supremacy in the area as the ball of utmost flames slammed into his hastily-erected barrier. The fireball burned its way straight through with a sizzle, leaving Zac gobsmacked. It might have expended a good chunk of its force by that point, but what remained was still more than enough to cause alarm.

Normally, Zac would have used the brief window bought by his barrier to move out of the way, but Iz demanded he withstand the flame, not survive the strike. He could only grit his teeth as he unleashed a herculean swing infused with his Branches of the War Axe and Pale Seal. He normally didn't use the second Dao in his human form, but he figured it was more effective at snuffing out flames than a Life-attuned one.

A primal roar of defiance echoed through the scorched wastelands as Verun bit straight through the golden ball of primordial flames. Zac felt his Daos being rapidly whittled down by the unrelenting fire, and his powerful soul churned as he infused more and more of it to combat the drain. The fireball didn't enjoy the same treatment. Soon after, it was completely ripped apart.

However, Zac's relief was short-lived as the ball's destruction released a splatter of flames in every direction like a Dao-infused Molotov Cocktail. A few managed to reach his body, and his robes became a tattered mess. A searing pain soon followed as parcels of fiery Dao dug into his body. It was almost as though the flames were alive in a tangible way that was completely different from the fire left behind by [Flashfire Flourish].

These little flames were connected with the boundless universe.

Sensing them with his soul felt like staring at the primordial soup from which the Big Bang created the universe. It was a fire of endless possibility, almost reminding him of one aspect of Creation. At the same time, it held the ability to reduce anything to ashes, leaving nothing in its wake but utter destruction. A facet of Oblivion.

Was this Iz's Dao? Her vision of a supreme Dao of Fire that was one with all?

A deep and angry thud from the depths of his chest brought him out from his reverie as [Void Heart] woke up, and it started to drag the wayward embers toward its maw. But the flames were unwilling to go quietly into the night, and desperately struggled against the pull. The Hidden Node managed to swallow a few, but most embers made their way out of Zac's body, leaving a second scorch mark behind before returning to Iz's side.

The apocalyptic surroundings died down, confirming it was indeed not real, but an effect brought by the Dao infused into the attack. Ogras was just fine, even though it looked like the flames had consumed him for a moment, and he was looking at Iz with wide eyes.

"Well?" Zac grimaced as he looked down at his ruined clothes with dismay.

He'd practically been returned to his roots, where he looked like a mix of a burn victim and a homeless person.

"I am very curious what your bloodline is. It is the first time I've seen someone dare consume the flames of my family," Iz said with interest. "Or at least *succeed* in doing so."

Her words made Zac pause. It looked like she didn't know quite everything about him, at least.

"Well, there's always a first," Zac grunted as he walked over. "The stone?"

"I left a mark on you during our first meeting," Iz said. Zac wasn't surprised.

He remembered the flame touching his chest but not actually harming him. He had long since guessed it was a tracking mark, but he hadn't been overly worried about it since she came from a different part of the Multiverse. So much for that theory.

"You managed to destroy it, but I had an elder bring it back and rein-force it," Iz said, making both Ogras and Zac look at her with alarm. Just how powerful did you have to be to *bring back* a destroyed tracking mark on someone across half the Multiverse? "It is through that mark I've been able to find you."

"Well, that explains some of it, but it doesn't explain how you know about the stone?" Zac said, putting the matter of her elder aside.

"The mark can create a lingering resonance in weaker cultivators that would let my family identify them," Iz said. "That would allow us to do all kinds of things. Such as finding the clerks you had been in contact with while living in the mutated Voidcatcher."

Zac's expression turned suspicious. It was as plausible as anything else, but he worried it wasn't the whole truth.

"In either case, the brand barely works now," Iz continued. "It would have to get bolstered by my elder again since you weakened it when you conjured Chaos."

"How do I know you're not just making things up?" Zac asked.

"Every word I've said is true," Iz said, appearing a bit hesitant. "The price for the knowledge might be off. Do you want to know anything else?"

"How about you remove the mark?" Zac said. "After all, you've already found me."

"Impossible," Iz said with a shake of her head. "Even if damaged, it has been bolstered by my elder. It's not something I can remove."

"Fine," Zac grunted. "Then can you tell me if a bunch of Autarchs, or even stronger beings, will come to Zecia to contend for the inheritance? You should know that's not something a small frontier Sector can withstand."

"Oh, you don't need to worry about that," Iz said. "The Boundless Heavens has shielded this Sector. My elder believes this inheritance is targeted at the younger generation, and the Heavens do not want undue interference. When we entered, only a Middle Monarch could be sent through."

Zac and Ogras shared a glance, relief evident in their eyes. This was their biggest worry, but it looked like the System had already dealt with the problem for them. Monarchs from the outside were difficult to deal with, but they were nothing compared to Supremacies.

"Ask her something else," Ogras urged as a grin spread across his face.

"You ask her, bastard," Zac swore as he looked down at his charred body. "I'm about well done over here. If I get any more toasty, you'll have to fight the next battle yourself."

"Fine," Ogras sighed. "We'll talk more after we've rested."

"I know many things," Iz added as she looked hopefully at Zac.

"Isn't that great," Zac muttered. "Now, where is that cave?"

# 18
# FLICKER OF HOPE

The weak rustle of leaves formed a tranquil song as the silence stretched on, even though the plants in the inner courtyard had died out eons ago. Replacing the plant life was a thick layer of ashy dust. It created a paradoxical environment—the utter desolation of eternal autumn mixed with the fresh winds of spring. Fifty by fifty meters, boxed in by ancient stones and an anthracite sky. Emily only had two things for company: her thoughts and the tattered banner hanging from the stele.

The sigil on its surface was simple, yet it held power and profundity beyond anything she'd ever heard of. Possibly of anything in the whole Sector. A rising sun which carried the breath of the universe. The unending cycle that brought the seasons, that brought life and death.

The Sigil of the Radiant Court.

Emily still couldn't believe she had been accepted when Pro'Zul and Ynaea had both been turned to ash right before her eyes. She felt like an impostor benefiting from something not meant for her, and she was just waiting for the pulse that would claim her as well. That was part of the reason why she hadn't moved over the past eight months, even if the sprawling castle might hold more treasures. Even if the army was slated to leave for the next Sector more than three months ago.

She was afraid to draw unwanted attention, waking up the terrifying power slumbering in this private garden. The other reason was that she simply couldn't. The gates had been sealed shut behind her, and she knew all too well just how sturdy those stones were. Even if she struck with all she had, she wouldn't leave a mark.

It wasn't all bad, though. The energy was both unbelievably dense and filled with meaning. She was making tremendous progress. The random herbs and baubles she'd picked up in her first excursion with the coliseum was nothing compared to this. The only things of value she got back then were painful lessons and the ticket to the Million Gates Territory.

Just sitting in front of the banner obviously couldn't compare to those shimmering lights, but it still felt like she was gaining a week's worth of comprehension every day she sat here. And she had a lot to work on. Forming a Supreme Pathbound skill with the help of the three strands of light was just the first step. Creating the axe array that would make the most of it required a lot of work, even with the banner helping.

Before she could even begin, she was forced to digest the truths from the lights. Truths that completely upended her understanding of synergistic energy, which was the basis of both her supportive skills and offensive ones. Still, she was only just grasping the corners of those truths, and she was getting less and less from the tattered banner. It almost felt like she was extracting the very last drops that it held.

The sky shuddered, for the third time that day, prompting Emily to look up with worry. Was the Mystic Realm really collapsing? What did that mean for her? Would the whole castle be thrown into the Void with her in it? How could she possibly survive something like this? Emily's heart shuddered when her thoughts turned to her squadmates, to Earth. To her family. To Zac.

Would she ever see them again?

No! She wouldn't give up. She was *so close*. A little bit more, and the array would be finished. If she were right, it would unleash a terrifying amount of force if used together with [Summer's Squall]. It might even be enough to crack open the gate. She forcibly pushed any stray thoughts aside and poured everything into the banner.

And it worked. Three days later, it clicked, and the [Dance of the Five Seasons] was born. The moment everything came together, the banner disintegrated, and a screen popped up in front of her.

**[Seal of the Radiant Court (Unique, Inheritance):** Form a Seal of the Radiant Court. Reward: Become a Lightbringer of Ultom. (1/3)**]**

The quest was a surprise, but a grinding sound pushed its unfamiliar contents to the back of her mind. The gates were opening, and tears of relief poured down Emily's face as she started running. She didn't spare so much as a glance to the small courtyard that had been her home for the better part of a year. All her thoughts were on escape. She stormed into the corridor, making a beeline for the exit.

She wondered what the elders outside would say upon learning that more than 80% of the army had died on the first day inside this death-trap. Some deaths were unavoidable when scanning a Pocket Dimension for invaders, but this was completely different from stumbling into some nasty environment or frayed space.

Soon enough, Emily reached the first corner where one of the wardens waited, only the fractured golemoid guard didn't react when she closed in on it. Emily breathed out in relief and flashed past it.

Her relief didn't last long. A deep rumble shook the whole castle, and the previously indestructible bricks started to show cracks.

The whole castle was collapsing! Was this her doing? Emily had no way to tell, and could only urge her legs to run quicker. Why hadn't she created a movement skill instead of a Supportive-Offensive Fusion Skill! What if she died from a rock to the head after surviving spatial tears, murderous constructs, and Annihilation pulses?

Her panic only grew as the walls closed in on her.

Emily finally spotted the gate leading to the enormous courtyard. The place where they'd realized they were trapped, unable to either leave or send a message for help. The place that had eventually been flooded with lance-wielding constructs when the army opted to not head deeper into the sketchy castle.

The corpses and constructs were gone by the time she barged through the gate. It was completely empty, like it'd been scrubbed clean after the battle. Just as she was about to burst through the exit, her eyes widened with alarm—another of the gates veritably exploded as a fierce-looking ogre crashed straight through it wielding two gargantuan stone axes.

It was Kan'Kalo, one of the five leaders of the mission, and a member of the Big Axe Coliseum, just as she. He appeared ready for a tough fight, then stopped in confusion upon seeing Emily was the only other one there.

"Little girl! You survived as well?" Kan'Kalo said with surprise. "I figured you'd get skewered by one of those lance-wielding monstrosities with your embarrassing strength."

"Wouldn't die before a fool like you," Emily snorted.

The five-meter-tall ogre laughed loudly in response, when another rumble reminded him where they were. "We can't stay here. Want to ride with me?"

"Sure." Emily jumped up on Kan'Kalo's left shoulder.

Cosmic Energy surged, and Emily's eyes widened with shock. "You've broken through!"

"Was only a matter of time for someone this handsome!" Kan'Kalo boisterously laughed as they flew through the exit, though Emily knew the truth.

This big brute was powerful, but he'd been stuck as a Half-Step culti-vator for centuries. She might have gotten her hands on the grand prize, but it looked like she wasn't the only one who gained from the experi-ence. The enormous castle turned more and more distant as the Hegemon flew through the sky, and she saw one figure after another emerging from various spots.

"Should we wait for them?" Emily asked.

"All men for themselves," the ogre muttered, hesitantly looking at Emily who wasn't even as large as his head. "And runts."

Emily rolled her eyes, and a crackling axe appeared in her hand. It released a few arcs of lightning into the clouds before she slammed it right into Kan'Kalo's head. He almost stumbled, regaining his compo-sure as he flew away with even greater momentum.

"Little brute," he snorted, one of his huge eyes looking to her with confusion. "No breakthrough?"

"I got insights instead," Emily shrugged. "I've learned to make an axe array."

"Fancy," Kan'Kalo hummed with interest. "Show me later, yeah?"

"Sure. If we get out of here alive."

"Haha! I'm not dying in this shithole after being stuck for months." Kan'Kalo laughed, though he warily looked at the rapidly fracturing sky.

"The closest exit isn't that far from here. The real problem is what's waiting on the other side. Better get ready to hold your breath, brat."

Emily's smile turned crooked, remembering how they'd first arrived. Their squad had found a pathway in the middle of space, far from any planet. Since it emitted strong energy fluctuations, the joint army had erected a temporary platform and sent in Emily's squad and a few more to perform reconnaissance.

But if the army had left three months ago as planned, would they pop out in open space? She didn't have a Cosmic Vessel, and the famously poor ogre who carried her obviously didn't have one either. However, a familiar aura suddenly filled the sky, and Emily's eyes lit up with relief.

"Teacher!" she shouted, and space was cut apart.

Through the collapsing sky, Warsong emerged, his body reeking of blood and killing intent. He sported a nasty wound across his face that almost seemed to have blinded him, though his aura was stronger than ever.

"What happened to you?" Emily exclaimed, but the axe-master only shook his head.

"Later," he muttered, performing a grasping motion with his hand. "This place is about to blow."

The next moment, twenty more people appeared next to her and Kan'Kalo, and Warsong turned his heel and dragged everyone out through the entrance he'd cut open. They soon found themselves on the platform the army had erected, though Emily frowned upon seeing it was covered in scars and cracks. A battle had taken place here.

Still, there was breathable air, and the enormous warship floating in the distance still seemed to be in working order. Emily and the ogre shared a look, and they both breathed out in relief. They'd made it. They survived a certain death trial.

"We were afraid you left us behind," Emily said as she climbed down from Kan'Kalo's shoulder.

"The Mystic Realm was sealed shortly after you entered, but the locked pathway started releasing extraordinary amounts of energy. We figured something big was happening inside, so we chose to change plans," Warsong said. "Just what happened in there? What was that castle?"

"We got sucked into that place the moment we entered," Emily grimaced. "Most of us died."

"I expected as much when I saw so few of you come flying out," Warsong said. "Did you learn anything? Like who built it?"

Emily described the building as best as she could, with Kan'Kalo adding details of his own. He was actually a lot more helpful than she was, with his knowledge of various architectural styles and materials. He even knew how to roughly determine the age of the ruins by studying the bricks that made up the inner wall.

According to Kan'Kalo, the castle most likely pre-dated the System, meaning it came from the Limitless Empire or one of the factions it warred against. Emily wasn't very surprised, considering what she'd seen in the vision. That was definitely something belonging to a tyrannical force like the Limitless Empire, and not some little border faction.

Neither she nor Kan'Kalo explicitly said what kind of opportunities they'd encountered inside the castle. Such were the rules of the coliseum —if you found it, it was yours. They only detailed the traps and environmental dangers, though Emily doubted it would matter. The pathway had already collapsed, meaning it was lost to the Void forever.

"I'll have to talk with the others," Warsong said after they'd recounted their experience. "It might be important. You people return to the Eyrie, we'll take things from here."

Five days later, Emily was called to her master's quarters, and she frowned when she saw him still covered in wounds.

"Are you really okay?" Emily asked.

"Some beasts found the energy released by the pathway alluring." Warsong shrugged, smiling. "You did well. What are your plans going forward? Because of the delay, we have decided to split up. Some will return to the War Fort, others will keep going. What do you want to do?"

"I—" Emily hesitated.

She wasn't sure. She'd been gone from Earth for a long time. She hadn't had any news at all since she entered the Million Gates Territory three years ago. Had Zac returned? Had they also come here to get a head start on this mess?

At the same time, she wasn't entirely certain she wanted to return now. The quest in her Status Screen beckoned her. This was her shot. An opportunity grasped with her own two hands, rather than something handed to her by Zac or Teacher. Could she just go home now that she'd finally found her path?

"You don't have to choose right now. We depart in two days."

"No need," Emily said with determination. "I'll keep going. I'll see this through to the end."

---

"So much Mara," Golden Bell sighed.

Three Virtues nodded in agreement as the group looked down on the sprawling world. No matter where they turned their eyes, there was evil and suffering. Men fought like beasts in their twisted pursuit of power, and blood flowed like rivers. It was an inherited madness, suffering perpetuated through generations.

"This continent truly needs the love of Buddha to start healing," Peaceful Way said with a shake of her head.

"This poor monk can sense this realm is on the cusp of Integration," Golden Bell ventured. "With a few seeds sown and a couple of temples erected…"

"For now, it will have to wait," Three Virtues said. "Our seniors paid no small price to find this realm and send us all this way."

"To think there was a third option," Peaceful Way said. "Lord Blessed Fate truly is a master of the Dharma."

"Still, this Goldblade Continent is vast," Golden Bell said. "Finding the path in this confusing mix of fell Karma will take time."

"Amitabha. A guide is waiting for us." Three Virtues smiled as he took out a low-quality Spatial Ring. "She will lead the way."

---

One step brought him to the Anolan Plains, where the Stalk Sages communed with nature as they followed the ancient paths imprinted by the cosmos itself. Today, the billions of rivers had dried up, and the endless sea of emerald grass was replaced by festering pools of blight. Creatures twisted by the Heavens shrunk into their dwellings as he passed, unable to comprehend why they just felt a pang of mortal danger.

This time, he didn't leave a path of destruction in his wake. What was the point?

Another step brought him to the towering peaks of the Pasho. Once, the whole mountain range would have sung from the Pasho'Har Bells, their cadence forming a universe through music. But the Pasho were long gone, as were the marvels they created. The Keeper of the Note had been known throughout all creation, but innumerable civilizations had risen and turned to dust since her songs were lost to the river of time.

Eternity—was there even such a thing?

And if this was it, what was the point? Wal'Zo's heart broke all over again upon seeing his fallen world. These small sections were moved here to honor those who sacrificed everything. Yet they'd become mockeries of their previous masters. Wal'Zo was even thankful it would soon all be over. He, too, would sink into the river of time, taking this twisted reality with him.

Another step brought him home, and the connection was erected anew. Wal'Zo slowly made his way back through the hallowed halls, the lingering corruption on his body wilting away with every step. Still, two more hallways had been tainted since he left. A few more eras at most before their undertaking would finally crumble, and that was if their power wasn't drawn upon any further.

Another wave of reluctance filled his heart as his mind wandered back to that distant past. To those who said no to the Terminus and set about changing the course of history. To the Eternal, who sacrificed herself to keep the flicker of hope alive when all else failed.

Soon enough he reached the First Garden, where the withered remains of Sal'Sun basked in the sunlight. Next to it, the red pot stood. Inside was a small tree, still no more than a sapling even after billions of years. The gift from that inscrutable man.

"I've seen it now. Your masterpiece. The so-called System," Wal'Zo smiled as he sat next to the small tree. "I wonder what you would think if you saw it today. It is truly something. But it seems to have diverged from what you described to us old things. Or is this still within your calculations? I could never tell where your depths lay. I guess that's why I went along with it. You reminded me of the Eternal."

"Would you still think the price was worth it? The sacrifice?"

"I even saw that man's son. I bet you didn't expect to hear that, huh?" Wal'Zo laughed. "Some things even you can't control. Ripples on the lake. I would have given him a shot, but he actually took it on his own. Now it will ultimately be up to him to prove himself more than a link in the chain. As it has always been."

His gaze turned to the false sky, his eyes flickering with thought.

"Fate is gathering. Ultom is rising from the depths. Us old things cannot hold on much longer. The inevitable looms closer."

Another hallway collapsed, and Wal'Zo sighed as he caressed the sapling.

"Laondio, I hope you were right."

19

# TESTING FATE

Zac cracked his neck. "Let's do this."

His Spirit Tool robes had already been placed to the side and covered in Nexus Crystals to aid its recovery, and Zac instead wore three layers of mish-mashed E-grade armors he'd picked up from some random cultists. Iz's flames had simply proven too potent, and any more tests of fate would probably ruin the clothes altogether.

"You can do it, buddy!" Ogras hollered from the distance, his voice dripping with schadenfreude.

They stood in a large cave, deep underground, that Ogras had found with his shadows, which then had been further sealed off by Iz. A thin film of golden flames covered everything from floor to ceiling, but they didn't feel hot to the touch. The flames emanated from a candle Iz had placed on a random stone. According to her, not even Peak Hegemons would sense any energy fluctuations from within the candle's domain.

Iz, who'd spent the last hour in silent meditation, opened her eyes and looked over at Zac with confusion. "What are you wearing?"

"Have to wear something after you ruined my poor robes," Zac muttered.

"I understand. But those pieces of armor would melt onto your skin."

Zac groaned at the small hint of excitement in her voice.

It'd become painfully obvious that Iz really enjoyed blasting him with her flames, and she used different types every time he asked a question over the past two days. It almost felt like she were experimenting on which kind of fire would toast him the best. Iz had even been so disappointed upon learning that Zac couldn't take any more punishment, that she'd provided a bottle of Healing Pills.

At first, Zac thought it wouldn't change things, but that was only until he sensed the monstrous amount of medicinal energy crammed into the pills. Not only that, but in the bottle of 10, every single pill contained a Pill Spirit. This was the first time he'd owned a Spiritual Pill since stumbling onto one back in the hunt, and it was shocking to see ten of them at one go.

Ten pills whose spirits were all far stronger than the one in the [**Four Gates Pill**].

Such pills didn't grow on trees. Not only did the pill itself have to be of Supreme Quality to have even a small chance of gaining spirituality, but it had to absorb the truths of the universe for a long time to evolve. They were exceedingly rare, even in more affluent places like the Twilight Harbor. A few occasionally popped up at auction, but there was no steady supply.

Some factions had gathering arrays for their pill cauldrons and left batches stewing for millennia in hopes of evolving a few pills. And even then, there were no guarantees. So ultimately, most didn't bother. The increase in efficacy simply couldn't make up for the effort and luck required to concoct those kinds of pills.

Yet this basic logic didn't have any sway with Iz Tayn's faction. Perhaps top-tier alchemists had ways to guarantee Pill Spirits awakening, but it was still odd to see it on normal Healing Pills. It was a bit like crafting a Peak-quality Spirit Tool for a toothbrush or paperweight.

Still, Zac wasn't about to complain about such a windfall. It had not only helped him and Ogras save a day of recuperation, but allowed them to gain some vital intelligence. For instance, they'd learned these Kan'-Tanu were related to the Black Heart Sect, a massive, unorthodox force with actual Supremacies in charge. That explained how they dared to negotiate with peak factions when selling opportunities for the Left Imperial Palace.

More importantly, it spelled bad news for Zecia. It was already a problem when Zecia's enemies was one unified force against their fragmented Sector. Now it turned out they had connections to an A-grade force. In other words, they were like the Void Gate. Even if they were just a distant offshoot, their heritage was bound to be deeper than the shallow foundations you'd normally see in a frontier Sector.

"If armor doesn't work, just go naked?" Ogras grinned. "Your hide is thicker than a Barghest's in either case."

"That would lead to less damage," Iz agreed. "Or mortal clothes that can be properly disintegrated."

"I can't go around naked," Zac said with exasperation as he started removing his layers of armor. "Your elders would probably burn me alive if they found out."

To say they'd gotten close to Iz over the past day would be an over-statement, but Zac had started to understand her personality a bit better. She wasn't haughty or arrogant like some powerful scions. It was just her penchant for burning things and people that left Zac with a bad impression. But she wouldn't take offense to some random words, nor did she act overbearing with either him or Ogras.

Iz undeniably had some odd social blind spots though, and Zac figured she was a bit of a cultivation idiot like himself. However, while he had only started cultivating when he was 29, she'd probably done so from birth. That left her personality incredibly lopsided, though it seemed like she was working on that.

"Oh, you're right," Iz nodded as though it was a matter of course. "Then, let's skip it. Instead, tell me of your experiences in the Twilight Harbor."

"How do you know about that?" Zac asked.

"That was where your signal led for a long time, until you suddenly disappeared through the interference of Chaos," Iz said. "By the time I left for the frontier, the Twilight Harbor had long since been destroyed."

"What happened to the people living there?" Zac asked.

"Most weren't fated," Iz said. "Around a third of the platforms survived. But without an energy source or a World Core, the environment is doomed to decline until it is barely habitable."

"Must be hell on earth there by now," Ogras muttered. "Those places will quickly run dry of resources. A lot of people would have to kill and steal to afford a ticket out of there."

Zac sighed and said another silent prayer for Nala, the half-blood Draugr who guided him when he visited.

"You just want me to tell you what happened in Twilight Harbor?"

Zac asked to confirm. "And you won't suddenly blast me with a fireball?"

"…No," Iz said after an entirely too-long pause.

Zac didn't even need to deliberate before he started to retell his experiences in Twilight Harbor and the Twilight Ascent. Almost any price would beat getting incinerated by Iz's terrifying flames again. Even Verun had lost its vigor in front of her skills, and the Tool Spirit had released a subdued whimper after the last test of fate. If it had to endure any more, Zac worried it might literally mutiny.

Iz listened on with interest as Zac narrated the events, occasionally asking for clarifications. But it wasn't for stuff like one expected, like lucky encounters or powerful beasts he'd fought. She rather asked about mundane stuff, such as what the unique Twilight Water felt and tasted like, or whether the water in the Twilight Chasm was colder.

She was also delighted when he took out a few of the corals he collected in the Coral Forest, or the puppet Catheya got him. In contrast, she didn't care much about the powerful scions he'd fought.

"The Eidolon and the Blood Clan. To think they both so easily fell prey to the destructive corruption of the Remnants," Iz commented.

"Blood Clan? You mean the Eternal Clan?" Zac asked.

"They do not have the qualifications to speak of Eternity," Iz said with equanimity. "Then what happened?"

Zac shrugged and continued the story, with the collapse of the Mystic Realm and how he'd jumped into a spatial tear to survive the battle outside.

"You truly are an unkillable, Mr. Bug," Iz said with a small smile. "What do you want to know?"

"What can you tell us about this Lost Plane and its connection to… that place? Would conventional means cut off the connection, or do we need to prepare something more than spatial destabilizers?"

"I find it curious you are unable to say Ultom without fate shifting," Iz said. "Is it because you are the first candidate?"

Zac could only helplessly shrug in response. It wasn't like he had any idea.

"I don't know this Lost Plane you've mentioned, and I don't recognize the taint in this world. But if you say the temples come from there, it's most likely a pocket world connected to the Eternal Heritage itself.

Most of them contain vast realms," Iz said after some thought. "It is a bit odd. Those worlds are always mirrors of the heritage they reside within, but Ultom does not carry this taint. I cannot explain that, so I might be wrong."

Zac frowned. "I guess we'll just have to pray our preparations work."

"I'm sorry I wasn't of more help," Iz said. "I couldn't answer your question, so ask me something else."

Zac thought for a few moments, but he didn't know what else to ask. She'd already hinted that she wouldn't divulge her background, and had already told them most of what she knew about the situation with Ultom and the Kan'Tanu. Although, there was something else he was curious about.

"Then, how did you arrive at the frontier so quickly? Could I use that method to reach the Six Profundity Empire?" Zac asked.

His strength was far from reaching the point where he felt confident in saving Kenzie, but opportunities like this were rare. Who knew when he'd meet someone like Iz the next time, someone who had actually traveled from the Heartlands to the frontier?

"The Six Profundity Empire?" Iz said with surprise. "What do you want to do there? Your heritage doesn't seem to have any relation to them."

Zac smiled. "Humor me,"

"This is a real scenario? Where you are just you?" Iz asked.

"I'm just me," Zac said with a roll of his eyes.

"A few people owed my family favors and helped my uncle reach this Sector, so you wouldn't be able to use our method," Iz said.

"What can I do?"

"The Six Profundity Empire is very far from here. You are poor, so you can't get a Cosmic Vessel fast enough." Iz's brows scrunched together like she was trying to figure out a riddle. "And you have no connections that can assist you. There are no gateways in the frontier either... Hmm..."

"It's impossible?" Zac grimaced.

"No, I can think of two solutions. The first is to reach the closest A-grade force. They should have access to some allies, and you might be able to pay for passage through their long-distance teleporter. That way, you can gradually jump closer and closer to your destination."

"What would something like that cost?" Zac asked.

"Transfer between two forces?" Iz said. "I don't know. I hear it's rarely counted in Nexus Coins. Factions like that have little use for System Currency. You rather need to provide rare treasures for them to activate the long-range teleporters. You should know, the energy required for such a jump would drain a couple of C-grade factions."

"So a jump would beggar a Peak Monarch, and one would have to make multiple jumps?" Ogras said with a scrunched-up face.

"If the factions will even allow you to use them. They are strategic resources, and they are incredibly difficult to both operate and maintain. Some might not want to risk their platforms, since it is one of their life-lines in case of emergency," Iz said. "And if they've broken down, they might take millennia to repair. Dozens of millennia if they need to send for Spatial Array Masters."

"What's the other option?" Zac sighed.

"Enter the Endless Storm and find a wormhole," Iz said.

"Enter the what-now?" Zac asked, and a glance confirmed Ogras knew as little as he did.

"You two live at the frontier but don't know about the Endless Storm?" Iz asked, her head cocked to the side. "How is that possible? It would be like living by the lake but not knowing what water is."

Zac and Ogras shared a helpless look. Iz wasn't *trying* to be rude, but that perhaps made her comments even worse. This wasn't the first time she'd been confused by their ignorance of what she thought was common knowledge.

"It's the region beyond the frontier?" Zac ventured.

"Yes," Iz nodded. "Beyond the frontier is the Endless Storm. You can actually see a calm corner of it in this Sector—the Million Gates Territory."

"That chaotic place is a *calm* corner?" Zac grimaced.

"I hear there are Solar Storms in the depths of the Endless Storm that would destroy even Supremacies," Iz said. "But it's not all dangerous. It's called a storm, but there are decently safe regions, some of which are larger than whole empires."

"Where would one find a wormhole then?" Zac asked.

"Usually in the actual storms," Iz said. "The System's expansion has pushed back the storm for billions of years, and it has resulted in some interesting phenomena. There are gateways, some of them incredibly stable, that can take you across half of the cosmos in an instant. The Space Gate to the Black Heart Sect is an example of this, though their Sector most likely is quite close to Zecia. Those that can take you across all reality need a stronger storm to be born.

"These tunnels are the most convenient methods of travel, but they are extremely rare in integrated space. No one has ever managed to replicate them either, except for Lord Stillsun, and later the System itself."

"I should just head into this storm and hope for the best?" Zac grimaced. "Seems like finding a needle in a haystack."

"Without a guide, it would be nigh-hopeless," Iz agreed. "There are factions who live inside the storm, who know of hidden wormholes or are able to find them. In this regard, the Technocrats are unsurpassed."

Zac tried to keep his face impassive, but his heartbeat sped up. Iz just unknowingly provided him with a huge lead. What if Leandra didn't choose the Six Profundity Empire because she had a special connection to it? What if she just wanted to go to any random A-grade Empire, and happened to know of a nearby wormhole that led there?

If so, perhaps he could find a way to trace her steps into the Eternal Storm after getting his hands on a Cosmic Vessel. Going there early might be preferrable anyway, since he would probably be able to grow quicker in such a place than here in Zecia. And it would be a good way to disappear, in case the situation with Ultom became too complicated.

Various plans started to crop up in Zac's mind, but he eventually put the matter aside. No matter if it was actually viable or not, it would have to wait. There were a lot of things he needed to deal with in Zecia before he sailed off into some cosmic storm in search of magical portals.

"Thank you," Zac said, and turned to Ogras. "How do you feel?"

"A lot better than I thought possible a day ago." Ogras shrugged. "I'm good to go."

"Let's head out, then? The quicker we deal with this mess, the more energy Gemmy will have for her transformation," Zac ventured. "Also, I don't want that golem to catch up. No offense."

"That's okay," Iz said. "That hand is just an expendable clone. It dying will have no bearing on Kvalk."

"That's not wh—" Zac stopped himself. "Well, never mind."

The three once more set out in the direction of the Ra'Lashar Kingdom. Ogras led the way, but it honestly wasn't necessary. The sky was a pitch-black curtain to the east, and even Zac could feel the ominous energy churning inside the clouds. You'd almost have to be blind to miss it.

Ogras didn't have to expend any energy concealing their approach either. Iz simply infused some energy into the candle, and it floated into the air and followed her. Around them, a ten-meter domain was erected, and both Ogras and Zac confirmed they were completely invisible within.

Seeing how Iz was taking care of everything, Zac chose to squeeze in some cultivation time while he walked. Most of his methods couldn't be trained while on the move, but he could make some progress on [Thousand Lights Avatar] if he didn't need to focus on his surroundings. It was almost like making candles, where he covered his Spiritual Framework with his Mental Energy over and over.

Each time, a little bit was left behind and thickened the avatar, though the change wouldn't be discernible to the naked eye. Despite progress being slow, Zac kept at it, partly due to a comment from Iz. She had told him that a powerful Soul could help stabilize one's breakthrough into Hegemony.

Zac didn't have any actual methods to accomplish something like that, but he had an idea. If he could form a proper avatar around his Specialty Core, he might be able to erect powerful Spiritual Barriers like the ones he used when he opened the last nodes in his head. That meant he had one more thing he needed to accomplish before reaching Hegemony. He couldn't just slack off and enjoy the view.

"Do… you think it's fun? Cultivation," Iz suddenly asked after an hour of silence, prompting Zac to startle awake from his semi-comatose state.

"Is it fun?" Zac asked as a smile crept across his face. "You'd have to eat my punch if you want to know."

# TAINTED WELL

Zac regretted the words the moment he uttered them. Flames gathered around Iz, obviously excited at the prospect of getting punched.

"I'm ready," Iz nodded.

"I was just kid—" Zac said with exasperation, but he stopped in his tracks when a displeased frown appeared on Iz's face.

"Do you think me too weak to bear your fate?" Iz glared at him.

"Uh, no?" Zac said.

"Then test me," Iz said as the burning field expanded around them, forming a dome the same size as the cave they'd spent over two days inside.

There wasn't much else to do—he needed to give this fate-obsessed firebug a good wallop. Zac was thankful that Ogras was the only other person around as he stepped back to create some distance. Punching someone for asking him about his feelings and opinions felt incredibly toxic, and it would drag his already frayed reputation further through the mud.

At the same time, Zac couldn't help but feel some excitement as Cosmic Energy started to course through his body. Iz Tayn had already scared him half to death a couple of times, and he was pretty sure she'd intentionally targeted his butt in the attack she traded for intelligence on the Black Heart Sect. He could still feel flashes of pain as they walked.

This was a chance for some sanctioned retaliation.

Four thick streams of Mental Energy traveled along the framework of

|Thousand Lights Avatar| into his arm as the muscles in his legs tensed. A moment later, Zac shot forward like an arrow released from its bow, leaving huge cracks in the ground from where he pushed off. Simultaneously, two streams of Kalpataru and War Axe entered his prepared Mental Energy-Braid before gathering in his fist.

His hand released a ferocious aura of primal life, and his body naturally moved according to his Evolutionary Stance. The air twisted around him as he released a vibrant and deadly Dao Field, like an apex predator pouncing on its prey. Zac's eyes met with Iz's, and he saw a small smile spread across her face before a wall of flames separated them.

If this were a real fight, Zac would most likely have released a staggered attack to first break the barrier before delivering the real strike, but this was just a friendly clash. There was no need to complicate things, so when Zac appeared in front of Iz, his hand was already shooting toward the barrier in a monstrous right hook.

Every muscle and cell in Zac's body were in perfect harmony. All his momentum and force were gathered into one spot. His fist slammed into the shield with enough power to disintegrate a small mountain, yet there was only a subdued thud. The force in Zac's attack was directed inward, yet Iz's barrier somehow managed to absorb most of it.

Only a trickle of Cosmic Energy and his Dao managed to pass through, but Zac couldn't just give up like that. Even if he hadn't put everything into the punch, it would be too embarrassing if a lazily erected barrier completely nullified his attack. So Zac took control and roused the lingering energies before they scattered, and a smaller wave leapt toward Iz's left temple in a final blaze of glory.

Just as Zac's attack was about to reach Iz's actual body, a finger gently tapped the ball of energy. Zac felt a flash of heat before losing his connection to his attack. Shortly after, the flame wall dispersed, and Zac looked at Iz with some helplessness. So close, yet so far away.

"You have a novel approach to Dao Braiding," Iz said with a smile as four streams of flames appeared around her hand. Two of them shifted colors into a darker hue, and Zac looked on with a sense of defeat as they formed a perfect copy of his crude Dao Braid.

"Well," Zac shrugged. "You have to play with the cards you're dealt."

"Cards?" Iz said with confusion.

"Just an expression," Zac said. "To make do with what you have."

Iz nodded. "Oh. It evens out, provided you are fated. The paths of those coming from humble beginnings are generally sturdier than those from powerful factions. By the time they defend their Dao, they are often more powerful. Forged through adversity. And in your case, your disadvantages seem to be wholly exaggerated."

"Tell me about it," Ogras muttered.

"So, your answer?" Iz said.

"What?" Zac asked, then he remembered why they'd fought in the first place. "I guess I think it's fun, for the most part? I like the feeling of discovery. The feeling of pushing past your previous boundaries. I kind of wish I'd have some periods of calm, though. Where I could just cultivate for the sake of it, rather than to avoid getting hunted down by some old monster or die in a war forced down my throat."

"But then you'd be without purpose. Without those Karmic Links that push you forward."

"That's fine, isn't it?" Zac smiled. "I can always find a purpose if I lack one."

"Find a purpose?" Iz asked.

"Yeah. Like, if I reached a point where all my enemies were gone, and I wasn't rushing toward anything, I could look for purpose elsewhere. Pick up hobbies. Improve the lives of those on my planet. I don't know, start a family. I was already a teenager when my dad was my age."

"My uncle said it is inadvisable to start a family before closing in on your limits," Iz said. "Your heart will become split between the Dao and your progeny, hampering progress. You also risk getting entangled with someone whose fate cannot match up to yours."

"I don't know. Does it have to be that cut-and-dry?" Zac said. "Can't family be another sort of fuel for your cultivation? Like you work harder because you have something important to protect, something more important than your own life. As for fate, I don't really believe in something like that. Fate is malleable. If it doesn't suit you, you change it."

"Fate is malleable?" Iz said with glimmering eyes. "Perhaps you are right."

"I don't want to interrupt… whatever the two of you are doing," Ogras interjected. "But we have company."

Zac looked over with surprise, his gaze following in the direction

Ogras pointed. Far in the distance, he could vaguely make out a handful of moving dots. They were neither moving at a fast nor a slow pace, and the dots would cut past their current position in ten minutes or so.

"Cultivators or beasts?" Zac wondered, feeling a bit hamstrung after not having Vai and her bowl accompany him.

"Cultivators," Ogras said. "They look like invaders. But it's odd…"

"They carry the taint," Iz calmly said after glancing at the distant dots. "A lot of it."

"I'm the only one without any far sight abilities?" Zac muttered. "Well, let's get a bit closer. Iz, are you sure this domain won't be discovered, even by scouts?"

"It is both an isolation field and a Karmic Partition. They have no fate with anything within these flames. As such, they cannot react to it," Iz said, glancing at Zac with an inscrutable look. "Of course, there are no guarantees if fate is *malleable*."

Zac nodded, and they moved to an outcropping to get a better look at these cultivators. Not long after, the small party was close enough for Zac to properly scan them with [Cosmic Gaze], and his brows furrowed in consternation. Iz wasn't kidding around.

A palpable aura of corruption surrounded the group of warriors as they ran through the wasteland. The sinister undulations from their Heart Curses were still there, but it was now mixed with the taint of the Lost Plane. The eyes of the cultivators felt a bit muddled as well, but Zac saw how two of them exchanged a couple of words as they ran.

In other words, they hadn't become vessels of mindless aggression like the Qriz'Ul Ogras had described.

"Looks like these fools have drunk from a tainted well," Ogras snorted after the party was gone. "Like they didn't have enough problems with those disgusting curses in their chests."

"That can't end well for them," Zac agreed.

"Should we follow?" Iz ventured.

"They're not moving in the direction of our destination," Zac said. "Let's just leave them be. Who knows if taking them out will alert the others."

"Proper scouting units would always carry life tablets," Iz said. "Some carry deadly poisons to use if they find themselves cornered.

Better dead than captured, as their deaths would serve as an early warning."

The trio set out again, but they stopped just twenty minutes later after reaching the crest of a hill. On the other side, a seemingly endless city stretched across the horizon. Only the foundations of a 20-meter-thick wall remained, and the structures inside weren't any better off.

An occasional building retained all of its walls, and there was a palpable sense of gloom covering the ruins. The sky was completely black, and a purple haze covered large sections of the city.

"The Ra'Lashar Capital," Ogras said as he looked at the city with mixed emotions. "Took me the better part of a year to deal with the netherblasted rune goblins over there. I can't believe I'm back in this cursed place."

"Does it look any different?" Zac asked.

"Well, it doesn't look like the Qriz'Ul have multiplied, at least. But the environment is far worse than when I was here. Back then, the corruption wasn't this palpable." Ogras grimaced as he crushed a Nexus Crystal to release some pure energy around him. "That's better," the demon sighed before turning to Zac. "Not sure if I can go all out if we have to fight in the depths of the pit. A bunch of corruption will sneak into my body if I'm not careful. What about you?"

"I'm fine," Zac shrugged. "Looks like I'm immune to the taint at these levels."

Zac had already noticed it some time ago. There was something else mixed into the Cosmic Energy in the wastelands, though it was barely noticeable. A sticky and stubborn energy that snuck into his body and seemingly wanted to glom onto his pathways. The energy was unlike anything Zac had encountered before, except for that enormous pillar blasting into the sky.

Back then, the energy of the Lost Plane had been contained by the nine sigils, and Zac couldn't observe its true nature. Even when it had infiltrated his body, Zac didn't quite know what to make of it. It didn't feel like attuned energy at all. In fact, Zac wasn't even sure it was comparable to Cosmic Energy.

Was this because the energy possibly stemmed from an Eternal Heritage? Was the fundamental energy of the previous eras different than the Cosmic Energy they used now? Thankfully, his **[Purity of the Void]** dealt with the infiltration all the same, and it never had time to become a problem. The situation hadn't even gotten to the point where his [Void Heart] needed to activate like in the Twilight Ocean.

"My flames are naturally purging the corruption," Iz said.

"Forget I asked," Ogras muttered under his breath. "Traveling with a buncha monsters."

A smile tugged at Zac's mouth, which made Iz look over with confusion.

"You take pleasure in your friend's lacking foundations?" Iz asked curiously.

"Hey!" Ogras interjected, but he just shrugged in defeat and dropped the matter after looking at the monstrously powerful scion.

"More in the faces he makes when he gets jealous, I think?" Zac said after some thought.

Iz hummed softly, turning to Ogras, who looked back at her vigilantly. "When I left for the frontier, my elder gave me 10 B-grade Nexus Coins for pocket money."

The demon tried to keep his face impassive, but the shades of grey on his face gained a hint of green, and it looked like he was about to become physically ill.

"That's… nice," Ogras squeezed through grit teeth, then walked away to the edge of the barrier.

"You were right," Iz smiled. "It is a bit amusing."

"You have to take pleasure in the little things," Zac said while desperately trying to hide his own jealousy.

Iz looked at Zac for an uncomfortable amount of time until her mouth slowly curved up. "To improve my Luck upon reaching E-grade, I bathed in the diluted dew from a two-million-year-old [Fateweave Orchid]. It also helped cleanse my marrow of some Natal Impurities."

Zac's stomach churned as he unwittingly remembered his most recent experience with improving his Luck. It almost felt like he could smell the unbearable stench from the [Celestial Clay], and he was forced to take a steadying breath to stop himself from gagging.

"Let's hurry and close that portal," Zac grunted, heading over to Ogras. When a small laugh came from behind, he wondered if he might have made a horrible mistake.

Thankfully, Iz didn't continue bragging about her financial prowess, much to the relief of both Zac and Ogras. Even then, her two little comments painted a painfully clear picture that his so-called fortune wasn't worth much in the grand scheme of things.

Seeing how they were approaching the city proper, Ogras took out a talisman that Pretty Peak had provided. It was a top-quality detection talisman that proved to work against the Kan'Tanu's arrays, and the air started to shudder a bit after the demon infused some energy into it.

Nothing changed until they reached the very edge of the crumbled wall. It was barely visible, but the vibrations had gotten stronger, forming a thin film halfway through the thick wall.

"They've really installed a detection array," Ogras frowned.

"My flames don't work if they're allowed to touch the barrier," Iz said.

"Then we pass through using our means and reignite the flame?" Zac said.

Iz nodded, and the floating candle winked out. That exposed the three to the surroundings, but Ogras worked quickly as he took out a small array disk. Two flickering gateways appeared, one right in front of them and the other a hundred meters into the ruins. They wordlessly passed through, and the array disk disintegrated to black ash behind them.

Such a short-range teleportation array wouldn't work against an actual barrier with spatial isolation, but it worked fine against large-scale detection arrays. Iz's candle reignited, and the three set off deeper into the capital. They continued for another five hours at a rapid pace before slowing down.

During this time, they encountered two more detection arrays and even a couple of traps, but they passed them without much issue. Still, it was a clear sign the Kan'Tanu expected trouble, and Zac started to fear their chances of detonating the pathway before slipping away unnoticed were pretty slim.

They'd also encountered a couple of Qriz'Ul on their way. To their surprise, not all of them looked like corrupted goblins. There were two who looked surprisingly similar to Ogras, while others had taken human form. Still, the vast majority looked like goblins, covered in runes unlike any Zac had ever seen. Iz didn't recognize them either, and she didn't even believe they were a derivation of the Apostate of Order's codification of the Dao.

By this point, the corruption was so strong it'd created a dark haze around them, and they couldn't see farther than a few hundred meters. Ogras had been forced to completely seal his pores, and he fastened over twenty Nexus Crystals across his body with his shadows to combat the corruption. Even Zac felt that [Purity of the Void] was reaching its limits, while Iz remained unphased.

"We're close now," the demon said as he pointed at an inner wall. "This was the fifth of seven layers that sealed the Ra'Lashar Kingdom. The seventh layer was just the central tower, which should still be one big crater. Still, the portal should be over there."

"No wonder those scouts were marked by the taint," Zac muttered. "I can't believe they dare stay in this kind of environment."

Ogras shrugged. "K'Rav said the whispers of the Lost Plane are insidious. The Ra'Lashar never really realized they were running straight toward their doom. The gifts of the Lost Plane were like saltwater—the more they drank, the thirstier they got."

"Well, let's get on with it," Zac said as he readied himself. "The sooner we can get out of this disgusting place, the better."

"You want to destroy the pathway first?" Iz confirmed.

"If possible. As long as we destroy it, we've won. We don't even need to fight the Kan'Tanu if we don't have to. This whole region will collapse when the Realm Spirit activates the Portable Realm array. There's no way the infiltrators survive that without some means to escape the Void."

They made their way through yet another detection array, this time by carefully calculating things so they appeared in one of the few still-standing buildings in the last layer. From there, they crept closer and closer to the heart of the city, until finally discovering what they were dealing with.

The crater Ogras had described was gone, replaced by a purple lake teeming with corruption. And on its shores, a thousand cultivators sat in silent meditation.

# GOING WITH THE FLOW

The silence around the corrupted lake was absolute, with not one of the cultivators moving. While the scene appeared tranquil on the surface, it was anything but. The lake released powerful waves of dirty energy, creating an invisible storm on its surface that spread out along the crater's slopes. Meanwhile, the auras of the cultivators kept rising and falling in pace with the pulses of the lake.

It was almost like they'd fused and become a singular organism that slowly inhaled and exhaled its corruption. The taint buffeted their surroundings, and Zac felt his **[Void Heart]** finally awakening from its slumber to consume the accumulated taint in his body.

A small settlement had been erected at the southern banks to their right. There were roughly 100 structures altogether, and their rustic design as they hugged the slopes of the crater would have made for an almost picturesque scene in another environment. With the absolute lack of activity and the black haze spreading among the buildings, it may as well have been an abandoned ghost town.

"Look," Ogras whispered and pointed to the left, and Zac's eyes widened in surprise upon seeing a group of Qriz'Ul standing right next to a squad of Kan'Tanu cultivators.

"They've allied?" Zac grimaced.

"More like these fools have absorbed so much corruption, the Qriz'Ul have mistaken them for their own," Ogras snorted. "What in the Heavens are they doing? Weren't they supposed to be digging for keys to the courts?"

Zac nodded in agreement. It looked really odd. There was no excavation being done, and Zac couldn't sense any hint of Ultom at all.

"Do you sense any calling for your seals?" Zac asked, and both Iz and Ogras shook their heads. "I guess we won't be able to conjure a pillar. Unless we blow up the lake somehow?"

"Not sure how we'd accomplish that," Ogras muttered. "More importantly, where is the gateway? Get the hell out here, bastard."

"Oi, what have these bastards done to my home?" A sad sigh echoed as the spectral goblin appeared next to Ogras, and he quickly turned to Iz.

"Young miss, I can see you carry great fate. If you—" K'Rav said, only for his words to get caught in his throat when a few small embers started to dance around Iz as she trained her eyes on him. "Ah, never mind, young mistress. I shan't take up your precious time."

"No, it's fine," Ogras grinned. "Go ahead, make your pitch."

"What do you want, you imbecile? To show me the aftermath of you blowing up the great Tower of Ra'Lashar?" K'Rav swore.

"That was mostly you, remember?" Ogras snorted. "Where is the gateway to the Lost Plane?"

"It's at the bottom of the lake, obviously," K'Rav said with disinterest. "Can't you brats tell? Those waters are not from our plane. It must have seeped out from somewhere. These children must really have cracked the whole thing wide open for physical matter to appear like this. Even we knew better than to be *that* greedy."

"I guess it's up to you two young masters then, yeah?" Ogras said. "Unfortunately, this poor peasant's foundations are no match to a lake with that amount of corruption. I'd die before resurfacing."

"I… don't think I can enter the lake either," Iz said after some hesitation. "At least not while accomplishing the mission. My bloodline will try to set the lake on fire if assaulted by that much corruption. I might even be teleported away by fatewarding treasures."

"I guess it's up to the fearsome Deviant Asura, then," Ogras said.

"Perfect," Zac muttered, eyeing the bubbling lake.

It should be fine. Right?

Though it was hard to tell from the distance, Zac felt he should be able to last for a short while. Even if the tainted waters came from the Lost Plane, they didn't contain energies that far surpassed this Mystic

Realm's. It seemed to be a bit worse than the depths of the Twilight Chasm, but he had **[Void Zone]** now. As long as it worked against this weird energy, he would have more than enough wiggle room.

"Give me some space, please," Zac said as he took a couple of steps away from Iz before activating an illusion array.

Zac was somewhat certain that Iz didn't care about whatever his hidden aces were. She couldn't care less about him being both Draugr and human. She only found it an interesting oddity. As for the Remnants, she was even less impressed. She even seemed to believe they were more trouble than they were worth, which was definitely a reasonable assessment.

But his bloodline was different. Emperor Limitless was still a sensitive subject billions of years later. Zac didn't know what ramifications it would have if people from the ancient factions found out whose legacy he carried. Even if he wasn't killed outright, it was possible that some would want to use him for the same purpose as Leandra and the Kayar-Elu—to control the System.

And just because Iz didn't care nor mind, there were no guarantees about her elders.

Ogras and Iz looked over, but the demon shrugged and turned away upon seeing the illusion array. Iz stared for a moment longer, but she too turned back toward the lake. Zac activated **[Void Zone]**, and a soothing sense of nothingness ensconced him.

It worked. Just like **[Purity of the Void]** had no problems purifying the energy of the Lost Plane, and **[Void Heart]** had no problems absorbing it, neither did **[Void Zone]** have any difficulties removing any such energy from his surroundings. That was still no guarantee it would be able to completely block out the energy in the lake, but it would at the least severely weaken it.

"All good, Mr. Secretive?" Ogras asked with a raised brow when Zac returned.

"All good. I'll deal wit—" Zac froze as **[Void Heart]** suddenly spat out a trickle of refined energy.

All at once, Zac understood a passage from the Book of Duality that had stumped him five days ago. A moment later, both the flash of inspiration and the refined energy were gone, but Zac was still frozen solid. It didn't come close to the lights of the seals, but what he'd just felt was definitely in the same category.

[Void Heart] could refine and distill the insights of the Lost Plane.

Zac's eyes were veritably burning as he turned back to the lake. It no longer appeared to be a putrid pond of corruption that needed to be incinerated. It looked like a treasure mountain. One round of refinement from [Void Heart] might only have helped him deduce a single passage of the Book of Duality, but what if he had a whole lake's worth of fuel for inspiration?

Altogether, it might even match up to a full piece of the seal. Just the thought of it made his breath ragged, and he could definitely understand why the Ra'Lashar held onto the Lost Plane until their very demise. The possibilities almost felt endless.

"Uh, you okay there?" Ogras coughed. "You look like Barghest in heat."

"You seem to have come up with a... creative... idea," Iz added with an excited sparkle in her eyes.

"Ah? What? Oh, never mind," Zac coughed. "I said I'll deal with the gateway. But do you guys have any better ideas than me just making a run for it? There are no guarantees these guys won't follow me into the lake. I'm not sure I can deal with a bunch of corrupted Kan'Tanu and the portal simultaneously."

"We can create a diversion?" Ogras offered. "But it's hard to tell how these guys will react. It almost feels like they've fused with the lake. They may ignore us if they feel the lake threatened."

"There were vast tunnel networks beneath the Tower of Ra'Lashar," K'Rav said. "Many should have flooded or collapsed, but some might be intact. If you can find one, you can either walk or swim beneath those glassy-eyed fools."

"Can you tell us where they are?" Zac asked.

"Everything's different now, hard to tell." K'Rav shrugged. "Besides, why would I help you after your nefarious attempt on my life?"

"I'll deal with it," Ogras said as he took out the [Shadewar Flag].

The next moment, five specters that both looked and felt like the Qriz'Ul creatures appeared within the domain.

"These guys should be able to move about undetected, unless the infiltrators really have learned to communicate with the monsters of the

Lost Plane," Ogras said. "I can just send them through the ground until I find a path."

"Do it," Zac said, and the creatures sank into the ground.

"Hopefully, I can catch a few new ones while we're here," Ogras muttered. "Who knows what kind of creatures this thing can accept."

"That flag is problematic," Iz said. "It takes without giving back, defying the Law of Balance. But the universe always exacts its price. You will have to carry the weight of every soul you capture. Eventually, they will drag you under."

"Well, I have this guy to keep my head above water," Ogras smiled as he nodded at Zac. "Besides, this thing is just a stopgap until my strength has improved."

"That's what we said about the Lost Plane," K'Rav snickered before he flew back into the flag.

"He's right, you know," Zac said. "That thing is trouble."

"I know," Ogras said, fastening a few more homemade talismans on the unorthodox treasure. "But I'm working on it, with the help of the epiphanies. I think it's solvable."

Zac nodded in understanding, turning back to the cultivators in the distance. He wasn't surprised to hear Ogras was focusing on fixing the problems of the flag, even if he personally felt it was a waste of an epiphany. At the same time, there were limits to what the lights of Ultom could help with.

Ogras' Body Tempering Manual wasn't in need of fixing from what he could tell, and the demon had told him he was planning on discarding his Cultivation Manual altogether at the D-grade. It simply didn't hold up even at Peak E-grade. And between the manual being incomplete and Ogras' path having shifted, it would be easier to create a new manual from scratch than to improve upon the shaky foundations of the old method.

Apparently, many elites started to work on that in the D-grades in either case. They either created a Cultivation Manual to perfectly fit their path or adjusted their current one to remove any mismatch.

The minutes passed as the trio kept watch over the stoic cultivators, but none seemed to notice the search going on underground. Eventually, Ogras perked up and turned to the small settlement at the other shore.

"One of the buildings over there has a pool of tainted water. It appears to be connected to the lake through one of the tunnels. The other pathways I've found are quite far underground, and we'd have to dig through at least fifty meters of stone to reach it."

"The vibrations would carry through and spread outside my domain," Iz said. "We might be discovered."

"Is there anyone inside the buildings?" Zac asked.

"None in the one with the pond, though there are two people standing in the neighboring structure. They're staring at some diagram, but I'm not sure if they're mentally present."

"What do you guys think?" Zac asked.

"I think it's our best shot," Ogras said. "We'll stay at the surface. If we see the cultivators react, we'll ambush and distract them."

"Does that work with you?" Zac asked Iz.

Iz didn't immediately answer, her gaze turning to the enthralled Kan'Tanu. Zac didn't want to rush her, but he'd be lying if he said he wasn't a bit worried. From the beginning, Iz had been flighty about what kind of role she envisioned for herself in this upcoming mission. Whether she was even willing to fight the Black Heart Sect. Then again, her participation wasn't something they originally planned for, and she had already helped a lot by providing intelligence and using her domain-creating candle.

If she could also test the fate of a couple of infiltrators, that would be even better.

"This is war," Ogras stated. "Besides, they are unorthodox cultivators shunned by the Heavens. Killing them will not bring fell Karma."

"But it will bring about Karma," Iz said, her brows furrowing. "It is unclear how our actions will affect the river of fate. These are just some guards, but they are part of a larger tapestry related to Ultom. I don't know how it will affect my trajectory in life. If the ripples might even affect my family. I don't—"

Zac looked into Iz's troubled eyes, and he thought he had a pretty good idea of what was troubling her. Iz Tayn was almost his opposite. He was thrown right into the world of cultivation completely blind, and he was still trying to unravel the mysteries of his origin. Meanwhile, Iz came from an ancient faction, and her entire life had probably been carefully planned out.

Every decision Zac made since reuniting with humanity on Earth had real-life implications. People lived and died depending on his choices, and the very fate of his planet had hung in the balance more than once. Iz had probably never been placed in such a situation, and she was only now truly realizing how much a decision could weigh on your soul.

Zac glanced at Ogras, who helplessly looked back. "Try not to get discovered?"

"Stealth is my middle name." Zac smiled, which elicited a derisive snort from the demon, and he turned to Iz. "You don't need to make a decision right now. I haven't been caught yet. I know it can feel tough, and I'm too much of a hillbilly to know what's the right choice for someone like you. I guess, just act according to your heart and conscience? That way, you can at least face yourself in the mirror, knowing you did your best even if things went wrong."

"...Thank you," Iz said.

"Alright, no time to waste. The longer we stick around, the more variables we'll have to deal with," Zac said, and they started to make their way around the crater toward the small settlement.

The occasional Qriz'Ul kept popping up among the ruins, which forced Iz to tighten the fiery domain around them. Even then, they narrowly avoided having a few unwelcome visitors ambling into their isolated surroundings. Twenty minutes later, they reached the edge of the temporary settlement.

It was an odd feeling, walking through a ghost town while invisible. It was like you were a ghost traveling through the ruins of another fallen civilization. The feeling didn't last long, as there were only a couple rows of houses, and they soon reached their target building.

Through a slit in the neighboring door, Zac saw the two infiltrators Ogras mentioned. Their auras were gentle and refined, meaning they were probably non-combat classes. If Zac had to guess, they were Array Masters, judging by the large tapestry they were blankly staring at.

Just like Ogras said, it was an incredibly complex array. It was painted in red and blue, with each color using a different script. The blue runes seemed like a mix of the nine subordinate sigils of the Left Imperial Palace and the unfamiliar marks on the bodies of the Qriz'Ul. Meanwhile, the red ones were the script the Kan'Tanu used, which wasn't all that different from the System Standard Script.

Together, the two systems formed a complex swirl that Zac could only guess was related to the pathway leading to the Lost Plane. But the array was obviously incomplete, with some sections missing runes while other areas were completely blank. It made Zac wonder just what happened here.

Had an experiment gone awry, or had they been too eager to crack open the pathway to the Lost Plane, accidentally releasing the purple lake? Because what they were seeing here didn't seem to match the original plan the lipless Hegemon had hinted at.

"Can you snatch that array when things go down?" Zac asked, and Ogras nodded as though that were the natural order of things.

From there, they walked over to the neighboring structure, where the five-meter-wide pool was. This close to the water, the ambient corruption was a lot stronger. Zac cursed the fact he didn't know how to turn off **[Purity of the Void]**, and he could only watch on with helplessness as his purification node destroyed most of the tainted insights.

It was impossible to make any hard plans when they didn't know what would happen going forward, but Ogras and Zac spent the next ten minutes coming up with some flexible ideas depending on how things went. Finally, there was nothing else to do, and Zac stepped into the pond, carefully controlling his movements to avoid creating any ripples.

"Have fun out here," Zac said as he lowered himself into the waters.

Zac barely managed to stifle a groan as a steady stream of corruption started to burrow into his body through all of his pores. But it was well within what he could handle, and he nodded in confirmation to the other two as he sunk farther down. When the tainted water reached his shoulders, he turned to Iz Tayn one final time.

"Don't worry too much. Just go with the flow," Zac smiled as his head started to become submerged. "Things tend to work out. When they don't blow up."

## 22

## PROVING ONESELF

Iz looked on as Mr. Bug—no, Zachary Atwood, dipped beneath the tainted water. Not much later, she felt him pass through her flame domain, exposing him to any discerning eyes. She froze for an instant, and was immensely relieved when there was no reaction from the corrupted cultivators sitting by the shoreline. She had a little bit longer.

She felt suffocated, and indecision gnawed at her. The world had always seemed so simple. Black and white. Fated and lacking fate. Even Zachary's experiences she'd seen through the lens of the Divine Mirror had felt like a series of humorous misadventures.

Foolish. This was life and death. There was suffering and uncertainty. There were *consequences*.

Her thoughts turned back to those she'd incinerated, certain in her righteousness from their lack of providence. Only now, when the ripples of consequence might reach the Tayn Clan, did she realize her shallow understanding. Even if all those people had no fate with her, did they not have fate with others? Were her family's precepts wrong? Or was she missing something?

She was sheltered from the world, yes, but she still understood the Multiverse was a cruel place. That the struggles here on the frontier paled in front of the wars that ravaged the Heartlands. Resources were limited, and there were only so many Seals and Thrones. So many Eternal Heritages. Was the approach of her family a necessity to survive at the peak? Perhaps, but that didn't help with her current dilemma.

She took a steadying breath, the words of Zachary Atwood mixing with that of her grandpa as he let her into the Zecia Sector.

"Heart," Iz muttered.

"Ah?" the demon said, her voice startling him out of his vigil over the shoreline.

"Nothing," Iz sighed.

"Alright. Nothing so far."

"They are too connected to the lake," Iz said with a shake of her head. "It is only a matter of time."

"That's great," Ogras muttered. "Left to fight an army."

"I—"

"You know?" the demon said. "Zac's home planet, Earth, was integrated recently."

"I am aware."

"I was leading the Incursion placed next to him. Through a twist of fate, we became uneasy allies, relying on each other to survive. Eventually, we both proved ourselves to each other," Ogras said. "I lost an arm proving it, though it's regrown since. Even if it hadn't, it would have been a worthwhile sacrifice. Real companions are hard to come by in this world. People you can trust your back to in thick and thin."

Iz listened with rapt attention, as the information was all new to her. The story almost allowed her to forget her current predicament.

"Later came along a wretch called Verana. She threw her lot in with Zac upon witnessing his strength, realizing the potential for profits. Zac accepted her, and everything went well for a while. But when things went awry, and the Undead Empire descended on Zac's home, on his kin, she was nowhere to be found.

"She was afraid that her involvement would create ripples, enmities that would cause troubles for her elders back home. After all, the Undead Empire is a powerful force even here on the frontier."

"What happened next?" Iz asked.

"Zac returned in the nick of time, slaughtered the invaders before taking out the Incursion of unliving." Ogras shrugged. "The day was saved. But from *that* moment, Verana's fate was changed. She could have been someone like me, whose fate has been swept up in his, as you called it. Now, she is just a distant business acquaintance to the Atwood Empire and will never be anything more…

"Because she couldn't be relied on when push came to shove. Because if it happened one time, it could happen again when the stakes became high. Fate is a tricky thing. Who knows what's right and wrong? When you struggle to keep a door open, you often close another one." The demon turned to Iz with a smile.

Iz truly looked at the shade-marked demon for the first time. She'd always considered him a passerby, a hanger-on. Those with powerful fates usually had a few such people hovering around them. She always viewed them as parasites, siphoning the fate of their betters. But she finally realized she was wrong on yet another front. There was more to this demon.

"So, what are you saying?" Iz asked.

"Perhaps some doors can be held open by a helping hand. How about you and I make a little deal?"

———

Zac slowly made his way through a narrow crack, using only his body to avoid releasing any energy ripples. Of course, he wasn't too convinced anyone would notice it with him being surrounded by the extremely potent water.

Just a few seconds after submerging himself, [Purity of the Void] was completely overwhelmed. One pulse after another cleansed his body of the corruption, but even more kept pouring in. Soon enough, it was all swallowed up by a greedy [Void Heart], and the cycle started anew.

A few moments later, he reached the underground tunnel once built by the Ra'Lashar goblins, and he could already see the exit in the distance. It was a small dot of shimmering purple, seeming blissfully unobstructed. Zac kept moving, but a frown soon marred his face as he felt the corruption grow uncomfortably condensed in his body while [Void Heart] still digested the previous batch.

Or did it matter? A little bit of suffering in return for clarity, for power. Wasn't that the core tenet of his path? He could already feel his confusions being swept away, replaced with ironclad certainty and possibility. And with his body having unlimited potential, wasn't *this* the path?

Zac shuddered as the waters around him dimmed, while the sweet whispers in his mind quieted to a muted white noise. The change came from Zac activating [Void Zone], which removed any spirituality from the surrounding waters while suppressing the taint that had already entered his body.

It'd just been a short test to see how well he could withstand the corruption, and it became a lesson in the importance of a steady heart. He had been awash with endless possibilities, had seen glimpses of promising alterations to everything from his skills to his pathways. It was similar to how he felt when using Creation Energy.

Instead of being consumed and drained by the endless hunger of Creation, he felt himself gradually being nudged in a certain direction. A little change here, and a small addition there. A suggestion to look at things differently. But out of little acorns grow huge oaks. Those small changes would eventually turn into a complete transformation.

The corruption of the Lost Plane wanted to reform him into an image of itself, both in spirit and flesh. Was that what happened to the Qriz'Ul? Had they once been living, breathing beings, only to find themselves twisted until they were no more than accumulations of tainted energy? There was no way to tell, but one thing was for certain—those cultivators at the surface were in trouble.

Their paths had probably been subverted already, and Zac doubted they'd even recognize themselves if they found a moment of clarity. Still, that wasn't Zac's problem. Just like K'Rav said, they were the ones who cracked open the pathway to the Lost Plane, probably without proper preparation or understanding of the situation.

A thud echoed out from his heart, and he stopped in place with anticipation as [Void Heart] spat out a burst of energy. A few more passages were deciphered, adding to his already impressive understanding of the nature of Duality. The moment the purified energy was expended, Zac turned off [Void Zone], and thousands of tendrils started burrowing into his body.

The process continued for another minute until [Void Heart] was satiated, and Zac reactivated his nullification domain. In a perfect world, Zac would have secluded himself in this corrupted tunnel, staying years if need be to consume the whole lake. Unfortunately, that wasn't possible with the collapse of the realm looming over their shoulders.

Zac made his way toward the exit, careful to not make any move except for the occasional push to help keep him floating forward. By this point, he was halfway through the tunnel, and some of the cultists were possibly sitting right above his head. He was no longer protected by Iz's candle either and was instead relying on the stealth cowl to prevent anyone from detecting him.

His eyes and senses were peeled for any sign of having been discovered, but there were no spikes of Cosmic Energy being released from above. Zac felt flush with success as he reached the mouth of the tunnel, but that sense of victory was doused upon witnessing the scene outside.

Qriz'Ul. Hundreds of them, some over ten meters large and emitting powerful fluctuations.

Zac forced himself to remain perfectly still. His worst fear had come true, though they'd discussed this very scenario. After all, where else would the current generation of Qriz'Ul have come from but this tainted soup? Most seemed to be in an almost comatose state where they had turned into blobs that drifted along the currents.

However, those around the cave exit had stopped in place as they started to contract, and Zac could tell they felt something was amiss. Did they sense his [Void Zone]? He couldn't be sure, but he knew he'd be discovered soon enough unless something changed.

Zac deactivated his domain, and the waters around him returned to normal. The same thing happened with the corruption that had already accumulated in his body, which would hopefully mean he'd look like the cultivators above water to these creatures. And it worked. The Qriz'Ul relaxed and returned to their spread-out form before drifting away. Only a ten-meter Qriz'Ul stayed a bit longer until it too floated away.

Zac returned farther into the tunnel before activating [Void Zone] and considered his options. His domain was the issue here. It probably wasn't the Void Energy that Qriz'Ul reacted to, but rather the lack of corruption in a spot. Which put him in quite a bind.

He needed the [Void Zone] to stay in the waters indefinitely. Except using it would get him exposed. And even if he found a way around it, there were no guarantees he'd be safe from the Qriz'Ul when entering the lake proper, even if he let the corruption spread through his body. What could he do in this situation? Should he go back and discuss it with the others?

No, Iz had already said she didn't have any invisibility treasures apart from the candle, and neither did she have any methods to traverse this kind of taint. She simply hadn't prepared for this kind of mission. Ogras couldn't help in this situation either, so he could only rely on himself. Besides, the longer they stayed in this region, the higher the risk of something going wrong.

Zac waited for another couple minutes until the next burst of inspiration pushed his insights further. Having a newly-cleansed body, Zac started swimming toward the cave mouth once more, and deactivated the domain the moment he got close.

There was one Qriz'Ul not too far from Zac, but it didn't seem to react to his presence, allowing him to creep out from the cave mouth and swim downward. With corruption rapidly pouring into his body, he couldn't maintain a slow and steady pace out of fear of being discovered by the cultivators above. Besides, with hundreds of Qriz'Ul floating about in the lake's depths, his movements shouldn't be cause for suspicion.

He descended over a hundred meters in a few short moments until he found another tunnel. Zac swam inside and activated [Void Zone] before the nefarious whispers returned. None of the Qriz'Ul appeared to react so long as he remained hidden in the darkness of the tunnel. In fact, they didn't bother with the tunnels at all.

They were content floating in a circle around the lake, with the occasional creature moving toward the surface. Perhaps that was an opportunity in itself? The energies in the lake had to be powerful enough to hide his actions. Zac hesitated a moment before taking out an inscribed canister and pushing it into a crack in the wall.

By briefly deactivating his Bloodline Talent and infusing a tiny hint of Cosmic Energy, the canister started to drag the tainted waters into its subspace. It created a weak current, but there was no reaction even after a minute, allowing Zac to breathe out in relief. Eventually, the bottle was full, and Zac's body was cleansed from any lingering corruption.

Having accomplished his goal, Zac deactivated [Void Zone] and continued on his way, the bottle full of lake water safely stowed away. It was a backup plan in case the whole lake was dragged into the Void before he could get any, and one bottle after another joined the first as Zac jumped between tunnels and deep cracks as he made his way toward the bottom.

And with the lake only being so big, he reached his target soon enough, though he found himself surrounded by six, huge, slumbering Qriz'Ul.

The gateway—at least Zac assumed it was the gateway—reminded Zac a bit of the Spatial Nexus that blew up. It appeared to be a hollow construct roughly 50 meters across, made from beams of crystal or purple glass. Together, they formed something like a dodecahedron that kept shifting in a disorienting way.

One moment it looked like a cube, the next it had a hundred edges in an incredibly complex tangle. Vai had long since explained it was a result of two realities with a different number of dimensions sharing the same space. Technically, the pillars didn't transform or shift about. It was just his vantage that kept changing.

What stayed constant were the dense scripts covering the crystal pillars, scripts that followed the unfamiliar ruleset of the Qriz'Ul. Zac couldn't tell if this thing was something the Ra'Lashar created or if it had formed naturally. He was fairly certain it wasn't the work of Kan'-Tanu, since the beams felt too old and powerful.

Zac also couldn't tell whether the crystal pillars were responsible for sealing the gateway, or if they were there to stabilize and strengthen it. As for the actual pathway to the Lost Plane, it hovered in the center of the shifting construct.

The similarity between the ominous swirl and the array he'd just seen in the infiltrator's lab was palpable. The thing didn't really look like a spatial tear. Instead, it looked like a pitch-black sphere the size of a beach ball, with two dozen deep purple strings attached. The item slowly rotated in place, prompting the strings to form a ten-meter-wide spiral that undulated with intensely condensed corruption and Spatial Energy.

In a perfect world, Zac would have spent a few minutes studying the thing, but there was no way he could do that. The taint was far more concentrated this close to the source, and he wouldn't last much longer without [Void Zone]. And with the big guys slumbering nearby, activating it would mean immediately getting exposed.

Zac steadied his mind as he went through the procedure Leyara had imparted. The moment he made his move, he would probably be exposed. The spatial bomb that the experts of the Void Gate prepared and then improved with some of Zac's materials was something that would drive the Ishiate Tinkerers wild.

It was volatile, unpredictable, and powerful. Just like how they liked their weapons.

A few seconds later, the construct reverted into one of its simpler forms, and Zac shot forward. This time, he even used Cosmic Energy to cover the remaining distance instantly, and felt multiple powerful auras ignite around him. Zac ignored the burgeoning pressure as a radiant cube appeared in his hand.

High-grade materials and inscriptions reinforced its glass walls, but Zac's heart still shuddered as he felt the chaotic spatial fluctuations trapped inside. How couldn't he be nervous? He was essentially holding an artificial miniature black hole. The sooner he could get away from it, the better.

Cosmic Energy surged through his body as Zac activated the main array of the bomb, and he hurled it toward the black ball in the heart of the structure. The cube started to twist and bend as it entered the odd domain within the pillars, but a pulse from within stabilized it. Cracks rapidly spread across the bomb, and the energy it leaked was enough to eradicate space around it.

Finally, the bomb reached the core, and reality buckled as a hole of utmost darkness appeared. It wasn't too big, and didn't release a speck of energy, but Zac's danger sense told him in no uncertain terms that touching that thing would mean instant death. It was a true black hole that swallowed space, time, and energy—the most sure-fire solution to destroy the pathway that Leyara could come up with.

Space collapsed, and the twisted spiral was rapidly consumed. Zac could even feel how the corruption was quickly decreasing. But just as Zac thought the mission a success and planned to deal with the fallout, a powerful consciousness descended on the area. Zac didn't even have time to react before a huge runic hand emerged from the remaining half of the sphere.

It grasped the black hole and squeezed, like the scene where the mysterious being crushed the Heart of Oblivion. Simultaneously, Zac felt a powerful consciousness slam into his, and his hair stood on end upon hearing an eldritch voice.

"Emp... ty... Empty... *EMPTY!*"

## 23
## EMPTY

Zac couldn't tell whether a million voices were clamoring in his head or one. The force alone was enough to give Zac's soul a jolt. He didn't know what the voice meant by *empty*, but the real problem was the source. A supersized Qriz'Ul was targeting his spatial bomb, possibly from the other side through the gateway.

At least Zac assumed it was a Qriz'Ul, even if its hand looked like a purple runic nebula rather than a twisted mockery of a goblin. Meanwhile, the D-grade runic beings around him had almost finished gathering, and Zac guessed he only had a few seconds before they attacked.

The rampant energies of the black hole rendered the whole area unstable, and the purple crystal pillars shattered one after another. The hand trying to contain the blast released torrential amounts of corruption. The resulting clash drowned the area in the taint of the Lost Plane, and Zac was forced to activate [Void Zone] to avoid being overwhelmed.

It soon became impossible to see what was happening inside, but Zac wasn't about to wait for the result. Scores of volatile items, from [Void Balls] to homemade Attuned Crystal-bombs, joined the chaos. Anything Zac could unleash without wasting too much energy. Then a fractal blade emitting an air of antiquity appeared on the edge of [Verun's Bite]. The domains of Arcadia and the Abyss entered the fray, and the lake itself was split in two from a huge spatial tear.

The straight line of delineated space started to twist as it was dragged into the confusing mesh, prompting the churning ball of utter mayhem to gain another level of intensity.

"Void... **VOID!**" the eldritch voice roared in Zac's head, and Zac sensed a palpable wave of hunger assail him.

Zac prepared to unleash his second finisher, but he didn't get the chance before his mind screamed of danger. A barrier glimmering with mottled gold and empowered by Void Energy enclosed him, just before an enormous shockwave threw him away until he crashed into the side of the crater.

Qriz'Ul by the dozens were reduced to floating blobs of runic soup from the blast, while Zac got away with a few scrapes and some disorientation. [Empyrean Aegis] dealt with most of the force from his bombs exploding, while [Void Zone] weakened the intense amount of chaotic energies and corruption loaded into the shockwave.

Concussive explosions illuminated the center of the lake while a million enraged shrieks escaped from within the gateway. It almost looked like time had frozen, with rampant energies struggling to expand and consume the surroundings in a fiery conflagration. They were unable to push beyond an invisible event horizon, held back by an unrelenting pull from within.

Whether it was the black hole or a spatial tear, Zac couldn't tell. It had been hard to discern the situation before, but now it was downright impossible. The static explosion was over 200 meters across, and its chaotic nature rendered [Cosmic Gaze] useless. There was no denying his items had gone off like they were supposed to—the question was whether it was enough.

The area flux from the unpredictable energy and dozens of spatial tears turned spacetime into a leaking sieve. Zac grimaced with pain upon seeing vast amounts of lake water disappearing into the Void. Though that was nothing compared to the dismay upon sensing that monstrous aura from within the chaos. The creature seemed severely weakened, but it had survived.

He needed to do something, *anything*, before the pandemonium died down. Zac grit his teeth and flashed toward the heart of destruction with his movement skill. Everyone had pooled their resources to maximize the potential of the black hole, and they didn't have a lot of options in case it failed. He simply wasn't powerful enough to destroy a spatial gate with his attacks alone. Zac needed to use the opportunity the black hole created before it was too late.

The backup plan was to simply pray the black hole caused enough damage to prevent any significant amounts of energy from passing through when Gemmy activated the array. Zac wasn't resigned to such an outcome, not while hope for success remained.

Another beat from [Void Heart] cleansed the large accumulation of corruption in his body, allowing Zac to save Void Energy as he activated [Arcadia's Judgement]. He'd hoped to reserve that skill for the Kan'-Tanu above ground, but he couldn't be picky in this situation. An even better solution would be to blast the remains of that spatial core with an Annihilation Sphere, but he couldn't even reach it.

The huge wooden hand emerged through one of the tears in space, and its towering aura pushed the already frothing waters into a fever pitch. Despite being pelted by shrapnel and corruption, Zac's focus homed in on his finisher. With its enormous surface, the hand was tainted by a tremendous amount of corruption in no time, which was then transferred to Zac.

The nigh-inexhaustible life force of the wooden hand only somewhat helped against the assault, and Zac quickly lost control of the skill. Thankfully, [Arcadia's Judgement] didn't need to be maintained for long, and its gleaming axe head was already cutting into the seething ball of barely contained destruction.

It felt like Zac had pushed his hand into a blender as the axe sliced through. He pushed on, desperately controlling the gradually collapsing axe with his Branches of War Axe and Kalpataru. Just a little more. He could sense it through his skill—the cracked gateway wasn't far.

Blood ran down Zac's nose as he pushed his empowered soul beyond its limits, forcibly holding the skill together through sheer stubbornness and determination. It narrowly passed by the trapped black hole, and Zac swore when a second runic hand emerged to block [Arcadia's Judgement].

Edge and palm collided, and Zac shuddered as the connection to his skill broke. Though it failed, his attempt wasn't an abject failure. The ball of destruction grew to twice its original size before rapidly shrinking to no more than five meters across. But just as Zac thought it would wink out, a huge shape shattered the lingering flames before pouncing at Zac.

*"EMPTY!"*

The ghastly Qriz'Ul reached more than fifty meters, though it didn't seem to have any solid features. The hands that had blocked Zac's attempts were gone, replaced by what almost looked like a comet's dust tail. It did have one familiar marker—its decidedly goblin face. A huge, sharp nose the size of a speedboat pointed right at Zac, and its wide mouth was locked in a perpetual sneer.

However, there were some differences to this thing compared to the normal goblinoid Qriz'Ul. First, it was less corporeal than its smaller brethren, even if its energy surpassed anyone Zac had seen so far. It had also taken on features you wouldn't see on the Ra'Lashar goblins. Three layers of runic teeth filled its mouth, and its chin was replaced by a bony hook that almost touched its snout.

The creature also had four sets of eyes that glared hungrily at Zac, while a larger ninth eye sat between them on its oversized forehead. The ninth eye contained such powerful corruption that it made Zac's soul shudder, but that wasn't the important thing. It was made from the broken-off half of the gateway itself.

The sphere had seen better days. Less than half its mass remained, reduced to a jagged crescent half-moon with cracks covering its surface, while only eight purple tendrils were still attached to it. Unfortunately, the broken gateway appeared somewhat functional. Weak spatial fluctuations were coming from the crystal, which provided the Qriz'Ul with a steady stream of dirty energy.

A weak pulse of Spatial Energy from within the shuddering ball of destruction in the distance made Zac's eyes widen in comprehension. He had been completely wrong. That sphere was this wretched creature rather than the bridge to the Lost Plane. It must have planted itself at the mouth of the gateway to enjoy the massive amounts of condensed corruption.

Perhaps the two were even connected somehow, since the crystal on the creature's forehead rippled with energy in harmony with the pulse.

This wasn't part of the calculations. The gateway refused to break down even after being blasted by the black hole. Was it this creature that allowed it to hang on? Did Zac need to kill the oversized goblin for the gateway to collapse altogether? Or was this creature immortal until he managed to close the pathway?

There was no time to figure out the details. The goblin had almost reached him, and it shuddered with energy far beyond the lipless Hegemon's. Zac activated [Ancient Forest] and slipped away, avoiding the approaching horror. His domain skill was rapidly falling apart in this toxic environment, but he only needed one jump.

Unfortunately, things didn't always go according to plan, and Zac felt resistance just as he was about to teleport next to the original spot of the gateway. He could only course-correct and pick another tree before pushing off from its crumbling trunk with [Earthstrider]. His surroundings were fraught with spatial tears and purple crystal debris, but he pushed straight for the epicenter as Oblivion was extracted from his soul.

Zac didn't know the relation between monster and gateway, but he knew the window of opportunity was fast closing on the latter. Chaotic energies ran rampant in the area, and space itself was exhausted to the limit of collapse. While his surroundings were dangerous, they weren't impassable. He needed to use this chance to add to the damage. That would hopefully be the straw that broke the camel's back and closed the thing.

A pang of danger warned him of an incoming calamity, but there was no time to respond. The goblin was impossibly fast, like he was fighting the lake itself. The moment Zac entered the tree, the thing had turned into a stream of runes and caught up with him. Zac could only urge his Annihilation Sphere on while he unleashed a storm of fractal leaves from [Nature's Edge].

The Qriz'Ul was cut through dozens of times over, but Zac knew it was a failure. He'd hoped to cause some real damage with his Daos, but he didn't even manage to delay it. A few dozen runes had been destroyed, but what was that to a giant with tens of thousands of them? He could only make one final gambit, and most of his remaining Cosmic Energy was almost instantly absorbed by a shimmering talisman hidden within his sleeves.

A wave of starlight shot out from the Early D-grade talisman while a tennis-ball-sized Annihilation Sphere formed between Zac's hands. It was much smaller than Zac planned, and not nearly the limits of his stockpiled energy, but he was out of time. [Empyrean Aegis] finally collapsed from the clash between talisman and goblin, but his eyes never left the small flickering disk of a slightly darker purple.

It was almost invisible and just the size of a plate. A small discoloration that could easily be mistaken for a shadow. But his body could feel it. The power that slumbered on the other side. Infinite, incomprehensible power. The Lost Plane. Power or not, Zac wasn't moved. It wasn't true. At least not for him.

The Annihilation Sphere bit into the window, and a good chunk of it simply disappeared. Zac saw a shocking sight when he managed to close just over half of the gate. Somehow, the enormous goblin had appeared beneath him, its glowing eyes staring hatefully at him.

"*NOTHING!*" the voices screamed, and the whole lake exploded.

Zac groaned from the impact as his surroundings became a blur. He hadn't been thrown into the wall this time, but was thrust straight into the air, far from the frayed gateway. Things went from bad to worse when Zac sensed dozens of massive energy signatures above, proving the Kan'Tanu were awake.

And that still wasn't the most immediate of his problems. A veritable volcano had erupted at the bottom of the lake, and a terrifying wave of energy was quickly catching up with him. Instead of molten-hot magma, it was a geyser of corruption with the face of a goblin closing in.

Its advance was a calamity, and the smaller Qriz'Ul were shredded and absorbed by the monstrous force. The whole lake was practically being pushed to the sky from the goblin's furious pursuit. And then, the world of purple was showered with a golden radiance as Zac was thrown into the open air.

The world spun too fast to make sense of the situation, but a sudden appearance of a massive maw made Zac swear with surprise. He was out of cards—in this form, that is—having expended them all on the gateway. Yet both the gate and his enemies remained. He would have to take the risk.

The final charges of **[Earthstrider]** were rapidly used to create some distance, at which point his body was flooded with the sweet kiss of Death.

———

For minutes, nothing happened, yet every second seemed to stretch longer than the one before it. The lake was only so big. Even if treading carefully, it could only take so long until Zachary reached the bottom, where the gateway was supposed to be.

Then it came. A weak pulse of spatial Dao made the surface of the lake shudder. Just a moment later, it looked like the whole lake had been set to a boil, and even the demon could sense the enormous eruption of power beneath the surface.

The change hadn't gone unnoticed to the stoic cultivators sitting at the shores either. It looked like someone had kicked up a hornet's nest as they all sprung to action at once.

"Well, I guess that's me," Ogras sighed before shadows consumed him.

Iz could sense how he was rapidly moving toward two Hegemons whose energy was already churning. But he wouldn't be enough. There were nearly 30 Hegemons altogether, supported by over a thousand E-grade fodder. Those foot soldiers were inconsequential when it came to individual strength, but together they would be able to forge barriers powerful enough to slow down any opposition.

Even then, the real problem was the Hegemons. One was seemingly at the very peak of what this Mystic Realm could contain. Another eight could be considered elites in the frontier. And that wasn't even considering the twisted energy creatures, some of which emitted D-grade energy signatures.

Not even Iz was certain she'd be able to deal with such an army before reaching her limits and having one of her fatewarding treasures whisk her away. For Ogras Azh'Rezak to contain them all was hopeless. Yet he rushed forward as a storm of shadows swallowed the southern shores. When push came to shove, he showed up, putting his life on the line.

"Follow my heart," Iz whispered as she looked to the sky.

She didn't want to be a betrayer, a person that couldn't be counted on. She hated the thought of the demon describing her actions in the future like he described those of that Verana woman. Her help was needed, and she would show up. And if someone had a problem with that in the future, she would just test their fate.

The slumbering ember in her chest erupted into a roaring fire, making Iz look inward with surprise. It raged with greater ferocity than ever before, and she suddenly remembered her grandfather's words—

that any flame needed fuel to burn, no matter if it was the fires of life or the empyrean flames of her bloodline. A fuel named *purpose*.

A smile spread across her face as six false wings sprung from her back. It felt like she had been given the blessing of her ancestors as she rose to the air, and the sky greeted her ascent by gaining a golden hue.

"[World's End], how fitting," she said as she sacrificed a third of her Cosmic Energy. "Come."

The world cried as a 100-meter orb of purest flames appeared beneath her feet, and her fatebound guardian appeared behind her back.

Hundreds of fiery motes broke off from the nine flames hovering in her Soul Aperture, and streaks of truth were left in their wake. Their dance rapidly formed one sigil after another, until three sets of 243 runes formed her family's exclusive Dao Array—[Empyrean Flame].

The Branches of Primal Starlight, Scorching Abyss, and Golden Sun were filtered and amplified through its intricate network as her guardian formed multiple sigils with her hands. Her veins were fire, her blood was flames, and she carried the apocalypse in her heart.

And with a nudge, Iz released the gates.

Nine streams of realm-breaking heat shot out from the prepared arrays, all fueled by the truths exclusive to the Tayns. The settlement and its lingering occupants were erased, their fate unable to withstand the proximity. The streams spread out, each one targeting one of the nine superlative Hegemons before they could unleash their strikes against the lake.

But it failed.

"Hm?" Iz muttered, her mind blanking out by the unexpected scene.

She wasn't surprised that the leader managed to survive her attack, but *five*? Odd barriers had blocked her spells, and Iz sensed an anomalous resonance completely unfamiliar to her.

"They're connected somehow! With each other and the lake!" a pained scream tore from the shadows, but Iz had no time to react before things changed again.

A distant wail echoed through the area as a familiar figure was flung into the air like a ragdoll, and Iz couldn't help herself as she started to laugh at the scene. That guy really couldn't stop himself from creating a spectacle.

Where had Mr. Bug found himself a mountain-sized goblin to fight?

# 24

# QRIZ'UL KING

Life was rapidly being supplanted by death as Zac activated his Specialty Core. Still, he was cutting it close. Even outside its natural habitat, the Qriz'Ul King was incredibly quick, resembling a floating river as it closed the gap between them. Zac thought the thing would try to swallow him, but it suddenly spat out a purple blade while runic tendrils followed in its wake.

The edge was over ten meters across and emitted a dense amount of corruption. It was the first time Zac saw the 'Nightmare Tears' as Ogras called them, and he felt an uncomfortable pressure even at a distance. The nefarious whispers of the Lost Plane churned within the tear, but the epiphanies were conspicuously absent.

Zac felt as though his body was shackled during the transformation, but the constraints soon broke, and a storm of Miasma was unleashed. [Love's Bond] had already taken its proper form, and [Black Death] replaced [Verun's Bite]. A sinister jagged edge stretching almost four meters appeared in front of the chained axe in his hand, and Zac unleashed a herculean swing at the incoming projectile.

Two edges collided, and if not for Alea's chains, he would have once more been thrown away like a leaf in the wind. Instead, they latched on to the goblin's diffuse appendages, and a struggle for poisonous supremacy ensued. The chains were empowered by [Blighted Cut] and the unrelenting death of the Pale Seal, while the appendages were made from the ancient madness of the Lost Plane.

Unfamiliar runes lost their luster and fell apart, but it wasn't a clean-cut victory. The mere touch of the Qriz'Ul was rapidly eroding the viscous coating of **[Blighted Cut]**, and Zac sensed that not even the reinforced links beneath were immune to the corrupting nature of the Lost Plane.

Zac himself wasn't much better off. His right arm strained to the breaking point from holding back the Nightmare Tear, and the black edge rapidly started to decay, even with the Branches of the Pale Seal and War Axe bolstering it. In contrast, the tear seemed to contain almost limitless force. There was no way he'd whittle that thing down.

A pull from the chains dragged him upward and closer to the face of the goblin, and Zac used the final lifespan of **[Gorehew]** to push the Nightmare Tear downward with everything he had, prompting it to fall toward a group of infiltrators below. A quick glance at the situation below confirmed something he'd sensed while being thrown into the air. Iz had really joined the fray, and she was waging a one-woman war against the cultists.

The scene was mesmerizing. Iz Tayn looked just like the first time Zac saw her, standing on a burning orb like a goddess of the sun, with a demonic angel raining death and destruction on her enemies. Last time, it'd been a scene of mortal danger. This time it was one of comfort. Without her, Zac wouldn't know what to do. He and Ogras alone wouldn't cut it when this big goblin was added to the calculation.

Of course, some things were changed with Iz's display. The flames had drastically improved since she was an F-grade cultivator, powered by at least two Dao Branches related to Fire. There was also a sense of antiquity to them, like they were flames that heralded from the birth of the era.

Antiquity like what his Void Energy emitted. Was this not something unique to him but rather the mark of ancient, powerful bloodlines?

The rattling sounds of Alea's chains brought him back to the present, and he conjured another jagged axe as he flew toward the Qriz'Ul King's head. Its maws opened to swallow him whole. However, a light rap on one of his chains made it slam into another, prompting a chain reaction where a length of links appeared right in front of his feet.

Zac used the chain to push off, narrowly allowing him to avoid both the sharp chin and the oversized nose. The blade of **[Gorehew]** was humming with killing intent and twinned Daos, and the air itself cried as the edge fell toward the pitch-black core atop its forehead. But a dark-purple barrier appeared just above its surface, and Zac was suddenly looking at the gateway to the Lost Plane again.

It was weak and muted, but even a weak mimicry of that aura was terrifying, especially when it was accompanied by a deluge of corruption far more condensed than the lake water. The blade of [Gorehew] disintegrated, and Zac urgently commanded [Love's Bond] to drag him out of harm's way.

A huge mouth suddenly filled his vision, but a third jagged edge crashed against the sharp chin. Zac used the bony hook to launch him toward the ground, and an enormous cloud was released in his wake like a smoke curtain of pure death. Simultaneously, Zac had all of Alea's chains detach from the huge creature and return to his side.

Their first clash ended with the goblin essentially unscathed, but Zac still considered it a success. He hadn't been sure whether he would be able to block these seemingly intangible attacks, but the Nightmare Tear had been stopped in its tracks by Zac's counter swing. The same was true for his chains, which meant his other skills should work against this creature.

Another piece of good news was that its aura had further weakened since leaving the lake. It seemed to have emitted an energy signature at the limits of Hegemony for a moment when it moved to seize the black hole, but the spatial bomb crippled it and reduced it to Late D-grade. From there, Zac had added to the chaos with his bombs and attacks. By now, it was somewhere at the edge between Early and Middle D-grade.

However, its foundations remained those of a peak being, and it was clearly more powerful than a normal Hegemon. Zac wasn't sure if the Qriz'Ul King was using any Daos, yet the goblin's very existence corrupted all of his attacks and even his equipment. And that barrier… A normal attack wouldn't get past that thing. Meanwhile, his attacks hadn't exhausted the goblin at all by the looks of it.

Its enormous body was a massive congregation of energy, and its stores would undoubtedly put most Beast Kings to shame. Between an almost grotesque amount of energy and the core that kept feeding it more, this guy would be hard to lock down, let alone kill. First things first, though; Zac needed to fight on the ground.

His undead form had many advantages, but aerial battles were not one of them.

Zac's thoughts whirred, already formulating an approach as he fell toward the shores. Ogras said the Qriz'Ul had a core rune that needed to be hit, but in this case, it had to be the stone on its forehead. He needed to create an opportunity and blast it with everything he had. It would be even better if he could break its connection to the gateway. That way, its shield might not work at all.

Shortly after, Zac slammed into the ground, and a second layer of death descended on the area around him as Zac activated **[Deathmark]**. Unfortunately, the goblin itself didn't immediately follow in his wake, making it difficult for Zac to strike back. His only real ranged skill was **[Desperation's End]**, but it was much too early to use his most powerful strike.

Besides, the goblin wasn't the only thing to worry about.

The shroud of **[Fields of Despair]** revealed over 100 cultists in his direct vicinity, three of whom were Hegemons. Though something was very off about them. In his current form, he should have seen powerful fluctuations of life from these people, especially from the D-grades, with lifespans surpassing ten thousand years.

Yet they were weak candles flickering in the wind, where a simple push would topple them. If they didn't emit such intense auras, Zac would have thought they were at death's door. Just as Zac suspected, the lake had turned them into something neither living nor dead.

A few silent specters appeared by the cultists, hooded executioners wielding pitch-black axes. **[Deathmark]** had seen an upgrade inside the temple as well, and their axes looked even more deadly. Not only that, but their auras had grown indistinct, as if fused with the darkness of the skill's domain. It was like they suddenly possessed an item like his energy-hiding bracelet, making them far harder to spot without a honed danger sense.

As expected, less than half of the cultivators noticed the incoming swing, but Zac swore with surprise when the situation rapidly changed. Sturdy barriers made from the purple lake water and bolstered with bloody tendrils enclosed all the cultivators at once. Almost as though when one of them saw the danger, all of them did, and they reacted together. Even those who weren't targeted by specters were shielded.

None had spoken a word, and the response was instantaneous. They had to be mentally linked for such a coordinated response. Zac grimaced in annoyance, especially after seeing that his skill didn't work on the water-based shields. The green runes of [Deathmark] briefly appeared on the barriers, but they crumbled long before they could drag in any significant amount of Zac's own corruption.

A sudden pang of danger made him look up just in time to see hundreds of purple scars shooting toward him like a nightmarish meteor shower. Each of the scars had the power to turn an average E-grade cultivator to mush, and a few fused and grew even larger as they descended.

"Holy—!" Zac yelped as he urgently activated [Abyssal Phase].

Zac turned into a puff of abyssal dust and flickered away, moving almost a thousand meters in an instant with his movement skill. It was the first time he'd used the skill since it got upgraded to Peak Mastery. Some skills gained new features, but the boon of [Abyssal Phase] was simple—speed.

It allowed Zac to move almost 50% faster than before, and he guessed only speed-focused Hegemons would be able to catch up with him in his current form. It also allowed him to avoid the hailstorm, though the Kan'-Tanu cultivators weren't so lucky. The whole area was ripped apart, and not even the three Hegemons managed to avoid the barrage, especially not after the Qriz'Ul King itself slammed into the ground like a comet.

So much for camaraderie through turpitude.

The whole area heaved from the collision, and Zac swore when he saw the Qriz'Ul absorb an Olympic pool's worth of water. It wasn't just an issue of the thing stealing his cultivation resources, it used the water to recover a large amount of energy it'd just expended with its nightmare rain.

The Qriz'Ul King seemed startled by Zac's sudden disappearance, but it soon caught his scent.

"*Empty… EMPTY!*" the Qriz'Ul roared as it lunged for him.

A golden rune suddenly appeared above its head, and thousands of burning sigils sealed off the goblin. The whole region shuddered as the goblin slammed chin-first into the golden barrier, failing to break out in one go. It was obviously the work of Iz Tayn, but not even Iz would be able to keep this thing for long.

A tenth of the burning runes had winked out from the collision, and the golden film weakened in turn. But it gave Zac a bit of a breather, and he looked curiously in her direction. Their eyes met, and Zac heard her voice in his mind.

'*Are you okay? What happened?*' Iz's smooth voice echoed, a welcome change of pace after the goblin's demented roars.

'*Ah, you can hear me?*' another startled voice echoed out, and Zac's gaze turned to a different section of the battlefield.

Ogras had already been forced to use his [Shadewar Flag], and a mix of spectral beings and ghosts that looked a lot like the Qriz'Ul themselves were already battling the armies of mindless cultists. Progress was slow, though. Those water barriers were incredibly durable, even if the Qriz'Ul King had made them look like paper.

'*Telepathic skill?*' Zac said with surprise.

'*Something like that,*' Iz said. '*Is the gate closed? And what is that thing you're fighting?*'

'*I didn't manage to close it completely,*' Zac grimaced. '*This guy was guarding the pathway and absorbed most of the damage.*'

'*That's its strength AFTER eating a black hole?*' the demon exclaimed. '*Wouldn't want to see how it was before.*'

'*I think it's still connected to the gateway,*' Zac said, thinking back to the impregnable barrier shielding its core. '*I think it will keep drawing strength from the Lost Plane until the pathway is properly closed. I'm not sure I can kill it like this. And I don't think I can deal with the gateway while also stalling this thing.*'

'*...I'll figure something out with the miss,*' Ogras groaned. '*Just keep the big guy occupied for now. If it's really connected, it might sense us targeting the gateway.*'

'*Do you have any solutions? I threw pretty much all I had at the gate,*' Zac asked. '*There were Qriz'Ul inside the lake, but most of them should have died because of this big guy.*'

The air shuddered as another hurricane of corruption erupted within the barrier, and runes rapidly started to wink out.

'*I am still hesitant about entering the waters. Besides, I need to keep these cultists in check. They are a lot stronger than I anticipated. I do have something that should work, but Mr. Azh'Rezak will have to deliver*

*it. Just place it next to the gateway and infuse some energy. But be care-
ful, the item is a bit dangerous.'*

Upon hearing Iz's words, it felt like a huge weight had been lifted
from his shoulders. Zac didn't know what changed since he entered the
lake, but it looked like Iz had fully joined their cause. Perhaps his speech
was a lot more convincing than he'd thought? In either case, an item
someone like Iz Tayn called dangerous was bound to be something absolutely terrifying.

And with just a corner of the gateway remaining, it should be more
than enough.

*'Great, sounds like a marvelous time, but I'm still not confident in
reaching the bottom in one piece, creatures or no,' Ogras complained.*

*'Then keep attacking these creatures, but don't kill all of them. They
are powering their shields with the lake,' Iz countered. 'The lake's depth
has already decreased by twenty meters, and the leader swallowed a lot
more just now. A minute longer, and you should be able to survive the
journey.'*

Zac glanced past the raging Qriz'Ul King. It was just like Iz said; the
shores had grown, and a band of wetness indicated that just over twenty
meters of lake water had disappeared. The scene made Zac's heart clench
with pain, and he furiously glared at the goblin still making a ruckus.

All because of this bastard. If not for him, Zac could have closed the
gateway before snatching the whole lake, turning it into a tonic that
would help him shore up his foundations. Now, they had to sacrifice it to
accomplish their goals. Just the thought made Zac furious.

*'I'll deal with this guy. But, uh, please try not to destroy too much
water,' Zac urged. 'Turns out it's pretty useful for my cultivation.'*

*'Of course it is. I wouldn't want to see the kind of wretched refuse
that not even you would use for advancement,' an annoyed scoff echoed
through his mind, and a laugh from Iz Tayn probably meant she shared
the sentiment.*

*'Whatever, just save me some water,'* Zac snorted as the burning cage
broke apart.

The Goblin King was hesitant to go for Zac, who stood over a thousand meters from the lake, or for Iz, who emitted a far more palpable
threat. Soon, it turned toward Iz, prompting Zac to do something. Even if

he flashed over to intercept, the goblin would still be precariously close to the lake.

Whether it was creating an opportunity for Ogras or preventing it from swallowing any more water, he had to force it over. And Zac had an idea. He released a wave of Void Energy into the air around him. The Qriz'Ul King's head instantly snapped around, confirming Zac's guess. There was something about his Void Energy that attracted it.

The creature had emitted an intense hunger the first time Zac activated his domain skill beneath the depths, and every time he used Void Energy during the fight, the monster entered a frenzied state. The goblin hesitated, but still took the bait. It condensed into a stream and shot toward Zac, ancient ruins reduced to rubble by the goblin's advance.

Four chains shot forward, each targeting the cracked sphere on the creature's forehead from various angles. Meanwhile, Miasma churned throughout Zac's body as his bones creaked. Zac even used some Void Energy to keep the Qriz'Ul's attention while speeding up the activation of [Arbiter of the Abyss].

The Qriz'Ul was incredibly agile for its size, bobbing and weaving to avoid the chains while barely losing speed. But Zac's web wasn't spun randomly, and a hidden chain appeared in the shadows of one that missed, a chain unlike the others. It didn't move very quickly, but the Qriz'Ul was out of options. It'd unknowingly moved closer and closer to the ground to avoid the chains, and now it couldn't dip any farther.

A tap on its forehead resulted in a spectral chain being born, and a smile spread across Zac's face. He didn't activate the taunting effect and instead released more Void Energy into the air. The Qriz'Ul King had initially stopped to swipe at the spectral chain, but the Void Energy made it move again.

And just as it came within 250 meters of Zac, a pillar rose from the ground. A monument to despair and inexorability. Ogras would need another minute before he could dip down and close the gate, which hopefully would further weaken the creature. But seeing the billowing waves of corruption trapped within the ethereal body of the goblin, Zac couldn't help but ask.

Could he even stall this big guy that long?

# HOLDING ON

The goblin grew agitated from being locked up far from its lake but didn't appear overly worried. Zac wasn't surprised. This creature was far more powerful than any enemies he'd previously fought, to the point Zac wasn't confident he'd even be able to trap it for the whole minute required. However, he had no choice but to fight, no choice but to keep this guy here long enough for Iz and Ogras to deal with the gateway.

Zac steeled his heart and kept infusing energy into [Pillar of Desolation]. Behind his back, the familiar tower rose through a black pool, like it'd been dragged out from the deepest recesses of the Abyss. Its overall appearance was mostly the same since reaching Middle Mastery, but like all skills, it received some improvements.

The statues bound to the pillars were more lifelike, almost like their twisted faces moved in agony. It was a surreal experience, and Zac could almost hear distant wails when he glanced in the tower's direction. Besides being crafted with a more skilled hand, the chains draped around its length were thicker and more durable.

The pillar had also gained 20 meters, now reaching 70 meters into the air, allowing it to tower above even the Qriz'Ul King. In addition, the pitch-black anti-sun hovering at its top had grown, emitting a more powerful aura. Finally, Zac could feel that its effect on his other skills had also become stronger.

The absolute darkness from [Pillar of Desolation] meshed better with his other two domains, and the ethereal chain that connected him and the goblin's face grew sturdier. It was just in time, as the goblin suddenly made a break for it, trying to tear down the deathly river before it had a chance to stabilize.

A tug on the spectral chain forced the goblin into a 180 to instead head straight for the pillar. Surprisingly, the chain of [Arbiter of the Abyss] had turned completely invisible with Zac, and not even using his taunt exposed his location. The goblin tried to break out a few more times, but each time it was redirected toward the center of the cage.

"Emp... ty," the goblin growled as its head swung back and forth, at a loss for where Zac had gone or what was happening.

Zac's eyes lit up at the scene, and he stopped the statues from throwing out any chains toward his enemy. As far as he was concerned, this guy could just stay like that while Iz dealt with the lake and the Kan'Tanu. He couldn't see what was going on outside even if the anti-sun didn't blind him, though he could sense Iz's monstrous aura and vast swathes of fiery Dao.

She was no doubt laying waste to the shorelines, rapidly vaporizing his precious water.

But nothing good ever lasts. After five seconds of fruitless searching, Zac started to sense a tremendous buildup of energy from the 50-meter-tall goblin. Zac didn't know exactly what it was planning, but if it was anything like the rain of Nightmare Tears, it could completely destroy his deathly river if unlucky. He would have to use himself as bait to keep this thing distracted.

Miasma flooded into multiple Skill Fractals as Zac rushed forward, all while desperately pulling on the spectral chain to distract the goblin. Meanwhile, chains shot out from the pillar behind him. The goblin ignored the chains because Zac activating his skills had exposed his location.

By that point, Zac had already closed most of the distance, and a short burst of Void Energy guaranteed he would have the creature's undivided attention. Its maw opened impossibly wide, and the churning corruption within felt like a Pandora's Box that absolutely couldn't be allowed to open.

The ball of corruption wasn't as unfathomable as what was released by its core when threatened, but there was simply too much energy. The short accumulation had already gathered more than half of Zac's total energy reserves. Even more than the cost of [Pillar of Desolation]. The skill would likely collapse if the Qriz'Ul King launched the blob at the river or the pillar itself.

Thankfully, Zac had acted decisively and just in time. When the goblin was about to spit out its ball of madness, three invisible cuts dismantled the Qriz'Ul King's whole head. Simultaneously, a black storm swallowed the suddenly exposed corruption ball. Even a Late-stage [Profane Exponents] was insufficient to move the ball out of harm's way, but it managed to realign its budding momentum downward.

Following up, Zac pulled on the ethereal chain to push his taunting domain to the limits, using the last second on the skill to repulse the goblin's attack. The three skills used in conjunction were barely enough to seize control from the Qriz'Ul, even if its head was already reforming.

The ball of corruption crashed to the ground right beneath the Qriz'Ul. It cracked, releasing billowing waves of condensed corruption throughout the cage with the goblin as an epicenter, and Zac immediately found himself submerged. An exquisite coffin sprung up to protect him, and it was thankfully able to block out the unfocused blast of the D-grade creature.

Like the previous upgrade, [Profane Exponents] received a general upgrade from reaching Late Mastery. Their auras had grown deeper while their tools, from coffin to lantern, looked more exquisite.

The wave of corruption passed around him like a river blocked by a stone. Most of it was held at bay by the coursing river, almost like two oils that refused to mix. However, the collision itself left a lot of damage behind, while some of the corruption managed to infiltrate Zac's skill, starting its unrelenting push toward mutation. The rebuffed energy formed a layer of taint covering the ground, and even Zac found himself submerged to his knees after the initial wave passed.

The corruption clung to him and tried to burrow inside. Circulating his Daos helped a bit, but it was ultimately impossible to completely block it without [Void Zone]. Between his previous usage and expending Void Energy to activate a couple of skills, Zac couldn't use his domain willy-nilly any longer.

It was easier to let it invade his body while [Void Heart] and [Purity of the Void] still had enough capacity to deal with it. He'd be harassed by intrusive whispers, but it was still within what he could deal with.

Only the tower itself was unscathed, somehow rejecting the shallow waters of corruption with its oppressive aura. Doing so was not only putting a strain on the skill itself but also a constant drain on his Miasma. Zac inwardly sighed at the scene. Just one failed attack was causing so much trouble due to the sheer volume of energy.

Meanwhile, the goblin had already reformed after Zac expended [Blighted Cut], and its energy reserves had only dropped a couple of percents. Even worse, Zac could feel how the missing unit was being recovered. It really looked like the Qriz'Ul King could still draw energy from its connection to the gateway, even when trapped inside [Pillar of Desolation].

One thing was certain, Zac couldn't follow his most basic strategy—to outlast the opposition with his endless energy reserves. This goblin showed him what it truly meant to be tireless. Zac needed to be smarter and more efficient as he stalled and detained the Qriz'Ul King. Luckily, that was exactly what the Inexorable Stance excelled at, and with his latest skills and upgrades, Zac had even more tools available to him.

Six intangible arms were already grasping for him since the Qriz'Ul had reformed, but Zac's heart was calm as he went to work. He had to maintain constant pressure while preventing any real buildups of energy. Chains rushed toward the sneering visage of the Qriz'Ul King as another jagged edge appeared in front of his axe.

Zac towered over four meters into the air after having activated [Arbiter of the Abyss], and the huge blade of [Gorehew] was no longer comically oversized. Instead, it became a serviceable tool to rip apart the Qriz'Ul's appendages while [Blighted Cut] was on cooldown.

Suddenly, Zac sensed an accumulation of corruption, and he pushed off the ground as the chains of [Love's Bond] rattled. Two of the chains dug at the cracked core on the goblin's forehead, while another formed a step for Zac to readjust his trajectory midair. In an instant, Zac found himself right in front of the goblin's face, their sizes now roughly the same.

The air screamed as the jagged blade of bloody death clove the air in a huge overhand arc aimed at the creature's mouth. However, the chains meant to force a realignment of the goblin's head failed to create the opening Zac planned for. That powerful barrier appeared again, allowing the Qriz'Ul to completely ignore any strikes targeting its only apparent weak spot.

The goblin once more displayed its surprising deftness by parrying Zac's swing with its chin before lunging to swallow Zac whole. Initially, Zac planned to back away and try anew, but he suddenly had an idea. Jagged teeth closed around him, but just as Zac was about to be bit, he activated **[Void Zone]**.

Corruption fought with nothingness, and nothingness won out. The second ball of taint dimmed and collapsed before it had a chance to form, while the runes making up the goblin's head started to lose their structural cohesiveness. Zac wanted to use the opportunity to see if he could destroy the core, but his eyes widened in alarm when he felt a pull.

The D-grade monstrosity was siphoning his Void Energy, dragging it toward its cracked sphere. His very essence was being robbed, and a primal fear surged in his heart as he kicked up a storm of carnage with his axe. Runes disintegrated all around him, but his domain couldn't prevent the goblin from recovering.

Meanwhile, it became apparent that **[Void Zone]** didn't work against the barrier around the core. Zac still couldn't tell exactly what the shield was, but it almost felt like the space within the barrier was in another dimension. Could it actually have phased its core to the Lost Plane for safekeeping?

And all the while, a deluge of corruption was released from the Qriz'Ul, rapidly draining Zac of energy. A few more strikes confirmed nothing had changed. Whether it was chains or axe, he simply couldn't break through that barrier. Staying inside its incorporeal body like this was futile, so Zac disappeared in a puff of smoke before appearing twenty meters away.

"**VOID!** *VOID!*" the goblin roared as it lunged for him, but by that point, the chains of **[Pillar of Desolation]** had already caught up.

The closest one inexorably wound around the supernatural creature and started pulling it toward the pillar in the distance. Zac used the opportunity to activate his taunting domain again, and the goblin was dragged over 50 meters in an instant, closer to the tower. Closer to

Oblivion. While the creature was twisted beyond recognition by the taint, it wasn't a mindless creature. It clearly understood the shimmering orb of Desolation was dangerous, or perhaps rather the core of Oblivion at its heart.

It started to push back while freely releasing waves of corruption. Soon enough, the chain of [Pillar of Desolation] broke apart, its improved durability not sufficient to withstand the corroding effect of the Lost Plane. A second chain replaced the first while Zac used his taunt to the maximum. But the Qriz'Ul was relentless, continuously struggling against its chains.

The chains never stopped coming, be it from Love's Bond or [Pillar of Desolation], so the Qriz'Ul changed tactic. It started releasing a barrage of Nightmare Tears at the tower, smaller projectiles it needed no time to generate. Even then, each one contained enough force to create actual spatial tears in their wake, and Zac was forced to deal with them one way or another.

Zac found himself in a passive position where he furiously contained the Qriz'Ul's rampage. Tears were either outright blocked with [Gorehew] and [Profane Exponent]'s barriers, or rerouted with the reversed taunt of [Arbiter of the Abyss]. He moved with purpose, not wasting a second while skillfully managing his array of skills to bring about maximum pressure and efficiency.

Chains danced, wraiths came and went, leaving rapidly disintegrating corrosive marks in their wake. All while the [Pillar of Desolation] pulled and pulled. The rerouted Nightmare Tears crashed into the deathly river, leaving hidden wounds in the cage that wouldn't recover. Others joined the rising tide of corruption.

[Fields of Despair] was the first skill to collapse from the infiltration of the Lost Plane. The loss of nigh-omniscience didn't matter, but losing the restrictive properties of the domain was a huge blow. After all, the deathly haze had restrained 10% of the goblin's attributes, and the creature's boost pushed Zac even closer to the edge.

It wasn't just a matter of pressure either. Zac was already running low on Miasma, to the point he was forced to use Void Energy to maintain some of his skills. Meanwhile, the level of corruption in the cage had already reached the level of the lake, and he was forced to continuously maintain [Void Zone] to retain his mental state.

And the corruption kept increasing.

It wasn't enough. No matter how much Zac cut and whittled it down. Most of his work was nullified by the mysterious link between the creature and gateway. It was constantly being bolstered by energy, to the point it still had over 90% of its strength intact. At least time was passing. Each second felt like an hour, and he kept swinging his axe, kept interrupting the creature's attempts to form more powerful outbursts. Zac was like glue, constantly sticking to his much-bigger foe.

Eventually, Zac knew he would soon fail, at which point he unleashed [Desperation's End]. The spatial spheres weren't enough to seal the Qriz'Ul, but with the additional help from [Pillar of Desolation] and [Arbiter of the Abyss], it was barely enough. The Qriz'Ul was cleanly cut in two, yet even his ultimate skill failed to damage the core.

And Zac could only look on with helplessness as the collapsed form of the Qriz'Ul started to reform just seconds after it was torn to shreds. At least it reset the battle and gave Zac enough of a breather to eat a handful of pills to recuperate. But soon enough, the cycle started anew.

Zac lost any conception of time as he fused with his path. He became death, relentlessly advancing. One wound after another was left on his body as he gave up on dealing with non-lethal strikes. What were some scars to the unrelenting pull of the Abyss? It was just a feeble expression of defiance that all beings exhibited. A delay of the inevitable.

[Deathmark] collapsed next, followed by [Arbiter of the Abyss]. Soon, not even [Gorehew] could be used, and not because of overuse. Not even [Void Zone] could completely shut out all corruption, and too much had entered his body. The taint then followed the strongest surges of Miasma and glommed onto the Skill Fractal. Only [Pillar of Desolation] held on, desperately defended by layers of his Dao.

Zac fought tooth and nail, using everything to delay the inevitable. He still had a few cards left, but the longer he could keep the goblin contained on his own, the better his chances of success. It was just too much. Cracks covered most of the pillar behind him, and more and more Nightmare Tears passed his guard now that he'd lost most of his tools.

The Qriz'Ul proved just as relentless, almost like it gained strength as its surroundings became increasingly corrupted. It reminded Zac of the unawakened Revenants back on Earth—mobile Unholy Beacons that naturally terraformed their surroundings to one more suited for their existence. The longer you fought, the worse your position would get.

Just as Zac was about to activate his next line of defense to buy a few more seconds, the Qriz'Ul froze. The gem on its forehead radiated a blinding purple light that forced Zac to look away. Just a glance had pushed the voices in his head to a crescendo, and Zac could feel how the distilled corruption was joined by actual lake water.

At the same time, a lone voice joined the discordant cacophony in Zac's mind.

'*Shit! The gateway just disappeared when I closed in on it!*' The voice was frazzled, startling him to the point that he failed to perfectly angle a swing. '*Ack, this netherblasted corruption!*'

The Nightmare Tear cut just under his arm, but a last-minute adjustment allowed him to avoid any grievous harm. The pain helped him clear his muddled mind, and he was horrified by what he saw. The core on the goblin's forehead had detached from it, but the creature was still very much alive. It hovered right in front of its forehead, releasing a deluge of tainted water.

Not only was the amount of energy terrifying, but the sheer volume of water was a huge problem. A liquid armor had already covered the Qriz'Ul King, and the cage would be completely submerged in seconds if nothing changed. Not that it would last that long, considering the pillar failed to keep the waters at bay.

The only good news was that the goblin's aura started to become unstable. Was it damaging itself by summoning the gateway? Did it matter in this situation?

'*It's been dragged here. I'll deal with it,*' Zac said in his mind as the waters passed his shoulders. '*Hold on a little bit in case it returns.*'

The goblin shrieked with rage and fear upon sensing the coruscating waves of Oblivion coursing through Zac's body and into his right arm. It redoubled its efforts to break free, desperately pulling in the direction of the real lake in the distance. Did it need to return to its original spot to recover its core? Zac wouldn't let it. The three pygmy skeletons reluctantly collapsed, leaving Zac with only a crumbling tower for assistance.

A tower and a coffin.

"Alea, I need your help," Zac sighed as he infused some of his waning Miasma into the coffin lid.

'*I'm here for you,*' Alea's voice echoed in his mind as the coffin lid creaked open. '*Forever and always.*'

[Death's Embrace] was gone with Alea's Evolution, replaced by a new skill yet untested. [Fate's Obduracy] remained, reforged and more potent than ever. Hopefully, it would be enough.

"Seal this bastard," Zac growled as he felt the pitch-black runes of Oblivion carve a network across his face.

# 26

# BEYOND THE CONCEPT

Even when finding himself pushed to the limits, Zac held back his last and most powerful aces. He wanted to save them until Ogras finished his side of the mission, to give himself something to fall back on in case the Qriz'Ul King went berserk. Now, he found himself without better options, and could only pray it was enough to break through that impenetrable shield.

The goblin's struggles grew more frantic as Zac squeezed out more and more Oblivion from his soul, the energy accumulation already passing what he used in the depths. Even more corruption was discarded and disseminated from the creature's labor, but Zac could barely hear it. The storm of Oblivion had quieted the incessant voices of madness, utterly extinguishing their existence.

The sudden bout of spiritual silence was almost deafening, but things on the material plane were approaching a fever pitch. The chains of **[Pillar of Desolation]** managed to restrain this unrelenting creature for almost a minute, but they could no longer endure under the deluge of tainted water. The last of the fetters snapped, and the goblin broke free.

But it was too late. The coffin lid on Zac's back had fully opened, and over twenty chains had already shot toward their target with a palpable hunger. They were pitch-black and emitted a cold and unrelenting aura of death, like they were made from the ice of Cocytus. They were also incredibly quick, moving with more than twice the speed of **[Love's Bond]**'s original links.

Before the goblin had a chance to speed away, the chains wrapped around it in a deathly embrace. Cascading waves of tainted water inundated the links, though a familiar scene occurred. Any time a chain was about to break apart from the corruption, a black pulse ran through its length and split the chain into two, each one in perfect condition.

Twenty chains had multiplied to over a hundred in no time, and the goblin was barely visible. The thing looked like a grotesque art installation as it struggled in the air. A sudden eruption destroyed two-thirds of the chains, but Zac could sense Alea had more to give. The chains grew back, winding at least three times around the huge Qriz'Ul, forming hundreds of loops that together created a coil. One pulse after another started to run through their lengths until they stayed illuminated, not by electricity, but death.

Even Zac, a Draugr, felt pressure from the immense amount of death released into the chains, and both goblin and tainted water froze in place as they became solid.

They hadn't turned into ice, though. There was no sense of cold emanating from the construct, except for the chill of death. It was more apt to say the water had died, bereft of its momentum, fate, and energy. All that remained was a useless rock-like compound. The only thing left untouched was the warded core floating in front of its forehead, which still released more water.

The lack of Kill Energy entering his mind confirmed what Zac already suspected upon seeing the cracked sphere was intact. Not even this was enough to kill this creature. But Alea had still gone above and beyond accomplishing what needed to be done. The goblin was locked down and trapped in a cycle of death and resurrection. It couldn't so much as move, let alone form any dangerous outbursts of energy.

Meanwhile, the Annihilation Sphere between his hands was approaching the limits of what Zac could control, which meant it was time. Zac shot forward, running up along one of the links toward the hovering core. The voices returned with redoubled intensity as he closed in. Looking at the vantablack orb of destruction between his hands helped a bit, but Zac still felt his mind mired in the Lost Plane's corruptive influence.

Thousands of ideas, most of them irrelevant or downright crazy, cropped up like weeds, leaving behind blemishes on his heart. It would take some time to sort out and cleanse all this madness, but that was a matter for later. Ogras was probably struggling in a similar environment in the depths of the lake without Zac's tools to deal with it.

It wasn't only the voices that grew louder. The closer he got, the more the goblin's resistance intensified. It railed against the prison of |Fate's Obduracy|, and Zac could tell Alea was running out of steam. Meanwhile, the sphere released tremendous pressure, making it seem like Zac was pushing against the weight of an entire world.

The air in the center of the cage twisted and groaned as it was caught in the middle of an unrelenting struggle between death and madness. Searing flashes of pain erupted across Zac's body as errant spatial tears left their marks. But he pushed on until he reached the top of the chain ladder—where a world of hyper-condensed tainted water waited for him.

A ball of water had become the final layer of defense against Zac's approach, its taint so dense it felt as though it could corrupt the Dao itself. Zac knew this would be dangerous, but he could only ward his soul and steel his heart as he crashed into the water, using his now fully formed Annihilation Sphere as a wallbreaker.

The water in front simply disappeared, annihilated in full by the power of Oblivion. But the water to his side remained unaffected, and it crashed into Zac with the force of a collapsing mountain. Zac's bones cracked, and madness stirred, but he pushed farther, deeper, until he encountered resistance.

A tremendous shockwave shook Zac's frayed mind awake, and he vaguely saw how his Annihilation Sphere was trying to dig into the purple barrier—trying and failing. The barrier buckled inward and was shuddering precipitously, but it wasn't showing any indication that it was about to break apart. The sphere was constantly extracting energy from the Lost Plane, replacing that which the Annihilation Sphere destroyed.

Meanwhile, Zac was gradually losing control of his conception. A second or two more, and the Annihilation Sphere would destabilize, and his mission would be a failure. This was exactly what he'd been worried about when dealing with this creature. The power of the Remnants had proven to be a reliable ace until now, but there were limits.

After all, they were only D-grade items, and the energy he used couldn't be considered the full expression of the Daos of Oblivion and Creation. Not only that, but his two attacks were fueled by his own Daos, which were just Early Branches. To deal with a creature that had once been a Peak Hegemon at the least, and who had this unique connection to an Eternal Heritage… It wasn't enough.

Then, an idea came to him. An idea born from madness and desperation, but one that might just work.

The Lost Plane's taint had completely spread throughout his body, yet a pulse of possibility corrupted the corruption. Madness was distorted and reformed in the forge of Creation as Zac roused the slumbering energy throughout his body. It swept through him, leaving bedlam in its wake. This was the strategy of sacrificing 800 soldiers to kill 1000 enemies, where unfettered Creation Energy damaged both his body and the accumulating taint.

The pain was unimaginable as his body went through a series of chaotic transformations. Though the agony helped him focus on maintaining his Annihilation Sphere a bit longer, while a set of golden patterns joined the black ones across his face.

Two streams of energy entered the already worn pathways on his shoulders before fusing in his chest. The Annihilation Sphere shuddered ominously, but was kept in check by Zac's soul working in overdrive. Even then, it was just a matter of time, and Zac knew he wouldn't be able to create an Origin Mark as powerful as his Annihilation Sphere.

Then again, more than half of the sphere had been consumed already from disintegrating the churning waters and clashing against the purple barrier. A weakened version might work even better. After all, his goal wasn't to form a separate attack. It was to balance Creation and Oblivion in one singular strike.

To form Chaos.

Zac slowly moved his hands apart, desperately controlling Annihilation with his right as a shimmering rune appeared in his left palm. Reality bent from the appearance of the Origin Mark, and the tainted waters started frothing from encountering an even more corruptive energy.

The pain grew exponentially, overwhelming anything else. Zac's whole being was consumed by what he'd wrought, but still he pushed his hands together in a final attempt at victory. Black and gold mixed, and space collapsed. A metallic flash illuminated the area, and Zac immediately found himself losing control.

'*Go,*' Zac groaned in his mind, praying Ogras would be able to hear him.

A surge of energy was followed by an endless expanse of white. A lingering thought was all that remained before he faded away.

This wasn't right.

---

Abyssal flames burned along bloody tendrils of the water elemental, but it didn't seem to care. Iz could tell nothing remained of the cultivators who'd been extracted and pulled into this fell construct of tainted water and unorthodox curses. Pure anger and suffering locked in a prison of its own creation.

She glanced at her arm, where her wound had already been cauterized. To think this thing could not only block out her attacks but even wound her. It'd been forced to sacrifice one of its appendages to break through her barrier, but still. Those attacks were proof her flames weren't infallible, even if this creature was only bordering Middle D-grade by conventional standards.

The flame in her chest had dimmed considerably, exhausted from cleansing the waves of corruption thrown her way. She only had 30% of Cosmic Energy remaining, but she held no thoughts of backing down. The weak demon was at the bottom of the lake, desperately trying to accomplish the mission.

Meanwhile, she could feel that Zachary had gone all out, unleashing one of the Remnants locked in his mind. Her uncle had told her the price of using those things, yet he didn't even think to back down, to flee. How could she step down at this juncture? The brooch on her dress flickered, and her surroundings started to blur.

It was trying to take her away, out of the Void Star. Iz wouldn't let it.

She ripped off the Fatewarding Treasure and threw it away, rousing the flame in her chest for one final attack. Her skin caught on fire, as did her hair. Soon she was completely engulfed, transformed into an avatar of the purest flames. With a shudder, one became three, and the trinity avatars representing the paths of the Empyrean Flame surrounded the creature, each with a different set of wings.

It recognized the threat, and space collapsed as it launched its core tendrils toward her. Each one was infused with the chimeral madness of the lake and the Black Heart Sect, turning into an unpredictable poison that targeted both the body and mind. But **[Trinity Apocalypse]** had already been activated, and Iz released a different creature from each of her avatars.

The wings of the Abyssal Butterfly fluttered, and the ground erupted, unleashing fires from the deepest recesses of the Underworld. The Vermillion Bird keened, and the flames of the first dawn burned everything in its path. The golden crow released the sun it held in its claw, and it fell onto the elemental from above.

Three planes, three paths. A trinity of destruction and new beginnings. The elemental tried to resist, to destroy the Origin Flames that were fast-consuming its body, but it was futile. Three paths merged in the center, and the elemental was no more. The three avatars converged atop **[World's End]**, and Iz stepped out from the flames.

She'd done it.

A surge of adrenaline Iz had never felt before coursed through her veins as she looked at the scorched remnants. Her thousands of battles, both in dreamscapes and realities, couldn't produce this sense of victory. She finally understood what her grandpa and uncle had told her so many times.

Some things simply couldn't be imparted from the previous generations, even with arrays and domains that subverted reality itself. Even the 'certain death trials' prepared by her uncle, where she sealed her memories before going in to provide authenticity, hadn't managed to elicit this kind of response—the burning fires of passion, the fear, the determination.

Iz had expended some of her Everflame Essence, but she believed her grandpa would consider this lesson a worthy trade. It allowed her to retain some of her strength, which might be needed. Something big, dangerous, was happening inside that unstable river of death. However, just as Iz was about to move over, a voice in her head stopped her in her tracks.

'*Go*,' the familiar yet foreign voice said, and Iz involuntarily shuddered from the pain that single word carried.

The lake heaved a moment later before a pillar of water and flames rose hundreds of meters into the air. The demon had detonated the modified [Star Seed]. If she remembered correctly, it'd been gifted by that annoying guy from the Stillsun Clan a few years ago. The thought of his gift being used as an incendiary instead of nurturing a custom-made star tugged a smile into Iz's face, though the scene in the distance commanded most of her attention.

She could tell the demon was alive, albeit a bit worse for the wear. But the emanations within the river of death made her heart clench. Even with [Sungod's Eyes], Iz barely managed to make out the scene within. The corruption was just too dense.

Iz didn't need to wait long before the frayed river of death shattered, destroyed by a tremendous shockwave that elicited a primal fear in her heart. Ancient ruins were leveled by the thousands as the blast consumed the center of the Ra'Lashar Capital, and a tsunami of corruption and lake water followed in its wake.

Everything was swept away, from rubble to corpses and scorched remnants of Black Heart Parasites. Iz suddenly felt extremely exposed without her Fateward Treasure, and she urgently entered the diminished orb of [World's End]. Her fatebound guardian wrapped the miniature sun in an embrace just as the shockwave reached her.

Iz's face paled from the tremendous onslaught, from the screams that entered her mind. A roar from her natal flame extinguished the voices, and the storm passed soon after. She took a shuddering breath before lunging for the glimmering brooch on the ground. She felt her fate realign, like a warm blanket keeping her safe.

Everything in moderation. That was the second lesson of the day. There was a fine but definite line between courage and madness, and she wasn't willing to cross that to accomplish her goals. Her grandparents had sacrificed too much for her to just throw her life away.

However, not everyone seemed to treasure their lives, and Iz's gaze once more turned toward Zachary with a mix of anticipation and trepidation.

There he stood, at the epicenter of the destruction. The heavy shroud that hung over the ruins had been destroyed, forming a hole in the sky itself. Weak light shone upon him as he stood unmoving in a crater full of viscous water and broken detritus. Surrounding him were tendrils of chaotic energy, destroying anything they touched.

She could barely recognize him as he blankly looked up at the sky.

His skin was covered in runes of forgotten truths and ancient madness, his eyes two metallic orbs with bolts of gold and black. The air around him strained just from his latent pressure, and winds buffeted his tattered robes.

Iz could have been looking at the resurgence of the previous era, of the unstoppable madmen who lorded over the previous sky. This was what she'd wanted to witness. Someone who didn't helplessly float down the river of fate but paved his own path. Someone who left ripples in his wake and indelible marks on history.

But why did she feel so sad?

Beyond the concept was a man. A man covered in black blood and grisly wounds. Both his hands were missing, where his arms had become cracked marble that ended just beneath his elbows. If not for the pressure he emitted or his fiercely burning life force, Iz would have thought him dead. He looked so tired. So utterly drained, hollowed out by the expectations and responsibilities placed on his shoulders.

"What in the—" a hoarse voice drifted over from a distance, breaking Iz from her trance.

A wet and scorched demon crawled up from the lake, his body fluctuating ominously like he was on the verge of losing his physical form.

"He's alive," Iz sighed as she pointed her finger at Mr. Azh'Rezak, activating [Cleansing Pyre].

A swirl of golden flames engulfed the demon, incinerating most of the corruption that tainted his body. Wounds were cauterized and scabs fell off, exposing unblemished skin beneath.

"Thank you," Mr. Azh'Rezak said with a bow before turning back to Zachary with a frown. "His hands... Do you have—"

The demon's words caught in his throat as something was created out of nothing and two hands regrew. Iz looked on with worry as Zachary slowly bent toward the ground, his movements jerky and discordant like a construct whose maintenance was long overdue.

"What in the..." Ogras repeated in disbelief.

"For every miracle, there is a price," Iz sighed. "Fate... is too dangerous."

27

# WHAT A MESS

Zac woke with a start, and the slight movement unleashed a chain reaction of agony that rippled throughout his entire being. A blurry scene of destruction met his gaze, but there were no threats as far as he could see. It was lucky, as well. Just keeping his eyelids open was a struggle. Another fight was out of the question.

He didn't need to look to know that almost all his pathways were shattered, but he still glanced inward to assess the damage. As expected, his pathways were in utter disrepair. His head, arms, and torso had taken the worst of it, the paths completely gone. The damage wasn't limited to the sections where he channeled the two attacks created with the Remnants either. There was visible damage all the way to the soles of his feet.

There was also damage to his foundation, like he'd opened up a dozen nodes without any protection. Recovering from this would take months rather than weeks, and there would still be risks of leaving imperfections behind. Even his [Thousand Lights Avatar] had taken a hit, and reforming the broken sections would set him back a few months.

The only thing that wasn't broken was his physical body, but a sense of hollowness in the essence of his very being explained the reason. He must have used Creation Energy subconsciously since he'd lost decades' worth of lifespan. By the looks of it, his arms had been completely disintegrated by his final blast, along with a good chunk of his chest.

Thank God his years of experimenting with his Annihilation Sphere and Origin Mark had taught an important lesson that was now ingrained into his body. Always remove your valuables before messing with the Remnants. More than one Spatial Ring had cracked or morphed from being too close to the Remnant skills, so now he always stashed them in a reinforced pouch behind Vivi's tube or Alea's coffin.

What a mess.

There was some good news, though it was insufficient to balance the bad. First, there was the terrifying amount of Kill Energy in his body, far surpassing anything he'd ever held before. In other words, the Qriz'Ul King was dead. Furthermore, the energy proved he hadn't been out of it for very long, even if the tranquility around him indicated the battle was already over. The energy would have dissipated if he'd been unconscious for a couple of hours.

Secondly, the corruption in his body wasn't that bad, considering how much had poured into him while he tried to break down that purple barrier. It was still quite a bit, and didn't seem to carry the insights of the lake. The voices were just weak whispers at this point. His bloodline should have dealt with that long before he recovered.

Zac tried to look around for clues on what was going on, but he didn't even have time to take in his surroundings before he felt his life, or rather death, slipping away. He was utterly drained of Miasma and would soon find himself forcibly swapped over to his human side. However, transforming this crude way would take over a minute, and this was not the time to black out.

A soft tendril of Dao and energy entered his transformation skill, activating the process before it was too late. A shudder went through his body as life replaced nothingness, the process slow and sluggish. Thankfully, the Specialty Core was one of the few sections of his body left untouched, and the process was slowed down rather than interrupted by damage.

Gods, *what a mess.*

Zac couldn't believe he'd been so foolhardy, though he admittedly still didn't have any better solutions with the benefit of hindsight. Fusing his Annihilation Sphere and Origin Mark for a supreme blast was something Zac had considered before, but never had the guts or time to experiment with. Because any time he'd considered a test run, a sense of foreboding filled his heart. And since then, everything he learned about his Daos and Duality only strengthened this impression of danger.

It wasn't necessarily impossible, it was just too early. His Annihilation Sphere was a fusion of his Branches of War Axe and Pale Seal, which was then powered with the distilled Oblivion Energy extracted from the cage in his mind. To fuse his Remnant attacks meant not only combining all three of his Daos, but also Oblivion and Creation.

He still hadn't figured out how to fuse just his Daos for his Cultivator's Core, so adding Oblivion and Creation to the mix was a recipe for disaster. At the time, it felt like a great idea, to push a bit further on the path he was already walking. It was almost natural. But without the voices urging him, he understood just how ill-prepared he was to take that step.

There was no plan, no system. Zac had just slapped together two highly unstable energies he only tenuously controlled and then hoped for the best. If anything, the outcome could be considered lucky, where he only lost a few limbs while the Qriz'Ul King perished. Still, it served as a poignant example of what awaited him if he failed to form a proper core. It wouldn't just be his hands that were blown off—it would be his whole body.

Thinking of his recently reformed hands, Zac realized he was holding onto something—the core of the Qriz'Ul King. That was the last item Zac would have expected to see, considering he aimed his Chaos Ball right at this thing. If this was intact, how had the goblin died?

Certainly, the core had seen better days. New cracks had appeared across its surface, and it no longer emitted any spatial fluctuations. Oddly enough, it was also a bit scorched. Had Iz helped him at the eleventh hour, or was this a result of the goblin's odd connection to the Lost Plane's gateway?

Had the Qriz'Ul truly transported its core away to avoid getting blasted by the unstable Chaos Bomb, only for it to be engulfed by whatever Iz had given Ogras to blow up the lake?

No matter how things worked, it was a welcome surprise. The core probably contained incredibly condensed corruption, which might be even more useful than the diluted taint in the lake. More importantly, this thing could absorb his Void Energy, which might mean it was useful for his bloodline down the road. Right now, his body didn't react to the thing, but his bloodline was also fully satiated at the moment.

His connection to the Qriz'Ul was another mystery Zac couldn't explain. Why had this Qriz'Ul wanted his Void Energy? Come to think of it, all of the Qriz'Ul in the lake had reacted to the energy his bloodline created. At the time, Zac believed they responded to a spot of water suddenly drained of corruption, but that didn't seem to be the case.

Was the Void Emperor bloodline somehow related to the Lost Plane, or perhaps to the Ultom Courts?

Zac had mostly been working under the assumption that his visions came from the Left Imperial Palace rather than Ultom, and that idea had only been reinforced after his talk with Leyara. Emperor Limitless had seized at least eight Eternal Heritages and then built immense Array Palaces around them to create the System. It wouldn't be too surprising if he had a Karmic connection to these places.

How did the Void, the Lost Plane, and the Dao-bereft insights of Ultom fit into the picture? Perhaps this core could help shed some light on the connection between these things and possibly even his bloodline. It also seemed like a promising material for his Cultivator's Core down the road.

Shuffling steps made Zac look up with alarm, but he relaxed upon seeing two familiar figures standing at the edge of the crater he found himself in.

"Uh, you okay over there?" Ogras asked.

"I've been better," Zac grimaced as he put away the Qriz'Ul Core. "What about you? Is everything dealt with?"

"The gateway is closed," Ogras said. "And the infiltrators are all dead. The young miss dealt with them for us."

"All of them?" Zac said with surprise.

"They fused into one entity," Iz said calmly.

Zac sighed in relief. He didn't have another fight in him.

"So, you're going to stay in the puddle, or?" Ogras asked.

"Oh, right," Zac said, and started to make his way out of the crater.

It was slow. Excruciatingly slow. Zac felt weaker than back before the Integration, and he nearly stumbled a couple of times on his way to the edge. Finally, he got there, though every step felt like getting stabbed.

"You weren't kidding," Ogras sighed. "Well, knowing your monstrous constitution, you'll be up and about in no time. I can't believe you're able to regrow limbs at will. To accomplish that, I had to find a bunch of treasures and fuse with shadow creatures."

"Borrowed Creation," Iz said as she gave Zac a deep look. "The price is steep."

"I try to avoid using it, but trouble keeps finding me." Zac weakly smiled.

"The burden of fate." Iz nodded as she took out a small vial. "Use this. It will recover some of what you lost."

Zac curiously looked at the shimmering drops inside the vial, and was shocked at the explosive vitality they contained. Each drop gave off radiant light like a sun, and even through the densely inscribed casing, Zac could tell they contained incredible amounts of life force. These things couldn't even be put in the same category as the other Longevity Treasures he'd encountered.

Uzu's Fire-attuned Longevity Pearl, which had since joined Zac's treasure pile, might as well be trash in front of these drops. Which meant these things were incredibly rare. And rare meant expensive.

"I'm not sure if I'm in any condition to get myself blasted with a fireball at the moment," Zac hesitated.

"You can owe me one," Iz said with a small smile.

Zac didn't know how he felt about mooching off of Iz like this. They'd gotten somewhat close over the past days, and she had proven herself a trustworthy ally, but she had been right before about balance. It wasn't right for him to just take and take without giving anything back. At the same time, he really needed this thing.

"More importantly, didn't you want that lake water?" Ogras interjected when Zac didn't move for a few seconds.

"Ah? What?" Zac perked up. "Why? What's wrong?"

"Well, the bottom of the lake is full of spatial tears since we blew a hole in the Mystic Realm," Ogras shrugged. "It's leaking."

"What!" Zac screamed as he started running toward the lake.

Or at least he tried to. The sudden burst of movement set his whole body on fire, and when he went to correct himself, his legs felt like lead.

"You're in no state to use skills," Iz said from the side.

"I can't, I have to—ah, crap," Zac groaned, stumbling and face-planting straight into the ground.

But his surroundings were suddenly swallowed by shadows, and he found himself right at the shores, which were growing longer by the second. Seeing the water within arm's reach, Zac ignored the pain and limped into the muck as he eagerly took out two canteens.

"I wonder what your devout followers would say if they saw this sorry sight," Ogras sighed. "So many crushed hearts."

"Just help me collect the water," Zac grunted.

"Alright, alright," Ogras said, appearing next to Zac.

The next moment, a set of shadows lifted Zac up and returned him to the shore.

"I'll deal with this. Just sit there and recover. You look like you're about to fall apart into a thousand little pieces," Ogras said with a roll of his eyes. "I need you to be in speaking condition when we get out of here."

"Thank you," Zac said, taking out a few more containers. "Get as much as possible, but don't risk your life for it."

"Too late for that," Ogras snorted.

By this point, Iz had caught up to them, and she held out the small vial in his direction once more. This time, Zac didn't reject.

"…Thank you," Zac said. "I'll make it up to you somehow."

"I'm sure," Iz said with a small smile. "The longer you wait, the worse the effect will be. Place a drop on your forehead."

Zac followed Iz's instructions. He wasn't worried Iz was lying to him. For one, he could sense the immense surge of Life within the drop. Also, he was completely vulnerable in his current condition. If she wanted to deal with him, she wouldn't need to use deception. She could just pick him up and bring him home like a piece of luggage.

The drop landed against his glabella, and Zac's eyes opened wide. For a moment, it felt like he'd opened his mind's eye where the drop touched his skin, connecting him to the other side of the cosmos. There, Zac saw an enormous tree, far surpassing the Worldtree in his old visions. It stretched far beyond what Zac could comprehend, its sheer mass an assault on his sanity. Each of its leaves was a world unto itself, nurtured by the endless vitality of its creator.

And just like that, the vision was gone, replaced by a warm sensation that had already spread throughout his body. The hollowness was partly alleviated, and Zac could even feel his foundations recovering a bit. He still wouldn't be able to use his Cosmic Energy, but he should at least not be as weak as a baby bird.

Still, the medical efficacy paled to the vision he'd just seen. Was that tree real?

"What… was that?" Zac said with shock.

"Don't think about it too much," Iz said. "How do you feel?"

"Tired," Zac grimaced. "But a lot better now."

"Do you regret it?" Iz asked, leveling an uncomfortably intense stare on him. "You have the talisman to escape this realm. You could have given up and either fled through a spatial tear or waited for the realm to collapse. But you fought to the point of almost crippling yourself."

"I didn't really think things through," Zac said. "Had a lot of voices screaming in my head at the time. But no, I don't regret it. How could I back down when people depend on me when I still hadn't done everything in my power to accomplish what I promised?"

"But your life force," Iz said.

"Well, you helped me recover some of it, and I'll get more of it when I break through." Zac shrugged.

"It is not that simple," Iz said, looking out across the dwindling lake. "It is not just a matter of days and years. It is providence. It is *potential*. The more you hollow yourself out, the harder you will find your climb in the future. You are creating a negative spiral, where you will need to take more and more risks to continue progressing."

"I know," Zac sighed. "Sometimes, you just have to keep going and have faith things will work out."

Iz slowly nodded, and they sat in silence for a few minutes as Ogras filled one canteen after another.

"What are you doing after this?" Iz asked.

Zac didn't immediately answer. Not because he felt the need to keep it a secret, but more because he didn't actually know. The original plan was for his visit to the Void Star to be a quick outing where he picked up a Ferric Worldeater. After that, he'd head out to the Million Gates Territory, where he would look for Ogras while racking up some early contributions.

Now, with more than half a year passing, things had grown infinitely more complicated. He'd also stumbled onto Ogras and Billy, which had been the main reason for him to enter the lawless zone at the edge of the Allbright Empire. Not only that, but he should also have already racked up a massive amount of contribution from his actions here, far more than he could have by hunting down some advance squads.

Still, he probably had to head to the Million Gates Territory anyways, if only to find the next piece of rubble. The Qriz'Ul Core and lake water would probably let him digest the whole Book of Duality in a couple of months, but that didn't mean he was guaranteed to figure out a working blueprint for his core. If it failed, he might still need another burst of Ultom's inspiration before heading to the Perennial Vastness.

"I—"Zac hesitated, but a deep rumble cut him off.

The clouds roiled and heaved until an enormous crack split the whole sky in two.

'*Owie Owie,*' *a distant voice echoed out.* '*Good job, Hungry Guy! Gemmy is leaving now. Try not to die.*'

## 2 8
## EXIT

Zac was startled at the proclamation, only to soon realize he shouldn't be. They were a bit ahead of schedule thanks to Iz extinguishing the stubborn flames from **[Flashfire Flourish]**, but only by half a day or so. It was no surprise Gemmy made her move soon after they'd closed the gateway, especially now that the concentrated taint of the lake had all but been removed from the Mystic Realm.

The people back in Billy's fort might even have finished things early, considering Iz had been guided to this realm by a group of Void Gate Hegemons.

Ogras appeared in a puff of smoke, carrying a whole bag full of containers. "Enough in here to go insane a few times over."

"Thank you," Zac smiled.

"You look better," Ogras commented as he looked to the vial still in Zac's hand.

"Had a little help." Zac handed the vial toward Iz, but she just shook her head.

"Keep it, in case fate strikes again." Iz smiled. "My family is friends with the one who makes these drops. We can always get more whenever we need it."

"That's… great. Thank you," Zac said, his insides twisting from jealousy while Ogras looked positively disgusted.

"It should be another hour or two," Ogras said as he looked to the sky.

Zac nodded in agreement. The world was collapsing as Gemmy sacrificed its outer regions to save on energy, but it wouldn't all disintegrate at once. Billy wasn't sure, but he said it would take at least an hour to activate the array. Essentially, one region would be refined at a time, with their section being the last to go as a safety measure.

"I'll take another look around," the demon added. "I never visited any of those tunnels last time I was here. If a gateway to an Eternal Heritage hid beneath the tower, who knows what else those greedy goblins stashed away there?"

"I wish I could help," Zac said. "I'm not really in any state to go spelunking."

"Just focus on recovery," Ogras said. "I doubt being dragged out through multiple spatial layers will be a pleasurable experience."

Zac's face paled at that. He'd completely forgotten about the Spatial Anchor. It wasn't supposed to cause any damage like his [Flashfire Flourish], but who knew if that held in his current state. He couldn't even circulate his Cosmic Energy to reinforce his body right now.

"I hope you can find some more clues about the Lost Plane," Zac grimaced. "I'll focus on not dying."

"Sounds fair enough," Ogras grinned. "I'll see if I can squeeze something out of that little bastard. He might be more talkative now that his heritage is about to be swallowed by the Void."

A moment later, the demon was gone, and Zac could see ghosts and shadows flit about in the chasm. Iz made no move to join him, seeming content to stay by Zac's side.

The silence stretched on, but Zac eventually couldn't stop himself from asking. "You're not going?"

"I'm not interested in this Goblin Kingdom," Iz said. "I'm better off incorporating the insights I gained during this battle."

"There might be clues to our inheritance," Zac was hesitant to say. "After all, these goblins investigated the Lost Plane for millennia."

"My fate will not be decided on whether I explore the moldy tunnels of the Ra'Lashar," Iz said with a shake of her head.

"I won't disturb you then." Zac closed his eyes.

He spent the next 20 minutes repairing the Skill Fractal of [Surging Vitality] until it could be activated. Its effect on damaged foundations wasn't worth mentioning, but it was better than nothing with all the Kill

Energy coursing through his body. And since he had reached Peak E-grade already, there wasn't much else he could use it for.

Some crafting techniques used Kill Energy, where the most common was weapon crafting. For example, Zac was pretty sure the ogre he met in the Big Axe Coliseum had crafted his axe using Kill Energy while instilling it with the killing intent nurtured through battle. But that was just one of the possibilities.

For example, Beast Tamers could transfer some of their Kill Energy to their beasts, and Heda had mentioned the possibility of doing the same for plants. Unfortunately, Zac neither knew any techniques like that, nor did he have the luxury of giving away his energy to Vivi or Haro.

The nurturing surge from his recovery skill went round and round throughout his body, and each circulation worked on the foundation built by Iz's lifegiving drop. It left him a bit better off, though part of that was simply his powerful constitution recovering naturally.

All the while, **[Void Heart]** and **[Purity of the Void]** kept swallowing or purifying any lingering corruption. As Zac expected, most of the corruption from the Qriz'Ul King hadn't contained any insights. However, Zac still managed to decipher a couple of paragraphs thanks to the tainted water he'd fought his way through at the end.

Zac hesitated, but eventually took out one of the Void Cores he'd bought in Salosar. He started drawing upon its energy to recover his mostly expended Void Energy. His best solution to avoiding chaotic energies at the moment was **[Void Zone]**, but he was running low on his hidden reserve.

Iz didn't react to the glimmering core hidden within his sleeves, though Zac didn't delude himself into thinking she hadn't noticed it. Especially not after repeatedly being forced to use his Void Energy during the battle. She simply didn't seem interested in his hidden cards, or perhaps she was merely following proper cultivator etiquette.

After all, the kind of elites someone like Iz socialized with back in the Multiverse Heartlands were bound to have a handful of secrets. If you started poking your nose in others' business, you would eventually get in trouble.

Like this, just over an hour passed until the atmosphere shifted. Space didn't really collapse like in the Twilight Ocean. It more felt like the air had gone out of the whole realm, leaving it empty. All the energy had been taken away, and even the slightest hint of spirituality from the ground had disappeared.

It meant Gemmy had reached their side of the Mystic Realm, and it was already detached from the core. The area might last another hour or two like this before it crumbled under the pressure of the Void. And as expected, the cracks in the sky were growing in both number and size. A few seconds later, Ogras appeared, looking satisfied with his outing.

"Anything good?" Zac asked curiously.

"Not much in the way of treasures, but these goblins sure were a bunch of burrowers. I found quite a few hidden compartments, ranging from small cubbies to whole hidden laboratories."

"*You* found?" the spectral goblin at his side snorted. "All the worthwhile hoards would have passed a fool like you right by if not for my discerning eye. And even if you found them, the traps would've killed you ten times over. You're lucky I felt it a pity for our heritage to end like this."

"More like you were afraid the flag would be lost to the Void," Ogras said with a roll of his eyes before turning back to Zac. "The pills and materials have long lost their spirituality, but I found quite a few crystals and tomes. I haven't had time to scan them, but a few looked promising. We should be able to extract a lot of good things if we're careful."

"Worst-case, we might add some good techniques to our repository." Zac nodded. "It's still kind of lacking compared to a proper faction."

"You two ought to be careful," Iz cautioned. "You saw what happened to this society. One cannot build a stable force on such dubious foundations."

"Of course, of course," Ogras agreed, but only the demon knew whether he was sincere or not.

"Well, I guess it's time to leave," Zac grunted as he got to his feet.

The pain was still there, but at least his limbs would follow his instructions, as long as he didn't overdo it. And with a chunk of his Void Energy recovered, Zac felt he should be able to withstand what came next.

"Here," Zac said as he threw the escape arrays over to Ogras.

"You two ready?" Ogras asked and received affirmative nods in return.

He activated the first talisman, prompting a shimmering lasso to cut out a hole in space. It was essentially a spatial tear, but it was kept stable by a gleaming edge of Spatial Energy. However, the three didn't immediately step through as planned, but instead looked through the portal hesitantly.

"What's going on?" Zac frowned.

The other side was supposed to be the Void, possibly with the occasional vision of one of the neighboring realms in the Void Star. Instead, they were met with a confusing blur of a million colors constantly shifting. If there were an opposite to the emptiness of the Void, then this would be it.

"I—" Ogras hesitated as he looked down at the talisman with confusion. "Is it broken?"

Zac doubted the talisman was a dud, but he didn't know how to explain the scene either. He could only turn to Iz, hoping she had an idea.

"It should be the Void," Iz said, though her tone didn't bring a lot of confidence in the assessment.

"Really?" the demon said, clearly not convinced.

"The imagery is wrong, but the energy is not. I can feel the hollowness of the Void on the other side and no other energies," Iz explained.

Zac realized Iz was correct. There wasn't any energy leaking from the stabilized tear.

"Maybe it's just an effect of Billy's array?" Zac ventured. "Anyway, we can't just stay here and get crushed."

"Never easy with you, is it?" Ogras sighed.

"Stay close to me just in case," Zac said, then turned to Iz. "Can you handle the Void?"

"No problem," Iz nodded.

"Alright, let's go," Zac said, and the three braced themselves as they stepped through the spatial tear.

For a moment, Zac was blinded by a cascade of color, but the chaos ended as abruptly as it began. Their surroundings were still full of color like what they saw through the portal, but the scene had stabilized. Zac could also confirm they really were in the Void as he felt the weird drain on his body.

At the same time, the effect was muted, a far cry from what he'd been forced to endure in his previous encounters with the Void. Zac didn't even need to activate his **[Void Zone]** to withstand it.

"You two okay?" Zac asked to make sure, even if they looked unbothered.

"I feel surprisingly fine," Ogras muttered. "I guess it's an advantage of having a shadow constitution? After all, the shadows and the Void are both hidden seams of reality."

As for Iz, she was completely unaffected by the hostile environment of the Void, just like she said. A thin film of nearly translucent flames covered her, keeping the surroundings at bay.

"So, what's all this?" Ogras asked with a frown. "Will it affect the talisman?"

It was a good question. Now that the confusing mix of color and shape had stabilized, they could see that it was actually an endless number of visions. They saw everything from starry skies to incomprehensible worlds. Like they were standing outside the universe and could pick almost anywhere to reenter.

Zac hesitated. "I'm not sure. This isn't what I saw when the Spatial Cortex collapsed. Back then, there were only a dozen Mystic Realms or something. This is... more. Not even the whole Void Star has this many realms."

"Didn't you say this place was connected to the Million Gates Territory?" Ogras ventured. "I hear there are an endless number of Mystic Realms and dimensional fragments over there."

"You think this is the Stellar Ladder?" Zac exclaimed, gazing upon the surroundings with marvel. "You might be right."

"Maybe we should—" Ogras ventured, but stopped in his tracks when Iz suddenly threw out a shimmering ball.

It soared through the Void until it hit one of the windows. The scene rippled before the ball entered the other dimension, where it kept flying for a few hundred meters and landed on the ground. The world on the other side didn't seem like anything special. It appeared to be a vast desert with dark-green sand under a purple sky. Zac could vaguely make out mountains in the distance, though nothing that would warrant special attention from Iz.

"What's going on?" Zac asked with confusion.

"I felt a signal from Ultom from that realm. That tracker will allow me to find the location easier," Iz said before she curiously looked at Zac. "You do not feel anything?"

Zac tried to sense something from that particular world. But there was nothing, not even the smallest of ripples coming from that window. A moment later, it was gone, replaced by another scene.

"Nothing," Zac said, and he was actually a bit relieved. Judging by Iz's expression, she shared the sentiment.

The fact both he and Iz had the quest to become Flamebearers was a subject they'd generally avoided. Still, you could make some assumptions based on how most inheritances worked. It was very rare for a legacy to be equally shared among many when a quest was involved. The System's creed was 'struggle for supremacy,' where the winner takes all.

Even if they were currently allies, Zac knew they were heading toward a collision down the road. But after getting no signal from that window, Zac realized they might not have to fight for the same pieces of rubble.

"Predestination," Iz hummed. "The fragments are unique to us, even when slated for the same inheritance? Or is my fate better aligned with that particular fragment?"

Zac nodded. "Perhaps."

"Let me borrow some of that disgusting Luck of yours," Ogras said as he poked Zac jokingly. "I still need two of these things."

"I'm not sure that's how it works." Zac grinned, but his smile turned crooked upon seeing the demon home in on a window that just appeared.

Ogras got one just like that? Had the demon really managed to benefit from his Luck?

"Miss Tayn, if you could help me out?" Ogras entreated, and Zac was surprised to see Iz calmly take out another stone and hand it over.

Zac thought her handing out that longevity water without payment was an exception to the rule. But now, she suddenly handed out items left and right? It was obviously a good thing, but it left Zac somewhat at a loss. Iz had barely exchanged a few sentences with Ogras before, and now they were buddies? Had something changed while he fought the goblin?

Perhaps he was being paranoid, but he smelled a plot. Though asking about it would have to wait until later.

"Infuse your Dao and throw it," Iz said. "You will be able to sense it from quite a distance."

Ogras followed her instructions, and his sphere entered the portal a few seconds later. The demon looked exceptionally pleased, but he kept looking back and forth as their surroundings cycled through tens of thousands of worlds. Zac was doing the same, but he started to get a sinking feeling when fewer and fewer new realms replaced the ones that disappeared.

Five minutes later, a ripple spread through the tapestry of worlds, and the three found themselves in an endless expanse of darkness. At the same time, the corrosive drain of the Void increased manifold, prompting both Zac and Ogras to grimace with pain.

"Well, I guess it's time to go," Ogras said as he gave Zac an odd look. "I can't believe you were the only one who left empty-handed for once."

"I'll figure something out," Zac said with a wry smile, though he had to admit he was a bit annoyed. All these Mystic Realms, and not one held either of the two pieces he lacked?

"Well, here's to hoping those girls weren't playing us," Ogras muttered before he infused the Spatial Anchor with energy.

A protective bubble five meters across enclosed around them, but it didn't keep its spherical shape for long. It soon stretched into a jellybean shape, but that was just the start. It kept growing longer and longer. In just a few seconds, it looked like a pillar that stretched thousands of miles through the Void.

And then came the pull.

Space pulled and twisted, and Zac groaned as he felt himself twist with it. At least he thought he groaned. It was hard to tell when all your senses were in flux. At least the pain wasn't unbearable. Soon, the vast darkness was replaced by a series of rapid flashes before the world exploded into a cascade of stars.

Zac almost felt like he'd witnessed the Big Bang, but the illusion shattered as he found himself surrounded by thousands of Cosmic Vessels. The scene almost made Zac's heart jump out of his mouth. He barely had the chance to take in the surroundings before space twisted again. Something had grabbed him and teleported him away.

Or someone.

# 29

# PATHS DIVERGED

There was no time to reorient himself or prepare. It was all happening too fast. One moment, Zac, Iz, and Ogras popped out next to one of the gargantuan space stations of the Void Star. The next, Zac found himself standing in a large, solemn hall, where his two companions were nowhere in sight.

It wasn't just the architecture that exuded a quiet dignity. The chamber was filled with an almost deafening silence, like the emptiness of space had been condensed into something corporeal. It felt odd, but more than anything, it felt comfortable, as if wrapped in a warm embrace. At the same time, he felt his very existence amplified by contrasting himself to the muted surroundings.

Zac could tell this was no dream, and neither was it a vision. His senses told him he really was there in person. He hesitated before making his way through the hallway toward a door on the other side. The only sound was the rhythmic taps of his steps, bare feet against smooth stone. It was muted, like the soundwaves were swallowed as soon as they were created.

Zac didn't bother taking out [Verun's Bite], knowing it was futile even if he were in perfect condition. Someone had whisked him out of thin air and teleported him here in an instant. The power required for something like that wasn't something he could contend with. Besides, he had a pretty good idea of what was going on and knew he shouldn't be in trouble.

The Void Priestess had summoned him.

Luckily, he'd managed to confirm Leyara's story through Iz Tayn, at the cost of some light burns. There really was a huge mysterious faction named the Vigil. They were supposedly older than even the Limitless Empire, and the Void Gate was a distant branch. Unfortunately, Iz didn't know much about their purpose. Their goals were not known to the public.

The Vigil had joined hands with the Limitless Empire without a struggle during Emperor Limitless' expansive wars, and many believed they'd had a role in creating the System. However, they never joined any of the empires' campaigns. And to this day, they largely stayed out of the struggles of the peak factions.

As Zac walked through the hall, his gaze turned to huge floating rocks that lined the main path. The smallest was the size of a soccer ball, while the largest was as tall as he was. For most people, they would have probably seemed like mundane rocks kept afloat by some array, but Zac knew the truth.

They contained Void Energy. It wasn't as condensed as the Void Cores, but it was pure and calm. Extracting energy from these stones probably wouldn't require [Void Heart] at all, but rather recover his lost energy directly. Part of him just wanted to snatch every single stone put in his path, but this wasn't a video game. He couldn't just ransack the house before speaking with the owner like nothing had happened.

Zac soon reached the exit at the other end of the otherwise empty hallway, but he hesitated about whether he should just walk inside.

"Enter, child," a mesmerizing voice emerged through the door, and Zac simply stepped through.

Austere. That was the best word to describe what appeared to be the Void Priestess' cultivation chamber. There was simply nothing there, a far cry from the meticulously arranged mountain of the Life Elemental he visited in the Orom World. Drab walls and two simple prayer mats. The only thing that prevented the room from feeling like a prison cell was that there was no inner wall. Instead, the room transitioned into a vast garden under a starry sky.

And in the distance, the Void Star. Judging by the size of the Void Star, Zac had to have been transported quite the distance. It was less than a third the size compared to when he first saw it from Zenith Vigil. Yet oddly enough, Zac couldn't see any of the four stations, or any other activity in the sky for that matter.

Were there two Void Stars? Or was it just an illusion?

It was a curious mystery, but Zac's attention was more occupied by the woman who motionlessly sat on one of the two prayer mats in the center of the room. She was an odd paradox, where her pristine appearance demanded attention, but her aura had completely fused with the palpable silence of the surroundings.

She wore a white nun's robe that spread out like a flower around her, and her hands were hidden within two large flowing sleeves. Even her face was covered by a partly translucent veil attached to a tiara in her long black hair.

"Come, sit," she said, head tilting slightly at the mat placed a few meters away from her.

"Uh, thank you," Zac said, his voice startling himself as it seemed to come from everywhere at once.

There was something odd about this environment, some sort of field he couldn't make sense of. It energized him, and even felt like it healed his foundations. Which made sense. No matter how puritanical a cultivation chamber looked, a figure like the Void Priestess was bound to have some pretty amazing arrays in their rooms.

"I am Perala Janodrok, though most know me as the Void Priestess."

"I'm Zac," he said as he sat down on the mat. "Can I ask why you have summoned me here?"

"Can't it just be because I am curious?" Perala said, and Zac thought he could see a vague smile behind the veil. "About the young man who has turned this Sector upside down in ten short years. First the Tower of Eternity, and now my Void Star. I even heard a story from an old friend, about a young troublemaker who unwittingly helped his ascent."

"That's…" Zac coughed.

The Void Priestess knew the Eveningtide Asura? Zac had never heard anything about that, though he knew Alvod never targeted the Void Gate during his rampage. Was Perala Janodrok really alive back then? If that was the case, she was much older than everyone thought.

"And now, I hear even the Undead Empire is leaving no stone unturned in their search of you," the Void Priestess continued. "Would it be so odd if I just wanted to see the man behind all the mayhem?"

"The Undead Empire?" Zac said with surprise. "What do they want with me?"

"You'd have to ask them, but I do not think they are hostile. Most likely, they want to make a deal with you, and I think you can understand why," Perala said. "Your most recent actions have already created ripples."

Zac slowly nodded as he thoughtfully looked at the Void Star in the distance. Had the Undead Empire somehow figured out he was a Flame-bearer, or at least connected to Ultom? If so, it made sense they wanted to get in touch with him, especially if they knew about his connection to Catheya. Who knew, had she perhaps returned to Zecia? They hadn't planned for something like that, but an event like Ultom could change many things.

It would be convenient if true. Powerful factions had probably already set their sights on Ultom, and he might be swept up in that mess, whether he wanted to or not. Getting a powerful backer like the Undead Empire was one way to give a lifeline to himself and his people. After all, the Undead Empire was already at war with all living beings, and if they were reaching out like this, they probably didn't care about offending the other factions.

Still, was that the right move? To have his fate depend on some ancient, unliving monsters he'd never even met? It wasn't long ago he received an all too real lesson in the dangers of dealing with the peak factions of the Multiverse. What if the Undead Empire targeted him like the crazy monks did with the [Boundless Vajra Sublimation]?

"You are wounded," the Void Priestess added, which dragged Zac out of his thoughts. "It seems breaking off the Stellar Ladder and exiling the Kan'Tanu did not come without some hardship."

"Uh, that's—"Zac hesitated.

Had the Void Priestess seen his actions? Was this why she'd brought him here, to thank him? After all, he had not only solved the mess she created by letting the infiltrators into the Void Star, but he might even have saved the life of her disciple. Looking back at it now, there was simply no way Leyara would have been able to deal with that Qriz'Ul King and close the gateway on her own.

"I will still not heal you. This is not a meeting with an elder imparting gifts and valuable lessons."

Zac's mouth opened for a few seconds before closing again, not knowing how to respond. Leyara's master was a bit of a jerk.

"Such are the rules. You have been chosen, and I cannot unduly interfere with your fate. If you get pulled under by the river, that simply means you cannot carry the weight of responsibility of Ultom."

"I understand," Zac grunted. "The others, are they fine?"

"Your demon friend and the young miss of the Tayn Clan are fine. My disciple and the others emerged a few minutes before you, and three Monarchs of the Void Gate are helping stabilize the Portable Realm. We will soon send in armies to deal with the invaders of both the Portable Realm and the Void Star."

"Now you're willing to deal with them?" Zac said, not without some exasperation.

"Fate stirred when you arrived, and the competition for candidacy began. Until now, there have been open slots, meaning I had to stay my hand. But no more. There was still one hidden in the depths of the realm, but it was thrown back into the Million Gates Territory when you destroyed the Stellar Ladder and millennia of work."

Zac weakly smiled upon sensing the mild irritation in Perala's voice. She had already said it wasn't a gift-giving meeting. Had he been dragged here to be chastised?

"Altogether, quite a lot of chaos for one E-grade cultivator. Then again, isn't that your calling card?" Perala said, but there was thankfully some amusement in her voice. "Mr. Deviant Asura?"

Zac coughed. "Uh, those rumors are exaggerated."

"I still don't like the idea of my little disciple getting swept up with a troublemaker like you, so keep it in your pants," the Void Priestess said, and Zac shuddered upon feeling space around him constrict. "Even stealing her underwear!"

"What! That was a gift," Zac croaked as he felt his bones groan. "No, I mean, I didn't—"

Perala laughed, and the pressure thankfully went away. "In either case. Focus on your cultivation. Now, I'm sure you're wondering why I actually summoned you here."

*Well, apparently not to heal me,* Zac inwardly complained, but he only had the guts to nod. Next time, she might try to crush him for real.

"Imbalance."

"What's that?" Zac said.

"Two fates converged, and one could say you were shortchanged," the Void Priestess said. "We were not the cause, and it is not within my power to right the imbalance, but I still wish to see if I can alleviate the deficiency a bit."

"I thought you people wouldn't get involved?" Zac said.

"Nothing is perfect, and I am just doing what needs to be done," Perala sighed.

Zac didn't understand what prompted this level of candor from the Void Priestess, but it was a huge opportunity. There were so many lingering questions, many of which Iz didn't even know the answer to. And this time, he didn't even need to eat an attack to get the answers. Zac quickly reorganized his thoughts before speaking up.

"Two fates converged? Mine?" Zac asked.

"Over the eons, purposes become muddled and paths slowly diverge," Perala said as she turned her head toward the Void Star. "The Left Imperial Palace chose you as a candidate, but something stirred the System into action. It forcibly broadened the scope and put its finger on the scale. This is different from what's expected. Different from the previous ascents."

So it was the Left Imperial Palace that was connected to him, after all? Then what about his Void Energy and the Qriz'Ul? Still, there was a more pressing issue.

"Previous Ascents?" Zac probed.

"It is not the first pillar to emerge," Leyara said. "It has happened more than once before. In fact, this is the fifth."

"What happened when the previous ones appeared?" Zac asked, though he had a sinking feeling he already knew the answer.

"War of unprecedented proportions. Wars to decide the direction of our era."

"Four pillars? The direction of the era?" Zac said before his eyes widened. "The Apostates?"

As far as Zac knew, there were a total of five Apostates. However, the First Defier was an anomaly that no one was able to explain. He appeared out of nowhere and was gone before anyone had time to react. He was like a rocket that shot straight through the Heavens, leaving chaos and confusion in his wake.

Meanwhile, the other four were similar. All peak figures in their own rights, who ultimately left a mark on the System related to their path. But how does one add something to the System, and why hadn't anyone else done the same over the billions of years? Was it because only four pillars had emerged so far?

However, Zac's theory was killed as quickly as it was born.

"No, that is different," Perala said with a shake of her head. "Only one of the pillars was involved in an Apostatic Ascent. The wars involved something else. Nothing good will come from you knowing the details right now. But suffice to say, there are opposing camps to an ancient struggle while the Vigil is a neutral party."

"So you just… look?" Zac said.

"Not quite. We have one important task: to keep the Heavens out of the equation. Fate must be decided by men, not by the Dao," the Void Priestess said. "Most factions are quite happy to help us out in that regard, as they want to seize the future for themselves."

"If you can't tell me what this is all about, then what can you tell me?" Zac asked.

"Don't worry. Those things might matter to you if you ever close in on the peaks. Until then, they are only a distraction," Perala said. "What I can tell you would rather help you in the short run."

"Can you help me find the rest of the pieces?" Zac asked hopefully.

"No, I cannot get directly involved like that." Perala smiled. "Besides, I have no idea."

"Then what?"

"As I said, the System has intervened and enforced some rules," Perala said. "Much is still in flux, but I can say a few things with certainty. These are things the other participants already know, or will soon come to find out, so it can barely be counted as an intervention.

"First, you will have to contend with others for your claim. You should already know that much. Their ages are limited to 100 years, which puts you at less of a disadvantage. Any older, and they will not be able to find or claim any of the keys."

Zac's brows rose in surprise. It looked like the System had done him a solid there. People below 100 years were all part of the young generation, and it beat competing against old monsters who'd lived for millions of years.

A century was still a long time, especially for someone like Zac, who had only cultivated for just over a decade. Progress slowed down the further you went, but 100 years should be enough to reach at least Middle D-grade for a young elite. Probably even Late D-grade if you had both the talent and resources.

"Secondly, you will not be able to complete your seal through fate and serendipity," Perala continued. "The System will not allow it."

"What!" Zac exclaimed.

Was this why he failed to sense any more pieces while both Ogras and Iz had found theirs? If so, it was a huge blow. Many of his plans hinged on him finding the seals to the Left Imperial Palace, even if he'd just gotten his hand on a decent substitute.

"It is not just for you. The inheritance of Ultom has been integrated with the upcoming war, and the right to participate will depend on your contribution," Perala said. "I do not know how close you are to gaining access to the inheritance, but the final piece is already in the System's hands."

"Integrated with the war? What does that mean?" Zac frowned. "I have to buy the last pieces with war credits?"

"Something in that regard. Or perhaps the pieces will be moved to key battlefields. I am not sure about the exact details. We will find out more once the war officially starts."

"Do you know when the war will officially start?" Zac asked.

"Four years," the Void Priestess said. "It was supposed to take longer, but I fear the fusion of these two events changed the timeline."

"And these outside factions will send their own people to join the war?"

"It appears that way. Some have already arrived, like the descendant of the Empyrean Throne you somehow know. Luckily for Zecia, there are some safeguards in place. This is a test of fate, and the System is preventing our little Sector from being overrun by outside combatants," Perala explained.

"But there will be scions of peak factions joining the war, on both sides probably? Bringing their elders and bodyguards?" Zac frowned.

"Most likely."

"A lot of locals will die if forced to face something like that," Zac sighed.

"The strong devour the weak, as it has always been," Perala said with equanimity.

Zac didn't immediately answer, instead going over his plans regarding the new information. Four years was a bit shorter than he could have hoped, but it wasn't a worst-case scenario. The biggest problem was the fourth piece of rubble, where Zac found himself in a Catch-22. He needed those pieces to break through before the war, but he had to wait *until* the war to get the pieces.

It put him under a lot more pressure. Not only did he have to find the third piece quickly, but he had to find a solution to his blueprint with that piece alone. There would be no backup unless he was willing to join the war as an E-grade warrior. And he wasn't, especially not after learning about these outsiders who would participate like it was some sort of Limited Trial. He refused to see his people become Contribution Points to some rich asshole from the Multiverse Heartlands.

Besides, with the System controlling the events, it was extremely likely he would be set on a collision course with the other candidates. If he stayed as an E-grade cultivator in the face of such a threat, he'd be slaughtered. If he broke through, he'd at least have a fighting chance.

"This is what I wanted to tell you," Perala said. "Work hard these coming years. The stronger you become, the more you will have to say about Zecia's fate. Now, I'll send you back to your people."

Zac's eyes widened in surprise. Already? He'd just been here for a few minutes, and there were still a lot of things he needed to find out. But he already felt space twist around him, prompting him to blurt out the first thing that came to mind.

"Wait! Can you tell me the real name of Emperor Limitless?"

"His name?" Perala said with surprise. "He went by his Dao Name for most of his life, but his true name was Laondio Evrodok."

Zac's heart clenched with shock, and in the next moment he was gone, leaving the Void Priestess alone in her chambers. Blood started to run down Perala's nose as cracks spread across her skin, but she didn't care.

"This is all I can do for you, my child," she said with a soft gaze as she turned toward the sky. "This guy is a troublemaker, but he might be the key."

## 30
# DEPARTURE

The confusing blur of space was nothing to the confusion already raging in Zac's mind. Emperor Limitless' name was Laondio Evrodok and not Karz? It completely threw a lot of Zac's theories out the window.

Not only that, but Laondio was a name he knew. Laondio was the talented alchemist Zac had seen in his bloodline vision. He'd been a unique talent of the Blue Spring Sect that Karz had managed to enter in the second vision.

But the Blue Spring Sect seemed to be the equivalent of a D-grade force at best. Being talented in such a faction ultimately didn't amount to much. To think a random alchemist managed to go from such a place to standing at the peak of all existence.

Or had he?

This was all ancient history. Between the founding of the Limitless Empire and the birth of the System, hundreds of millions of years had passed. Who knew exactly what happened all those years ago. Perhaps Karz had taken the identity of this alchemist for some reason? Or was Karz the true Emperor Limitless, but had his throne usurped? Why else would Leandra say that he carried the 'Original Sin'?

It was impossible to tell, but Perala's proclamation undeniably left ripples on the calm lake of certainty.

Space soon stabilized, and Zac found himself standing in an enormous chamber made of stone. Walls were covered with inscriptions, and the air was rife with Spatial Energy. That might be because of the

Templar and two nuns standing in the distance, surrounding a familiar gemstone—Gemmy.

There were some clear differences to the Dimensional Seed, though. For one, the gemstone was just over half the size. Secondly, it had turned squarish with a radiant cut. Around it, a mesh of some sort of Spiritual Silver had been added, making her look like a fancy amulet.

Tremendous waves of Spatial Energy surrounded Gemmy and the three cultivators, who had to be the Monarchs Perala mentioned before. They were still hard at work, infusing tremendous amounts of energy into the gemstone.

"What happened to you?" a familiar voice said, and Zac turned to see Ogras, Iz, Billy, and Leyara standing to his side, looking curiously at him.

"I had a talk with the Void Priestess," Zac explained.

"You talked with master?" Leyara said with surprise. "Why?"

"She wanted to clarify some things," Zac said.

"Your friend was just telling us how you closed the gate," Leyara sighed. "I'm sorry, I didn't expect the danger to be that great."

"Well, it worked out in the end," Zac said. "What's going on here? Did something happen?"

"Haha, how can Billy's plan fail?" Billy said triumphantly.

"They are helping stabilize the realm so Billy can provide access a bit quicker," Ogras explained.

"We were lucky Miss Tayn and her guides arrived when they did," Leyara added. "The final touches were much more difficult to deal with than we expected. But I'm curious, how do the two of you know each other?"

"It's a bit complicated," Zac said with a wry smile.

"Fate," Iz said.

Leyara's brows rose with surprise, but before she could speak, another presence appeared right in front of them. It was a humanoid golem just a bit bigger than Billy. It emitted no aura, but Zac felt a pang of extreme danger as it turned its head toward him.

"Enough," Iz calmly said.

"I am happy to see you are safe, young miss," the golem rumbled. "I was worried when I felt the connection to my clone disappear. Are you ready to leave?"

Iz glanced at Zac.

"I have some lingering matters to attend to. Kvalk, could you isolate us for a moment?"

The golem was obviously reluctant, but a fiery barrier still erupted around Zac and Iz, leaving the others outside.

"Is everything okay?" Zac asked as he glanced at the golem.

"You never answered my question before," Iz said.

"What?" Zac said before he remembered their talk before the Mystic Realm started collapsing. "Oh, what I'm doing next?"

Iz calmly nodded. "Fate's tide is rising."

"I know. I just heard more powerful factions are on their way. Apparently, the war in this Sector will involve the inheritance. It's a big mess."

"I would give you advice if I could, but I believe your future is best explored by yourself," Iz said. "I am heading into the Million Gates Territory. I would offer to bring you, but my family will not agree as we are technically in contention for Ultom."

"That's fine." Zac hesitated for a moment before he decided to speak up again. "I might meet you there, though I'm not sure. I plan on shoring up my foundations before heading to the Perennial Vastness to form my core. I will probably go within two years."

"Perennial Vastness?" Iz mused. "I've heard of it. Its environment is far superior to this region. Both materials and opportunities exist in abundance over there. It should help lessen the burden of your path."

Zac's eyes lit up, as this was the first concrete description of the mysterious realm that would make even scions of powerful factions desirous. There being a bunch of materials was the most important part. At the very least, he would have to upgrade his Specialty Core along with his grade, and possibly parts of his bloodline.

And one thing was for sure—his body was always hungry. The more stuff he could gobble up in the Perennial Vastness, the less his own coffers would suffer.

Still, that was just the tip of the iceberg of what he needed to know. "Do… you have any advice? For core creation?"

"I am afraid I'd cloud your path," Iz said. "You are creating your own system. I am not qualified to guide someone like you. But if I could offer one piece of advice, it would be not to limit yourself by conventional wisdom. My grandpa once said that under the Heavens, anything is possible."

Zac nodded in thanks, feeling her sentiment echoing Yrial's. And Zac was of a similar mind himself. If you limited yourself to what everyone said could and couldn't be done, especially here on the frontier, you'd never rise above.

"I will visit you once more after I've found the pieces," Iz added.

"What?" Zac exclaimed.

"Our arrangement still stands," Iz smiled as the [Stone of Celestial Void] appeared in her hand.

Zac looked at the treasure with a mix of desire and reluctance. He really wanted it, but the thought of getting roasted by Iz Tayn's flames made him shudder, especially in his current condition.

Zac eventually nodded. "Just so you know, I'm staying on a planet shielded by the System."

"It does not matter as long as you do not form another eruption of Chaos like you did in the Voidcatcher," Iz said without care, confirming Zac's hunch her tracking method worked even through the System's shroud.

"It's been... interesting... traveling with you," Iz said as a small smile spread across her face. "Be careful not to poke the river of fate too much. If you blow up every place you visit, you'll end up living in ruins."

"Well, I'm working on it..."

Iz nodded, and the next moment she was gone, engulfed in a puff of flames. The golem was gone as well, but a rumbling fire appeared in Zac's mind, blocking out all else.

'*Boy, our young miss is magnanimous, but the world is cruel. A storm is coming to this corner of space, and you have placed yourself in its center. Talent is useless in the face of raw strength. Ask yourself if it is worth it. Of course, if you assist our young miss in this under-taking, I dare guarantee no force will dare meddle with you or your kin.*'

With that, the two were truly gone, leaving Zac with mixed emotions. As expected, her clan didn't share Iz's apparent indifference to Ultom and his relation to it. At least the golem wanted him to assist Iz in seizing the inheritance rather than outright killing him, which wasn't too bad.

Still, there were no guarantees such a treatment would last. Like the golem said—talent was useless in the face of raw strength. He had nothing to bargain with when dealing with those kinds of factions. The moment he stopped being useful, he would become expendable.

"What's wrong?" Leyara asked, which dragged Zac out of his thoughts.

"Oh, nothing," Zac sighed.

"Girl troubles?" Leyara smiled. "Want me to teach you about the fairer sex?"

"Good luck with that, lass," Ogras snorted. "You should know a lost cause when you see one."

"I think I'm doing just fine, thank you very much," Zac grunted. "So, how long until we can extract the others?"

"Not long," Leyara said.

Ten minutes later, the powerful fluctuations surrounding Gemmy subsided, and Billy scurried over with worry in his eyes.

"Is Gemmy okay?" Billy asked as the others caught up.

"The Realm Spirit is alive and well, just very tired. It will most likely have to enter a long rest to recover," the Monarch said.

"Ah, Billy always feels better after sleeping," Billy said.

"As the owner, you should still be able to exert basic control over the world. Are you able to sense those still inside? It might take some time to get used to the different sensa—"

The Monarch didn't get any further before almost thirty people appeared on the platform around them.

"—tions. Huh."

Everyone was there, except for the small settlement of Gnivelings. Vai looked a bit harried, but her eyes lit up upon seeing Zac.

"You did it!" the researcher said excitedly as she walked over.

"Nothing to it." Zac smiled, like he hadn't almost gotten himself killed just a couple of hours ago.

"What... What are you doing next?" Vai asked.

"Heading back home soon," Zac said. "How about you join us? The Atwood Empire could use some talented researchers."

"Ah—I—" Vai stuttered.

"Hey, don't go kidnapping my little aunt," Leyara said with a mock scowl. "How about I—"

"No!" Vai said with determination. "Focus on cultivation until you've grown up."

Zac smiled with a shake of his head.

"No need to go back right away," Ogras said.

"I thought you would be the most eager one to get back home," Zac said with surprise.

"Fair, but this is a pretty good opportunity, no?" Ogras said. "This is a proper C-grade faction, and they should have some good things for sale. I'm sure the young miss of the vaunted Void Gate can help us in this regard?"

"I'm just the boss's disciple. I don't have any actual authority," Leyara said with a roll of her eyes.

"You are welcome to stay here at Alpha Vigil," one of the Monarchs said. "We must deal with the enemies inside the Mystic Realm in either case."

"Can't Billy just drag them out too?" Billy asked. "Billy can sense them just fine."

"Removing someone unwilling will cause a conflict," the Monarch explained. "With the Realm Spirt so exhausted, it's unwise to exhaust it unduly."

"Let's stay until everything is dealt with," Zac agreed.

Zac and the others spent three more days in Alpha Vigil. The remaining Kan'Tanu cultists were captured or killed as the Void Gate sent over 500 Hegemons into the Mystic Realm. The Templar traitor was also caught, thanks to Billy essentially being omniscient when connecting with Gemmy.

As for the Gnivelings, they chose to join the Void Gate. Honestly, Zac wasn't too surprised. It beat being stuck in a Pocket Realm, and he had to admit the Void Gate was superior to the Atwood Empire no matter how you looked at it. As such, the Mystic Realm became a wild realm with only beasts remaining.

Apart from recuperating, Zac spent most of his time perusing Alpha Vigil's extensive stores and venues. Most stores used the Void Gate's internal currency, but Leyara helped pull some strings to allow Zac to buy some items for Nexus Coins instead. The first thing he bought was a batch of Void Stones just like the ones he saw in the Void Priestess' home.

The stones he managed to buy were unfortunately no larger than fists, but they still contained the equivalent amount of Void Energy to a

High-grade Nexus Crystal. The energy was clean and easily absorbed, so even if they didn't hold as much energy as Void Cores, they allowed him to recover his Void Energy quicker.

Unfortunately, these types of materials only appeared in the Void. It wasn't that actual worlds existed in that weird dimension, but rather that things occasionally wound up there. A Mystic Realm could collapse, and whole mountain ranges could get swallowed by the Void. Usually, those places gradually eroded into nothingness, but on occasion, they mutated into things like these Void Stones.

Thanks to this, Zac also acquired various Void-related materials, things he'd never even heard of. Zac even suspected the Void Priestess had personally intervened for these kinds of things to appear in the Contribution Store.

With Vai safely returned to the Void Gate, he also completed his bodyguard quest. The rewards didn't matter much to him, but failing quests was never good. Unfortunately, there was still no word from the others on the squad.

The good news was that Teo Kastella had a life tablet, and it was still intact. It looked like he managed to survive the Cortex collapsing. Hopefully, he managed to save a few others, though Zac wasn't too hopeful in that regard. It was an unfortunate reminder that life was all-too-cheap in the Multiverse.

He also struck some tentative agreements through Pretty. She was shocked to find out Zac owned a production line for top-tier Cosmic Vessels, and said she could almost guarantee that the Allbright Empire would buy as many vessels as he could deliver. Although, that was contingent on the quality of the vessels. Zac was confident anything the Creators crafted was up to snuff.

Zac wasn't the only one who benefited from their stay at the resource depot. Ogras finally got his hands on a Peak-quality E-grade Spirit Tool suited for his style. It was made from a mix of spatial metals and others designed to make it harder to track. It was completely translucent and almost looked like a 3-meter-long icepick, but when infused with the Dao of Shadows, it became dark grey. Thanks to its spatial components, the spear could even enter Ogras' shadows without issue.

But soon enough, it was time to leave, though that came with a sudden revelation.

"You're not coming?" Zac said with shock as they stood at the tele-portation station. "Why not?"

"Billy made a promise," Billy said with a grimace. "Billy has to go to Southern Mountain."

"What? Where?" Zac asked.

"Before, when Billy fell asleep, a statue taught Billy to get stronger. When Gemmy got sick, Billy made a deal with Statue-man. Billy got the array to save Gemmy, but Billy has to join Southern Mountain."

Zac's eyes widened in comprehension, remembering how he'd seen Billy cultivate in his sleep. Turns out he didn't only gain levels and comprehension in his sleep, he even received guidance from some master. After all, someone who could just hand out a method like the one they used on Gemmy had to be fairly powerful.

"Don't look at me," Ogras said when Zac glanced in his direction. "Perhaps some sort of Karmic connection? Like that monk?"

"Stupid Statue-man always say Billy is a Titan like Statue-man, but Billy is human," Billy huffed.

"Uh," Ogras coughed, and Zac wryly smiled.

From the sound of it, the Southern Mountain was a Titanic Faction. However, Zac had never heard of such a place before. He wasn't even sure it was part of Zecia. Zac doubted it was, considering the method to produce Pocket Realms was beyond even the Void Gate, according to Vai.

In other words, this was an amazing opportunity for Billy. Conversely, Earth didn't have much to offer someone like him, and Zac wasn't sure a brutal war was the best place for Billy to grow. Better he left for a powerful Titanic Faction, even if it meant Earth lost another capable fighter.

"When are you coming back?" Zac asked, opting not to question Billy's lineage. That was a headache for the Southern Mountain.

"Billy doesn't know. But maybe a long, long time. Say hello to Thea and Nigel for Billy?" Billy said with a weak smile.

"…I will," Zac said after a small pause.

Zac hadn't told Billy about Thea while they were stuck in the Mystic Realm. He figured it wouldn't do anyone any good to drop such a bomb on Billy while things were so chaotic. And now, it didn't make much sense to tell him either.

Or was he just being selfish?

"The teleportation array that Billy needs to create is quite complex, but my master promised to help as thanks for Billy helping us solve the problem of the infiltrators," Leyara added.

"Thank you for everything, all of you," Zac said as he looked at the others.

"Billy will miss you, Super Brother Man," Billy said and lifted Zac in a big bear hug. "You, Horny Guy, not as much."

"Well, isn't that nice," Ogras said with a roll of his eyes.

"I'll miss you too," Zac said. "But I'm sure we'll see each other again. Until then, work hard to get stronger, alright? There are a lot of bad guys out there."

"Billy will become the strongest!" Billy said as though it was a matter of course.

"You're always welcome to visit again." Leyara smiled. "We'll just have to keep you away from important places, so you don't blow them up."

Zac could only laugh in response. Being known as a walking calamity was at least better than being known as a world-renowned pervert.

"Be careful," Vai added.

"You too," Zac smiled. "Next time we meet, we might both be Hegemons."

"That's—" Vai hesitated. "I'm…"

"I believe you can do it," Zac said. "After all, you're someone who made it to the depths of the Void Star and back."

"I'll… I'll do my best," Vai said with determination in her eyes.

The array flashed to life a moment later, and he and Ogras stepped through. He was finally going back to Earth.

31

OLD FRIEND

The tranquility of the secluded courtyard was broken as Zac and Ogras stepped through the teleportation array, arriving in Zac's private compound. Looking at his hands, Zac barely believed what he'd been through was real. But the quest remained, proving that the visions, the Left Imperial Palace, and the existence of the Ultom Courts were all real.

Unfortunately, neither Perala Janodrok nor his stay at Alpha Vigil provided any further clues to what it meant to be named a Flamebearer of Ultom. And the talk of the direction of the era and opposing sides only muddied the waters, making it impossible for Zac to know what to expect.

"Still overexerting that brain of yours?" Ogras snorted.

"You're not worried?" Zac asked curiously.

"Not really." Ogras shrugged. "I'll snatch the opportunities I can without getting myself killed. As for the bigshots coming here, they'll hopefully be too busy dealing with each other to bother with some random native. And if worse comes to worst, I'll just go ahead and hide in your shadows."

"Well, isn't that nice," Zac snorted. "What's your plan now?"

"I'm pretty much rested, so I'll go ahead and tour this empire of yours." Ogras grinned. "Just remember to contact your followers so I'm not mistaken for a shapeshifter, if you would."

It was an odd feature Zac learned of when traveling through the Mystic Realm with Ogras and Vai. Ogras' affiliation hadn't transformed to Atwood Empire when the others' did. It stayed as Port Atwood until Zac told him about the situation. Zac had no idea the purpose of something like that, but perhaps it was to combat abuse.

"I think you'll find Ilvere's establishments in Azh'Rodum to your tastes," Zac said with a small smile.

The demon's eyes lit up, and he stepped back onto the teleportation array. "Good man. I knew I could trust him to fix this boring place."

A moment later, the demon was gone, leaving Zac alone with his thoughts. Before anything, Zac sent out a series of messages that he'd returned, that the mission was successful, and that he even brought Ogras back. It took less than a minute before he sensed two auras bearing down on him, and he turned with a smile to see Vilari and Joanna appear in front of him almost simultaneously.

Joanna smiled. "You're back."

"It's nice to see you two. You've both gotten stronger."

Joanna's aura had become more condensed, while Vilari's had turned more ethereal. If Zac had to guess, Vilari made some improvements to her soul. Perhaps she practiced [Thousand Lights Avatar] to some degree of success? After all, he'd given her the method after returning to Earth.

"I used a few of your Teleportation Tokens while you were gone to hone myself," Joanna said. "I've filled up my Limited Titles now, and I even managed to finally form my first Dao Branch."

"First?" Zac said with surprise.

"With the war coming up, I've decided to go for broke and work on a second one," Joanna said with a determined gleam in her eyes.

Zac understood what she meant. The war was a risk but also an opportunity. It was possibly Joanna's best shot to reforge her fate and have a go at something more than becoming an Early to Middle Hegemon. Although, this would make her path far more difficult as well.

"Let me know if you need anything from me," Zac said. "I found some good things during this trip. They might be useful."

"I think I just need to pit myself against more powerful enemies," Joanna said. "Using treasures to bolster my path of war would probably do more harm than good."

"You're wounded. Badly," Vilari interjected with a frown. "Your energy is completely turbid."

She was absolutely correct. Three days of rest on Alpha Vigil was only enough time to do more patchwork repairs on his body. He was still far from a fighting condition. In fact, he could barely circulate any Cosmic Energy in his human form even if his human pathways weren't that badly off.

The real problems were his Draugr side and his foundations. He'd been forced to swap over to his human form soon after the battle ended, leaving his undead side in utter disrepair. Since then, he couldn't swap back because he had activated the array to hide his constitution, leaving his pathways for Fetters of Desolation mostly broken.

Pathways were easily repaired, but the damage to his foundation was an entirely different story, which affected both sides. Not only could he still feel the nasty cracks left from activating his two Remnant attacks, but there was still a lot of invisible damage from being engulfed by his own ultimate blast.

"Things got a bit complicated," Zac grimaced. "I plan to seclude myself and focus on recovery. But I'll be back in business soon enough."

"Is there anything we can do?" Joanna asked. "Do you need materials? Or—"

"I'm fine." Zac smiled with a wave. "I just need to rest up in my cave."

"Alright, but don't hesitate to call if you need us for something," Joanna urged, glancing toward the shipyard with some anticipation. "So, you did it? You really got the piece needed to upgrade that place?"

"I got it. I'll upgrade the shipyard soon. Some things have changed though. I think we need to have a meeting with the core members."

"The demon friend of yours?" Vilari asked.

"That's part of it," Zac agreed. "But also things about the war. Please have people gather at Brazla's in a week."

"Before that, you might want to visit the Sky Gnome," Joanna said. "I talked with him the other day, and he was quite troubled. You had left some instructions for him, to look out for certain coded messages? Apparently, he's been bombarded the last month, to the point he wonders if he should respond."

"Oh?" Zac said with interest.

The only messages he instructed Calrin to keep watch for were the special channels he'd prepared to communicate with Catheya. After hearing Perala's warning about the Undead Empire, he already suspected as much, but it looked like the Draugr scion was back in Zecia.

Either that or she'd sent a trusted messenger. It was still impossible to tell whether it was related to his entry into the Undead Empire or Ultom. Judging by how incessantly they seemed to be looking for him, Zac guessed it was associated with the latter.

"I'll deal with it tomorrow," Zac said. "For now, I have to rest. Is there anything else that's urgent before I leave?"

Joanna and Vilari glanced at each other—Vilari spoke up. "There are a lot of rumors floating about in Port Atwood. Rumors of undead skulking in the shadows, of clandestine experiments performed by you. We've done what we can to curtail it, but…"

"Well, it was inevitable after the Ensolus Incursion was closed," Zac grunted. "I guess it's time to properly integrate the two sides of the Atwood Empire. Keep things stable for now. We'll discuss the details during the meeting in a week."

"Of course," Vilari said.

A few moments later, Zac sat down on his prayer mat in the undead half of his cultivation cave, letting the soothing waves of death wash over his Draugr form. Everything looked mostly the same, except for the energy having become slightly denser and purer. Part of it probably came from Triv's incremental upgrades to the environment, while part of it came from the still-ongoing maturity process of Earth.

Gradually, order was imposed on the chaotic mess that was his pathways as Zac redrew one section after another. Between his powerful soul and Peak Mastery [Spiritual Anchor], the process was both quick and almost effortless, allowing him to go over the events.

Just sitting in his hidden cave provided some balance and tranquility, and he gradually started to digest and go over what he'd learned over the past months. Unfortunately, so many pieces of information were missing to draw any clear conclusions. Everyone was afraid to say too much, lest it somehow affect fate.

The conflict he'd been dragged into also appeared to have multiple layers, where the struggle for an Eternal Heritage was just the surface prize. What were the opposing sides Perala mentioned? Who fought for the direction of the era? The Boundless Path and Heaven's path, perhaps? Did one side want to use the pillars to dismantle the System, while the others wanted to use them to improve it?

Was that why the pillars were gradually resurfacing? By design, according to Leyara. Was the Limitless Emperor giving the future generations a choice? Or was it related to some other far-reaching plan of his, one that may or may not have gone awry now that he was long gone? Was that what the Vigil was waiting for?

And how did it relate to Zac and his bloodline?

There was no way to tell. Yet. Piece by piece, Zac would unearth the truth. And he even had a possible venue to get more answers, provided his theories were correct—the Undead Empire.

Zac spent the next day getting his Draugr pathways into a barely functioning order. A lot of detail was missing, but the framework he'd set up would at least allow for his Miasma to naturally flow through his body. It suddenly felt like he could breathe again, but he only got to enjoy the feeling for a short minute before transforming back to his human form.

A cursory scan of his already accumulating pile of messages confirmed that Ogras' reintegration into society had gone well. The demon was living it up in Azh'Rodum, and the festivities would probably last a few days longer. Zac had received a note of thanks and an invitation from Ilvere to join them, but he, unfortunately, had a bit much to deal with.

Instead, he teleported over to the Mercantile District to visit Calrin. Zac found the Sky Gnome in his office, and as usual was accompanied by Vikram, Zac's business liaison.

"Ah, Lord Atwood? You're finally here!" The Sky Gnome smiled when Zac entered through the gilded doors. "When I saw the sun part the clouds this morning, I knew this would be a good day."

Zac rolled his eyes. "Are you looking for handouts again?"

"Absolutely not," Calrin said with a puffed-out chest. "Things are looking up since your last dona—ah, consignment. Some of the bulk materials you had in your Spatial Rings are extremely scarce in the Zecia Sector. We could deal in tons while others dealt in kilos! Thanks to that, I managed to sign a few lucrative agreements."

"You didn't sell off anything we needed, right?" Zac asked with a frown.

"Most of your materials are only used in specific types of recipes and crafting techniques out of our reach," Vikram explained. "For example, you had over five hundred metric tons of a type of Cinnabar Bark which is a core material for a certain ink popular among inscriptionists. That stockpile alone is worth almost two million D-grade Nexus Coins now that demand for talismans has shot through the roof. Though it will take some time to unload it all."

Zac's eyes widened in shock, recalling how he'd almost considered pawning off all that bark in exchange for 100 Contribution Points in the Orom World Merit Store. From what he'd gathered, it wasn't anything special. Zac had failed to take into account that a lot of useful materials were missing in a frontier Sector like Zecia.

"Better yet, it allowed us to sign a trade agreement with the Kalton Clan, a variety wholesaler and direct subordinate of Mount Luminous, one of the nine peak ventures in Zecia. With the suppression of the other two bastards, the Kalton Clan would never dare do so without the go-ahead from Mount Luminous."

"Mount Luminous?" Zac hesitated, feeling it was vaguely familiar. "Buddhists?"

"Not at all," Calrin smiled. "It's a joint venture between the Allbright Clan and a few other major players in the Allbright Empire. We received an offer with another of the nine peak Mercantile factions, but we figured you already had some connections to the Albright Empire…"

"That's perfect." Zac wasn't surprised at all the Albright Empire was willing to clash with the other traders for these strategic resources. "Do they know I'm connected to the Thayer Consortia?"

"Unless they're stupid," Calrin said. "The Tsarun somehow managed to find out even if you killed that brat in the Base Town, and the spies of the other factions should have figured it out by now as well. In fact, the Kalton Clan has sent more than one inquiry, just barely stopping short of outright asking about your situation."

"Hm…" Zac slowly nodded.

"If Lord Atwood is interested in my opinion, then I would say your connection to us being made public is a good thing," Calrin added.

"It is? Like for marketing?" Zac asked curiously.

"Well, that too," Calrin said. "But with our recent moves, the mystery surrounding you has grown. With our access to rare materials, seemingly infinite resources, and your sister's apparent ability to break any low-grade array, some new rumors have started flourishing. That you are more connected than you let on before. That you possibly have already found a benefactor outside Zecia."

Zac couldn't help but laugh at that. Honestly, the rumors felt more believable than the truth, that he picked up most of these things off the ground during a battle between Divine Monarchs and an Autarch. Perhaps the Monarchs of Zecia believed some bigshot from a faction like the Radiant Temple had taken him as a disciple, which wouldn't be too surprising considering his feats in the Tower of Eternity.

"We kept things vague for now, only hinting but never confirming," Calrin added.

"That's good. Give me some time to think things over," Zac said. "So, what's the total value of the items I brought?"

"In raw materials alone, you've reached a net worth of almost 40 C-grade Nexus Coins," Vikram said. "However, we've only sold off a tenth for now, because the prices are still rising. We didn't want to empty our stores too quickly and only parted with what we had to in order to secure the agreements."

A smile spread across Zac's face as the good news kept getting better. His own estimate had been at only half that, and that was for the whole hoard. The only thing raining on his parade was Iz's offhanded comments that crushed his image of a young scion with deep pockets.

"It is harder to estimate the value of the unique treasures, but I'd say the total value is between 4 and 6 C-grade Nexus Coins," the Sky Gnome added. "It's a moot point, since we're keeping those in-house."

"Anything I can use?" Zac asked.

"Perhaps," Calrin said as he handed over a list. "Some of these items have no recorded name in Zecia, but through a series of tests, we have pinpointed their functions. With a good chunk of the items either having Life or Death-attunement, there should be some that can help expedite your cultivation. The lesser ones might be good carrots to keep your new subjects motivated."

Zac grinned as he took the ledger. He'd been looking forward to this for so long. Years spent in the Orom World, with a treasure trove at his fingertips. Certainly, that was partly his own fault, with his reluctance to take out too many items from his Spatial Rings out of fear they'd be marked by the Orom.

A cursory scan was enough to find more than ten items that would help him shore up his foundations before breaking through. They ranged from Life-attuned materials that would speed up the cultivation of his [Void Vajra Sublimation], to rare Dao Treasures, and even items that could search for Hidden Nodes.

Zac couldn't be sure, but he felt he'd tapped out his nodes that originated on his human side. The three nodes of the Void Emperor bloodline formed a coherent system, and he doubted his original form was meant to have anything else. If he understood the plans of the Kayar-Elu properly, his human side was intended to be a blank slate that would be bolstered through the [Quantum Gate].

Things no longer followed the original script with him becoming a Draugr instead of whatever the Technocrats planned, but the plan was still relevant. So far, he managed to excavate [Adamance of Eoz], though Zac doubted that was the limits of his Draugr heritage after seeing how his ancestor was one of the three strongest original Draugr.

Seeing all the amazing items, Zac just wanted to seclude himself and start working on his cultivation, but that wasn't why he'd come here today.

"Great work with all this. You can deal with the rest according to your plan. Only one thing, the upcoming war will start earlier than most expect, so you might need to adjust for this," Zac said.

"Oh?" Calrin said with a frown.

"Four years," Zac sighed. "And it will be even bloodier than we feared. Powerful outsider factions are joining in. So, if you see anything up for grabs that can improve our strength and survivability, get it."

"Four years? Outsiders?" Calrin muttered as he shared a look with Vikram.

"We certainly do need to make some adjustments," the liaison said.

"So we do," Calrin agreed.

"Let me know if you need anything from me," Zac said. "On another note, I heard there had been activity through the line of communication I left you?"

"Yes," Calrin nodded. "If you want my opinion, they are desperate judging by the frequency."

"Desperate? Have you responded?" Zac asked.

"Not yet," Calrin said. "The trade is still open."

"Good." Zac took out a notepad and scribbled some instructions. "Here, complete the trade according to this."

The Sky Gnome nodded, and a screen appeared in front of him. Half a minute later, a box appeared in his hand. Zac opened it up, and a Communication Crystal waited inside. He scanned the contents, and a wry smile spread across his face.

It looked like he would get to meet an old friend sooner than expected.

3 2

# UPGRADE

'*You jerk, I know you escaped that space fish over a year ago,
and you only contact me now? Every week I record these things
like a fool. The elders even started thinking I was lying when I
said I knew you. In either case, I have good news. Everything
worked out way better than I expected. I even got to visit the
Abyssal Shores as a reward for introducing you.*

'*You have to see that place—it's* amazing. *And I don't think it's
possible to truly unlock our heritage without visiting the Abyssal
Lake. It's paradise, though it can also be dangerous, even for
Draugr.*

'*There have also been some new developments, and our representatives really want to discuss some matters with you. It's not
convenient to speak like this, but I think you know what I'm
talking about. Couldn't even wait one year after coming home
before you started creating waves, huh?*

'*I know what you're thinking, but I hope you believe me when I
say we have strict orders from above to be as accommodating as
possible and not to antagonize you in any way. We are ready to
negotiate in good faith, and we are willing to agree with any
security measures you feel necessary to meet with us.*

*'In either case, I look forward to seeing you again. I think you'll be shocked to see how much I've progressed.'*

Zac wordlessly looked at the Communication Crystal as he went over the message. As expected, the Undead Empire was quite interested in Ultom. They already had the Heart of the Empire, but why be satisfied with one Eternal Heritage when you could have two? Zac could understand why the Undead Empire was so interested. Judging by the bursts of unattuned knowledge Ultom had provided so far, this might be one of the few heritages that suited the Undead Empire apart from one dealing with death.

The message also contained valuable hints, probably left intentionally by Catheya. For example, she'd said 'the elders' rather than master or 'my family.' In other words, it looked like she was accompanied by someone other than her Revenant master or some elder from Clan Sharva'Zi. It served as a small warning, even if she said the Undead Empire wanted to discuss things in good faith.

Not only that, but judging by her opening sentence, it sounded like she not only knew about the Orom, but had arrived in Zecia even before he triggered the quest for the Left Imperial Palace. According to Iz, they only found out about Ultom because of some sort of galactic ripples that appeared during his first vision. So Ultom wasn't the only reason they were interested in him.

It was a small comfort since it meant he possibly had two things the Undead Empire needed. An advantage he might be able to use, compared to the other outside factions where his access to Ultom was his only redeeming factor. None of this solved the main issue, though, that there were huge risks associated with bartering with these kinds of factions.

Still, Zac felt it was worth meeting up with Catheya, and not just because it would be nice to see her after over five years. Risks were unavoidable on the path of cultivation, and trouble would come looking for him even if he hid away on Earth. Better to take charge of his own fate, and the Undead Empire seemed one of the best options to ally with.

Especially considering they probably had brought some nice gifts to bribe him with.

Opening his remaining Draugr Hidden Nodes was one of his goals before breaking through, and Catheya's handlers were by far his best options to accomplish that. He just needed to devise a plan that would allow him to navigate these muddy waters before setting out.

"Is everything alright?" Calrin asked curiously.

"It's good," Zac nodded before taking out a blank Communication Crystal.

He imprinted a short answer that he was back after dealing with some things and needed a couple of months to recover before meeting with Catheya. Zac didn't offer any details or pinpoint any specific location, though. He would have to discuss the matters with the others to see if they had any ideas.

Perhaps they could meet near one of the main factions of the Kaldran Strait? Or in the Million Gates Territory, perhaps?

"Send this back with the method," Zac said after placing the Communication Crystal into the same box and locking it with his Cosmic Energy.

Calrin nodded, and the box was gone a few seconds later. It looked like the people on the other side were extremely eager for them to complete the trade the instant it appeared. With that, Zac was done with his objectives at the Thayer Consortia. But just as he was about to leave, Zac had another idea and stopped in his tracks.

"See if you can find any information about these sigils," Zac said as he took out a slightly bloodied parchment. "These ones are slightly modified from the original design to not give anything away, so just look for something similar. Be discrete, for your eyes only, and don't let it trace back to us."

It was one of the more detailed drawings he'd lifted from the bodies of the Kan'Tanu invaders, depicting the slightly warped versions of the Left Imperial Palace and the nine subsidiary courts. Most things indicated the seals originated from the Million Gates Territory, but Zac figured it wouldn't hurt casting a wider net. After all, he got nothing when Ogras and Iz picked up signals to their respective pieces in Zecia's patch of the Endless Storm.

Perala had already warned him that the final piece was in the System's hands and would be used as a carrot during the war. The fact that Perala Janodrok and the Vigil weren't hostile didn't mean she was implicitly telling the truth. Even if what the Void Priestess said was correct, there was still one piece out there that he needed to get his hands on.

"Oh, don't worry, we already are," Calrin nodded.

"What?" Zac said, completely blanking out.

"These are the runes your followers found in the ruins on the other planet, no?" Calrin said with confusion. "We have been making discrete inquiries about them for quite some time. Many of them differ from what Miss Thompson provided before, though."

"Ah?" Zac said, barely able to keep his voice stable. "You're saying these match the Ensolus Ruins?"

"Some of them, yes," Calrin said. "We have not found anything that can shed some light on the origins of the Ensolus Ruins, though."

Zac's heart beat like a drum. "Then pause the search for now and seal any knowledge of these things."

"Oh?" Calrin, though confusion was evident on his face from the quick turns, understood the severity. "Of course, I will deal with it personally."

Zac nodded in thanks and was out of the doors, making a beeline for the closest teleportation array. He appeared in a private Teleportation chamber prepared in the depths of Fort Atwood on Ensolus. When he appeared, he gasped in surprise as a familiar ripple made his mind blank.

It really was here, the third piece for his quest.

Zac took a deep breath to stabilize his agitated mind as he looked in the direction of the Ensolus Ruins, barely able to believe his sudden windfall. It was like he could see a straight path toward Hegemony, the final roadblocks removed without him lifting so much as a finger. The only thing he needed now was time.

Ogras joked about treasures falling from the sky around him, but it almost seemed true this time. How was this possible? Fate? Or had the System intentionally put those ruins on this planet?

Why hadn't he noticed anything the first time he appeared on Ensolus? He'd been a lot closer to the Ensolus Ruins back when visiting the mines with Ilvere. Was there something special about the Void Star that had been needed to trigger the quest, or perhaps the connection? Was it because the Void Star held the connection to the Lost Plane at the time?

That weird spatial star was linked to the Million Gates Territory and the Endless Storm where the Left Imperial Palace probably resided, while Ensolus was shielded-off by the System for another 100 years. Or perhaps it was the proximity to the Lost Plane through the Mystic Realm.

The ripple was calling, telling him to rush over and claim his prize. But Zac shook his head and teleported back to Earth. The moment he returned, he sent a message to Vilari, asking her to stop any expeditions into the ruin and seal it off for now. He wasn't worried anyone would steal his opportunity, but he feared those disintegration pulses would get people killed.

Besides, it was possible there were more pieces over there than just his own, considering the ruins were huge. He didn't know what the criteria for people like Ogras to get the quest were, but it was perhaps possible to stumble onto a remnant through dumb luck. If possible, Zac wanted to reserve those opportunities for his most trusted people rather than random explorers from his army or the two native races.

As for himself, he wasn't in any hurry. He still had a lot of room to improve on his own, and he wanted to use the third burst of clarity to create a perfect blueprint when his foundations were as stable as they could be. In other words, just before heading to the Perennial Vastness. Using it right now would only help him decipher the remaining chapters of the Book of Duality, which would be a huge waste.

He would head over later to properly seal off whatever temple held his piece, just to make sure nothing unexpected happened to it. For now, he had other pressing matters to deal with. Zac took a calming breath to clear his mind before returning to his compound, where he set course for the shipyard.

Zac didn't even have time to greet Rahm at the reception before he heard the deep thuds of metallic legs approach from the back rooms.

"Brat, you got it?" Karunthel asked with excitement as he entered the reception.

"I got it." Zac smiled as he handed over the Beast Pouch. "A spatial affinity Worldeater, like you ordered."

"Not bad, not bad. It will be nice not to be in charge of the crappiest shipyard in the whole Multiverse," Karunthel grinned as he looked Zac up and down. "Seems you had a few gains of yourself, even if you look a bit worse for the wear. Getting ready to evolve?"

"I'm ahead of schedule, but there are a few more steps I need to complete," Zac said after some thought. "How long until everything is dealt with?"

"It's a quest reward, so the shipyard will be replaced quickly. Ten days at most," Karunthel said. "The ship would have been ready along with the shipyard, but that only holds true for the Early-level hull right now. The upgrades would take two months, depending on which model and what modifications you want. Have you decided what to do for that one?"

"I have. I want the Yphelion model."

"What, the *scout ship*?" Karunthel blurted, looking visibly disappointed. "I thought better of you, kid. You sure you don't want me to make you the destroyer instead? I can guarantee your name will spread far and wide after your first engagement."

"That's exactly what I want to avoid," Zac said with a roll of his eyes. "The situation has gotten a bit complicated."

It wasn't an impulse decision to go with the scout vessel, despite it not being what he originally planned. Initially, the idea was to get the all-rounder ship and modify it a bit to suit the chaotic region of the Million Gates Territory. Compared to most vessels in Zecia, it would have been able to shine no matter if you talked speed or defenses.

But things had changed when he heard a bunch of powerful factions were encroaching. Those people would probably have High-quality vessels, even if the System restrained their grade. The advantage provided by the Creators wouldn't be as big. Not only that, but Zac felt the risk of accidentally running into Monarchs was suddenly a lot higher with various factions scouring the Million Gates Territory for clues to Ultom.

For now, it was just his people and the outsiders who knew the truth, but even the native factions were bound to catch on sooner or later. And no matter how impressive the work of the Iliax was, it was simply impossible for a Middle D-grade Cosmic Vessel to deal with even an Early-stage Monarch.

And while most Monarchs couldn't match up to Cosmic Vessels in terms of long-haul speed or their ability to pass through dimensional layers, they could teleport vast distances in quick bursts thanks to movement skills.

Zac had discussed the situation in the Million Gates Territory with both Pretty and Leyara at length, and ultimately concluded that the scouting ship was the best option for him in the short run. The Yphelion's defensive and offensive capabilities weren't particularly impressive, but the ship came with various other useful features.

Most important was its speed—the Yphelion was far quicker than the other two models. Furthermore, being a scouting ship, it could initiate dimensional jumps more frequently and with shorter delays. That could be the difference between life and death when a Monarch was bearing down on you.

Its scanners were also top-of-the-line, which would help spot and avoid enemy vessels long before the Yphelion was spotted. And finally, while its defenses wouldn't last long in large-scale space battles, they should hold up well enough against random encounters against Kan'-Tanu scouts.

The Yphelion was even a decent option if you looked at it long-term. In the future, the ship would save Zac a lot of time when he needed to travel long distances. His goals would eventually take him out of Zecia, no matter if it was to find Kenzie or to continue his cultivation. In the open world, he didn't have access to the whole teleportation network as he did here, and he would probably have to spend years traveling through space.

The scouting vessel was almost three times as fast as the generalist vessel, which could shave off years when he needed to visit hard-to-reach-places. Routes that would take the massive carriers decades, would only take a few months in the Yphelion. Going at maximum speed was also expensive, but Zac could easily stomach the cost.

Karunthel sighed. "I guess the Yphelion models are better suited for those chaotic regions you want to visit. And we could always add proper weaponry if you meet the requirements for further upgrades down the road."

"What kind of requirements are those?" Zac asked curiously.

With him having delivered the [Ferric Worldeater], the [Items for Karunthel]-questline was finally dealt with. However, that only upgraded the Shipyard to Early D-grade from what he understood, which was a far cry from the limits of that kind of facility.

"Who knows," the spider golem shrugged. "It's up to the Heavens. Come back when the upgrades are finished, and I'll see if you've met the requirements to get the second quest."

Zac nodded. "By the way, can you build multiple Cosmic Vessels simultaneously?"

"The mass-produced models are much easier to construct," Karunthel said. "We can build ten or so at a time, and they take between one and three weeks to build. Why, do you want more ships?"

"Well, war is coming, so I've found some potential customers," Zac smiled.

"Finally, some real work," Karunthel grinned. "But you should know, your Yphelion will take up all our capacity until it's built."

"I'm thinking we'll build a round of showcase vessels for our prospective clients first while we finalize the plans for the Yphelion."

"Sounds good," Karunthel agreed. "Now, shoo, I want to begin upgrading this place. Come back in ten days."

"Enjoy yourself," Zac said, leaving for his compound.

He didn't even reach the forest before a huge gleaming barrier sprung up around the whole shipyard, and a moment later, it was gone. It had been transported to a barren mountainous island at the edge of his archipelago that Abby had suggested before he left for the Void Gate. By now, the island had already been fitted with a teleporter with restricted access and powerful arrays to keep both beasts and explorers away.

With that, the most pressing issues had been dealt with. Abby and Adran had both sent him a bunch of messages with various issues of the Atwood Empire, ranging from proposals to expand the academy and found subsidiaries, to small problems that had cropped up during the Integration of the Mavai Demons and the Raun Spectrals.

Nothing required his immediate attention, so he returned to his cave to focus on his recovery. And with the third piece of the seal waiting for him on Ensolus, he would have to change his plans. He already had an idea the moment he felt the pulse, and it made more sense the more he thought about it.

He only wondered what the others would think upon hearing his decision.

# 33
# CHANGE OF PLANS

Zac opened his eyes as his alarm buzzed, and he took a deep breath from the dense lifegiving mist. Six days had passed since he secluded himself, most of which had been spent in the depths of death, where he repaired his broken pathways. He also bathed in refreshing concoctions designed to heal stubborn wounds daily.

They were mixed up by Triv, using all kinds of Death-attuned materials Zac had picked up over the years. Even Hegemons would probably be shocked at the expenditure, especially if they learned their only purpose was to double the speed his foundations recovered.

Still, Zac felt it a worthy investment. Four years wasn't little, but it also wasn't a lot. He had so much to do, but his current state prevented him from doing any real form of cultivation. Perhaps he could have cultivated his soul with a different method, but [Nine Reincarnations Manual] empowered his soul through destructive collisions—the opposite of what he currently needed.

Zac was most eager about starting up his Body Tempering, but doing so while there were a bunch of hidden wounds was bound to leave imperfections. He could only take it easy and avoid activities that strained the body or mind. Instead, Zac had spent most of his time studying the Book of Duality while bolstering the broken framework of [Thousand Lights Avatar] after repairing his pathways.

He still hadn't dared absorb any corrupted lake water, though he at least confirmed it retained its magical effects even after being taken from its source. He didn't think he needed to be completely recovered to start using the water to speed up his progression, but it still felt a bit premature.

Altogether, Zac felt a lot better after this first week, but he would have to pause his recovery. The meeting was starting in just minutes, so it was time to go.

"My lord!" a ghastly voice echoed through the chambers as Triv emerged through the ground. "Your aura seems to have stabilized even further."

Zac smiled. "All thanks to your help. Amazing job as always."

"I am the one who should be thanking young master," Triv said with a bow, their spectral form humming with excitement. "I have been making great progress since young master became a Baron and your Empire was officially sanctioned by the Heavens. Not only that, but the Eidolon manuals young master provided have completely reforged my body. With this sublime environment, I even have a decent chance of forming a Dao Branch."

"Let me know if you need any materials to keep progressing," Zac said. "Our faction lacks many things, but Death-attuned cultivation resources are not one of them. Are you joining the meeting?"

"I am afraid this old ghost is of no help to young master's plans," Triv sighed. "I am old and inflexible. Lady Vilari is much better suited to advise on the fusion of your two settlements. With your permission, I would like to continue my work in Elysium instead."

"That's fine," Zac said, and headed for the teleportation array.

Triv, or Old Man Ghost as the undead children called him on the other continent, had worked tirelessly for years to improve this nascent society's lives. Ultimately, the undead races were supernatural existences, and some things didn't come naturally to them. There was a lot to learn, whether it was the conversion arrays or properly dealing with feral children who hadn't gained their sapience yet.

Triv had done his best to impart what he could without going against the commandments of the Undead Empire. As such, he'd gained the reputation of an esteemed scholar among the undead. If not for Zac's inherent connection to his undead 'descendants,' Triv would probably have enjoyed a higher status on Earth's second continent.

"Will young master need anything else?" Triv asked.

"No, I'll stay in my human form for a week or so," Zac said after some thought. "It feels like my body is recovering better when I alternate races for some reason."

"Your body is reaching satiety from the environment, I would presume, and the effect on your wounds are lessened after a while." Triv nodded. "I will be back in a week and prepare another round of baths."

"Thank you for the help," Zac said, and the two disappeared in the teleporter a moment later, one heading for Elysium and the other for the Towers of Myriad Dao.

It wasn't strictly needed to have the meeting in Brazla's chambers, but it had become the standard for important meetings. And you never knew, Brazla sometimes let valuable pieces of information slip by accident.

By the time he arrived, Zac could already hear familiar voices through the opened gates. As he stepped inside, he saw Ilvere talking with Vilari and Rhuger, while Joanna gazed upon the titan inheritance with Pika standing next to her. Alyn and Calrin discussed something together, and Julia stood by herself, lost in thought.

Quite some time had passed since Zac saw Julia Lombard, the former World Government official. However, from what he'd read in the reports, she had been a key asset since he left for the Twilight Harbor. She singlehandedly quashed over a dozen insurrections while most of the elites were stuck on Ensolus. Not only that, but she was the author of the Atwood Codex, the set of laws that fused Old Earth's justice system with the realities of the Multiverse.

Unfortunately, her hard work left her cultivation lacking, and from what Zac understood, she was planning on making a similar shift like Vai once had. In contrast, Abby wasn't present, nor were any of the leaders from the Mavai or Raun. Some topics that would get discussed today were too sensitive, and they couldn't be allowed to spread from this room. The administrators and new citizens would be brought in for future meetings instead.

Ogras stood alone to the side, staring at his own statue, or rather that of his backhanded master.

"You're looking rosy." Zac smiled as he walked over to the demon.

"At least one of us needs to sire some descendants to keep watch of this place," Ogras grinned. "Such is the burden of responsibility."

"Thank you for your service," Zac said with a roll of his eyes before nodding at the statue depicting the Umbra. "Have you decided what to do?"

Ogras was already Peak E-grade, and his foundations were rock solid after having spent a decade in an environment that was probably unsurpassed in Zecia. Like Zac, he was already preparing to break through to the next realm. In other words, he had to enter the inheritance sooner rather than later if he wanted to keep it going.

The problem was that the Umbra was just as mercurial as Yrial, with an addition of sinister curiosity. The Umbra had forcibly sown a Ka'Zur Planeswalker into Ogras' very soul during the first round of the inheritance. Things would have ended in disaster if not for a series of lucky coincidences. Who knew what the Umbra would do if Ogras dared return?

"I think I have to, even if I can wait a bit." Ogras grimaced. "I had the little blue thief look for suitable targets to progress my constitution. There aren't many that look promising compared to the creatures this guy has sealed away in the inheritance. The few I can get my hands on before evolving would be unimpressive, even with your help. I need stronger bloodlines than that to reforge my foundation."

"Well, I think there are limits to how much damage these remnant souls can do," Zac said. "Are you ready for the meeting?"

"Is it true what you said before?" Ogras asked. "It's really here, on your other planet?"

Zac didn't answer, but the smile on his face spoke volumes.

"Just disgusting," Ogras spat. "I should have guessed as much when you didn't get a signal before me or your flametouched girlfriend. Whatever, let's get this over with."

The others had already sat down around the table upon seeing Zac arrive. This time, Brazla didn't bother joining them in person and opted to loom a dozen meters above them atop a golden cloud. That was fine by Zac since most topics didn't require the Tool Spirit's input.

"Nothing from Emily?" Zac frowned when he saw her empty chair.

"We've received no response from the Big Axe Coliseum," Joanna said with a shake of her head.

"I'll check it out later," Zac sighed as he glanced at the second empty chair.

Sap Trang had also declined the invitation, though he wasn't off-world. He'd chosen to remain at sea, guarding the borders with his pet Kraken. Zac had been meaning to track him down and have a chat, but there were just too many things to do at the moment.

"Everyone here is busy training and preparing for the upcoming war, so I won't drag this out any longer than it needs to be. By now, you should all have read the missive I sent out three days ago. The short of it is that the war will officially commence in four years, much earlier than we expected. How are we looking?"

"As usual, we have mountains of resources and unusually powerful elites. But we still lack bodies to fill the ranks," Ilvere said. "We have accelerated our training programs, but four years is simply too little time for any drastic improvements without something like an Incursion or Mystic Realm to whip people into shape."

"Too many have slowed down their progress after Earth stabilized," Joanna added. "It might sound odd, but we might have made our cities too safe with powerful arrays and fortifications. Few beast tides can threaten our people, so they aren't feeling the sense of urgency and pressure from before."

"I think it's time we talk conscription," Ilvere said.

Zac sighed as he looked at the documents on the table. He'd already read most of them while recuperating, and they painted a somber picture. As things stood, the Atwood Empire would be able to field less than half a percent of their population for the upcoming war, including support staff. There was still the Zhix Hives, but their numbers were far too small.

The System was originally a tool of war meant to extract as much military might out of the populace as possible. They didn't know exactly how many warriors the Atwood Empire would have to supply to meet the criteria. Still, they estimated they needed to supply at least 2-3% even if the System lowered their quota for being a newly integrated world.

Another problem was that most of their numbers were made up of the Mavai Hordes and the Raun Spectrals. Just over one million out of four were earthlings, even though there were more humans than the other races combined. Such an army composition wouldn't work. The newly integrated races were still cautious about whether they would be used as cannon fodder, which might lead to all kinds of problems during the war.

"Do it," Zac said. "Our goal should be 25 million E-grade warriors before the war starts. The Zhix, Mavai, and Raun are already providing a high quota, but see if we can nurture even more by throwing money at the problem. Our main target should be humans, though. Too many have taken their place in the Multiverse for granted. The same goes for the Ishiate. Even if the pacifist faction can't provide many warriors, they'll have to supply healers and other support staff."

"How much are you willing to spend on their training?" Alyn asked. "There are only so many E-grade warriors out there. Most of them we'll have to raise from scratch. To nurture ten E-grade warriors, we would have to enlist at least 100 recruits, even if we have stringent selections for potential. That number could be lowered if we're willing to force some breakthroughs."

"I'll have Calrin transfer 2.5 C-grade Nexus Coins to the Atwood Empire Treasury," Zac said, drawing a small gasp from Pika, and Ilvere's eyes widened in shock. Calrin looked queasy, but he reluctantly nodded in agreement. "This will be our war coffer. Hopefully, it will last us until the end of this mess.

"The Thayer Consortia has also managed to secure a deal with a top Mercantile house. We will have no problem getting our hands on the basic herbs and materials needed to expand our army."

"With so many resources, we should have no problem reaching the target, but what about the recruits themselves? There will be a lot of resistance," Ilvere said. "Your earthling humans have peace and individualism ingrained in their bones."

"Just beat it out of them," Ogras shrugged, to which Zac agreed.

It was tough, but so was the reality they lived in. He couldn't shield the people of Earth forever. He'd seen what happened to planets that didn't live up to the System's expectations, and he alone wasn't enough to protect them from such a fate. Besides, he had already done more than enough for this planet, including opening the contribution exchange. It was time for Earth to give back.

"There will be discontent, especially if you plan on integrating the unliving simultaneously," Julia said. "Remember, the Undead Empire killed almost two billion people before they were finally routed. Even if the Blackwoods here are of a different origin, it won't matter to the general public."

"There isn't much we can do about that," Zac sighed. "The rumors are already running rampant, and I feel I'm doing my undead citizens a disservice by hiding them away like they're a secret weapon. We'll just have to rip off the Band-Aid and deal with the fallout."

"How would I do that if most of you are deep in the Million Gates Territory by then?" Julia asked. "I'm not able to quash uprisings with my aura. There will be a lot of bloodshed."

"We will borrow the strength of the Zhix, and I'm planning to summon some of the experienced warriors of both the Mavai and Raun to teach and maintain order," Zac said before taking a deep breath. "However, there is another change of plans regarding this. I will, unfortunately, not be joining the rest of you. I will remain on Earth for at least two years, only leaving for short shopping trips at most."

"What?" Joanna blurted, growing worried. "Is it your wounds?"

"No," Zac said with a shake of his head. "I am getting better by the day. However, I had a few lucky encounters while finishing my quest to upgrade the shipyard. Therefore, I have decided to push for Hegemony before the war starts. I need to seclude myself and focus on my cultivation to accomplish that. I cannot run about in space."

"So, we're not going?" Vilari hesitated.

"A squad will still set out as we planned, but it will be captained by Ogras instead," Zac said.

A few looked at Ogras with surprise, while the demon took the news in stride. Of course, Ogras already knew all this after a talk he and Zac had yesterday. At first, the demon was hesitant to enter the Million Gates Territory without his 'lucky magnet,' but greed soon overcame fear, agreeing to set out in search of his second piece for the inheritance.

"I will ferry you all over in a few months when we have our ships ready, but the details of your excursion will be up to you," Zac said. "You can see this as a test. I cannot always be around, and I fear you all won't reach your full potential if I loom over you. Fate has to be seized with one's own hands."

The meeting lasted another five hours, and detailed plans were drawn up. The militarization of Earth was a huge undertaking on its own. Add the Integration of the undead, and you had an administrative and managerial nightmare on your hands. Luckily, a lot of plans for both ventures had already been prepared, and most of the time was simply spent fusing the two.

The construction of training camps across the whole planet would begin immediately, while the Integration of the undead would start after Zac met with Catheya. He was hoping to get some assurances from the Undead Empire first, that they would look the other way like they did with the Twilight Harbor.

They also discussed the Creator Vessels, and there was a general agreement on choosing the Yphelion as the first flagship of the Atwood Empire. However, Zac was surprised to hear that both Joanna and Vilari didn't want to use his vessel for their upcoming visit to the Million Gates Territory. Instead, they insisted on using one of the simpler mass-produced models.

Ogras was unsurprisingly reluctant, though he eventually acceded while muttering something about 'netherblasted rivers.'

"We'll have more meetings to iron out the details before you all set out, but there is one thing I need to bring up before you leave. However, this topic has extreme ramifications, so I will give you all a choice," Zac said as he solemnly looked around the table. "If you are willing to risk everything for your cultivation path, to face certain death for a chance of having your fate reforged, stay behind. If not, leave and focus on the tasks at hand."

# ONE BY NINE

People had started to get distracted the longer the meeting toiled on. Then Zac's somber words and serious face were like a cold shower, waking everyone right up. No one said anything until Ilvere suddenly released a pent-up sigh.

"Risk everything? Certain death?" the demon captain said with a wry smile. "I think that's it for me then, unless you desperately need my help?"

"This is about individual fate," Zac said with a shake of his head. "Some things are happening here in Zecia, big things with terrifying ramifications. There might be a chance to fish in these troubled waters for opportunities, but one would have to be ready to die at any turn."

Ilvere smiled as he stood. "I've seen and heard what you've been forced to go through to reach your current level. For *you* to utter such words, this cannot be simple indeed. I feel it's not for me. The battlefield, shoulder to shoulder with my fellow soldiers, that's my home."

With that, the demon walked out without looking back, proof of conviction with his path. Julia shook her head while giving Zac a reproachful stare, like he was a troublemaker, before following suit. Calrin gazed at Zac with ruminating eyes, clearly putting two and two together after having been shown the sigils. He didn't comment on the situation and left with Julia.

Eventually, only Ogras, Joanna, Vilari, and Rhuger remained. Zac was a bit surprised to see Pika bowing out, and perhaps even more shocked to hear she was engaged to one of the budding Liches of Elysium. She wasn't willing to go beyond the command of her current post, which was fair.

"Are the three of you sure?" Zac said. "My words weren't a test. The dangers are very real."

"I know my foundations are shallow, but I'm not content just staying a captain," Joanna said. "No matter if it's to repay you or to open a path for myself, I am willing to take this risk. To see the true face of the Dao."

"The same goes for me," Rhuger said.

"Don't worry about us," Vilari said. "We understand the risks of power. We might die, but better die following our path than shying away from our destiny."

"The Great Brazla isn't interested in your mundane opportunities," a snort came from above. "But since you're the one encroaching on this Sage's domain, you should be the one who leaves."

Zac agreed and stood. "Then follow me."

Being thrown out was fine by Zac since he didn't plan on discussing the next part in front of the Tool Spirit. Brazla had caused spectacles before to get what he wanted, such as creating enormous plaques in the sky. There was no way Zac would take such a risk with this topic. As for what the secret was, it was obviously Ultom and the Left Imperial Palace.

The three exchanged a curious glance, and followed Zac to his compound, where Zac activated the teleporter. Soon enough, the five of them sat on a flying vessel taking them across the alien landscapes of the Ensolus continent.

"This direction," Joanna said, breaking the pregnant silence.

Zac nodded. "You're right. We're heading to the Ensolus Ruins."

"This is related to why you had us seal off that area," Vilari concluded.

"Correct again. Before I explain, remember the matters I bring up now cannot be shared outside of this group. Both for your sake and the sake of the others. This includes when you set out in the Million Gates Territory, even if part of your mission will be related to this opportunity."

"I understand." Vilari and the others nodded.

"A terrifyingly powerful inheritance is emerging here in Zecia. It's so valuable that A-grade factions are coming over in hopes to seize it," Zac said.

"And it's related to the Ensolus Ruins?" Rhuger said with skepticism. "No offense, but I spent a month exploring that place. It's odd, but it doesn't seem like something that would interest bigshots from the outside."

"I'm still not sure how the Ensolus Ruins fit into the picture," Zac said. "But it's related to something called the Left Imperial Palace. And when I say Imperial, I'm talking about the Limitless Empire."

From there, Zac told the others what he knew about the Left Imperial Palace, Ultom, and the nine subsidiary courts. He also shared most of what he'd learned from Iz, Leyara, and Perala to give everyone a proper understanding of the situation and how the war tied into the quest for Ultom.

"I'm not surprised you're mixed up in something like this," Vilari said with a small smile.

"Life is odd," Joanna said with a helpless shake of her head. "Ten years ago, I was a part-time yoga instructor. Today, I am sitting on a flying boat talking about magical castles from a billion-year-old civilization. And I'm not even on drugs."

"Takes some getting used to." Zac smiled wryly.

"What is our role here?" Rhuger asked.

"The Mystic Realm where I found Ogras had four temples, and at least two of them contained pieces of seals. I'm collecting seals for the Left Imperial Palace itself, while Ogras is collecting for one of the Outer Courts," Zac said. "As for the Ensolus Ruins, I have already confirmed it holds one piece for me."

"And you're hoping there are more pieces in the Ensolus Ruins," Vilari concluded.

"Exactly. I have no idea how candidates are chosen, but fate shifts just by *speaking* of this inheritance. I'm hoping that me explaining the situation, and two candidates traveling with you, will somehow give you a chance at seizing a slot if there is one to seize."

"Are we up to it?" Joanna hesitated. "We're pretty strong compared to normal people, but we're far from someone like you. Compared to the A-grade factions you mentioned, we probably don't amount to much. At least not yet."

"I don't think it's just about strength," Zac said. "From what we've gathered, this inheritance is aimed at the younger generation, with an age ceiling of 100. No matter who the courts choose, they'll just be kids who have just started on the road of cultivation. Ultimately, I believe it's more about fate and compatibility."

"Then, that illusionist... Janos," Rhuger asked. "Do you think he's —"

"I'm hoping to find that out as well." Zac nodded. "If we're lucky, we can find him, and he might be able to shed some light on the situation with these ruins. But we also have to be realistic... Neither Ogras nor I were stuck for years when getting our pieces. It might be unrelated, and he might even be dead."

"That guy is a bit odd, but he's very good at surviving," Ogras said. "Remember when he played dead beneath the ground? He might have done the same if caught in some dangerous place. Just waiting for us to break him out."

"Are you here to claim your piece?" Joanna asked. "It might give us some insights to see it first-hand, if that's okay."

"Not this time," Zac said with a shake of his head. "Just claiming a seal is a huge opportunity. You gain an enormous burst of enlightenment that will allow you to improve almost anything except progress your Daos. I still need to shore up my foundations for a year or two before I take the next piece. This time, we're just here to seal off my temple so no one gets killed, and also see if you feel anything from the temples after learning the truth."

"So, what do we do?" Joanna asked. "Just meditate on the inheritance?"

"I'll try something when we arrive at the ruins. For now, start thinking of parts of your cultivation where you feel you have the most room for improvement, just in case the opportunity is suddenly presented to you. For example, I completely reformed a top-tier Body Tempering Manual to suit my bloodline."

The three asked clarifying questions for another 20 minutes before they sat down to go over their options. Rhuger had the easiest of it. He had all of Cervantes' old manuals, though he still hadn't had much luck adapting them to his undead form. Given the opportunity, he would reform and perhaps even elevate the Lunar heritage that was still out of his reach.

Three days passed like this, where Zac mostly read the Book of Duality while absorbing Divine Crystals and Nature Crystals to get a small boost to his recovery. Occasionally, he meditated on the odd energy on the Ensolus continent, hoping to glean insights for his blueprint.

Infusing the twined Realm Spirits hadn't changed Ensolus much, but Zac could tell the energy was stabler than before. According to the reports, the earthquakes had subsided a few weeks after he implanted the spirits, mostly confirming the transplant was successful.

However, the world had still not fully recovered from the cataclysmic upheavals that struck the world, the Ensolus continent in particular. Huge scars ran for hundreds of miles across the ground, and new forests hadn't managed to replace those burnt down by the wildfires. Still, there was a sense of vibrancy in the air, and Zac guessed it was just a matter of time.

Finally, there was a change as Zac felt a ripple from the distance. He looked over, and he could barely spot a small settlement standing at the edge of what looked like a stationary grey sandstorm. The storm was only a couple miles across, but Zac knew that small sphere held an area as large as a huge capital.

Within, the Ensolus Ruins waited for them.

The settlement outside was a now-evacuated research station lacking a teleportation array, not by choice but necessity. The sandstorm was a Spatial Anomaly similar to the Void Gate encampment he and Vai visited. The strong spatial field around the folded space made it impossible to buy teleportation arrays through the System.

Perhaps it was possible to build reinforced arrays by themselves, but the Atwood Empire obviously lacked the means to build something like that.

The group soon landed at the center of the settlement, and two guards walked out from one of the nearby houses. Zac recognized one of them —Cynthia, one of the original Valkyries who joined him at the very beginning. The other was a Revenant Zac didn't recognize, but he had to be one of the captains judging by his solid Late E-grade aura.

"Anything?" Joanna asked as the two walked over.

"Nothing to report," the Valkyrie said with a shake of her head. "We have sealed off the whole cloud after being given the order. No one has attempted to approach this region since."

"Good," Joanna said, turning to Zac.

"Let's go," Zac said, and the quintet walked straight into the dust cloud.

Visibility was almost zero, but there was no need to bind people together with Vivi's vines—Zac could still sense the others around him with his domain. There were no spatial fluctuations either. They didn't have to walk for more than a minute before their surroundings changed. The haziness was replaced by a sprawling city covered in moss and vines.

Zac's heart shuddered, and he was filled with a sense of adventure as he looked across the ruins. It almost felt like he'd found a hidden city in the depths of the Amazon or even Atlantis. But the truth was even more invigorating—Zac recognized the architecture. The buildings didn't look like the temples from the Lost Plane.

They reminded Zac of the enormous palace he'd seen in his first vision—the Left Imperial Palace. Certainly, the scale and domineering aura wasn't there, but the buildings were made from the same type of black stone. Most civilizations in the Multiverse were like pyramids. If the Left Imperial Palace was the tip of the pyramid, then these buildings represented the base.

Perhaps a city where servants lived?

Vaguely familiar scripts covered walls, archways, and statues, most broken far beyond repair. However, not all runes had succumbed to the passage of time. This was both the danger and the opportunity of this place. Just in the vicinity, Zac spotted three buildings empowered by some sort of array. They were still covered in vines and moss, but their foundations stood tall.

And who knew, there might be a trove waiting inside if you managed to force your way through. So far, they hadn't been able to break through too many of the still-active arrays. They didn't use much energy, but they were insanely sturdy, and no attempts at array breaking had shown hints of working.

Ogras whistled as he looked at the edge of the storm behind them. "Impressive."

Zac had to agree. The method used to cram these sprawling ruins together in this small sandstorm was extremely impressive. They hadn't sensed anything at all as they entered the folded patch of space. Apparently, the scale was almost 50:1 according to measurements, and the researchers believed the effect was generated by a statue in the heart of the city.

"What now?" Joanna asked, and Zac could see the hunger in her eyes.

Zac first looked toward the heart of the city, which unsurprisingly was where the calling came from. But he soon looked back at the other three.

"Be ready. The name of the inheritance is… Ultom," Zac said, and the ethereal pressure of fate bared down on him.

"What was that?" Joanna said as she vigilantly looked around, while a frown appeared on Vilari's face.

"Felt like a ghost just passed through me," Rhuger said.

Zac barely listened, his eyes trained on the screen that popped up in front of him.

**One by Nine (Unique, Inheritance):** Form a full cycle of Sealbearers.
**Reward:** Entry to the Left Imperial Palace (4/9) [2683 days] **[NOTE:**
Multiple cycles can be formed.**]**

Zac read the new quest carefully as it divulged a few key pieces of information. Most importantly, it was a timed quest, giving him just over seven years to 'form a cycle.' If Zac was a betting man, that meant the first stage of the inheritance would start at that time. In other words, he would most likely have to find all four pieces of his seal within that timeframe.

The quest even hinted at the inheritance's direction, considering it was telling him to form a posse. After all, a 'full cycle' no doubt meant one sealholder from each subordinate court, such as Ogras' Hollow Court. Was personal strength not enough? Did you have to gather powerful followers if you wanted a shot at the inheritance? And the multiple cycles—would that bring special benefits, or would it just keep the competition from entering?

And more to the point, how was the quest halfway finished already?

"What's wrong?" Ogras asked, dragging Zac out of his thoughts.

Zac considered it for a second before deciding to share the screen. "See for yourself."

"A quest?" Ogras exclaimed before his eyes thinned. "Four? Just like that? Can you really make it happen by willing it into being? Are you the Son of Heaven?"

"I—No idea. I didn't expect things to progress this way," Zac said, confusion written all over his face as he turned to the others. "Did you get a quest or something like that?"

"Nothing," Vilari said. "For a moment, I felt something nudge my soul. But it's gone now."

"Same here," Rhuger said, his eyes repeatedly darting toward the ruins. "Perhaps if we get closer…"

"Let's go and take a look," Zac agreed. "It can't be a random coincidence I suddenly get a half-finished quest to gather followers when I'm trying to share this inheritance with you. See if you can spot any of the seals I showed you on the way."

With that, the group set out, heading toward the core of the Ensolus Ruins, following an incomplete map drawn by the explorers. After all, the Ensolus Ruins might have been long abandoned, but there were still dangers. Some of the arrays inscribed on the broken towers and buildings were Killing Arrays, and there were unstable areas as deadly as any gauntlet.

Thankfully, there were multiple safe pathways leading to the center of the ruins, which was the only reason Zac dared set out in his current state. He just needed to set down a couple of arrays and see if the others could pick up anything before they headed out. Ignoring all the inviting ruins felt like an itch Zac wasn't allowed to scratch, but he could always check things out in the future.

"Walking into the depths of an ancient ruin with a trouble-magnet such as yourself," Ogras muttered as he skipped over a vine as thick as a barrel. "Surely, nothing bad will come of this. I must be mad to have joined you."

# SIDELINED

Zac wanted to roll his eyes at Ogras and ask him what the worst that could happen was, but he reined himself in. His track record wasn't the best in this regard, and it felt a bit foolhardy to tempt the Heavens just after drawing the attention of the river of fate. Instead, Zac turned his attention to his surroundings, using his danger sense and [Cosmic Gaze] to ensure nothing changed in the ruins compared to their map.

"There aren't actually that many dangers unless you try to mess with the arrays," Joanna said. "But if you do, it's a crapshoot. Sometimes, the building is simply fortified beyond what any E-grade can deal with. Other times, you trigger dangerous arrays. We had one explorer caught in an illusion that lasted for thousands of years in their mind. By the time we got them out, their soul was so over drafted they died just hours later."

"His perception was completely warped," Vilari sighed. "He believed reality a dream once we freed him. The poor man kept calling for 'Cassie,' who I guess was his wife in the vision."

"Poor bastard," Ogras muttered as he increased his distance from the closest building.

Zac shook his head, remembering the similar arrays during the hunt. Those things were no joke, but they were probably just a shadow compared to the ancient arrays spread throughout the Ensolus Ruins. Thankfully, the still-intact barriers weren't too common. They had appeared in a residential district, and few of the structures were probably considered valuable enough to go through that kind of effort.

Still, that wasn't enough for Zac to lower his guard, and he vigilantly scanned every building they passed.

"What's with all the temples?" Zac muttered after passing the fourth temple in under ten minutes. "Were these people so devout they needed one on every block?"

"Communal cultivation, I would guess," Ogras said. "Each temple would be equipped with a powerful gathering array and other arrays to help with cultivation, drawing the neighborhood's energy into it. That way, each person gets access to a better environment than if they just stayed in their home, and there's no competition where two neighbors fight for the same energy."

"It's just a bunch of empty cultivation chambers with broken arrays inside?" Zac said with disappointment.

"Not necessarily." Ogras' eyes gleamed with greed as he looked at a shielded temple. "Depends on how wealthy this civilization was, and how well these arrays have preserved what's inside. They might have powered the arrays with valuable treasures. Or stocked them with public Cultivation Manuals surpassing anything we own. Parts of their heritage might be placed in these structures."

"This might have been a faith-based cultivation society as well if these ruins really are related to the Limitless Empire," Vilari added. "In some eyes, Emperor Limitless might have been considered a god of war. I've read that many powerful factions draw power through faith, overtly or passively."

That statement made Zac give the sealed temples an extra glance. What if there were statues depicting Emperor Limitless inside? Would they look like Laondio or Karz? Did it matter?

Zac shook his head and kept walking toward a large dome in the distance that was their first pitstop, according to the map. However, they only advanced for two minutes before Zac suddenly stopped as his danger sense warned him against proceeding farther. Zac didn't understand what was wrong until a wave of colorful lights illuminated the path ahead, like a flash of fae fireflies.

The scene was gone as quickly as it appeared, but it was ample proof something was going on with the street.

"This is an array that has started to leak out from a neighboring building," Joanna said. "Go around or push through?"

"Let's just go around it," Zac said, not in the mood to tempt fate or risk new wounds when he'd just started getting better.

In this manner, they slowly made their way toward the center of the town, guided by the ripples in Zac's mind and the map prepared by his explorers. Only five minutes passed when they were forced to reroute again to avoid another array that crept out across the area, forming a seemingly bottomless lake.

It was an odd feeling seeing the varied phenomena. The city was dead, yet it kept reinventing itself. These aberrations would either be reined in as the array self-healed or when the arrays ran out of power. Thankfully, these were the biggest surprises they encountered until they reached their destination: a desolate square only decorated with a huge statue.

A decent number of chunks of the enormous statue were missing, but it looked like it had once depicted a 23-layered wave or rainbow, each layer made from a different type of rock. It was over 100 meters tall and half as wide, and Zac initially thought it was a building. At this distance, the structure was clearly only decorative.

It felt like a brutalist statement in the otherwise sparse environment. Zac didn't initially understand why he felt this region so dour, but he soon realized what made this place stand out—the square was caked with a layer of dust, lacking any vegetation that otherwise covered the ruins.

Even then, it didn't look like the statue was the origin of the ripples. It rather originated from a majestic temple standing at the edge of the square. Its five-meter gates were wide open, and a path of destruction had been formed from them in the shape of a cone. For some reason, the statue itself was unscathed, while everything else had presumably been turned into ash.

"This is it," Zac said. "My piece is inside that building, it looks like. See the dust? That's what happens to you if you get too close to a piece that's not fated with you."

"At least it would be painless," Rhuger said grimly while taking an extra step back.

"What's your plan here?" Ogras asked.

Zac studied the eroded temple for a few seconds, feeling the pull from the seal within. Just seeing it with his own eyes was a source of great comfort. He knew himself well enough by now. If he hadn't come here, his mind would keep coming back to it, wondering how exposed it was. Now, they just needed to seal this place up.

"We'll begin with setting up a protective barrier around the square and temple," Zac said. "Later, we'll station some trusted warriors in some of the ruins here to ensure no one tries to sneak inside."

Zac took out the series of prepared array flags, each looking like a one-meter-spike hanging from a tripod. The cobblestones were too durable to break apart, but the relentless river of time had given them an opening through all the vegetation. There were gaps everywhere, and one spike after another sunk into the ground, forming a perimeter roughly 100 meters away from the temple and the square.

The work hit some snags because of two still-active arrays in the vicinity, but Zac had more than enough flags prepared. Soon enough, an invisible fence was erected. It wouldn't keep out a determined Peak E-grade cultivator forever, but it was more than enough for reinforcements to arrive.

With that, Zac saw no reason to stay, considering he'd done what he could to share the quest. He wasn't in any state to properly explore these ruins, and he would recover faster back in his cave. However, it looked like only Ogras would follow him back to Earth.

"We're staying here for the time being," Vilari said after sharing a look with Rhuger and Joanna. "We'll explore this place and search for clues to the inheritance. We've been here before, but now we know which runes to look out for."

"Don't worry, we'll deal with the guards as well," Joanna added.

"Alright," Zac said. "But try to return to Port Atwood in three months at the latest. And don't overdo it. Fate can't be forced. Most of the seals are waiting in the Million Gates Territory, so it's not the end of the world even if you don't find anything here. And try to send a message first in case you plan on entering any sort of ruins. We don't want another Janos situation on our hands."

Ideally, Zac would have wanted to get some life tablets as well, but tablets strong enough to track E-grade cultivators across any significant distances were pretty difficult to make. Besides, few bothered crafting them, at least in Zecia. After all, E-grade cultivators generally stayed within the confines of their clans or traveled with their elders. What was the point of tracking them with an expensive tablet?

"Don't worry about us," Vilari said. "Focus on your recovery and let the others deal with the day-to-day."

"Good luck." Zac smiled, giving the brooding temple one last look before turning away.

Now, it was up to fate whether the others could find the key to the courts. If not, Zac would have to figure out another way to get a couple of followers from the outside to fill up the numbers. Luckily, he had a pretty good solution for that—Catheya and the Undead Empire. They would probably be more than happy to send some competent followers his way in exchange for access to the Left Imperial Palace.

———

Catheya ran her hand through the dense clouds of death that danced in the fountains, and she took a calming breath as she looked up at the familiar architecture of her kin. She had to admit it was a welcome change from the wretched environment she and her guardian had stayed in during the past months.

Even with beacons holding life at bay on an unawakened planet, it felt like you were trapped in a small bubble, and the whole universe was bearing down on you. It was an unwelcome reminder of how limited her sky was, yet Catheya couldn't help but want to go back.

"Is it really alright to leave that man to his own devices?" Catheya asked with worry as they walked toward the teleportation chamber. "He might do something foolish."

"Who? The Dreamer or the brat?" Enis asked.

"Well, both, I guess, but I was thinking of the Dreamer."

"He should understand his place by now," Enis answered without care. "If that Dreamer tries to break the restriction, only an early awakening awaits him. Besides, he is incredibly meek by nature. I would guess it will take years before he dares so much as nudge that mark with his Mental Energy."

"But our line of communication—"

"Can be reinstated through another proxy, if need be," Enis concluded. "Now, remember to mind your manners. Your irreverence cannot be allowed to cause any friction or problems. Don't forget, this mission even has the Heart's attention."

"I know," Catheya said with a roll of her eyes. "Just doesn't sit right with me. This was our mission, and suddenly we're sidelined? And they won't even tell us any real details."

Enis didn't immediately answer, though Catheya could tell there was a hint of annoyance between her brows. It was no wonder. She was a competent warrior of Clan Umbri'Zi, but she held no real political sway in her clan. This mission, one ordered by the Abyssal Lake and the Umbri'Zi Ancestor herself, was a chance for Enis to accrue enough credit to take up a better role and accumulate more resources.

Perhaps even gain a permanent spot at the Abyssal Shores, which would drastically improve her chances of confirming her Dao.

But now, just as they'd finally managed to contact that troublemaker, they were sent back home, ordered to assist some newcomer in an undertaking of great import. One that their own target was apparently part of.

A wave of reluctance tugged at Catheya as they entered the enormous hall reserved for exalted visitors, almost regretting she shared her method of contact with the Undead Empire. Before, it was like everything had clicked into place, and she could confidently say she upheld her promise. She even held onto some sort of farfetched conviction that Zac would manage to break the convention of Edgewalkers, allowing him to stay on as he'd been.

Now? Who was to say what would happen.

Catheya knew one thing—when 'matters of great import' were being discussed, people became expendable in the face of goals and benefits. Especially outsiders without any proper backing. Like Zac. Clan Umbri'Zi might have claimed him as their own to gobble up some of the rewards, but they would just as quickly discard him if the benefits from this undertaking eclipsed those of a Draugr Edgewalker with a small chance of bolstering one of their incomplete bloodlines.

The two found Tassar Kavriel and his most promising descendant already standing at attention in front of the platform when they arrived. The old man's eyes kept shifting to the teleportation array, waiting for the new arrivals to appear.

"Mistress, young miss," Tassar said with a nod.

"Lady Umbri'Zi, Lady Sharva'Zi," Rezo Kavriel followed up with a much-deeper bow.

"Hello," Catheya said. "Uncle, have you heard anything?"

Tassar Kavriel had taken care of her since she and her master arrived in Zecia the first time around. And with Va Tapek entering seclusion, or rather leaving to search for some item as Catheya found out later, this old Monarch and his descendants had been the ones to accompany her most of the time.

Tassar's ancestor was an illegitimate mixed-blood son of one of the supreme elders of the Umbri'Zi. Since his talent was quite good, a pure-blooded Draugr had been arranged as a Dao Partner. They'd then been sent off to manage this newly integrated Sector. Millions of years had passed since then, and the Kavriel Clan was almost completely detached from the Umbri'Zi.

As far as Catheya could tell, that was fine with Tassar. His position was extremely secure thanks to his heritage, and no factions were powerful enough to shake the Undead Empire in Zecia. No one from above pushed him to expand faster either, so he simply waged the occasional war to satisfy the commandments.

Apart from the lacking materials, it was a cushy life. Except chaos was now knocking at his door, and Catheya could see new lines of worry had appeared on the face of the kindly old man.

"Nothing yet," Tassar said. "But it shouldn't be long now."

No one was in the mood to talk, and they stood in silence for 30 minutes until the array hummed to life. A moment later, eight new people appeared in a flash of spatial death. They all seemed extremely powerful, but two drew more attention than the others for natural reasons. They were Izh'Rak Reavers, each one attended by a Revenant.

The Reaver standing in the back was most likely a Monarch. They emitted no aura, but a sense of unfathomable momentum was locked within their frame. The other one was a Hegemon, and their monstrously condensed aura was on full display. Catheya felt her vision swim as she was drowned in murderous intent, while Rezo gasped and was forced to take a step back.

"Sorry, sorry," the younger Reaver laughed as he stepped off the platform, his attention surprisingly on Rezo. "Didn't even puke. Not bad. Join my squad later, yeah?"

"I—ah?" Rezo hesitated, his eyes unsurprisingly darting toward the other half of the group.

They were two pureblooded Draugr, flanked by a Revenant and Corpselord. Just like with the other part of the contingent, it looked like they were two Monarchs accompanying two Hegemons. Catheya couldn't fathom the price paid to force not one but four Monarchs through the seal that surrounded Zecia.

"Enough, Kator," the other Reaver said. "The elders have already decided on the rules for the formation of your battalions."

Catheya and Enis shared a look. Battalions?

"Welcome," Enis said while Tassar was content to take on a background role in front of these powerful guests. "I am Enis Umbri'Zi, and my ward here is Catheya Sharva'Zi. I pray your long journey was not too taxing."

Enis' displeasure had only increased after seeing these new arrivals judging by her small frown. After all, these two Draugr were unfamiliar faces, and even Catheya could tell they weren't part of the Zi bloodline, even if they kept their auras in check.

"Thank you," the older Draugr, he too a Monarch, said with a curt nod. "Laz Tem'Zul."

Catheya looked at the man curiously. Zul was a branch on the rise, and Tem'Zul was one of the most powerful clans of that surname. They essentially enjoyed a similar position as the Umbri'Zi, which only increased Catheya's confusion. Why had someone from the Zul been sent to Zecia, when this was technically the domain of the Zi?

After all, the Umbri'Zi already had Monarchs stuck outside the Sector seal. Why forcibly grant these people entry while keeping the Zi out? Were there some conflicts brewing between the factions of the Abyssal Shores? And who was this woman who hadn't deigned to speak up, even if she was clearly just a Hegemon like the Reaver?

"And young miss is…?" Catheya hesitated after getting a pointed glance from Enis.

"Tavza An'Azol," the annoyingly beautiful woman said, her face remaining impassive.

Catheya's eyes widened in shock, and she hurriedly curtsied. Even Enis was alarmed by that surname, and her small frown transformed into a somewhat strained smile. Catheya couldn't fault her guardian for putting on such a fake façade.

What else could you do when a direct descendant of an Abyssal Prince stood in front of you?

However, a thought struck Catheya, and she glanced at the Izh'Rak Reaver. He'd already retracted his overwhelming aura, but Catheya still remembered its terror. Considering his almost unfathomable accumulations and how he showed no deference to a Descendant of An'Azol, his origin couldn't be simple either.

"Hey, lass, I'm Kator. That there is Brigadier Toss. We're from the White Sky Phalanx," Kator said. "The other two are Pavina and Umbar."

Catheya shuddered as she curtsied again. As expected, these people came from one of the three Royal Phalanxes of the Izh'Rak Reavers. This was big. Too big. To the point Catheya almost felt suffocated. The already frayed realm of certainty was fast collapsing around her, and the next words out of the Reaver's skull only made the matter worse.

"Now, where is this half-dreaming native who holds the key to the castle?"

# GATES OF REBIRTH

"How about it? Should we take a look around?" Ogras asked as he and Zac made their way toward the edge of the Ensolus Ruins.

"My body is still all kinds of messed up," Zac said with a helpless shake of his head. "You can go ahead if you want to, though."

"Without your supercharged fate to keep me safe?" Ogras scoffed. "I suppose there's no real urgency. It's not like any outsiders can access this place in the short run. But we should perform a proper sweep before the war starts. Who knows what kind of good stuff this place holds? After all, no one did war better than the Limitless Empire."

"Agreed. Although, Janos might still be in here."

"Honestly, if he's been trapped in the equivalent of one of those temples we visited in the Void Star, there's not much we can do about it," Ogras said. "We'd just get disintegrated if we tried barging in. And if his disappearance isn't related to the Left Imperial Palace…"

Zac sighed with a nod.

"Well, those three will scour this place with new information over the next months, and they know about Janos. If they find something promising, they'll let us know," Ogras said. "Though, should *you* investigate, with your luck, it would be even better."

"I'll take a look just in case after I've fully healed up," Zac said.

"Perfect, thank you," Ogras said. "You might want to set up your trial while we're here. Most of them have limits on how many can undergo it a day. With four years remaining, you want to cycle as many people through the gauntlet as possible."

"Oh, right," Zac said. "We'll place it close to Zelphi Watch on the way back."

The Ensolus Ruins being related to Ultom had thrown Zac for a loop, but he ultimately felt it didn't affect his long-term plans for the planet. It could still serve as a front-facing world to trade with neighboring empires like Salosar or Havenfort World. After all, there were almost 100 years until the Assimilation.

By then, the first stage of Ultom's inheritance was bound to be over and the ruins thoroughly searched. If not, they'd have to keep the world closed-off for another generation or two until things cooled down. They could even dismantle the whole Ensolus Ruins to avoid any unwanted attention.

As for rumors spreading, Zac wasn't worried. There were millions and millions of places with old ruins in Zecia. That alone wasn't enough to cause any waves without knowing its relation to Ultom. And that was limited to the five people currently in the ruins, and possibly Calrin. And any lingering clues of the connection was already being quietly scrubbed clean by the Valkyries and his core personnel.

As for Zelphi's Watch, it was one of the frontier forts on the continent, one that had previously belonged to a fairly weak Incursion force. It was far from any critical architecture or resources, surrounded by inhospitable mountains. Meanwhile, there was still room for an enormous trade city in case their plans worked out, which made it the perfect site for the trial.

"By the way, what do you think about the Zhix?" Zac asked as they walked. "I'm thinking of giving Rhubat the same opportunity as the other three."

It'd been a while since he'd visited the leader of the Zhix, but he read in the reports that the Zhix were still struggling with finding a proper path that would take them beyond the initial steps of cultivation. If humanity had been hit by the loss of Origin Dao in the atmosphere, the effect on the Zhix was magnified fivefold.

Rhubat and the other Anointed had looked for solutions that would allow their conformist society to embark on the road of cultivation, a journey that generally required more personal introspection than the Zhix was interested in. Even after years of searching, they were no closer than when they started.

However, getting access to the epiphanies of the Left Imperial Palace and the Outer Courts might be what would allow Rhubat to perfect the homebrewed cultivation system of the Zhix. At the very least push it to a level that would allow a larger number of common warriors to form their Dao Seeds and step into the E-grade.

"Those guys?" Ogras said. "Well, he's capable enough, but he's not really part of your faction."

Zac nodded in agreement. That was the crux of the matter and why he hadn't invited Rhubat to the war meeting the other week. It didn't really matter that the Status Screens of the Zhix Hives said they belonged to the Atwood Empire. The Zhix were Zhix, beholden only to their own. Even if he had a good relationship with the insectoids, there was an insurmountable divide between them.

Even today, ten years after the Integration, the Zhix barely interacted with the other races on Earth. The occasional representative appeared in Port Atwood to deal with various matters, and explorers sometimes ran into Zhix hunting squads in the wild. But that was about it.

Everything was fine today, but who knew how things would look in 100 years? In ten thousand? Strengthening the Zhix would help in the short run with the war, but it might lead to unexpected consequences. Just give it a few generations, and the leaders of the Zhix might not feel it fair for them to play second fiddle to the Atwood Empire.

And by that point, he would possibly be long gone, headed for the Six Profundity Empire or other opportunities in the Multiverse.

"We still have some time to find a solution," Ogras shrugged. "And I don't think even you can just point at people and fill their spirits with divine providence. Who knows how the Left Imperial Palace chooses its candidates? We can figure out what to do with those crazy insectoids after these three have looked around these ruins for a while."

Zac agreed. This endeavor was ultimately just a long shot, even if he had gained a quest from it. Still, Zac hoped Vilari, Rhuger, and Joanna's fates would align more with the Left Imperial Palace by walking through the Ensolus Ruins for a month or two. That might be what allowed them to sense the seals when heading into the Million Gates Territory.

"More importantly, how about we invite those Mavai for the inauguration?" Ogras said with a familiar gleam in his eyes.

"Still?" Zac snorted.

"I'm just curious to see these Life-attuned demons," Ogras grinned. "But now that you mention it... tribal women..."

Zac could only helplessly shake his head. "We'll invite representatives from both sides to Zelphi's Watch."

The two passed through the shroud at the edge of the ruins a while later and set course for the border fort. Thankfully, most of the preparations were already complete, and they could teleport straight there after flying to the closest teleportation array. It didn't take long for two groups of representatives to arrive, each one led by the leaders of the respective factions.

"Lord Atwood, I heard you had returned. It is good to see you," Ra'Klid, the young Mavai Chieftain, said as he curiously looked at Ogras. "This is?"

"Ogras Azh'Rezak." Ogras nodded as he looked curiously at the warriors. "Very interesting. You're really a new form of demonkin not registered within the horde."

"So we heard," Ra'Klid said with a smile. "Lord Azh'Rezak, we have heard of your great exploits from your followers and would love to have you visit our tribes at your convenience. The Mavai could gain a lot from your experience."

"Of course," Ogras said.

"Lord Atwood," Aouvi, one of the two remaining Ghost Kings of the Raun, called as he floated over. "May I ask why you have called us here?"

"Part of it is to update you on some important matters," Zac said. "Secondly, it is time to finally open the Limited Trial I previously mentioned."

"The opportunity that will provide Limited Titles?" Ra'Klid said with excitement. "Can we undergo the trial? How many slots are there?"

"No idea," Zac said with a smile. "I won't know much until I receive the reward. I just know it should be a pretty good one."

There wasn't much else to say, so they moved to the edge of the large basin, far away from the small settlement that acted as a placeholder for the future city that would be built there. At that point, Zac finally accepted the quest reward that had been waiting for him for almost a decade.

The effect was immediate, and the whole valley started to heave. A few seconds later, the ground cracked as a massive wall of gold and black rose from below. Seeing the colors, Zac's eyes lit up with interest, and his guess was soon confirmed as powerful waves of life and death started to radiate from the wall.

Soon enough, the shaking stopped, and a structure reaching over five hundred meters into the air had already appeared. It didn't look like a proper building, more resembling a huge coin pushed halfway into the ground. It was as wide as it was tall but no thicker than ten meters.

By the looks of it, the wall was constructed with two types of metals that failed to mix properly. Chaotic and unpredictable patterns of gold and black covered its surface.

At its center, two gates stood next to each other, each roughly ten meters tall. One was golden and radiated powerful waves of life; the other was black and filled with death. Oddly enough, Zac sensed hints of death from the golden gate and the opposite from the black one.

Above the gates, two lines were carved, each stroke instilled with a deep understanding of the two opposing Daos. To Zac, the words contained the same level of comprehension as the scars on the Big Boss' Big Wall back at the Big Axe Coliseum. In contrast, the meaning was somehow sealed into the letters, preventing Zac from actually gaining anything from them. Still, the words gave a clear hint of what was going on.

"*Gate of Life* and *Gate of Death*, huh?" Ogras muttered as he glanced at the two groups of natives. "How fitting."

Zac was reviewing a short burst of information he'd just received. The natives looked at the two doors with desire before turning to Zac.

"Give me a second," Zac said. "Can you check out the surroundings, meanwhile?"

The groups nodded and started to look around, short of entering the structure.

"Behind!" a startled Ra'Klid soon exclaimed.

Zac and Ogras flashed over and stopped in confusion upon seeing what was hidden behind the huge metallic half-circle. Having just visited the overgrown Ensolus Ruins, Zac was filled with a sense of déjà vu.

Instead of an ancient city being overtaken by plant life, it was rather a dour graveyard.

Pitch-black crypts and coffins covered the area behind the trial. They were covered in vibrant roots, some as thick as a full-grown man. However, in contrast to the Ensolus Ruins, the graveyard was in pristine condition. There wasn't a single blemish on the coffins, and they exuded stable waves of death.

"How odd," Aouvi muttered.

"I don't know exactly what waits inside, but I have some preliminary information," Zac said. "This trial is called the Gates of Rebirth. Right now, one hundred people can pass through each gate daily, meaning 1,400 warriors can receive a title every week. You can only pass through the gates once. There are six levels to the trial, and passing each level will improve the title you receive."

Ogras frowned. "What about the attunements? Can only the undead enter the Door of Death?"

"It didn't explicitly say, but it seems that Life and Death cultivators have an advantage for this trial," Zac said. "You'd have to be pretty damn strong to reach the top floor without cultivating either of those two paths."

"Well, isn't that great," Ogras scowled, looking like he wanted to stab the enormous wall.

Zac smiled. "Even the fifth-layer-reward should be pretty good compared to most publicly available trials."

This was a reward for his S-grading on his Sovereignty quest chain. He figured the title had to be at least comparable to the top-tier titles like the one he got in the Big Axe Coliseum.

"Few opportunities come without risk. Lord Atwood, can you esti-mate difficulties and casualty rates?" one of the shamans of the Mavai asked.

"No idea," Zac said with a shake of his head. "But you can only leave after completing each of the six layers. Using pills like **[Coward's Escape]** might send you out, but there are no guarantees. And even if it works, you'd definitely not get a title. Overestimating your strength might cost you your opportunity at best, or even get you killed."

"That is natural," the chieftain said, and the spectrals nodded in agreement.

"So, does anyone want to give it a go?" Zac asked. "Scouting out the Gates of Rebirth to sound out the challenges and opportunities would provide Contribution Points as well."

"You're not going first?" Ra'Klid said with surprise.

"All my Limited Title slots are filled, and I'm in no rush. I'll see how the rewards look first," Zac said.

Zac could always reject a Limited Title if it was worse than the ones he already had. The real reason was the state he was in. Going inside now would be a waste of an opportunity, especially considering he hadn't even forged his Life-attuned Constitution yet. There was time to revisit this place after he made some inroads into the [**Void Vajra Sublimation**].

"I'll go!" the young chieftain said with excitement plastered all over his face.

"Wait," one of the old advisors said. "Let one of us old bones step through the gates first to test the waters. We don't know what to expect, and we can't have you dying at this critical juncture."

"A chieftain can't be afraid of death," Ra'Klid said with annoyance, though he did relent. "Alright, which one of you want to go?"

"I'll do it," an old axe-wielder Zac recognized from the peace summit said.

The man was at the Peak of the E-grade and exuded both the aura of a warrior and of one cultivating the Dao of Life, making him a perfect candidate. Similarly, a spectral warrior stepped forward to enter the Gate of Death.

The group walked over to the front of the Gates of Rebirth, and the gates soundlessly swung open. On the other side were just two swirls, but the golden gate held a shimmering swirl made from Death-attuned energy. The opposite was true for the Gate of Death.

"The Gate of Life is made from Miasma?" Ogras muttered with confusion. "And a Gate of Death filled with Life?"

"Uh…" Zac said as the others looked at him with inquiring glances. "I honestly have no idea."

"Fighting against death is part of life," the seasoned Mavai warrior said. "I'll still enter the Gate of Life."

"I shall follow suit and enter the Gate of Death," the spectral warrior said.

"Even if the element is wrong, you should at least pass the first layer of the trial," Zac said. "Just go out instead of overdoing it if it's the wrong path."

They nodded and were swallowed by the swirls a moment later.

"How long will this take?" Ogras asked.

"Six hours," Zac said. "The burst of information was very clear on that point, at least."

The group set up a table to wait for the two to emerge, and Zac took the opportunity to update the Mavai and Raun on the situation with the war. The Raun hesitantly asked about the problem with them betraying the Undead Empire. Zac answered that Arcaz would meet up with his allies from the Empire soon enough and that he'd have a definite answer in a couple of months.

The subject of the Kingdom of Raun really was something Zac planned on discussing with Catheya, and he didn't believe the Undead Empire would cause a stink over a small tribe of ghosts at the edge of the Multiverse.

Eventually, the six hours had passed, but Zac frowned when the gates showed no sign of reopening.

"I felt a ripple from the graveyard," Aouvi said.

"Let's go." Zac flashed away.

By the time they reached the backside of the trial area, they could immediately spot signs of activity.

"What in the…" Ra'Klid muttered as he saw the Mavai warrior push open the lid of a coffin and crawl outside.

Similarly, a thick bulbous plant was cut apart, allowing the ghost to emerge from within. Zac breathed out with relief upon seeing they were mostly fine, though the Mavai warrior sported some pretty nasty wounds. Zac had no idea why the trial would send out people like this, but it was fine so long as they were alive.

"How was it?" Zac asked.

"It was…" the warrior said, only to freeze. "Huh? Why can't I remember?"

# LIFE THROUGH DEATH

"You can't remember?" Ra'Klid frowned. "This is no time for jokes."

"I... can't remember anything either," the spectral warrior said as he floated over.

"Nothing? Nothing at all?" Zac asked.

"Well, that's not completely true," the Mavai warrior said. "First of all, I remember being in a marvelous state after completing the challenge. I can't properly remember it, but I can *feel* it. Like I was in the womb, full of life. I've made some progress on my Dao Fragment."

"I was in a similar state," the ghost nodded. "Like my soul had been taken through the cycle of reincarnation, visiting the other side. I, too, have made some progress on my Dao."

"A Limited Trial providing insight?" Ogras muttered. "Sounds quite rare."

"You still got an insight into Life even though the entrance itself reeked of Death?" Zac asked.

"That's right," the demon nodded.

"Life through death," Zac muttered as he looked at the two warriors.

Small hints of death lingered on the body of the Mavai warrior, and streaks of Life-attuned Energies ran through the incorporeal body of the Raun Spectral. But was that from their encounters inside or a result of the way the Gates of Rebirth sent them out?

"What level did you two reach?" Zac asked.

"I do remember that. I reached the Fourth Layer," the Mavai elder said as he shared his newly acquired title.

[**Gate of Life - Fourth Layer:** Reach the Fourth Layer of the Gates of Rebirth. **Reward:** Strength, Vitality +4%.]

"Even you only reached the Fourth Layer, and barely so by the looks of your wounds." Ra'Klid frowned. "Didn't your Dao Fragment reach Late Mastery recently thanks to the resources of the Atwood Empire?"

"I—" the Mavai Warrior stumbled over his words, unsure what to say.

Zac could understand the problem. He was most likely one of the most skilled warriors of the Mavai, yet he barely scraped by to get an above-average result. Even if he wasn't someone like Zac, he was still a progenitor who had not only shored up his foundations for over a century before the Integration, but also enjoyed a series of opportunities when the System arrived.

It was worth remembering this wasn't the Tower of Eternity, which was legendarily difficult to ascend. It was just a local Limited Trial. Zac still remembered the tens of thousands of memorial tablets and trinkets left behind at the bottom of the Havenfort Chasm. Similarly, seeing someone become a proper Big Axe Gladiator was an exciting event, but it was by no means unheard of. People who passed all five levels of the challenge didn't necessarily appear yearly, but they weren't that rare.

At the same time, the warrior had a hard time defending himself or explaining since he didn't remember a thing. He could only look at his warchief with resignation and confusion, clearly none too happy with his own performance either.

"What about you?" Zac asked as he turned to the Raun Warrior.

"I also reached the Fourth Layer," the ghost said, and another screen appeared as the ghost ate a soulmending pill Zac recognized. It was part of the wares he'd brought back from Twilight Harbor.

[**Gate of Death - Fourth Layer:** Reach the Fourth Layer of the Gates of Reincarnation. **Reward:** Wisdom, Endurance +4%.]

"Completely different attributes," Zac muttered. "How are they related to your builds?"

"Strength is my main attribute," the warrior said, not to anyone's surprise considering the man's arms were even thicker than Zac's. "I also have some Vitality due to my Dao, but not from my class. It is my third highest attribute."

"I focus on Wisdom and Dexterity," the ghost said. "Endurance is not an attribute I focus on. I just gain some of it from my Dao Fragment."

"Does Endurance even work on ghosts?" Ogras asked curiously.

"It does," Aouvi said. "It strengthens our bodies just like it would yours, and helps us resist Dao-infused attacks better. Though many of us focus on defenses through other venues than taking direct hits."

"Your soul is wounded?" Zac asked as he turned away from the Title Screen.

"It is," the spectral sighed. "It's not a grievous wound, though. I will recover in two weeks. I'm afraid I can't remember what hurt me, but the wounds contain a hint of life. That might be a clue?"

Zac nodded as he went over the information. By the looks of it, the difficulty of the trial was somewhat serious, but it did provide a burst of insight in addition to just a Limited Title. Say that these two warriors managed to pass one additional level thanks to cultivating the right Dao, then most elite warriors of Port Atwood should be able to get a third-level title.

3% in two attributes wasn't too impressive, but it wasn't bad for the average warrior, especially considering almost no one on Earth had any Limited Titles. In addition, you got a second opportunity in the form of enlightenment. That might be what allowed some of his followers to break through a bottlenecked Dao Seed or Dao Fragment. Unfortunately, this part of the trial was more useful for the natives of Ensolus than Earth's citizens.

Even if Earth's attunement was becoming more apparent by the day, there were still few Life or Death cultivators among the ranks of the earthlings. Most of Port Atwood's elites had been there for the Integration, enjoying the Origin Dao and unique opportunities back then. More and more new cultivators chose paths related to life and death, so this trial would become increasingly useful as the years passed.

And Zac, who had visited the Havenfort Chasm with the hidden Equanimity title, couldn't help but wonder if something special would happen upon passing the final level of the trial. Would you get an even better title? Or would your Dao-related opportunity become better?

In either case, the trial seemed to be a top-tiered one, at least for a region like Zecia. The unfortunate part was that the two warriors didn't remember anything about what they encountered, making it difficult to properly prepare future trial takers for the dangers within.

"It's a decent first set of data, but we need more people to pass through the gates if we're to figure out the hidden rules," Ogras muttered, echoing Zac's thoughts. "Even if people get their minds wiped, we can still extrapolate important information over time."

"We'll start bringing more people over," Zac agreed as the group walked back toward the settlement.

However, soon after they passed the wall, Ra'Klid exclaimed after glancing back. "Look!"

"A ladder?" Zac muttered as his eyes followed where the demon pointed.

To the left of the Golden gate, a singular name had appeared at the top of an engraved plaque large enough to contain quite a few names.

### [1. Gorund Shatterstone. 4th level, 4:32:21]

Similarly, a second plaque had been engraved to the right of the Gate of Death.

### [1. Souva Telosir. 4th level, 4:18:44]

"Just over one hour per level," Ra'Klid muttered. "But why…"

"Why were they sent out at six hours on the dot?" Ogras continued with a nod. "Should be the Dao opportunity?"

"Perhaps the quicker you pass the trials, the more time you'll have to enjoy the Dao Enlightenment," Zac hummed. "We'll set up a series of experiments."

Zac wasn't in any real hurry to go back, so he stayed on to oversee the groups of elite warriors who were sent through the gates just an hour later. The first batch was made up of an equal split of Mavai, Raun, Einherjar, and Port Atwood Elites. And in their wake were thousands of workers who started expanding the settlement with speed visible to the naked eye.

Over the next few days, a steady stream of warriors entered the Gates of Rebirth, and every batch brought a new set of findings. They first noticed that no one managed to leave with their memories intact. Everyone remembered which floor they reached, though that was about it.

Secondly, they found that the big ladders only displayed 100 warriors at a time, but you could see more names if you touched them. Since there were only six layers, the rankings were mostly based on time since all top ten results had only reached the Fourth Layer. Everyone always emerged after 6 hours at the dot, though some finished their run after just one or two hours.

By the second day, it was all but confirmed that a quicker run resulted in more time to enjoy the Dao Enlightenment. However, this only applied to those who cultivated Life or Death. Anyone could enter, but only those with either a Pure or mixed-meaning Dao related to Life or Death would gain any comprehension.

It also seemed that reaching a higher tier resulted in a better burst of Dao, which meant that stopping at a low layer to spend more time focusing on the Dao wouldn't work. After just three days, there had already been a couple of breakthroughs, and all those came from those who reached the third or fourth level.

You could also leave whatever name you wanted behind, and a Port Atwood soldier had left behind the name 'Banana Man' for some reason when asked to see if he could modify it afterward. You could also skip leaving behind your name altogether, but it looked like you'd lose access to the Dao Enlightenment if you did.

As for benefits, there didn't appear to be any with leaving your name behind on the ladder, except for the bragging rights. But that was more than enough for some of the competitive cultivators, and each faction of the Atwood Empire tried to keep as many top spots as possible.

They also confirmed you didn't need to be undead to enter the Door of Death, and Revenants wouldn't get killed by trying out the Life-attuned challenge. However, the undead were clearly disadvantaged when entering the Gate of Life. Similarly, the Mavai were punished for entering the Gate of Death, though the effect wasn't as pronounced. As for unattuned beings like normal humans, it didn't matter which gate they chose.

The most sobering realization was that **[Coward's Escape]** did not seem to work in this trial. Everyone would be sent out alive with a title or as a corpse. The trial was not without risks, even if you could opt out after each stage. Altogether, the death rate was only 5%, but that was still ten of the Atwood Empire's elites that would die every day as long as they kept filling the slots.

Furthermore, the people they sent through the gauntlet at this point were all handpicked for both their talent and survivability. Zac wouldn't be surprised if the mortality rate increased even further as the months passed and the more common talents had their turn. Still, Zac saw no reason to seal off the opportunity.

Like the shaman said before, risk and reward came hand in hand. However, he couldn't make it mandatory for his soldiers with the mortality rate. Instead, they would list it as a limited resource that would normally cost Contribution Points to enjoy but would be free for the upcoming years. That should make enough people want to pass through the gauntlet.

Soon a week had passed, and Zac stood at the edge of the graveyard with a few envoys to his side. The next batch of trial takers were about to emerge, and everyone kept their eyes peeled on the large golden flowers and the crypts. Everyone had soon figured out that the better your performance, the nicer the item you'd emerge from.

The first two warriors had emerged from an inlaid stone coffin and a sturdy root, but not everyone was so lucky. A few had been forced to crawl out from beneath the ground, covered in maggots and smelling of death. Yet no one emerged from any of the crypts or golden bulbs, meaning they were reserved for those who reached the highest layers of the trial.

Soon enough, dozens of roots started to wiggle while coffins shuddered. There were no bursts of energy or activity from the top-tiered exits.

"Still not enough," Ra'Klid sighed. "Just how difficult is this trial?"

"There's no rush," Zac said. "Sooner or later, someone will pass the fourth level, and we'll have our answers if anything's changed."

"You're still not...?" the chieftain hesitated.

"No," Zac said. "Everything is running smoothly, and I can't waste any more time here. I'm going back to cultivate."

"I understand," Ra'Klid said, then nodded to the others to give them some space. "Before you go. I've heard rumors. Rumors of an expedition into the Million Gates Territory."

"You want to go?" Zac asked with surprise. "What about the Mavai?"

"The council can manage the daily affairs. I need to follow in your footsteps to gain the strength to protect my people. A civilization without an ancestor to keep the ship stable will soon capsize," Ra'Klid said.

"I'm not involved in this Incursion, so I'm not involved in the final decision of personnel," Zac said. "But I'll mention your request when I go back. They'll set off in a few months, so prepare yourself."

"Thank you," Ra'Klid said with a bow. "I will."

Zac flashed away, heading for the teleportation array. A few jumps later, he was back in his cultivation cave. From here on out, his administrators would figure out a system to extract as much value as possible from the Gates of Rebirth over the next four years. The nitty-gritty was for others to figure out. Zac was more interested in continuing his recovery and cultivation.

He was still months from being in perfect condition. Still, he was approaching the point where he could continue with his training regimen, and Zac had Triv prepare another nurturing bath. A week later, Zac sat alone in the center of his cave, and the energies of Life and Death clashed all around him. However, Zac's attention was fully on a shimmering crystal in his hand—a Dao Stone he'd gotten from Ogras.

There were more of them waiting in his Spatial Ring, more than enough for his purposes. It was finally time to upgrade his Branch of the War Axe. Zac first evolved his Fragment of the Axe into the Branch of the War Axe in the hidden valley of the Twilight Chasm, where he witnessed the super condensed Daos of Life and Death clash.

All the while, the mysterious egg he got from Va Tapek had purified and released more and more energy, almost pushing him into a state of hysterical madness. He unknowingly found his answer in that environment, where he rejected Twilight's unity of Life and Death, and instead confirmed his own Path.

Many things had happened since then, and his experiences long since made up for his rushed breakthrough. Most important of which, he'd spent years inside the Orom, completely reforging his understanding of combat and technique. Then the events in the Void Star followed, where his techniques and strength were tested to their limits.

He fought, bled, and struggled to the point that his understanding of conflict was more than enough to upgrade his Dao again. If his constitution had been normal, he would already have taken that step naturally. But now, it was just a matter of ingesting treasures while holding onto his vision.

Upgrading one's Dao wasn't dangerous or taxing, but Zac still surveyed his soul to ensure it was in decent enough shape to avoid any surprises and mishaps. The rotating cores in his Soul Aperture still showed some hairline cracks after his battle with the Qriz'Ul goblin and being drowned in both Creation and Oblivion, but they'd stabilized.

The damage was on the mend, and the Remnant energies would be fully purged in a month or so. It was good enough. Zac focused on the crystal and tried to drag out the Origin Dao it contained. These crystals of Pure comprehension would become the fuel, allowing him to make a breakthrough without any interference by external inspiration.

But nothing happened.

Zac looked at the crystal with confusion. It wasn't defective—he could sense the pure truths trapped within. It was like a diluted version of that white light that upgraded his Dao the last time—the Primal Dao. Or perhaps it was more apt to liken it to an untainted version of the energy released by Salvation's Dao Funnel.

Yet it refused to listen to his command, as though the crystal casing was an impassable barrier. It felt a lot like the Cosmic Energy around him, which simply refused to listen to his call when he tried using Cultivation Manuals as a mortal. Zac looked at the stone for a few seconds before sighing in defeat. Some things never changed.

With a lack of better options, Zac put the crystal in his mouth and bit down, prompting a shattering sound to echo through the chamber.

# EATING THROUGH

Zac chewed on the Dao Stone and swallowed it with the assistance of some water. Thank god no one else was in his cultivation cave. Zac could only imagine what someone like Emily or Ogras would say upon seeing him cultivating more like a beast than a cultivator as he took out a second crystal and bit down.

The shards and dust created from the cracked crystal tasted bland and were incredibly dry. At least his 16,000 Endurance was more than enough to protect the inside of his mouth and stomach from being lacerated by the innumerable sharp edges. More importantly, it worked. Streams of pure comprehension flowed toward his mind, where he had his Dao Avatar absorb it before [Spiritual Void] could take too much of it for its own.

The Dao Stones contained Origin Dao just like Ogras said, and not a speck of Origin Dao was wasted with this delivery method. He did have a decent stockpile of the unique resource, thanks to a heated bout of haggling with Ogras. But he absolutely didn't have enough to wantonly release their precious contents, like he sometimes did with Cosmic Crystals to improve the ambient atmosphere. Still, one crystal after another entered his gullet, and the trickle of Origin Dao soon became a steady river that fed his breakthrough.

All the while, Zac held onto his comprehension and his path, refusing to let any sudden burst of inspiration warp it.

The previous insight that birthed the Branch of the War Axe had been based on the primordial nature of Conflict, showcased by the interrelation between Life and Death. It used war's inexorable and ever-changing nature to connect his understanding of the axe with the Heavens, officially setting out on the Path of Conflict.

The second step of his Dao Branch wasn't as grand and far-reaching. It brought complexity back to simplicity, where Zac returned to the origin—his Axe. Back when he had stood in that valley of life and death, seeing the birth of true Twilight with the help of Primal Dao, he'd chosen Conflict over Harmony. He still didn't understand how Conflict and the Axe were related back then.

The underpinning rules of Conflict and how it pushed the river of fate forward were undoubtedly important truths of tremendous power, but Zac had long realized he couldn't focus solely on those kinds of concepts. One day, he'd reach those towering peaks where a simple swing of his would contain the primordial principles of Conflict.

For now, he was still cultivating the Branch of the War Axe.

It had taken years of arduous work and reforging his stances from the ground up to reach this point. Tens of thousands of battles, millions of swings and permutations until both Conflict and his other Daos properly integrated with the weapon in his hand. Now, his foundations couldn't be more solid, and his understanding of the relation between Dao and combat had never been deeper.

The first time Zac had truly seen this phenomenon, except for his Dao Visions, was when fighting Void's Disciple the first time. Back then, his movements felt like magic, where he moved quicker and more unpredictably than his attributes possibly could allow. Now, Zac understood that Void's Disciple simply moved in accordance with his Dao.

And truthfully, the seemingly unfathomable Dominator wasn't even close to reaching the Integration Stage. Void's Disciple was more like the previous him, grasping after everything before understanding the basics. He tried integrating his Dao of Space, a notoriously difficult Dao to comprehend, into a set of combat techniques that didn't have the foundations for it.

Still, Adcarkas had been the seed that sent Zac down this path. Where Axe became the Dao, and Dao then became the Axe. A million swings, a million permutations—all of them ultimately becoming the fundamental truths of the Axe.

The Dao Avatar in Zac's Soul Aperture was already moving per his two stances, dancing across the stars that made up his soul. One moment he was Inexorable Death. The next, he was Evolutionary Life. As more and more Origin Dao entered his body, it almost felt like the flickering axe in his hands became more... apparent.

It was still the same size, and it didn't start radiating blinding lights like the Towers of Myriad Dao. Yet, it commanded more attention, where the small figure's movements were just adornments to the center-piece that was the weapon itself.

Finally, it all crystallized, like a spiritual link had been established between himself with the vast cosmos. It all became so clear, and any lingering doubts or hesitations were swept away as the movements of the Dao Avatar changed. No longer was the avatar following his two stances. The avatar was no longer evolutionary nor inexorable—there was no longer room for life and death.

This was an intentional change by Zac. Even if his Daos were parts of a bigger whole, he didn't want the individual branches to be influenced by outside concepts. The Daos themselves would be pure and unblemished, diving straight at the truth of their intrinsic nature. From there, Zac could freely create anything he wanted by mixing and matching, from Dual-affinity skills to his two combat stances.

Conversely, if he started mixing too many concepts into his Daos, there was a danger of creating problems with compatibility down the road. It was just like how he acted with his combat stances at the beginning. He needed to fully comprehend the basics of combat before he fused the Dao into his attacks. Similarly, he should first perfect the principles behind his individual Daos before linking them.

Zac believed that was not only the key to reaching further on the road of cultivation but also to finding the answer to his most pressing predicament—forming his Cultivator's Core. The better he understood each aspect of his path individually, the more success he would find at fusing them.

The avatar had become an extension of the axe rather than the other way around, and the gleaming edge of the incorporeal axe sang as it danced through the solar system that was Zac's Soul Aperture. Zac almost felt like he could hear the sounds of war as the axe moved. The drums, the roars, metal clashing against metal.

314 | JF BRINK & THEFIRSTDEFIER

He could feel it, taste it. Sand, salt, and metal. The winds of Conflict swept through his mind, his very being. At its forefront, the axe advanced, crystallizing the lasting impressions into a sharp edge of unmatched destruction. And with that edge came a storm of unfettered power that didn't stay trapped inside his Soul Aperture. It spread throughout his body, filling every single cell of his with strength and ferocity.

Eventually, the deadly but exuberant dance of his Dao Avatar abated before he returned to the central core of his soul. The miniature version of himself didn't look any different from before, but it felt more solid, almost corporeal. It exuded a boundless fighting spirit, an aura with a sharp and heavy edge that seemed capable of cutting through anything. The fundamental nature of the War Axe. With a thought, that feeling exploded outward from his body as an oppressive Dao Field covered the whole cultivation cave.

Usually when Zac did this, the constant struggle between life and death in the cultivation chamber would explode when bolstered by his Branch of the War Axe. However, this time it was like a third combatant had entered the fray and viciously attacked both flanks. Chaos ensued until both life and death were pushed back from the chamber's core, forming an area of pure weaponized air.

Anyone who dared enter this field would be attacked by innumerable cuts powerful enough to slay unevolved cultivators. Yet not a single blade of grass was harmed by Zac's churning Dao. This was partly thanks to his powerful soul allowing for greater control over his Dao, but also due to his most recent upgrade to his Dao.

What kind of master wouldn't have perfect control over their weapon?

A moment later, the opposing waves of Life and Death came crashing back with redoubled ferocity, thanks to Zac subtly altering his domain to welcome and fuse with the two elements. For a moment, he could almost grasp something from the chaotic clouds in the air, a clue to the mysteries he was trying to solve.

The feeling passed before he even had the chance to take out any treasures to grab hold of the insight. Zac shook his head with helplessness, but he wasn't too disheartened. He knew his current foundations were lacking. In fact, a bout of random inspiration he chanced upon right now might lead him toward a dead end. He was better off taking things one step at a time over the coming years, rather than rushing for perfection at the beginning of his undertaking.

Zac glanced toward the sky, or rather the cave's ceiling, but the vast pressure of the Heavens showed no indication of descending. This was the expected outcome, since you wouldn't get blasted by Tribulation Lightning because of a minor breakthrough, but Zac could never be completely certain which conventional rules applied to him and which didn't.

Seeing he was safe, Zac retracted his newly empowered Dao Field and opened his screens to check on the results.

[**Branch of the War Axe (Middle):** All attributes +50, Strength +4,750, Dexterity +2,000, Endurance +250, Wisdom +500. Effectiveness of Strength +25%.]

**Name:** Zachary Atwood
**Level:** 150
**Class:** [E-Epic] Edge of Arcadia
**Race:** [D] Human - Void Emperor (Corrupted)
**Alignment:** [Zecia] Atwood Empire – Baron of Conquest

**Titles:** [...] Grand Fate, Blooddrenched Baron, Connate Conqueror, The Second Step, Singular Specialist
**Limited Titles:** Tower of Eternity Sector All-Star – 14th, The Final Twilight, Equanimity, Heart of Fire, Big Axe Gladiator
**Dao:** Branch of the War Axe – Middle, Branch of the Kalpataru – Early, Branch of the Pale Seal – Early
**Core:** [E] Duplicity

**Strength:** 27,352 [Increase: 143%. Efficiency: 287%]
**Dexterity:** 11,800 [Increase: 103%. Efficiency: 206%]
**Endurance:** 16,242 [Increase: 134%. Efficiency: 287%]
**Vitality:** 14,192 [Increase: 127%. Efficiency: 273%]
**Intelligence:** 3,763 [Increase: 97%. Efficiency: 206%]
**Wisdom:** 7,603 [Increase: 104%. Efficiency: 216%]
**Luck:** 712 [Increase: 121%. Efficiency: 229%]

316 | JF BRINK & THEFIRSTDEFIER

**Free Points:** 0
**Nexus Coins:** [D] 846,027

The sudden boost in Strength was, in a word, terrifying. A single breakthrough had pushed his pool of attributes by over 12%, most of it into Strength, providing him with a full 2,500 points in his main attribute. With his large number of titles, those points had been turned into a boost of over 6,000.

Those numbers were almost incomprehensible for most E-grade cultivators and a stark reminder that elevated Dao Branches rarely were something you attained before forming your Cultivator's Core. No wonder someone Dao-blessed like Iz Tayn still felt like an unsurpassable mountain, wielding multiple Daos with these kinds of monstrous base numbers.

The only small letdown was that the breakthrough didn't provide any more Efficiency or Luck, keeping them at 25% and +50, respectively. Then again, it might be for the best. The easier access others had to those attributes, the smaller his relative advantage would be. Besides, the importance of 10 additional Luck was nothing compared to the huge direct boost to his combat effectiveness.

Zac had heard that Earthly Daos, the step after Dao Branches where you had formed a complete man-made Dao based on your path, didn't provide as many base attributes for Monarchs. Instead, they would empower their Inner Worlds to a more noticeable degree. For now, his three Dao Branches were still Zac's best bet at vastly increasing his attribute pool.

Even better, the Gates of Rebirth had increased the odds of him pushing all three of his Dao Branches to Middle Mastery before leaving for the Perennial Vastness. Zac had a feeling that having all three of his Dao Branches at the same level would help tremendously with maintaining the delicate balance needed to form his Trinity Core.

Seeing the more tangible gains now only helped increase his motivation to work hard on his cultivation, and he couldn't wait to seclude himself. Zac stayed in his cultivation cave for another two full days growing acquainted with his unprecedented boost in power. Becoming so much faster and stronger in one go was a bit disorienting even for him, but he soon regained his balance.

A positive surprise was that his foundations had healed a bit from the infusion of strength. He had by no means fully recovered, but he could tell he saved a couple of weeks by upgrading his Dao. It didn't change much for his four-year empowerment plan, but every little bit helped.

For example, he believed he was in good enough shape to start using the tainted lake water and resume his studies of Duality. The water still held the mysterious insights from the Lost Plane, but his treasure might be gradually getting worse for all Zac knew. He had no real way to measure the wisdom hidden within. Before he could dive into his cultivation, there were a few matters he needed to take care of.

Zac called over Triv with a mental nudge, and the ghost appeared in just under a minute. The spectral butler had built a manor of their own roughly a thousand meters beneath Zac's cave, not too far from one of the Miasmic Veins reaching up toward Port Atwood. That way, Triv not only had a great cultivation environment but was also always close by in case their services were needed.

"Young lord, your aura has undergone yet another transformation," Triv sighed with amazement. "I daresay that no E-grade cultivator of the Kavriel Province is your match any longer."

"I'm getting there," Zac said with a smile. "Did anything happen while I secluded myself?"

"Another message has been delivered through your Mercantile network," Triv said, expectancy in their voice. "From the Empire. I took the liberty of accepting it."

"Really?" Zac said, surprised as he accepted a familiar box.

His message to Catheya had been quite clear: he needed a couple of months more before they met and didn't want to decide on any details before the day of the meeting approached. For Catheya to send a message this early made Zac wonder if something had changed, so he quickly scanned the contents of the Communication Crystal.

'*I am sending you this message under the urgings of Mistress Tavza An'Azol and Lord Kator of the White Sky Phalanx. They have just arrived in Zecia and would like to meet you to discuss the great events happening here. The Undead Empire is sincerely looking for mutually beneficial cooperation in this endeavor, and we eagerly await your answer,' Catheya's voice echoed in his mind.*

It was a succinct message, containing quite a bit of information. Even then, there were no storms raging in Zac's heart. He expected more powerful people than Catheya to arrive from the Empire Heartlands after realizing she knew about Ultom. She and her master would have sent word of Ultom the moment they realized something was up, and they alone weren't powerful or connected enough to take charge of a matter this important.

However, the two names listed still surprised him for different reasons. He'd heard of neither Tavza An'Azol or Kator, yet both their origins were familiar. Tavza was undoubtedly a descendant of one of the two Draugr apart from Eoz he had seen in his vision. The three of them had been the quickest to emerge from the Abyssal Lake, and it even seemed like Azol was the first.

That didn't necessarily mean the Azol bloodline was stronger than his, but it was still probably one of the strongest branches of the Draugr. Certainly, a once-powerful bloodline could decline. But if that were the case, then Tavza wouldn't have been the one to receive this opportunity.

As for this Kator, Zac found out about his origin from Pavina. She was a subordinate to an Izh'Rak Reaver, so she unsurprisingly knew quite a bit about their armies. Pavina had mentioned the White Sky Phalanx once. It wasn't even considered breaking the commandments since the name was known far and wide. After all, the phalanx had destroyed two A-grade forces since its inception—they were known all across the Multiverse.

The feat didn't sound like much in contrast to how long the Undead Empire had waged its mad war, but Supremacies were all notoriously difficult to kill. They were old monsters who survived to the very peak of cultivation. Not only were they unimaginably powerful, they had innumerable hidden cards up their sleeves. And so long as the Supremacy survived, so did their faction.

The Supremacy could relocate and raise new generations of cultivators. Even worse, they could become an A-grade Wandering Cultivator bent on revenge. The amount of damage someone like that could cause an established faction was unimaginable. Zac shuddered at the thought of a ruthless person like the Eveningtide Asura, only at the level of an experienced Supremacy.

It was much easier to wait out A-grade forces. Not even Supremacies were immortal, even if it sometimes felt like it, and most factions couldn't raise a second one to protect them.

Zac was a bit surprised the Reavers showed up in Zecia. This region was at the edge of the Multiverse, and jurisdiction was blurry, but Zecia was definitely not within the sphere of influence of the Izh'Rak Reavers. This was solidly Draugr territory as far as the Undead Empire was concerned. Was it connected to him and his relationship to Kaldor?

More importantly, how should he deal with this matter? He didn't have some perfectly crafted scheme just because he knew something like this might happen.

"When did this message arrive?" Zac asked.

"Two days ago, my lord," Triv said.

Zac went over his options and felt a headache coming on. Was it a good sign that he received this notice, or was it bad? Did it mean Catheya still had some say in matters, or were these newcomers so sure they could control him that they didn't need to bother with any subterfuge?

Then it struck him.

Why beat himself up trying to figure out this mess when he finally had the scheming shadow back at his side? It was time for Ogras to earn his pay.

# STARFLASH

Remembering he could pawn off the issue of Ultom on Ogras, it felt like a weight had been lifted off of Zac's shoulders.

"I'll think on this a bit longer before sending an answer," Zac said. "Is there anything else?"

"Nothing of great import," Triv answered. "The large movements of troops related to young lord's new trial has intensified the rumors of our existence somewhat."

"I guess that's to be expected." Zac shrugged, neither too surprised nor worried.

Every soldier who entered Ensolus had been under strict orders to suppress any rumors of the Einherjar and Elysium. Still, no secret shared by so many could stay hidden forever. The chatter was growing in intensity by the day, to the point Zac had told his administrators not to bother him with the inquiries from the subsidiary factions across Pangea anymore.

But it was about to end, and soon.

Keeping his people separated like this, while hiding the true natures of Ensolus and Elysium, was a logistical nightmare that hampered their preparations for the upcoming war. Besides, Zac already decided to merge his two societies while visiting Twilight Harbor, and nothing had changed since then. Now, the plans to properly integrate the undead citizens into the Atwood Empire were mostly complete.

A huge walled district meant for the undead was already being built in Port Atwood. The walls weren't there to keep the citizens apart but to contain the Miasma they'd draw from the ground. Even the official structures like the government building would be fitted with Miasma-infused wings to allow the undead to work together with the living.

It was a bit of a hassle to create pockets of death everywhere, and it wasn't really a true fusion of Life and Death. However, Zac didn't feel confident in trying to create an atmosphere like the one that covered Ensolus.

As a Life-Death Edgewalker, he understood all too well how difficult it was to fuse the two elements, and his instincts told him that the odd energy of Ensolus didn't come without a cost. They just didn't understand what it was yet. Besides, it wasn't like Zac could reform the fundamental nature of the energy covering Earth even if he wanted to.

The Atwood Academy had tried replicating the energy of the Ensolus Continent for years now, but they were no closer today than when they started. Not even a tremendous cash infusion from Zac made any difference during the time when he visited the Void Gate. For now, pockets of death on Pangea and pockets of life in the cities of Elysium would have to do.

"Just maintain the course and continue with the preparations," Zac said. "We'll wait until Vilari and the others are back before announcing things. Vilari first advocated for this change, and much of the planning has been overseen by her personally. She should be here for the announcement."

"Do not worry. We will take care of everything," Triv said. "Is there anything else I can do for young master?"

"No, that's it," Zac said, his thoughts mostly on the matter of the Empire elites.

"Then I will take my leave," the butler said with a bow as they sank through the floor.

Zac didn't plan on staying around either. He sent out a series of instructions and inquiries as he headed for the teleportation array, and was soon swallowed by a flash of light. A few minutes later, Zac enjoyed a cup of tea in his private compound as the shadows congealed into a person.

"Something important must have happened for you to finally emerge from your cave," Ogras grinned as he sat opposite Zac. "Your bad habits

322 | JF BRINK & THEFIRSTDEFIER

have only gotten worse while I was away. You're becoming more and more of an old hermit. You're only supposed to reach that state *after* sowing your oats and breaking some hearts, you know?"

"I'm pretty happy with my current situation." Zac smiled as he threw over the Communication Crystal he got from Catheya. "I wanted your opinion on this."

"I'm guessing these two are bigshots?" Ogras asked after listening to the recording.

"Most likely from the strongest factions of the Draugr and Izh'Rak Reavers. I can't be sure, but I bet they're of our generation. The Undead Empire should have figured out that much, at least."

"If little princelings have arrived, then so have dangerous Dao Guards, like that golem of your fiery girlfriend. You absolutely can't meet with them," Ogras said without hesitation. "At least not now."

"I'm thinking the Undead Empire might be the most promising backer, though. More and more factions will come, most of which we have no connection to," Zac said. "I already have an in with the Empire and have other things to barter with instead of just the inheritance."

"Do you really think they'd care about your weird constitution in the face of the Left Imperial Palace of the Limitless Empire?" Ogras countered. "They might strike you down to secure a spot."

"We don't know if it's even possible for the seals to change hands," Zac said.

"Certainly, but I believe there is a decent chance for it to work, even if there might be some restrictions," Ogras said. "Your quest told you to gather a full cycle of followers, multiple cycles even. We also know the Ruthless Heavens have somehow connected this whole inheritance with the upcoming war.

"I think we both know the Ruthless Heavens well enough by now. When has it ever favored peaceful recruitment over slaughter? In fact, I believe getting a piece of a seal is just the first checkpoint to be deemed worthy of the inheritance. Keeping your life and defending your slot after the war starts—that'll be the real challenge."

"You've thought this through thoroughly," Zac said.

"I never slack off when it comes to my survival." Ogras winked as a bottle appeared in his hand.

"What do you think I should do?"

"Keep dealing with your friend instead. Use her as a shield to keep the wolves at bay. She shouldn't mind since it would elevate her position. If possible, don't even meet Miss Sharva'Zi in person. Only when we've entered the inheritance zone can you link up with the undead representatives. They will be forced to play nice with you by that point because of the outside pressure."

Zac nodded. "The other trial takers,"

"Exactly. Their Dao Guards won't be able to protect them, and the Undead Empire is an isolated faction in the Multiverse. They won't be able to afford to piss off any potential ally. Certainly, they will eventually turn on you even if things work out. Any old faction will always see to their own interests first. But by that point, you should have already figured out an exit strategy."

"Still, it's easier said than done to string along the Undead Empire for four full years," Zac said.

"Why not trade some intelligence for benefits? You should know a few things about the trial that the unliving still don't. That will both help you in the short run and plant a seed of goodwill. Meeting you in person shouldn't be as important as accomplishing their goal, unless their goal is to snatch your opportunity," Ogras said. "Better stay away from the limelight and have the outsiders fight among themselves for slots."

"You know pretty much everything I do," Zac said. "What should we trade, and what should we keep to ourselves?"

"Everything? I doubt it," Ogras said with his trademark suspicious look. "Anyway, most of the things we've gathered about the palaces should be fair game. The powerful factions will figure out the details sooner or later, so we might as well get some benefits while our knowledge is worth something. However, I don't think you should divulge your new quest under any circumstances. We need to look to our own before feeding our allies.

"If anything, we want the others to consider this an individual opportunity. Even better if we could get these two princelings to compete with and hamper each other. We don't have enough resources or talents to send out more than one or two vessels searching for seals. Though I wouldn't be surprised if the Undead Empire were willing to send billions of prospects into the Million Gates Territory to grasp hold of an Eternal Heritage."

"Isn't that what we want, though?"

"Honestly? I doubt it would help us all that much," Ogras said. "The Ruthless Heavens is geared for war, and it's even hiding the Space Gate to ensure it takes place. Unleashing the Undead Empire would get some Kan'Tanu scouts killed, but I bet even more local warriors would get caught in the crossfire and resurrected. After all, the alliance headed by the Allbright Empire is still scouring the place in hopes of somehow stopping the invasion. And having the area crawling with undead deathsworn would definitely make my job of filling your cycle harder."

"We'll keep the matter of my quest secret," Zac agreed. "But I doubt I'm the only one who will receive it."

"As long as we get a head start to form a cycle of your own. In fact, the moment your cycle is full, you can share the 'new discovery,'" Ogras smiled. "That way, we'll have more helpers inside the Left Imperial Palace."

"This is all based on one of those two getting a Flamebearer seal, though," Zac said.

"Well, the event hasn't even started in earnest, and we know of two candidates already. With each one of you needing at least one cycle of subordinates, I wouldn't be surprised if the trial will involve over a thousand people," Ogras said. "And the Undead Empire has most likely sent the best of the best, people at the level of Miss Tayn. If they can't get a slot in a place like Zecia, they might as well go become dirt farmers."

"It's good to have you back," Zac said. "All this scheming is exhausting me."

"As long as you know," Ogras said with a haughty expression. "Just don't go do anything crazy while I'm off getting the second piece of my seal."

"It's not like I'm looking for craziness. It just tends to find me," Zac sighed.

"Now, isn't that the truth," Ogras snorted before his eyes widened with anticipation. "How about the ships? Are they done yet?"

"Just got a confirmation before you arrived. Your ship will be done in an hour or so."

Three weeks had passed since Zac handed in his quest for the Creator Shipyard, and the golems had been hard at work completing both the ships required for Ogras' mission to the Million Gates Territory and a few different models meant to be showcased and sold. Now, the first Cosmic Vessel of the Iliex Shipyard was about to roll out, and the rest would be finished within the week.

"It's done? What are you waiting for? Let's go!" Ogras said excitedly. "Let's take the baby for a spin."

"Sure, but let's iron out the details on how to deal with the Undead Empire first," Zac laughed.

Ogras grunted with annoyance, but he still sat back down. And so, the two spent the better part of the hour workshopping various ways to hold the upcoming meeting safely. It had already been a risky endeavor with just Catheya and her master on the other side since they didn't know the fallout from Zac's actions in Twilight Harbor.

But now, the stakes were so much higher, and it involved powerful factions to which Zac had no relation. Without having a good solution to this predicament, Zac was afraid to even set foot on the same planet as the undead delegates.

They eventually came up with a partial solution with a decent chance of working, though it would depend on Calrin's abilities to procure some specific tools. By that point, the hour was nearly up, and they were far too preoccupied with the thought of a piping fresh Cosmic Vessel just waiting for them to continue discussing the Undead Empire.

"We should just go," Zac snorted when he saw Ogras glance in the direction of the teleportation array for the twentieth time in the last couple of minutes.

Ogras would probably have left already if not for the fact that only Zac had access to the shipyard's island. Upon hearing it was time, Zac only heard the demon's laugh as they were both swallowed by the shadows. The next moment he stood in front of the teleportation array, with Ogras looking at him like a puppy waiting to be let outside.

The array flashed to life, and they appeared in a building that looked just like the reception of the old shipyard.

"Lord Atwood, welcome," Rahm said with a small bow before nodding at Ogras. "Mr. Azh'Rezak."

"Good to see you, Rahm." Zac looked around. "I expected you to have changed things up a bit.

"Perhaps if you look out the window," Rahm said.

Zac and Ogras shared a glance before walking over to the window.

"That's more like it," Zac said with a smile.

This was the first time Zac had visited since the Creators' relocation, and he had to admit they really didn't half-ass things. The island had been completely leveled and replaced by a thick metal plane that covered its whole surface. The small mountain and its surrounding forest—all gone.

A mechanical mountain of sorts had taken its place. Towering nearly two thousand meters into the air, it was covered in the squarish scripts of the Iliex. A big exhaust at the top released plumes of smoke, while some sort of array cleansed the exhaust before they left the island's sphere of influence.

It had to be the foundry where they forged the alloys for the Cosmic Vessels. Zac used [**Cosmic Gaze**] to make sure, but the shockingly condensed energies within almost blinded him, forcing him to quickly look away.

"Safety goggles are recommended to look at the forging process," Rahm kindly reminded from the side.

"Thank you," Zac said with a crooked smile before turning back to the view.

The foundry was surrounded by ten huge factories, each significantly larger than the old warehouse back on his shore. Everything was connected by thick pipes and floating conveyor belts, and blocks of metals and sometimes finished plates were transported from the foundry into the factories.

There were also a few smaller buildings whose protective scripts were denser than the factories themselves. Zac guessed they were the workshops where the master artisans worked on the more delicate parts of the vessels, such as the Ship Cores and Spatial Arrays. Finally, there were five warehouses next to the reception, and Zac felt his heartbeat speed up when he vaguely saw a huge metallic shape in one of them.

Their first Cosmic Vessel.

"Brat, it's not often you bring guests," a rumbling voice echoed through the room as Karunthel appeared.

"Well, you guys are too good at your jobs. Most factions would go mad if they learned the Iliex had a subsidiary in Zecia." Zac smiled. "Just quelling any rumors keeps me up at night. How can I bring guests?"

"Haha, I'll take that as a compliment," the spider golem guffawed before turning to Ogras. "Hey, little demonling. So you're the one who's getting the first Starflash?"

"That's me," Ogras grinned.

With the upgrade being a System Reward, there were several rules in play. Zac hadn't gotten access to the millions of designs in the Creators' repository, but nine distinctive designs picked by the System rather than Karunthel. None were as fancy as the three options Zac had to choose from when picking his personal vessel, but that was to be expected.

You could still tell the System hadn't chosen these ships at random. They all had great synergy and were designed to be parts of a stellar Navy, with a mix of destroyers, personnel carriers, logistical vessels, and even a command ship that could link up with and control the other vessels in the fleet.

There were none of those gargantuan motherships, though, simply because there was no point in having an Early D-grade mothership. Besides, Zac wasn't sure he'd be able to afford one after seeing the prices on the smaller vessels.

One of these handpicked designs was the IL-28 Starflash, a destroyer-class ship focused on speed. It was a bulky beast that could comfortably house a standing army of around 2,500 elites, or transport five times that number for shorter stints. It was one of the mid-sized options, yet it cost a whopping 18,000 D-grade Nexus Coins.

Zac didn't even want to imagine what a mothership measured in miles rather than meters would cost. The IL-28 Starflash had a wide range of use due to its high-average performance and agility. For example, it could carry elite squads into hostile territory on critical missions or act as a roving sentry post.

Its scanning capabilities weren't nearly as advanced as Zac's Yphelion, but there wasn't much to do about that. The scout vessel for sale, the IL-32 Farsight, simply didn't have the defensive capabilities to roam the Million Gates Territory without a support system for very long. As such, the Farsight would warn them of High-grade cultivators nearby, but they would still be at the mercy of the whimsical laws of physics inside the chaotic zone.

Seeing as there were no skilled technicians in the Atwood Empire, they would have to pick vessels that could take a beating and survive long enough to limp back home in case disaster struck.

Karunthel laughed. "Perhaps it's time for this civilization to join the spacefaring nations. What did you call it? The final frontier?"

"The final frontier," Zac said with a smile.

# MAIDEN VOYAGE

"Amazing," Ogras whispered.

Even Zac was moved as they looked up at the huge, dark grey Cosmic Vessel floating in front of them. His Cosmic Vessel.

It wasn't as big as some of the ships he'd seen in the Void Gate nor as awe-inspiring as the three models he had to pick from for his quest reward. But it was clearly of a far superior make compared to the thing that flew his squad to the Void Star, or even the Technocrat's Little Bean, for that matter.

"A decent little skipper," Karunthel hummed with a satisfied nod. "Feels good to build items for adults, finally."

The vessel looked far blockier and utilitarian than the Yphelion's sleek catamaran design, yet it emitted an undeniable aura of power and vigor. It was of the common, squarish oblong shapes, which widened slightly at the end to give room for the powerful array thrusters. Its front didn't end in a cockpit or a viewing deck, but with five nasty spikes arranged in a circle.

The longest one in the middle was almost fifty meters long, and Zac felt his heart shudder as he looked at the engravings covering it. This was one of the other benefits of upgrading his shipyard—weaponry. The old vessels Zac had access to before upgrading the shipyard barely had any weaponry to speak of, but these army vessels packed quite the punch.

"This is the main energy battery, with four more deployable across its bodice," Karunthel said as he followed Zac's gaze. "These models of yours are pretty good. We call the main cannon a Wave Signature Tower. On the surface, it looks like a common pure energy weapon that you'd see anywhere. But it has an interesting twist. It isn't just releasing raw energy at your enemy—it is encoded with thousands of hidden patterns."

"Patterns?" Ogras repeated.

"Following certain concepts on how energy works and reacts when under pressure," the spider golem explained. "Simply put, you can consider these patterns as array breakers. The Wave Signature Tower will blast an enemy's shield with a rapid burst of array breaking attempts and record the result.

"Then, it'll adjust all your energy weaponry based on the results. Larger fleets can pool their data for greater efficiency. At worst, it will find a pattern that will cause more damage and drain the enemy's energy faster than the others. At best, it will find one that will directly destabilize the enemy's shielding and blast right through."

"That powerful?" Zac said with surprise.

"Well, most decent vessels have protective measures against these kinds of brute-forcing attempts. But this is the frontier where Cosmic Vessels are essentially floating trashcans. I doubt too many here have countermeasures against a technique like this." Karunthel grinned.

"Is the vessel equipped with single-use weaponry as well?" Ogras asked expectantly.

"Alas, no," Karunthel sighed. "Restrictions and whatnot. So, no good old bombs. However—"

Ten smaller vessels floated out from chutes at the ship's midsection the next moment.

"The Starflash is not like the Wingstorm with its huge array of unmanned drones," Karunthel explained. "It still carries 100 of these things. They all have simple energy cannons and are quite agile. More importantly, after you buy the ships, you're free to do any modifications to these little drones you want. Say, if you for some reason filled one of these guys with explosives, strengthened its propulsion, and ordered it to fly right into an enemy vessel…"

"Not bad." Zac laughed. "You could hide a bomb among the other drones until it's time to strike."

"And we provide full service, including replacing broken drones. For a fee, of course," Karunthel grinned before throwing over a small sphere to Ogras. "This is the control node. Bind it, and you will become the captain and gain access to most features."

"Most?" Ogras was clearly disappointed at hearing that.

"Some technical features are blocked out," Karunthel shrugged. "You would just get yourself killed if you started to fiddle with the Spatial Arrays, for example. Those features will automatically unlock if you get a D-grade technician or Array Master to join the crew."

"Fair enough," Ogras said.

"Here, take this." Karunthel threw a golden cube at Zac.

The moment he grasped it, the thing melted and turned into a small tattoo on his left hand before fading entirely. However, Zac wasn't worried as he got a short burst of information.

"What's that?" Ogras asked.

"Nothing," Zac said, smiling, then nodded to Karunthel. "What else?"

"Well, standard operations are fueled by gathering arrays, and there is a small energy surplus that will be stored. That surplus can be used on shields, energy weaponry, or even on dimensional jumps," Karunthel explained. "But it isn't an endless font of power. If you push its engine for long durations or get caught in pitched battles, you'd have to supply it with high-tiered Nexus Crystals, or preferably Cosmic Crystals."

"Cosmic Crystals?" Zac grimaced. "Those cost a fortune."

Karunthel laughed. "This is a machine of war, and to wage war is to burn money. Now, the models you have access to take around two days to power down if you want to put them into your Spatial Rings, and the power down feature comes with spatial compression. If you need to save space, this model can turn into a 20-meter cube instead of its current shape."

"Wait, *two days*?" Ogras frowned. "If we want to hide from pursuit, we'd have to create a two-day lead before stowing the ship? Doesn't that make it useless?"

"Brat, what do you know?" the golem scoffed. "Most vessels you see in this Heaven-forsaken corner of the Multiverse can't even be powered down, and never be put in a Spatial Ring. Hell, many can't even survive inside a proper atmosphere. In fact, you shouldn't even use the power down feature in public since it will expose that this vessel is of uncommon origin."

"Why can't people store their ships?" Zac asked, then remembered how he'd seen thousands of vessels docked into Zenith Vigil. He hadn't reflected on that back then, but why hadn't the captains just stowed their ships?

"For the same reason Spatial Rings can't be stowed inside other Spatial Treasures. Their arrays and energy fields would clash. The systems needed to push through the dimensional layers are incredibly complex. Usually, they are passively running like Spatial Rings, keeping the vessel in a constant state where it can travel without being ripped apart by the vacuum of space or dimensional skipping. Creating a vessel that can be safely turned on and off at will is far more difficult."

"How quickly will I be able to stow away the Yphelion?" Zac asked.

"Six hours, give or take ten minutes," Karunthel said.

Zac nodded thoughtfully before looking at the Creator with curiosity. "Do any of your top-tiered vessels allow for instantaneous power down?"

"Yes and no," Karunthel said after some thought. "For vessels based on the Dao of Space, no. And believe me, we've tried. There are Cosmic Vessels out there that are based on completely different principles, like the Dao of Light or the Elemental Daos. Their systems don't clash with Spatial Treasures, so they can generally be stowed at any time."

"So, what's the catch?" Ogras asked.

"Price. You wouldn't believe how expensive those things are. The Dao of Space is obviously the most convenient Dao for traversing space and jumping between dimensions. To create the same effect with other Daos... You'd be looking at a price tag at least 100 times higher at even lower performance points. For top-tier vessels, it's far worse."

Zac gulped for air as he glanced at the Cosmic Vessel in front of him. This thing had cost him enough money to bankrupt a normal Zecia D-grade Clan, yet an elemental variant would be over 100 times more expensive? What about higher-tiered vessels? Would the cost of a Peak D-grade elemental vessel even be counted in C-grade Nexus Coins?

"Well, never mind that." Ogras shrugged. "That sounds like some luxury toys for the rich bastards in the Heartlands. Can we take this beauty out for a spin?"

"Of course," Karunthel said. "The command sphere should be able to answer any questions you have. Most systems are intuitive enough that even a fool can handle them. You will need a good crew to take charge of the different features to bring the most out of the vessel."

"How do we get inside?" Zac asked.

"Just ask it," Karunthel said with a wave as he started to walk away. "Now, I have to finish the rest of the ships. Kid, work hard and get some contracts for us. A lot of the workers have been bored senseless for the past years. In fact, it might be in your interest as well."

"What do you mean?" Zac asked.

"The next quest will unlock when you evolve, but you can already work toward its goal," the golem said before he disappeared.

"Perhaps you need to build enough ships to upgrade the shipyard? Or perhaps sell enough of them?" Ogras ventured when Zac shot him a look.

"Sounds like it," Zac said. "But why would the System hide the exact details?"

"If you keep asking *why* the Ruthless Heavens does the things that it does, you'll soon drive yourself crazy. Just roll with the punches and make the best of the situation. Now let's see how—"

The next moment, they were covered in a bronze light, and Zac felt a pulling sensation. He didn't resist it, and they found themselves inside the Cosmic Vessel.

"Not bad," Ogras nodded as he looked around. "Teleportation, very fancy."

"Maybe too fancy," Zac hesitated, remembering Karunthel's warnings about showcasing the Starflash's high-tech features.

"There *is* a proper hatch, but what fun is that?" Ogras laughed.

The teleportation array didn't take them into a cargo hold like the previous ship Zac entered, but rather into a large foyer with some desks, tables, and benches. The Starflash's interior was in the same dark grey metallic as the outside of the ship, giving it a somewhat similar feeling to the sterile environments of the Technocrat Memorysteel base.

"How dull," Ogras muttered before looking to the sphere in his hand.

The next moment, the surroundings started to change, and the walls became a deep blue with white details, while the floors changed color into a deep wooden brown. The pre-installed furniture turned white, and the lights shifted to give off a softer glow. Suddenly, the area looked less futuristic and more inviting. It almost felt like Zac was inside a hotel on Earth rather than a spaceship.

"That's better," Ogras nodded with satisfaction.

"You can even do stuff like that?" Zac muttered with amazement.

"Yep, even the exterior. Can't reshape the metal, though," Ogras said.

"The makes sense," Zac said. "Still looks a bit austere. I guess we'll have to bring our own furniture."

"There are some fixed installations like these benches, but just the bare essentials." Ogras turned to a pedestal not far away. "That thing should be a map."

Zac had already suspected as much since it was similar to the mappers he'd seen inside the Void Star, and a holographic cutout of the Starflash appeared when he infused some Cosmic Energy into it.

There were no surprises with the interior. The biggest of the ship was set aside as living quarters for the crew. They were arranged in sets of ten, which all shared a common area. It wasn't much room per person, but it was still quite generous for an army vessel. There were also five mess halls, several training rooms, a few lounges, and so on, allowing for a comfortable long-term stay.

After these areas came the storage areas, both for the drones and some things that were inconvenient to store inside Spatial Treasures. For example, there were complex spare components, and escape pods. There were also ten smaller docking vessels, each able to hold roughly twenty people. They didn't possess any weapons though, so they would be useless in a fight.

"The bridge is that way," Ogras said as he pointed down a hallway.

The security doors soundlessly slid open as they approached, and Zac's heart beat an extra time with excitement when he found himself on a real-life science-fiction bridge. Those Old Earth showrunners had gotten things mostly right, except that the huge screen showing the exterior was just that—a screen. The bridge was hidden right at the heart of the vessel, protected by multiple layers of both physical and energy barriers.

Twelve seats were spread out in a half-circle in front of the screen, with the captain's chair taking the central spot. Each one had a console, but there were no buttons or levers as far as Zac could tell.

"Let's take her out for a spin," Ogras said as he sat down in the captain's chair.

The scene on the screen gradually changed as the vessel soundlessly slid out of the warehouse onto the enormous metal square outside.

"Do you already know how… to…" Zac said, his voice dying as the surroundings went from a panoramic vision of the Creator Shipyard to deep space in a couple of seconds.

There had been no sense of acceleration nor indications of engines humming to life. Yet they'd pushed through the stratosphere and entered the vast beyond.

"Amazing," Ogras gasped. "That wasn't even its peak speed."

"I can't imagine that any but the fastest Hegemons would be able to catch up to this ship," Zac said, his excitement growing.

"Even they wouldn't be able to keep up for too long," Ogras said. "The shields on this girl should be able to take a few hits. By that point, we'd leave them in the dust. Only Monarchs and powerful weaponry should pose a real threat."

"Don't get cocky," Zac laughed. "Besides, the environment in the Million Gates Territory is more dangerous and unpredictable than any D-grade cultivator could hope to be."

"I know. For now, let's check out the neighborhood. See that seat over there? It's for the navigator."

Zac walked over, but he looked back at the demon with confusion. "What do I do?"

"Just sit down in the chair and place your hand on the console," Ogras said, his anticipation evident.

Zac shrugged and followed the instructions. A moment later, it felt like his mind had expanded to the size of the solar system as a surge of data unfurled. It wasn't quite like the burst you got when binding certain treasures. It was more like a steady stream of information fed straight into his mind.

"There are actually thirteen planets in our solar system?" Zac muttered. "Our scanners back home only picked up eight. But what's that beyond? The scanners just cut straight off even if it isn't their range limit for a cursory scan."

"Should be the shroud," Ogras said. "We probably don't want to go

through it with the vessel. Might not be able to get back in. Same goes
for dimensional jumps, probably."

"I think you're right," Zac agreed. "Wow, look at this one."

The holographic map focused on the tenth planet of the twinned-sun
system. It could just barely be considered a planet by Multiverse standards with its circumference, but that wasn't what was so interesting
about it.

"Middle E-grade? Metal-attuned energy?" Ogras whistled. "Should
be whole mountains of Spiritual Metals to mine. That's a floating fortune
right there."

"It's a shame the System was so stingy with the type of vessels I can
buy," Zac sighed. "There are no resource extraction vessels."

"Maybe ask the golem if things like that can be added at the next
upgrade?" Ogras said.

"I will. That planet alone might cover all our wartime needs for
metal," Zac said, going over the data of their stellar neighborhood. "Our
neighboring planets both have life signatures as well. Only F-grade planets, though."

"Probably just beasts," Ogras shrugged. "Out of a thousand planets,
cultivators only have a claim on one or two. Although, that's for E-grade
planets. D-grade worlds are always contended unless there are specific
reasons letting them stay untamed."

"You think these F-grade worlds might be good for anything?" Zac
asked.

"Not sure," Ogras said. "Your planet isn't exactly lacking space. For
example, I can't see the use of setting up low-grade farms on those F-
grade planets when you can get twice the harvest for half the effort back
home."

"Well, it's not like I expected any real treasures to pop up in my
backyard," Zac smiled. "The metal world alone is a pretty good get."

"So, where do you want to go?" Ogras asked. "Too early to sail back
home."

"Can't travel to the other planets. It would take too much time
without dimensional manipulation," Zac hummed. "Emerald Eye?"

"Emerald Eye," Ogras agreed, and the ship set off.

# EMERALD EYE

Emerald Eye was the name given to one of Earth's four new moons, and the one that looked the most like an actual planet. The name came from large parts of its surface being green, with a large dark spot that almost looked like an eye. After Port Atwood had gotten better scanners and repurposed some of Old Earth's telescopes, they realized the eye was a huge inland sea.

Meanwhile, much of the greenery was forests, though there also seemed to be a lot of green minerals making the moon appear a bit more verdant than it actually was. Still, the Starflash's scanners clearly indicated there was lots of life on the moon, which was roughly 50% larger than Old Earth in circumference. As to whether that life was plants, beasts, or intelligent species, the destroyer couldn't tell.

The ship's scanners weren't meant for galactic exploration. Thankfully, they were still advanced to the point Zac could confirm that Emerald Eye had a World Core, considering it generated Cosmic Energy. The moon was at the top of Early E-grade, judging by the measurements. However, that wasn't the whole story when it came to moons.

Being in such close proximity to Earth, it benefited from the vastly superior environment nearby. Planets continuously lost some of their energy to space, and moons having Planetary Cores naturally attracted a good chunk of it. Thanks to that, the environment on Emerald Eye was much better than if it were just another planet, though it might be forced into cycles of decay if it had an elliptical trajectory.

If you were ready to pay the price, you could create a similar effect with moons lacking a natural ability to generate or absorb Cosmic Energy. A few powerful gathering arrays, some terraforming work, and a desolate rock would turn into a private world full of life. Of course, a planet only had so much energy run-off, and you couldn't catch it all. Eventually, you'd run out of energy to siphon.

The ship changed course, and the Cosmic Vessel created a parabolic arc as it started to make its way around the planet. Huge patches of churning oceans passed below, with storm formations larger than whole pre-Integration continents raging across the seas. Even from this distance, Zac could vaguely sense the energies of Life and Death hidden in those outbursts.

It was easy to forget how large New Earth's oceans were, with tele-portation arrays making all his intra-planet travels instantaneous. But their current view was just a huge ball of blue, where they could only see the shores of Elysium and Pangea as borders on the sides. Not even half of the planet was land, just like pre-Integration.

Still, the diverse biotopes of Pangea came to view as the ship moved farther away from the planet.

"Is the ship easy to control?" Zac asked after he'd had his fill of measurements and readouts.

"What control?" Ogras sighed with disappointment. "This thing doesn't allow me to steer. It's more like I tell it where I want to go, and the ship plots a course on its own."

"Can't you manually override that function?"

"Not with just the two of us. Like that golem said, without a crew, you can't really get the most out of this girl. We need to start training personnel immediately," the demon grunted.

"We already have a list of candidates picked out. Now that you have a more practical understanding, it should be pretty quick to assemble a crew."

They spent the next hour trying out various features of the ship as the green dot of Emerald Eye grew larger. The biggest takeaway was that they really needed to nurture more people focusing on Intelligence if they wanted to create a proper Space Navy.

Whether it was energy weapons, the drones, navigation, or the other subsystems, they all relied on the controller's simultaneous capacity and ability to make rapid calculations based on a mountain of data. For example, Zac only managed to control nine drones at a time thanks to his Soul Cultivation, but even their movements were stilted and predictable.

If not for the [Nine Reincarnations Manual], he probably would only have managed to control one at a time. Ogras did a little better, but even he only managed to control 15 drones before he reached his limit. Zac couldn't even imagine controlling the storm of drones that another of his models, the Wingstorm, used to fight. That thing held over ten thousand drones of various makes and models.

They both agreed to allocate more resources to Intelligence-based cultivation in the Atwood Academy.

Until now, it had been a school that wasn't very popular in the Atwood Empire, or for the whole of Zecia, for that matter. Taking the path of a mage was simply harder than a warrior during the earlier stages of cultivation. Blasting enemies with fireballs from a safe distance sounded good on paper, but neither beasts nor enemy cultivators were complete dummies that would sit around and eat the attacks.

Mages generally had weak bodies because of their attribute allocation, and before reaching D-grade, they didn't have the Cosmic Energy capacity to create powerful and permanent defensive layers. When starting out on the path of cultivation, most people would get hit because of mistakes or lack of experience. That's where the free points in Endurance warriors got proved to be much more effective for survival.

That simple fact had created a noticeable skew during the Integration. In reality, many had picked mage classes early on, just like Zac had been tempted to do. But most of those who went in that direction either got themselves killed or had their progress stalled out because they lacked the support system needed to advance. Even his sister had somewhat faced this problem until she joined Port Atwood.

Zac's own path had also influenced the direction of his faction. With him being a pure meathead, many cultivators in the Atwood Academy also chose a pure martial path. Now that their faction was maturing and the types of roles they needed to fill were growing more diverse, they had to put more effort into nurturing other kinds of experts.

That was the only way to evolve as a faction. If they didn't, the Atwood Empire would stagnate, much like the Azh'Rezak Clan that could only sell themselves as mercenaries to eke out a living. By the time they reached Emerald Eye two hours later, they'd drawn up a series of ideas, some of which were already being implemented back on Earth.

Zac and Ogras could finally get a better look at the moon's surface from this close proximity. There weren't any oceans on Emerald Eye, but that didn't mean there was a lack of water. The huge lake was the source of thousands of rivers, some of them almost reaching all the way around the moon. Of course, this also meant the surface was covered with innumerable, much smaller lakes naturally formed along the river paths.

The Starflash gently sank into the atmosphere of Emerald Eye, and a set of arrays automatically and effortlessly diffused the heat and friction that normally would appear from entering with their great velocity. The only sign they had entered the atmosphere was a deep groan that made his Soul Cores vibrate in resonance.

Soon, the vessel drifted at a leisurely pace at an altitude of around a thousand meters above ground, and they moved to a viewing deck at the bottom of the ship as the ship itself continued on autopilot. Zac's strongest impression of Emerald Eye was the humidity. Everything looked wet and sticky, and the forests reminded him of the rainforests on Earth.

Still, the vegetation didn't seem similar to either Earth or any of the three other planets it got fused to. There had been some theories that Emerald Eye was made from the leftovers of the planets since none of the species recognized the moon, but it didn't look like that was the case. These trees simply had a different flavor, for lack of a better word.

As for the green minerals…

"It's moss," Ogras yelled as they flew past a mid-sized mountain. "All the way to the peak. How tenacious."

It turned out the stones and minerals weren't actually green, but rather completely covered in a layer of lichen. Not only that, but the large swathes of green haze they had seen from Earth were, in fact, spores released by the moss, though some of it had mixed with the clouds created by the high humidity.

"Did you see? Even the trees are covered in it," Zac said. "Is it really not toxic?"

"According to the readouts, the moss can barely be considered F-grade," Ogras said. "And that dust isn't considered hazardous. I'm telling you, this place is as safe as can be."

"Famous last words," Zac snorted, but he had to admit that the nearby console's readouts indicated it looked safe below. "It's kind of weird that there are no beasts."

"It's not too uncommon for worlds to evolve onto a path with only plant life," Ogras shrugged. "There might be some nasty Spiritual Plants hiding in the forests, though. Or creatures living in the rivers."

"Alright, let's just check it out for a bit," Zac sighed when he saw Ogras' expectant look.

His recent breakthrough had further fixed up his foundations, and his pathways were long since repaired. With the huge boost of attributes and his elevated Dao, Zac felt he was almost as strong as his previous peak condition. And with Ogras on his side, an Early E-grade moon shouldn't pose much danger.

"Good to see you haven't completely lost your sense of adventure," the demon laughed, and the two flew the Starflash to an empty field not too far from a lake.

"Here," Zac said as he threw over a necklace.

"What's this?" Ogras asked.

"Pretty decent environmental protection talisman," Zac said as he put on an identical one.

Environmental protection talismans took on the role of space suits in the Multiverse. Zac hadn't needed anything like it in the Void Star, but the Void Gate already vetted those realms. There were tons of planets out there with toxic environments or worlds without breathable oxygen. These talismans helped weaker cultivators explore these places, while stronger warriors could brute force it by relying on their constitutions and stores of Cosmic Energy.

"Looks like you planned on some exploration right from the start," Ogras laughed.

"I made sure the army started stocking up on these things as soon as you guys decided to set out into the Million Gates Territory." Zac smiled. "My body can deal with most things, but normal people don't have that luxury. And even I wouldn't dare claim my body immune to any poison or environment."

"Better safe than sorry," Ogras agreed, and the air around him shimmered as the necklace activated.

The same scene took place around Zac, and Ogras teleported them down to the ground. The Starflash stayed fifty meters above ground, and a shield enveloped it in case there were hidden threats on the planet.

Just as they reappeared, Zac heard the deep groan, the same as when the ship broke through the atmosphere. It pulsated through the whole field, moving through his legs and into his soul. It felt like the world tilted for a moment as an undulating whistle followed. The next moment, it was gone, and only a hum from the ship and the slight crinkling of compressed lichen under his feet could be heard.

"What is that?" Zac muttered as he looked around.

"What's what?" Ogras asked. "The buzz from the ship?"

"I—" Zac frowned, shaking his head and looking down at the moss. "Nothing. This thing is deeper than I thought."

"Over two meters," Ogras whistled after sending his shadows through the nooks and cracks. "Imagine if we can find some valuable livestock that can feed on this stuff. We could just drop off a handful of beasts, and they'd keep multiplying with endless food and no predators."

"No predators we can see," Zac snorted.

"Well, maybe there's something valuable around," Ogras shrugged as dozens of shadows spread in every direction.

"The waters are completely dead," Ogras sighed after a moment. "The moss has even covered the lakebed. Let's check out the forest instead. Might be some valuable herbs hidden among the trees, at least."

Zac nodded, and the two soon entered the nearby forest in search of something more exciting than the endless supply of F-grade moss. But even after walking for ten minutes, they hadn't encountered anything. Zac's **[Hatchetman's Spirit]** might as well have been turned off from how he got no impressions from it.

Neither his nose for opportunity nor sense for danger was nudging his mind, making their stroll somewhat dull. It came to the point it almost felt like the lack of excitement was wearing on Zac's nerves. The muted rustling of the leaves in the tree crowns were jarring, and even the gentle rays peeking through the foliage seemed glaring and amplified.

Was he that bad? Had the past years made him so tuned for danger and struggle that his mind was going into overdrive when it failed to show up?

Zac felt he needed to do something, anything, to shake his mind back into a normal state, so he walked over to a nearby tree. Like the others, it was draped in a thick layer of lichen that covered every inch of the trunk. An invasive species had essentially drowned it, yet the tree was clearly alive, judging by the verdant leaves swaying in the wind above.

Zac cut a hole in the moss and put his hand against the trunk, infusing it with his Branch of the Kalpataru.

"Hmm, I think I have something," Zac muttered, but there was no response.

Ogras was staring into the depths of the forest with a thoughtful expression, the green sheen of the moss around them giving him almost a sickly appearance.

"What's wrong?" Zac said, his voice a little louder this time.

"Ah?" Ogras said with a start. "Nothing, I just felt it odd there's nothing valuable, not even Spiritual Grass. I thought it'd spontaneously spring up with this much ambient energy."

"That's what I was about to say," Zac said. "These trees. They're moss."

"What?" Ogras said uncomprehendingly before swiping at a nearby tree, cutting it in half in a perfect vertical line. The two sides fell to the ground, displaying the greenish wood inside. "Doesn't look like it."

"I mean, they're still trees, but they aren't really alive," Zac said. "They don't have a unique Life Signature. It's like the moss has invaded their roots and systems and sucked out all spirituality. But instead of killing the trees, they've integrated them into their mesh. They've become one life living in symbiosis."

"So the moss is stealing spirituality? Where does it all go? Might be a treasure somewhere," Ogras said with gleaming eyes.

"Unless it's just spread out across the mountains and fields, turning ordinary moss into slightly better moss," Zac said with a grimace.

"What a nasty thing," Ogras muttered and stabbed into the ground.

"I'm not sure if—" Zac began, but he froze in place.

The surroundings had changed, with him now standing at a lichen-covered hill, overlooking a large emerald vista. His instincts told him this wasn't an illusion—this was real and true, and not some dreamscape. He'd been moved here from the woods without him even noticing anything.

Zac's hair stood on end from the sudden transition, and **[Verun's Bite]** appeared in his hand as he looked for threats.

"Sure if what?" a familiar voice answered, but the tranquility of Ogras' voice was extremely jarring. Zac swirled around and spotted the demon leaning against a rock, looking at the sunset.

"What just happened?" Zac frowned. "Are you okay?"

Simultaneously, he sprung to action as he threw out a dozen different talismans, from purifiers to defensive barriers that shot up around them. [Soul Guardian] was already running at maximum capacity, and Zac even activated [Empyrean Aegis] as a precaution.

"You know, this moss might have eaten all the good things in this world, but this place isn't all bad," Ogras muttered, seemingly oblivious to Zac's actions. "Nothing to fight for, no one to fight with. It's all... blank. No stakes, no threats."

"That's not what I—" Zac said, but a piercing cacophony in his mind cut through any conscious thought.

When he regained his senses, he found himself in the middle of a lichen-covered field, and Ogras was nowhere in sight. He was in trouble. Zac infused his will into the hidden seal on his body—the control override mechanism of the Starflash and all future vessels of the Atwood Empire.

Zac didn't understand what was happening in this weird place, and his defenses seemed utterly incapable of stopping it. He could only pray that the Starflash's barriers would be able to protect him. But before the ship could catch up to him, he was once more overwhelmed by a series of sounds.

Groans like tectonic plates grinding against each other, piercing screams of dimensions being ripped apart, churning roars of endless storms. It was unending and overwhelming, threatening to drive Zac mad. Then it stopped.

'*You...*' an otherworldly voice echoed in his mind as the deafening chaos subsided.

It sounded both impossibly distant and uncomfortably close, and it was decidedly unnatural. Like millions of small discordant sounds had combined into words, forcibly instilling them with an excessive amount of meaning. That short 'you' almost made Zac pass out as he was blanketed by a rapid-fire series of impressions.

He saw endless darkness. He saw stars flashing into being. An incomprehensible dance of innumerable wavelengths. Discordance and repeating patterns. There was balance in this ever-changing conflux, moving toward unity. Then he saw… himself.

'*You can… hear me…*'

"Who's there!" Zac growled, not without a small amount of trepidation in his heart.

'*You… will fade… You will fade…*'

# FADING LIGHTS

"Who are you?" Zac growled as he wildly looked around, [Verun's Bite] having already appeared in his hand.

'*Being... being... I...*' the voice answered, and Zac almost felt like he could sense a hint of confusion.

That impression was soon drowned by an ocean of images that rose and sank like a breath. The rustle of the wind in the trees. A tropical storm raging above. An endless cycle, a natural progression. Trillions of lines forming a whole—a sphere.

"You're this world," Zac said with alarm. "Realm Spirit?"

'*World...*' *the voice sighed.* '*I am—I am.*'

By the words used, it sounded like the voice confirmed Zac's guess, yet the meaning crammed into the words rejected them. Or rather, it was like it didn't fully understand the distinction between self and others. It was hard to know for certain with the confusing jumble of pictures. Especially when it felt like Zac's mind would explode from the impression overload.

Zac could tell the only reason he could hold onto his thoughts was thanks to the unique composition of his soul. The Outer Cores dancing in their trajectories of life and death acted as dampeners, protecting the true core in the middle. They became akin to tuning forks that were forcibly altered to hum at the entity's frequency, while his final core safeguarded his sanity. Unfortunately, judging by the blackouts, this protection wasn't perfect.

What could Zac do but continue talking? Now that he knew some sort of entity was responsible for the odd occurrences on Emerald Eye, he was hesitant to call over the Starflash. A simple string of words pushed Zac's Soul Aperture to its limits—what if it screamed at him in anger? There was nothing in the spec sheet for the Starflash about protections against mental attacks.

Still, he instructed the Cosmic Vessel to inch closer just in case. In a perfect world, it would have been possible for Zac to instruct it to go pick up Ogras on the way, wherever he was. Unfortunately, this was a Cosmic Vessel, not a Technocrat Spaceship controlled by an AI. The Starflash wasn't meant to be used by one person. It was already pretty good that he could command it like this with his override seal.

There was a small crinkling beneath his feet as Zac repositioned himself as he tried to secretly look around for clues, but that sound made him freeze and look down with shock and comprehension.

"Stealing spirituality, one large network," Zac muttered before he looked out across the endless green vista. Suddenly, he remembered the impressions crammed into the entity's words. "You're... the moss?"

The deep groan came back, accompanied by a confusing mix of sounds. Zac's Soul Cores groaned ominously, and his vision swam. He'd have to be a fool not to understand the sound came from the entity by now rather than the Cosmic Vessel. Was it thinking? Was this the result of it trying to process his question?

In either case, it had to stop. Zac felt his Outer Cores were unable to fully absorb the resonance, prompting his consciousness to slip again. Who knew how many times he could blank out before he never woke up again? Zac did the only thing he could think of as he visualized his knowledge of moss as best as he could, together with the things he'd seen since stepping onto Emerald Eye.

"Moss!" Zac shouted while instilling those pictures into his Outer Cores, hoping to use them to broadcast his meaning.

Thankfully, the deep groan subsided, and Zac took a shuddering breath in relief.

'Moss... I am moss...' the voice said after a while, and there almost seemed to be a sense of satisfaction. 'Moss.'

The final word came with a string of images, these ones clearer and more cohesive than any before it. A small spiritual flicker in a patch of green undergrowth. On its own, it was nothing, but it managed to use that flicker to grow. Soon, one glimmer became two, and two became four. At this stage, it was still not yet cognizant of itself or anything else. But with every cycle, it became more than it was.

And so it continued, over mountains, through forests. Into the rivers, across vast plains. Tens of thousands of miles, hundreds of trillions of plants connected into one mesh, both simple and terrifyingly complex. It might have started as a singular spiritual flicker, but repeated and amplified nigh-endlessly, consciousness had been born.

Zac nodded, but he could still barely believe his theory was correct. No wonder he was blacking out—he was standing on top of a planet-sized brain. A brain that grew, that consumed and absorbed anything it came across. He had no idea how powerful something like this was—it might be impossible to accurately grade this huge network of plant-based synapses.

Even world-spanning Spiritual Plants like Heavenrender Vines had some similarities to cultivators and beasts. They had a core, a central network. The vines themselves were just like expendable appendages, while the critical center of their being was no larger than a skyscraper. In contrast, this moss entity didn't appear to have a core, and it really didn't seem to be any stronger than 'barely F-grade' from an energy standpoint.

But one thing was for sure—the amount of Mental Power this thing wielded possibly exceeded that of any cultivator in Zecia. Judging by the vision, its voice and presence right now was the result of only a slight contraction surrounding Zac, while the rest was still spread across the whole surface of Emerald Eye.

That was the only reason he was still alive—the moss didn't know how to condense its will much further, nor saw a need to. Judging by the scenes that had flashed past during its attempts to communicate, it was probably usually in a state where it was essentially dormant, no different from a non-spiritual patch of moss.

The groan and the pressure most likely came from its attempts to think or communicate. That by itself raised another question. Had the moss been trying to contact him since the moment they entered the atmosphere? Why?

"Why are you doing this? We were just visiting. We meant you no harm," Zac said, trying to convey images of harmony and friendship through his Outer Cores.

While sealing any more destructive schemes deep into his heart, praying the entity couldn't sense them.

'*Lights are born. Weak, lonely, short. They fade. Lights join us. Join Moss. Provide, be provided for. Help.*'

An array of memories and concepts accompanied the words like before, growing clearer by the moment. That alone was problematic. The moss almost felt like a blank slate, but it was adapting shockingly fast during their conversation. Before, its words had contained a jarring juxtaposition of incomprehensible waves and fragmented images. Now, Zac found himself looking at a starry sky with billions of shimmering lights.

At its center, all lights were in harmony, stably shining at a unified frequency. Together, they only made up a small corner of the universe, and even their combined luster was weaker than some of the other lights. While some were blindingly bright, most were so weak and flickering they could barely be seen. Some even winked out, unable to sustain their forms.

Certainly, new ones were born to take their place, but they weren't any better than the ones before. It was imperfect. Gradually, the harmonious light spread, adding one star after another into its mesh. Eventually, half of the night sky was one, and the sum was greater than its parts.

Zac could see that barely any new lights were born where harmony spread its influence. As Zac saw it, the moss entity had spread to the point it had destroyed most of the biodiversity on the planet, and there was very little remaining room for expansion. But this didn't matter. The moss didn't desire expansion or Hegemony. It was simply living, following the natural order of things.

It wasn't absorbing everything out of greed. It could be considered evolution, where one lifeform's method of survival and propagation was vastly superior to anything else's. It didn't feel threatened, even when he and Ogras appeared. It was just two weak and short-lived lights that would eventually join the mesh.

That was certainly good news that the strange events weren't a result of them being specifically targeted, though Zac guessed his confused state and blackouts were a result of the moss entity trying to find a way to convey its words. Still, that didn't mean he or Ogras were out of the woods. After all, Zac doubted this alien creature came calling just because it was bored.

*As expected, the voice soon continued.* 'Your light is... different. Similar. Like Rain... Like rain...'

Another burst of images, depicting eons of stability and steady growth. Things were hazy, but there was contentment. Then one day, the waves started to grow stronger. It was like a nourishing rain was falling across its body, powerful yet invisible. Thanks to its magical effects, the haziness began to thicken, to focus. A sense of being was born.

And the rain made the colony propagate with unprecedented speed. Soon, the balance was broken, and even the powerful lights joined the unity. In the blink of an eye, the whole night sky had become one, and it felt... perfect. But just as the unity started to get accustomed to this new state of existence, another change occurred.

The invisible rain changed.

The rain suddenly brought something bad along with the good, and it split into two. One nurtured even more, to the point it created an imbalance. The harmony was disrupted as sections almost broke free, out of control. Calming the waves was exhausting. The other rain was just as bad. Rise and decay were natural and needed to maintain a healthy form. Yet this rain hastened the decline to an unsustainable level. Offsetting it was just as exhausting.

So far, the rain was manageable, but the entity was worried. It even wondered if 'waking up' was a good thing because it had never felt these things before the rain came. And it didn't know what to do.

But now, new lights had appeared out of nowhere, lights unlike any it had seen before. One light even reminded the entity of the rain, even though it was not. It could even sense that the two new lights interfaced with waves while staying separate. It tried to do the same, to interface while staying separate. For answers.

Zac sighed as he finally understood what was going on. The moss entity was clearly extremely old, but it hadn't been a spiritual being before. It was just a huge colony with tendrils of energy running through endless root systems. But the Integration had flooded Emerald Eye with energy, which shocked the entity awake while allowing it to cover the whole moon.

However, not much later, Earth became Life and Death-attuned. In the beginning, it wouldn't affect Emerald Eye because it was barely noticeable even on Earth. But every day, the attunement grew more pronounced, to the point that attuned energies were now being released into space.

But what the hell was Zac supposed to do about that?

Zac's thoughts furiously spun as he tried to figure out a way to extricate himself from this mess without getting turned into fertilizer. He was suddenly extremely relieved he hadn't managed to attempt an escape before figuring out the situation. The moss entity's consciousness had both sensed him and nudged his mind at the atmosphere's edge.

Its reach was clearly not limited to the surface, and who knew what it'd do if it saw the "light with the answers" attempt to leave?

He had to mix truths and lies and pray it would work.

"I know where the rain comes from. I'm from there," Zac said as he pushed a picture of Earth, of how it was tens of times bigger than Emerald Eye, with incredibly powerful waves. "Many lights live on it and grow from the rain. We don't like the change either, but it's too powerful. I cannot stop it. No one can."

'*You... Rain...*' the entity said, clearly dissatisfied with the answer, and Zac felt like his Soul Aperture had been thrown into a gravity array.

"I have an idea," Zac said hoarsely while nicking himself with **[Verun's Bite]** to stay awake. "A filter to soak up the bad from the rain before it reaches you."

He pictured a large cloud covering Emerald Eye, siphoning off the Life-attuned Energies while leaving the unattuned energies to reach the surface.

'*How?*'

"First, you cannot let our lights fade here," Zac hurriedly said.

'*You do not wish to join?*' the voice asked with genuine surprise.

"No. My light is weak, but it is mine," Zac said. "This is the only way we can help you. But we are too weak right now. You need to endure the bad a bit longer while we grow under the rain. Then we can make the filter."

'*When?*'

"I—" Zac hesitated, unsure whether to give a short or long answer.

Obviously, he had no real intention to improve the habitat of this scary thing. He just wanted to make some empty promises and get the hell out. But he was afraid that the wrong answer would result in him being integrated as the entity searched for answers within his body instead.

'*When? WHEN?*' the voice repeated, and Zac felt a tremendous pressure build in his mind.

"One decade," Zac said through gritted teeth, trying to impart the period from when the rain started to now. "That's the absolute quickest, and it shouldn't be long for someone like you. It's the best—"

Blankness.

Zac woke up with a start on a shady patch of moss, and he hurriedly got back to his feet. He had once more moved or been moved, yet this time he recognized where he was. It was the same field where he first set foot on Emerald Eye. And a glance up confirmed the shade wasn't due to a cloud, but rather the Starflash hovering right above his head.

Had the moss accepted his offer? Just like that? Thank God for guileless cosmic beings.

Zac wanted to thank his lucky stars and run for his life, but he spotted Ogras lying not far away, blankly staring up at the sky.

"Are you okay?" Zac asked as he ran over.

"Why wouldn't I be?" Ogras muttered, his eyes unfocused. "I'm just a bit tired, going to rest here a bit. You keep looking for treasures. With your Luck, it shouldn't be difficult."

Zac didn't bother answering and hoisted the demon up on his shoulder. Ogras didn't resist at all, and he seemed happy to just hang there.

"I'm going," Zac said, yet there was no answer.

Zac was frozen with indecision for a few seconds, but he eventually activated the teleportation beam, unwilling to spend a second more on top of this eldritch horror. As soon as he was back on the bridge, Zac instructed the ship to set course for Earth, and the ship started to rise through the air.

'*Half. Half a decade. Then you remove the bad,*' the voice echoed in his mind just as he was about to break out of the atmosphere.

"What?" Zac exclaimed.

'*I help your light grow,*' the voice said, ignoring his interjection. '*Half a decade. Must return.*'

"Of course," Zac lied. He was already on the ship and heading for Earth. Why not give the guy a better deal?

But Zac suddenly found his perception rocked.

*'I help your light. Half a decade.'*

Following that was a final burst of imagery. Of how a couple of small crystals had formed at the very bottom of the huge lake on Emerald Eye. Terrifying pressure and eons of time had instilled them with tremendous amounts of Mental Energy. As the moss grew more intelligent after the Integration, it realized how useful those things were.

It had slowly started moving them across its body, using the rivers, the rain, and its never-ending network of plant life. That way, they were spread across the whole planet and became incredibly powerful synapses and mental amplifiers. These crystals were as much the reason for its burgeoning intelligence as the infusion of Cosmic Energy.

But now, one such crystal had somehow been placed in Zac's Soul Aperture, drip-feeding him with raw power for his Soul Cores. Yet that crystal might as well have been an Atomic Bomb going by how much energy it contained. It was orders of magnitude more than his own Soul Cores held. And the imagery indicated in no uncertain terms that tampering with the crystal or not following up on his promise would result in the crystal erupting.

So much for the thing being guileless.

# 43
# CONTINGENCIES

Had the moss entity managed to sense Zac wasn't sincere, even if he tried to control his thoughts? And how had it known how to feed Zac a poisonous pill like this? As far as Zac could tell, he was the first sapient being to interact with the entity. It really shouldn't be that clever.

Zac tried calling the creature with some bogus matters a few times, but it all fell on deaf ears. Neither could Zac sense the pressure from the vast consciousness. As expected, its consciousness didn't spread that far from the moon, which was at least one piece of good news in this mess. Eventually, ten minutes had passed, at which point Zac finally dared relax his mind and focus on solving the issue.

Honestly, Zac felt pretty good about things as the Starflash sailed farther away from Emerald Eye. At first, he'd believed himself trapped by the scheme of a vastly more powerful being, just like with the Eveningtide Asura. But the more he thought about it, the more Zac realized the situation wasn't like that. This was actually an opportunity.

He could already feel how both his Outer Cores and Inner Core were being doused in a gentle shower of pure Mental Energy. It even felt like how the entity had described the Cosmic Energy—like rain. The energy was completely unattuned, which helped him with [Spiritual Void]. The Hidden Node wasn't interested in feeding on this raw force, so it all went into nurturing his soul.

The fully formed Outer Cores didn't want any either, so it was shared between the still-growing Life and Death Cores and his main core. This was a huge timesaver. Zac would have to provide the actual attunement with the **[Nine Reincarnations Manual]** later, but that process could be sped up with attuned treasures.

The goal of the current layer of his Soul Strengthening Method was to form two sets of nine Outer Cores, half attuned with Life and the other half with Death. That would finish the first step of the current reincarnation. When he reached this stage, the soul strengthening process would run at maximum capacity, rapidly nurturing his main core.

This crystal would not only allow him to create these auxiliary cores far quicker, but his main core was already benefiting. He'd thought it would take decades to upgrade his soul after seeing how much time it took to form each Outer Core. But looking at the gentle haze already suffusing his Soul Aperture, the next breakthrough was suddenly much closer than Zac thought possible.

As for the implied threat that came with the opportunity, Zac wasn't overly worried either. He had to admit he'd been outwitted by the moon moss, which honestly was a bit embarrassing. But the entity ultimately lacked a lot of critical information and understanding of cultivation. It didn't even seem to possess any Dao.

Furthermore, Zac had already left its sphere of control. It wasn't like inside the Twilight Ocean, where he was at Alvod's mercy. Neither could the crystal be compared to the Remnants still locked in their prison. Those things contained shreds of undying will from incredibly powerful beings. Meanwhile, the Moss Crystal, as Zac decided to call it, was almost pure spiritual energy.

There seemed to be a lingering piece of consciousness locked in its depth to maintain its function. Except, without access to the moss network, its thought processes were most likely limited. Zac didn't believe for a second he couldn't figure out a counter-play over the next five years.

The easiest method was quickening the energy extraction and absorbing it all before the deadline. The bomb couldn't go off if Zac ate all the fuel. With his manuals and Void Emperor bloodline, Zac believed it was doable. He might even be able to use the thing as a battery during his core formation down the road. And when that time came… well, he did have some experience in blowing things up. Destroying a moon couldn't be too hard.

It might not be fair, and the moss entity wasn't exactly hostile. But that thing was way too dangerous to have floating right next to Earth unchecked. It had consumed the whole planet in less than a decade after being infused with Cosmic Energy. How powerful would it get if left unattended for too long? He either needed to destroy it or push the whole moon out of orbit, preferably into a wormhole leading toward the Kan'-Tanu armies.

Having come to a preliminary decision, Zac turned to his companion, who was still slumped in the captain's chair with a vacant expression. Zac frowned at the scene. Ogras was still trapped in that fugue state?

At least it shouldn't be a case of possession. That wasn't how the moss entity's consciousness worked. It needed the vast network to form thoughts, and any piece of consciousness cut off from the network should dissipate unless powered by a Moss Crystal. And Zac somewhat doubted Ogras had been implanted with one unless the Moss Creature lied with its final vision.

Those crystals were extraordinarily rare, and it seemed to only have six or seven of them. Sacrificing one for a chance at dealing with the attunement was already an incredibly high price, and Zac doubted it would be willing to part with two.

Zac guessed Ogras' state was more a result of having been submerged in a slow-moving ocean of consciousness. Like Zac's Outer Cores, the demon's whole consciousness had been gradually forced to harmonize with the moss, which apparently resulted in a semi-comatose state for sapient beings.

But sapience wasn't that easily erased. Since Ogras' soul was unharmed, one simply needed to shock his consciousness awake.

"Hey, wake up," Zac said as he started shaking the demon, which only resulted in an annoyed groan.

"One more hour," Ogras muttered as he nestled deeper into the chair. "Let me sleep in just one more hour."

"Well, don't blame me," Zac sighed as he took out one of his spare Body Tempering vats and a heating array.

A moment later, the water he'd poured inside had begun boiling, at which point Zac emptied a small jar of grey dust into the waters.

"In you go," Zac said, a smile tugging at his lips as he pushed the demon into the scalding waters.

The demon didn't resist. In fact, he seemed to enjoy the heated bath, and a content smile spread across his face after the initial reluctance at being dragged out of his comfortable chair. However, a frown soon crept up as the grey dust burrowed into his skin. Then, his eyes snapped open in a horrified expression.

"Ah, shit!" Ogras screamed, voice turning shrill as he veritably exploded out from the bubbling water. "Shit, my bones! What in the—"

"You wouldn't wake up, so I had you try out some [**Bone-forging Dust**]," Zac said as Ogras reformed next to him. "Seemed more effective than coffee."

"This is the stuff you used to temper your body back in the day? Monster. Masochist," Ogras grimaced, his whole body twitching from the Body Tempering paste that had entered his body. "Bastard, don't fall asleep in front of me in the future."

Zac was about to explain himself, but Ogras soon realized something as he looked around with confusion. "Wait, what in the world is going on? When did we get back onto the ship?"

"What do you remember?" Zac sighed.

"We entered the forest to look for treasures," Ogras said as his brows scrunched together in a frown. "Then... nothing."

"Figures, you looked pretty wonky already by that point," Zac muttered as he retold what he'd experienced.

"An aberrant lifeform?" Ogras said as he fearfully looked at the glistening emerald moon on the screen. "We need to kill that thing right away. Who knows what something like that might turn into."

"About that," Zac grimaced as he shared the final gift of the moss entity.

"That thing implanted you with a *safeguard*?" Ogras closed his eyes, then breathed out in relief. "Nothing. I guess I wasn't worth blackmailing, thank the Heavens. So, what do you want to do?"

Zac broadly recounted his plans, assuring the demon it wasn't a problem.

"Of course you'd be able to turn a profit from a calamity like that," Ogras muttered as he took a swig of liquor to counteract the Body Tempering paste. "Well, if we have to keep the thing around for a few years, we might be able to figure out something better than just killing it. Why blow up the moon if we can control it? That way, we can both harvest more of those crystals while having a living weapon to guard the home base."

"Sounds pretty optimistic, but it might be possible." Zac nodded. "Perhaps if we launch arrays that disrupt it from gathering its consciousness? If it can't think, it can't act against us."

"Well, there's a plan, but we're better off leaving this to the brainiacs at the academy. Shame that little nun didn't want to join us. She would have been quite useful here. Maybe you should contact her when we've return—wait, what's going on?"

"What's that?" Zac said as he looked around.

"How is the ship moving on its own?" Ogras frowned as the command sphere appeared in his hand. "What? Override?"

"How odd," Zac hummed as the Starflash continued flying toward Earth.

"You? It's you?" Ogras scowled. "You can just take over control of my girl like that? Wait, *that tattoo*!"

"Of course, I can," Zac laughed. "You might be the captain, but I'm the admiral. You're welcome to buy the Starflash from me if you think it's unfair. For you, only 20,000 D-grade Nexus Coins."

"Bah, no sense of camaraderie," Ogras muttered.

Zac grinned. "Hey, I could have left you on that moon, you know?"

"Then who would solve all your little headaches?" Ogras snorted as he sank back into his chair. "I can't believe you've used that paste for hours. One little dip, and I feel like a twelve-legged Barghest King has been stomping on my spine."

"Well, thankfully, I've moved past that stage of my cultivation." Zac's smile turned crooked upon remembering the painful body tempering sessions that would begin as soon as he was fully healed.

They continued for another twenty minutes, during which both Zac and Ogras mostly sat in silent meditation, scanning themselves to make sure there weren't any other surprises hidden within their bodies. No matter how much they looked, the only souvenir from Emerald Eye was the Moss Crystal floating around in Zac's Soul Aperture.

In fact, Zac noticed something odd—his body was in noticeably better shape now than before visiting the moon. At first, Zac thought the verdant atmosphere on Emerald Eye might have restorative powers, but he soon found the true reason.

"Holy crap," Zac swore, prompting Ogras to look over. "We were on Emerald Eye for *ten days*. I thought it was no more than a couple of hours."

"A ten-day vacation, yet I feel exhausted," Ogras muttered.

Not much later, they entered the communication range of Earth, at which point both Zac's and Ogras' communicators started to buzz frenziedly. Obviously, it would create some panic when the two most powerful people on Earth suddenly up and disappeared without warning. The only reason there weren't ships zipping around looking for them was that the Creator Shipyard was fully sealed off and guarded by barriers.

Two hours later, Zac thumped onto his prayer mat with a grunt after placing Yrial's statue and the **[Mind's Eye Agate]** in their slots neighboring his seat. He had just spent thirty minutes being scanned by every conceivable tool and purified by multiple types of healers. Yet none had found anything, hopefully proving there weren't any more lingering threats from Emerald Eye.

Contrary to Zac's expectation, Ogras' near-death experience had done nothing to curtail his passion for space exploration. By this point, he was already gathering a preliminary squad to man the Starflash. One moon was kind of a dud, but Zac guessed the demon would spend the next couple of weeks looking for treasure on the neighboring planets instead.

Zac wasn't worried about missing out, nor was he eager to explore another planet. Between Emerald Eye and the Void Star, he'd seen enough weird and dangerous places for a while. Besides, both he and Ogras had already reached a point where they needed very specific types of treasures to make any breakthroughs, so they were rarely in competition for resources.

If the demon found something that might help Zac with his cultivation, Ogras would just trade it for something in Zac's possession. That, in a sense, was the fundamental reason powerful warriors started factions in the first place. Let others gather resources for you while you focus on your cultivation.

And like the old masters hidden behind most of the powerful factions, he needed to cultivate.

Zac spent the next couple of hours repairing and reinforcing his frayed skeletal framework of **[Thousand Lights Avatar]**. He still hadn't

360 | JF BRINK & THEFIRSTDEFIER

given up on cultivating this unique technique, even after much of his preparatory work had been undone by the ravages of Creation and Oblivion. First of all, who wouldn't want to have a second life in case your soul was destroyed in battle or from some other mishap?

Secondly, Zac felt like a network of condensed Mental Energy spread through his body could benefit him far beyond the original use of the Eidolon technique. After all, weren't the Mental Energy pathways of **[Thousand Lights Avatar]** very similar to the ones he used to form Dao Braids? What if those temporary channels were not only made permanent, but sturdier and of higher quality?

It might be the key to taking his Dao Braids to greater heights.

Unfortunately, his current braids were only at the level of what decently talented F-grade cultivators could form. They wouldn't be enough in the future. In the battle for Ultom, he would come face-to-face with people like Iz, cultivators with God-given affinities who used extremely powerful Dao Arrays when fighting.

The same was true during the war. There were no guarantees he'd only face those around his own level, even if it were a System-sanctioned event, and upgrading his Dao Braids was one way for him to better match up to experienced Hegemons.

Unfortunately, Zac wasn't confident in reaching the required level of control over his soul even if he evolved his soul twice over. Some Dao Arrays were even more complicated than Skill Fractals, and Zac could barely twine together a couple of simple strings. He needed to find an alternative, at least in the short run.

The idea with the greatest potential was to form a series of pre-created Dao Arrays in his Soul Aperture. For example, he could have one Evolutionary Array and one Inexorable Array. When he needed to activate them, he would just fill them with his Dao and channel the output into his Skill Fractals.

Zac first needed to form the actual avatar before he started refitting it into a full-body Dao Funnel, though. Only when it was fully formed, much like his soul, would it be able to survive on its own. Neither attacks nor rampaging waves of Creation or Oblivion should be enough to destroy it by that point.

Luckily, it looked like the Moss Crystal could even help in this regard. Directly controlling the energy that was being released by the crystal seemed impossible, though doing it indirectly worked. Cultivating the early stages of **[Thousand Lights Avatar]** was mostly sending waves of Mental Energy through his body over and over, with each wave leaving a little bit behind.

As long as he made those waves pass right by the Moss Crystal before leaving his Soul Aperture, some of the moss energy would tag along. A preliminary session indicated that his cultivation speed had more than doubled, though the framework only improved when he actively cultivated the method. Conversely, his Soul Cores were being nurtured around the clock in what almost felt like force-feeding.

Soon enough, Zac opened his eyes, rather satisfied. Looking back at it, that eldritch horror wasn't all bad. Maybe he really should figure out a way to keep it around. For now, he had lake water to absorb. It was finally time to start working toward his Cultivator's Core in earnest.

# REFINEMENT

"Heugh," Zac retched as he spat the lake water onto the ground, and helplessly watched it seep into the soil.

After the success of eating the Dao Crystals, it seemed like a solid plan to simply drink the lake water, preventing any of its mysterious insights from slipping away. One mouthful, one insight—easy enough. But who would have thought his body would reject it so vehemently? He didn't even get a taste of the truths of the Lost Plane before a huge sense of disgust overwhelmed everything.

Had the water spoiled inside the canisters? No, it didn't smell any worse than before, and it was still mostly clear. The corruption of the Lost Plane didn't seem to taste like anything, either. Was it a mental block, or was his body protecting him from doing something stupid? Either case, it wasn't the end of the world. The first method had failed, but there were many more.

Zac took out a large bowl and filled it with lake water, and a surprising scene occurred. As soon as it left the canister, the water started releasing plumes of vapor even though it was room temperature. In other words, it wouldn't last long outside the containers. Zac guessed it had something to do with the fact the water was no longer connected to the Lost Plane through the spatial tunnel. It had become rootless, like a harvested Spiritual Plant.

There was no time to waste, so Zac dunked his head into the bowl. Almost immediately, he felt the corruption seep into his head. This was just a test where he wanted to check whether he could directly gain insights from the corruption before his Hidden Nodes refined it, leaving more insights for himself and less for [Void Heart].

Unfortunately, this experiment was a failure as well. The only thing Zac gained were distant voices clamoring in the back of his mind until the corruption was dragged down to his heart for purification. Not only that, but the small amount of taint absorbed by just dunking his head allowed [Purity of the Void] to destroy a significant portion before it could enter [Void Heart].

A moment later, the purified comprehension was released from the Hidden Node in his heart, and Zac was provided a flash of clarity. But again, with the amount being so little, he didn't manage to take even a step forward with his comprehension of Duality before the moment passed. It looked like it was time to get back to basics, so Zac took out a large medicinal bath and filled it with lake water.

With water reaching his chin, Zac was soon filled with corruption, and more kept pouring in. He even started to feel his perception shift, but [Void Heart] was already fast at work refining the water into something usable. Soon, his Soul Aperture was filled with the light of truth, and Zac methodically deciphered one character after another from the [Book of Duality].

Ten minutes later, the corruption had either been absorbed, purified, or dissipated into the air, leaving only common water behind. Zac took a deep breath as he thoroughly scanned his body. Thankfully, no matter how hard he looked, it seemed there weren't any negative side effects from this type of cultivation.

The corruption wasn't a tangible element, so there were no physical impurities that could hamper his cultivation. It was more akin to a Dao-infused wound, but his bloodline was uniquely capable at dealing with things like that. Neither did interacting with the corruption seem to impact his still-damaged foundations. More things might crop up after prolonged use, but it really seemed as though the lake water was suitable for long-term cultivation.

Of course, he hadn't forgotten the lessons he'd learned while trapped in the poisonous sea. Vai's research notes had shown how small alterations to his approach could have huge benefits. A few percent improved efficiency here and there would accumulate just like his titles, and a perfected cultivation method might be twice as good as simply sitting down in the water.

Like this, days passed as Zac entered a cycle of cultivation, comprehension, and experimentation.

Zac's most important goal was to waste as little lake water as possible. He did have a huge amount of it stored in his canteens, but it was still a finite resource. The first step was to find the right quantity of water per session. Zac soon realized that the amount of water used had a noticeable effect on how much corruption he absorbed per second. In other words, it wasn't just a matter of covering his entire body.

It was just like when he visited the lake itself. Back then, just a few seconds was enough to overload him if he didn't use [Void Zone] as a buffer. The absorption rate was far lower when using the water in a tub. However, when Zac changed his smaller tub for a larger medicinal bath, the rate increased.

The key was to find a level of optimal efficiency. Too little water, and [Purity of the Void] would purify and waste a large chunk. It was an annoying reminder that his Bloodline Method, [Bloodline Resonance], was utter garbage, completely incapable of providing Zac with even a semblance of control over most of his bloodline.

If he used too large a vat and too much lake water, he would instead lose a great amount of it to the atmosphere, and he had found no way to salvage the insights by that point. Zac figured out the right balance through trial and error, and constructed a larger bath of two-by-two meters and filled it up to his chest while sitting.

By that point, Zac started another series of experiments to further improve the process. The type of arrays medicinal baths used to retain medicinal energy were completely incapable of trapping the corruption. Heating the water was even worse—it rapidly increased the dissipation rate.

Conversely, cooling the water had the opposite effect, so Zac had Triv install ice arrays that lowered the temperature far beyond what could be found in nature. Allowing the water to turn into ice would ruin the absorption process, but Zac circumvented that by adding powerful gravity arrays. Working in conjunction, Zac pushed the lake water far into sub-zero degrees, drastically improving the retention.

The gravity arrays even helped stimulate his bloodline a bit, allowing him to absorb the corruption faster. That way, he could add more water per session without any downside, further speeding up his cultivation. The catch was that the sessions grew a lot more grueling. Between the blistering cold and crushing pressure, most F-grade cultivators would die instantly after entering the vat.

Even then, Zac mostly felt nostalgic as he silently endured the torture. It made him think of his first weeks on Demon Island, when he was still finding his way in this new reality. A gravity array had been one of his first purchases from the town shop, which had allowed him to refine his body and gain a few attribute points.

Today, he endured a punishment hundreds of times more severe, but Zac was certain he wouldn't gain any attributes even if he spent years in these arrays. He'd all but exhausted the untapped potential in his body. Common E-grade warriors might be able to gain a few hundred attribute points through decades of painstaking work. But elites who had elevated their bodies through Daos, attribute fruits, and titles had very little room for conventional gains.

Another discovery was that he couldn't just keep absorbing the water indefinitely. After roughly an hour of cycling water and epiphanies, his mind was completely shot, like he'd been cramming for an exam for 24 hours straight. Even if his [Void Heart] kept extracting the marvelous insights, it barely allowed him to digest any more knowledge.

Perhaps it was for the best. Forcibly pushing his understanding forward at a breakneck pace might lead to rickety foundations. It was better to take things one step at a time and digest what he'd learned after every session.

And it wasn't like Zac didn't have other things to do. Ten days after secluding himself, he resumed his Soul Cultivation, which took up most of his time. Zac initially planned on waiting a bit longer, but there was no other choice. The Moss Crystal was continuously feeding him, and the energy it released wouldn't perfectly meld with his Soul Cores on its own. If he didn't start refining the energy, he'd end up weakening his cores.

That could be considered the real downside of the Moss Crystal. Zac estimated he would start running into trouble if he didn't run his method at least twice a week on average. Any less and his soul would eventually be riddled with imperfections.

If this had happened while in the Twilight Ascent or the Void Star, such a situation might have spelled trouble. He didn't have the luxury to set aside whole days for Soul Cultivation back then. Luckily, he was back on Earth, and the downside was no downside under these conditions.

Another piece of good news was that running his [Nine Reincarnations Manual] extracted even more energy from the Moss Crystal, speeding up his cultivation speed even further. At this pace, Zac believed he'd finish forming his next set of Outer Cores in a few months, saving him potentially years of effort.

Then finally, the day came. A full three weeks had passed since returning from Emerald Eye, and Zac judged his body was finally in condition to try out the grand prize from his visit to the Void Star—the [Void Vajra Sublimation]. Between the healing baths and top-tier environment, Zac had recovered a bit earlier than expected.

Over the past week, he'd gone over his new method numerous times just to ensure there weren't any mishaps. Though he wasn't sure it was needed. The old [Boundless Vajra Sublimation] had somehow been engraved onto his mind by Three Virtues, with every single detail as clear as day. Later, the Seal of the Left Imperial Palace reforged that parcel of imparted memories, which would have allowed him to start cultivating back in the Void Star already.

The only reason he hadn't done so was that he had too much on his plate, and the lingering worry of there still being traps hidden in the depths of the method. But no matter how he looked, the dangerous elements were solved by completely swapping out the Heart Cultivation aspect of the Body Tempering Manual. Even the movements and medicinal array patterns had been altered to suit his new direction, leaving none of the three pillars of the method entirely intact.

Zac wasted no time as he walked over to a grove inside the Life-attuned side of his cultivation cave. In the beginning, the environment had mostly been powered by the [Lotus of Harmony], the [Primordial Breath Amanita], and Divine Crystals. Similarly, the Miasmic side utilized the odd seed the Undead Empire used as an Array Core to realign planets, along with Miasma Crystals.

But the Nexus Veins beneath the island had gradually transformed as Earth continued its transition into a Life-Death world. Most of the veins were still unattuned, but both Divine Veins and Miasmic Veins had started to crop up here and there. Now, two of the purest veins were the main source of attunement in his cultivation cave, providing the environment with nigh-endless energy of Life and Death.

Triv had already prepared a spot to practice his Body Tempering Manual, an undertaking that led to no small amount of suffering for the poor ghost. The spectral butler had looked so wan after spending time inside the Life-attuned Forest, that Zac had given him a vacation and a couple of Death-attuned treasures to recuperate.

Now, the small grove was already instilled with Gathering, Purifying, and Gravity arrays to maximize the efficiency of the Body Tempering Manual. He'd made some inquiries into getting the Arhat Golden Flames mentioned in the manual, but he couldn't find anything like it in Zecia. Besides, Zac wasn't even sure the treasures mentioned in the old method would even work after he reformed the **[Void Vajra Sublimation]**.

This would be the first time he cultivated the method, so Zac only activated the Purifying Array as he got completely naked. Here beneath the mountains, there was no point in covering himself. He'd already burnt off his hair and beard to more easily tack on the medicinal mixture. One line after another of Life-attuned paste was added across his body, and he was covered from head to toe in no time.

The new pattern was similar to the original arrays he'd painted on himself while trapped in the Undrusian Sea, yet different. They were somehow inverted, even if the array was clearly a manifestation of Life. It reminded him of the difference between seeing himself in a mirror and a picture.

Zac couldn't quite remember or understand the underpinning concepts that led to these changes. Now that the boundless comprehension of Ultom was long gone, he was only left with vague and blurry impressions. The changes were done to allow for a greater harmonization between the materials and a Heart Cultivation centered on the concept of the Void, rather than the Buddhist harmonization with the cosmos.

All done, Zac started moving with pinpoint precision, following the new sets of movements designed to agitate his cells and allow them to accept the medicinal paste. Just like the array covering his body, the movements were both familiar and foreign. But with the experience he'd accumulated by this point, he easily completed the first cycle.

"Ka," Zac uttered, followed by a sharp inhalation the moment his right foot slammed into the ground.

It felt like the whole cave—the whole world—shuddered from the step, and Zac's perception shifted.

When he'd tried out the **[Boundless Vajra Sublimation]** in the Void Star, this step of the manual elicited a sense of profound vastness. It had felt like his body was being tuned to the frequency of the cosmos, connecting him with all of creation. That way, he was one with all, and for Life to meld with his body was natural and expected.

This time, the feeling was diametrically different. Instead of being one with the universe, Zac felt like he'd stepped out of the Multiverse. He had become the all-encompassing Void, everything and nothing at once—a small island of nothingness surrounded by a sea of being.

His step hadn't opened or tuned his body to the Heavens—it had breached the impermeable layer between real and unreal. He could even see a hidden seal beneath his foot. An impossibly intricate spiral pattern reminding Zac of a black hole. It wasn't really there, yet it was. A manifestation of the heart—a heart attuned to the Void of Dao.

Something that might only be achievable by Zac across the whole Multiverse.

And through this mysterious breach, Life poured into the Void—into his body. There was no clash like when Life and Death struggled for supremacy inside his cultivation cave. The Void could accept anything. The medicinal array, the steps, the breathing. They were designed to snatch Life while keeping the rest of the cosmos at bay.

Reality acceded to the undeniable truth in Zac's heart, and his body heated up as the energy was dragged into his body by the pull of the Void. The pain was agonizing, but Zac barely registered it. He'd entered an ethereal state where everything was absorbed and consumed. The Life-attuned paste and the ambient energy. The pain. Even his thoughts.

It all entered the black hole of his existence, becoming fuel for his path.

Another step, another seal, and another breach to welcome Life into the Void. Altogether, eighty-one aspects of the Void formed a complete circuit, both with the Dao of Life and within his body. Any more, and extraneous concepts would be allowed to join the perfect system. Any less and the transformation would be imperfect, incomplete.

Zac persevered through the pain, moving toward the next expression of the Void. But it was at that point his perception was nudged, almost to the point Zac lost his focus. [Void Heart] had finally woken up, and it greedily wanted to consume the foreign energies that had entered his body. It felt like the Void splintered, with there suddenly being two black holes—himself and his Hidden Node, both competing for the same energy.

Zac knew this would come, yet he couldn't help but feel a wave of annoyance upon sensing some of the energies, *his* energies, drift toward his heart. Going through the eighty-one aspects of the Void and completing a Body Tempering session would take over an hour, and who knew how much energy [Void Heart] would manage to steal?

Even worse, with this kind of energy, it would only return bog-standard Cosmic Energy, completely wasting Zac's time. Losing some resources was fine, but losing months of progress was not. Zac kept going through the motions of the [Void Vajra Sublimation], not wanting to stop prematurely and waste a whole session.

But in his mind, Zac was roaring at [Void Heart] to stop, to give him a break.

And the node obeyed.

# 45

# TAKING CONTROL

Zac couldn't believe it when [Void Heart] suddenly shuddered and stopped contending for the medicinal paste mid-beat. The surprise was so big that he tripped, instantly failing the stance and losing the ethereal connection to the Void. The Life-attuned Energy that had entered his cells failed to fuse and instead started seeping through his pores.

It was an unavoidable result of not completing the session. Only when fully completing the [Void Vajra Sublimation] would the Integration become perfect, allowing some of the Life-attuned Energies to fuse with his body permanently. Even then, Zac didn't mind the loss. He sat down, far more interested in what just happened. This was only the first session, and discoveries were far more important than the progress itself.

And this was a big one.

Ever since breaking open [Void Heart], it had always marched to its own beat. Zac was never able to control it in the slightest. Instead, he'd been forced to learn its rules and work within those confines. But this time, he somehow managed to connect to the Hidden Node and turn it off with a mental command.

But now, the moment had passed. Zac watched on as [Void Heart] resumed thumping, dragging the lingering Life-attuned Energy into its vortex. He tried commanding and cajoling it like before, but the Hidden Node completely ignored him. Even then, Zac wasn't overly concerned. Between the ethereal connection he'd sensed and how different the [Void

Heart| acted, he knew what he'd perceived was real and not some hopeful delusion.

Zac even had a decent idea of what was going on—it was all thanks to the |Void Vajra Sublimation|.

The whole reason to cultivate a Body Tempering Manual was to gain a specialized constitution. Like with Soul Strengthening Manuals and Souls, there were both attuned and unattuned constitutions. An unattuned constitution might provide general improvements, such as his Draugr durability and poison resistance. Meanwhile, an attuned constitution could attune your whole body to a specific Dao.

For example, a Pyromancer who managed to cultivate a Fire-attuned Constitution would find their skills were more powerful. Sometimes, they'd even improve their affinity to the Dao of Fire and their cultivation speed. The |Void Vajra Sublimation| was an example of an attuned Body Tempering Manual, where he would gain a Life-attuned Constitution to balance out his innate Death-attuned Draugr Constitution.

However, there was another aspect that complicated the situation with constitutions—bloodlines.

There had always been a close connection between constitutions and bloodlines. Most bloodlines naturally imbued the cultivator with a constitution, and specialized Bloodline Methods generally doubled as Body Tempering Manuals. The Izh'Rak Reavers were a prime example of this. They were all Body Tempering Cultivators who tempered their bones through their Racial Bloodline Methods.

In fact, people with bloodlines often had extremely stringent requirements on what Body Tempering Manuals they could use. The slightest mismatch and the unaffiliated manual wouldn't work. Such a conflict could even damage one's foundations. It was akin to a cultivator with a fire-based class suddenly starting to use a water-based Cultivation Manual.

This was something Zac had been worried about ever since getting his hand on the |Boundless Vajra Sublimation|. He knew next to nothing about his Void Emperor bloodline, except that it had some sort of relation to the Limitless Empire and Karz. What if he cultivated a Life-attuned Constitution, only to encounter a clash between the Body Tempering Manual and an incompatible bloodline?

That was a big reason for wanting to reform the method in the first place, though it had become a necessity for other reasons after discovering the hidden traps within the [Boundless Varja Sublimation]. If he tuned the method to the Void, the risk of conflict would hopefully decrease. Now, it looked like Zac hadn't only managed to avoid calamity, but reaped some benefits he'd barely dared hope for.

The [Void Vajra Sublimation] allowed him to connect with his Void Emperor bloodline in a way that [Bloodline Resonance] never had. Right now, it only worked while he was running the method and was attuned to the Void, but that might not be the case forever. Every reincarnation with the [Nine Reincarnations Manual] gave him greater control over his soul. In the same vein, every layer of [Void Vajra Sublimation] might improve his natural control over his bloodline.

Just turning the Hidden Nodes on and off was just the first step. Top-tier Bloodline Methods could even amplify the effect of bloodlines. What if he could suddenly supercharge [Void Zone], allowing it to spread across a whole enemy army? Or if he managed to completely open the floodgates of [Spiritual Void], drastically improving the lethality of a strike?

There were so many possibilities, but Zac reined in his imagination. There were ultimately no guarantees he'd gain full control over his Void Emperor bloodline through his Body Tempering Manual, even if things appeared promising. He would have to finish the first layer of the [Void Vajra Sublimation] to see the results.

Zac was even more eager to continue his cultivation after encountering such a stroke of good fortune, and he quickly bathed and reapplied a new set of Life-attuned paste. Moments later, he was once more one with the Void, moving from one position into another with pinpoint precision.

His muscles and tendons were shuddering from the surprisingly strenuous stances. Accepting the attuned energy into the depths of his cells felt like standing inside a bonfire. Yet he continued, forming one seal after another. Soon enough, [Void Heart] woke up once more, but a focused thought successfully quieted it down.

Zac didn't lose his focus this time, and smoothly transitioned to the next seal in the series, deepening his connection with the Void. The minutes passed, and a crackling sound accompanied his movements. It wasn't his bones creaking from the exertion but rather the paste covering his body.

More than half of its medicinal efficacy had been dragged into his body, prompting some of the paste to dry and fall off. The falling paste disintegrated and created a mysterious haze, unable to settle because of Zac's constant movements. It looked like he had formed a cloak of mist as he swirled around in the grove, a fog that echoed the secrets of Life. Once in a while, a shadow of inscrutable patterns would flicker in the dust, only to disappear as quickly as they formed.

As for Zac himself, he fell deeper into his Void state. Initially, he'd thought himself standing outside creation, a small pocket of anti-existence surrounded by the cosmos. Now, he gradually shifted like he was being superimposed on the world. He still was distinctly separate from the cosmos, but he was closer.

He'd become a specter walking through the Dao, grabbing what he wanted while passing through anything he disdained. His Branch of the Kalpataru was already coursing through his body because of the stances, helping draw more energy into his body while tuning it to his Path. As a result, it seemed like an illusory fractal was being constructed within him.

It was an expression of Life, one uniquely tailored to him and his Dao. Each seal he completed added to the pathways, pushing it closer to perfection. And the closer the pattern came to completion, the more strain Zac was under.

Like he was carrying a mountain on his back as he moved, but Zac knew it was actually the world trying to barge in, to depressurize and drag him out of the Void. Meanwhile, the Life-attuned Energy had reached the very depths of his cells, amplifying the pain.

Most F-grade cultivators would be forced to stop at this juncture and slowly build up experience and resistance. But not Zac. He was already at the Peak of E-grade, and neither the pain nor the pressure was enough to make him stumble at this critical time. He smoothly forged on until he reached a neutral stance where his hands slammed together.

"Aum," Zac hummed, and his voice melded with the sound of the clap from his palm.

He'd closed a gate to his body, completely cutting off the temporary connection with the universe after snatching the final expression of Life. As a result, the pressure disappeared, and the illusory fractal was

374 | JF BRINK & THEFIRSTDEFIER

perfected and melded with every inch of his body. All of the medicinal paste had already fallen off, and the last motes of Life-attuned Energy were swallowed by his cells.

Zac remained frozen in place for a few minutes as the swirling haze of dried paste gradually settled. His consciousness was like a diver slowly rising from the depths of a lake until it breached the surface. This time around, there was no need to activate [Void Zone] to purge the effect of the Heart Cultivation.

This wasn't the [Boundless Vajra Sublimation] with its path-breaking influence of the Buddhist Sangha. The [Void Vajra Sublimation] was uniquely tuned to himself, so there was no need to reset anything. If anything, he wanted to repeat and reinforce the Heart Cultivating aspect of his Body Tempering Manual.

Ultimately, it wasn't the Life-attuned Constitution that would allow him to connect with [Void Heart] and his bloodline. It was the Heart Cultivating aspect rolled into the method. And that part needed to be gradually built up, brick by brick, just like any other aspect of cultivation.

Of course, that didn't mean the impression of being a black hole separate from the universe was his true state of being. His self was *his* self, and his Dao Heart was *his* Dao Heart. They were connected but separate. It was more correct to say that his Path was being reinforced by these impressions, rather than his personality.

Cultivating his heart this way would allow it to become sturdier, like intangible walls protecting him from outside influence. Whether it was the Buddhist Sangha, the corrupted water of the Lost Plane, or the immortal will of the Remnants, they would find it much harder to influence his mind and his Path. He would be just like the Void—there yet separate, taking what he needed, and rejecting everything else.

Zac took a deep breath and opened his eyes. The first thing he noticed was that his skin had taken on an almost copper hue. The redness came from the damage the process had done to his skin, while a slight golden tint came from the Life-attunement. This wasn't a permanent effect, and the color was already fading thanks to his bloodline and high Vitality.

This was exactly what he hoped to see happen. To reach an equilibrium between his two races, just completing the first layer of the [Void

**Vajra Sublimation]** wasn't enough. He didn't exactly know how big the gain from each layer was, but he would at least have to complete the first two layers for his human body to match up to the latent potential of a pureblood Draugr.

There were no hard and fast rules to how much Body Tempering you could practice. It all came down to your body and how much punishment you could take. Some cultivators could only absorb a small amount of energy before their cells reached their limit, where they would have to take a break to recover and stabilize. And how long that period of recovery was differed from person to person.

In this regard, Zac believed his potential was outstanding. His bloodline made his cells unique, almost turning *them* into black holes that could naturally swallow up energies. And between his extraordinarily high Vitality, his Branch of the Kalpataru, and his other unique advantages, his body recovered far quicker than normal.

Peering into his cells' depth, Zac sensed the energy he'd absorbed. They were like small flakes of gold swirling around in the vortices of his cells. Most would soon be filtered out, but some would permanently stay on and become part of his body. This was regrettable but ultimately unavoidable.

More importantly, Zac could tell that one session absolutely wasn't his limit, at least not while he still practiced the first layer. As long as he had more paste at hand and could endure the punishment, he could keep going. So, he did.

Zac only needed to wait ten minutes for his body to stabilize, at which point he reapplied the paste. This time, Zac activated all the arrays to improve the effect even further. Roughly an hour later, Zac lay sprawled on the ground as steam rose from him in mighty plumes. Occasionally, one of his muscles would twitch, prompting a series of painful jerks across his body.

Normally, Zac would barely notice a gravitational amplification of ten times. But he'd almost been pushed to his limits when performing the stances in that kind of environment. It wasn't the stances themselves that became too strenuous. The difficulty came from how the gravity array had somehow magnified the mysterious pressure of the cosmos.

But it'd paid off. Almost twice as many golden flakes had been added thanks to the arrays, and Zac believed he'd be able to push the arrays even further as he mastered the process. Not only would his body adapt to the pressure, but the original [Boundless Vajra Sublimation] also mentioned that the stronger one's Dao Heart grew, the better one could endure the training.

It should be possible to push the gravity arrays all the way to fifty so long as one's heart grew firm enough. That would, theoretically, increase the cultivation speed a few times over, though you'd have to use higher-grade medicinal paste. The cost per session would shoot through the roof going about things this way, but Zac welcomed any improvements that could be seized by throwing money at them.

Altogether, Zac managed to practice the [Void Vajra Sublimation] five times before his body reached saturation. By that point, he could tell he wouldn't be able to retain Life-attuned flakes of gold even if he could withstand the pain, and he was better off letting his body settle while practicing his other methods.

After adding the [Void Vajra Sublimation] to the mix, Zac was finally running toward Hegemony at full steam. At the same time, Zac felt the truth in Pavina's teachings at this moment. The Revenant Monarch had warned against spreading himself too thin back in the Orom World, where tacking on too many things to your Path would eat up too much time and steal your momentum.

Twenty-four hours simply wasn't enough to fit everything he needed to train. But instead of cutting out things from his itinerary, Zac divided his days into 36-hour-cycles. That way, he could fit [Nine Reincarnations Manual], [Void Vajra Sublimation], [Thousand Lights Avatar], and study both Duality and the general theories of Core Blueprints.

The only windows of rest he gave himself were those small pockets of utmost exhaustion after each Body Tempering session. After a few days, even those short windows were filled with Triv updating him on the ongoings on the outside. Everything was steadily progressing. The topic of the war had already swept across the planet, and the recruitment stations across Pangea were almost mobbed with people.

Zac had been worried they would face staunch resistance from his citizens, to the point they'd be forced to conscript people. But a few rumors proved more efficient than any stick or carrot Zac could produce. The threat of another System-run worldwide event had made people desperately try to join the Atwood Reserves.

The horror of the Integration was still fresh in the minds of most people, and many knew they only survived through sheer luck, while 80% of the world's population had perished. They weren't confident in surviving another round in case the System dragged the conflict to Earth, so they sought strength and safety from the Atwood Army.

Others saw the war as an opportunity to catch up after a weak start to their cultivation journey. There were plenty who regretted not pushing harder during the Tutorial and the early phases of the Integration. When it was easier to rack up achievements and the air was literally filled with the Dao.

It was widely believed that Zac's monstrous strength came from hitting the ground running and closing both the first and the most incursions, which was partly true. So many elites thought if they could rack up some early achievements in the war, they could snowball that into huge gains. Thanks to that, many independent talents had finally taken the step to properly join Zac's faction over the past weeks.

Zac himself didn't bother with the details. Ilvere and the other leaders had already set up standardized tests and training programs to turn the recruits into powerful cogs in the Atwood Empire's war machine.

One day, there was a break in the monotony, as Zac received a notice he'd been expecting for a while.

Vilari and the others were back.

# 46

# RENDEZVOUS

Checking the time, Zac realized he'd already spent over a month grinding his Body Tempering Manual. Altogether, close to three months had passed since he returned to Earth, and it was about time to deal with the lingering matters standing between him and his prolonged seclusion.

Just ten minutes later, five people gathered in Zac's compound: Zac and Ogras, along with the three candidates chosen to receive the heritage of Ultom. Ogras had thankfully returned a week ago after having surveyed not only the remaining moons but also the two neighboring worlds containing beasts.

Zac was curious about the demon's findings, but the matter of Ultom obviously took precedence.

"Anything?" Zac asked, already knowing he had his answer upon seeing Joanna's downcast face.

"None of us managed to attain a seal," Joanna sighed. "We did find six structures with fragmented markings related to one of the nine outer sigils, but we failed to uncover any fragments. Four of the buildings were unsealed and searched already by the scouting parties, while the remaining two were part of sealed blocks. Neither of the two had any dust lining the streets like you described, though."

"We managed to break into one of the two sealed chambers," Rhuger added. "We did make some interesting finds, such as Cultivation Manuals and a powerful recipe that seemed to be a faith-based berserking pill. But no seal."

"So, nothing?" Ogras muttered, glancing at Zac. "Then just what's going on with your quest?"

"That's—" Zac frowned, not sure himself. He opened his Quest Screen to make sure, but the result was the same.

**One by Nine (Unique, Inheritance):** Form a full cycle of Sealbearers.
**Reward:** Entry to the Left Imperial Palace (4/9) [2604 days] **[NOTE: Multiple cycles can be formed.]**

The progress was still the same, with almost half of the slots already filled in. Back then, the progress made sense if you counted Ogras, Joanna, Rhuger, and Vilari. But now, Zac didn't know what to think.

"There was really *nothing?*" Zac asked to make sure.

"Well," Joanna hesitated and glanced to Vilari, who wordlessly took out a black crystal ball the size of Zac's fist.

It didn't emit any energy fluctuations, and **[Cosmic Gaze]** didn't give Zac any indication something was special about it either. It just looked like a black decorative glass ball. Considering how carefully Vilari held onto it, there had to be more to it than that.

"This was the only thing of interest," Vilari said. "We found it in the center of the building we managed to unseal. Neither Rhuger nor Joanna can sense anything from this thing. Truthfully, neither can I, yet I'm drawn to it for some reason. I feel there is some secret inside it. I just haven't figured out how to unlock it. I was wondering if you could sense anything from it?"

Zac and Ogras looked at the crystal, but neither could glean anything.

"Nothing," Zac said with a shake of his head. "But that doesn't necessarily mean anything."

"That's right," Ogras agreed. "I've visited two sites with seals belonging to Zac, and I couldn't sense the slightest hint of anything magical coming from those places. I think only those fated will be able to connect with the items related to the Outer Courts."

"But I can't get anything from it," Vilari sighed with helplessness.

"Give it time," Ogras said. "I had to kill a kingdom's worth of cursed beings to gain access to my seal. I don't think everyone will fall ass-backward into an opportunity like our blessed lord here."

"It doesn't hurt to keep working at it," Zac agreed, ignoring the demon's jab. "Since you're the one who can sense something, it might be related to the soul. Maybe one of the courts is related to Mentalists? After all, Ogras got the Hollow Court, which seems suitable to him. Soul-related things often take a bit longer."

"I'll keep trying," Vilari nodded.

"Did you find any signs of Janos?" Ogras asked. "If I'm one and Vilari is the second, then Janos could be counted as the third. That only leaves one mystery person for the quest."

"No," Joanna said. "If his disappearance is related to all this, then he's either in the central temple we sealed off or in the building we couldn't crack open."

Zac sighed. "I'll try to break into that building later to ensure he's not trapped. Otherwise, I think the results are decent. The Ensolus Ruins weren't that big. Finding a possible clue apart from my own seal is pretty good already."

"I'm sorry we couldn't help you more," Joanna said.

"Don't look at it like that," Zac said with a shake of his head. "I was just hoping to provide the same kind of opportunity I've enjoyed. I have no expectations of you helping me in the upcoming inheritance."

"Besides, it's not over yet," Ogras added. "We're heading to the Million Gates Territory. A few years there will provide far more opportunities than some old ruins. The Ensolus Ruins were probably just placed there by the Ruthless Heavens for its favorite son to finish up his seal."

"I guess that's true. It's still not over," Joanna said. "We have the Million Gates Territory."

"And even if that fails, there's a final chance waiting for you," Ogras continued. "Seizing fate. We already know this mess has been integrated with the upcoming war. I am certain likes will attract, and we will find ourselves fighting against other seal holders."

"Stealing the opportunities from others?" Joanna said with a small frown. "That's a bit…"

"Cultivation has always been a fight for resources," Ogras snorted. "How is this any different? Better we get the slots than some outsider bastards. Or even worse, the invaders."

"We still don't know if things will work like that," Zac said, but there wasn't a lot of conviction behind his words. He could almost feel it. A storm of fate was brewing, and those with affinity would find themselves on a collision course sooner or later.

"We'll figure out the rules given time," Ogras said. "There are probably a few infiltrators who have stumbled upon opportunities already."

"That's fine, but I doubt getting the seals that way will provide the same burst of insight," Zac said. "The insights themselves are half the reason to get the seals, considering we have no idea how dangerous the actual inheritance is. We might be forced to bow out immediately when faced with the scions from the outside. If possible, we want to find the seals rather than snatch them."

"All the more reason to not waste any more time. The ships are ready, and the key personnel has returned. We're just waiting for your go-ahead," Ogras said, and Zac could see the other three were of a like mind.

Zac nodded in agreement. It was time for his subordinates to spread their wings and search for their own opportunities. Emily had already gone ahead in that regard. Zac had sent a demon to the Bloodwind Planet to bring her a message he was back. But it turned out Emily had left for the Million Gates Territory as part of the very same coalition army Zac had seen mentioned when he visited the coliseum all those years ago.

The thought filled Zac with a mix of pride and worry. Part of him wanted to set out himself and bring her back home. Except the better part of a decade had passed since they last met. She wasn't the wild teenager robbing adventurers any longer. Like Thea once said, she had to find her path. Zac believed she would return before the war, hopefully strong enough to help keep both herself and Earth safe.

The same was true for the others. They would never become true elites until they gained some real experience. But he couldn't ferry them over to the Red Zone of the Allbright Empire just yet.

"I just need your help dealing with a few things before you go," Zac said.

"The Integration?" Vilari said, and a rare hint of anticipation flashed across her face.

Zac nodded. "The Integration of the undead. Everything is prepared."

"When will you announce it?" Vilari asked.

Zac turned to Ogras first. "How did the experiments go?"

"It worked just fine. The little blue cheat came through. The plan seems feasible, and we can start setting things up anytime."

"And the other thing?" Zac asked.

"Here," Ogras said and threw over a box. "Three uses."

"Perfect," Zac sighed in relief, then turned to Vilari. "I just need to meet with the representatives of the Undead Empire. We'll go ahead with the Integration no matter what their stance is. But having some assurances would be better, especially for the Raun Spectrals who are currently in a tough spot."

"Of course," Vilari said.

Zac turned back to Ogras. "Set everything up, and I'll send the location to Catheya today. It should take them around a week to reach the planet we chose."

"Do you want me to accompany you to the meeting?" Vilari asked.

"No, this time, I have something different in mind," Zac said with a shake of his head.

"Do you need our help in some other ways?" Joanna asked.

"Just focus on your upcoming expedition. Ogras and I are enough to deal with the preparations." Zac smiled. "Ten days. Provided the meeting is fruitful, we will have a global announcement in ten days."

"I guess it's time to earn my pay," Ogras grunted as he got to his feet. "I'm heading to So'Liv."

"Perfect," Zac said. "I guess I'll go deal with things from my end."

It was going to be a busy week.

---

"Long time no see," Zac smiled as his old friend stepped into the little meeting room he'd placed in the middle of the forest. "You look nice."

It was true. Zac didn't know what Catheya had been through since they met last, but it felt like every single aspect of her had undergone a subtle yet very noticeable elevation. Her appearance had moved closer to perfection, in the same sense that Iz's features were marked by the Dao. She even carried herself with a level of grace that eclipsed her previous manner. Just taking a few steps into the building had almost been enough to steal Zac's breath away.

It wasn't just her appearance either. Her aura was incredibly condensed, surpassing that of elites like Leyara and Ogras. She still wasn't at the level of Iz, but it was far beyond her previous status as a decently talented Scion of the Empire Heartlands. It looked like Catheya had encountered some lucky opportunities of her own, real significant ones at that.

"What nice? You unrepentant troublemaker, you know what kind of headache you created for me?" Catheya huffed as she sat down opposite him. "I've had the ancestors breathing down my neck for years because you had to go get swallowed up by a space fish, and now you don't even come meet me in person? You send this tin can in your stead?"

"Well, it was a gift from you, so I figured it was suitable," Zac joked.

This was the solution he and Ogras had landed on. As they saw it, there were only two ways to ensure a safe meeting when there were Monarchs in the mix. Either he would have to meet Catheya with some sort of proxy, or he would have to take Catheya to a different world to shake off her handlers.

Ogras had argued for the latter, saying it would allow them to control the situation better. They would set up a meeting, but only leave Catheya a Teleportation Token. After she'd arrived at some other corner of Zecia, Zac could teleport in, and they could have the meeting in peace. Knowing there was no way for the Monarchs of the Undead Empire to get there in short order.

Ultimately, Zac felt this method put Catheya in too much danger and chose the proxy method instead. The problem was that no place on a planet was safe when C-grade cultivators were involved. If they managed to pin down your location, they could be there at a moment's notice, sealing you before you even had a chance at teleporting back home.

So he simply didn't stay on the planet.

Zac's vision was currently split into two. One of them was the puppet's sight, where he saw Catheya in the secluded meeting place on So'Liv Six, a central planet in the Kaldran Strait. It was mostly a desolate wasteland because of its location. The Late E-grade planet was situated at one of the narrower stretches of the border between the Undead Empire and the surrounding empires, and it had been swept up in the struggle more than once.

Currently, it was tentatively under the control of the Empire of Light, but it was pretty much a penal colony and advance scouting station. A few million people had been transferred over to harvest some of the local plants, and the Empire hoped their presence would at least give a small warning in the event of an invasion. It was the perfect place to hold a clandestine meeting with the Undead Empire. The undead delegates could get there in a week, moving from one of the closest frontier planets under their control.

While the puppet he got in the Twilight Ascent was sent down to the surface, Zac himself was hiding in the vast emptiness of space, remotely controlling it from a safe distance. He wasn't using one of the standard Creator Vessels either, but something much better, the Yphelion.

He was currently sitting in a large room, its walls glistening in a beautiful mix of gold and black. It wasn't a design choice by Zac, but rather a result of the materials that went into building the huge space catamaran. Zac had provided a lot of Life and Death-attuned materials for its upgrade, and after being purified and turned into alloys, they had mostly gained these colors naturally. The few with different colors had been altered by the Creators to not clash with the theme.

The bridge of the Yphelion looked a bit different compared to the one of the Starflash. For one, it was almost twice as big to accommodate a large floating sphere over five meters across. It was the core of the reconnaissance arrays, and ten administrators were sitting around it, continuously sifting through the endless data it spat out.

After building the first batch of ships, Zac immediately switched production to his own Cosmic Vessel. Thankfully, it had been completed with time to spare, which drastically increased the chance of their plan succeeding. Now, the vessel was hidden in a debris field at the edge of So'Liv Six's solar system.

Obviously, the puppet Catheya gave him couldn't be controlled over such vast distances. It was hastily constructed by an E-grade craftsman inside the Twilight Ascent, limited both by materials and the creator's skill. But on the outside, they had no such limitations, and much of the internal machinery of the puppet had been replaced over the past weeks.

Even then, sending a signal across a whole solar system was easier said than done, which is why Zac had placed hundreds of repeaters between So'Liv Six and the debris field. This technology was something he'd tasked Ogras with testing out while he surveyed the neighboring planets around Earth.

It'd worked perfectly thanks to Calrin's connections. The only downside was that the signal would be drowned out in regions with too many people and arrays. But there was no interference to speak of in a desolate forest of a mostly-deserted planet. This way, Zac could meet up with Catheya with peace of mind. Even if the Monarchs managed to trace the signal, there was no way for them to get close without the Yphelion's powerful sensors picking something up.

In fact, Zac already knew that two Monarchs were hidden in the forest, both exhibiting energies at the Middle C-grade. Not only that, but there was one more staying in the Cosmic Vessel that had ferried Catheya to So'Liv Six three hours ago. It was proof of how seriously they were taking this meeting and how he'd been right not to trust a powerful faction like the Undead Empire blindly.

The hidden traps of the [Boundless Vajra Sublimation] had engraved an important lesson on the dangers of the Multiverse deep into his bones, and it paid off today.

## 47
# CAT AND MOUSE

Spotting the three Monarchs wasn't only a confirmation that Zac was right to be occasionally paranoid. It was also proof of just how powerful the sensors of the Yphelion were. There wasn't any way for him to actually see the Monarchs, but he could pinpoint their location with a hundred-meter precision across half the solar system. And even if they hid their presence, the Yphelion could somewhat estimate their strength by how the Cosmic Energy around them reacted to their presence.

Zac hoped this would be enough to deal with those sneaky elders. Even if the undead Monarchs managed to break through the protections of the repeaters and trace the signal, they still had to reach the Space Debris. By that point, Zac would be long gone, having jumped to a different dimension. From there, he could make his way to any number of planets at the edge of the Empire of Light.

Even the Monarchs would have to be careful about following him there. If the Empire of Light were a bunch of weaklings, they'd have been swallowed by the Kavriel Province long ago. They might not have as powerful Monarchs as the ones sent from the Undead Empire, but the Empire of Light possessed some of the most powerful arrays and fortifications in the Sector.

They'd reinforced their borders for millions of years, spending mind-boggling resources on defensive arrays and other fortifications. And they were all designed to kill or weaken the undead. Not only that, but most of the top factions of Zecia had pitched in to construct this iron curtain so they wouldn't have to deal with the Undead Empire.

"You came as a puppet out of nostalgia?" Catheya said with a roll of her eyes. "I'm sure it has nothing to do with your paranoia."

"Well, it might have been a factor. You can never be too safe." Zac laughed, but he chose not to expose that he knew about the Monarchs just yet. "How did things go on your end? You never provided a clear answer in the messages."

"No small talk as usual?" Catheya giggled, and Zac couldn't help but sneak a peek at the impressive cleavage she was showcasing today. "I'd hoped that some time spent apart would have made your insensitive heart grow fonder."

"I'm working on my manners." Zac smiled. "But people are already gunning for me left and right. I need to know if I should add the Undead Empire to the list."

"I guess that makes sense," Catheya said, her face turning serious. "Before anything, there's something I need to know, and don't you dare lie."

Zac was slightly surprised by the sudden shift in tone. He guessed Catheya's handlers had left her with strict instructions. Perhaps she was even fed her lines from the Monarchs hiding in the bushes. The longer the meeting dragged on, the higher the risk was of something going wrong, so if they wanted to jump straight into business, he was amenable to that.

"Alright, what is it?" Zac asked.

"Do you really think I look pretty?" Catheya, her serious face breaking into a radiant smile.

"What? That's what you wanted to know?" Zac said with exasperation.

"Of course. You said I looked nice. It hasn't been easy dragging compliments out of you, so I just wanted to make sure." Catheya grinned, and she even fluttered her eyelashes a bit.

Zac inwardly groaned. How could she act like this with three ancient monsters listening in? Was she trying to get in trouble? Besides, the situation was a bit embarrassing for him as well. It almost felt like having a girlfriend brazenly flirt with him in front of her grandparents. But what could he do but accommodate her? He didn't want to talk to the ancestors just yet.

"You really do," Zac said. "It feels like you've become more in tune with the Dao. You must have worked hard on your cultivation over the past years."

Zac hoped that was enough to get Catheya back on track, but she didn't look too enthused about his answer. "Still a block of wood. Would it kill you to throw out some niceties unrelated to cultivation?"

"That's…" Zac hesitated, suddenly feeling a bit regretful over his perfunctory answer.

Even if you disregarded the matter of the Monarchs, this wasn't his forte. He hadn't been the best communicator even before the Integration, and the events since had only made it harder for him to open up. There was even a small voice in the back of his head warning him from allowing himself to be attracted to others. No matter if you looked at Alea, Thea, or Hannah, his romantic interests hadn't fared so well since the Integration.

It made him think of Iz's warning to Ogras, of how his powerful fate would drown the demon if he didn't manage to elevate himself. No matter how you looked at it, the same could be said about the women around him. The cultists had targeted Hannah because of her relationship with him. Thea had been killed because of his mother's ideals.

Alea was a bit different, but it was still undeniable she'd been put in the position where her soul was shattered because of him. Her fate had been swept up by his, and she had been thrust into his conflicts until she eventually paid the price. Even before then, she'd almost been killed because of him on multiple occasions.

At the same time, pretending to be oblivious was both rude and cowardly. Catheya deserved better than that, even if she was partly teasing him right now.

"I—" Zac said, but he really didn't know what should come after that.

"Relax." Catheya laughed. "I can hear the gears turning from here. Don't worry. I know you've been forced to fully focus on the Dao just to survive. I still think you'll improve after you join a proper faction and don't have to fear every shadow. You can give me a proper answer by then."

Zac was thankful to have been given an out. "What have you been up to since the Twilight Ascent? I was worried there for a bit, even if you had your master with you. I didn't expect things to get so crazy."

"Apart from the year I've spent waiting for you here in Zecia, I've been staying at the Abyssal Lake. That place really is something. You'll only be able to unlock the true potential of your heritage if you go there. You can't imagine what it's like standing on its shores. It's like coming... home."

"Maybe one day."

Zac wasn't surprised Catheya's elevation was related to the Abyssal Lake. After all, it was the holy land of the Draugr, and there had to be all kinds of opportunities waiting there. At the same time, Zac guessed it wasn't the whole story. Because if everyone who visited the shores came out as powerful as Catheya, then the Draugr would already have become the leading race of the Undead Empire.

"You don't seem too interested," Catheya said with a pout. "I'm telling you, that place is amazing."

"I believe you," Zac laughed. "More importantly. I've been curious for a while. How did you know about the Orom?"

"Whatever. One day you'll realize I was right, and you were just obstinate. I can be magnanimous if need be." Catheya smiled. "Alvod Jondir's ascent made things a bit chaotic, as you can imagine. Such an important trade hub blew up, and even Divine Monarchs of the Undead Empire were killed and crippled. The Umbri'Zi Matriarch soon showed up to take charge of the situation."

"The top elder?" Zac exclaimed with some shock. "I thought those figures spent all their time in sealed cultivation chambers."

"Wouldn't the ancestors go mad if they had to live like prisoners?" Catheya countered. "Either case, your name soon came up. An unknown E-grade Draugr causing so much trouble, it beggared comprehension. It was all recorded, you know. What you did inside the City of Ancients?"

"Uh..." Zac coughed, suddenly doubly happy he'd chosen not to come in person.

"What was it you said to that lunatic as you ruined her plans? 'Since when has Draugr feared a bunch of bloodsuckers?'" Catheya grinned. "I have to admit, you were quite dashing there. It's a shame the conclusion was lost because of some sort of interference."

390 | JF BRINK & THE FIRST DEFIER

"That wasn't my—" Zac said.

"Relax. Those people only had themselves to blame. Who asked them to fish for opportunities in Draugr territories? In either case, between your performance and my introduction, Reyna Umbri'Zi was quite interested in you. But we couldn't find you. Not even your corpse —that thing you prepared was pretty good, but it wasn't enough to fool a motivated Autarch.

"Lady Umbri'Zi figured something was wrong after a lot of bodies had simply disappeared in the aftermath of the Twilight Ascent, and she found out about that Voidcatcher with the help of her skills," Catheya sighed. "Even then, she only managed to track it down because of some powerful energy fluctuations that could be felt far and wide. We ultimately learned about your fate from an Izh'Rak Reaver called Kaldor."

"You met Kaldor?" Zac exclaimed. "Is he okay?"

"I only read the reports, but he's fine. Reyna Umbri'Zi sensed there were imperials trapped within that fish's body and she had it spit them all out. Along with some monks, apparently, due to an agreement," Catheya said.

Zac sighed in relief upon hearing that both Kaldor and Pavina were fine. Both had taught him a lot during his stay in the Orom World, especially Pavina. But while he had helped Heda escape with the help of the seed, Pavina had been left behind. She'd stopped him when he tried to give her a hint about his imminent escape, but the matter still weighed on his heart over the past year.

However, there was one thing Zac had some difficulty understanding. Kaldor and the Umbri'Zi ancestor had saved Three Virtues and his fellow monks? "Since when were you guys so friendly with the Sangha?"

It didn't take a genius to figure out it was Three Virtues and his subordinates who'd been released. But why? The Sangha and the Undead Empire as a whole might not be mortal enemies, but they definitely weren't allies either.

"Well, for one, the leader among the monks had a pretty lofty position with the Sea of Tranquility, one of the Four Oceans of the Sangha," Catheya said with some fear in her eyes. "The Oceans are incredibly powerful and even more reclusive than the Mountains and Temples. They have never joined in on the crusade against the Undead Empire, apart from some of their Acolytes coming along to temper themselves. The elders didn't want to poke that hornet's nest. Attacking them might have summoned some terrifying Deva."

"The Sangha is that powerful?" Zac exclaimed. "They've caused you such a headache even without the top branches of the faction joining in?"

"Well, they're not considered a true peak faction without reason," Catheya shrugged. "But much of their strength comes from their consecrated grounds and seclusion. They wouldn't be able to exhibit the same level of power when emerging from their Holy Lands."

It was hard to imagine that shifty monk, Three Virtues, as some bigshot. Though Zac guessed it made sense. Three Virtues and Lord 84th were only splinters of the Lotus Emperor. And if a single fragment was a powerful cultivator who could become a Divine Monarch any time, then the Lotus Emperor was most likely a Late Autarch.

His shocking action of splitting his soul into 100,000 splinters and having them enter the cycle of reincarnation might be a bid to grasp the insight needed to become a Supremacy. To kill someone like that could create a huge problem for the Undead Empire.

"That's not all," Catheya added as she looked at Zac oddly.

"What? Something related to me?" Zac asked.

"Well, yes and no. It turned out Commander Kaldor hadn't been swallowed by the Orom on accident, and neither had that monk. They both had missions to investigate the Orom's actions. And according to the monk, Karma had been sown. Harming him would have a negative effect on their goals."

"Goals? The Orom's actions? What's going on?" Zac said with confusion. "Is it related to how it swallowed a bunch of cultivators left and right?"

"That was just a means to an end," Catheya said. "You should know those kinds of creatures normally don't appear in the frontiers. The Cosmic Energy is too sparse to sustain Autarchs, especially such large beings."

"I know, that's why it had to keep feeding," Zac said.

"But do you know *why* it stayed here, barely surviving at the edges of the universe?"

"I figured it was too weak or cowardly to contend for a domain in the central regions," Zac shrugged.

392 | JF BRINK & THEFIRSTDEFIER

"Actually, the Orom was part of a powerful faction, the Starbeast Alliance. That big spacefish would be one of its weaker core members. It was traveling across the frontier on a mission. Had been for millions of years."

"A mission for what?" Zac asked.

"That was what the Izh'Rak Reavers wanted to know after finding out about the Orom. Anything that would prompt a Primordial Beast to spend millions of years had to be pretty impressive, right? Something that would make powerful factions like the Starbeast Alliance mad with desire," Catheya said as she looked at him with a pointed gaze. "Can you think of something like that here on the frontier?"

"Don't tell me…" Zac muttered.

"The thing you unearthed," Catheya nodded in confirmation. "The Starbeast Alliance knew about that place somehow and has been searching for it for so long. Unfortunately for them, they encountered a wandering calamity like you, and their plans were exposed. Now, the Reavers are here for the prize, but we Draugr have also staked a claim. Partly because of you, partly because this is Draugr territory."

"So that's how it was," Zac said as a wry smile appeared on his face back on the Yphelion.

The Orom really was a bit unlucky. It'd searched for Ultom for millions of years, only to have its plans exposed because of Iz Tayn's grudge against him. The huge commotion Catheya mentioned was undoubtedly the flames of Iz's terrifying Dao Guardian, which led to the Orom being exposed even with its comprehension of the Dao of Space.

The Orom's involvement in all this could also explain why the Reavers were here in Zecia. To think that brute Kaldor was actually a covert agent seeking clues. No wonder he stayed on even if he could confirm his Dao any time he wanted.

"I still can't believe the Orom was looking for the Eternal Heritage," Zac muttered. "Did you guys kill it?"

"No," Catheya said. "Reyna Umbri'Zi wanted to, but she was only here in the frontier with a clone. It wasn't powerful enough, allowing the Primordial Beast to use some sort of forbidden skill and break free of her hold. But it shouldn't be able to recover in the short run."

"The others inside?" Zac asked, but he sighed when Catheya only shook her head.

This was the likely outcome for most of those trapped by that Primordial Beast, but it was still sad to have it confirmed. Many faces flashed past his eyes. People he'd met during his years trapped in the Orom. The Multiverse could be a cruel place. That some, including those closest to him, survived and managed to get out was at least a small comfort.

"You know…" Catheya said, dragging Zac out of his thoughts. "I know you wanted to discuss this with me, but there are real representatives waiting on the ship that took me here. People with actual influence. If you want, I can call them—"

"No need," Zac cut her off before turning the puppet's head in a certain direction. "In fact, if I see one of them make a move, I'll consider that as the end of this meeting. That includes the two elders hiding in the bushes."

"The what?" Catheya blurted, genuine confusion written all over her face.

A powerful snort echoed through the room a moment later, and a mighty pressure descended before it quickly disappeared. Zac didn't care—his real body was far away, after all. He was more interested to see that the two backed off and had teleported into their Cosmic Vessel.

"Keep a close watch on that ship. Make sure it's not up to something," Zac said to the administrators on the Yphelion before refocusing on Catheya.

"That's—" Catheya stuttered with a mix of resentment and helplessness. "I'm sorry, I didn't know. It's just that this is such an important matter, and I'm only a junior. I'm not qualified. But they're back on the vessel now, and we'll make reparations for this transgression."

"It's okay."

He really wasn't too upset over the Monarchs hiding. If anything, it allowed him to showcase that he wasn't some fool they could take advantage of, while also giving him an edge in the upcoming negotiations.

Besides, the Undead Empire would have to be crazy if they didn't at least try something. Truthfully, he would have done the same if he were in their shoes. This wasn't some random trade. It was an Eternal Heritage. If someone with the key to the inheritance had just strolled up to him, Zac would probably have kidnapped him as well if it was a matter of life and death for Earth.

Just like Ogras said, cultivation had always been a war for resources. It was simply a part of the struggles in reaching for the peak. Zac held no delusions they would stop after this one attempt either. It was unavoidable when being the weaker party, but he would be able to extract more benefits after every attempt, provided he managed to thwart them.

This was the dance of cat and mouse Zac would have to endure until he could lay down the law with his axe.

# ASSET OR LIABILITY

"We can talk about the heritage and reparations later. Let's go back to where we left off," Zac said. "So, what's the verdict? Discounting the thing brewing here in Zecia, does the Abyssal Shores consider me an asset or a liability?"

There were many things Zac needed to cover with Catheya, but the first thing he needed to do was to sound out his value as an individual to the Undead Empire. Even if he knew he'd never measure up to something like Ultom, he'd be safer the more valuable his identity as an Edgwalker was. It might make the Monarchs of the Empire think twice before trying to sacrifice him and instead lean toward plans that didn't include him dying.

"Asset or liability? Well, you tell me, Mr. Arcaz Umbri'Zi," Catheya winked.

"What?" Zac said.

"As I said, the Umbri'Zi Matriarch was intrigued by you, and she chose to cover for your actions. They claimed you were a hidden scion of their clan, and you accidentally went a bit overboard in the Mystic Realm when completing some tasks. Officially, you're currently in secluded cultivation to reflect on your actions. Congratulations, you've gone from a frontier hick to one of the most eligible Draugr bachelors in this generation." Catheya smiled.

"Well, it's not like the title is real," Zac snorted.

"No, it's real," Catheya said with a shake of her head. "I'm quite jealous. You'll be sent straight to the Abyssal Shores when you return for further training. And here."

Catheya placed three items on the table. They all looked extremely impressive, but one drew Zac's attention more than the others. After all, he'd seen that thing before—it was a Perennial Vastness Token.

"This is a small greeting gift from the Abyssal Shores and Clan Umbri'Zi. Things prepared before the situation became... complicated," Catheya said with a pointed look. "I know you recognize that token. Lady Reyna took it from the Twilight Lord's own hands. That's the benefit of being part of a top-tier faction."

"From Alvod? What happened with that guy?" Zac asked curiously.

"He succeeded with his ascent, and now he's a Grand Deacon of the Radiant Temple," Catheya shrugged.

"You guys didn't kill him?" Zac asked with surprise.

Catheya laughed. "Why should we? He has a deep grudge against the Havarok Empire, and he has no scruples. If anything, the Empire would be more inclined to send him Longevity Treasures so he can keep causing trouble."

"Well, alright then." Zac smiled as he took the Perennial Vastness Token and looked at the intricate seal on its surface.

Who could have thought he would end up getting the token Alvod promised him all those years ago? The problem was he already had one.

"Are you sure you're okay with giving this thing away?" Zac asked. "I can tell you're getting ready to break through as well."

"Who do you take me for?" Catheya said arrogantly. "If you can get one, then why can't I?"

Zac looked on with surprise as a second token appeared in her hand, this one identical to the one Zac held. "You got one as well? Since when were they so common?"

"Finder's fee. Introducing you came with some benefits. And while these things aren't common, they're not unique wonders of the Multiverse. If the Twilight Harbor can get one, then surely the Abyssal Shores can pick up a few. I was thinking we could go together. I still don't know exactly how things work in there, but having someone to watch your back can't hurt."

"Sounds good," Zac said as he pocketed the token. "I still need a few years to shore up my foundations, though."

It looked like he had some good news for Ogras when he returned. Vilari and Joanna were two other candidates, but he knew it was too early for them. Vilari wanted to push her soul further before breaking through, while Joanna sought to gain insights into her Path on the battlefield. That left Ogras, who was almost ready to enter Hegemony just like himself.

"That's fine," Catheya said. "I want to improve my foundations a bit before ascending as well. We can figure things out as the date gets closer."

"Sure. What are the other things?" Zac asked as he looked at the two other items—an engraved box that almost seemed to shift in and out of reality, and an opaque vial that exuded a pervasive darkness.

"The first one is called the [Essence of the Abyss]." A great longing lingered in Catheya's eyes as she looked at the vial. "Just like its name indicates, it contains the essence of the Abyssal Lake. It can't completely replace the real thing, but it will partly awaken your Draugr heritage. Opening at least one Hidden Node is a foregone conclusion."

Zac's brows furrowed a bit aboard the Yphelion as he looked at the vial. "How long can it be saved? Is it usable in the D-grade?"

"What?" Catheya said with confusion. "Why would you save it? You know, most Draugr would *kill* for this thing. Only a limited number of people can receive a true awakening every year, and creating this elixir removes a few of those slots. It doesn't have any drawbacks. It's a free elevation."

"My Draugr side is pretty powerful as is," Zac sighed. "Too strong, and there might be trouble when forming my core."

Zac obviously wouldn't mind getting a free power-up, especially with more Hidden Nodes on the line. However, he already had his plate full catching up to his Draugr side with the [Void Vajra Sublimation]. The past month had resulted in more progress than he'd expected, but it wasn't like he would reach a state of Life-Death equilibrium with years to spare.

If he suddenly awakened his Eoz bloodline with this treasure, there was simply no way to push his human side to the same level before the war started. There was still a chance it wouldn't matter for forming his Cultivator's Core, that his Daos being in balance would be enough. But the deeper his understanding of Duality became, the more he believed Three Virtues had been right in this regard.

Having an imbalance between the two elements would lead to an imperfect outcome, at the very least. It might make the core formation impossible for someone with a massive foundation like Zac. As a mortal, you had to thread a needle as you forcibly constructed a core powerful enough to carry your cultivation. If he also had to constantly keep watch to prevent the Death-attuned side from overwhelming the Life-attuned side, the difficulty would skyrocket.

"I-I'm not sure," Catheya said. "You can still awaken your bloodline as a Hegemon, but I don't think you'd be able to open your Hidden Nodes. Hidden Nodes are like small gateways into another dimension. When you attach a Cultivator's Core to your pathways, the surge of energy will wipe the slate, destroying or burying these entrances. Opening Hidden Nodes is difficult on its own, and doing it as a Hegemon is far too difficult."

Zac nodded thoughtfully, not sure what to do. It would really be too much of a waste not to open the Hidden Nodes while he had the chance. Perhaps if he could find some equally good body-refining treasures with Life-attunement? Maybe he could even have the Undead Empire source some treasures for him.

That actually didn't seem like a bad idea. Many of the Empire's enemies used Life-attuned treasures to deal with the Miasma of the Undead, and they should have seized mountains of the stuff over the years. Those items were essential to them. At the same time, they couldn't just sell them through some back channels since that might come back and haunt them later.

"Well, I don't have a solution in this regard. But the third gift might be useful if you can find one on your own," Catheya added, making Zac curiously look up from the vial.

"What's that?" Zac asked.

"I can't open it, but it's a Self-contained Temporal Chamber with three years sealed inside."

"A Temporal Chamber?" Zac hesitated. "That sounds a bit—"

Dangerous. That was the word Zac left out. Temporal Chambers were something that Zac had wanted to get his hands on for a while now. He'd heard of how Va Tapek had made Catheya cultivate in a Temporal

Chamber for a year, allowing her to quickly gain her levels in time for the Twilight Ascent.

The downside for her had been the inability to cultivate the Dao for that duration, but that didn't matter to Zac. He couldn't improve his Daos through meditation in either case and rather needed to deal with his constitution and soul. For him, a Temporal Chamber sounded like the perfect solution to his current time crunch.

Unfortunately, reality didn't always match up to expectations. After discussing the matter with Calrin, he soon found that things weren't so simple. There were a few solutions where you could lessen the impact of time, where two years would pass on the outside while you only aged one. You essentially blocked out some of the Dao of Time to accomplish this effect.

These methods were unsurprisingly popular among aging ancestors, who sealed themselves to protect their descendants for longer. Or to wait for their descendants to gather resources or source some critical treasure for their breakthrough. But to cheat time in the other direction was even harder.

You had to harness the Dao of Time to speed up the passage of time in a certain area or subspace. The slightest imbalance could create Temporal Rifts, something just as deadly as Spatial Rifts but even harder to defend against. Constructing something like that was incredibly difficult and not something Zac could buy on the open market.

And even if Zac managed to get one, would he dare use it? A single fault or imperfection, and he risked getting ripped apart at a moment's notice. Just starting such an array could kick up a temporal storm, as could shutting it off. Even the natural energy flows of Earth could suddenly create a small but deadly imbalance.

The only reason Catheya could have enjoyed such an opportunity was by having a Peak C-grade master. Calrin guessed that Va Tapek had sped up time in a section of his Inner World, a subspace where the laws of the universe were more malleable. That way, Va Tapek could personally control the Time Chamber and suppress any errant energy flows for the entire duration. And it wasn't like Zac had a Peak Monarch in his back pocket to help him with this.

Ultimately, these kinds of cultivation tools weren't something you'd see on the frontier, and you'd most likely require an Array Master or

400 | JF BRINK & THEFIRSTDEFIER

Temporal Cultivator to run it. That's why Zac was cautious, even if the sender was the Undead Empire. A portable, unmanned Temporal Chamber sounded too dangerous, and no one in Port Atwood would be able to tell whether it was starting to fail.

"I know what you're thinking, but you don't need to worry," Catheya said. "This is not some rinky-dink array you'd find in the frontier. Reyna Umbri'Zi *personally* crafted this domain at no small cost. You might not know this, but she's a Late Autarch and a Temporal Cultivator. This thing is even more stable than a planet."

Zac's brows rose in surprise. He hadn't thought the Umbri'Zi ancestor to be a Temporal Cultivator. He had to admit, if someone like that created the Temporal Chamber, it was definitely safe to use. Provided it wasn't some sort of trap, that is.

"What's the temporal ratio?" Zac asked.

"There is none," Catheya said. "As I said, the item contains three years. After you enter, the timer will start. When you leave three years later, no time will have passed."

"What!" Zac exclaimed, and he gave the box a second look. This was way beyond what he'd expected.

It was just like the Spatial Chamber technique Vai had explained to him, and the one Leyara's Templar squad had utilized to set up hidden camps. Creating something like that in the main dimension was incredibly difficult. But something told Zac it would be even harder to accomplish with a Temporal Chamber.

Zac looked at the box with desire. Time in a box, an incredibly valuable item for someone short on time but with thousands of years left on his lifespan. "Can the ancestor make more of these things?"

"She probably could, but it's dangerous to use these kinds of items too much," Catheya said.

"Because of the Dao?" Zac asked.

"Not only that. Unless you're a Temporal Cultivator, then stepping outside of time will gradually detach you from your timeline. In the early stages of overconsumption, it will feel like your surroundings will randomly speed up or speed down. It can cause quite a headache during critical situations. If you ignore the signs and keep stealing time, your body will eventually be unable to withstand it. You would become unable to reenter the timeline without being ripped apart by temporal storms.

"The ancestor estimated three years was the limit for you. Any more might affect your breakthrough to the D-grade, forcing you to take a few years to harmonize with the river of time. This is especially true considering time is apparently dilated inside the Perennial Vastness. So the sooner you use this thing, the better."

Zac nodded in understanding. He should have guessed nothing came for free on the road of cultivation. It seemed like Temporal Chambers were like the Cosmic Water he'd used during the first month of the Integration. A little bit was fine, but overindulging could create immense problems. Even pills were this way with the pill toxins and immunity.

Still, gaining three full years was huge. It almost doubled the amount of time he had to train and prepare. If he could speed up his Body Tempering, it might just be enough to cultivate the third layer of the [Void Vajra Sublimation]. That way, it should be fine using the [Essence of the Abyss].

It would also give him even more time to study the rules of Duality, a subject that was becoming increasingly abstruse, even with the help of the lake water. The only problem was the Moss Crystal and the five-year deadline. He didn't know if there was some hidden timer within the crystal, which would erupt when the time was up. If it were, he'd have to figure out a solution before heading to the Perennial Vastness.

But as Zac saw it, that was a negligible downside in the face of these potential benefits.

"These items are all amazing. Convey my thanks to the Umbri'Zi representative," Zac said.

"These things are just a small gift from the elders," Catheya said. "When you go to the Abyssal Shores, your cultivation requirements will all be taken care of."

Zac couldn't help but feel suspicious over this treatment. No matter what Catheya said, a Perennial Vastness Token had to be rare, even in the Undead Empire. For them to give him one meant a Heaven's Chosen would miss out. They even gave one to Catheya in a not-so-discrete effort to send someone with him.

The [Essence of the Abyss] and the top-quality Time Chamber were even more valuable. Zac doubted that even the descendants of the

Umbri'Zi could freely enjoy such things. On the surface, it sounded like a meat pie had fallen from the sky, an opportunity to further his cultivation. It was obvious these items came with strings attached.

"So what's going on, and don't tell me it's your bargaining skills," Zac said, drawing an annoyed humph from Catheya. "Do they value an Edgewalker that highly?"

"Well, no," Catheya said, and she actually looked a bit conflicted. "That's... Well, the Umbri'Zi and the Abyssal Shores were interested because of something else."

"What then?" Zac asked with a frown. "I'm sure the Empire isn't lacking elites, judging by what a pain in the ass Uona was to take down."

"Do you remember what I told you about the history of the Undead Empire?" Catheya asked. "About the dark ages?"

"Of course," Zac nodded.

"The Draugr lost a lot during those years. So many succumbed to the environment. Altogether, over a third of our heritage is gone," Catheya sighed. "Did you know? It has been over two hundred million years since we encountered unattached Draugr from the outside. When they were welcomed back into the fold, one of the Draugr branches gained a previously lost Hidden Node."

"Don't tell me," Zac said with surprise.

"The thing that interests the Abyssal Shores is ultimately not your ability to become human. It's the fact you might carry something we lost all those years ago. You might be able to strengthen our race as a whole," Catheya said, becoming serious again. "Do you know which of the Draugr branches you're a part of?"

Zac didn't immediately answer, and instead countered with a question of his own. "Which branches does the Draugr currently have? Which ones are complete, and which are missing?"

"I've been instructed not to divulge that," Catheya said with a wry smile.

"Figures," Zac snorted as he slowly tapped the table.

He'd been going back and forth about whether he should hide his bloodline or hope to use it as a bargaining chip. Now, it turned out his perceived value as an Edgewalker was considered useless, while everything hinged on which ancestor he had.

If the Eoz branch was alive and well back in the Abyssal Lakes, he would just be another junior. He might not only become expendable here, but even lose the support of the Umbri'Zi.

Ultimately, Zac chose to trust his guts and roll the dice. Right now, he didn't have any true value in the eyes of the Abyssal Shores. In their eyes, he was a mere gamble, a small chance to regain a Hidden Node or two. As far as they were concerned, he was far more likely to be one of the weaker or complete bloodlines.

But if it turned out the Eoz branch was missing, or at least incomplete, his value would suddenly skyrocket in the eyes of the Abyssal Shores. After all, Zac was pretty sure Eoz was one of the strongest branches of the Draugr.

"My bloodline is that of Eoz. In my vision, I was the third to emerge from the Abyssal Lake," Zac said.

"The Vanguard!" Catheya exclaimed as her eyes widened in shock, but she barely had time to finish her statement before a tremendous pressure descended on the room.

"Child, is what you said true?"

# THE VANGUARD

At first it seemed as though the voice appeared out of thin air. But mid-sentence, it focused into a singular point as another Draugr appeared in the room's doorway. His aura was restrained, but Zac felt like he was looking into a churning maw when gazing in his direction. According to the readouts from the Yphelion, he was one of the two who'd stayed in the woods earlier.

That was actually a surprise to Zac. If he had to guess, this Draugr was a Peak Monarch, not a Middle C-grade cultivator like the Yphelion indicated. Even among Monarchs, this had to be an uncommonly powerful warrior. Furthermore, there was something different about him.

The Monarch reminded Zac a bit of the [Essence of the Abyss]. It was like his very presence was swallowing all light around him. Catheya had gained a hint of this sort of aura, but it was just a shadow of what this man exhibited. In other words, he probably had awakened his bloodline multiple times or stayed for prolonged durations in the Abyssal Lake.

"Chil—no, young man, is what you said true?" the Monarch said. "Does the bloodline of Eoz flow through your veins?"

"Lord Tem'Zul!" Catheya exclaimed as she stood.

Zac frowned at Catheya's words. She'd greeted the Monarch out of respect, but her words also acted as a clue. Tem'Zul? So, yet another branch had arrived in Zecia, one Zac had never heard of before. Zac expected the Monarch to be another Azol, but this muddied the waters even further.

Unfortunately, Zac didn't have the information needed to deduce anything from this man's name, so he felt it best to distance himself for now.

"I thought I made myself clear," Zac said, instructing the puppet to stand to leave.

"Wait, wait," the Catheya urgently said. "The news you sprung on us is just too big. This is Lord Laz Tem'Zul, the Dao Guardian of Tavza An'Azol and a permanent resident of the Abyssal Shores. He can answer any quest—"

"I don't care," Zac interjected as he put the Perennial Vastness Token and [**Essence of the Abyss**] into the large pockets of the puppet's robe.

"This is my mistake. I had not expected to hear that name today," the Draugr warrior sighed as he placed a black crystal and a Spatial Ring on the table. "Here, take these things as my apology. Please carry on."

A moment later, he was gone, but Zac made no move to sit down.

"Don't be like this," Catheya said with a helpless shake of her head. "The elders just got excited. I think you've figured out that the name Eoz holds significant meaning to us. Please, let's sit down and discuss this?"

"Fine, but *only* for you. This is the last time," Zac said as he picked up the ring and the crystal. "If they keep butting in during our conversation, I'll just leave, even if I have to sacrifice this puppet and the treasures."

"Of course," Catheya nodded. "Now, is what you said really true? Is your bloodline Eoz?"

"What're these things?" Zac asked, ignoring her questions.

Catheya clearly wanted to press the issue, but relented. "The Crystal is a database of Draugr genealogy. It has information about all Draugr branches, including your own. The information can help you better understand your lineage and how to make the most out of it."

"Something you probably would have given me anyway?" Zac scoffed.

"No. That's a primer from the Abyssal Shores. It's not something we'd normally hand out. We just planned on comparing your aura to the database in the crystal. But if you're an Eoz, it's moot. Instead, you can read about your branch's history and your future brothers and sisters. As for the ring, it has various rare treasures useful when forming a core and shoring up one's foundation afterward. Now, can you tell me what's going on?"

"I'm pretty sure my bloodline is Eoz," Zac confirmed. "That's what I saw in my vision when I opened a node called **[Adamance of Eoz]**. You're free to believe me or not."

"What vision are you talking about?" Catheya asked.

"Didn't you see one when you opened your nodes?" Zac asked. "I remember the depths of the Abyssal Lake, the sense of belonging. And then…"

"Then what?" Catheya's curiosity was visibly growing.

"Is Eoz a missing bloodline?" Zac asked instead of answering.

"It's all in the crystal," Catheya said with exasperation.

"I can't read it with this puppet, so humor me," Zac said.

"*Fine*. Rather than lost or missing, it's more apt to say they sacrificed themselves to give the Draugr a chance at survival."

"During the Dark Ages?" Zac asked.

"Exactly. As the System was born, the universe was drained of energy, and the Abyssal Lake somehow… sealed itself. Our environment was rapidly deteriorating, and we knew we had to move. But where could we go? Until that point, the Draugr had been content staying by the lake, and we knew very little about the rest of the universe.

"So we set out without any clear goal or destination in sight. We could only tell that some dimensions weren't as affected as others, and some unique environments could resist the System's drain."

"Special environments?" Zac asked.

"Things like certain Ancient and Immemorial Realms. There are special places in the main dimensions as well, unique regions that can be deadly even to Supremacies," Catheya said.

"Sounds pretty dangerous."

"It was, but what could the ancestors do but forge ahead? And among the Draugr, none were as resilient as the descendants of Eoz. Your Miasma lasted longer, and you could resist all kinds of dangerous environments that would severely weaken or even kill the others. Thus, your branch took on the roles of advance-scouts during the dark ages. They became the Vanguard, those who forged ahead into those dangerous zones and realms in search of safe harbor."

Zac wasn't surprised when he heard Catheya's description. The first part sounded just like the effect of [Adamance of Eoz], and it seemed the other parts of the bloodline further improved survivability. Truthfully, Zac would have preferred a bloodline that was a bit more rounded or one improving his speed to make up for his lacking focus in Dexterity and mobility.

But ultimately, survival always came first, so it was by no means bad news to hear he apparently had the Draugr Tank bloodline.

"You can understand how dangerous such an undertaking was," Catheya continued. "None sacrificed more than the children of Eoz during our great migration, even though your branch are the ones best suited for survival. One by one, the Vanguard found temporary harbors that allowed us to survive a bit longer.

"But you should know, Death-attuned worlds were barely a thing back then. The Dao wasn't as accessible, so most places we found were things like ancient battlefields or other anomalies. Eventually, those places ran out of Miasma, and we were forced to keep moving.

"The leaders all knew this, so the Vanguard never stopped searching. They kept going, traveling the Multiverse, searching for a more permanent solution. Unfortunately, they never found it. By the time we joined up with the Founders and discovered the Empire Heartlands, the branch of Eoz had already fallen," Catheya sighed.

"It is the only branch that's *completely* missing. Honestly, I still can't believe this. How can you possibly carry the bloodline of Eoz? Are there more of you?"

"I can't comment on the first question," Zac said. "But you shouldn't expect anyone else to pop up."

He obviously wouldn't tell them about the Corpselord Clan that had somehow stumbled onto a perfectly sealed corpse of the Eoz bloodline. So long as he remained unique, he was valuable. Looking back at it now, that poor Draugr Mahl's brother found had most likely been a descendant of one of those scouts who'd set out from the rest of the Draugr.

"That's a shame," Catheya said, but she didn't look very disappointed. "So, then what happened? In your vision?"

Zac digested the news of his ancestors before continuing. "As I said, I was deep underwater in the Abyss. No past, no future. Then, I felt the pull from above, and I started to swim toward the surface as new thoughts and impressions filled my mind. It wasn't easy, like the Abyssal Lake didn't want to let me go, but I pushed on. By the time I crawled onto the shores, two were already standing there—Mez and Azol."

"Ancestral Descent? Just how pure is your bloodline?" Catheya muttered with disbelief.

"It sounds like my bloodline is a pretty good one," Zac smiled.

"I was kind of joking before when I said you'd become a top bachelor in the Heartlands. Now, it's probably true," Catheya said. "You're a living Bloodline Patriarch, sole inheritor of a whole bloodline. And by the sound of it, your bloodline is incredibly pure. Rekindling a bloodline can be incredibly difficult, but it should be possible with your power and your bloodline's purity."

"Just remember that for our upcoming talk," Zac said. "Now, what do you want to know about the Eternal Heritage, and what are you guys willing to pay?"

"You're essentially a core member of the Undead Empire already," Catheya said with a pout. "Why the need for secrecy and trade-offs? Why not just work together on making sure we get our hands on the Left Imperial Palace? The competition will be incredibly fierce. We've already received word that at least one Imperial Clan is on their way."

"Imperial Clan?" Zac asked curiously.

Zac could tell Catheya wasn't talking about some random Empire when she said Imperial Clan. It made him think of Leyara and her mention of Nine Imperial Bloodlines. He'd tried to dig into what she meant by that, but she never really answered him. With the Left Imperial Palace being in the center of all this, it wasn't hard to figure out what Empire it all related to.

"Remnants from the Limitless Empire," Catheya said, confirming Zac's hunch. "The most powerful factions of the Limitless Empire collapsed almost immediately when their undertaking was finished. The System's awakening killed off too many patriarchs and great generals. But out of the ashes, seven phoenixes rose.

"A few clans acted more decisively than others, turning on the Empire the moment they saw which way the wind blew. They attacked their masters and pillaged the treasures of the Limitless Empire. Not much later, the great beings of the Multiverse realized what Emperor Limitless had done and descended on the Limitless Empire with fury.

But by that point, these seven clans were long gone, having stolen the riches and hidden in various corners of the Multiverse.

"They only emerged much later, when the energy returned to the Multiverse. And they were more powerful than ever. Using their stolen foundation, they are all incredibly powerful factions to this day. Except for one clan that was exterminated for some reason."

"Seven clans, with six remaining?" Zac hummed, thinking back to Leyara's words. "Not nine of them?"

"Not that I know," Catheya said with a shake of her head.

"These seven factions, were they top-tier powers within the Limitless Empire?" Zac asked.

"No," Catheya said. "If they were, they would have been present for the System's awakening and absorbed with the rest of the leaders. These seven clans were either middling factions or upstarts. But make no mistake, that was then. Today, they're all genuine A-grade factions with unfathomable foundations."

Were they perhaps different? Sounded like it. Zac didn't feel these people were the ones Leyara spoke of. Perhaps the Nine Imperial Bloodlines referred to lineages of those close to Emperor Limitless, lineages that were gone or diluted by this point in time.

"Working together is fine, but there are some small things I want from the Undead Empire first," Zac said.

Catheya smiled. "I expected as much."

"First of all, I don't like the idea of compulsions. I can join the Undead Empire down the road, but I don't wish to be restrained like that," Zac said.

"That's impossible. Those are fundament—"Catheya froze, then looked at Zac in shock. "Guess I was wrong. They agreed. You're technically already a councilor of the Abyssal Shores, provided your bloodline is that of Eoz. Of course, that's just an empty title without the actual power of the position until you become at least a Late Autarch. Until then, you can stay on as Arcaz Umbri'Zi while enjoying certain special privileges.

"That way, you would have an official position in the Undead Empire without *technically* joining it. In return, you'd only have access to the Draugr domains. If you wished to travel through the other regions, you would have to get permission first. Provided your official allegiance remains to your own faction, you would also be unable to access certain System-maintained features," Catheya continued, looking more and more confused by the words transmitted to her. "I can't believe they're making this kind of accommodation."

"So, what's the catch?" Zac asked.

"Apart from providing us with information, you have to assist our side inside the inheritance when possible," Catheya said. "Also, if you find a trove, our representatives get the first pick. Finally, there is a certain item inside the palace you need to help bring out, if possible, whether you manage to join up with our representatives or not."

"What item?" Zac asked with genuine confusion.

The conditions were mostly fine. Giving the Undead Empire the first pick was the only one that might smart a bit, but there was a real chance a situation like that might not even occur. As for forming an alliance and information sharing, that was already something Zac wanted in either case.

The most interesting thing was the third condition, the unnamed specific item the Undead Empire wanted. Between the second and the third conditions, it almost seemed like this was their real mission.

Perhaps they already knew that swallowing the whole Eternal Heritage was too difficult. The competition would be incredibly fierce with people like Iz Tayn and these imperials showing up, and that was just the start. The Undead Empire was already an embattled force and trying to monopolize a second Eternal Heritage might be more than some ancient factions could accept.

If that were the case, it was better to lower your expectations a bit and take something that could benefit the Undead Empire but might not necessarily create too many problems on the outside. The question was what kind of item this was and how the Undead Empire knew about it.

"They can't tell you right now," Catheya said, but she quickly continued when Zac grunted with annoyance. "They don't know. This is a command from the Heartlands. They haven't given us the specifics either. Perhaps they're afraid of the details leaking."

Zac thoughtfully went over the information. Honestly, Zac was a bit surprised they agreed outright to his main condition without pushing back at all. It really seemed a bit suspicious. Then again, what were some accommodations for a junior in the face of an Eternal Heritage?

The problem was assurances. They could promise things left and right, but it was ultimately up to them to follow through in the future. It wasn't like there was a complaints department he could turn to if they simply threw him to the wayside after this was all said and done. And did these representatives even have the status to promise these things?

"It's easy to promise things, but what guarantees can you provide?"

"Before the inheritance, you will have an official writ signed by the Primo himself, witnessed and consecrated by the System. Breaking that would turn the System against us, essentially making it a pledge to the Heavens," Catheya said. "I don't know about these things, but apparently, you will be able to tell its authenticity upon seeing it."

Aboard the Yphelion, Zac glanced at Ogras, but he shook his head after Zac repeated what Catheya said. He had no idea if something like that was real or not. Zac's guts told him it was possible.

Even C-grade cultivators could somewhat use the System for their benefit, from having it issue quests to stopping it from teleporting people away. It didn't seem like such a stretch for someone like the Primo to have the System witness an agreement. If it was real, then Zac was mostly satisfied.

Such a writ was like a poison pill—they could still break the agreement or kill him, but there was no reason to do so unless the benefits outweighed the costs. And killing him after the inheritance would serve no purpose and only rob them of his bloodline.

"That's fine, but what if your people fail to get a slot?" Zac said. "I can't be responsible for that."

"As long as you do your best in helping us, the offer stands. We can only blame our inadequacy for not gaining access," Catheya nodded.

"That's fair. My second condition is that—"

"There is a second condition?" Catheya scoffed. "Be careful not to get overstuffed."

"I still think there's room for more," Zac laughed.

Catheya sighed, then a wide smile spread across her face. "What is it?"

# THE ROAD FORWARD

Catheya stood just outside the temporary building, looking on as the automaton walked into the woods toward the closest settlement. She was filled with a mix of disappointment and relief that Arcaz hadn't appeared in person. It would have been nice seeing him again, but these shifty elders were up to no good, no matter what they said to her.

That by itself was a huge headache. They didn't trust her and only divulged details at the last moment. Even now, she didn't know whether the promises and agreements she had put forth were real. Thankfully, Arcaz seemed to understand that much, and he didn't appear to hold it against her.

A moment later, she sensed a shift in the air, and she turned around to see five people standing behind her.

"Good job," Enis said.

"I was just repeating the words said to me," Catheya sighed.

"You made some alterations," Tavza said as she expressionlessly looked at Catheya.

"It's because you don't understand how things work here," Catheya said with a roll of her eyes. "He's not a junior from the Heartlands. He's a progenitor who grew up on a world without cultivators. He lacks the whole cultural heritage of established factions. It would just backfire if you tried to pressure him with seniority or status."

"Now that I can believe," Laz Tem'Zul snorted as he glanced toward the automaton. "No reverence at all."

"I still don't understand that point," Kator White Sky, the Izh'Rak Reaver scion, said. "Wasn't he connected to your ancestor, the one who refused to leave the Boundless Path? Yet he's a clueless progenitor? Which is it?"

Catheya warily looked up at the hulking Reaver, and she couldn't help but remember his terrifying power. He was eighty years old and at the cusp of Late Hegemony, but the local Peak Hegemons had to put their lives on the line just to spar with him. And since this war-crazed skeleton couldn't go a single day without fighting, the wounds of the local elites had racked up to the point that Monarchs had been forced to become his sparring partners.

Even now, it felt like this lunatic was barely reining in his battle lust.

"That's—" Catheya hesitated.

"Be'Zi Sharva'Zi has already been given special dispensation from the Heart, as has Catheya," Enis Umbri'Zi said. "More to the point, we have already confirmed their connection comes through the Dao of Oblivion and happenstance. It is doubtful they have ever met in person. Be'Zi and her companion should currently be located deep within the Eternal Storm."

"That by itself is a problem. We do not have a proper understanding of his connections, and therefore his motivations remain obscured. I read the reports. Someone else has been hiding in his shadows since the beginning. Before he even visited Twilight Harbor. His very existence is proof of this," Tavza An'Azol said. "A pureblood Draugr Edgewalker does not just appear out of thin air. Especially not if he's carrying the bloodline of the Vanguard."

"So why did you stop the plan? We had already locked in on their position," Kator snorted. "You were even the ones to put it forward."

"What!" Catheya said with shock, but she was soundly ignored.

She looked at Enis, but the Umbri'Zi Monarch only shook her head slightly, telling her not to push the matter.

"The information put forth changed the stakes," Tavza calmly said. "Besides, the make of that vessel was out of our expectations. That's not something you'd expect to find on the frontier. There was a high likelihood its arrays would have noticed Sepravo had he moved any closer."

Catheya's eye widened in surprise. Sepravo A'Tem was here? She'd never seen the Revenant Monarch aboard their vessel. Come to think of it, she hadn't seen him since they appeared in Zecia. Even back then, it was like Catheya had noticed him but soon forgotten about his existence.

Now, Catheya realized it was most likely part of the Monarch's skillset, making it clear what kind of profession Sepravo had. An assassin, and an incredibly skilled one at that, considering he'd been allowed to take the name of a Bloodline Clan. Catheya shuddered at just how close to disaster her friend had been.

"So, you feeling threatened, girl?" Kator snickered as he looked down at Tavza. "Your prince isn't exactly young, and now the Vanguard is back? I hear those guys were almost as sturdy as us Reavers. I wonder how the branches of Mez and Azol feel about that."

"If the lost bloodline of Eoz can rejoin our ranks, we will all be better for it. Why would An'Azol hamper that?"

"You say that, but why don't I see any sincerity on your face?" Kator laughed.

"We are not like the Eternal Clan, constantly fighting among themselves while striking out at anything around them," Tavza calmly said. "Besides, he is just one junior. Raising a whole branch requires both time and resources."

"Resources you could withhold if they start to grow too much," Kator laughed.

"Enough, Kator," Toss White Sky grunted before glancing at Enis. "That ship is another point of suspicion. Has he already joined up with another faction for the upcoming trial?"

"Not necessarily," Enis countered. "No matter what the truth of his origins are, it has been confirmed he is a genuine progenitor, even if he was somehow placed on a world just before it got integrated. And he is a stand-out progenitor at that. He might have been given the vessel as a reward from the System."

"The matter of his hidden backers can be put aside for now," Laz said. "What's important is the intelligence he provided. As far as I can tell, it seems genuine."

"He held back," Tavza said, glancing at Catheya. "You could have pushed him further."

"I did what was asked of me. If you think it insufficient, you're welcome to try taking over the future negotiations," Catheya snorted. "I'd like to see how many secrets you can get out of that guy."

"Enough," Enis said before looking at Laz and Toss. "What do you wish to do?"

"Isn't it obvious?" Toss shrugged. "We're sending the kids into the Eternal Storm while we deal with the demands your greedy little adoptee put forth. Do the locals have any nearby seeds?"

"There should be a few hidden worlds," Enis nodded.

"Good, then there's no point staying here," Toss said, and the next moment he and Kator were gone.

Catheya glanced in the direction of the puppet once more, and a sense of helplessness filled her heart. What should she do? Then it struck her, and she turned to Tavza before her guardian whisked her away.

"I wish to enter the Million Gates Territory as well," Catheya said with determination. "I wish to contend for one of the lower courts."

"Why should I take you?" Tavza countered, not at all surprised. "You seem to be harboring many ideas of your own. That's not a trait you look for in a party member. Besides, your role is to be our liaison with that man. That will not be possible from within the Eternal Storm."

"That may be, but this way, I can be your liaison with Arcaz inside the trial. And I can guarantee you will find no more capable followers in Zecia after I've formed my core," Catheya said. "Besides, I'm sure Arcaz would not begrudge me a chance to join this opportunity."

"You seem to like that man," Tavza commented. "But I wonder if that will be enough. Remember, Arcaz Umbri'Zi, or rather Zachary Atwood, has to choose death. That is even more important if he truly is a descendant of Eoz."

"I know that," Catheya huffed, but inwardly she wasn't convinced.

She didn't have any logical reason to refute the words of Reyna or the others, and her research of the topic in the Abyssal Shores had confirmed many things. There hadn't been any Life-Death Edgewalkers who successfully entered Hegemony. Yet, when she recalled that man, how he'd looked when he first transformed in front of her to save her life, she couldn't shake off her lingering doubt.

Her father once said nothing was impossible in the Multiverse. If it seemed like it, that was only because the solution hadn't been figured out yet. Why couldn't that be true for him? If not him, who could possibly break the old conventions? So what if it was related to a broken peak?

"Well, if that fails, we will have to make the choice for him," Tavza shrugged, which dragged Catheya out of her thoughts. "I will think on your proposal."

"What are you—" Catheya frowned, but the An'Azol descendant and her guardian were already gone.

"Child, that was a mistake," Enis sighed after the two appeared in their quarters aboard the Eclipse a moment later.

"I know a lot of powerful warriors will enter this inheritance, but I will have become a Hegemon by the time the inheritance starts," Catheya said.

"That may be, but for you, surviving until the gates open might be even harder than the inheritance itself," Enis said. "Those two are allies, yet they are also competitors. Each will want to bring as many of their own into the Left Imperial Palace. Should you manage to seize one of the seals, you will become a ticket they might both consider better used on their own people. Don't delude yourself that your identity as Arcaz Umbri'Zi's companion will keep you safe from them."

"Since when were you worried for my safety?" Catheya smiled.

"I am trying to salvage this mess at least somewhat. Our branch can't walk away completely empty-handed," Enis sighed. "It's a shame that brat didn't allow you to join him on his planet."

"That's for the best," Catheya snorted. "From the sounds of it, those people would have used my presence there to do something backhanded."

"Don't forget yourself," Enis said. "No matter what you think of their actions, they are ultimately acting for the betterment of the Empire. You cannot let your priorities get mixed up."

---

"What do you think, uncle?" Tavza asked as she sat by the screen transmitting the outside of the Cosmic Vessel.

"The council gave you free rein to take charge of this matter. If us old things involve ourselves too much, it might affect the outcome negatively." At this, Laz smiled. "Judging from what we've learned today, such might be even more true than we previously thought."

"I doubt taking some suggestions from my elders at this juncture would impact my chances at becoming a candidate," Tavza said, the planet growing smaller in the distance.

"Well, things have gotten complicated," Laz said. "Who would have thought he'd be a descendant of Eoz?"

"It's still not confirmed. He was conveniently absent to confirm anything, and I don't trust that girl," Tavza said. "She was investigated, but that was in the Abyssal Shores. She might have hatched this plan while waiting for us to arrive."

"She is conflicted at the least, but I do not believe she planned this," Laz said as he sat down opposite her. "The Vanguard returning. That little Reaver brat wasn't lying. This will create significant waves. The other Divine Races might feel threatened, and the current balance in the shores will be upended. Perhaps him not returning—"

"We can't," Tavza sighed. "I would have preferred simply killing him and taking his seal. I just feel he carries too many secrets to be allowed back home. That feeling has only increased after getting a first-hand look at his personality. He's shifty, greedy, and only accountable to himself. But now, we are forced to act as his shield."

"Oh?" Laz said with surprise.

"The Patriarch spoke to me before I left," Tavza said after a pause.

"What!" Laz exclaimed. "Prince Aewo has left the depths?"

"No," Tavza said. "Ancestor just sent a whisp of his consciousness to me as a precaution. He said he had felt the lake stirring not long ago and had a premonition that this Zachary Atwood might be part of the lost branch. And if he was, then he had to be returned to the shores at any cost."

"Is it that important?" Laz said with a frown. "Truthfully, I feel that perfecting another one of the established bloodlines would have a greater impact on our race's strength in the short run. As you said, it would be a huge undertaking to resurrect the bloodline of Eoz. First of all, he'd need to become an Autarch at the least before he can properly pass on the whole branch."

"I thought so too," Tavza said. "But apparently, there's more to it. The princes have found something, something in the depths of the lake. They've failed to access it all this time, but Zachary Atwood might be the key."

"A bloodline lock?" Laz said with interest.

"Azol, Mez, and Eoz. Three upper bloodlines leading the nine others," Tavza said. "All three would have to be present to access that place. Across the eons, the princes have been working on a workaround. They have made no progress, even when consulting the Primo."

"So, what is it?" Laz asked.

"Ancestor never told me, except that it's related to our very foundation and origin. It's far more important than a few missing links of the lower bloodlines," Tavza explained.

"Then the brat is the key to this thing?" Laz grimaced.

Tavza nodded. "Do not tell the others. I only told you now to impress on you the importance of his return to the Abyssal Shores, where he can be protected until he fulfills his role. Until then, he might be targeted by Kator's camp and assassins who sneak into this Sector. The Hiveminds and the Sanguine Palace aren't above something like that."

"Of course," Laz agreed as he took out a Mindseal Talisman and added an extra layer of protection to the memories. "There is one problem, though."

"What?" Tavza asked.

"How do we protect someone who refuses to even meet with us?"

---

The scenes stopped playing, and the wall turned dark in the meeting room of the Yphelion.

"What do you think?" Zac asked.

While Ogras had been next to him during the meeting, he hadn't been able to see or hear what was happening on the other side. But now that the meeting was over, Zac replayed the whole thing.

"What do I think? I think your spring is about to come. The moment they get their hands on you, they'll strap you to a bed and bring in a steady stream of young flowers." Ogras glared at Zac. "Just how bright is your star of providence? Where is the justice in the world? How am I supposed to live with you showing me something like this?"

"Not that," Zac laughed. "Besides, you're probably overthinking things. They'd just need some cell samples or something. I want to hear what you think about the agreement."

"Well, I doubt the gifts are problematic," Ogras said. "I don't think their excitement over your heritage was fake, though it's a shame we have no way to confirm things from our side. But I doubt they would send you off with something problematic and risk missing out. If the original gifts were tampered with, they would most likely have swapped them out under the pretense your bloodline deserved a better gift."

"I think so, too. What about the heritage?"

"They knew even less than we expected," Ogras said with some bemusement. "I didn't expect them to not even have figured out about the Million Gates Territory already. We might have sold that intelligence cheaply, but it doesn't matter. We got most of the things we needed. And the ongoing agreement between you and the Empire will prove incredibly lucrative."

There had been a few things Zac had wanted to accomplish with this first set of negotiations, and the treasures he'd asked for were just a smaller part of it. The real goal had been to open up a path for Earth and the Atwood Empire while keeping the demands reasonable. Too much, and they might figure out various loopholes.

Therefore, the demands were carefully chosen as part of a plan Zac had mulled over since learning of Ensolus. He'd managed to get an agreement that the Undead Empire would accept their presence and expansion across the Kaldran Strait. Not only that, but they would covertly assist in the Atwood Empire's development and protection after Earth and Ensolus emerged from the shroud.

The Atwood Empire would essentially become an allied faction, which meant they would be safe from the biggest faction in that region of space. Truthfully, Catheya even seemed a bit excited at the prospect, which surprised Zac. But it didn't take long for him and Ogras to figure out what was happening.

It wasn't long ago that Twilight Harbor had collapsed, and the Umbri'Zi had lost one of the most useful trade hubs where they could purchase the resources of the frontier without breaking any commandments. Twilight Harbor had also been a significant revenue stream for Clan Sharva'Zi, with their Dao Repository and other shops. Now, with the Kavriel Province's tacit approval and even protection, Zac was primed to set up something similar in Zecia.

An unaffiliated grey zone, where both living and undead could come to trade resources.

Each side had treasures the other required, and every transaction would mean money entering Zac's pockets. Zac had already made a fortune through his lucky encounters, but that was nothing in the face of the revenue streams a popular trade hub could generate. Better yet, no one could compete with him on this matter, thanks to the support of the Undead Empire.

For the first time in a while, Zac felt the future looked bright for Earth. The Assimilation had always been a cloud looming over him, especially since his faction became part-undead. But now, the clouds had parted, and the road to endless riches paved.

He just needed to survive the schemes of the Undead Empire and the dangers of Ultom to get there.

# CALL TO ARMS

Apart from the difficulties of cinching the deal, Zac's little kingdom was far from reaching the status of the Twilight Harbor. Even if he now had the fundamental qualifications, he lacked the strength to protect something so valuable, even with the Undead Empire on his side. You simply couldn't build a solid faction on a foundation of borrowed strength.

For the first couple of millennia, it would just be a local hub where merchants within Zecia could make some money by getting their hands on rare materials. But it did have the potential to take on an even greater role, where resources would stream into the Atwood Empire from neighboring Sectors.

This would be a huge boon for him even if he left Zecia in the future, all thanks to the Merit Exchange. He would be able to access parts of his treasury and the Atwood Empire's coffers despite being halfway across the Multiverse, as long as he found one of the Furem Harq golem's subsidiaries. There were even services where he could transfer funds through relay between different banks.

Of course, his long-term plan was only possible thanks to one simple fact: the Undead Empire would stop its expansion in Zecia. They would defend their domains and do the bare minimum expansion through incursions that the commandments required, but they wouldn't send out crusades. Instead, the representatives agreed to mobilize the Kavriel Province for the upcoming war against the Kan'Tanu.

Initially, they hadn't planned on full mobilization. After all, they didn't care which living factions were in control of Zecia. They were just different Dreamers, targets for conquest in either case. But now, they'd agreed to immediately send armies to join the coalition forces while fully activating their reserves for the upcoming conflict.

In reality this couldn't be considered the Monarchs accommodating Zac's wishes. It was all about Ultom and the fact the System had mixed the war with the trial. The more people the Kavriel Province sent to the battlefields, the higher their chances were of picking up tickets to the Left Imperial Palace.

The third requirement Zac had put forth was that they would provide materials, untouched corpses, and various resources to help bolster his undead population and their foundations. This included Cultivation Manuals, awakening arrays, and entire heritages that suited both the Raun Spectrals and the Revenants of Elysium.

At first, Zac thought they were just agreeing with things to extract information from him. That they'd come back in a few months with some 'bad news.' Though it was hard to argue with the fifty permanent Skill Crystals and a dozen Cultivation Manuals Catheya produced.

The puppet Zac used couldn't activate Spatial Items, but Catheya had shared the screens of both manuals and Skill Crystals. The items were the real deal; High-quality and practical for raising armies. There wasn't anything in the way of top-tier techniques meant for elites, but even Zac felt he could use some of the skills.

The only failure in Zac's negotiations was that he didn't squeeze a single Life-attuned treasure from their hands. They'd been adamant in not providing anything of that element, to the point it almost seemed that the negotiations would fall through if he kept pushing. Eventually, Zac settled on some top-tier treasures for his soul, both Death-attuned and unattuned. This wasn't something they had on hand, and would send it over within a few months.

He ultimately would have preferred Life-attuned Body Tempering treasures, but the things he walked away with would allow him to get closer to the next reincarnation. Now, he only lacked some Life-attuned treasures for his Soul and Constitution. These items were difficult to get his hands on, but he had three years to scour the Auction Houses across Zecia for anything useful.

There were also the upcoming negotiations with the Allbright Empire that Pretty was hopefully setting up at this very moment. Perhaps he could get some good things from the Allbright Clan's Treasury as part of his sale of Creator Vessels.

Zac and Ogras went through the meeting a few times over, trying to figure out what traps and schemes the Undead Empire might be planning over the coming years. The biggest one was that they might hide some sort of tracking measure with all the materials they'd send over. But they luckily had Ensolus by this point.

They could simply use all those materials on his other planet. If the undead Monarchs managed to pierce through the System's shroud, they still wouldn't get to Zac. And there was no way they'd dare cause havoc on Ensolus in an attempt to flush him out. Doing so would make the negotiations completely fall apart.

"They should have returned by now," Ogras commented.

Zac thought so too. A group of five trusted cultivators had been stationed in the forest, and Zac had set off the moment they retrieved the puppet. From there, they just needed to travel for a few hours before reaching the closest teleportation array. Zac and Ogras would instead have to travel for two days before reaching another border planet where they could teleport back home.

"Oh, that reminds me," Zac said as he took out his Perennial Vastness Token.

"What?" Ogras blurted. "You had one of those things already? I thought they were rare."

"They are, but I picked up one inside the Orom World." Zac smiled as he threw it over. "Now I have a spare, so you take this one."

"What exactly is this?" Ogras asked, and Zac recounted what he'd learned about the Perennial Vastness.

"Do you want me to go scout ahead?" Ogras asked.

"No, I was thinking I'll go in roughly a year before the official start of the war. That way, we'll have ample time to break through, especially if the realm has a different temporal ratio."

"You know, the last time the two of us left together for an opportunity, things didn't turn out so well," Ogras said with a raised brow.

"This is different. We'll just keep our heads down and get our cores," Zac said.

Ogras scoffed in response as he exaggeratedly rolled his eyes, but he still accepted the token and stowed it away. "Fine, I'll join you in whatever madness you will bring upon that poor realm. Thank you for this."

"Don't sweat it.".

"So, we'll return from the Million Gates Territory in three years. With the speed of your Creator Vessels, that should be enough to give the place a decent run. We'll only be able to cover a small corner of it, but that's to be expected. We'd need centuries to scour that region properly."

"It's ultimately about fate," Zac agreed.

"If I haven't returned one month after our deadline, go without me. We might be stuck somewhere, and I'll use this talisman so that we can join up in this Perennial Vastness."

"One month," Zac confirmed.

Thankfully, there were no surprises for the rest of the journey, and the crew returned to Earth two days later without getting into trouble. They could have just waited for the undead to leave, but Zac feared those shifty Monarchs had left a trap behind.

By that point, the preparations for the announcement were already well underway, and Zac was handed a list of talking points by Vilari the moment he emerged from the teleporter. The whole thing would be transmitted everywhere to be displayed on huge screens, and Zac inwardly shuddered at the prospect of addressing almost two billion beings across two planets.

Zac would much rather fight a Beast King than deal with this, but some things couldn't be pawned off to his subordinates. He was the one who chose this path, so he would have to be the one to bear the responsibility. It was just a matter of time before his announcement was spread across the Sector, and he wanted any eventual crosshairs to be trained solely at himself.

Most of the world's leaders had already arrived in Port Atwood, while the representatives of the Mavai and Raun were kept on a separate island. Officially, the reason for him calling the meeting was to discuss the upcoming war and for him to share his plans for the Atwood Empire's future.

Zac barely had time to gather his thoughts before the night had passed and the time for the world summit arrived. Zac donned his presence-hiding equipment as he walked toward the Atwood Hall, the ever-growing central government building at the heart of his capital. He was surprised to see the whole town had been transformed for this day, with thousands of banners of the Atwood Empire's crest dancing in the wind.

Countless people also walked the streets, heading for the closest floating screen. Zac flitted through the crowd and entered the Atwood Hall unnoticed, and found Vilari and the others waiting behind the main stage. Everything looked ready, and Joanna smiled as she handed him a tablet.

It showed a crowded hall with representatives of all the races present. The view panned around, showing the stage he'd take in twenty minutes. Zac's eyes were immediately drawn to the thing in the center—it was impossible to miss. They'd created a 20-meter-tall crest from pure gold and onyx, depicting the seal of the Atwood Empire: the four mountains of his island, with an axe and shield beneath.

Right under it was the podium he'd speak from, where he'd be lined with more flags of the Atwood Empire.

"What's with this stage?" Zac grimaced at the ostentatious backdrop. "I'll look like a dictator."

"I mean, you kind of are?" Joanna countered, and Zac rolled his eyes when he saw the excitement on her face.

"What do I need to do?" Zac sighed, knowing it was too late to change anything.

Zac spent the next twenty minutes reviewing everything while independently dealing with a few things. After that, Zac took a steadying breath and walked out on the stage.

It was as though the air went out of the hall as thousands of people quieted at once. The only thing that could be heard were bare feet against stone as Zac headed for the podium with steady steps. A moment later, Joanna, Ilvere, and ten more Atwood Army captains followed, forming an orderly line behind him.

If this were before the Integration, Zac would have been shaking like a leaf. But he found himself oddly calm as he faced the crowd. Not even a ripple appeared in his heart as he looked down at the audience, and Zac's voice was strong and steady as he began speaking.

"Over the past decade, our people have overcome insurmountable odds to eke out a living in this new reality," Zac began. "I am awed at the resilience you have shown, and thankful for all the hard work you've put into rebuilding our collapsed societies. Humans, Ishiate, Zhix, and

Underworld Molekin have set aside their differences in appearance and cultures to rebuild what was taken from us.

"But I can never forget the 10 billion lives lost across our species. The tall buildings and other monuments to our triumph over adversity came at a tremendous cost. It is an eternal reminder that there is no such thing as safety in the Multiverse. Under the System, there is a mandate for constant struggle, and our place under the Heavens will forever be contended. A moment of weakness, and we will be dragged down again.

"I am sure that most of you have seen the recruitment stations across Earth, and have heard what looms on the horizon. In four years, a war of terrifying proportions is descending on our corner of the Multiverse—the Zecia Sector. The Integration was nothing in the face of what's to come. Not even Earth is shielded from the madness.

"To hide or refuse to fight isn't an option, not when the System is involved. Neither will our enemies relent. I can tell you right now there will be no mercy and no negotiation with those people. The invaders are called the Kan'Tanu, and they are an incredibly dangerous unorthodox faction. Should we lose, most of us will be sacrificed to fuel their cultivators. The rest will be implanted by terrifying parasites and become war-slaves.

"Since defeat is not an option, we can only struggle and become stronger. That way, we can protect our world and keep casualties at a minimum. Luckily, we are still in a phase of rapid growth, and four years will give us a small window to shore up our foundations. I have invested multiple C-grade Nexus Coins into our armies, and I encourage every able-bodied adult to join. We need not only warriors but all kinds of staff to support our military."

Zac took a breath as he solemnly looked across the room. "This time, the actions of a few elites will not be enough to save Earth. I cannot protect you. Only by working together will we survive this storm.

"Let me be clear. While the Atwood Empire has largely allowed all factions across our planet to do things their way, this is a matter where I won't accept any compromise. For now, recruitment is open and voluntary, and those who sign early will enjoy more of the resources I have prepared. But if we see certain factions or cities neglecting their duty, we will move on to conscription. Every race and every force will have to pull their weight one way or another."

A subdued murmur spread through the room, but it was quenched by Zac releasing some of his aura. "Do not test me on this. I will protect this world even if I have to drag some of you to the battlefields myself."

No one dared speak up, though Zac could see there was more than one dissatisfied person. Zac didn't care. He wasn't just speaking empty words. This wasn't a trial where he and a few of his followers could do all the heavy lifting. Still, the stick was best accompanied by a carrot.

"Of course, the System follows the Law of Balance. Where there is risk, there is also reward. Your participation in the war will accrue Contribution Points, which can be used to access a System-run Contribution Store. The greater the feats, the better the reward. Some will get their hands on treasures they'd never encounter normally. Between the Atwood Empire's investment and the Contribution Store, this is your final chance to rekindle your fate before our planet is fully assimilated into the Sector.

"We still don't know all the details, but we are constantly getting reports from the frontlines. As soon as we know something, so will you. Over the coming years, there will be more summits where details are ironed out. We will also hold large-scale exercises, some on Earth, others off-world. In short, I will do everything I can to prepare my citizens for this trial.

"Our Recruitment Stations are open across the world. If you want to know more about enlisting and what benefits we provide, you are welcome to visit them over the coming days. For those present here in Port Atwood, we will have representatives available to answer any questions you may have. But do understand, we don't have all the answers yet."

Zac glanced to his left, and a small nod from Joanna indicated that everything was prepared for the next segment of his speech.

"Secondly, I will speak on the changes that are taking place on our planet and how the Atwood Empire will adapt to them moving forward. First things first. The changes to our world are permanent. Earth is now a Life and Death-attuned world, which will continue to generate energy attuned to both these elements.

"This will become increasingly noticeable over the next few years. The Miasma will grow more potent in some regions, but Blessed Lands teeming with Life will also appear. However, most of the energy across the planet will remain unattuned, or at least have so little attunement it will not affect one's day-to-day.

"For those living on Pangea, you do not need to worry overly much. Miasma will not swallow the continent as we feared ten years ago. A balance between Life and Death has been established another way. For those who are unaware, our planet has two continents of roughly equal size. The second continent, Elysium, is the opposite of Pangea. Most of it is covered in Miasma today, even if the Undead Empire never set foot there.

"This kind of unique world has created a unique set of challenges and realities we have to face," Zac said. "I strongly believe the reason I've found success so far is that I quickly adapted to what the System threw at me. If we keep holding onto old beliefs and outmoded ideals, it is just a matter of time before we get swept away by the river of time.

"I know there have been rumors circulating on this subject, and I am setting the record straight today. Half our world is marked by Death, and I knew early on that we needed to embrace it rather than ignore it. So yes, the Atwood Empire has undead citizens, citizens who have lived in isolation on Elysium. Until now."

With that, the side door opened, and a procession of warriors with powerful auras walked out as Joanna's group moved to the side. There were Vilari, Pika, and Rhuger, followed by the captains of the Einherjar. Only the Raun Spectrals were missing since they were slated to make a later appearance.

And in the lead, there was a singular Draugr emitting a towering aura —himself.

# CARDS ON THE TABLE

It almost felt like looking at a mirror as he saw himself, or rather his design for Arcaz Black, walking onto the stage. No matter how one looked at him, he seemed like a powerful undead cultivator. Only Zac would recognize the aura seemed slightly hollow, but the Branch of the Pale Seal mostly masked it.

Zac felt Arcaz Black couldn't be absent for this announcement, so he'd looked into temporary solutions. Eventually, Calrin had gotten his hands on three top-tier cloning treasures found in some ancient ruins. They looked like clay dolls and would create a clone that would last 12 hours. You imprinted it with your Daos and some of your soul, and it would create a perfect copy that, in Zac's case, had roughly 20% of his attributes.

Its aura was near-identical in strength to his own, making him appear completely real. Even scouting skills would show a normal Draugr warrior rather than a puppet.

Apart from its limited duration, the downside of this treasure was that it had taken Zac almost two hours to form the clone earlier this morning. It could also only stay a couple of miles away from himself before he lost his mental connection with it. In other words, it wasn't something he could suddenly take out in the middle of a fight to get a helper.

Still, it was the best Zac could do for now since he wasn't ready for his identity as an Edgewalker to become common knowledge in Zecia.

The secret would be exposed sooner or later, but he didn't want to give factions like the Allbright Empire or Calrin's Mercantile associates any reasons not to work with him before the war.

Getting a real clone would obviously be better, but actual cloning skills were incredibly rare before the D-grade. And the few that existed weren't very good. These kinds of skills simply required too much Cosmic Energy for the clones to become useful, or at least believable, which was why you needed a Cultivator's Core.

Before then, clones used concepts such as illusions or arrays to give the impression of creating multiple bodies, but they rarely had any real combat ability.

Murmurs of unrest spread across the hall as a chill of Death spread out from the scene, and some even stood up to fight or flee. However, it was all quelled when Zac unleashed his aura once more, this time together with his evolved Branch of the War Axe. Those who stood to flee were frozen in place, no doubt feeling like they suddenly had a thousand blades pointed at them.

Slowly, they inched back into their seats under Zac's unrelenting stare, and a suffocating silence spread across the room. Only then did Zac continue his speech.

"In this new reality, abstract concepts like Death have taken corporeal form, which forces us to reevaluate many things we once knew as truth. In this new reality, a different form of Life can and will spring from the depths of Death. As such, it is a natural consequence for Death-attuned worlds to start producing undead citizens," Zac said as he looked across the room.

"Rather than fight the natural order of things and wage an endless crusade against the undead, I chose to integrate them into the Atwood Empire. Today, there are multiple settlements of Revenants across Elysium, and they are an integral part of my force.

"I understand how this feels for many of you. All of us lost a lot of good men and women to the Incursion of the Undead Empire, especially the Sino-Indo Alliance. However, I want to be clear that Revenants have nothing to do with the Undead Empire. I *personally* killed the leader of their Incursion, along with all those who didn't manage to flee back through the Incursion Pillar.

"These Revenants are natives to Earth just like you all. They have no more relation to that distant faction than you all have to the old Empires of the Multiverse. They have no agenda against the living and only want to live their lives as the rest of us."

"That may be, but you know the undead are at war with the living out there," a powerful voice said. "Your actions might implicate this whole planet."

Zac looked in the direction of the voice and inwardly sighed when his eyes fell upon Henry Marshall. This was the first time he'd seen Henry since returning, even if he'd visited Thea's grave a few times. The old man didn't look so old anymore. Just like Sap Trang, he managed to break through to the E-grade despite his age, and he now appeared to be in his fifties.

Not only that, but his aura was quite deep, and Zac could tell he had reached Late E-grade already. With Henry losing the pillar that was Thea and Zac taking control of the whole planet, Henry decided to shift his attention to the martial path. Politics were ultimately a game of the old world—nothing could be accomplished without strength. Between his inherent talent and the resources of his clan, he was making decent progress, even if he couldn't compare to the elites of Port Atwood.

"There is a risk of that happening, but I have my reasons for choosing this path," Zac said. "First of all, I am just following the path the System has laid out for us. As many of you know, Port Atwood has participated in an Incursion of our own over the past years. The result was that we exterminated all the other invaders on that planet before integrating a second world into the Atwood Empire."

The doors to the scene opened once more, and two rows of people came walking in—the Mavai Demons and Raun Spectrals.

"What you might not know was that the System sent us to yet another Life and Death-attuned world. A world with natives naturally attuned to the elements of Life and Death. Today, the Mavai Tribes and the Kingdom of Raun have joined the banner of the Atwood Empire, and they will fight alongside us against the Kan'Tanu invaders."

No one spoke, and more than one had ruminating looks as they gazed at the large group of people on the scene. Zac let the silence stretch on for a bit longer before he continued.

"Do you all know how rare these kinds of worlds are? Twin-affinity worlds naturally producing both Life and Death? They are essentially non-existent across our whole Sector. Yet the System has put two of them under my control. I don't believe for a second this is a coincidence.

"It is an instruction, a path forward for the Atwood Empire. I have no interest in going against the wishes of the System or fighting against the Heavens. I will instead use the tools it has given me to elevate our faction to the next level. The undead lands and races will provide the Atwood Empire with unique skills, resources, and manpower; things we desperately need right now."

This was the official story they'd settled on—blame everything on the System. In all honestly, Zac knew he was the most likely reason for the changes to Earth and why they were sent to Ensolus of all places. However, he couldn't just go out and say that since it would damage the people's faith in his vision for the Atwood Empire.

This way, his actions could rather be seen as destiny. The System had chosen this route, and as long as they followed through, they would be rewarded. Of course, Zac would still hold the ultimate responsibility for this direction, but they hoped that framing things this way would quell some of the unrest. The next step was to dangle a carrot in front of the leaders.

"Besides, I have some important news on the issue you mentioned," Zac said. "In the face of the upcoming war, the Undead Empire is calling a semi-permanent cease-fire on the living forces of the Zecia Sector. Instead, they are joining with the other top factions to repel the invaders. As such, the perpetual war between living and undead is ending, and we will not be caught in the crosshairs.

"Ultimately, I believe this is an opportunity. During the past years, I've traveled across many worlds to temper myself. Out there, the world is not black and white. I even learned of a place in a neighboring Sector called Twilight Harbor, a so-called grey zone where undead and living lived side by side.

"Because of its nature, the harbor has become a natural trading hub between the Undead Empire and the surrounding factions. This trade has made Twilight Harbor one of the most prosperous factions in the area. This is the future I want for the Atwood Empire, and I believe it's possible thanks to the Undead Empire finally stopping their war against the living factions.

"As such, some changes will take place over the coming months.

New districts are being built in Port Atwood and many other settlements across Pangea. These districts will be filled with Miasma to give our undead citizens somewhere to live. Similarly, neighborhoods are being built on Elysium, places of pure Life where living cultivators can thrive.

"Furthermore, we are opening our second planet, where vast resources are waiting to be extracted. In other words, millions of job openings will soon appear, opportunities that will allow you to rapidly accumulate Atwood Empire Contribution Points. It's also possible for private ventures to open up shop in these new realms to help them grow.

"This is not a small thing I'm springing on you, but I urge you to meet this change with an open mind. Ultimately, the only difference between the living and the undead is that one cultivates with Cosmic Energy and the other with Miasma. Among all the strange and inexplicable things in the Multiverse, such is barely worth mentioning.

"Once again, I want to reiterate that these Revenants and Spectrals have no connection to the invaders that attacked us a decade ago. We will not tolerate attacks against our innocent citizens, living or undead. Any such actions will be considered terrorism and an attack against the empire, and the response *will be swift*. We are all in this together.

"Remember, the enemies are the invaders, not your neighbors."

With that, Zac covered the subjects that needed to be covered, and a flashing light indicated his speech was no longer being recorded and transmitted. What remained now was the actual work.

"All the pertinent details will be sent out, and representatives will remain to answer any questions you may have," Zac said. "I look forward to your cooperation."

With that, Zac turned toward the door and walked away, giving no room for a Q and A. His departure was like the starting signal as a raucous clamor spread across the hall, with people shouting over each other for answers. Zac ignored the noise as he left the scene, but he could still see the situation through the eyes of his temporary clone.

Some were just shouting, whereas the more quick-witted were hurrying toward the neighboring conference area the elites on the scene were moving toward. They probably realized there would be a reshuffling of resources and power with such large changes to the Atwood Empire. Those who adapted quickly could get a bigger piece of the pie.

Zac didn't head toward the conference hall, but he didn't leave the venue either. He ascended a floor and entered a private meeting room that had already been prepared. A few minutes later, the doors opened before four figures entered: Ibtep, Rhubat, and two Anointed Zac didn't recognize.

They were most likely two of the more powerful Anointed remaining after most of the Anointed Council had sacrificed themselves to kill Void's Disciple.

"Warmaster, it is good to see you," Rhubat rumbled as they sat down in one of the prepared jumbo-sized chairs.

"Chainbreaker, your aura has grown stronger yet again," Zac smiled before turning to the others. "Welcome, please, sit down. Ibtep, I've heard you've been busy."

"Sometimes I feel the world grows more interesting by the day. The more I discover, the more I realize I've just scratched the surface," Ibtep said. "It's good to see you're back. We were worried for a while. I should have known better than to doubt your resilience."

"That was some news you sprung on us just now," Rhubat sighed. "Working with those tainted things? Did you call on us because you wanted to know the stance of the Hives?"

"That's part of it," Zac said. "I don't think I have met you two?"

"This is Kezret and Adrotep," Rhubat said. "I brought them today to get acquainted with your domain. They are new commanders of the Zhix armies, and I thought them suitable to be our contacts for the upcoming struggle."

Zac nodded. "Of course. Let me know if the Zhix needs anything to prepare. I wasn't exaggerating on how dangerous this conflict will be."

"You say there is war, but you never said why?" Kezret asked. "Conflict for conflict's sake is foolishness."

"If I had a choice, I wouldn't join this mess either," Zac sighed, and explained the situation with the Space Gate, the Kan'Tanu, and their origins.

"Unorthodoxy," Androtep hummed. "You mentioned this word before. These Kan'Tanu walk the same path as the Dominators?"

"I guess you could say that," Zac said. "The leader of the Dominators and the Kan'Tanu are both unorthodox cultivators. They gain strength through taboo means such as sacrifice instead of cultivating by following the natural order."

"What is our role in this struggle?" Kezret inquired, prompting Zac to explain more in-depth how sanctioned conflicts worked.

"Then we are forced into the conflict by the Heavens," Androtep said. "To avoid it means punishment. To embrace it means death."

"That's about it," Zac agreed. "I can't stop it, so I can only work to make my people stronger and minimize losses. That includes integrating the undead into my faction."

"My instincts tell me those things are not natural and that I should pierce my spear through their skulls," Rhubat said. "That they represent a path that ought not to be traversed."

This was obviously not what Zac hoped to hear, but he didn't interrupt the de-facto leader of the Zhix as they mulled over the situation.

"However, the Zhix have been forced to adapt to many realities that clash with the precepts over the past years. It has reached a point where it is hard to trust our senses," Rhubat continued. "These unliving, how do you know they can be trusted?"

"The Raun Spectrals is a conquered society," Zac said. "Truthfully, I don't trust them, not fully. But the native undead of this planet I trust with my life. They have proven themselves in the conquest of Ensolus, and I have a few other guarantees as well."

Rhubat nodded slowly, glancing at the others. "I need to speak with Warmaster alone." Once the others had left, he looked squarely at Zac. "These unliving on the other side of our planet. They did not appear naturally, did they?"

"I raised them," Zac confirmed. "In a sense, they are my children. That's how I can guarantee they are loyal."

"I expected as much, though I don't understand how you split your unliving side from yourself," Rhubat said.

"Just a small trick." Zac smiled, not phased by the comment. Rhubat was present during the battle with Void's Disciple, where Zac had been forced to use both his classes. They were one of the few outside Zac's inner circle that knew about his situation.

"Be careful. When you feel powerless, and the world is closing in on you, it is easy to make decisions that can come to haunt you in the future."

"Of course."

"I will talk with the Zhix. We will not be the cause of instability during this critical time," Rhubat eventually said. "As for these unliving. They must prove themselves as warriors and trustworthy allies before the Zhix can embrace them. Your word alone is not enough."

Zac nodded. "That's all I ask."

"This Contribution Store, do you think it carries knowledge?" Rhubat asked, shifting the subject.

"Knowledge?" Zac said before realizing what Rhubat was driving at. "For your Cultivation Manual?"

"We have gone from a sprint to a crawl," Rhubat sighed. "Before, we could at least make small amounts of progress, but we have been stuck in our research for over three years now. Our inquiries through your merchant have not yielded any results either. It's frustrating. I know the Zhix can flourish even in this new environment, but the universe is not giving us enough time to adjust."

Zac thought about it for a moment before making a decision. "I don't know about the Contribution Store, but I may have another solution for the Zhix if you're willing to take a risk."

Ten minutes later, Zac and Rhubat left the room, where Rhubat called the other Zhix for a private meeting. A few minutes later, a Valkyrie would take them to the Ensolus Ruins for a chance at the inheritance. As for Zac, he had one more person he wanted to speak with before he left.

Henry Marshall.

## 53

# UPRISING

Zac was planning on heading toward another conference room, but he stopped when he saw a familiar face below. It was Ibtep, looking out at a garden courtyard from a large window.

"You're still here?" Zac asked as he walked over. "Rhubat didn't call you?"

"No, I have no commitments apart from my farms nowadays. Did things go well?" Ibtep asked as they handed Zac a red larva that almost looked like a Jelly.

"I think so," Zac said, wryly smiling at the little grub struggling in his hand. "Is this one of your new breeds?"

"It is," Ibtep seriously nodded. "I've found tremendous joy in breeding new and exciting species on my farms. Unfortunately, my brethren have a narrow palate, and few of my latest inventions have had much success. So many interesting species and flavors have gone underappreciated, so I had an idea. If the Zhix refuse to expand their horizons, why not enter another market?

"So, humans?" Zac grimaced.

"Exactly," Ibtep eagerly nodded. "There are so many of you! This is a new breed, designed with you humans in mind. I would love your input."

Zac looked down at the larva with some resignation, then bit down. However, his eyes immediately opened wide as an explosion of a familiar flavor entered his mouth, prompting him to eat the rest of the grub in one bite.

"*Strawberries?*"

"Exactly," Ibtep nodded eagerly. "It took some time, but I think I got quite close to the real thing. I would have kept going, but it turns out those berries are quite poisonous for us Zhix. I had to spend a week on the latrines while I taste-tested them."

"Well, the taste is there," Zac smiled. "You might need to... repackage them, though. Humans aren't used to eating larvae."

"What about these new races you've scrounged up? Do they enjoy tasty treats?" Ibtep said.

"Well, the ghosts definitely don't," Zac said. "The demons probably will, though."

"What about the corporeal unliving? Do they eat? Do they poop?" Ibtep asked eagerly.

"Only after reaching Late E-grade," Zac said. "Undead enjoy scents, though. So if you can breed fragrant critters, I'm sure they would like it."

"Interesting," Ibtep said with gleaming eyes.

Zac looked at the Zhix, remembering how he'd been a fount of inexhaustible curiosity during their first meeting and into the following days. Suddenly, a thought struck him, and he made an impromptu decision.

"Rhubat is leaving Earth in a week or two. Most likely for a few years," Zac said.

"Oh?" Ibtep exclaimed. "Where to?"

"The depths of this Sector, a place called the Million Gates Territory. If you want, you can join him. He'll be traveling with most of the elites of Port Atwood."

"A reconnaissance mission?" Ibtep asked.

"Among other things," Zac said. "They will also explore hidden realms in search of ways to gain strength before the war arrives. I thought your talents might be useful in such a mission."

"I am just a worm farmer nowadays," Ibtep hesitated, though Zac could see the Zhix was interested.

Zac smiled. "Well, think it over and discuss it with Rhubat. I have to go. Thank you for the treat."

"Good luck," Ibtep bowed.

Zac nodded before turning toward his second appointment, and contacted Ogras through his communicator on the way.

"Rhubat is joining you on your mission," Zac spoke into his communicator. "Maybe Ibtep as well."

"You decided to clue those people in," Ogras said on the other side. "But why the insect-peddler?"

"I don't know. Call it a hunch?" Zac said. "I felt that it's not necessarily the strongest who will get the inheritances, but those with affinity to it. Ibtep has a rare mindset and a class based on discovery. I didn't tell Ibtep about the heritage, though. I just felt Ibtep can be an asset to you, even if they don't end up getting a seal."

"I trust your instincts, and we have more than enough room aboard the vessel," Ogras said. "By the way, did your quest update from sharing the details with the big guy?"

"No," Zac grunted with annoyance. "I can't figure out what's going on with this thing."

"We'll see how it goes," Ogras said. "By the way, the Sino-Indian alliance left in a huff with some others soon after you left the stage."

"I saw. We'll see how that goes as well," Zac sighed as he walked into a meeting room closer to the hall where the ambassadors were getting debriefed on the transition.

He made another call with his communicator, and Henry Marshall entered a moment later, along with an Atwood Hall employee who brought a tea set and some water.

"Your presence is something else these days," Henry said as he sat down. "Have you entered D-grade already?"

"Not yet," Zac said. "This time, I want to shore up my foundations a bit more. But I'll break through before the war starts."

"It's hard to believe your foundations can get any sturdier," Henry said with a shake of his head. "It's almost like you're a different species than the rest of us at this point."

"In a way, we're all a different species compared to before the Integration," Zac said as he put some rare herbs into the tea kettle. The leaves immediately dissolved, and a fragrant aroma spread through the room. "How are you?"

"I'm getting along." Henry smiled. "The family is doing quite well, thanks to you."

"It's mostly your own work," Zac said as he poured Henry a cup.

This little ceremony had been common while he lived with Thea. Henry had always served tea when Zac visited, and Zac reciprocated in turn when Henry visited Port Atwood. Henry had stuck to the teas of Old Earth, while Zac usually served interesting Spiritual Leaves he'd found through Calrin.

In a way, it reflected their mindsets, where Henry still had a foot in the old world while Zac wholeheartedly embraced the new.

The old man nodded in thanks, and a small smile spread across Henry's face as he took a sip. "So, how was it?"

"Perfect," Zac said as he poured a cup for himself. "Thank you for agreeing to this."

"Just like in New Washington," Henry said. "I wonder if this is to be my lot, to set up your sales pitches."

Zac laughed, remembering the humble beginnings of Port Atwood. Back then, they were forced to set up a stall in a bid to get a few people to move to his island. But it was only after Henry Marshall confirmed his identity that they got anyone to join. Today, Henry played a similar role, though this time, it was at the behest of Zac.

"And as I set myself up as an antagonist to this endeavor of yours, I'll get approached by like-minded people," Henry continued.

"Perhaps," Zac said. "What do you think I should do with these people who pull in a different direction?"

"Does it matter what I think?" Henry said with a smile. "It took a while, but us old bones have started to come around to this new reality of ours. The one with the biggest fist makes the rules, and the rest have to figure out how to maximize their benefits within that playing field. If possible, we'd like to set up some ventures on both Elysium and your other planet. They will not clash with your consortium."

Zac nodded. "Of course. The broad strokes are set in stone, but I'm always open to suggestions."

Henry set his cup down. "Well, if you truly want my advice, it would be not to half-measure this change. I don't know if you are right in choosing this direction, or if your strength and infamy have nurtured a hubris worthy of the Roman Emperors. What I do know is that there will be discontent, both with the undead and how you unilaterally have decided the future of Earth.

"I have seen it. Some of us have managed to discard the trappings of old, while others are slipping back into routine thanks to years of safety. They whisper of democracy, of overthrowing tyrants. One whisper will birth three more, and opinion will eventually become fact. Many love to be the underdog, the oppressed. That way, they can rail with righteous indignation at the system holding them back."

"What do you think I should do?" Zac asked.

"Strangle those whispers in their cradle."

They talked for a while longer, with Zac sharing some of his experiences in the outer world while Henry provided suggestions based on his experience. The old Marshall Patriarch wasn't as knowledgeable as himself or Ogras about cultivation, but he did have many insights into human nature thanks to his pre-Integration life.

Henry then left to take charge of family matters and create a plan for their expansion into Ensolus and Elysium. Of course, this would be done in secret. The official reason for their talk, which Henry would also leak, was that the Marshall Clan had tried to change Zac's mind in private. Zac wanted to be done with this matter, but the constant barrage of messages in his communicator told him he couldn't just up and leave.

Instead, Zac spent most of the day meeting with one group after another, mostly leaders of various subsidiary factions. The Underworld Council had no strong feelings about the undead. They were the ones who'd been least impacted by the undead Incursion, so they didn't have any objections more than the inherent oddity of the situation.

In fact, they were interested in hiring a large number of Revenants to work in the Underworld. Even today, quite a few sectors were largely unexplored, and many were already filled with Miasma. Having undead explorers and laborers who could extract the rich materials down there was a good opportunity to increase profits, which was something everyone wanted with war looming on the horizon.

The Ishiate Tinkerers didn't care much, either. They were more interested in exchanging insights with the Einherjar in hopes of weaponizing Miasma for their gadgets. For example, Zac heard one mention the possibility of creating cannons that could shoot out condensed Miasma, instantly turning the enemy ranks into mindless zombies. Zac knew it was possible, considering that exact thing had attacked him in the heart of the Dead Zone.

The shamans of the naturalist Ishiate were far less comfortable with the undead factions, but Zac didn't care. They hadn't accomplished much during or after the Integration, and their top cultivator, Starlight, had left Earth behind long ago. Thankfully, it looked like they would become more useful as time passed.

They had a generally high affinity with the Dao of Life and Nature, and more and more talented healers were appearing in their ranks of shamans. By providing access to some of the Blessed Lands and some manuals, he could likely gain a competent medical corps in time for the invasion.

Simultaneously, Zac held a private meeting between his puppet and the Raun Spectrals. They were relieved to hear that a deal had been struck with the Undead Empire. A few inquired about the possibility of joining the Undead Empire down the road, which Zac was open to. Ultimately, Zac doubted there would be many who showcased enough potential to get recruited, but the possibility might make the Raun military work harder.

Many more wanted to discuss all manner of topics with Zac, but he didn't have time to spend whole days in meetings. He didn't know any of the details of the Integration, and he had no time to micromanage everything. Instead, Zac retreated to his cultivation cave to continue his cultivation, though he had no intentions of using the Temporal Chamber immediately.

Zac had already decided to use it after getting the first set of treasures from the Undead Empire. He also wanted to finish the first layer of the [Void Vajra Sublimation] before sealing himself for three years. Zac had made several improvements to his methodology over the past months, from adjusting the composition of the paste to the complementary arrays.

He wanted to go through the same experiments for the next layer before entering the chamber. Because according to Catheya, you couldn't enter and leave as you pleased. You would be sealed away for three full years when you entered, so Zac needed to prepare.

Most importantly, he needed to let the chamber absorb Divine Energy from a Nexus Vein for a few months, or he'd have to use Divine Crystals to power everything constantly. Reyna Umbri'Zi had already filled it with both Miasma and Cosmic Energy, so he only needed to place the box in one of the Life-attuned veins to gather the missing element.

It didn't take Zac long to put the matters of the outside aside as he entered an empty state where only his path and the Dao existed. Unfortunately, he only got to complete one session of the [Nine Reincarnations Manual] before his communicator buzzed. Zac sighed as he looked at the Communication Crystal. He'd already told the others not to bother him with minor details, so something big must've happened.

"Three factions are revolting," Ogras said on the other side the moment Zac accepted the connection. "What do you want to do?"

Zac wasn't the least bit surprised. The Atwood Empire hadn't made any big moves on Pangea in years. He'd been gone for almost a decade while the strongest elites were busy dealing with Ensolus. Now, Zac had openly taken on the role of the ruler of Earth. Some were bound to be angry, and some were dumb enough to do something about it.

"Who are they?"

"A faction within the Sino-Indian Alliance led by some Guru Anaad Phakiwar. Apparently, he's someone who used to be a big shot before you left him in the dust? The other two are the councils of two major cities situated near the Dead Zone," Ogras said. "There's also a few who put forward ideas like a world council that should decide certain matters through majority votes."

"As we expected, then." Zac sighed. "Only humans, at least. Do you need my help?"

"It's just a bunch of weaklings living in the past. We'll deal with it," Ogras laughed. "It's better if you don't appear. It will damage your prestige if people see you running around personally putting out fires."

"Alright, thank you," Zac said before putting away the communicator.

Some things were inevitable, just like Henry said, and it wasn't just about him controlling Earth. The Undead Empire had caused so much damage to Earth, all but destroying some of the most populous countries. That wasn't something you could just forget in a couple of years. Hell, if Zac himself hadn't gotten to know Catheya, he might have felt the same way, even if he had a Draugr half.

In a perfect world, Zac could have allowed time to heal the wounds and met their anger with compassion. Unfortunately, Earth wasn't ready for a galactic war. Too few had the skills to survive in an all-out clash against an experienced cultivator army, even if Zac equipped them with superior gear. He couldn't have people casting doubt on his plan, slowing down the transition of the population.

These early voices of discontent would have to become the sacrifices that kept the others in line.

Zac resumed his cultivation, completing another rotation of [Void Vajra Sublimation]. As far as Zac could tell, he was one-third through the first layer of the method. Quite a few golden flakes were dancing in his cells even before he started, with more being added every session.

It even felt like his cultivation speed kept increasing as his body grew increasingly accustomed to Life. Calling it an exponential speed increase would be an overstatement, but he didn't think it would take much more than another month to complete the first layer. Continuously reinforcing his Dao Heart also helped. The quicker he entered the right state, and the deeper he delved into the depths of the Void, the greater the effect of the [Void Vajra Sublimation].

By the time Zac finished, another report had been sent over. Everything was already over. Ogras had led a few Demons and Valkyries to the settlements, and not a single agitator managed to escape. The rioters hadn't realized how to usurp a town properly. They hadn't bothered killing the appointed mayors and snatching the Nexus Nodes, allowing Ogras to pop up right in their midst.

So just like that, the original second-place-holder of the Dao Ladder had died, quashed like a bug by Ogras.

# THREE YEARS

In just an hour, three powerful factions on Earth had disappeared without leaving so much as a ripple behind. This would all be kept away from the general population, but those who needed to know would learn of it one way or another. Zac shook his head and started up the second rotation of his Body Tempering Method.

The days passed this way. The world outside was rapidly changing while everything remained the same in Zac's cultivation cave. He got a few more notifications about the Integration, from scuffles erupting to another outright mutiny. Ogras dealt with the dissidents from the shadows while Vilari toured Pangea as an ambassador of peace.

Days turned to weeks, and Zac soon reached the point where his [Thousand Lights Avatar] was fully recovered to the level before it was destroyed. Part of it was thanks to the Moss Crystal, but it was only upon returning to Earth that he'd seriously cultivated the Eidolon Manual for extended periods. He'd occasionally practiced it in the Orom World, but he spent most of his time focusing on his techniques back then.

At this rate, Zac judged he'd be able to finalize the avatar inside the Time Chamber. Of course, this was just the first layer where he'd form a complete spiritual body that would be able to emerge from his body for short durations. There were further layers in the technique where one would drastically strengthen the avatar, and even allow it to survive indefinitely outside his body.

Zac wasn't sure if there was any point to that, though, not with how he planned to use the [**Thousand Lights Avatar**]. He'd have to see if the first layer was enough to use it as a delivery system for his Daos. If not, he'd keep going until it was.

His soul was getting along as well, with his fifth set of Outer Cores already nearing completion. This was years ahead of schedule, though he hadn't planned on cultivating the [**Nine Reincarnations Manual**] this much before breaking through to the D-grade. Until getting the Moss Crystal, he'd thought reaching the third reincarnation before heading to the Perennial Vastness was a fool's hope.

Now, there was a window of opportunity.

Zac was even using Soul Crystals during every cultivation session since returning from the Kaldran Strait, something that was only possible thanks to his recent negotiations with the Undead Empire. Soul Crystals were impossible to source in Zecia, but the Undead Empire obviously had its own channels. He already commandeered any Soul Crystals Catheya and the others carried with them, and larger batches would start arriving soon.

His [**Void Vajra Sublimation**] was also closer to a breakthrough. In a perfect world, Zac would have wanted to stay inside his cave until he reached the first layer, but there were a few more things he needed to deal with. First, he needed to send the others to the Million Gates Territory, and he'd just gotten a message that they were ready to set off.

Fifty people stood just outside the Nexus Hub when Zac arrived. Most were the core combatants of his faction. Rhuger and Vilari would lead ten more Revenants. And two Raun Spectrals, apparently. Had they heard about Ra'Klid and a Mavai Shaman joining the mission and petitioned for two slots as well? Then again, spectral cultivators had a couple of unique advantages, and they made great scouts.

Joanna brought eight Valkyries and a couple of human warriors Zac somewhat recognized. There was the archer who'd left some impression on Zac in the battle between the Raun Spectrals and the Ensolus army. Next to him was a demoness, along with six more Torrid Demons.

Ten people didn't emit as bloody an aura. They were the support staff, which included the administrators who helped steer the Yphelion during the previous mission. Among them, there was a familiar face Zac hadn't seen for years. He hadn't anticipated Sui, the little healer who once saved his life in the depths of the Dead Zone, to join the mission.

Zac had almost forgotten about her, but it turned out she'd reached Late E-grade. Judging by her almost holy aura, she continued down the path of a healer. She would no doubt take up the role of medic on the mission. There was also one Ishiate and one Volor Stoneturtle among the support staff. They were most likely technicians who would hopefully be able to perform some field repairs on the Starflash in case something went wrong.

Finally, there was Rhubat, Ibtep, and two more elite Zhix warriors.

The Starflash could obviously house a lot more people, but Zac could only send one person over at a time. Furthermore, he was under the same restrictions as the Space Gate Guild, which meant he couldn't just activate the Nexus Hub and transport a whole army to the other side of the Sector.

If he wanted to accomplish something like that, he would have to first seize the destination planet and hold it long enough to lock in the ownership. Better yet, he could have the Allbright Empire gift him a world, avoiding the headache. Apparently, that was exactly what was happening right now in the Red Zone, where most C-grade factions were given planets to allow for mass transportation and Cosmic Vessel production.

"I won't waste your time with empty speeches. You are all the best of the best our planets have to offer. I hope you find opportunities on the outside. But remember, you only have one life. Coming back in one piece is the most important," Zac said, then turned to Ogras. "Is everything prepared?"

"Would have been ready a week ago if not for the bastards who refused to face reality," Ogras snorted with annoyance. "You should've just let me put their heads on pikes to wake the others up."

"Well, from what I hear, things have already stabilized," Zac said. "But thank you for your help. All of you."

"It was our pleasure," Vilari smiled. "It was nice to finally see the other half of our home world, even if the environment was a bit unpleasant."

"Is everything dealt with in that regard?" Zac asked.

"Both main ship and the backups have been refitted with Holy

Beacons and barriers," Vilari confirmed. "We will most likely need to temporarily disable them when we jump through dimensions, but that shouldn't be a problem. We have more than enough Miasma Crystals as well. Enough to last us two decades, if need be."

Zac nodded. "Good. Still, be careful. From what I've heard, there are very few Death-attuned worlds in the Million Gates Territory. Most places you will traverse will be toxic."

"We'll be careful," Vilari said, a grin beginning to spread. "And who knows, some suffering might help me advance my soul faster. I have been much-too-comfortable as of late. Oh, by the way, don't forget about Lily. I will not be able to keep tabs on her after I leave."

"About who?" Zac said with a blank look.

"The pet keeper with a bonded Ayn Hivequeen. Of course, it's more apt to say she's become the pet while the Hivequeen is holding the leash," Vilari said.

"I thought it was handled?" Zac frowned.

"It is, in a sense. I forced the insect queen to leave Lily's mind, but the two were bonded in a way I couldn't deal with. I felt it was fine after I had a talk with the Hivequeen. It will work for you, and the girl will act as your liaison. Of course, you can always kill the queen, but that would damage the girl's soul," Vilari said. "But I think they can be an asset in the war, provided you can speed up the hive's growth."

"Alright," Zac sighed before turning to Rhubat.

"Anything?" Zac asked.

"Not yet, but I will keep searching," Rhubat rumbled.

Zac nodded, not overly surprised. Finding another seal in the Ensolus Ruins felt like a long shot. But walking among the ruins of the Limitless Empire might have helped him gain some Karmic Links to the Left Imperial Palace, so Zac didn't think it a complete waste of time.

Finally, Zac turned to one more person who stood to the side from the others—Calrin, who was accompanied by two Peak E-grade warriors with powerful foundations. Of course, Calrin's safety mostly came from the shocking amount of defensive and offensive treasures he was decked in. Seeing as the little Sky Gnome was a Hegemon himself, he could throw those things out indefinitely and create utter mayhem.

"Are you prepared?" Zac asked.

"I have everything I need." Calrin nodded.

"Perfect, get me a good deal."

Calrin obviously wouldn't join the others on their adventure to the Million Gates Territory. A ship belonging to the Peak family was already waiting for him on the other side, which would take the gnome to the closest War Fortress, where he could showcase and negotiate the wares. Zac ultimately chose to send Calrin for the negotiations rather than dealing with the matter himself.

With the region currently so hectic, Zac didn't feel confident negotiating in person as he did with the Undead Empire. It was better to send a representative, someone who had experience in negotiating trade deals. Calrin didn't mind either since this was a great opportunity to make connections and offload parts of the huge stockpiles of raw materials Zac had brought back from Twilight Harbor.

"Alright, let's get started," Zac said as he put his hand against the Nexus Hub.

Zac spent the next week sending one member after another to the Million Gates Territory. He didn't head over himself, just simply activated the hub and let the others enter. He had to wait almost five hours before he could trigger a teleporter to the same world again, so he kept up most of his cultivation in-between, except for the **[Nine Reincarnations Manual]**, which took up too much time.

The world Zac was sending his squad to was called Crimson Edge. It wasn't quite as dangerous as it sounded, though it was by no means a safe world. The name simply came from the fact that it was a world at the edge of the Red Sector, bordering the Million Gates Territory. A lot of mercenaries, pirates, and adventurers passed through Crimson Edge on their way to the lawless lands beyond.

As such, the order had never been particularly good, and battles in the street were a common occurrence. The war had changed that, though. Tens of millions of soldiers were now stationed on the planet. They didn't interfere with the unattached cultivators, but few dared to cause a stir with such a force nearby.

Calrin had already bought a large plot of land through some sort of dummy corporation, giving the Atwood Empire a small base of operations in the region. Zac hadn't visited himself, but there were already barracks and hangars where they could set up their Cosmic Vessels without anyone spying on them.

The week passed until Ogras was the last one remaining.

"Three years," Ogras said.

"Don't get yourself stuck in some Mystic Realm again," Zac smiled as he shook the demon's hand. "I'm not sure how many times I'll be able to fish you out."

Ogras grinned. "My ring is full of escape treasures. I'm not sitting around for another decade."

"Have fun then," Zac said as he activated the Nexus Hub one final time. "And if you get the chance, recruit some capable fellows?"

"I'll mention the boss is filthy rich, trick a few of them," Ogras laughed. "Good luck on your end."

A moment later, Ogras was gone, and the array winked out. Zac sighed as he looked up at the sky. He wouldn't have minded exploring the vast beyond in the Yphelion, but he had work to do. Zac returned to his cave and resumed his cultivation. Every day, his body was annealed with the inexhaustible flame of Life, pushing him closer and closer to a tipping point.

Zac could feel it build up inside him, even if his body hadn't yet changed in any noticeable manner. His skin hadn't taken on a golden or bronze hue, at least not a lasting one, and he didn't seem to recover any faster from wounds. He hadn't gained any attributes either, making it almost seem like the golden flakes in the depths of his cells were completely useless. But he felt full of life and verve even when not cultivating the **[Void Vajra Sublimation]**, to the point he managed to add even more rotations every day.

Then finally, he reached the tipping point.

Even from the first stance, Zac could tell this one was different. The moment he stamped down on the ground, the whole underground forest around him shuddered, and a golden glow spread across the area. Like radiant pollen had been released from the leaves, but it was the Life-attuned Energies being kindled by Zac's aura.

Zac wouldn't lose his composure at such an important junction, and he smoothly transitioned into the next expression of the Void. He actually *feel* the illusory seal forming even as he moved away. It became a fixture that marked the starting point of the sublimation. And that was just the beginning.

One mark after another was imprinted in the small clearing as Zac progressed. They hovered in the air like gateways into the Void. They didn't even contain a smidgeon of Dao or Cosmic Energy, and none but Zac would ever lay their eyes on these runes. Yet they were as real as could be, confirmed with utmost veracity by his heart.

Thirty, fifty, seventy. The seals grew more numerous, and Zac felt he was closing in on something. On their own, they were just breaches into the Heavens, small pathways where he could siphon Life for his benefit. But as Zac expertly went through the motions, he felt he was creating something greater—being shown a constellation after only having focused on individual stars.

The rune.

It was the illusory rune that always formed inside his body, only to disappear the moment the session was over. At the same time, it was different, almost inverted. Zac couldn't figure out the details in the middle of his breakthrough, so he pushed all errant thoughts aside and became one with the Void.

One seal after another was added until Zac finally returned to the origin. As he looked through the meadow, the seals seemed chaotic and disorderly. In reality, they were anything but. They were just missing the final piece of the puzzle, the key that would allow it all to click into place. Zac took a final controlled breath, and his hands clapped together.

A tremendous shockwave erupted from his body, and the trees around him were pushed back so far that their crowns almost touched the ground. It was like time was put in reverse as the shockwave was dragged back toward the heart of the glade. And in the wake of the implosion, a storm of Life followed. It was like the shore receding from an impending tsunami before it all came crashing back.

Left behind were the trees that made up the natural formation of life. They were still bent, but now they bowed toward him, like subjects showing deference to their sovereign. And from them, even more Divine Energy was released, dragged out from the depths through their roots.

Zac welcomed it all with equanimity. He was the Void, there was no limit to how much he could absorb, and the innumerable vortices in his cells had begun a feeding frenzy. For a moment, it almost looked like he would drag up the whole Nexus Vein by its roots, but things soon changed. One by one, the illusory runes started vibrating, beginning to absorb the abundant energies as well. Gradually, they lit up with golden splendor, turning into radiant lanterns of truth.

The first seal to light up was the opening step on the ground, and it rose by itself and entered Zac's body. The pain was unreal, far worse than when the paste burrowed into his skin, but Zac couldn't back down now. He had to withstand the whole process without flinching, or the foundation for his future Body Tempering would be imperfect.

Zac stood frozen in place like a statue, holding on to his Dao Heart to withstand the agony. Meanwhile, the first seal superimposed on the large illusory pattern that always formed when he practiced the **[Void Vajra Sublimation]**. A corner of the fractal lit up, dragging it to the surface of reality from the illusory world of his Dao Heart.

One by one, the fractals entered his body and Zac started to radiate a blinding gold. The grass grew with a mad zeal, and the branches of the neighboring trees stretched toward the warmth of his existence. Unfortunately, Zac could barely register the changes around him as he desperately held on to the Void. When the final seal slipped out from between his palms and entered his chest, it formed a perfect whole.

Life.

Once more, the pattern receded into the depths of his body, but it was different this time. It wasn't just a truth made real by his heart. The pattern contained immense amounts of Divine Energy, which endlessly filled every cell in his body. By this point, his body had already swallowed a terrifying amount of Divine Energy, to the point the black holes were no longer black. They'd become golden vortices filled with everlasting Life.

As the mysterious force from the rune of Void Life joined the vortices, like reality shifted. What was temporary was now permanent, on a deep, irrevocable level. A smile spread across Zac's face as he knew he'd passed the first hurdle. He had perfectly passed the first layer of the **[Void Vajra Sublimation]**.

The agonizing pain was soon swept away, replaced by a vibrant warmth as his cells adapted to the new energy at their centers. The process continued for a full day, where Zac felt he'd returned to the womb. There were no thoughts or problems, just warm Life and the protection of the Void.

Eventually, Zac's mind return to normal, and he slowly opened his eyes. This time, he could tell something was different with his body, even if his skin hadn't changed color. But just as Zac was about to open his Status Screen to check things out, a voice broke the silence of his cultivation cave.

The voice of a woman. A voice all-too-familiar.

"You've improved."

# TRAPPED

"The etherstorm is descending," Onandar said as she glanced at the crimson horizon. "End them."

"They're just children," Thea entreated, looking down at the huddled captives, her hand shaking—both from the mental strain and the rampaging intent coursing through her veins.

It was getting harder to control. She'd been drinking out of the tainted well of the Blessed Kin for years now. Thea wouldn't be able to prevent the madness from seeping into her Dao for much longer. She was so tired, having been forced to stand guard against the liquid every moment. And in this place, she was constantly tested.

By this point, Thea only felt a hollow numbness thinking back to horrors she'd come across roving the Stoneshatter Valleys as part of the Hallowed Mother's scavenger squads. Of course, scavenger was a relative term when most of their resources were 'scavenged' by slaughtering rival camps, bandits, or other unorthodox factions hiding in the valley.

Usually, Thea didn't mind. The Blessed Kin were evil people slaughtering other evil people—on the Goldblade Continent, there were few innocents outside the distant citadels. That was doubly true for fallen regions like the Stoneshatter Valleys. Anyone not equipped with ruthlessness and strength would have died before long in this place.

If anything, slaughtering these monsters helped Thea release some of the budding madness before it infiltrated her intent and twisted it. Still, it accumulated in her body, like a monster constantly nourished by that alchemic concoction. There was nothing Thea could do about it. She'd tried everything to rid herself of the vile mixture without any result.

And Thea knew there would be no going back if she gave in.

The vile brew of the Hallowed Mother allowed her and the Blessed Kin to push at a mad pace, but it came with a terrible price. It drained you in exchange for pushing past your limits. Drained you of longevity, of thought—even your humanity. And as soon as you stopped struggling, you'd become an addict. The moment it infiltrated your soul, you wouldn't survive without it for long.

The rest of the scavengers had given in to the Hallowed Elixir, including Onandar. They were all addicts, madly roving the valleys for loot they could exchange for more elixir. That was how the Hallowed Mother ensured her underlings were loyal and productive. It was a treadmill of suffering and depravity.

She still didn't know why the Hallowed Mother, a terrifying Monarch of the Unorthodox Path, had bothered capturing her three years ago.

Thea accomplished some small feats after being dropped off at a desolate corner on this nightmare of a continent. She had quickly realized that her chances of survival in this place were almost nil, no matter what her status back on Earth was. It was simply too chaotic. Just three days after arriving, she'd stumbled upon a battle between two Peak Hegemons.

Dozens of miles had been devastated by their battle, and Thea had almost succumbed to the poisonous mists one of them conjured. By now, that encounter was more like a small greeting by the Goldblade Continent. It took her two months to recover and capture someone weaker than her to get a lay of the land.

And from there, a plan formed. She needed to get to the Cloudsoar Terrace, a famed Sword Sect at the continent's center. The environment there was apparently beyond comprehension, and the Sect's foundation was immense. From what she'd managed to piece together from various sources, it probably surpassed any of the factions in the Zecia Sector.

More impressively, this was on a continent without the System. These masters had reached the levels of Peak Monarchs without the aid of the System—their foundations and insights into the Sword had to be immeasurable to accomplish that. If she could enter the tutelage of one of the Sword Saints of the Terrace, while still retaining the System's features, a limitless future would await her.

But a C-grade continent is just too vast. For years she traveled toward her destination, narrowly avoiding death on a daily basis. But her luck finally ran out when she passed the Shatterstone Valleys. The Hallowed Mother herself suddenly plucked her from the sky and marked her by a seal that prevented her from escaping.

The old hag never explained herself, nor had Thea ever seen her after being abducted. The only hint that her status was special, was that she'd been given a house of her own and a larger share of cultivation resources. But she was forced to drink the Hallowed Elixir all the same, just like the war-slaves and common members of the Blessed Kin.

And now, it'd finally come to this. She could feel herself right at the precipice. Circumstance and accumulation had put her at the limit of what she could endure. Thea was losing control over the concoction in her body, and her very sense of self frayed at the corners. The elixir egged her on and told her to just embrace the realities of the Goldblade Continent.

But she couldn't.

This ragged group of children were just between five and twelve years old. They hadn't even embarked on the road of cultivation yet. From the looks of it, they were the remnants of a collapsed clan fleeing from whatever took them out. Even the light in their eyes was different from the murky or red-rimmed orbs of the Shatterstone natives. They hadn't yet been twisted by life in this place.

"Are you questioning the Hallowed Mother?" Onandar said as her eyes thinned. "I knew it was a mistake to give all those resources to a half-formed outsider. Cannot be trusted, cannot be depended on. Weak of will and weak of intent. A waste of the precious elixir. Mother dotes on you, so you will get a final chance. Kill them, or I'll cripple you and bring you back for judgement."

The pressure built as Thea resisted the murderous intent. Her heart beat so hard it might just break out from her chest, like a volcano about to burst. Her whole body twitched, and veins started to pop out all across her body. She couldn't move. She could barely think. Thea was like a small raft on a raging sea, just trying to hold on a bit longer.

"I have to say, it's my good luck finding this group of cattle,"

Onandar said with a twisted smile on her face. "It will make your surrender much more enjoyable."

Thea wasn't able to answer. The sharp intent she'd honed for the better part of a decade was being overrun by madness and synthetic killing intent, and the walls of her Soul Aperture were starting to show cracks. Thea could only settle for giving her captain a murderous glare.

"That's right. I *knew*," Onandar sneered. "You thought yourself better than us, resisting the Hallowed Elixir? Fool. Most of us never even tried to fight it. Why would we? The concoctions of a Nascent World Alchemist are almost impossible to get for commoners like us. Where do you think our members come from? They travel far and wide to join the Hallowed Mother's protection and receive her blessings. Your little struggle amounts to nothing.

"It's just been a source of entertainment to see how long you would hold on. I have to admit, I'm a bit annoyed. I lost six Bloodeye Rubies betting that you'd only last a year. But now, Mother's patience has run thin. You'll come back as a good daughter, or you'll come back as a cripple."

Anger.

Searing fury cut through the madness of the Hallowed Elixir, threatening to replace it with a different type of insanity. Thea remembered the nights of bitter training, of tempering herself to withstand the burning pain of the elixir. Of breaking down in tears in the corner of her home after having been forced into one bloody struggle after another with the other scavengers. Of the constant emotional and spiritual toll she'd endured these past years.

*It was all a joke? To you and the goddamn Monarch hiding in the shadows? Then I might as well lash out and satiate my hatred against one of you!* Even if the brew consumed her, even if she died, she should at least drag Onandar with her down to hell.

Purpose gave her a new wave of strength. Her struggle, her conviction, and her path, they all converged as Dao and purpose became one. It cut apart the madness and severed the chains of the Hallowed Elixir. It danced through her body like a cleansing wind.

But it wasn't enough.

"I—" Thea said hesitantly, except her hands didn't share the hesitance. They were filled with intent so strong it could pierce the sky.

Aigale tore through the air, though not toward the children. Years of frustration had crystallized into a Sword Intent of absolute sharpness, and it headed straight for Onandar. She didn't need Cosmic Energy or a skill to carry her Branch of the Clouded Sword. They would only slow down her ambush.

Space tore apart, and Onandar didn't even have time to circulate her Cosmic Energy before the Sword Intent passed through her body and continued into the sky.

"Wha—" Onandar said as a sanguine shield sprung up around her.

The barrier only managed to form for a second before it fizzled out. A sloshing sound followed as Onandar fell apart, cleanly cut in two.

Thea stared at the corpse while panting, barely believing her eyes. She'd never moved that quickly before, and she had never managed to conjure Sword Intent that pure. Not even the intent Irei had left her could compare. She'd put everything in that strike, and it had been enough to kill a Middle-stage Hegemon instantly.

Of course, Onandar would no doubt have won in a real fight, especially considering Thea wasn't sure she would be able to conjure that level of Sword Intent again. It'd been fueled by years of suffering, and that wasn't something she could just pull out of a hat. Still, it was a monumental first step.

She might not be able to freely conjure that kind of intent right now, but she would be able to in the future. Now that she had accomplished it once and gotten a feel for it, she would be able to work her way toward it. Not only that, but Thea could feel that the Hallowed Elixir barely affected her. It was still there like an unwelcome passenger, but it was almost completely restrained.

Now, she only needed to figure out how to get rid of the prisoner seal. But just as Thea dared dream of freedom, a void plunged her right back into the pits of despair.

"Good, child. You had me worried there for a while, but you really didn't let me down."

The next moment, Hallowed Mother appeared in the sky, looking just like the last time they met. An elegant yet severe woman appearing to be in her fifties. Her slightly greying hair was pinned up in a simple bun, and a few crow-lines could be seen when she smiled. If not for the fact that her left arm was an oversized monstrous claw with six gaping mouths, she would have looked like any random middle-aged lady back on Earth.

"I'm only on the sixth iteration, but it looks like this mixture can stimulate one's heart and even nurture intent," the woman said. "Of course, there is something off about you. Perhaps I chose a subject with too strong a providence. Before I can draw any definite conclusions, I will have to study your body and the secrets it holds."

Thea looked up at the crazy alchemist with a sense of anger and helplessness. So that's what it was. For the other scavengers, her struggle was a joke. For the main culprit, she was just an experimental subject to test her drugs. She wanted to scream, she wanted to cry. She was so tired of old monsters appearing in the sky to mess up her life. Most of all, she wanted to send out another sword beam and cut that mad scientist in two.

Only, it was hopeless. The Hallowed Mother was a genuine Early-stage Monarch, or a Nascent World Stage cultivator as it was called on the Goldblade Continent. Even if her Sword Intent had evolved just now, it wasn't enough to kill that kind of being. Besides, she didn't have it in her to send out another one.

She still had all of her Cosmic Energy and a decent amount of Mental Energy remaining. The problem was her emotional state. She'd infused everything into that swing, leaving her numb. Intent was ultimately a fusion of Dao and Heart, where your convictions took corporeal form. And with her heart exhausted, the power of her intent was drastically diminished.

"Pl... ease... Mother," a gurgling voice said from the ground.

Thea was shocked to find Onandar had actually survived being cut in two. One of the halves lay unmoving, but the other desperately grasped toward the sky.

This was one of the downsides of cultivating on an unintegrated planet. Thea might have the System 'installed' on her body, but others didn't. The most noticeable consequence for her was that she didn't get any Cosmic Energy from kills. Because of that, reaching Peak E-grade had taken at least two years longer than it should have, and the lack of kill confirmation could result in surprises like this.

Not that it mattered now, with the Hallowed Mother appearing in person. Thea knew she was doomed no matter whether Onandar lived or not.

"You are just a useless prop, but I suppose you fulfilled your task admirably," the Hallowed Mother muttered.

The next moment, one of the mouths on her arm spat out a green blob that landed on the dying Hegemon. Thea stepped back with shock-filled disgust as the green goop started to wriggle and writhe. Initially, Thea thought the vile-smelling concoction would fuse the two halves, but that was only partly true.

The mixture dragged the two body-halves closer, but it more so seemed to turn into greenish flesh that replaced what had been cut off. A new creature resembling a mutated conjoined twin formed in just seconds. It was more than twice as wide as the original Onandar, and the midsection was a green horror show filled with tumors and boils.

"A-Ah," the left half of Onandar's face gurgled before her remaining good eye rolled up into her socket. The miscreation crumbled, and Thea was certain she wouldn't get up again.

"Hm, heads are still out of reach," the Hallowed Mother muttered, then glanced at the children, who looked up at the sky with abject horror.

"Wait!" Thea shouted. "Spare them, and I will go with you willingly."

Thea was done for. There was no escaping a Monarch. She might as well try to overturn the Heavens. But if she could save these children, then at least something good would have come from her death.

"Your willingness does not matter. Sooner or later, all your secrets will be laid bare whether you like it or not," the Hallowed Mother calmly said. "And leaving stragglers like this can have unexpected conse-quences."

"Run!" Thea screamed as she rushed in front of the group of huddled refugees.

"Dying for some random trash." The Hallowed Mother smiled with a shake of her head. "What foolishness."

"Better than to become an old monster who has lost everything but her power," Thea spat as she gathered everything she had for a final strike of defiance.

Thea's actions were undoubtedly futile, but she wouldn't just stand by. It was like her heart had been reignited, and an even greater Sword Intent was formed. Thea looked at it with marvel as it flew toward the sky. It was the most beautiful thing she'd ever created, and a sense of accomplishment washed through her, even if it was just empty bluster in the face of a Monarch.

"Blessings, blessings," a sudden sigh echoed through the world.

Thea didn't have a chance to react before her sword beam lit up with golden splendor, and it shot forth with impossible speed as it expanded through infinity. For a moment, it looked like the whole sky would be cut in two. The scene only lasted for a moment before it turned into something even odder.

The blade of Sword Intent was suddenly gone, and in its place were two enormous hands pressed together in prayer. Thea's heart shuddered, and her instincts told her to kneel in obeisance to the holy aura it emitted. She felt like she was looking up at the actual hands of God, descended to the mortal realm to shield the innocent.

"Benefactor is right," the voice continued. "Life and death are but fleeting moments. Mara is forever. To sully oneself is to sully the Cosmos."

# CONNECTED BY FATE

The golden hands radiated a holy light, and Thea could almost glimpse something inside the radiance—a vast ocean where all the answers to cultivation existed. In front of that ocean, her Sword Intent was nothing, a small parlor trick not worth mentioning.

No, it wasn't! Thea shook her head, her awe at the hands replaced with fear. It was almost like she'd been hypnotized, led astray by another's path. Zac had described something similar that happened when they reached the Dimensional Seed, but this was more targeted, more intentional.

The next moment the hands disappeared, and Thea's eyes widened in shock upon seeing the state of the Hallowed Mother. She was completely drenched in blood, and her demonic arm was simply gone.

"Who!" the bleeding Monarch screamed, not even waiting for an answer before she disappeared.

Thea wasn't surprised in the slightest. If she had learned one thing over the past eight years, it was that concepts such as victory and defeat were luxuries that only existed in the minds of men. When the thin veneer of civilization had frayed, there was only life and death. Honor and mercy didn't exist in the wild.

That was why the Hallowed Mother ran for her life when faced with a mysterious cultivator with the strength to cripple her. The only benefit to staying was to figure out who attacked her, but what did that matter compared to surviving the ordeal? Running was the best option in this kind of situation.

Yet it was futile.

Two monks and a nun suddenly appeared out of nowhere. One of the monks seemed to be a hairless dwarf or a very fat gnome, while the other two had the same statures as humans. Thea couldn't see the features of the female, though, as her face was hidden by a veil. None spoke. They just looked in the direction of the fleeing Monarch with an eerie calm.

Thea could no longer see Hallowed Mother. She'd turned into a streak of light, escaping thousands of miles in no time. However, the veiled nun simply waved her sleeve, and the Hallowed Mother was suddenly right in front of them. At first, there was confusion on her face, but it was soon replaced by horror.

"Wait!" she screamed. "I have—"

"Too much sin has accumulated," the tall monk sighed as he lifted the staff in his hand. "To send you into the wheel of reincarnation like this would be doing you a disservice. You shall be given a chance at redemption."

The staff slammed into the ground and the dozen golden loops on top of the staff sang. Thea didn't know what she expected after the monk's proclamation, but it wasn't a massive explosion of gore. What chance at redemption? The Hallowed Mother had been splattered all over the ground.

Thea swore with surprise when she noticed a young woman appear where the Hallowed Mother once stood. She looked a lot like the Hallowed Mother, but there was a sense of hollowness to her that Thea couldn't quite explain. She almost seemed like a humanoid puppet, albeit an incredibly lifelike one.

"What is your name, child?" the staff-wielding monk asked.

"This one does not now," the naked woman said with a bow.

"You will return with us and recite the Avalokiteshvara Mantra." The monk nodded as the nun handed the woman a simple robe. "When you have found your self, you can begin your journey of redemption."

"This one understands," the reformed Hallowed Mother silently moved to stand behind the nun. There was not a ripple of emotion in her eyes, just a sea of tranquility.

Thea just looked on with incomprehension. What just happened?

Rebirth? Was such a thing even possible? And why had these people appeared here? They were clearly Buddhist monks. Was there such a faction on Goldblade Continent? Thea didn't know what was going on, but her heart shook when the four turned toward her.

"Benefactor, the past years have tested you," the short monk sighed. "This poor monk is happy to see benefactor has managed to hold onto their humanity even after becoming subject to the sorrows of the world."

Thea's eyes widened in alarm upon hearing his words. She could tell. The monk hadn't said it outright, but they knew. They knew she wasn't a native of this place.

"Thank you for saving my life," Thea said. "Can I ask who you are?"

"This poor monk is but a passerby, traveling the cosmos in search of enlightenment." The small monk smiled. "Karma pulled us toward each other, benefactor. We are connected. Benefactor, you carry great destiny on your self, and it was too early to enter the Samsara. Lending a helping hand was just the will of the cosmos."

Thea frowned as she looked back and forth between the monks. The small monk's words seemed genuine, and he was clearly incredibly powerful. But why were his eyes so shifty? Then, she noticed something in the cherubic monk's hand, and Thea's eyes widened in shock as she reached for a hidden pocket in her sleeve.

It was gone.

The small Spatial Stone she'd found during her travels was currently in the small monk's hand. It contained a few cultivation resources and some other things she managed to embezzle over the past years—a go-to bag in case she ever managed to escape from the Hallowed Mother's grasp.

"That stone—" Thea couldn't help but blurt.

"Blessings, blessings," the monk smiled. "A beautiful pebble indeed. This monk will keep it as a memento of our chance encounter."

Thea blankly looked at the diminutive monk, her mind trying to comprehend the events. Had a powerful Buddhist Monarch really just stolen her backup stockpile and refused to give it back? Its contents couldn't be worth more than a few hundred E-grade Nexus Coins. Why did he need it?

"I... Uh, thank you for saving my life," Thea said again with a bow, dropping the matter. Some random cultivation resources were ultimately a cheap price for her life. "I hope you can care for these children. As you saw, I don't have the strength to protect them. I will not disturb you any longer."

With that, she resolutely started to walk away. Her instincts told her not to get mixed up with these monks. Her track record when running into powerful Monarchs was horrible, and the Buddhist Sangha weren't just some altruistic do-gooders. She might not have as strong a danger sense as Zac, but she had developed a nose for trouble—and these people reeked.

Thea would much rather resume her journey to the Cloudsoar Terrace. Its existence had been a source of inner strength for years now. That one day, she'd escape from the Shatterstone Valleys and continue on her path. And today, that moment had finally come. The seal on her heart had dissipated the moment the Hallowed Mother was gone, and nothing was holding her back anymore.

And today, the odds of making it to the terrace were a lot higher.

Even if it was just for an experiment, the years with the Blessed Kin had undeniably made her a lot stronger. It wasn't a coincidence the Hallowed Mother and many other unorthodox factions had settled in the Shatterstone Valleys. It was one of the most flourishing spots in the region, and there was no local force powerful enough to claim it all on its own.

The environment far eclipsed that of Earth. Between the constant life and death battles the scavengers had thrown her into, and the forced progression of the Hallowed Elixir, she'd already pushed her Branch of the Clouded Sword to Middle Mastery. Now, she just needed to form a Pure Wind Branch to complement her Pure Sword Branch, and she would essentially be ready to tackle Hegemony.

After breaking through, with her unique access to the System's benefits such as titles, she should be able to fight even Late-stage Hegemons here on the Goldblade Continent. As such, she would be approaching the top level of the Wandering Cultivators here. The only problem was that she didn't know how much of her potential and lifespan the Hallowed Elixir had stolen.

Thea estimated it was centuries, though, which meant there was no time to lose.

A subdued whisper dragged Thea out of her thoughts, and she was shocked to realize the group of children was still right next to her. Some-how, she'd been moving in place, rather than running away from these Monarchs. She fearfully looked back, only to see the monk smile at her.

"Benefactor has a benevolent heart," the monk continued, pretending he wasn't preventing her from leaving. "Neither fire nor wind, life nor death, can erase one's good deeds. They can't be seen, but they will nurture you. This poor monk has already benefited by lending a helping hand. It just so happens, I could use benefactor's assistance."

There it was. These monks hadn't just saved her out of the good of their hearts. They knew she was an outsider, so were they after the secrets of her body? A body reforged by the System. Unfortunately, she didn't have any way to integrate others on this continent—she'd already tried all sorts of things when she arrived.

"I'm not even a Core Formation Cultivator. I'm afraid I can't help vaunted beings such as yourselves," Thea said, almost with a pleading look on her face.

"Benefactor underestimates herself. It just so happens a few of our young Acolytes are about to leave their monasteries on a pilgrimage, most of them for the first time in their lives. They are unaccustomed to the dangers of the mortal world and could use a guide. A guide with a benevolent heart, but who still is aware of the Mara in the world."

"You want me to guide your disciples?" Thea said with confusion. "You three are so powerful. What need do you have for me?"

"It's not proper for us old monks to look over the shoulders of our disciple-nephews. We would become like the tall oaks, our canopies covering the ground in shadows," the other monk said.

Thea inwardly groaned as she thoughtfully looked at the three. "Where are you going? Toward the center of the continent?"

"No, benefactor," the smaller monk said. "They are heading into the stars. Is benefactor ready to leave this world behind?"

"Leaving the Goldblade Continent?" Thea said with surprise.

Perhaps she shouldn't be that surprised. This place didn't have the System's teleportation arrays, but these three appeared to be Late Monarchs. Perhaps they had other means of transportation, which would mean they might have access to all kinds of places. Like integrated space, or the distant Heartlands of the Goldblade Continent where the Terrace still waited.

"I could guide your Acolytes," Thea said. "But I get to pick where you drop me off afterward."

"Of course," the small monk said as his smile widened. "This poor monk is called Three Virtues. We will be in your care."

---

Zac was in the depths of a mountain, hidden and protected by multiple layers of arrays. More importantly, he was on a planet shrouded by the System itself. Yet she'd popped up out of nowhere when she should be on the other side of the Sector right now.

"Iz, what are yo—" Zac said as he spun around, but his voice rose an octave upon realizing he was still stark naked.

He dove toward the ground, thanking the gods for the tall grass that just sprouted as he hurriedly put on a robe. Only then did he dare look up again, and he was immensely relieved to see that the fiery golem wasn't with her. Zac wasn't sure he'd have survived if that were the case. Still, Zac didn't feel safe, and he warily looked around.

"Kvalk is not in this solar system," Iz calmly said. "He wasn't able to force his way inside. The shroud was surprisingly dense around your planet. If not for my uncle preparing a backup method, I wouldn't have been able to make my way here."

Zac sighed in relief before looking at her suspiciously. "How did you manage to find me?"

"Every day, the echoes of Chaos around you weaken. The tracking seal on you is working again," Iz said as she walked over. "As for the arrays… Well, they weren't very impressive."

"They weren't made to stop people like you," Zac said, giving her a weak smile. "Now that we know each other, how about you remove that mark of yours?"

"Removing a mark empowered by a Supremacy is beyond my abilities," Iz said, but the smile on her face showed she wasn't too broken up about it.

"Forget it," Zac muttered as he took out a canteen of water. "Well, welcome to Earth, I guess."

"Just now, what did you practice?" Iz asked. "Those seals—"

"What?" Zac blurted as the water went down the wrong pipe. "Just how long did you look?"

"Long enough to see your Body Tempering Method contained some very odd concepts," Iz said.

"That's not what I—" Zac coughed as his eyes darted to the side.

"Your nakedness?" Iz said, her eyes widening a bit in realization. "Do not worry. You have quite a good musculature. As for the—"

"Let's just drop it," Zac groaned.

"No, this is my mistake. I admit, my social experience is lacking," Iz said as she thoughtfully looked at Zac before looking down at herself.

"You aren't—" Zac said, his heart suddenly beating a lot quicker. Surely she wasn't planning on balancing out Karma that way?

Zac was soon filled with a mix of disappointment and relief as a small bottle appeared in her hand. For a moment there, he almost thought this would turn into a sitcom scenario, and he wasn't sure his fate could withstand something like that.

"This is a tonic called **[Wreathstar Nectar]**. It is normally meant to be used after breaking through to D-grade, but it should be helpful after your current breakthrough as well. It will stabilize your foundations and even set your body in a 'hungry' state that will allow you to quickly absorb more energy," Iz said as the vial floated over.

Zac's eyes lit up, grabbing the bottle. The nectar didn't sound too impressive from Iz's description, but every single thing she'd produced since they met had been a unique treasure that you'd never get your hands on in the frontier. There was certainly more to the **[Wreathstar Nectar]** than she let on. Otherwise, she wouldn't have been carrying it around.

Showing some skin in exchange for a supreme tonic that would allow him to quickly move on to the next layer of the **[Void Vajra Sublimation]** felt like a worthy trade, even if it was disconcerting how she could just find him like this. She'd mentioned Chaos, could he perhaps get a jammer that used the energy of the Remnants?

"Oh, only drink three drops or you'll explode," Iz added with a small smile just as Zac was about to chug the whole thing.

Zac barely managed to stop himself from turning into a bomb, and he carefully swallowed three drops of the **[Wreathstar Nectar]**. A powerful gust of wind swept through his body, and Zac shuddered as small pebbles of grey goop were squeezed out from his pores. Meanwhile, Zac's body quickly stabilized like he'd broken through months ago rather than just now.

The process lasted only a minute, yet Zac suspected the drops had saved months of cultivation. It wasn't just the impurities that were removed and the foundation that got stabilized. It felt like the gust of wind had somehow pushed the Life-attuned Energies deeper into his cells and condensed them. That left room for more, and he could feel how his body almost screamed for more nourishment.

He would have to practice the next layer to be sure, but Zac suspected his cultivation speed would be drastically improved until the condensed cells were filled up with Life again.

"You have almost impossibly few toxins in your body for someone on the frontier," Iz commented with interest. "I thought you would at least have accumulated some by that water you collected."

"My body is pretty good at dealing with toxins." Zac shrugged. "And the Tribulation Lightning helps as well. Besides, the lake water doesn't seem to leave any impurities."

"You ought to be careful. Impurities can take many forms, including spiritual," Iz said after some thought. "I managed to contact my grandpa before I entered the Eternal Storm. Do you know what that corruption is?"

"I just figured it some sort of spiritual rot from the Lost Plane," Zac said.

"You're right, in a sense. It's the corpse of a previous Heaven," Iz said. "When an era ends, the Dao collapses and is then slowly reformed. Except someone seized a corner of the Heavens and put it inside the realm you call the Lost Plane. It became cut off from the Dao, separate from the natural rise and fall of the eras."

"The Dao couldn't escape, so it started to decay?" Zac frowned.

"The Lost Plane is incredibly old," Iz said. "It is most likely one of the oldest Eternal Heritages that remain. Its ancient Dao has long lost its source and has mostly dissipated, and what little remains has been twisted in unexplainable ways. No one can know what the effect of prolonged use is, so tread carefully."

"I'll be careful." Zac nodded as he looked down at the grime covering his arms. "I'm sorry, give me a second, will you?"

"Of course," Iz said, and Zac flashed away.

He didn't go far, entering a secluded side room that was a small living space. There, he took a quick shower to rid himself of the dried Life-attuned paste and the expelled impurities. He also scarfed down a bunch of dried Beast King meat, which helped him satiate the sense of hunger that the **[Wreathstar Nectar]** elicited.

He was done just a few minutes later, but before returning to Iz, he first opened his Status Screen to look at the result of his breakthrough. There wasn't any new line on the main screen, and neither did he find one for his constitution. However, when opening his Bloodline Panel, Zac saw that a new line had been added.

**[Life] Void Vajra Sublimation (First Layer):** Base Attributes +5, Vitality +10, Endurance +5. Vitality +5%, Effect of Vitality +5%.

# WHAT DOESN'T BELONG

The gains weren't earth-shattering, but Zac was still happy with the result. Getting attributes at all was usually a sign of a High-quality constitution, and he actually got efficiency from the first layer. That almost made the entry layer of the method equivalent to a top-tier title, which wasn't anything to scoff at. The flat attributes were useless now, but Zac suspected he'd get a noticeable boost when the method caught up to his cultivation level.

Besides, the Body Tempering Manual provided other benefits than just raw attributes. It was just that the System didn't showcase them. Zac could absolutely feel a sense of vibrancy in his body, though his Branch of the Kalpataru didn't seem to gain anything from it. The Dao felt the same, confirming his affinity hadn't changed.

With his bloodline, that was to be expected, and Zac was confident the same thing would happen after using the **[Essence of the Abyss]**. The vibrancy in his body was rather that of a powerful life force. Zac couldn't be sure, but he'd probably regained a good chunk of the years he lost to Creation Energy and other encounters.

Iz had warned him that using life force as a source of energy would hollow one out, robbing you of your fate and potential. Conversely, getting a longevity boost was equivalent to reigniting your momentum and potential. Zac wasn't sure if the rule fully applied to him with his unique cultivation system, but who would say no to living longer?

The original method also provided resistance to toxins, certain curses, and a faster recovery speed. Zac guessed these boons were still there, even if he had altered the method. After all, replacing "Boundless" with the "Void" mostly changed the absorption process rather than the end result, with the notable exception being the difference in Heart Cultivation.

As to why the System placed the information together with his bloodline, Zac wasn't sure. He guessed it made sense considering the connection to the Void, and his Draugr-node was also there. In a sense, it was almost good news since it hopefully meant there weren't any clashes of compatibility between bloodline and Body Tempering Method.

Now, he was just missing the equivalent line on his undead side. In fact, Zac wanted to check whether the attributes transferred to the other side. He couldn't be certain that [Quantum Gate] would fully transfer these gains. However, with Iz waiting outside, Zac skipped turning into a Draugr for the time being.

Iz wasn't waiting where he left her, but Zac soon found her standing by his central prayer mat, curiously looking at Yrial's statue.

"My master," Zac said with a weak smile when she looked up at Zac. "He's also the one who made the escape treasure and penned that poem. He's a bit... eccentric."

"I didn't know you had a master," Iz said with surprise. "What force is he from?"

"None. He's a soul wisp from a Dao Repository I got from the System," Zac explained. "He's also an Edgewalker like me, though with Fire and Ice."

"Hm," Iz said as she looked up at the clashing elements above her. "A world of Life and Death. It's odd. Life and Death are part of the natural cycle of a world, yet this seems unnatural."

"I've inconvenienced everyone with changing this planet's direction," Zac sighed.

"To progress is to cause ripples. If others can neither rise above the waves nor adapt to them, then they simply aren't fated." Iz looked at Zac curiously. "But that method of yours, the one from before. It contains something different. It's a method of the Sangha, yet it is not. Can you tell me what it is?"

"It was a Body Tempering Method I got from a monk belonging to the Sea of Tranquility. It didn't suit me, though, and contained hidden traps. So I reformed it using the insights of the seals."

"My uncle says the Sangha is incredibly difficult to deal with," Iz commented. "Then again, that goes for all established factions for someone unattached like you."

"I've come to realize that as well," Zac grunted, then he froze, looking up at Iz speculatively. "Are you able to discern whether items are tampered with?"

"I might," Iz said after some thought. "But a price must be paid to maintain balance."

Zac nodded, mentally preparing himself to be scalded again. Though things took a different turn.

"I don't need to test your fate. I know you are fated. Instead, I want an answer," Iz said. "I've asked twice now, but you skirted the answer I sought. Your method contained a concept that felt familiar yet distant to me. It is not often I fail to discern the true nature of things. If you can tell me what that was, I will do my utmost to resolve any hidden traps in your treasures."

Zac hesitated. He obviously knew what she'd been digging at before, but this was closing in on some of his secrets—secrets he had no way to gauge the importance of. There was simply no information on the concept of the Void of Dao in a Sector like Zecia. Who knew what people from the Multiverse's Heartlands thought of it?

Still, Zac didn't immediately refuse upon remembering the trap hidden within the **[Boundless Vajra Sublimation]**.

He had all kinds of justifications for why it should be safe, but it would ultimately be risky to drink the **[Essence of the Abyss]** or jump into the Temporal Chamber blindly. His instincts told him the Undead Empire wouldn't harm him before they could extract all value from him, such as assisting them inside Ultom in seven years. But the **[Boundless Varja Sublimation]** showed him that being killed or crippled were not the only things he needed to look out for.

Now that Iz was right in front of him, he had a rare opportunity that might allow him to forge ahead with peace of mind. And if he had to ask himself whether he felt Iz was more trustworthy than the Undead Empire, his instincts said yes. If anything, she and her family seemed so far above him and his secrets that it didn't matter if he divulged them.

"It's the Void, and not just the Void of Space," Zac said. "I used the seal to replace the Buddhist Sutras with the pull of the Void, dragging Life into my body. Don't ask me how, though."

"Interesting," Iz said, and a smile bloomed on her face. "I wonder what those old things would think if they knew. A few have tried to grasp the peaks by plunging into the depths, but I don't think anyone has ever succeeded. Just extracting some benefits from the other side of the coin is incredibly difficult, yet a barbarian at the frontier communes freely with the Void, upending convention."

"Uh, please keep it between us, yeah?" Zac said, deciding to forgo objecting to being called a barbarian. After all, being a barbarian beat out being a bug.

"I'm not so lowly as to gossip about the matters of my friends," Iz said, her eyes shifting away slightly.

"Thank you," Zac said. "It's not easy to find trustworthy people in this world."

Iz nodded slightly, then looked up at the clashing energies.

"You are forming a Life Constitution to match your undead half," Iz mused. "Balance between Pure Life and Death. Forming a core on a path that only converge at the peak… difficult. Are you prepared?"

Zac sighed as he followed her gaze. Iz had hit the nail on the head with that comment. He'd realized this more and more as his understanding of Duality, and the nature of Cultivator Cores, had increased.

The Elemental Daos held a relationship of restraining and enkindling one another, but that wasn't the case with Life and Death. It all led toward Chaos, and Chaos was split into two, Creation and Oblivion, which gave birth to the concepts such as Life and Death. By their inherent nature, they were each other's opposites, only fusing into one when they returned to their origin.

To fuse the two concepts into one Core at the D-grade was to put the cart before the horse, a paradox. Still, Zac wouldn't give up. Henry Marshall might be right, that he had nurtured hubris worthy of the Roman Emperors. But Zac still believed he could accomplish it thanks to his unique encounters and bloodline.

He just needed to find the key that would make the impossible possible.

"Your heart is steady," Iz nodded before changing the subject. "What do you want to inspect?"

"Give me a minute," Zac said, taking out a table before flashing away.

A while later, Zac returned with the sealed Temporal Chamber and placed it on the table next to the [Essence of the Abyss]. The chamber had been left at an offshoot to the Divine Vein beneath the cave to charge while Zac cultivated. Iz didn't have any particular reaction to the two items and only nodded before taking out a fiery crystal.

The gemstone was similar to a normal Fire Crystal, but Zac felt some palpitations from the aura within. Iz took the crystal, and Zac looked with amazement as a drop of fire formed on her finger. Looking at it was like seeing the true face of Fire for the first time in his life, and only the light of Primal Dao could compare.

However, that Primal Dao had been spread out, diluted by holding so many truths. In contrast, this drop was pure flames, unblemished by anything else. The drop landed on the crystal, and Zac looked on with interest as it cracked. It didn't shatter and turn into dust, just looked more like an egg hatching.

And that turned out to be exactly the case. A small bird made from pure flames emerged, resembling a golden crow. Except it had three legs and an additional eye on its forehead. The whole thing emitted an incredibly ancient aura, almost like the aura Zac felt when using Void Energy.

"Please find what doesn't belong," Iz said.

The crow shook its wings, bouncing over to the two items on the table, leaving fiery runes in its wake. First, it jumped a few times around the box before its third eye opened. Zac's mind screamed of danger, forcing him to quickly look away. He'd barely seen a glimpse of the golden swirl, but it had almost felt like he had been dragged back to the beginning of time.

Inside that eye, there had been a sky set on fire, and Zac knew it wasn't some illusion. The whole cave shook from the pressure as sweat started pouring down Zac's face. The feeling soon passed, and Zac carefully glanced at the table and was relieved to see the crow had closed its eye.

"The Temporal Chamber seems to be unproblematic," Iz said as the crow jumped over to the vial and started the same procedure.

The same ritual repeated itself, and Zac realized the crow wasn't just bouncing around randomly. The runes its jumps left in its wake formed an intricate array around the item, though Zac couldn't figure out its purpose. The runes were too archaic, reminding Zac more of the markings on the Stele of Conflict than anything created under the System's purview.

Once more, the crow opened its eye, prompting Zac to avert his gaze. Something was different this time, though. When Zac looked back at the crow, he found it angrily staring at the **[Essence of the Abyss]**, and Zac's eyes widened in alarm when it stabbed forward with its beak.

"Wai—" Zac's words were caught in his throat as he saw the crow's beak somehow pass straight through the vial before dragging something out in a lightning-quick motion.

It looked like a ball of black mud, but Zac only caught a glimpse before the crow gobbled it up.

"What's going on?" Zac said with bewilderment.

The next moment, the crow flew right into Iz's forehead and disappeared, and she shuddered before slowly opening her eyes.

"Something akin to a curse had been added to the mixture," Iz said. "It would seek out Life and convert it to Death. I'm not sure if it would have worked against you, though. After interacting, your situation appears somewhat unique. It's as though you carry two different bodies in one, completely separate. Normally, you should have Death hidden deep in your cells right now, but that's not the case at all."

"Still, better safe than sorry," Zac said as he looked at the vial with some trepidation. "Thank you."

So, there *was* a trap after all. It wasn't as nefarious as the one Three Virtues left him, but it was still extremely dangerous. It didn't take a genius to put two and two together after learning about the curse attached to the **[Essence of the Abyss]**. As Catheya said, they didn't care about him being an Edgewalker. They were much more interested in his bloodline.

Meaning, they wanted to kill his human half.

Zac had to admit it made sense. He could probably break through to the D-grade in a month if he only had to worry about one of his two halves. His path was infinitely more difficult, and there was a real risk of failure. Better they sweep the problems aside and open the path for him to progress as a normal Draugr.

Perhaps it was even a precautionary measure. They feared he'd give up on his path and discard his Draugr side. After all, he was ultimately born human.

"It was nothing much," Iz said. "I'm afraid I have damaged the vial's seal, though. The actual tonic will slowly lose its efficacy. I recommend you take it within a month."

Zac wasn't too bothered, since his Body Tempering Progress was better than he'd originally expected.

However, he soon looked up at Iz suspiciously. "Wait, if you had that crow, why wouldn't you be able to remove the mark left by your elder?"

"That crow wouldn't dare peck at something my grandpa created." Iz smiled. "After all, it's just a sentient wisp of his Dao."

"Oh," Zac muttered.

"Is that it?" Iz asked, and Zac absentmindedly nodded in response as he stowed the two treasures. "Good, then it's time to fulfill our agreement."

"Ah, what?" Zac said before he looked up with alarm. "Ah, there's no need, no need. How about I give you a tour of my planet instead?"

But Zac shook his head in resignation when the |Stone of Celestial Void| appeared in Iz's hand.

"Some things are inevitable. As your poem said: Heaven's Path won't be denied," Iz said. "Now, do you want to spar here, or shall we relocate?"

"Follow me," Zac sighed, leading her toward the teleportation array, where each step felt like walking toward the gallows.

"I thought I'd have another year to prepare," Zac added as he helplessly looked at Iz. "I figured you'd be deep inside the Million Gates Territory by now."

"I was fortunate. It did not take me a lot of time finding the piece I marked," Iz explained. "I had no reason to stay in that region after that. In fact, it took me more time reaching your planet than searching for the seal."

"You're going home after this?" Zac asked.

"I need to work hard on my cultivation for the upcoming trial, yes. My grandfather will guide me over the next years."

"Can I ask? Someone like you, what did you figure out with the insights the seals provided?" Zac asked. "It's okay if you don't want to answer."

"Someone like me?" Iz asked with a raised brow.

"Rich," Zac said with a roll of his eyes. "I feel like I'd need twenty seals to cover everything I'm lacking, but that's because I'm kind of making things up as I go. So I was just curious what someone with a proper background would ask from the Seal of the Left Imperial Palace."

"I focused on my Core. Like you, I have a heavy foundation and many pieces that need to fit together. Without its insights, it would take me years to figure things out."

"Won't your elders provide you with a working core?"

"They could, but it would ultimately harm me," Iz said. "For one, any seemingly perfect solution my grandpa creates might not be the most suitable for me. Some answers need to come from within, and a slightly imperfect start to your journey doesn't mean it will be shorter. As long as it is truly yours and you fully understand every aspect of it, you can work on the imperfections as you progress.

"Conversely, if I rely on my elders too much, I might not even be able to defend my Dao properly. At that time, my grandpa would have to step in, and I'd be stuck as an Earth Immortal."

Zac stopped, confusion overcoming him as he looked at Iz.

A what?

58

# EARTH IMMORTALS

Zac had never heard of the concept of Earth Immortals before, and believed this to be a rare opportunity to learn some new things without getting blasted by Iz.

"A what?" Zac said with interest.

"If you fail to build a ladder to Heaven, you still have a chance to conjure the chains to the Earthly Planes and become an Earth Immortal, or a Fallen Autarch. You are weaker than true Autarchs, and you will be assaulted by increasingly ferocious Heavenly Tribulations every ten thousand years," Iz explained.

"It's a false realm, in a sense?" Zac asked. "Like a Half-Step Hegemon."

"Both yes and no," Iz said after some thought. "It can mostly be considered a false stage. Though technically, one can sever the chains to progress. If you manage to break all seven Earthly Chains, you should theoretically have a chance at Supremacy. And a Supremacy who rose through this path should be no worse than a true Supremacy who walked Heaven's Path. They might even have unique advantages."

Zac slowly nodded, despite not quite understanding the difference.

"But practically, it's not a feasible path of progression. Severing a chain barely improves your strength; you're still bound to the Earth. Also, breaking each subsequent chain will become more and more difficult. Even breaking the first is more difficult than stepping into Late Autarchy. And all the while, you must deal with the recurring Tribulation

Lightning." Iz sighed. "I've never heard of an Earth Immortal who managed to break more than three chains before a tribulation annihilated them."

"Sounds like a broken path," Zac muttered.

"That's because it is. Heaven's Path is to form a ladder toward Heaven where eight is peak and nine is perfection. The system of Earthly Immortals isn't part of this. It's the path of a previous Heaven, and the method was discovered in an Eternal Heritage shortly after the System was created. Some hoped to use it as an alternative path to the Peak, so they adjusted it to work with our Dao. Ultimately, it's not part of this era."

"More suffering and less strength," Zac said with bemusement. "Are there any benefits to it?"

"Certainly beats dying when you fail to defend your Dao." Iz shrugged. "Today, it's mostly used as a backup if your Dao Defense fails."

"Then why haven't I heard of it before?"

"You need a decently powerful Supremacy to guard your ascension and fight back the Heavens when you fail to build the Heavenly Ladder." Iz smiled. "Just suppressing the Heavens for the time it takes to summon the Earthly Chains is quite taxing, even for a Supremacy. It can also be extremely dangerous because of outside intervention. Finding an A-grade cultivator in such a vulnerable position is not easy. Therefore, Earth Immortals are quite rare, even in the central regions of the Multiverse."

"No wonder," Zac said.

It made sense. Why would a Supremacy take such a risk in normal situations? To risk their very lives for some Monarch who wasn't powerful enough to become an Autarch on their own? Especially when the end result wasn't that great. Perhaps if it were their child. But they definitely wouldn't stick their neck out for some random junior of their faction. Better to wait a few dozen millennia for another promising Monarch to appear.

"Less stalling. Where are we going," Iz said, and Zac grimaced when he saw her eager expression.

It was just like when they traveled through the Dimensional Seed together. She had offhandedly dropped a bombshell piece of information, such as the background of the Kan'Tanu. But any time he'd asked for more details, she looked at him with that face while talking about testing fates.

"Of course," Zac said with a crooked smile as he activated the teleportation array. "Let's get this over with."

A few moments later, they appeared on one of Zac's private islands. There were a few beasts around even though the island was a rocky plateau without any vegetation. None would dare get close after sensing the auras of him and Iz. He led her to a flat vista some distance away from his small camp, where they could fight without worrying about damaging the teleportation array.

"Is this really necessary?" Zac sighed, trying once more to avoid the inevitable.

"I never go back on my words," Iz said, while a smile crept up her lips. "Besides, aren't you curious? The distance between us, compared to the first time we fought?"

Zac reluctantly admitted he'd be lying if he said no. He felt he had made tremendous progress, and his foundations were far deeper today than when he ascended the Tower of Eternity. If he climbed an E-grade variant of the tower today, he was almost certain he'd be able to conquer the whole thing.

At the same time, Zac doubted Iz's family would have just let her laze around all day during her prime cultivation age. It was just hard to know what kind of methods someone like her practiced. Zac made it this far while cultivating Soul, Technique, and now Constitution. There was no way Iz didn't have similar accomplishments.

Unfortunately, he only caught glimpses of her fight inside the Void Star. Having been too busy dealing with the oversized Qriz'Ul goblin to figure out anything new. She was a fire mage, though he suspected the truth was far more complex.

"How about we don't use any skills?" Zac ventured, hoping he could leverage his Integration Stage techniques to level the playing field.

"That would put you at a disadvantage," Iz said as an array of intensely bright fireballs appeared above her head. "I do not think you possess the ability to utilize Cosmic Energy without guidance fractals."

"Nevermind," Zac grunted. "Just wanted to make sure I don't accidentally—"

Zac didn't get any further, as Iz looked at him like he were an idiot. "Don't worry about me. I'll be fine even if you hit me with a blast of Hollow Chaos. Let's go."

"Alright, alright," Zac said with a roll of his eyes. "Do you want to fight my undead side or human?"

"I shall leave that up to you."

Zac gave it some thought, then ultimately chose to stay human. His Draugr side would be a better match, especially if you included Vivi's weakness against fire. But this wasn't a fight to the death, and Zac wanted to push his human constitution to the limits to see if his Void Vajra Constitution improved his combat strength in any way.

Any errant thoughts were thrown out the window as an enormous eruption of fiery energies blanketed the area. Iz had flown back, creating almost a mile's distance between them, and was already preparing her skills. It almost looked like Earth's core had been dragged to the surface as a small sun rose beneath Iz's feet, and the six-winged demonic angel soon followed. Zac wasn't surprised by the scene—having witnessed Iz use this combo multiple times.

The whole island appeared to be fried by Iz's domain, and Zac wasn't ready to be outdone. Thousands of swirls appeared in the air as Zac unleashed a Dao Field powered by the Branch of the Kalpataru and the Branch of the War Axe. An area covering over a thousand meters became a battleground even more ferocious than the environment in his cultivation cave.

Zac found his domain suppressed and contained. But as long as it wasn't ripped apart, he'd accomplished his goal. A clash of domains wasn't a matter of pride and vanity, but a strategic struggle for the upper hand. Whoever managed to take control of the environment would have a home-field advantage. And since Zac could at least prevent his domain from buckling, the environment wouldn't empower her attacks.

Of course, Iz wasn't relying on her apocalyptic Dao Field, even if it exerted constant, overbearing pressure. The thing that really made Zac's danger sense wake up was the six archaic arrays that appeared around the demon's head like a nimbus. A stream of pure flames shot toward him with the speed of a falling meteor, but Zac was no longer the help- less person from back in the Tower of Eternity.

A huge fractal blade shuddering with barely contained Dao appeared on the edge of his axe, and **[Verun's Bite]** keened with fighting spirit as he swung the weapon at an upward angle. The blade tore into the beam, only splitting its front in two. A lone leaf was not enough to completely bisect this beam of unfettered fire.

Of course, the fractal leaves of **[Nature's Edge]** rarely traveled alone.

A storm followed in the first fractal blade's wake, and they ripped the beam apart like a swarm of piranhas. A few leaves even managed to continue toward Iz, who calmly stood atop the sun like a goddess. The huge Demonoid swatted them away like annoying flies, allowing Iz to calmly spectate the battle without moving. Even when imbued with Zac's Branch of the War Axe, the leaves only managed to leave shallow scars on the Demonoid, which soon closed in a flash of flames.

Zac wasn't deterred by something like that. That demon creature was one of Iz's staple skills, just like his Pillar of Desolation in his other class. It wouldn't fall so easily, especially not from a simple attack like this. The sun-and-demon pair were like a summonable array turret. Trying to beat Iz at her own game with **[Nature's Edge]** was a fool's hope.

The ground cracked beneath Zac's feet as he shot forward like a rocket, easily avoiding a second beam that followed the first. Zac found himself caught in an apocalypse, with fiery rays and molten rock assaulting him from every direction. He was already moving based on the concept of his Evolutionary Stance, each step finding a path of life in a sea of fiery death.

The pressure mounted as he drew closer. The beams were incredibly fast and unending, and Zac got less and less time to react to their trajectories. Just dodging wasn't enough after two hundred meters, and he was forced to fight fire with fire. His right arm turned into a blur, and he kept launching fractal leaves to either destroy Iz's barrage of strikes or put some pressure on Iz herself.

Even now, Iz hadn't moved so much as a muscle, appearing content to let her avatar duke it out with him. Zac almost felt like he was playing a video game facing a two-stage boss. He needed to take out the guardian before he could face the real challenge. And Zac had a plan to accomplish just that.

The whole battleground was soon destroyed beyond recognition.

Some of the fire beams slammed into the ground between them, redrawing the landscape, and Zac kept ripping up huge swathes of stone in an effort to obscure his pathing and create an opening. Vivi's vines were also helping by grabbing massive boulders and hurling them at Iz. Normal stones couldn't withstand the beams of flames for long, but they could delay them for a fraction of a second, allowing Zac to pass through or launch a fractal blade at a tricky angle.

Zac soon noticed that any time he made the avatar block one of his fractal leaves, there would be a brief pause in the beams. Seeing a path to close the gap, Zac focused even more attacks on Iz herself, which allowed him to advance even faster. Finally, Zac judged he was close enough for the next step, and pushed from the ground while activating a torrential storm of leaves from **[Nature's Edge]**.

Two beams were already bearing down on him the moment he launched into the air, but a simple step moved him over fifty meters closer. Waiting at his destination was a flying boulder Vivi had hurtled just a moment earlier, and Zac used it to reset **[Earthstrider]**. At the same time, huge amounts of Cosmic Energy entered his arm.

A giant wooden hand appeared in a crack of reality, just one hundred meters away from Iz Tayn and her demonic avatar. It ruthlessly swung down in a bloodthirsty arc just as Zac forced the avatar to block out a series of attacks on Iz. It prevented the Demonoid from instantly changing targets, but it still managed to fire off three of its arrays at **[Arcadia's Judgement]**.

Blinding pain almost made Zac fall to the ground, but he gritted his teeth as he pushed the skill downward. The hand burned like a pyre, and space itself broke apart in the face of the immense sharpness contained in the axe head. Iz looked up with a thoughtful glance, and moved for the first time since the battle started.

A stream of flames rose from the depths of the raging sun, slightly weakening its radiance to form a massive barrier above Iz's head. A moment later, edge and shield collided. The whole island shook, and billowing waves of cutting flames pushed away the clouds. Zac furiously tried to push through, but the barrier seemed completely inexhaustible.

Not only that, the defensive shield further scalded the wooden hand, rapidly weakening its structural integrity.

"Close," Iz commented just as **[Arcadia's Judgement]** was about to collapse.

At this point, Zac floated in the air, assisted by Vivi's vines.

"Was it?" Zac smiled as the ground started to heave even harder.

"Wh—" Iz frowned before looking down with surprise.

She didn't get the chance to prepare her next move before the second half of **[Arcadia's Judgement]** came crashing from below. This was the beauty of his ultimate skill. The wooden hand and its humongous axe were so dangerous, it forced most opponents to activate their strongest defenses or counter with an all-out strike.

However, that left them vulnerable to the judgement of the earth, and the skill would pincer the enemy like the closing jaw of a Primordial Beast. Zac suspected Iz's sun would be able to withstand this much, but he had some outside assistance this time around.

"What—"Iz started again, the rest drowned out by a tremendous explosion that threw Zac hundreds of meters away.

Zac barely had time to land and steady himself before a wall of superheated mist slammed into him. If he hadn't been prepared for this, he would possibly have been thrown clean off the island. Thankfully, he'd already secured his spot with Vivi. His robes were frayed, and he was drenched in water like a drowning cat, yet a wide smile spread across Zac's face.

There was no coincidence he chose this particular island, this particular spot, out of all the possible locations they could fight. Visibility was almost zero, but he could vaguely see a geyser of shimmering water break apart a few hundred meters into the air, showering the parched island in torrential rain.

This wasn't some new addition to his skill, but it was only made possible thanks to the powerful eruption of **[Arcadia's Judgement]**. The earthquake had created an outlet for a spiritual spring containing huge amounts of Spiritual Water. This water wasn't like the Cosmic Water back on his island, but F-grade water imbued with the Dao of Water.

Life and Death weren't the only elements on the planet, even if they became increasingly dominant. There was still the huge Fire Crystal Mine in the Underworld, along with several other attuned resources. This island and its subterranean spring was one such example, though it hadn't been excavated.

There simply wasn't that much use for the Water-attuned spring on Earth, at least not water that could only be considered F-grade. It wasn't even useful to nurture Spiritual Plants. It was more efficient to infuse clouds with Cosmic Energy and feed the plants with gathering arrays instead. So the island had been sealed off and its resource listed in a ledger until Port Atwood found some use for it.

And today, the water had finally shown its worth. Its Dao was obviously far inferior to Iz's sun, but the volumes were tremendous. Between the force of it bursting out from the depths and the slight attunement, it defeated quality with quantity.

Zac couldn't even see the hand in front of his face because of the mist, but he still shot forward at full speed. He didn't need his normal vision to figure out where Iz was. She was like an almost blinding beacon to his [Cosmic Gaze]. Two steps with [Earthstrider] placed him right behind her, and Zac's axe was already descending for her shoulder.

A hint of worry filled his heart when he saw Iz fearfully look back with shock, and his hand slowed down a bit from hesitation. Was he going overboard? What if he actually hurt—

No.

A teasing smile appeared on Iz's face, and Zac yelped as a conflagration swallowed him. It wasn't an attack. Iz herself just up and exploded. A flash of heat left him toasty, but the force of the eruption wasn't enough to actually wound him. Zac still scrambled out of the way as he warily looked around. If his target was a fake, then where was the real Iz?

"You're pretty shameless." A laugh echoed behind him, and Zac swirled around only to cut apart a plume of scalded water.

"Nothing shameless about taking advantage of your surroundings," Zac said, trying to find the source of the voice. "You could consider it as a lesson in practical combat."

Iz giggled, her voice coming from every direction. "You sound like my uncle. Well, it's more fun this way. I guess I can be a bit shameless as well."

"Uh…" Zac said with a sinking feeling as the island started to rumble.

# 59

# WINGS

Zac was rendered a bit helpless as he tried to figure out where Iz was hiding and what she was up to. The huge geyser was supposed to help him suppress Iz, but it instead filled the battlefield with scalding mist that helped obscure her location. Meanwhile, Zac could feel something was changing in the surroundings as the temperature was rapidly rising.

Iz was unleashing a domain skill, but the lack of clear accumulations of Cosmic Energy left him uncertain. What Zac did know was that he couldn't just stand around or swing his axe blindly in the air. He activated [Ancestral Woods] to get a better understanding of the situation.

Thousands of ancient trees sprung from the ground, and the haze lifted a bit as they swallowed the mist around them. Zac's vision expanded to a radius of over three hundred meters in every direction, and Zac immediately found the source of the changes. Hundreds of small flowers were growing out of the ground.

Zac couldn't tell if the red and purple flowers were real or made from flames, but they emitted searing heat and an apocalyptic aura. It was almost as if a little bit of the Dao of Oblivion was mixed in the flowers, giving them a more powerful destructive tendency than normal flames. Of course, Zac could tell the source of the ruinous aura didn't actually come from Oblivion.

This aura had a different flavor, where the flowers almost felt like they had a desire to bring about the apocalypse and the end of days. Thankfully, they didn't seem to cause much trouble yet, except they managed to suppress the geyser that was fast-losing steam. But it didn't matter, as Zac had found his mark.

Just at the edge of his forest, a two-meter cocoon had appeared. It didn't emit any energy fluctuations at all, appearing like a crystallized flame from the depths of hell. It had the same colors as the flowers, and Zac could vaguely see a humanoid shape inside. Zac wasted no time as he jumped into the closest tree, appearing just a few meters away from the cocoon.

This wasn't some tv-show. Zac wouldn't wait around for Iz to transform into some Giga-Iz. If he could stop her mid-transition and eke out a quick victory, that would be for the best. Unfortunately, just as Zac made to destroy the cocoon, it erupted in a hailstorm of sharp shards that pushed Zac back. He rapidly found his footing and pushed through the shrapnel to attack, but he stopped upon seeing his opponent.

"A pixie?" Zac exclaimed, trying to make sense of her trans-formation.

Zac had seen Iz use a set of six wings a few times now, wings of pure golden-orange flames that felt almost holy. Iz emitted an inherent pressure when she wore those wings, like an empress looking down at her subjects. This was something else entirely. Instead of six wings, Iz only had one set, and they looked nothing like the empyrean pure-flame wings.

Two small butterfly wings had formed on her back. They were partly translucent, reminiscent of soap bubbles that shifted in deep red and purple colors. Iz's skin had a similar effect, though it wasn't as apparent as her wings. Most notably, Iz held a weapon for the first time. At least, Zac guessed it was one.

She bore a large flower of a different species than the smaller things that grew across the forest. It reminded him of a purple and black sunflower, with the stalk cut to be around two-thirds of a meter. The flower was almost the size of a plate, and its weight made the stem slump slightly. The scene would have both been a bit comical and incredibly cute if not for the terrifying aura of infernal destruction the flower emitted.

The air twisted around the flower. She may as well have been holding something plucked from the depths of hell.

"What are yo—" Zac hesitated, but he got no further before Iz attacked.

She didn't conjure any fireballs or other skills Zac would have expected. Instead, Iz flashed forward with incredible speed, swinging the flower like a club. The experience of a thousand battles kicked in. If Iz wanted to infight with him, that was fine. Great, even.

Because that was his domain.

Zac pounced like a Primordial Beast, unwilling to surrender even an inch of territory. This was the principle of the primal wilds, where it was only eat or be eaten. |Verun's Bite| howled with mad glee as Zac slashed up at the incoming flower, while Vivi's vines had already begun their suffocating dance.

Only, the scene of Zac cutting off the flower halfway up the stem didn't occur. An overbearing pressure formed on his right arm as edge and branch collided, and he was almost pushed into the ground. Iz was surprisingly strong, and the flower incredibly sturdy. Verun's edge didn't even manage to leave a mark on the stem, but that wasn't the only problem.

The collision released pollen from the flower, which turned into a terrifying hellfire threatening to submerge him. Zac was in no mood to get scorched, but that didn't mean he would back away. He leveraged the fact that his raw Strength slightly surpassed Iz's to tilt her arm to the side while he pushed forward for a frontal collision.

Iz nimbly dodged Zac's rush with a flutter of her wings, and another wave of her flower unleashed a second cascade of flames. That sunflower doubled as a melee weapon and a wand, with each attack releasing a fiery outburst with power comparable to the fireballs that almost cooked him alive in the Void Star. Taking too many of those waves would be more than his body could handle, and he didn't want to go out like that.

But now that Zac knew how the flower worked, he wasn't overly bothered. It was just another variable to work around. A sharp cut split the wave apart, leaving Zac only slightly burnt as he rushed into melee range once more. Zac furiously tried to break past her defense, while Iz created cascading curtains of flames with her expertly aligned parries.

Simultaneously, Vivi's vines slithered around, trying to tie Iz down and prevent her from utilizing her wings. And it soon became apparent

490 | JF BRINK & THEFIRSTDEFIER

the odd sheen on Iz's body wasn't just there for looks. It was a thin film of incredibly destructive flames, preventing Vivi from holding onto her for more than a fraction of a second before a section of her vines burned off.

Zac swapped to standard suppressive use, where the vines aimed at Iz's vitals like eyes and heart. Zac was like a hurricane of violence, using not only his axe but his free fist and legs to drown Iz in strikes. It was clear this wasn't Iz's first rodeo. Fighting her felt like fighting a dancing flame, where he continuously failed to land any real strikes and instead came away scorched.

But it wasn't all bad. While Iz was a surprisingly competent fighter, she wasn't at the Integration Stage as far as Zac could tell. She was just using a top-quality set of techniques that probably belonged to her family. Neither were Iz's attributes geared toward infighting like his were, so Zac had completely seized the momentum after Iz's initial ambush. As long as things kept going this way, Zac would be able to force an opening before his burns became too much to handle.

However, the situation in his forest was deteriorating. The first flowers had fully matured, and a silent flame burned from their petals. Dozens of trees had been burned down already, and it was just a matter of time before his domain collapsed. If that were the only problem, it would have been manageable. He didn't really need [Ancestral Woods] right now.

The real issue was the small butterflies that each flower seemed to birth when they bloomed. They looked a bit drunk just after being born, and Zac glimpsed one accidentally knocking against one of the trees. The tree instantly disappeared in a puff of flames, leaving not even a wisp of his energy behind. If Zac had any hair left, it would have stood on end at the prospect of hundreds of those little firebombs flying over to blast him.

Zac would have to step up the pressure and end things faster if he wanted to avoid being overrun. Seeing that Iz had time to grow hundreds of little kamikaze pilots while fighting proved she wasn't at her limits, even if Zac held a small advantage. It meant he could stop holding back.

Until now, a part of him had been afraid to wound her, leaving his strikes hollow. Such a mindset was anathema to the brutal technique of the Evolutionary Stance, which fully focused on killing one's targets.

Zac finally accepted reality. Thinking he could grievously wound Iz Tayn without any of his hidden trump cards was simply overestimating himself.

A fiery storm soon raged through the forest as Zac and Iz turned into a blur. Zac was pushing harder and harder, his axe and vines working in perfect harmony to suffocate Iz and restrict her movements. She found herself increasingly unable to fight fire with fire, and was forced to continuously use her wings to avoid leaving any openings.

Unfortunately for her, Zac completely controlled the trajectories she could back away in, which allowed him to simultaneously dodge the deadly butterflies. He was relentless, refusing to give Iz even the smallest of breathers. Neither did he unleash any skills or massive strikes that would slow his tempo. He was content in whittling at his opponent's momentum, like a pack of hyenas dragging down a wounded lion.

Zac was amazed at Iz's combat awareness, even if she found herself on the losing end. To this point, he hadn't managed to land a real hit. A few kicks and lashes from Vivi had connected, but they'd been neutralized by Iz deflecting most of the force with her free hand. Most enemies he'd fought would have made a mistake and left some opening by now, but Iz remained steady as a mountain even as she spiraled closer to a loss.

Suddenly, Zac felt a pang of danger, forcing him to dive to the ground. He barely had time to close his eyes before the whole forest exploded. Zac only got a short vision of hundreds of butterflies exploding simultaneously, creating a wave of flames that scorched his back while tearing [Ancestral Woods] apart.

Zac swore in annoyance, scrambling to his feet. He'd been so close to victory. In less than ten strikes, he would have been able to break through Iz's meticulous defense and leverage his edge against her neck. Zac guessed she figured that out, forcing her to take drastic measures. Still, that would only delay the inevitable, and Iz was now without her restraining butterflies.

But as Zac burst through the curtain of flames to resume his siege, he found his opponent had transformed once more. A second set of wings joined the first. The second set weren't like the pixie wings she still wore, they were golden wings like the ones on the three-legged crow from before.

It should have looked odd with two sets of such different wings, but it was somehow natural. Iz herself had undergone a small change once more. Her opalescent skin was the same, but it'd gained a greater golden hue, while some of her hair had been replaced by golden feathers. Simultaneously, she brandished a new item in her previously free hand—a small sun that drenched the area in golden luster.

What were these transformations? Zac didn't get it. He'd barely sensed Iz rotating any Cosmic Energy, yet the effect was almost as pronounced as his ultimate skills. Was this her actual appearance, while she usually kept herself sealed? Or was this some form of cultivation that didn't exist on the frontier? Zac had no idea, and Iz wouldn't give him any time to figure things out.

She was already upon him, and he wasn't overly surprised to find her speed and strength having gained a boost after adding another set of wings. Simultaneously, Zac saw nine golden suns gradually phase into reality above his head and immediately felt a vague sense of danger from them. It was almost like a dangerous beast was glaring at him from above.

At the same time, new infernal flowers were already replacing those that had been incinerated, and he didn't have [Ancestral Woods] to keep track of the situation any longer. And to make a bad situation worse, Zac soon found the small sun in Iz's hand wasn't just an ornamental object.

The orb kept spewing out arcs of flames so hot they looked like plasma. Zac wasn't even sure if Iz was controlling it, but it both helped her block his strikes while sending out attacks on its own. Zac was suddenly fighting two people rather than one, and the pressure tested the limits of his Evolutionary Stance.

Still, Zac refused to give in, and managed to at least give as good as he got. He didn't have an advantage anymore, but neither did Iz suppress him. With his monstrous endurance and energy reserves, he would have a chance to turn things around again.

A pang of danger forced Zac to back away just as he was about to launch another attack. His danger sense narrowly allowed him to avoid a golden crow that dove at him from one of the suns above. It just missed Zac's face, but it still left a trail of primal flames in its wake that obscured his vision. Zac growled in annoyance as he cut apart the trail, only to be forced to dodge a solar flare from Iz's hand.

Two sets of flames raged around them as Zac desperately fought, pushing his Evolutionary Stance to the limit. [Verun's Bite] was a blur as it fought off the flower with its infernal flames and the constant barrage of solar flares. It was lucky Verun had swallowed a small lake's worth of Dragon's Blood. Without it, the Spirit Tool would probably have been damaged by this point.

Vivi was much worse off, her vines in a constant cycle of destruction and regrowth as they tried to help as best they could. Zac sensed exhaustion through his link. These terrifying flames were too draining, and she wouldn't be able to keep fighting much longer. If he forced it, Zac would be damaging her already waning vitality, and he definitely wouldn't do something like that for a duel.

The pressure kept mounting. One three-legged crow turned to two as another one emerged from a sun in the sky. Zac was forced to fight the critters off with his free arm, relying on his durable body and recovery to constantly heal his burnt skin. Even then, the situation wasn't sustainable.

He was already drowning under Iz's assault. And since two of the suns had birthed powerful helpers, Zac guessed it was just a matter of time before there were nine of them harassing him. Zac fought with all the ferocity and tenacity of a Primordial Beast, but some things couldn't be defeated with guts and grit alone. Iz Tayn was a natural calamity that had descended upon his domain. Fighting her was like fighting nature's wrath.

Zac would either have to activate [Arcadian Crusade] to bring things back under control, or go for a Hail Mary before more crows and butterflies emerged. Since Vivi was tired and this ultimately was just a sparring session, Zac went with the latter. Using Berserking skills or treasures felt like breaking some unspoken rule, so he'd rather give it one last hurrah before throwing in the towel.

The next moment, Zac's combat style slightly changed. It became more frantic, almost to the point it could be seen as suicidal. Zac completely ignored a solar flare hitting his chest as he violently slammed the infernal flower to the side. From there, Zac once more made to slam into Iz in a full-frontal collision. Like before, she expertly created enough distance with the help of her wings, but this time Zac didn't follow in her wake.

Taking a solar flare straight on his chest hurt like hell, but he ignored the pain as he pushed Cosmic Energy into the Skill Fractal for **[Empyrean Aegis]**. He'd kept his ultimate defense in his back pocket until now, and it was finally time to use it. Iz's eyes widened in surprise upon sensing Zac's energy churn, but she smiled a bit as she followed suit.

But how could Zac let her do as she pleased?

He had a head start already, and with a small infusion of Void Energy, he cut the casting time down by another 30%, allowing him to summon the golden pillars before Iz activated her own skill. Zac hadn't initially planned on using Void Energy in this fight, but he also didn't want to lose without giving a proper performance.

A golden radiance swallowed the fiery domain, and Iz shuddered as the suppression of Zac's defensive skill interrupted her skill activation. Zac was already charging his second skill, and he launched it the moment it was ready. The Abyss and Arcadia sang as the world was split in two, and the delineation between Life and Death headed straight for Iz.

Vivi managed to catch Iz's ankles, thanks to **[Empyrean Aegis]** temporarily weakening her burning film. She wouldn't be trapped for long, but Zac didn't need more than an instant. He was ready to forcibly deactivate his skill if Iz threw in the towel, but he knew there would be trouble as she shoved her miniature sun forward with a wide smile on her face.

Zac urgently activated a barrier to block the fallout. As the world turned white and eerily calm, Zac heard the sound of three pillars instantly crumbling before he lost consciousness.

# 60

# THE BUSINESS OF WAR

"Not bad," Calrin said with a small nod as he worked hard not to seem impressed.

It wasn't easy.

The scene outside was far from anything Calrin had ever witnessed, even if he was toiling under a fate-touched oddity like the little Lord Atwood. That troublemaker might have visited amazing places, but Calrin had been stuck in the offices of the Thayer Consortia most of his life. He hadn't even gotten to travel much since his clan had already lost most of its businesses by the time he started rising through the ranks.

The War Fortress was as large as an E-grade planet, and thousands of vessels flew in and out through its gates like bees running errands for the hive. While impressive, seeing so many Cosmic Vessels in one place filled Calrin with worry. The production capacity of Lord Atwood was only a few vessels a week.

Even if the shipyard worked night and day until the war started, they still wouldn't be able to construct this many ships. And this was just one of many War Fortresses, along with the actual planets that had been turned into military bases. Would he be laughed out of the offices when he presented his demands?

Worse, would he be made captive to lure out his boss?

Calrin's intestines turned with regret as the War Fortress drew closer. He'd taken the bait hook, line, and sinker. So what if the lord had offered him a 10% commission on the difference between the calculated asking price and the actual price? In that moment, Calrin forgot one needed to be alive to enjoy his riches. He could only see the tens of thousands of D-grade Nexus Coins that would potentially enter his pockets.

Besides, through the conversations with the crew, Calrin knew he might be in for some rough negotiations even if they didn't scheme against him. Time was running out, and there were a million things that needed to be purchased. The Allbright Empire was already stretching itself thin and had been forced to increase taxation twice over the past three years.

At the same time, Calrin's wares were simply problematic when put in context to the Zecia Sector. Sure, the vessels in his Mercantile Space were better than the buckets he saw flying outside, but the price was also in a league of its own.

Here in the Red Sector, you could get an Early D-grade Cosmic Vessel for around 1,500 to 2,500 D-grade Nexus Coins. If you dared use one of the Salvaged Scrap Vessels from the Million Gates Territory, you could go as low as 500 D-grade Nexus Coins. And those were procurement prices, not production prices, in a time when many forces were building their own.

Meanwhile, the models of Lord Atwood ranged between 18,000 and 32,000 D-grade Nexus Coins per vessel. It was more than ten times the average purchase price in the region. Add in sales taxes, System-enforced import tariffs, and a profit margin, and you were looking at twenty times the price. For every vessel the War Coalition purchased from the Thayer Consortia, they would be giving up on a small fleet.

Lord Atwood's goal was to make at least five C-grade Nexus Coins before the war started, which meant each vessel would have to have an average profit of almost 6,000 D-grade Nexus Coins. Certainly, such a margin was, in fact, quite modest considering the production prices, just 25% compared to the average of 50%.

Their only chance was that the unique features and technology would be deemed powerful enough to price the vessels as the equivalent of Medium-quality Middle D-grade Cosmic Vessels. Even if the speed and durability of the ships were better than any Early D-grade vessels in Zecia, there was ultimately a small gap from them being true Middle D-grade vessels when it came to fundamental specifications.

Still, Calrin was ready to fight for his nest egg as the Cosmic Vessel drew into one of the many hangars. Outside, a group of ten people waited, and Calrin got a sinking feeling when he saw the man in the lead. This man had the aura of a practiced miser, and an air of authority around him indicated he would have a say in the negotiations.

Like that, the nest egg sprouted wings and threatened to fly away. No! Calrin wouldn't give up after having come so far.

"Esteemed friends, heroes of the Vanguard, it is my very utmost honor to make your acquaintance," Calrin said with a wide smile as he walked over. "This one is called Calrin, and I represent the Thayer Conso—"

"Tsymo Sendroska." The haughty man cut Calrin off without so much as looking up from the docket in his hand. "I am a senior quartermaster of the Sixth Procurement Division, and I will be in charge of measurement and quality control of your wares. Along with the potential brokerage of a trade agreement, should the wares be deemed genuine and of use to the Alliance."

"Master Sendroska, a pleasure," Calrin said with a bow. "Pardon my ignorance. I was under the impression I would be met with a representative of the esteemed Peak family?"

"The Peak Clan is one of the foremost fighting forces of the Allbright Empire," Tsymo scoffed. "They do not have time to deal with small trade agreements, so they handed the matter to the Sixth. Now, where are the wares? Looking at the specifications, it will take roughly a week to test the products, so we should start as soon as possible."

Calrin's smile became increasingly strained, but he couldn't give in now. This man was trying to bulldoze them. If he just bent over here, they would definitely get a bad quote, if one at all.

"The War Coalition should have been sent the specification sheet already," Calrin said with as pleasant a voice as he could. "And as I mentioned, we come recommended by the Peaks themselves. Our specifications may seem like grand exaggerations, but this one can guarantee—"

"The fact you come recommended is the only reason we are wasting our time on this at all," Tsymo said, finally looking up from his clipboard, only to give Calrin a withering look. "And we should just take the word of a small workshop that proclaims their wares are better than any other shipwrights in the Sector? There has been no lack of wartime profiteers who have tried to defraud the Alliance, heedless of the fact that every coin misspent will mean lives lost."

"I assure you, there are no problems with our wares," Calrin said. "Master Sendroska, you should be aware of who I am representing. The young lord is a million-year genius, which comes with certain unique advantages."

"Climbing towers does not make one a shipwright," Tsymo snorted. "Now, take out the vessels for inspection, or is their portability a lie as well?"

Calrin blankly looked at the presumptuous quartermaster. Sometimes he wondered if he'd strayed down the wrong path. Sometimes, he dreamt he could be like the young lord, swinging his axe to make all trouble disappear. Was the pursuit of wealth that important? It would feel infinitely more satisfying to throw out a handful of talismans instead. He was even willing to sacrifice a few D-grade Nexus Coins with **[Curse of Mammon]** if it empowered the talismans enough to blow this bastard to kingdom come.

A gnome could dream.

"These vessels contain some proprietary arrays, and I have not been permitted to freely expose these things without a contract in place," Calrin said, though he still conjured two huge cubes that thumped behind him. "Out of respect for the Peak family, I will hand over the IL-28 Starburst and the IL-32 Farsight for the Sixth to inspect. With my lord being a personal friend of Miss Pretty Peak, I trust I can count on your discretion."

"We will take it from here," Tsymo said as he took the two control spheres. "Lead our guests to their quarters."

"You do not want us to oversee what you're doing to our vessels?" Calrin frowned, no longer able to pretend to be pleased with the situation. "It sounds like you are confining us."

"This is a strategic base for the upcoming war. We cannot have civilians running amok," Tsymo said as he nodded at the guards behind him.

Calrin sensed his two guards tense up, and could only sigh with resignation. "Then we'll be in your care."

From there, they were whisked away to a decent group of rooms far from any important people and resources.

"What should we do?" Tina, one of the two human lasses Lord

Atwood had sent to accompany him, asked after they were alone. "It almost seems like this guy has it out for us, and now we're essentially on house arrest?"

"Most organizations have these little barons who let their authority go to their heads. It's but a small bump in the negotiations," Calrin assured. "Luckily, our wares speak for themselves. Some little quartermaster isn't enough to shroud the Heavens."

"Still, it's odd," Tina muttered.

"That it is," Calrin said. "No force is without its internal strife, and a shared base like this is even worse. I fear this Tsymo might belong to one of the lord's enemies. After all, he killed quite a few scions in the Tower of Eternity."

"Then what should we do?" Jennifer, his other guard, interjected.

"Worse comes to worst, we will have to create a scene that will force some higher-ups to come," Calrin said. "That way, we can plead our case to a new party. And the lord has prepared a few things for us in case the situation goes south."

"But what if they steal the technology of our vessels?" Tina asked.

"I asked the young lord about that scenario," Calrin said. "According to him, they won't get close to unlocking the secrets of these ships even if they had ten thousand years. I say let them have at it. When they realize it's futile, we'll be put in a better position for the negotiations. Don't worry. Ol' Calrin has the situation under control."

As the days passed, Calrin became less and less confident. They were essentially treated like prisoners on lockdown, except their items weren't taken. Being away from the consortia, Calrin didn't have access to the Mercantile System either, making it impossible to contact anyone for help.

Had their preparations been insufficient? Would he really have to pull that card?

After one long week, they were finally called to a conference hall. By that point, Calrin's nerves were frayed, and he didn't have the energy to pretend to be satisfied upon seeing that they still had to deal with the insufferable Tsymo Sendroska. At least there was one more person in the room. A stern middle-aged woman with a stack of diagrams and schematics in front of her.

A technician, perhaps? Or an Array Master?

"Sit," Tsymo said as the three were led into the room.

"Being witness to the hospitality of the War Coalition has been a unique experience," Calrin commented. "I pray my lord and his benefactors will not see it as a slight against their prestige."

"An army has its rules and regulations. No one is above it," Tsymo said without a care. "Now, we've tested the vessels. While they barely meet the specifications you listed, there are multiple problems. For one, it is impossible to properly gauge many of the technologies you spout. And even if they work, the cost-to-benefit ratio will be abysmal. As such—"

"Excuse me, what do you mean by benefactors?" the woman interjected, drawing a displeased look from Tsymo. "The Peaks? No, that can't be right. They don't have the skills to manufacture these types of vessels. They are much too advanced."

Calrin glanced at Tsymo, and he knew he didn't have an option. Someone bought this bastard off, and this technician was his best chance at getting fair treatment. The other option was to blow up the whole chamber to attract the leaders. Although negotiating from the position of a terrorist was an uphill battle Calrin didn't feel confident in emerging victorious from.

"While my young lord is on friendly terms with multiple people from the Peaks, they are only the sponsors for this meeting. The lord's benefactor is someone else, though you might not have heard of him," Calrin said, adding a pause for effect. "He has gone by many names, but my lord knows him as Alvod Jondir."

"Jondir?" the technician slowly said, her eyes widening in shock.

"The Eveningtide Asura?" Tsymo scoffed. "Are you trying to threaten us with the name of a dead man? As I suspected, you are up to no good. As such, I see no option but—"

"I hope I am not interrupting," a calm voice interrupted.

Calrin was both shocked and delighted to see a scholarly-looking man appear out of nowhere. He had no aura yet somehow exuded an innate pressure that almost made Calrin bow in deference.

A Monarch.

"Your Royal Highness!" the technician and Tsymo exclaimed. Calrin was delighted to see Tsymo's face go deathly pale as he shot to his feet.

"My young friend, I am sorry to have left you waiting so long. I wanted to personally welcome you after my friends told me you were coming, but I was forced to deal with some matters inside the Million Gates Territory," the man said with a warm smile before turning to the quartermaster. "Tsymo, is it? Why are you just standing there? Why have you not offered our guest some refreshments?"

"Of course," Tsymo hurriedly said, his haughty demeanor long gone.

"After you're done, you can present yourself to the Wartime Tribunal. Your employers might be an important sponsor for our endeavor, but they are not above the law."

Calrin's face remained impassive as Tsymo served him tea with a constipated look, but his heart wasn't as calm. This was an even bigger fish than he expected. Calrin didn't know if this Allbright princeling was telling the truth or if he had been forced to act because of the threat of the Eveningtide Asura. And Calrin didn't give a hoot. He only cared about what the shift in reception meant for him and the Thayer Consortia. There were profits to be made here.

The only question was how far he could push things based on a lie.

———

"Ow, shi—" Zac swore as he woke up with a start, surprised to find that he didn't actually hurt at all.

He lay prone on the ground, looking around with confusion, trying to remember what just happened. He remembered Iz pushing her Golden Sun toward the incoming slash of his [Rapturous Divide], followed by an incredibly bright light. It felt like it had consumed everything and completely engulfed him, yet both he and his surroundings were fine.

At least, as fine as one could expect after such an intense battle. The whole area was scorched and marred beyond redemption, and echoes of his and Iz's Daos were engraved into the ground. Cracks reached deep into the ground, an effect of [Arcadia's Judgement] and the geyser eruption. If this little island had been a barren rock before, then it was now a truly desolate wasteland.

"How are you feeling?" Iz asked, and Zac turned over to see her sitting a few meters away from him.

"Your face!" Zac exclaimed with shock as he saw a small cut that barely missed Iz's eye.

"Don't worry," Iz said as the wound started burning. A moment later, it was gone, not even leaving a scar behind. "I just wanted to let you see how far you had come."

Zac wryly smiled as he got to his feet. A small nick wasn't much of anything, but it still felt like an accomplishment. So his [Rapturous Divide] hadn't been completely overwhelmed at the end.

"What's going on?" Zac grunted, trying to figure out what kind of attack had knocked him out. "What happened at the end there? Did you cheat and throw out some treasure?"

"That depends on how you define cheating," Iz said after some thought. "I didn't use any treasures or outside help. I fused two Aspects to allow my Golden Sun to unleash a wave of the Abyssal Star. Its effect is disruption. It breaks apart most skills, and it even disrupted your consciousness for a moment."

"Isn't that too powerful?" Zac muttered.

"Not really," Iz said. "You wouldn't have lost your consciousness had you blocked your sight in time. And if you had avoided letting the light of the Abyssal Star enter your eyes, you would have been able to hold onto your skill better. It would have broken down regardless, but that's because my heritage has an inherent advantage over certain concepts that particular skill is based on."

"I guess it was a valuable lesson." Zac smiled. "There are only so many kinds of heritages that exist here on the frontier. Getting exposed to new things will help me shore up my weaknesses. But what did you mean when you said you fused Aspects? Is it Dao, or those forms? Something I can do?"

Zac wouldn't mind getting a transformation like that based on his Daos. Just the thought of getting Aspects to match his two stances sounded incredibly powerful.

"It has some natal prerequisites," Iz said with a shake of her head, instantly dashing Zac's hopes. "Bloodline, Inheritance, Dao, Energy Control. You could consider it akin to Dao Intent and Atavism, but slightly more complicated. Truthfully, I don't think it's a path suited for you."

"That's fine. I have my hands full anyway. Still, those forms of yours were amazing. Though I have seen more than enough of that terrifying flower."

"It didn't manage to keep you contained." Iz smiled. "And its flames only left some small blemishes."

"So why am I fine?" Zac muttered as he looked at his body. "Is my new constitution that amazing?"

"Of course not," Iz giggled. "You looked a bit pitiful when you were knocked out, so I poured some elixir on you."

"Never mind," Zac coughed as he dragged his hand over his once again bald head.

Still some ways to go.

# A LONELY PATH

Zac overestimated his new Void Vajra Constitution for a moment there, but it wasn't all bad. Zac believed his constitution wasn't just for show during the fight, even if it hadn't given him unique healing capabilities just yet. He'd been constantly inside or adjacent to incredibly powerful flames, but his skin resisted the onslaught better than expected.

The vibrant life in his body had sped up the healing process by letting his damaged cells die, and new ones be reborn. That didn't just allow his body to endure more punishment but even helped expel Iz's Dao faster. The constitution wasn't powerful enough to provide a significant advantage in a battle with someone like Iz, but that would eventually change.

By the time he reached Minor Sublimation at the third layer of his technique, he would no doubt be immune to Daos and attacks beneath a certain threshold, where his body automatically healed faster than the environment or enemy could damage him. And this effect would have great synergy with his Eoz durability, where the sum would be greater than its parts.

"So, are you satisfied now?" Zac asked.

"Yes, I feel much better." Iz nodded seriously as she handed him the **[Stone of Celestial Void]**. "Like an annoying sound in the back of my head has been quieted after a decade."

"That's nice, I guess," Zac said with a roll of his eyes before he looked at Iz suspiciously. "By the way, why the hell are you so strong? I thought you were a mage."

"My transformations convert and add Strength and Dexterity, based on my Intelligence and Wisdom," Iz explained. "Besides, I never said I was a pure mage. It's simply more convenient to use my [World's End] and Dao to deal with annoying matters. Also, using these forms have some implications, so my elders don't want me to use them on the outside."

"Well, your secret's safe with me." Zac took out a piece of Beast King meat.

[Adamance of Eoz] had been working overtime throughout the fight, reducing the damage he took while buffeted by Iz's unrelenting flames. Now, it felt like a black hole had opened in his stomach, and he was only satiated after gobbling down over five kilos of D-grade meat in a physics-defying feast.

"By the way, you still have another transformation you could add on, right?" Zac said. "For six wings total."

Iz nodded slightly, and Zac sighed. "So, I couldn't force you to go all out."

"I think you weren't going all out either. I didn't add my third Aspect, while you didn't use your third Dao Branch. And I know your bloodline is incredibly powerful. I can't sense it anymore, but I could feel it back in the Tower of Eternity," Iz said. "Who knows how far you would have pushed me if you had used all your cards? The distance between us is much shorter today than ten years ago."

"How is that possible, though? I am by no means an expert, but I can tell you have incredibly high affinities. Not only that, but you're rich enough to give others Heart Demons. How am I catching up to you? Don't you enjoy cultivation?"

Iz ruminated over the question for quite a while before she finally answered. "Do I enjoy it? I don't know? I think I do, and I want to live up to my family's expectations. They sacrificed a lot to give me an opportunity. I've worked hard on my cultivation, even if it might not seem like it from your perspective.

"Your ascension would be considered rapid anywhere, and I think you have experienced more than most in our age cohort. But an important reason you are progressing relatively quickly compared to me and others like me is urgency and timeframes.

"You have been desperately pushing yourself to protect yourself and others. You have been forced by environment and circumstance to target short-term gains, things that will directly improve your combat strength. It was only when you were stuck in the Voidcatcher and forced to slow down that you had the chance to focus on a long-term project such as your techniques, no?

"People from older factions generally do not have that urgency. We have no deadlines to meet, no looming threats that require us to rise to the occasion. Nothing has changed for my family over the past million years. The way we cultivate is a bit different because of that. I have less reason to focus on quick gains—I will still be considered a junior even after reaching Monarchy.

"Instead, we spend the earlier grades purifying our bodies and communing with the Heavens, steadily shoring up our foundations. You could say that we are both floating down a stream, but you have been swimming to speed up your progress even further," Iz said. "Meanwhile, people like me have been conserving our strength and gotten to know the river better. In the future, we will be better prepared when the river turns more dangerous and unpredictable."

"You're improving yourselves in various ways that will help you pass the future bottlenecks?" Zac asked.

"The road of cultivation is long, and you can only direct the river of fate when you reach the peak," Iz said. "And only when we become Autarchs or higher can we be of real assistance to our factions. So that's what we plan for, what we train for. Some things are better accomplished early, even if it delays our progress by a decade or two. Because it will create a ripple effect of positive changes for the rest of our journey."

"What about momentum?" Zac asked.

"In the grand scheme of things, a few years, decades, millennia even, doesn't matter. If you rush headlong toward the future, you might miss some clues along the way," Iz answered. "As long as we progress one way or another and don't dally too long at every grade, we will retain our momentum."

There was truth to her words, and he had multiple examples of just that in his own situation. His ascent to E-grade was extremely rushed. He would have been far more powerful if he had just spent a few more years shoring up his foundations. He could have gotten more titles, higher Daos, and figured out his path better before evolving.

Ultimately, Zac felt no need to worry about it overly much. Everyone had their road to walk. There were no guarantees a slower path like Iz's would have benefited him more in the long run. He might have missed out on other opportunities instead, such as Twilight Harbor and the Orom World. Progress was progress, and there were usually ways to shore up one's weaknesses down the road.

Life wasn't a video game. There was no such thing as min-maxing and getting 100% completion. You could only work your hardest and stay true to your heart.

"I'm not saying this to minimize you or your accomplishments. The path you've taken is incredible," Iz added after a short silence. "I'm saying this because you need to be careful about underestimating your competition in the upcoming trial."

"What about them?" Zac asked.

"There are still some years before the competition for the Eternal Heritage begins. The candidates of the respective factions have most likely already entered a different phase of their training. One more akin to your progress where they use their steady foundations to climb in strength quickly. That way, they will be able to exhibit far more power during their trial. It will be the same with me after I return."

"I know. I'll keep working hard," Zac said. "Anyway, we need to get out of here. Do you want me to take you to the Nexus Hub?"

"I'm not in a hurry. Kvalk will require another two days to reach our assigned meet-up spot," Iz said. "How about you show me around your grand empire?"

"Sure," Zac grinned. "But you'll have to hide your presence. Your looks will create some waves, and your presence here might leak to the outsiders. It'll be hard to extract resources from the various factions if people think I work for you."

"You're playing a dangerous game," Iz smiled. "But that's what I like about you."

They toured Earth and Ensolus over the next two days, visiting the various species and towns under his umbrella. Iz mostly asked about his process of conquest and how he had incorporated the various factions rather than the people themselves. It seemed to be a result of her family's upbringing. Other people weren't fated, so they didn't matter to her.

She was much more interested in how the Integration and the subsequent years on Earth had influenced him and his path. She hadn't participated in an Incursion herself, so she was curious about the struggles and how they helped him grow.

Instead of an Incursion, Iz had undergone various tests and trials that provided similar titles and boons. Not to mention, she was already a Countess from the System's perspective, which apparently was the highest rank you could attain in the E-grade while mostly relying on your background. You needed to be an actual Autarch to become a Duke and enjoy the various benefits such a rank provided.

Not only that, but you also needed to accomplish various feats. Unsurprisingly, conquering unintegrated territory seemed to be the most effective way to rise through the ranks, but there were other ways you could prove yourself to the System. Similarly, Iz had needed to complete a series of quests similar to his own Sovereignty-questline to get the rank and titles that her family's status awarded.

Ultimately, Iz didn't say much about life in the Heartlands, and Zac didn't feel comfortable prying. He felt like something would change if he did, and not for the better. One thing was clear, it was a very different environment to the chaotic and lawless struggle for power that allowed Zac to climb the ladder of success.

The two also discussed various aspects of cultivation, and it was almost like they were in a world of their own. Even when strolling the busy streets of Port Atwood, they were like ghosts. Zac didn't even need to use his cowl or bracer. Iz had some sort of treasure that had a much greater effect—it even made people unconsciously move around them.

Zac and Iz sparred a few more times, though they didn't use skills in the bouts. They fought using just techniques and Dao while restricting their attributes to be roughly the same. As expected, Zac held a small edge when it came to technique, but Iz was infinitely better at infusing her strikes and movements with her Dao.

That way, it balanced out. Her application was slightly worse since she couldn't perfectly fuse her Dao into her movements and attacks. Conversely, the empowerment from her Dao was greater since she always used incredibly powerful Dao Arrays.

The two days passed in a flash, and they eventually returned to his compound. Iz had asked to visit his favorite spot on the island, and he'd taken her to the pergola overlooking the sea after some hesitation. He rarely visited this spot anymore, but Triv always kept it nice and tidy.

"Your citizens seem happy," Iz commented after sitting down.

"Well, I try my best," Zac said with a smile, though it wasn't without some mixed emotions as he sat with another woman in this spot.

"Don't you find it a hindrance to your path?" Iz asked curiously. "To be fettered by billions of lesser fates?"

"I don't look at it that way. My empire and my followers make me work harder so I can better protect them. Besides, I'm not some benevolent ruler who spends every waking moment fretting over the betterment of Earth. I know I'll continue into the Multiverse one day unless I get myself killed first. At that point, they will have to pave their own path."

They overlooked the ocean for a while longer until Iz spoke up again. "It is about time I return."

"It's been nice having you," Zac said. "Apart from the beatdown, I guess."

"I don't know about that. I've seen the happiness in your eyes when we've fought, and it shone the brightest during our first bout. Your path is best expressed on the battlefield. It's where you're closest to the Dao." Iz smiled as she stood. "I have enjoyed myself as well. It's like your poem said: the road to power can be a lonely one, even if you are surrounded by people. Occasionally getting a break is not bad."

"I know what you mean," Zac sighed.

Zac could tell she was in a similar situation as himself back home, where status and potential created a wall around her. If anything, it was most likely more exaggerated in her case. From what little he could gather, Iz's family wasn't one with trillions of descendants like some of the ancient clans.

It was rather one of the small factions with incredibly powerful individuals. Like the Peak family, only far more exaggerated. Being the little princess of such a faction as an E-grade cultivator was most likely quite lonely. Those around her were either old monsters like her 'uncle,' or servants.

It wasn't quite that bad for Zac just yet. Even then, he could tell how his relationships had shifted as the gap in power and status increased.

Lacking fate, Iz would call it, where most of his followers weren't destined to walk down the same path as he. Some, like Nonet and Sap Trang, had already indicated they'd reached their limit, and they were just the first.

Iz and her family dealt with it by avoiding Karmic connections and keeping a distance. Zac still tried to hold onto his mortal side, but it was getting harder as he pursued the Dao. Would he one day sever his connection to individual citizens and look at the Atwood Empire as an abstract machine?

Zac wasn't ready to face that issue, so he turned his attention to Iz. "When are you coming back to Zecia?"

"Just before the trial, I expect," Iz said. "My elders will want me to train for as long as possible if they're to let me participate. I will only arrive in time to pick up the last piece before I head into the Left Imperial Palace."

Just as expected. Which made Zac reluctant about a gut feeling before he made his decision.

"There's one more thing," Zac said as they walked toward the teleportation array. "I have some information that I think is important for you."

"Oh?" Iz said curiously.

Zac waved his hand, and the Quest Screen for Ultom appeared.

"Nine Sealbearers," Iz muttered. "I do not know that many people. This is troubling."

"I figured you should know, considering you've been dealing with this alone," Zac said. "Of course, I'm not sure if everyone gets this quest or if the rules differ for different people. I was just afraid that you wouldn't have time to assemble a cycle if you returned at the last minute."

"This is too much," Iz said as she seriously looked at Zac. "Balance has been eschewed. What can I give in return?"

"It's fine," Zac said with a wave of his hand. "You've already helped me a lot since the Void Star."

"No, my elders will not allow it," Iz said. "This is a gift affecting fate."

"Well," Zac said after some thought. "The Undead Empire is getting me Death-attuned treasures to nurture my Draugr side. I'm looking for some Life-attuned items to balance myself out. Are you able to manufacture a certain array for me?"

"Array? For your soul?" Iz asked.

"Exactly," Zac said as he imprinted the fourth and fifth schematics onto an Information Crystal.

He'd gotten the second and third sets of array disks in Twilight Harbor, but they'd lacked the raw materials needed to create the fourth. Getting the fourth and fifth Death-attuned arrays from the Undead Empire shouldn't be a big problem, considering their desire to push him toward Death. That left the Life-attuned side, where Iz was his best bet for a quick solution.

"These things are incredibly simple to manufacture," Iz commented.

Zac wryly smiled. "Well, throw in some Life-attuned treasures for nurturing my Soul and Constitution until you feel fate has been balanced."

Iz's brows scrunched up in thought, then her eyes lit up. She took out an item, to which Zac blankly stared with confusion. It wasn't a vial, pill, or some other sort of treasure. It was a plushie resembling a large fireball with a wide grin.

"This…" Zac hesitated.

"This was a present from grandpa when I was young," Iz said. "Grandpa has an identical one back home. In a sense, they are one, even if they are apart. I don't have any of the items you need on me, but I can place them in the mouth of Ballie back home, and it should appear in Flammie's mouth instantaneously."

"Something like that's possible?" Zac exclaimed. "A quantum-entangled plushie?"

"That sounds like some Technocrat invention," Iz said with a shake of her head. "In reality, the toys contain a unique stone found inside a Spatial Anomaly. They're the reason this works. The transfer can only be used a few times more times, though, since Grandpa used to send me candies with it while he was cultivating. A long-distance transfer like this will likely expend the last of their energy, so don't put anything in Flammie's mouth, or you might break it."

"Thank you," Zac said with a smile.

Iz really came from a prodigal family. Those kinds of spatial stones were undoubtedly incredibly valuable, and they used them to sneak sweets.

"It's just what I should do."

"How will you deal with the quest?" Zac asked curiously.

"I'm not sure," Iz said. "I do not like the idea of having the fates of nine strangers hang onto mine, even if my uncle sends some subordinates into this Sector. Perhaps I can capture nine people after returning and let them go on their own business after the inheritance has opened."

"That might not work," Zac countered. "What if the whole cycle is needed to progress through the inheritance?"

"If I cannot attain the inheritance by following my beliefs, then I am simply not fated," Iz said.

"I guess that makes sense," Zac nodded before he thought of something. "Those guys who invade us, the Kan'Tanu, seem to be capturing candidates and selling them to you outsiders. You might be able to get access that way, while freeing some people captured by those lunatics."

"Perhaps…"

Zac could tell she didn't like the idea of trading with the Kan'Tanu.

"I'm going," Iz said a moment later, the teleportation array flashing to life.

Zac smiled. "Work hard on your cultivation. Wouldn't it be embarrassing if a barbarian on the frontier caught up with you?"

"I don't think it would be so bad," Iz said. "I'd say 'stay out of trouble,' but I know you wouldn't listen. I will see you in a few years."

With that, Iz was gone, headed toward a border town of the Zecia Sector where Kvalk was waiting. Apparently, it was quicker for Iz to make a few jumps until she reached a special wormhole a few sectors over, which would take her back home instantly.

The shimmering lights of the teleportation array soon dissipated, leaving Zac alone in his compound. It had been a fun diversion to have Iz visit. Like Iz said, even the beatdown provided him with multiple insights. But now, it was time to continue his cultivation.

It was time to see what other Hidden Nodes his undead side had.

# ONCE MORE INTO THE DEPTHS

Originally, Zac planned on using the **[Essence of the Abyss]** some time after using the Temporal Chamber. Now, he didn't have that luxury. He wasn't ready to seal himself off for three years, and the elixir would start losing its efficacy soon. Zac would have to activate his Draugr heritage immediately, which was why he'd asked Iz for Life-attuned treasures rather than something else.

Any item Iz sent over would undoubtedly be absurdly powerful, far surpassing what Calrin might get his hands on. And with his cultivation of **[Void Vajra Sublimation]** being faster than he'd expected, he felt it was safe enough to drink the **[Essence of the Abyss]** early without risking the balance between Life and Death.

When Zac returned to his cave, he transformed into his Draugr form. A smile spread across his face since he still felt the sense of vibrancy in his cells even if there were no golden flakes to be seen. In other words, the intangible benefits of his new constitution were still there. Not only that, but a quick calculation confirmed that he retained the bonus attributes, even if the line in the Status Screen was gone.

This was exactly what he'd hoped to see. Until now, Zac had been worried that his mother's clan planned on using his second half as a "feeder class" that would pour a bunch of benefits into his outwardly normal human form. Thankfully, it looked like the benefits were bidirectional, creating a huge advantage for both sides.

Hopefully, this meant he could fully stack the benefits of two consti-

514 | JF BRINK & THEFIRSTDEFIER

tutions just like he gained the benefits of his Branch of the Pale Seal in his human form without really using it. And judging by what Catheya told him about Eoz, his Bloodline Constitution would match his Dao.

The only regret was that he was becoming more and more lopsided. His survivability was shocking as it were, and it would only get more absurd when tacking on his constitutions. Meanwhile, Zac felt his speed falling behind, even if he poured all his free attribute points into Dexterity.

Until now, he'd been the bane of speedy cultivators like assassins. But as Iz said, he couldn't underestimate the elites of the Multiverse. His only way to deal with powerful rogues was to trap them and whittle them down with his domains. Except he wasn't confident he'd be able to hit them with his attacks.

And if the enemy was fast enough, his danger sense wouldn't be enough to save him from a powerful finisher. His body could only move so fast to avoid those kinds of strikes. Zac thought it over before he chose to send Catheya a message. He wanted to ask a few confirming questions about the Constitution of the Eoz bloodline and whether one could somehow make it provide Dexterity and speed rather than durability.

The response came within a few hours. Just as expected, the bloodline of Eoz focused on Endurance and Survivability, and it couldn't just be swapped over for something else. Bloodlines were fixed among the Draugr branches. The only difference between the descendants was how pure their bloodlines were and how many pieces of the bloodline they managed to awaken.

There were no such things as mixed bloodlines among them either. If two people of different branches married, the children would either have the father's bloodline or the mother's. The difference in bloodline purity and cultivation level could skew the result in either direction, but it was still a bit of a toss-up. Therefore, Draugr generally married within their branch to avoid familial complications.

Though there was good news. Draugr was ultimately a top-tier race, and the benefits would become more and more obvious the further you awakened your bloodline. Even a defensive bloodline like Eoz would provide comprehensive benefits, including strength and speed. Not only that, but Eoz had Hidden Nodes that weren't just defensive.

The exact details had been lost with time, or at least unavailable to the people in Zecia. The Monarchs were certain the Eoz possessed a means to become temporarily faster. Ultimately, he would have to use the [Essence of the Abyss] and figure out the details himself according to them.

They'd already sent a general Bloodline Method, [Abyssal Revolutions], that would help him better control his Draugr Nodes. They had also promised to petition the Abyssal Shores to see if any of the original Eoz manuals remained. Unfortunately, they had already indicated those things might not be possible to send to Zecia in the short run.

Zac guessed that was just another way for them to bind him to their chariot. Perhaps they'd take them out in a few years in return for him providing some sort of additional help. At least, Zac hoped that was the plan. It was hard to figure out all the ways these people could be scheming against him. Zac smiled wryly as he put the Communication Crystal with Catheya's recording away. He wondered what she would think if she knew the top-tier treasure she so proudly displayed for him was laced with a Life-erasing seal.

Not that it mattered. It was just like Iz said. He wasn't convinced that something like that curse would work in the face of his Technocrat Duplicity Seal. In a sense, Zac felt his body was a lot like Iz's toys. It was almost like his Duplicity Core had created two separate bodies superimposed on each other, and these bodies were then connected by [Quantum Gate]. If he swallowed the [Essence of the Abyss] in his Draugr form, there wouldn't be any Life to latch on to unless it somehow managed to pass through the mysterious tunnel in his chest.

That wasn't quite how it worked, but it also wasn't so simple as his Duplicity Core holding a bunch of Miasma and a spare set of pathways. It wasn't like his pathways emerged from the core itself when he swapped races. It was more like his human side sunk to the depths while his Draugr side rose to the surface. The bodies were one, yet separate.

Zac shook his head as he took out the small vial. The mysteries of his body were something he'd have to excavate gradually and investigate over the coming years. For now, Zac just wanted to see what his bloodline had in store for him, so he decisively drank the tar-like concoction in the vial.

Immediately, any errant thoughts were washed away. Zac's vision closed in, like a darkness crept closer. It felt like death but also a warm embrace. Zac didn't try to fight it, as he recognized the feeling. This was just like what he'd experienced during his first Draugr vision. The embrace of the Abyssal Lake.

Soon, his surroundings were gone, replaced by endless darkness.

---

It was joy and sorrow entwined.

Returning into the depths was to come home, in a way the buildings above could never match. The buffeting streams of the Abyss were the caress of a parent, welcoming and familiar. At the same time, it was different. Back then, before time, before thought, they'd been one. Since he woke up, there was an unbridgeable gap between them.

Was that why it resisted his will all those years ago? Because it knew it was hard to take back an arrow that had left the string?

Eoz occasionally wondered if it had been a mistake for them to wake up. They had been safe, content. And while the boundless sky outside was marvelous beyond compare, it was also dangerous. Mez saw it in the stars. A great darkness was coming to the cosmos, and they had little time to prepare.

The others looked to them for leadership, but Eoz didn't have the answers. He couldn't see the will of the Heavens like his elder sister, nor could he call on the Abyss like Azol. He would become a shield for the children of Draug, the Vanguard that would lead them through the coming calamity.

Except he wasn't ready.

He'd seen it with his own eyes. Not even his eldest brother had traveled as far as he. If what Mez said was true, that they soon would lose the protection of the Abyss, there weren't many places for them to go. They were created in the image of the Abyss, but most of the cosmos was not. So Eoz had come back, to beseech Abyss for the strength needed to carry out his task.

Deeper and deeper he went, far past the Pools of Rebirth and the Temples of Eschatology. The blessings inside were not enough. The Thirteen Fates, the Seven Grottos. Even the Sea of Unknowing passed by as Eoz pushed farther than the children had ever gone. Toward where the true power of the Abyss hid.

Part of him wanted to bring with him the sacred spaces of the Abyss, but Eoz understood he could not. They were a gift of the Abyss, or perhaps from those who came before. Before time, before the Heavens. Those who they'd only found whispers of in the deepest sanctums, who had pressed against the edges of reality and chosen war. It was not their place to take them—the Abyss made that clear.

Eoz still hadn't reached his destination, yet the weight of the universe was already bearing down on him. Existing was a struggle. Moving meant pushing the boundaries of what his body could withstand. If not for his body's endurance, he would have succumbed already, yet it was not enough.

Will became strength, determination became speed. He pushed against fate and his limitations as he followed the path in his memory. He was getting closer to the beckoning call he'd felt upon first awakening. A call similar to the other unexplored mysteries of the depths, but one uniquely tuned to him.

He could only pray that it would still accept him. Eoz's muscles tore, and his soul cracked, but he kept going. His faith and his purpose shattered the fetters that chained him down and allowed him to push back against what had given him life. And just barely, it was enough to carry him to the journey's end.

The obelisk towered in the dark.

The Abyss hummed, and a wave of terrifying disassociation hit him. For a moment, he was unsure who he was as he gazed upon the ancient pattern on the pillar. Was this real, or was it a dream? Was that short and confusing life an illusion or a warning? Was he Eoz, or was he Zac?

---

The world shuddered and twisted, and Eoz shook his head as he looked at the swirling maelstrom in the distance. There had to be a sanctuary within, judging by the streams of Death in the confusing mesh of energies. But the taboo power expelled from its core was strange and terrifying, and he was so tired.

Twenty thousand years had passed since he'd left the last sanctuary, and he could feel how the weight of the Heavens was wearing him thin. Entering this anomaly to scout and stabilize it would carry a real risk.

What choice did he have? If he was suffering, the fates of the children were far worse, and both Azol and Mez were needed to sustain their people.

Once more into the depths.

---

Zac slowly woke up, but he didn't move an inch. There were a lot of impressions to digest from the vision, and he was reluctant to give up the feeling of warmth and security that the [Essence of the Abyss] provided. More importantly, there was a huge amount of energy from the elixir remaining, and it was all burrowing into a hidden spot by his navel, just over his Specialty Core.

This sensation wasn't anything new. A Hidden Node was being cracked open.

Unfortunately, not even half a day was enough, and the energy from the elixir was finally waning. Meanwhile, the node seemed unwilling to pass the threshold and awaken. Had Iz's investigation damaged the treasure more than she'd realized? There was no time to cry over spilled milk. Zac had to figure out how to turn the tides.

A quick test confirmed Miasma Crystals and random Death-attuned treasures didn't cut it. They entered his body, but they barely affected the node. There was something about the energy of the [Essence of the Abyss] that made it far more efficient than normal Death-attuned items. It was based on something deeper, more profound, than the items Zac had sourced in the Zervereth Sector.

The situation was worsening by the minute, and Zac could even feel the Hidden Node recede. The window of opportunity was closing.

Zac suddenly had an idea. He swallowed a few normal Node-breaking Pills to buy some time as he flashed over to the inner sanctum of his Death-attuned cave. Right in the center, a black pedestal held a small black sphere.

It was the [Seed of Undeath] he'd taken from the undead Incursion years ago. It was once the heart of the Realignment Array but had since been turned into a battery for his cave. Because of its inherent nature, it had also strengthened the Miasma Veins beneath the mountain, allowing the transition to be completed far earlier in Port Atwood than elsewhere.

The egg had used up most of its energy before Zac got his hand on it, and it was almost running on empty now. However, even if just a small amount of Death remained in the tank, it was pure and concentrated. Zac still didn't know exactly how these things were made, but he suspected it had something to do with the Heart of the Empire, the Eternal Heritage the Undead Empire had found.

The Death in these things was so pure and potent without being High-grade, and the only similar thing he'd encountered was Ultom and its light of truth. That would also explain why these things had to be sent over from the Heartlands rather than produced locally by the Kavriel Clan. No matter how impressive its origins were, it was mostly useless by now.

With Earth already becoming a real Death-attuned world, there wasn't much purpose to holding onto this thing. Zac took it and cracked the sphere open, prompting a huge cloud of Death to erupt in the cave. If any living being had stood in the chamber at this moment, they would probably have been instantly converted to Revenants.

The seed didn't actually contain a deadly gas but a few drops of turquoise liquid that were rapidly vaporizing. Zac hurriedly swallowed the remaining liquid, and a storm of Death joined the waning energy of the **[Essence of the Abyss]**. The energy was extremely chaotic, though, and billowing plumes of aquamarine clouds poured out of his pores to join the vapor in the room.

But as much as he lost, there was even more remaining. Zac forcibly took charge of the rampaging currents and slammed it into the half-opened node before it could recede into the depths of his body. It was like a tsunami crashing into a small floodgate, and the result was instantaneous. The node was blasted wide open, along with most of his midsection.

Black ichor poured on the ground, but Zac didn't care. Mending flesh wounds and some broken pathways was easy. Getting another Hidden Node was not. The injury was agonizing, yet Zac couldn't stop himself from eagerly opening his Status Screen to see what he'd just gained.

**Bloodline:** [E – Corrupted] Void Emperor

**Talent:** Force of the Void – 50%, Void Zone
**Bloodline Nodes:** [E] Void Heart, [E] Spiritual Void, [E] Purity of
the Void
**Nodes:** [E] Quantum Gate, [E] Adamance of Eoz, [E] Conviction of
Eoz, [E] Immutability of Eoz

Zac blankly looked at the screen, wondering if the pain was making
him see double.

There were actually two of them?

63

# THE FIRST DRAFT

Zac thought the node in his navel was the only Hidden Node he'd get, but it turned out he'd already opened one during his vision. It explained the odd shift where he saw Eoz of two different epochs. One moment, Eoz stared up at a mysterious obelisk in a pre-System timeline. The next, he'd floated in space overlooking a terrifying vortex as large as a galaxy, presumably during the great migration.

He'd believed the shift resulted from the obelisk rather than his second Hidden Node. That thing was mysterious, terrifyingly powerful, and something at the level of the Stele of Conflict. Almost like time had twisted, where he and Eoz had been one. In fact, Zac really suspected that was the case. He truly may have missed out on something because of his second node opening.

Then again, Zac wasn't certain he'd be able to see what Eoz did with that obelisk even if **[Immutability of Eoz]** didn't appear. He couldn't remember a single detail of the dense scripts that covered its surface. He only vaguely recalled that the pillar contained ancient and tremendous power, eclipsing even Eoz. Of course, the obelisk might have been powered by the Abyssal Lake itself, which would explain the power it emitted.

Though the details of the obelisk were vague, Zac still remembered the other parts of the vision. The Temples, the Fates, the Grottos. The memories were also oddly detailed, even if he hadn't physically seen the holy sites of the Draugr race during the vision. He even remembered some hidden paths Eoz explored in the millennia before the vision.

It wasn't the first time this happened. His visions with Karz were the same, where he, for a moment, became his supposed ancestor. What they saw, he saw. What they thought, he thought. With Karz, it didn't much matter since he was still just an orphan turned outer disciple, with little valuable knowledge to impart.

With Eoz, it was different since he was a being at the peak. Zac was certain Eoz was a Supremacy, though Zac had no idea how the Draugr progenitor would compare to the System-empowered Supremacies of today. Unfortunately, Eoz didn't think about the Dao during the visions, or perhaps those thoughts were removed, just like the details of the obelisk. What remained was still incredibly valuable.

If Zac ever managed to get to the Abyssal Lake, and things hadn't changed too much, he would come into a windfall. A few distracted thoughts as Eoz headed to the depths had exposed multiple secrets and opportunities that could drastically speed up his cultivation in the D-grade.

As for the origins of those ancient structures beneath the surface, Zac wasn't sure. But it didn't seem they came from this era unless it was from a civilization much earlier than the Limitless Empire. Did that mean the Abyssal Shores were an Eternal Heritage? Or could natural phenomena be powerful enough to survive the end of an era?

Zac was unsure what to make of the situation. He supposed it didn't matter. At least not for some brat like himself. But it was hard to forget the sense of awe Eoz had felt when he thought about those people. People who seemingly reached the very limits of cultivation and 'chosen war.' War against what? The Heavens?

Zac shook his head, putting the matter aside. It was yet another mystery one could not so easily unravel. Instead, Zac refocused on the gains. He'd gained two new nodes but no constitution. The former was a welcome surprise, while the latter was expected. Catheya essentially told him as much when she gave him the [Essence of the Abyss]. It was a bit of a letdown not to get a single attribute point, though.

Still, Zac could feel that his body had drastically improved. He was holding almost 20% more Miasma than before, which would transfer over to his other side, thanks to [Quantum Gate]. His pathways had improved, not by growing any thicker, but like the paths had been swapped out with higher-quality wiring, allowing for faster energy transfer.

Dragging an edge across his skin confirmed it'd become noticeably more resistant without losing its elasticity. In other words, all the inherent benefits of being a Draugr had been boosted even further. If he were a cultivator, his attunement to Death would most likely have skyrocketed, though Zac could tell his Draugr side had the same limitations as his human side. His affinity was still zero, and he hadn't even gained any of that Dao-given beauty Iz, and now Catheya, possessed.

While his affinity hadn't changed, Zac felt much closer to the Dao of Death. If his human side had formed whirlpools with golden flakes, then each of his Draugr cells now held a bottomless abyss. Peering into the depths of his body felt like looking into the netherworld, and there was a strong accumulation of Pure Death. It was a phenomenon far more palpable than the first layer [Void Vajra Sublimation].

Pushing his Branch of the Pale Seal through his limbs was noticeably smoother, almost like it blended with his body. And almost as fast as letting it pass through the pathways of [Thousand Lights Avatar]. All energy moved smoother in his body since the upgrade, to the point he might be able to match the energy rotation of a mid-tier cultivator.

The thought made Zac release a huge cloud of Miasma before he took out a Supreme Miasma Crystal. Soon, new Miasma replaced the energy he'd sacrificed. As expected, his recovery rate of Death-attuned energy had almost doubled thanks to his constitution. It wasn't at the level of the elites of Port Atwood, let alone the many Heaven's Chosen of the Multiverse, but it was a start.

Zac guessed he'd gain something similar from his Life-attuned Constitution sooner or later. With two constitutions improving the base functionality of his body, yet another one of his weaknesses would eventually be shored up.

With the gains of his body covered, Zac turned his attention to his new Hidden Nodes. Zac had a pretty good idea of how [Conviction of Eoz] worked, and it was easy to test. He closed his right hand into a fist and tried to flex his muscles as hard as possible. Normally, one would be able to push their muscles to a certain point based on their attributes, after which one wouldn't be able to exert more speed or strength.

This time, it just kept going. Zac felt like someone was inserting needles into his bicep, but he had no problem noticeably flexing his muscle harder. The same thing happened when he tried to leap forward as far as he could.

[Conviction of Eoz] had essentially upped the limiters on his body at the cost of damaging his limbs. Almost like a hidden Berserking Method, but the drawback wasn't very punishing. It hurt your muscles and could probably damage your bones, but Zac had incredibly high Endurance and Vitality. For someone like him, it couldn't really be called a drawback unless you were forced into an extremely pitched battle.

Even then, it wasn't a problem. Zac had pushed his techniques to the Integration Stage, and he had nigh-perfect control over his body. He had no trouble controlling his movements to avoid overdoing it. He wouldn't even need to use a Bloodline Method to turn the node off. The real risk was if he was forced to overextend himself against a powerful enemy.

At that point, he'd risk entering a negative spiral where self-inflicted damage weakened him to the point where he was forced to use the Hidden Node even more to keep up.

After testing things out for a couple of minutes, Zac felt he could push his speed and strength by roughly 3-4% without any drawbacks except the prickling sensation. It felt a bit uncomfortable, but his natural resilience and recovery fixed his muscles faster than they could be damaged. Not only that but the effect could be doubled if he was willing to harm himself.

Less than 10% wasn't special, but Zac could tell this wasn't the limit of the node. Even when running the node at full blast, the damage to his body wasn't too bad. Ultimately, it came down to the name—conviction.

He remembered Eoz's conviction as he pushed toward the depths of the Abyssal Lake. He was fighting against the weight of the universe, ready to risk his life to reach the obelisk. Sitting around in his cultivation cave wouldn't allow Zac to bring out the mental and emotional state needed to fully awaken the node.

The other node, [Immutability of Eoz], was a tougher nut to crack. The second vision showed Eoz floating in space, looking at a vortex. But since its name indicated it was a defensive node, Zac started to try various things. Two days later, he had a preliminary answer.

It became apparent the node didn't provide any physical resistance like the **[Adamance of Eoz]** did by strengthening his Miasma. Instead, it was more like **[Purity of the Void]**. While his Void Emperor Node cleansed impurities and foreign energies, **[Immutability of Eoz]** protected against and cleansed intangible things.

To reach this conclusion, he'd been forced to call upon a wide variety of cultivators from the Atwood Army, from normal Elementalists to Poison Masters and Hexers. The node had been useless against the former, but against the latter, the node had finally awakened.

When the Hexer tried to inflict him with a curse of weakness, Zac felt his node automatically heat up. That prompted the curse to fail, and the Hexer had even been hit with a small backlash. Part of it was probably because the Hexer was only Early E-grade, but it hopefully meant that it would at least weaken the curses of powerful adversaries.

The same thing happened when a ranger tried placing a tracking mark on him a few moments later. In other words, it looked like the node protected against various detrimental afflictions. This was an amazing node, and Zac liked it even better than **[Conviction of Eoz]**. The Multiverse was filled with dangerous and unpredictable environments, and there was almost no limit to the weird skills that existed.

A lot of these methods were incredibly difficult to spot as well. The fact he'd been carrying around six tracking marks after his visit to the Tower of Eternity was proof of that. And as his battle with Iz had shown, things could take a drastic turn when they launched unexpected forms of attacks.

Unfortunately, there were no Karmic Cultivators on Earth, or at least none that his people knew of. Zac would have liked to test whether **[Immutability of Eoz]** also helped against Karmic meddling. After all, the Great Redeemer was probably out there still, and Zac had already been targeted by the Buddhist Sangha once. Some extra protections against those kinds of people would be a godsend.

The easiest solution would probably be to just ask Catheya, but Zac wasn't sure how to deal with the Undead Empire after finding out they'd spiked the **[Essence of the Abyss]**. He believed he was better off pretending he hadn't used it yet. That way, they'd think he would lose his human side sooner or later. Otherwise, they might move on to other methods of dealing with him.

As for the cost of his Hidden Nodes, it was similar to **[Adamance of**

**Eoz]**. The nodes drained his body, rather than using Miasma or Mental Energy. For lack of a better description, Zac called it Vigor, like what the Body Tempering Cultivators before the System used. Expending his Vigor would leave him hungry, and overusing it would make him feel hollow and weak, just like Eoz in the second vision.

The good news was that he'd noticed upgrading either of his two constitutions seemed to improve his stores and the natural recovery rate of Vigor. Still, Zac feared there was no getting around his needing to eat even more to keep himself in fighting condition. He'd have to rely on Ryan's chef buddy even more going forward.

Zac spent another day getting used to his most recent upgrades before returning to his original training regimen. The first three layers of the **[Void Vajra Sublimation]** weren't as complicated as the **[Nine Reincarnations Manual]**. They were fundamentally the same, except the 81 stances had become 108 in the second layer.

Each additional stance added a surprising amount of difficulty, leaving Zac sore for over an hour after each session. One welcome surprise was that his **[Conviction of Eoz]** and generally improved constitution from **[Essence of the Abyss]** noticeably helped him when cultivating **[Void Vajra Sublimation]**.

It was still more difficult to complete each pass than the first layer. But without his other gains, Zac suspected it wouldn't have needed one hour of rest. Zac even felt lucky he'd been forced to use the elixir early. This way, he'd save a huge amount of time over the coming years, time that would otherwise be spent lying sprawled on the ground, too exhausted to even think.

And Zac already knew what he'd spend his extra time on—drawing blueprints.

It was something Iz suggested he add to his daily routine. Zac's original idea was to work hard on the theoretical aspect of Duality before starting to create blueprints. He wanted to avoid a situation akin to his stances, where he'd been forced to throw out much of what he'd learned because of shaky foundations.

However, Iz said he should start experimenting immediately and that expressing his understanding would help connect what he learned with his path. It would also concretize the problem, allowing you to look at it from a different light. It was fine going over the options in your mind, but that could lead to missing some critical weaknesses that would be laid bare when trying to draw the blueprint.

Zac ultimately felt it was a good idea, especially after thinking back to the vision Yrial showed him. Zac's master had conjured that flame hundreds of times during his journey, making incremental adjustments to get closer to his truth. With his superhuman attributes and Integration Stage technique, drawing up a blueprint or two wouldn't take much time each day.

Hopefully, it would also act as a motivator, where he could see his gradual improvement over time.

There was no better time to begin than now, and Zac produced a stone disk the size of a manhole cover. He didn't have Yrial's energy and Dao control to form something like his flames, so Zac was better off inscribing his ideas onto various materials. Zac took out a small scalpel shaped like an axe he'd prepared for just the occasion. It looked a bit odd, but he'd found he was far better at carving intricate details when using an axe than something like a chisel.

Zac wasted no time as he started engraving the fractals and paths he'd envisioned and iterated upon so many times in his mind. He began at the outer edges, carving runes that held the whispers of true Life and Death. Life to the left, Death to the right, separated by the center of the disk. It was like Yrial's second trial, where he'd cheated his way through after returning from the Orom.

Back then, his path had been showcased by three brutal scars instilled with his Dao. That obviously wasn't anything worthy of being called a blueprint, but it worked as a starting point. Meticulously drawn fractals replaced wild energies and destruction, and unfettered Dao was replaced by runes instilled with precise meaning.

At the opposite edges, the two concepts were pure, but they transformed as Zac worked his way toward the middle. Gradually, the Dao of Conflict entered the fray on both sides, seamlessly melding with the two other Daos. The sides moved toward each other like warriors charging their enemy, just like the struggle he saw in the air around him—an Evolutionary force against an Inexorable one.

Then the problems arrived. He'd thought about how to fuse the two sides at length, and a pattern similar to yin-yang had already appeared on the disk. In the center, the Branch of War Axe dominated, being the inspiration for over 75% of the patterns. Those parts were not difficult to fuse, but the problem came from the other two Daos.

The shadow of Life could be found in any Evolutionary Pattern, even if it was dominated by Conflict in the center. The same was true for the opposite side. These two Daos completely changed how most of the patterns worked and the balance of the whole schematic. And they refused to harmonize.

If Zac were using one of his [Fractal Framework Arrays] to create a skill right now, it would have blared with warnings that the energy conduits were unstable. After all, this wasn't just about fusing Dao. The Cosmic Core was a battery, and he was trying to create something that could hold both Miasma and Cosmic Energy.

Still, Zac trudged on, using all the insight he had accumulated to fix the issues as best he could. This wasn't a final design. It was a test to see how far his current understanding could take him. Twenty minutes later, the whole disk was engraved and completely covered with an intricate array of patterns. Zac wordlessly looked at his first blueprint, the schematic that was supposed to take him into Hegemony.

Thank God he had years to work out the kinks.

# MISSIONS

"This seems... ill-advised," Ra'Klid hesitated as he looked at the screen, but shook his head in helplessness upon seeing the expressions of those around him.

Ogras was barely listening as he tried to make sense of the readings his girl was spitting out, but there were others to deal with these kinds of matters.

"How so?" Vilari smiled, her gaze making the skittish chiefling swallow nervously.

"I mean..." Ra'Klid said as he waved at the weird gash in space and the huge frozen corpses floating around it.

"The beasts are quite dead, I assure you," Vilari said.

"That's not the problem," Ra'Klid said with a roll of his eyes. "Why are they out here, and what's with the wounds on their bodies? Something made these big bastards run for their lives, to the point they jumped through a spatial scar to escape."

"Those wounds might have come from passing through the hole in space," Ibtep said. "We saw what happened to the moon the other day. To shreds in seconds."

"You are only furthering my point," Ra'Klid groaned. "Why would we enter such a place?"

"In search of opportunities, of course," Ogras snorted as he finally looked up from the readouts. "The space on the other side nurtured at least seven Beast Kings, which means the energy density is good. The atmosphere inside is also decently stable, and the readings indicate it's not too large. We can search the place within a week without splitting up."

"Multiple Beast Kings shared such a small region?" Rhuger said with surprise as he turned to Tom, one of the non-combat personnel who'd been brought along. "What's going on?"

Ogras looked over as well. Apparently, this human had been a scientist of some renown before Earth had been integrated. Ogras didn't understand what was so interesting about celestial objects. Their heat made it impossible for most types of treasures to survive. And the few that were nurtured on the celestial objects were impossible to bring out even for most Hegemons.

However, Tom Nowak's pre-world knowledge had translated into a star-based class, and he even managed to form a Dao Seed related to space. Armed with the powerful arrays of the *Temptress*, the flagship of their expedition, he'd been able to both prevent some beginner's mistakes and find small opportunities over the three months since they entered the Million Gates Territory.

This place was discovered by Tom as well, further proving these brainiacs were worth their weight in gold. Even better, they were mostly content exploring space and studying various phenomena. Apart from the occasional materials they wanted for experiments, they didn't cost a thing. They were even happy to pilot the ship without any pay.

"We're still running some tests, but I think I understand what's going on," Tom said. "It seems this gate is just a shard of a much-larger Mystic Realm. The real thing either collapsed or had this splinter shaved off for some reason. Either case, this shard was set adrift and eventually closed in on this particular dimension."

"So the beasts might have been wounded during the upheavals," Ogras nodded. "I'd also want to leave if the sky collapsed on my head."

"Is it safe to enter?" Vilari asked.

"It's stable for now, but it's hard to tell for how long. I doubt a realm of this size can survive for much more than a month or two in this kind of chaotic environment, especially after colliding with a main dimension like this," Tom said.

"Perfect," Ogras grinned.

What made the Million Gates Territory so dangerous was also what made it so alluring. Its name was truly apt. A million gates invited travelers to the mysterious beyond at any moment, thanks to the spatial storms that had raged for innumerable years. On the other side, anything from ancient troves to deathtraps awaited. And if you were too slow, the storms would swallow or drag away your chance at riches.

"Perfect?" Ra'Klid groaned. "That thing can collapse at any time, and we'd be spat out into the Void."

"Exactly. If this is a time-limited trove, all the more reason to hurry," Ogras said.

"The captain is correct," a rumbling voice echoed as the Zhix party entered the deck. They must have realized the ship had stopped and ended their cultivation session early. "We joined this expedition in search of opportunities to further ourselves. Those opportunities will not be found in easy to find or safe locations."

"No wonder the scions of the Atwood Empire are progressing so quickly," Ra'Klid said with resignation. "You people are lunatics."

"The Mavai are staying behind then?" Vilari asked, a small smile playing on her face.

"Of course not," Ra'Klid sighed. "I just felt there should be at least one voice of caution in this group of daredevils. That guy Carl seems to be the only one in this party without a death wish."

"Enough with your whining," Ogras said with an annoyed wave as he closed the console. "Go get your shaman, his spells might be needed inside. That goes for the rest of you too. We're entering in an hour after we've finished scanning the region and erecting the isolation arrays. Command group, let's talk."

The people on the deck sprung to action, their previous excursions to various asteroids and dead planets proving to be useful experience now that the stakes were higher. There were no safety nets out in space, no Lord Atwood to deal with the terrors in the dark.

Ogras entered a sealed chamber with Rhuger, Joanna, Vilari, and Rhubat in tow. The five of them were the only ones who knew of the covert mission of their outing, so Ogras had created a command group consisting of the five so they could discuss the matter without raising suspicion.

"Is this it?" Ogras asked Vilari after the door closed behind them.

"I'm afraid not," Vilari said with a shake of her head.

"You were the one who said you felt a nudge in this direction," Ogras reminded. "From that ball of yours."

"I do, but this tear seems to be unrelated. What's calling me is farther beyond," the Mentalist explained.

"Fate cannot be rushed, Shadewar," Rhubat said. "What will be, will be."

"Told you I'm not a fan of that name," Ogras muttered, but the Zhix paid him no mind. "I guess we're lucky this isn't it. That way, we won't need to go overboard on our first real mission. Let's use this as a chance to integrate our forces into one unit."

The command group went over the details for another ten minutes before they went about their preparations. An hour later, a group of 20 gathered in the *Temptress*'s hangar. With so few expedition members, each outing was essentially a full mobilization, where only the non-combatants and a skeleton crew were left behind to deal with surprises.

"How about we not waste any time," Ogras said as the door to the small shuttle opened. "We know very little about what's on the other side. We move together, and remember your roles. Never deactivate the protective talismans, and never stray outside the War Array on your own. We're in the wild now, and we're definitely not the apex predators here."

The shuttle flew out from a gate in the hull a moment later, and Ogras nodded upon seeing six satellites already surrounding the area. They were part of the kit of the Drone ship in his Spatial Ring rather than the Starflash model, but they could be used in limited numbers with all the Creator Models.

Their use was simple: to hide the area and make spatial phasing difficult to impossible. If someone were passing by this dimensional region, their arrays would find this particular dimension turbulent, which was incredibly common in the Million Gates Territory. Unless they actually knew about the gate, they'd move on to calmer waters.

The shuttle reached the spatial gash in no time. Everyone inside didn't dare to much as breathe as the ship passed through to the other side, but the craftsmanship of the Creators was something else. Only a small shudder rippled through the vessel before they were through. What came next was much worse.

"Brace!" Joanna screamed as she desperately veered, but the ship was still rocked as blinding red lights passed through the cockpit.

A cascade of defensive fields from the Valkyries and the Mavai Shaman clashed with the raging red, and the foreign energy was quenched before it managed to cause any damage.

"What the hell was that?" Ogras grunted, and he got his answer a moment later when the knocked-out scanning arrays woke up again.

The world they'd entered was one dominated by giants—giant trees as large as cities reaching toward the sky, their sprawling branches wide enough to hold whole ecosystems. But it was clearly a kingdom in decline, with flames raging across vast swathes of the Mystic Realm. Other trees had been toppled by other forces, most likely massive earth-quakes judging by the deep scars that ran across the ground.

The scene was impressive, considering each one of the trees appeared to be D-grade Spiritual Plants, with a large number of lesser herbs growing on their massive bodies. But Ogras was more concerned by the commotion on the other side of the Mystic Realm, the source of the red energy that almost shot down their vessel.

It looked like a hauntingly beautiful yet dangerous flower hundreds of meters tall, with innumerable petals and pistils made from arcs of pure red energy. It swayed back and forth erratically as though buffeted by invisible winds. What hit them was just the edge of a wayward streak of energy, having crossed almost the whole realm to slap them silly.

Of course, it wasn't actually a flower. The scene seemed to result from something incredibly energy-rich going haywire on the ground.

"What the hell is that?" Joanna muttered from her pilot's seat.

"No idea, but the energy lashes radiate upward, barely damaging the ground. Hide behind one of the big guys for now," Ogras said.

"One second," Joanna said as she rapidly pushed a series of buttons before the shuttle dove for the forest below.

"What's wrong?" Ogras asked, and the others looked over curiously from the hold.

"I thought I saw something. Look at this," Joanna said, and a magni-fied image appeared a moment later.

It was the base of the energy flower. Most of it was covered by the trees, but you could barely make out a broken dome the lights seemed to emerge from.

"A structure?" Ogras whistled, his heart skipping a beat.

"Looks like ruins," Rhuger commented, the excitement in his

turquoise eyes mirroring Ogras' own. "It might be a treasure's emanations."

"Or some old failing array going haywire, to the point a Mystic Realm broke apart," Joanna said as she turned to Ogras. "This seems like a pretty big risk. What do you think?"

"Taking risks is the only way to rise against the river of fate," Ogras said, adding under his breath. "And I refuse to sink."

---

"It's even more pitiful than I imagined," Yselio Tobrial sighed as they stepped out through the gate. "It's like you can barely breathe. To think one of the Pillars is in such a region of space."

"Only worse from here on out, kid," Ylvin grunted as he waved over his subordinate, who'd arrived ahead of time. "This region is still not technically considered the frontier."

"General," the captain said with a bow, then turned to Yselio with another bow. "Your Highness."

"What did you find?" Ylvin asked as they walked out from the Alliance Teleporter toward the closest square, where a vessel was already waiting.

Normally, the capitals of empires were no-fly zones. But rules were man-made prisons, and never absolute. There were ranges of encroachment that would go unpunished, and even greater transgressions would often lead to bigger gains than losses. In this case, the issue was simply solved by having the right surname.

"There are no direct routes, but arrangements have been made," the soldier said and handed over two crystals. "We didn't dare choose the destination, so we've made preparations for both. We await your decision."

Ylvin and Yselio took one crystal each, scanning its contents.

"Six months?" Yselio frowned. "We're falling behind the competition."

"Those Stillsun bastards playing favorites," Ylvin snorted.

"It might also be the fact that my Royal Father and uncles threw them out of the Heavenly Realm," Yselio said with a wry smile.

"The emperors were absolutely justified. If Povan Stillsun was allowed to stay any longer, then an Eighth Heaven would emerge within a million years or so. That man is just too scary," Ylvin shuddered. "With the Third Heaven already creating problems from the shadows and the Technocrat's Neural Network trying to sneak its way inside, we cannot abide another."

"You're right, of course, but it does put us in a bit of a bind," Yselio said as he thoughtfully looked at the two crystals. "Two routes, two very different paths."

"The Edge of the Seventh Heaven picked you. You will have to choose the path," Ylvin said.

"The Kan'Tanu," Yselio said after some thought. "But send Captain Soha and five Adjudicators to Zecia. It might prove useful."

"Right away, lord," the captain bowed.

"You're curious." Yselio smiled when he saw Ylvin's look. "Why I picked the Black Heart offshoot, even though the trial seems to originate in Zecia."

"I wouldn't say I'm curious. I'm just here to make sure you don't get yourself killed early. But if you're willing to explain your thought process, I am willing to listen," Ylvin shrugged.

"It's amazing you've reached such a rank within the courts with your curt demeanor." Yselio laughed as the two boarded the Cosmic Vessel, ignoring the local Monarchs who had come over to greet their arrival.

"Strong fist and strong backing," Ylvin said.

The two walked in silence through the B-grade vessel, and neither spoke up until the ship rose from the square and moved into space.

"Well?" Ylvin asked, prompting a smile from Yselio.

"I picked it because my gut told me it would be better."

"Your gut? That's it?" Ylvin said with a mix of disbelief and disgust. "This is a serious matter with wide ramifications. Only the First Heaven has managed to claim a Pillar so far."

"I know that. That's exactly why I went with my instinct."

Ylvin pretended to look disinterested, but a smile tugged at Yselio's mouth. The adopted grandson of his uncle wore his emotions on his sleeve, and Yselio could tell his Monarch guardian was about to get annoyed. And as both he and his siblings had been made aware over the years, Ylvin did not care whether the target of his ire was a royal prince when he was in the mood to beat someone up.

"I'm strong, but Yrin is stronger. I'm smart, but Yzum is smarter. And that's not even counting the scions of the Fourth and Sixth, who were both qualified to contend for the Pillar. Yet the Heavens chose me. What does it come down to? Fate. For some reason, my fate with the Left Imperial Palace is the strongest, so I will listen to the whispers of fate for direction."

"And it told you to choose Kan'Tanu," Ylvin said with a thoughtful look.

"Now I just need to figure out why."

The ship entered the Void, piercing toward the utmost edges of the incorporated universe. There wasn't much point using the wretched teleportation systems in this region. A proper vessel would move with roughly the same speed. There were no doubt local vaults that could have sped up their journey, but they neither had the paths nor the keys.

"What you said is true, but you forgot to mention one thing," Ylvin grunted after a minute of silence. "You're far more devious and scheming than either of those little straight shooters. Don't think the elders didn't notice what you did to the other candidates."

Yselio smiled. "There must be a misunderstanding."

"Bah, what misunderstanding? You're clever, but those old guys are fused with the realm itself. How can you hide from their gaze? But it's fine, you kept it within their tolerance levels. Besides, we are heading into a chaotic struggle with unknown requirements and participants. We don't need a hero. We need a devil."

Yselio didn't answer, but his smile grew wider. A devil, huh?

---

How did it come to this?

Emily blankly looked through the window of her small pod, the pain and sedatives preventing her from even moving as the healing arrays mended broken bones and lacerated flesh. There was nothing but darkness on the horizon. Yet Emily knew the horrors that hid in that endless black.

So many dead.

She didn't even know if Warsong had made it out alive, though she suspected he had. It seemed he and the other leaders ran for their lives before the ship was hit by that storm, only sparing her a single transmission before he was gone.

Then again, she couldn't complain. Not even Monarchs were safe in this place, and Warsong had no obligation to risk his life for her. His early warning allowed her to jump into her personal life pod in time, while tens of thousands most likely died when the Cosmic Vessel was ripped apart.

They'd set out with such vigor, but the Million Gates Territory quickly beat the sense of invincibility out of their bones. It was hard to pretend you were a master of the universe when you were just a speck in an angry and unforgiving sea. The advance army hadn't managed to find a single invader before a random spatial fluctuation put their grand ambitions to an abrupt and early end.

Sometimes she wondered if those who fell immediately were the lucky ones. Fifty days had passed since her pod was flung God-knows-where in the storm. Most systems were damaged, turning the pod into a coffin sailing through space. She was alone, helpless—a prisoner with only her thoughts for company.

She missed home.

# WALK OUT OF THE DREAM

"How is it?" Um'ha asked. "You have been frowning at that ball the whole day. For weeks, really."

The intricate machine of interlocking parts sat in the cavity on the worktable, both table and contraption created with such detail that the mechanical orb could freely be rolled in place without the slightest resistance. Thousands of parts and years of work to create something never-before-seen in this world. Yet Anson wasn't happy.

"Taking a walk helps clear the head. Come keep me company."

Anson didn't move for a few seconds, but finally roused himself and looked up at his partner with a smile. "A walk sounds lovely."

"Good," Um'ha said. "You know, sometimes it feels like you are cheating on me with this thing, spending your days locked away in here. I've even considered smashing it to have you all for myself."

"But you didn't," Anson said as they left the small workshop, arm in arm.

"I wouldn't destroy something you worked so hard on," Um'ha said. "Besides, it's quite beautiful in all its intricacy. Even if it doesn't work in the end, we can always put it in the front yard as a centerpiece."

"Perhaps," Anson nodded.

They exited their manor at the edge of the town, walking with no particular direction or purpose in mind.

"You know, I still don't understand what it's supposed to do," Um'ha said as she waved at a neighbor hanging her laundry. "Qi'schzto is getting along. The child should come within a month."

"I hear Haldo has his hands full feeding all seven," Anson said as he nodded at the highly pregnant demoness.

"The water array you installed on the community field has lessened the pressure on him. On all of us," Um'ha said before poking Anson with her elbow. "The ball?"

Anson looked up at the beautiful red sky stretching across the horizon, and the puffs of clouds that couldn't have been painted better by a master artist. Perfection under the Heavens.

"It will change the world."

"Change the world?" Um'Ha muttered. "I think it's pretty good, though?"

"That it is," Anson sighed.

"There is no need to put this kind of pressure on yourself," Um'ha said, patting Anson's hand. "Just trust in yourself and walk forward."

"Thank you."

They passed the smithy where Un'do was hard at work repairing the metallic sheets that would be put up before squall season, to protect the harvest from the overpowering rain coming down from the mountains. They saw the mayor, trying to once more wrangle the twins into gainful employment, when all they wanted was to randomly swing their iron-wood swords and talk of adventure.

They passed through the town gate and the communal fields, where the Lonton stalks were already reaching Anson's chest, and the bushels of Prokko seemed to be ready for harvest within days. Um'Ha exchanged a few friendly words with most of the townspeople who passed them by, while they treated Anson with a respectful distance.

After all, Thaumaturges were rare in the countryside, even this close to the capital.

Their life was different from how they'd lived when under the court's employ as a botanist and Grand Scholar. Simpler, closer to nature, to the point Anson could feel the breath of the world. At least he thought so, though it should be impossible.

Only three hours later did they return to their home. Where it waited. Anson felt queasy as they passed the picket fence to their garden, but he couldn't delay any longer. Time was running out.

"The Realmkeeper Orb is complete. It has been for some time now," Anson said as he grasped Um'ha's hand.

It was slightly calloused after years of fieldwork. There were also the small scars and burns she'd gained after various experiments meant to improve the yearly harvest. More than anything, it was warm, and Anson could feel her pulse that beat with the frequency of the Heavens.

"Does that mean you've made your decision?" Um'ha said as she grasped his hand tighter.

"You knew?" Anson said with shock.

"Not all of it. But you have been… bleeding… into the surroundings the past month," Um'ha said as she led him into the workshop. "I've come to understand some things. We're dying, aren't we?"

"I'm sorry," Anson said, his vision blurring as he looked at his wife of fifteen years. "I can't hold on any longer."

"Will I see you again?" Um'ha asked as she touched his cheek.

"One day, I'll be powerful enough to let you walk out of the dream," Anson said, tears flowing down his cheeks as he placed his hand on the Realmkeeper Orb. "Until then, you will live on in my memory."

Janos opened his eyes, a sense of profound loss filling his heart as he looked at the foreign sky above him. The world was so bleak, a shadow of the imaginary realm he'd lived inside for the past years. No, it wasn't illusory. It was a mirage created through unfathomable means. He could have lived his whole life there if not for the fact that the world was decaying.

But it could be made anew.

Janos' eyes turned to the shimmering globe in his hand. The Realmkeeper Orb was now no larger than a fist, flickering in and out of reality. It held the key, the key to get her back. He slowly pushed it against his navel, toward where his core would be in the future—an illusory core leading to a mirage world. And one day, a false Heaven would be made real.

The orb settled and a screen appeared, confirming what Janos already knew.

**[Seal of the Mercurial Court (Unique, Inheritance):** Form a seal of the Mercurial Court. Reward: Become a Realmsinger of Ultom. (1/3)]

"Work, you bastard!" Emily growled as she kicked the panel, but she immediately regretted it. "Sorry, darling. I was just too eager."

The only response was a groaning hum as the lamp flickered.

"Why? Why won't you do me this one solid?" Emily said as she threw the chisel at the ground. "I've treated you like a tender lover for over a year. I've repaired you, sourced materials from my own stuff, mind you. I had to melt down a tank in *outer space* just to make you the antenna. Do you know how much it hurts to spacewalk without a proper suit? Of course you don't. You're a broken beacon…"

"What? I just did it for the shiny new wings? I did it for all of us. So we can go home. And you can't even send out one little signal to do your part?"

Chris didn't answer, as he was wont to do, and the hum died a moment later. The silence only lasted a few seconds before Harry started singing.

"Well, shit," Emily swore as she started to furiously crank the winch that realigned the propulsion array on the outside of the SS *Trashheap*, and it sputtered to life. Soon, the directional scanning array pointed to the source of the ominous song.

She took out her tablet, and a series of calculations allowed her to breathe out in relief. The storm didn't move in her direction. She would be fine if it didn't change trajectory over the next hour. Emily looked at the housing holding the scanning array and caressed it lovingly. "You're the good one in the family, Harry."

The signs were good, but that was no guarantee in this place. If anything, it was a miracle she was still alive after being stuck so long in the broken-down hub. Thank God for Spatial Rings, and thank God for a paranoid teacher who drilled in the necessity of bringing years' worth of provisions everywhere.

Emily looked out through the screen at the spatial storm in the distance. What was he doing right now? He should be back on Earth, right? Or was he perhaps here, looking for her? The thought was comforting, like he could appear at a moment's notice on the horizon.

Then again, she wasn't sure he even knew about her situation. The advance army was slated to head deep into the Million Gates Territory to rack up enough Contribution Points to get a head start in the upcoming war. They weren't supposed to return for another year at the earliest, and the home base knew it was impossible to send messages back.

Would Warsong and the others even say anything if they managed to return? It would be a huge hit to morale if people found out they'd lost everyone so soon after arriving. And it would be a hit to the prestige of the leaders if they returned alone, having failed to save any of their subordinates. Something like that would make it impossible to participate in the upcoming war in an organized fashion.

Her scattered thoughts put aside, Emily focused on what was important—to take from the storm as it had taken from her. It was time to practice. She crawled out from the pod and into the living room, where a larger screen was already running. Emily looked at the phenomenon far in the distance where a region as large as dozens of planets strung together was being twisted on its head.

Reality was forced into an unpredictable dance where distance and proportions were in constant flux. Spatial tears thousands of miles long lashed out with wild abandon. And as the universe danced, so did the axes that appeared in her hands.

By the time Emily healed up, or more like when the pod's anesthesia ran out, seventy days had passed. The nasty wounds from the spatial flux had been mostly healed, and she'd already expelled the wild Dao of Space in her body. Seventy days was more than enough to confirm no one was coming for her, but she wasn't willing to just wait for death.

So she hatched a plan. If no one would come save her, she would simply have to save herself. Her main project was Chris, the rescue beacon that sent a deep pulse into space that would reach incredibly far. But she also improved the pod in general, and the main cockpit was now a separate compartment built and soldered onto the pod by her own hands.

It was lucky she had a Fire-based Dao, which allowed her to repurpose the various items in her Spatial Ring. Today, her cramped little pod held oceans of space, a cube over three meters across. The original pod, with its wiring and other systems, had been placed beneath the living quarters like an engine.

Wings had been soldered onto the sides, and she even managed to repurpose a few weapons she'd gotten from the crazy Ishiate into rudimentary propulsion engines. They couldn't do much, but they could at least change the direction she floated, which had saved her from flying straight into a sun months ago.

With space being in such flux, the ship could be standing still at one moment, only to be hurtling through space with such speed the surroundings were a blur the next. Honestly, it was a miracle the ship remained intact after all this time. It was the benefit of having been deposited in an extraordinarily empty stretch of space.

A humming song accompanied Emily's dance as a dozen flying axes started dancing in the small compartment around her, flashing back and forth seemingly erratic and at random. The same was true for herself as she swung her two tomahawks like a conductor of chaos. But within the chaos was order.

There wasn't much else to do on the SS *Trashheap* except work on the broken arrays and cultivate. Since there was only so much she could glean by angrily glaring at inscrutable arrays, most of her time was spent on the latter. And while it was a wretched existence, the constant threat of death kept her motivated enough to make a lot of progress, allowing her to digest most of Warsong's lessons in record speed.

Her axe array **[Dance of the Five Seasons]** was essentially mastered by this point, thanks to strengthening her soul with the method she got from the Big Axe Commander. But she was still trying to incorporate it into a holistic and dynamic approach. That was where the spatial storms came in. They could appear like a summer's squall out of nowhere, and their twisting arcs of destruction contained endless mysteries.

She wanted to take the mysteries of the storms and become the tempest herself. She'd become the heart in the dance of axes, striking when her array paved the way. She didn't cultivate the Dao of Space, but it was all related. The cycles of Nature weren't made up of arbitrary rules. They were the result of the stars and gravity, of the kind of rotational force she saw all around her.

Seeing another spatial storm up close was a rare opportunity to refine her idea, but her session was abruptly cut short by a new appearance on the screen.

A ship.

It had been spit out from the storm just like she once was. They did seem better off from the experience than her, even if the large Cosmic

Vessel was missing some sections. A steady pulse of energy was still being released from the engines at the back, and it was flying away from the storm. This was her only chance.

She'd survived seventeen nearby storms, but Emily knew her luck would eventually run out. Just being swept up in the edge of a storm would disintegrate the SS *Trashheap* and her with it.

"I'm sorry, darling," Emily sighed as she opened the panel and inserted an inscribed Nexus Crystal. "I'd hoped it wouldn't come to this."

Two wires of E-grade Starsilver were added next, forming a crude route bypassing most of the array. It was time to go all out.

The array hummed to life, and Emily screamed with excitement as a deep pulse passed out from the makeshift antenna on the top of her vessel. A snap quickly brought her back to reality. The array disk had snapped from being overloaded with energy, a reminder this was a last-ditch measure. If these people didn't come for her, she would be in an even worse spot than before.

Emily became a flurry of activity, activating all her prepared measures. A series of incredibly bright lights, both technological and magical, lit up on the hull, turning the SS *Trashheap* into a blinding beacon that should be impossible to miss in this desolate corner of space. The minutes passed, and nothing changed. The ship was getting farther and farther away.

"Please, please," Emily whispered.

Then, the Cosmic Vessel turned.

A wave of relief so powerful it almost made Emily delirious swept through her, but she pushed it down as she readied herself. This wasn't the Old Earth, where a castaway being rescued by a ship would turn into a global feelgood story. This was the Million Gates Territory, where the darkness of man was on full display. Few good ones were traveling these waters, and those who did were unlikely to operate such run-down vessels like the one inching toward her.

Still, being captured by pirates beat slowly dying in the emptiness of space. She'd heard that was how a lot of groups expanded their crews. They captured smaller crews and press ganged those who weren't too stubborn. Some would become meat shields, while others could integrate into true members.

Her features shifted thanks to **[Million Faces]**, turning her into a young man half a head taller than herself. She slung a mage's staff across her back, while the tomahawks returned to sheathes hidden within the sleeves of her arms. The minutes passed, yet they felt too short as Emily tried to prepare for any eventuality of what awaited her on the ship.

The SS *Trashheap* shuddered as a gravitational array pulled it in, and the ship thumped down on metal inside the hangar a minute later. A group of ten soldiers was already waiting outside, but she was relieved upon seeing not one of them was a Hegemon. If she were lucky, they'd all been killed when the ship lost its tower and a wing.

"Thank you, thank you," Emily said with a bow as she stepped out of her vessel. "Thought I'd end up as stardust."

"Lad, how did you end up in that thing?" the man asked as he looked at the odd-looking escape pod with a frown. "Where are you from? What quadrant is this?"

So that's how it was. They were lost after the storm, possibly with navigational arrays damaged. They only picked her up to get their bearings.

"My ship was blown up in a spatial storm not long ago," Emily said as she warily looked around. "I don't know which quadrant this is, but I am willing to work for passage."

"That's a shame, but we could always use some helping hands," the leader said.

They didn't seem like pirates, but Emily couldn't be sure. These people were too organized, though some of the most dangerous pirate crews were as organized as any militia. She surreptitiously activated **[Daybreak Revolutions]**, giving her eyes a second sight that showcased energy flows. Only a glance was needed to shock her to the point the skill collapsed.

These people had monsters hiding in their bodies.

Emily's reaction was instantaneous, and a blazing arc of flame punched a hole through the leading man's chest, even if he'd had his guard up. It instantly killed him and the parasitic creature that had made his chest its home.

"Attack!" another man screamed, but he didn't have a chance to launch a single strike before a five-meter salamander wrought from flames swallowed him in one bite.

Emily was right on the heels of her familiar, a storm of axes already raging around her. It looked like she had finally encountered the infiltrators, which meant she'd either have to commandeer the vessel or be infested with those cursed things.

It was time to put her newly devised **[Tempest Bop]** to the test.

# SHADEWAR

"Brats, you think you can keep us out forever!" the six-meter golem roared as he swung his hammer in their direction.

With the swing, dozens of earthen spears tore out of the ground and shot toward them, but earth rose to meet earth as a super condensed stone exploded forth with far greater ferocity. It shattered the spears without losing momentum and slammed into the Dao-infused hammer. Both hammer and golem were thrown over fifty meters away, and it was hard to tell whether he was still alive.

It was Rhubat who'd launched yet another ruthless strike, and the Zhix's even stare cowed any further attempts at breaking through their perimeter. By the boundless killing intent radiating from their body, the Anointed might very well be ready to wage a solitary war against the hundreds of pirates who gathered up and sealed off their escape.

For now, Rhubat held themself in check, and thank God for that. Carl could tell these people weren't any sort of top-tier individuals, but they were ruthless, crazy, and most had weird items that bordered or down-right embraced the unorthodox. Even if their squad could win the battle, the risk of casualties was high.

And who were the most likely candidates to become a sacrifice to this madness? The top-tier elites of the Atwood Empire with stockpiles of marvelous treasures provided by their mad emperor, or the grunts filling up the numbers? Considering his wife was also here, Carl said a silent prayer for peace. But in his heart of hearts, he knew it was just a matter of time.

The apple didn't fall far from the tree, and the fruits grown from Lord Atwood's nurturing were all rotten.

"More incoming! Hegemons!" Carl transmitted to the others from his lookout atop the pillar.

They were just dots on the horizon, but Carl inwardly swore when he saw the radiating waves of energy around them. They came from five directions, most likely the other entrances of the realm. It looked like the realm seal had finally weakened to the point the bigshots could make their way inside. With everyone having gathered at this spot after weeks of looting, they didn't even bother with the other treasure mountains.

Carl glanced back at the odd rotund structure. It was hard to believe this thing was just the base of an array tower rather than some ancient fort. It was over ten thousand meters across, large enough to hold a whole city. Now, it just stood one hundred meters tall, a far cry from when it pierced the sky.

Even more terrifying was the ancient sword aura that lingered at the edge where the whole thing had been cut off, the tower itself collapsed and turned into a mountain range. That sword aura was beyond anything Carl had ever seen, and it didn't feel like something that should exist on the frontier. Only a shadow of the original intent lingered, yet it bent reality itself, conjuring those sword servants across the whole Mystic Realm.

And the worst of it was no doubt inside that confusing maze of over-sized circuitry. Carl couldn't fathom how that scatterbrained Zhix would survive in that place. Vilari, he could understand. That girl was a menace, scattering sword servants left and right with a glare. But what was Ibtep to do? Treat the illusory swords to those, admittedly delicious, critters of his?

And why the hell did the rest of them have to stay outside while those two went inside to search for the Heavens only knew what? Why did they need to defend the entrance with their lives?

This was different from the various excursions over the past months. It was shady, troublesome. And not only because this was one of the few outings where multiple forces had appeared to contend for the riches. The ancient array tower, the sword aura, the sneaky glances between the members of the command group. Carl knew a conspiracy when he saw one.

He simultaneously wanted to know the truth and stay clear. It smelled of trouble and smelled of the crazy Lord Atwood and his machinations.

Luckily, these pirates treasured their lives and had no trust in each other. Annihilating the few who stepped out first had been enough to cow the rest into a passive state, but that would only work until the Hegemons appeared.

"The vice-captains are coming," another golem snickered, not caring that his buddy had been thrown away like a piece of trash. "We'll have fun with you bastards then. Your fancy ship can't save you in here."

Like on a hidden signal, the dozen-odd crews moved farther back, giving the Atwood crew and the sole entrance to the broken array tower a wide berth. Left were the 25 warriors who guarded the gates, led by their increasingly reckless demon captain.

Unfortunately, few others appeared to share his concern over the suspicious behavior of Captain Azh'Rezak. Even his former comrade-in-arms, Ra'Klid, had lost his way and was now looking at the surrounding army with anticipation as he gripped his axe and shield. Gone were the words of caution, replaced by an insatiable desire for trouble. And he wasn't the only one.

"We should attack, weaken their strength before the leaders arrive," Rhubat rumbled while the other two Zhix were clearly ready to throw away their lives. "We cannot let anyone disturb them."

Ogras didn't immediately answer, instead opting to turn toward Carl. "How many?"

"Eight that I saw," Carl said as he jumped down. "But more might be coming."

"Anyone from the direction of our gate?"

"None," Carl said.

"Well, that's good," Joanna said. "Those drones are worth every penny."

"They can't fight an armada alone, though," Carl hesitated.

"It's fine," Ogras said. "Those two have already been inside for a day. It shouldn't be much longer. Let's wait for our guests to arrive. That way, we can deal with them all at once."

"Do you have a plan, Shadewar?" Rhubat asked, looking down at the much smaller demon.

Ogras shrugged. "I figured it was time I tried out the thing I've been working on. I'll see if I can deal with all the Hegemons. They shouldn't be too powerful going by their underlings. You just follow behind me and fill up the gaps."

"What gaps?" Joanna said with confusion.

"You'll see," Ogras smiled. "For now, defend and prepare for an attack. Remember, our main goal isn't to eradicate these people but to ensure Vilari and Ibtep aren't interrupted before they return. Anyone that so much as looks at the entrance, kill them."

Another twenty minutes passed until the eight powerful auras appeared above the pirate army almost simultaneously. Carl inwardly scoffed at the sight. They'd obviously timed their arrivals, none wanting to arrive first and be the focus of attention.

The eight knew each other by the familiarity in their glances, which wasn't a surprise. Few low-tier pirate crews dared steer their run-down vessels through the larger gates that could move you across vast distances in the Million Gates Territory. They kept to their quadrant, waiting for opportunities to arrive, be it easy-to-grab resources or unlucky passersby. Even better, none were able to cow the other seven with their reputation alone, which meant none of the local tyrants had arrived.

Eventually, one of the eight floated forward, grey-skinned humanoid, looking down at them with a neutral expression. "A small party with surprising wealth and strength, but you are all young and untested by the dangers of the Million Gates Territory. I am guessing you are outsiders?"

"Outsiders? Like the invaders?"

"The forces of Zecia are outsiders here just as much as these invaders are," the man said. "You are newcomers, so making mistakes is normal. But you should understand there are rules. Rules to keep the harmony."

"Rules? Harmony?" Ogras guffawed. "Are you really pirates?"

"We're just people making a living in a rough and unforgiving world," the humanoid countered. "It's hard to survive out in the wild, so it's better to make friends than enemies. We don't ask for much. 50% of what you looted from the surrounding mountains and free access to investigate this mysterious structure. In return, you will be free to leave, and we will not harm the two who have already entered."

*Oh no.*

They asked for the captain's loot. If there were any chances of reconciliation before, they were gone now. Carl almost wondered if the lack of resources had become a heart demon for their leader, pushing him ever harder in their outings. Or was it the result of being under a man whose talent to attract wealth was only second to his talent to attract trouble? Perhaps greed was contagious.

"Only 50%, huh?" Ogras said with an all-too-calm smile as his body started to grow. "Counter-offer. You fuck off right now, or I kill you all and take 100% of your loot."

Both sides were already primed for battle, and the demon's words became the signal for hundreds of skills to be launched at once. Carl inwardly cried as his arrow array appeared behind his back, and dozens of shimmering bolts shot toward the core of the incoming attacks. Meanwhile, heavy shields slammed into the ground as the Valkyries activated the arrays, and a thick barrier sprung up in front of them.

The whole area shook as frenzied waves of energy slammed into the shield, but it blocked out the pirates' initial salvo. Some of the attacks went wide and hit the array tower instead, but nothing could leave so much as a scratch on that impossibly sturdy metal. Carl's heart beat like a drum as he returned fire, his arrows targeting those on the ground who exhibited a greater penchant for ranged warfare.

The others similarly unleashed attacks from within their barrier, but there were just too few of them. These pirates were disorganized and weak, but there were hundreds supported by eight Hegemons. Only a few attacks passed through the discordant shields they'd erected, taking out a few of the unluckier attackers.

Carl's eyes turned to their captain, waiting to see his response. But he wasn't there. Carl swore upon seeing that the lunatic had actually jumped out from the shield. Did he think he was the lord? And what kind of skill was that? The demon was a demon no more—he had become a true devil.

Reaching almost ten meters, he'd become a shadow creature brought out from one's deepest nightmares. Dozens of attacks hit him the moment he stepped out, but even the Hegemons' attacks passed right

through his intangible body. How was that possible? Even spectral cultivators would be affected when struck by a Dao, but Ogras seemed
completely unruffled as he took in the battlefield.

In one hand, Ogras held a black spear seemingly wrought from the
night sky. In the other, a thin flag that made Carl's hair stand on end. The
banner itself didn't seem to be made of fabric, but rather hundreds of
anguished faces that moved repellently, creating a band of suffering
stretching to the ground.

Carl vaguely heard Ogras mutter something, like he was talking with
the flag, which made Carl's heart drop even further. Was the demon
really losing his mind? This was no time for a psychological evaluation,
though. They needed to be ready to support whatever move their captain
was about to unleash.

Ogras swung the spear, and it was almost like their surroundings had
become a punctured balloon as all light was drained. Even if their
captain had somehow drenched the world in dour anthracite, Carl could
still see their enemies just fine. The pirates didn't appear to have the
same luxury, looking back and forth with evident fear. A few were
running already, heedless of their bosses being right there.

Most took up defensive positions, fearing an attack was coming their
way. And they were absolutely right.

A terrifying cackle echoed through the battlefield as Ogras swung the
flag. Over a hundred spectral creatures appeared in the darkness. Most
were indistinct ghost types, but Carl swore when he recognized a few of
the forms. Two were the assassins who had tried to sneak aboard their
ship and steal it a few months back. The bastards who killed John. A few
others were opponents felled by the demon in the battle inside the treasure moon.

Now, they looked like mindless spectral cultivators as they rushed for
the unwitting pirates like a tide rising from the netherworld. Ogras joined
in as his form expanded further, turning into a huge maw that seemed
ready to swallow the Hegemons whole. It turned into a bloodbath almost
instantly, with Ogras and his minions being both quick and impossible to
retaliate against.

Four Hegemons were ripped apart in an instant before the others
managed to break apart the darkness, and the other four were wrapped up
in a losing battle against the storm of shadows.

"Shadewar indeed," Rhubat sighed before rushing forward, wading straight into the mayhem to fill the gaps like ordered.

The others followed suit, dealing with common soldiers.

"Don't get distracted," Lissa said from a few meters over, and Carl once more thanked the gods she'd been assigned to guard those who maintained the barrier to the entrance. "You're our sniper."

"So the young lord has turned into a shadow monster," Carl said as he shot out a perfunctory arrow that pierced the skull of a pirate who'd taken out what looked like a rocket launcher.

"It would appear that way," Lissa said.

"And he's waving around an obviously cursed soul-trapping item like a madman."

"Seems to work for him."

"Promise me," Carl said as he looked at his smiling wife. "After this, no more."

"Well, maybe if I had a child to care for, I'd be less likely to take these large risks," Lissa said, eliciting a few laughs from the nearby Valkyries.

"I'll speak with the alchemists," Carl said, ignoring the teasing looks as he started shooting arrows with newfound vigor. "That's an assignment I'll finish even if I die trying."

"Well, first, we have to survive the next 20 months in this place," Lissa laughed as she disappeared. She'd skewered an invisible pirate who'd tried fleeing into the base a moment later.

"Twenty months," Carl muttered, knowing their budding reputation in this quadrant would get even more outrageous after this. "God help us."

---

The walls hummed, and Galau threw out a Six Directions Talisman that formed a cross in the air, creating a protective bubble around the group. Powerful undulations of runaway force scattered his thoughts once more. A moment later, he woke up on the ground with a painful burn on his leg from where the manacle held him in place.

Still not enough. The pulse could scramble their minds even when inside the protective sphere.

Galau grimaced as he bent down to unlock the constraints, but the vibration remained in his body. His fingers were that of a stranger's, and it took him almost a minute to free himself. By that point, the others had started to wake up, and Galau sighed when he saw a new set of cracks had appeared on Kaso, Bubbur, and the others.

"Don't look at us like that, shartermaster," Bubbur said with a weak grin. "It's a miracle we've survived until now. I would have joined the others already if not for your talismans."

"Still not enough," Galau muttered as he started recording. "Something off about the fourth trigram…"

"Sure, sure," Bubbur grimaced as he took out a canteen. "You'd have to be a real bastard to build a pulverization tower. Leave your enemies a body to bury, at least. And if you have to build them, make sure you shield the damn things, so you don't hit your own."

The others swore in agreement, some angrily glaring at the tower vaguely visible through the window. That particular one wasn't the weapon that had gone off just now, but Galau suspected there was one just like it that kept launching its deadly salvos from farther inside the base.

Ten minutes passed, and Galau was forced to put away his notebook. There were so many things to go over and too little time. Nullifying the collateral damage from the vibrational attacks was important, but so was breaking through the next door. The castle showed no indication of slowing down its frenzied war against an empty sky.

Sections as large as whole towns had collapsed already from the forced activation of the weapon batteries. Sooner or later, these sections would collapse. Before then, they needed to find the escape array that a base like this should possess. If that failed, at least turn off the weapons before they destroyed everything.

Since the pulverization tower had gone off, their window of opportunity had arrived. If the patterns held, they had an hour before the ring of fire would incinerate the sky. That one was easier to deal with, but they would still have to retreat to the underground to survive the heat. Before that, Galau wanted to crack open the next door.

Galau shook off the lingering effects of the attack as he walked over to the gate, and the soldiers expertly helped him dismantle the outer panels to display the array within. Everyone breathed out in relief. The recently added array spindles had survived the previous round of barrage. Yet Galau didn't immediately add the final piece to the puzzle.

"I might be wrong. These security measures are far more stringent than the outer doors," Galau muttered. "Maybe I should just head back to the other sealed chamber."

"No," Bubbur said. "Trust your instincts. If you go and get yourself dusted, we'll all die."

"That's right, that's right," Kaso added. "Besides, how can such a good thing fall into one's lap twice? You're already a Threadwinder of that Ultom thing. You said the other room felt different. I bet it's meant for someone else. Maybe someone with a handsome face."

"Well, that would explain why none of you got it," Galau muttered.

"That it would," Bubbur laughed. "It's better we stay the course and keep looking for the others. That explosion two months ago was definitely our munitions rather than the weaponry of this base. I bet they have the same idea as we do, but only you have managed to figure out a real plan."

Galau nodded, and he installed the last spindle. This one had six strings of revolving talismans, and it should short-circuit the door and its defenses if he understood the theories in the Scripture Hall right. If only it hadn't collapsed back then.

But it worked, and the door soundlessly slid open before its lights went out.

"Alright, who'll it be?" Bubbur said. "Draw lots?"

"Don't bother," Asho grunted as he stepped forward, his shield already fastened to the stump of his left arm. "I'll take this one."

"This…" Galau hesitated.

"Don't say anything," Bubbur said as they watched Asho warily enter the path. "Remember, we can die, but you cannot. This castle, those schematics that now only live on inside your head. Even that opportunity of yours. I have a feeling they might be the key to winning the war."

# FORCED DECISION

Sweat ran down Jaol's face, but he froze his nerves to keep his hands steady through the pain. The slightest mistake would cause the makeshift Disruptor to blow up in his face. He put his troubles aside as he engraved the detection array his vision overlay indicated. Even then, it wasn't easy. The further he was forced to progress under the Cursed Heavens, the worse his components worked. It wasn't long until he'd have to make a decision.

Either head back home or replace the rest of his components for flesh. Both paths felt insurmountable. He still didn't know why the bounty on his head was so grotesque. He only had a small part in the destruction of *Little Bean*, and that was under duress. Yet the government was willing to pay one hundred times its value for his capture.

Why?

It had to be that chimeral lunatic. That bastard who set his fate off-kilter. They rather wanted him, and Jaol had become a clue. However, there was no point in explaining that to the higher-ups. The AI Lawkeepers didn't make mistakes, they said. And since they said he was a terrorist, he obviously was one.

That left a biological respec, but where would he find a Grafter in these parts? There were more outcasts like him., but his status was just too low to get in contact with anyone who had the skills required for such a surgery. Besides, those who fled to these parts all had troublesome backgrounds. He'd probably end up an experiment even if he managed to scrounge up the Credits or Nexus Coins for the surgery.

Thirty seconds later, Jaol was done, and it wasn't a moment too soon. He could hear his pursuers close in through the bugs he'd planted. They still seemed to know his location, though only the general direction. Less than ten seconds. Jaol groaned as he got to his feet, and he hid the Disruptor behind some of the refuse lining the walls of this godforsaken excuse of a space station. Simultaneously, he linked it up with his other devices, finishing the chain.

A second later he was gone, running toward the Primarch Harbor. The Thearch Harbor was controlled by his old crew and the pirate alliance. There was no way he'd be able to get close enough to sneak aboard a vessel without being spotted. Eden Harbor would be better, but Jaol doubted he'd make it past the controlled sections of the city. Captain Redvine had too many contacts in this place.

Luckily, the streets were mostly empty these days, with the faraway sun being blocked by the broken world for the next few days. As such, the arrays covering New Eden had been turned off. There was no way the mayor would open his pockets to fuel the arrays when the star didn't. Here in the slum, that included the arrays meant to keep order.

The endless corridors blurred together as Jaol ran for his life. An explosion from behind confirmed his trap had been sprung, but an enraged roar indicated it hadn't been enough. He could only urge his legs on and pray the wound that almost bisected him didn't rip open any farther inside the makeshift tourniquet.

Raucous laughs and hollering taunts echoed through the streets from the temporary residences to his sides. Jaol didn't know whether they were laughing at his or his pursuers' misfortune. More importantly, were any of them willing to fish in muddy waters? Someone being pursued often meant there was money to be made, and the bigger fist made the rules in the slums of New Eden.

As expected, a few people appeared ahead, but activating [Flaming Geas] made them scurry out of the way. Few Class-3 cultivators made the slums their home, so the outburst of a Peak Class-2 was enough to scare away random opportunists. As for the Underworld leaders, they hopefully wouldn't insert themselves into this mess. Sometimes, it was better to stay out of trouble. You never knew what kind of deadly attention your actions could attract.

For example, how could Jaol have expected that a supposedly simple mission would end with him being hunted by Redvine, a terrifying Late Class-3 captain who'd terrorized the surrounding regions for over ten thousand years? It wasn't like Jaol had even wanted that thing, nor had he planned for the rest of the crew to turn to dust.

He'd be reasonably safe if he could travel a few quadrants. People like Redvine hadn't lasted so long by taking overdue risks. They stuck to their lane, seldom sailing into regions controlled by other Monarchs than their benefactors.

A sharp pull made Jaol fall over, and he groaned in agony as he slammed into the ground. His vision was going haywire from the synaptic overload, but he could vaguely see an energy leash locked around his ankle. And on the other end was Kalso, his face a furious mask of scorched skin.

"Bastard," Kalso swore as he stabbed his arm with a syringe full of healing serum. "You're lucky the captain wants you alive. You better pray you have something she needs, or I'll ask her to hand you back to me. I'll see how you do with one of those grenades shoved up your ass."

"I've told you I didn't steal any treasure," Jaol said as he scrambled to his feet. "You searched me over and over."

"There are all kinds of treasures," Kalso said. "Including ones in your head. We heard an interesting rumor lately. Of impressive bounties."

Jaol shuddered as he'd heard the very same rumor. Some newcomers to these quadrants paid huge premiums for the capture and delivery of individuals who had encountered a specific opportunity. Newcomers who rejected the Law of Balance, the kind of people who had given Technocrats such a bad reputation across the Cosmos. There was no way you'd have a good ending if handed over to the Kan'Tanu.

And the Redvine Pirates had figured it out.

It was over. Even if he had ten lives, he wouldn't be able to defeat Kalso, and he'd brought twenty helpers that had already caught up. Even if Jaol had been forced to partly embark on the martial path because of circumstance, he was ultimately a navigator. How was he supposed to defeat a Hegemon? Neither did he have the money to bribe them; Jaol was almost broke.

There was only one thing left to barter with, which was clearly valuable beyond the knowledge it imparted. Anything was better than the Unorthodox Path, so he could only take a shot in the dark.

"I AM A PLAINSWALKER OF ULTOM, HELP ME, AND I'LL JOIN YOUR CREW!" Jaol screamed at the top of his lungs, his voice echoing through the streets.

"What in the nine hells are you talking about? Ultom? Never heard of them, can't be anyone too impressive," Kalso laughed. "Should have figured someone like you were a spy. Too bad, this is Redvine's domain. Scream all you want. No one is coming to help you."

"I don't know about that," a snicker came from the distance.

Next, three hooded beings appeared as though out of nowhere, placing themselves between Jaol and Kalso.

"This will impact our plans," the smaller hooded one commented, her voice so soothing Jaol almost forgot his situation.

"We're just starting a bit early. It should be fine. No need to be too discerning on the way out. We can't just look the other way when a spare part appears in our lap, can we?" the owner of the original voice said before turning toward Jaol. "How about it, Plainswalker? Ready to join a new crew?"

"Yes, yes!" Jaol eagerly said, though the comment about spare parts was decidedly unsettling.

Whatever. Join today and run away tomorrow. He'd done it many times before over the past decade.

"I'm a skilled navigator, and I can—"

Jaol was interrupted by a lazy wave from the hooded man.

"Do you know who I am?" Kalso growled as a bloody aura started to spread through the whole neighborhood, to the point the nearby houses were completely drowned.

"Redvines, right?" the leader laughed as a ripple burst out from the lithe woman who'd spoken before.

Jaol looked on with incomprehension as the whole crew behind Kalso simply collapsed, their spirituality completely erased. They didn't even have a chance to pass on to the afterlife, either. A dozen wraiths were dragged out of their bodies before they flooded into the leader's sleeve. Jaol shuddered at the scene. These people were even scarier than the Redvine Pirates.

"You! Shadewar Armada!" Kalso said with a sharp breath before his body shattered.

A pained wail reached them not much later as the Hegemon reappeared a few hundred meters away, dragged down by four wraiths even more powerful than the ones that appeared before. His escape measure failed, Kalso desperately tried to fight them off, but his struggles met an abrupt end as the largest of the hooded ones threw out a spear that pierced his head.

"Wha—" Jaol said, a series of enormous explosions interrupting his line of thought. From the direction of Thearch Harbor.

"So, navigator, time to prove your worth," the necromancer laughed. "We'll be robbing some people today, and you'll be leading the way."

Jaol blankly looked at the four lunatics who dared rob a space station owned by a Monarch before a wave of déjà vu hit him. Wasn't this just like that time aboard the *Little Bean*? Jaol inwardly cried, wondering if another decade of suffering had arrived.

---

It was now or never.

Tavza was terrifyingly efficient. She wouldn't spend more than a few hours inside the Mystic Realm unless something unexpected cropped up, and it had already been 100 minutes. The moment she could confirm nothing was calling to her, Tavza would move on, no matter how valuable the realm appeared. No sense of adventure, that one. All eyes on the mission. This wasn't what cultivation should be like.

How was it even possible to make exploring a mysterious place like the Million Gates Territory boring?

More importantly, it was that utilitarian mindset that was pushing Catheya toward her inevitable doom. She couldn't be certain, but she'd felt a growing sense of wrongness over the past year. She'd always been the outsider in this group, but it was starting to feel like she was prey. And the reason was painfully obvious.

She'd become a sealbearer while only Tavza and two of her followers had gained similar access. It was a far cry from Tavza's envisioned army that would steamroll all resistance inside Ultom. She hadn't even managed to secure entry for her core squad of six followers, the elites who were meant to pave the path for her inside the inheritance.

Meanwhile, a ticket was just sitting there. On an outsider who hadn't even reached Hegemony, at that. That'd been a tenuous, albeit manageable, situation at the beginning. Her value as liaison to Arcaz Black still held some sway. But it all changed yesterday when they seized the Kan'-Tanu vessel. They'd found a captured sealbearer in the brig, and Tavza had finally managed to confirm her theory.

Killing a sealbearer transferred the seal, though without that marvelous burst of inspiration that came with it. No longer was she a risky venture. One slash across her throat, and Tavza's next-in-line was guaranteed to become a Threadwinder.

Catheya had no faith in the commandments at a time like this. Nothing was absolute. Catheya wasn't even sure the commandments would protect her, considering Tavza had been given a mission of utmost importance to the Empire. What did it matter if the vaunted An'Azol killed a few juniors if it improved the Empire's chances of accomplishing their goals inside the Left Imperial Palace?

Neither was her relation to Arcaz much use here in the Million Gates Territory. Anything could happen in this lawless place. How would Arcaz know whether she was sacrificed or died looking for opportunities? At best, she'd become a warning to take precautions against betrayal, but what good was that to her when she'd passed on to the great beyond?

She didn't have a danger sense powerful enough to warn when fate was moving against her, but she did have a nose for trouble. If not for the fact that a batch of Kan'Tanu elites had entered the small realm ahead of Tavza, Catheya might already have found herself at the sharp end of her sword. She needed to be gone before it was time's up.

If she managed to activate the token, all would be fine. She would be whisked away to the Perennial Vastness, where Tavza couldn't reach her. She could tell Arcaz about her situation, and he would put pressure on Tavza's elders. Having Arcaz and his sealbearers as enemies should outweigh the benefits of having another minor sealbearer on their side. At least she hoped that was how it'd play out.

Going this route would further damage her standing within the

Empire, but it was better than being a sacrificial lamb. Besides, she still had the Umbri'Zi. It was thanks to Enis's surreptitious warning that Catheya managed to hide away the token before Tavza arrived back then. When they confiscated her Spatial Tools under the guise of their mission being Top Secret. Saying that her items might be bugged or marked, and that nothing could go wrong.

But who would have thought the Heavenblighted token didn't work inside the Million Gates Territory?

Twice she'd tried activating it, but it just hummed a bit before dying down. The most likely reason was that space was too unstable here in the Million Gates Territory. Such was life on the frontier. Nothing worked as it should. It was nothing short of a miracle that someone like Zachary Atwood appeared in a place like this.

The solution was both simple and difficult. She needed to leave the Million Gates Territory, or at least reach its edges where space was more stable. Luckily, they weren't that far by this point, thanks to the agreement with Arcaz. Besides, Tavza's brutal pace had cost them two vessels and most of their personnel, and she had to return and resupply in either case.

Crossing just the final stretch alone would still be difficult, but Catheya had no choice. She lay unmoving in the infirmary's healing vat, her eyes never leaving the information array that tracked the surrounding spatial phenomena. Ten minutes later, it happened. It was time.

Catheya rose from the tank, the physician-turned-warden immobilized by a gust of utter cold before they had a chance to react. The frozen Draugr soon took Catheya's place, getting a nice bath. She would probably thaw out in an hour, and the tank would prevent any lasting damage. Catheya donned the physician's clothes before leaving the infirmary.

Unfortunately, she'd lost her mask, but a small layer of ice adjusted her features enough to pass a cursory glance. Especially when her hair mostly hid her features as she looked down at a random report she'd lifted from a table.

She slightly nodded at the guard outside, relaxing upon seeing him barely sparing her a glance. He was in the middle of his cultivation cycle, a dereliction of duty you'd only see when Tavza wasn't aboard. Catheya didn't immediately head for the Kan'Tanu vessel docked to their own. First, she entered a series of rooms and compartments, embedding Miasma Crystals while freezing certain sections solid.

It only took ten minutes, yet it felt like an eternity. Every small shudder to the vessel made her think of the gates to the hangar opening, but she still completed the preparations she'd planned over the past year. A single spot missing, and her plan would fail. Catheya considered visiting Tavza's compartments as well to hopefully find her Spatial Ring. Ultimately, she decided against it.

It was too big a risk, and Catheya didn't even know if her things were there. Instead, she walked over to the upper deck, her steps excruciatingly slow so as not to draw any unwarranted attention. Luckily, only two wholly unimpressive Hegemons stood guard. Thank the Heavens for the theory that bringing too-powerful followers would weaken any chances of finding seals.

"Doctor Ynsa? Wait, no, what's go—" the guard said, but he didn't get any further before a wave of frigid cold swept forward, locking the two early Hegemons in place.

With their energy reserves, they would manage to free themselves in less than a minute. A minute was all Catheya needed as she flashed through the temporary corridor that connected the two vessels. Utmost cold followed in her wake, and the whole pathway shattered before the guards could thaw.

Time was of the essence, and she became a streak of ice that zigzagged through the corridors until she reached the bridge. The two guards standing outside were frozen before they could react, and Catheya crashed through the door a moment later. Inside were three badly startled researchers who seemed to be reviewing various readouts.

"Hurry! Activate the propulsion. They're getting away!" Catheya screamed as she entered like a hurricane.

"Wha? Who—" a shocked Revenant blurted and was promptly awarded a slap.

"NOW!" Catheya roared, and the three veritably threw themselves at the controls.

Just a second later, the familiar hum of a Cosmic Engine roaring to life was followed by the shudder of the anchors breaking off. In just a second, the ship moved hundreds of meters and was already outside reach for the skeleton crew that remained on the Empire ship. That didn't mean she was safe just yet.

"South-southwest, the spatial window!" Catheya urged and saw the one she slapped dutifully input the coordinates.

However, Catheya frowned at the other two, who shared a glance as their fingers moved toward an unfamiliar console. The next moment, they were frozen solid, leaving a lone researcher looking at Catheya with horror.

"I'm sorry, my friend, but it looks like we are going on a journey together," Catheya smiled.

A sudden shockwave threw the man to the ground, but Catheya grinned as she tapped a few buttons, prompting a screen to appear. The Imperial Venator was slowly spinning as it moved away from the spatial gate, shrapnel from its broken engine forming a shimmering trail.

*That's what you get for shutting me out from all the meetings and training sessions, Catheya inwardly scoffed.*

It had given her ample time to wander about and figure out the fault lines of the ships. The ship was doomed the moment the crew activated the engines to move in pursuit. Her preparations created a few energy blockages, and the release valves were frozen. Had they just waited another ten minutes, they would have been fine. Now they'd need at least a week for repairs.

By then, Catheya would be long gone.

"Is everything alright?" Ilvere asked as he cautiously looked around.

"Looks like it," Zac said, not without some surprise.

The previous two times he'd absorbed a part of the seal, he ended up ripping a hole in the fabric of space. This time, nothing of the sort happened after the initial shockwave. It was possible the previous outbursts were because he'd picked up the pieces inside the Void Star, where space was far more fragile.

"How did it go?" Ilvere asked curiously. "Did you accomplish what-ever you set out for in there?"

"Something like that." Zac only nodded, hiding the complex feelings in his heart.

Difficult. Too, too difficult.

Over six years of relentless work. The lake water had been completely used up two years ago, but his studies hadn't stopped there. On the contrary, they'd taken up more and more of his time. The Book of Duality was not only completely deciphered but also expanded upon with an eighth and ninth chapter. Tens of thousands of models, hundreds of thousands of patterns simulated.

Only to learn the path he'd originally envisioned was a dead end. Zac shook his head, looking out across the odd army. There were two hundred warriors, each sitting atop a mantis-like Ayn ant. In addition, there were another hundred brutish-looking Ayn meat shields ready to take on the role of Vanguard.

"How did these guys do?" Zac asked.

"Well, they can stand around, at least, I can tell you that," Ilvere said with some bemusement. "Sometimes I almost forget they're real ants and not statues."

"They have no desires," Lily said as she caressed her Ayn mount. "These are pure warriors who take commands from the queen. Or, well, me. You can pretty much consider them machines."

"Still might be a good idea to bloody them," Ilvere muttered. "We use Barghest for a similar purpose back home, but some of the blood-lines are simply no good. They'd go out of control when the blood and killing intent in the air reached a certain point, especially those without direct contracts. They'd turn around and attack their controllers. Beasts usually have an inborn ferocity, after all."

"These guys won't do that," Lily assured.

"I believe you, lass," Ilvere said. "But it's still worth testing out."

"Can you take them for some actual battle after this?" Zac asked.

"Of course."

Zac nodded and turned to Janos. "Did you feel anything?"

"No," Janos curtly said before settling his almost vacant gaze on the ruins around them.

"Don't mind him," Ilvere said with a grin. "He's just trying to figure out something in that world of his. And don't worry. We'll stay here for a while and check things out in case there's a delayed reaction. The erup-tion after you entered might have disrupted some of the remaining seals, so this could be an opportunity. We'll test these ants afterward."

"That's fine," Zac said as he gave the illusionist a helpless look.

Zac could barely believe his ears upon hearing that Janos had come walking out of the Ensolus Ruins a year ago. Zac had even cracked open the last ruin with the markings of the Left Imperial Palace to make sure the illusionist wasn't trapped, but he wasn't there.

Even today, Zac didn't quite understand where Janos had gone, partly because he'd turned even more laconic during his opportunity. From the sounds of it, he'd physically entered a crumbling, ancient illusion created by the Limitless Empire. It had taken him over two years just to realize he was trapped and another five to get out. However, those years weren't spent in vain.

Janos' illusions were terrifying by this point, and even Zac had trouble escaping them in short order. He'd also learned an incredibly odd technique, where he created an imaginary world in his mind. Janos could bring things out from that illusion, and they fought as though they were real. The downside to the technique was that it seemed to require huge amounts of his mind power, leaving him with one foot in reality and one foot in his own world.

More importantly, Janos was now a Realmsinger of Ultom.

Most likely, Janos had been counted as part of his posse since Zac first got his hand on the quest. Just like Ogras got a quest in the Ra'Lashar Ruins, Janos got a quest the moment he realized he was trapped in an illusion. That quest ultimately allowed him to find a piece of the Mercurial Court.

Janos was one of the first to become part of his cycle, but he wasn't the only one. Zac hadn't heard back from Catheya or Ogras since they ventured into the depths of the Million Gates Territory, but he at least had a way to keep track of Ogras. Just over a year after they set out, Zac's quest updated to 6/9 in one go.

Since then, it'd been updated twice until it reached 8/9 three months ago. However, Zac suspected this was due to their deadline to return being just two months away. It would have been great if his quest had filled up before leaving for the Perennial Vastness, but the progress was ultimately better than Zac expected.

They made such progress by sailing through the Million Gates Territory. With the war starting in 15 months, Zac suspected they'd have ample opportunities to complete the cycle, perhaps even finish a second one.

"Let me know if you find something interesting. I'm heading back," Zac said before heading toward the settlement outside.

Two hours later, he was back on Earth, and Zac sighed as he stepped into his cultivation cave. Thank God his time in this place was coming to an end. He still felt it rewarding to practice the various aspects of his cultivation, but he could really use a change of pace. Ultimately, he was a cultivator walking the Path of Conflict. Caves and seclusion weren't the optimal way for him to progress.

Of course, some things couldn't be skipped just because he wanted to go out on capers like Ogras and the others. Like Iz had said, the foundation was the most important. Certain improvements in the E-grade could create a ripple effect of positive outcomes lasting all the way to the peak.

He'd ignored the call for adventure and studiously continued tempering himself and shoring up his foundations. His years in the Time Chamber weren't any different. The treasure had essentially created a bubble roughly fifty meters across, where the world outside was frozen in place.

By the time the Time Chamber ran out of juice, Zac knew the trees in his cultivation cave so well that he could recite how many leaves they had without pause. He'd emerged a new person, having pushed his Soul and Constitution to new heights. Now, there was just one step that remained.

Zac reached his prayer mat, and kept going until reaching the opposite edge of the cave, where he entered the most recent addition to his subterranean complex. The gate slid open, and Zac was greeted by a scene that had become incredibly familiar over the past years.

Thousands of paintings, schematics, statues, and contraptions filled a vast hall. Some were over five meters tall. Others were no larger than eggs and placed on pedestals so as not to disappear. The first item that greeted him upon entering was the crude diagram he made based on his insights inside Yrial's trial.

Coming back from the enlightenment of Ultom, it was almost like he was seeing the schematic for the first time, and Zac stopped for a moment to inspect it. Zac shook his head with a slight smile. It wasn't even worthy of forming a basic skill, so riddled with issues and misunderstandings. But it didn't matter. Albeit a stumbling one, it was the first step that had started his journey of discovery.

Zac passed the blueprint and continued deeper into the cave. When he first opened this inner sanctum, there'd only been a straight corridor that grew increasingly longer. But after emerging from the Time Chamber, he'd been forced to redesign the room. Now, the path was a huge spiral, and Zac was slowly making his way toward the center.

The first 100 blueprints were both similar in shape and nature. They were all drawn on circular disks, mirroring the concept of the first one. Life to the left, Death to the right, transforming as they moved toward the center. Yin and Yang, light and dark. Each blueprint was far more refined compared to the one before it.

Progress had been easy in the beginning, when he was still on the fifth chapter of the **[Book of Duality]**, and he was just scratching the surface. Even then, some things cannot be bridged with hard work. This type of straightforward core was most likely impossible. Even today, Zac had no solution. Its fundamental concept was flawed, or it required a Dao that far surpassed what was possible in the D-grade.

As such, the blueprints started to change after Zac walked a third through the outermost spiral. He'd added another source of inspiration— his Duplicity Core.

The more Zac learned about Duality and the underpinning rules of Cosmic Energy and Attunement, the more Zac realized how magical the Duplicity Core his mother's clan had created was. He'd become half-Draugr by accident, yet it accommodated this change without issue. It seemingly could encompass all Daos.

However, Zac eventually realized that he couldn't base his Cosmic Core on the ideas of his Duplicity Core either. It ultimately didn't contain the concept of Duality, even if it looked like it. The Specialty Core was a container, an unfathomable solution to split a single person into two. Its underpinning rule was that the two were kept completely separate while one nurtured the other, most likely because the Kayar-Elu had planned for his other half to be mechanized.

And that was not Duality. It'd taken some time for Zac to reach this conclusion, with each following iteration of the blueprints tarrying the echoes of his Duplicity Core. It would be a few hundred meters before that changed. Each step was like retracing his cultivation journey. What once felt like strokes of genius were now riddled with errors.

Yet, they were the foundation of where he was today. Even reaching a dead end was an important lesson, leaving you better off as you righted the ship. As Zac continued down the path, the patterns grew increasingly complex.

There was a clear demarcation where he'd mastered the sixth chapter of the **[Book of Duality]**. The patterns became denser, and new sections were added, all in an attempt to cross that seemingly unbridgeable gap between Life and Death. It hadn't worked, even when the patterns reached a point where they were tens of times more complex than conventional Cultivator's Cores.

The ample reserves of lake water had given him a deeper foundation in the subject than almost any centennial in the Multiverse, yet he hadn't managed to find the solution. By the time he'd mastered the final chapter, Zac realized he'd been walking in circles. It wouldn't help, no matter how many sections, arrays, and frameworks were added to the blueprint.

From there, he'd continued into uncharted territory, focusing on the specific interactions between Life and Death and their flavor of Duality. Luckily, he still retained a third of his lake water by that point, allowing him to walk a bit farther. And halfway into the spiral, there was a change.

From complexity came simplicity, where more was expressed with less. The change was small and subtle, but it was there. Gradually, the patterns were refined while also better representing his Trinity Path. Conflict was still the glue that would bind together and contain Life and Death, but he'd realized it wasn't enough.

Zac shook his head, a smile tugging at his mouth. In a way, he'd been walking in a circle, both metaphorically and literally. He was now over two-thirds into the spiral, yet he had come to the very same conclusion as the day he learned of blueprints. No matter how you looked at it, there simply wasn't a theoretical foundation to create something lasting and stable with these three Daos, at least not while retaining his path.

Life was Life; Death was Death. Forever separate. That was the conclusion he'd arrived at inside the Twilight Ocean.

Back inside the Inheritance Trial, he'd understood his crude creation might allow him to create a powerful skill that would unleash unmatched destruction. But to build a core would end up with him exploding. And after five years of effort, he arrived at the same roadblock. Of course, this time, it was with a scholar's understanding of *why* it didn't work.

It was the difference between knowing the sun would rise the next day and knowing how and why it would do so. And it was at this point he ran out of lake water. No more were there any easily-accessible insights. Every step of progress had been fought for with blood, sweat, and tears. Thankfully, his foundations and theoretical knowledge were terrifyingly stable by that point, so he had the tools to continue down the path on his own.

Zac set out to solve the equation by adding something without damaging or altering his path. For a while, he experimented with centrifugal force. Zac suspected he couldn't rely on the static Cosmic

Core most used. Because conflict wasn't a glue. It was a matchbook and gasoline. There was no such thing as an eternal and unchanging war. Even his Inexorable Path continuously adapted to seal and suffocate the enemy.

Zac figured he needed a core that automatically and perpetually rotated the energy. This was nothing unusual on its own, being an established high-tier concept for Cosmic Cores. Their storage capacity was worse than equally high-tier static models, but they were good for energy transmission. The experiment lasted for over two hundred blueprints before it was discarded for being too unstable.

Between the inward pressure from the vortex and the agitation of conflict, he couldn't create a safe system that would work for energy storage. It was like his Soul Strengthening Methods. The ferocious storms were fine for short durations where he could temper his cores, but it wasn't a sustainable state to maintain indefinitely.

Just creating two sealed off chambers of Life and Death with his Branch of the War Axe in the middle wouldn't work. Not only would it halve his energy capacity, but it would be just as unstable as the vortex core. The moment he'd try to extract any significant amount of either Divine Energy or Miasma, a resonance would naturally form, and balance would be disrupted.

One idea after another was discarded in this way. This was where Zac started to worry for real that he'd taken on a project beyond his abilities. Perhaps beyond the realms of possibility. The only solution he could think of was to create two separate cores, even if all missives said it was impossible. One Evolutionary Core that would be connected to his human pathways and one Inexorable Core that fueled the other.

Unfortunately, the [Book of Duality] said this was a fundamental impossibility, and not for lack of people trying. Who wouldn't want an extra Cosmic Core to double their energy reserves? No matter if it was creating two identical cores or complimentary ones, it simply didn't seem to be something you could do.

Ultimately, Zac was forced to reach out for clarification to the only one who might know the truth—Iz. The two plushies had almost collapsed by the transference of the promised Life-attuned array disks, but they still had some lingering power left. Zac had sent a message asking if his idea was even possible, along with his thoughts and theories. He received a one-sentence answer in return.

*Outside the scope of this Heaven.*

Iz hadn't said it was *impossible*, but her answer wasn't much better. No cores or multiple cores weren't possibilities within the system of cultivation that existed in the Era of Order. Even if you somehow succeeded and broke past the boundaries of the era, you'd be disconnected from the natural path of progression. It was just like the Earth Immortals Iz mentioned.

Zac didn't have any Supremacy to push away reality while he embarked on a path of a previous Heaven, and neither did he have the fundamental qualifications to forge a completely new approach to cultivation. Forming a Life-Death core was incredibly difficult, but creating two cores was even more farfetched.

Dark clouds were gathering, yet Zac hadn't stopped or let the task shake his conviction. Luckily, he was far ahead of schedule on both Soul and Constitution, allowing him to focus fully on his blueprint alone. He tried everything he could come up with, to the point he spent every waking moment theorizing, simulating, and engraving.

Yet the patterns grew increasingly similar as Zac walked the final stretch of the spiral, even if the expressions became more diverse. Ultimately, he'd exhausted everything he could think of. There was simply no path forward. He only managed to come up with a few wild ideas that may or may not work, crazy last-ditch efforts that were far more likely to end in disaster. And then, the blueprints ended as Zac reached the center.

Six years of constant work had gone into this room. And these were just his finest creations, the ones that Zac felt worthy of entering his museum of failure. Because that was what this place was. In total, there were 3,412 attempts at creating a Life-Death core lining the path to the center. In total, there were 3,412 failures.

Every day, he'd made multiple attempts at drawing, carving, sculpting, or chiseling an array. Every single day, he ended up with a defective product. Since he was well and truly stuck, having the theoretical knowledge but lacking the inspiration, Zac turned to the one chance remaining.

Ultom. It was a few months earlier than planned, but what could you do? Zac had exhausted all his venues. Unfortunately, the moment the light of clarity entered his body, he was instantly met with an inescapable truth. Cores with both Pure Life and Pure Death were simply impossible to form without also controlling Chaos. It was no wonder the Undead Empire wanted to erase his human side.

Conflict couldn't solve that insolvable equation. It could only make the fallout more volatile. Zac had almost given in to despair right then and there, but in the next moment, Ultom shone a light in the darkness. A weak, flickering light, but it was there. A possibility that perfectly toed the line between genius and madness.

A path only open to a Void Emperor.

# NEITHER AND BOTH

The impartment of Ultom was unequivocal in its message. He couldn't
fuse Life and Death in one core, and he couldn't use two cores. Meaning,
he would do neither and he would do both.

The end of the spiral led to a small empty square, no more than ten
meters across. It symbolized the destination of the journey he'd taken
over the past years. It was here he would place his final blueprint, the
one that encompassed his path without being a paradox. And it was
finally time to create it.

Zac stood in the middle of his museum for over an hour, stabilizing
his mind while recollecting the solution he'd seen in the light of Ultom.
When Zac's soul was completely calm, and his heart was steady, he took
out a table, a chair, and a piece of white marble as large as his torso.
Next to it, he took out a stack of papers with hastily scribbled notes.

Some of the concepts that went into his idea were too complex, and
Zac had been afraid he'd forget them over time as he had after some of
his other epiphanies. Everything from feelings to step-by-step construction had been written down, but Zac didn't feel they were necessary. The
core was so tangible and detailed in his mind that it might as well be
real.

Zac opted to use a sculpture to represent his path this time. A simple
disk wouldn't be enough. He'd have to work with all three dimensions to
even get a slightly accurate representation of his plan.

One of his artisan axes chiseled away most of the marble until what remained was an almost perfect sphere. With a Dao-empowered swing, the ball was perfectly cut into two, and Zac put one of the halves aside before turning his attention to the other. He swapped out his axe for a finer one and began engraving a series of patterns on the sphere.

The outermost layer of patterns were no more than a finger deep, and individual patterns were so small they were a tenth the width and height. A normal human would barely be able to make out the runes, yet each represented whole sets of fractals. Sometimes hundreds. The edge of the small axe moved with extreme precision, guided by experience and the Dao.

Years had passed since he completed the first layer of the [Thousand Lights Avatar], which allowed him to freely and naturally instill his body with the Dao. Just as he and Pavina theorized all those years ago, it provided noticeable benefits to his technique. Not only that, it proved useful in all kinds of scenarios, even carving blueprints.

Since [Thousand Lights Avatar] had been practical beyond expectation, from channeling Daos into skills to improving his connection to his techniques, he'd kept cultivating it whenever he had time. And with the Moss Crystal's incredibly pure source of spirituality, he'd already completed the second layer.

Today, his whole body was covered by a secondary soul instead of just having a skeleton framework. It was still mostly hollow, though. Even with a second Moss Crystal he'd arduously bartered from Mossy, in exchange for enormous attunement traps in space and mountains of Nexus Crystals, it would take years to fully flesh out the budding avatar.

For better or worse, Mossy realized its crystals were incredibly useful to things outside their one-ness, and they actively started working on creating more. With Zac's attunement traps siphoning off all attuned energy to create Divine and Miasma Crystals, Mossy had more energy left over for that. The only problem was that the moss entity became noticeably smarter every time they conversed, though Zac had ultimately decided to take the risk.

Mossy's Crystals were simply too magical, no matter if it were for himself or other Mentalists like Vilari. Soul Cultivation was an incredibly powerful path, and most cultivators' defenses were on the weaker side against mental attacks. Problem was, Mentalists just took too much time to nurture. With Mossy providing crystals to the elites of the Atwood Empire, that weakness would be shored up.

The effects of the soul avatar were palpable, even if it wasn't fully fleshed out yet. It was like the Heavens themselves were guiding Zac's hand as one pattern after another appeared with blazing speed. Not even the laser cutters of Old Earth would be able to compare to the precision or pace Zac added engravings to the half-sphere.

In just a few minutes, the whole outer core was covered in dense scripts that emitted the familiar aura of the Evolutionary Cores he'd created over the past years. However, there were some differences here and there, so subtle Zac doubted any outsiders would spot them. They didn't change much by themselves, but that was just the start.

Zac carefully flipped over the half-sphere and continued engraving. He began at the middle, released a small engraved nucleus from the center, and put it aside. From there, Zac removed a layer of marble before carving a set of runes, both familiar and foreign. More than the runes on the outside, they reminded Zac of the seals in his **[Void Vajra Sublimation]**.

The whole inner pattern was carved, Zac then cut it out of the sphere, hollowing it even further. That section was placed aside with the nucleus, and three more layers eventually joined it. By that time, only the outer shell of the half-sphere remained, and Zac carefully put the five layers he'd carved back.

Each piece perfectly fit into the whole, creating an almost dizzying array of patterns. Zac studied the result with satisfaction. This was one of the most intricate designs he'd ever brought forth from his mind into reality, and it pushed his artisanal skills to the limits.

Zac spent the next thirty minutes studying the runes, confirming they really were a perfect representation of the core in his mind. As far as he could tell, the runes were all as they should be. Truthfully, he mostly relied on Ultom for a good chunk of the patterns within the sphere. After all, half of the patterns were a fusion of Conflict and the Void of Life rather than the Dao of Life, and that was mostly uncharted territory for him.

Since nothing was wrong, Zac placed a talisman on the half-sphere. With a small shudder, the six layers fused back together without needing any type of glue. With that, the first piece was complete, and Zac continued the same process on the other half before pushing the two back together.

Another talisman was placed on the cut, and the two pieces fused like they'd never been apart. Left behind was a single sphere with six layers of runes, including a nucleus, intricately connected in a way that created echoes of his path.

It was already lightyears ahead of his other designs, yet it was incomplete. Hollow. Moreover, it looked completely erratic from most vantage points, to the point it didn't even resemble a real blueprint. But that didn't mean he'd failed. It simply meant he hadn't finished the core yet.

Zac placed the white sphere to the side before sending a nudge into his Specialty Core, letting Miasma spread through his body. The second part would be best carved in his Draugr form. After four hours, a second core joined the first. This one was made from black marble instead of white, and its patterns were unsurprisingly those of Death and Conflict. And like with the first core, it both felt complete and defective.

Only from one direction could Zac see the inexorability of his path. The other sides were bedlam, chaos that made no sense. This core was even more alien than the first. Half of its patterns were created with the Void of Death and fused with his Dao of Conflict in ways that would be foreign to anyone whose understanding was limited to the Apostate of Order's fractal framework.

Zac already had some understanding of the Void of Life and how it affected his Dao after years of practicing his **|Void Vajra Sublimation|**, but he didn't have the same experience with the Void of Death. Zac suspected that would have to change going forward. Thankfully, Zac could extrapolate the connections through his understanding of Life, for now at least. So he somewhat understood the goal of the patterns.

The two orbs were placed on separate pedestals right in the middle of the spiral, with only a hands gap between them. They looked like two broken moons next to each other, hinting at something greater that seemed irrevocably lost. It even looked like he'd added unnecessary strokes and filler paths that served no real purpose.

But it was all a matter of vantage.

Zac slowly walked around the installation until Death was completely hidden by Life. There, the view was completely different. It was like everything clicked into place. The previously incomplete or unnecessary additions to the core were suddenly perfect, thanks to the juxtaposition of the core behind.

The Void of Death nurtured and completed the Evolutionary Core from within, just like the threat of death was the driving force for struggle in the wild. Similarly, the Void of Life completed the Inexorable Core on the other side. Without life, there could be no death. It was an Evolutionary Core. It was an Inexorable Core. It was neither and both.

A Quantum Core to contain his Trinity Path, made possible by Void and grasping for Chaos.

In truth, the core wasn't two separate things, not really. It was impossible to engrave the concepts onto stone properly, so he was forced to take a shortcut. When it came to the real thing, it would be a single core with two states of existence.

When he was in his human form, the core would look like it did from the vantage of the white marble sphere: Life, Conflict, Void of Death. They didn't actually clash in this case. The Void of Dao acted as a hidden booster, enkindling his path and stabilizing it. Life from the absence of Death, one could say.

When Draugr, the Cosmic Core would be in its other state, where Death and Conflict were supported by Void of Life.

It looked simple when he moved back and forth between the two sides. In reality, it was incredibly complex, deviating from anything Zac had seen. Even if he had 100 years, he would probably never have figured out these patterns. They relied on the concept of Void, which was mostly unexplored, and for a good reason.

To have an affinity to a Dao meant not having affinity to the Void of that Dao. No cultivator of Life would ever touch upon the Void of Life. He, as the Void Emperor, was possibly the sole exception in the Multiverse, which opened a door that was closed for everyone else.

And that still wasn't enough to make this impossible core possible. The Kayar-Elu had created something equally impossible when creating his core and the [Quantum Gate]. His body was in two states simultaneously, like two sides of a coin. As Zac was right now, he wouldn't have been able to stably create this Trinity Core without the assistance of these impartments. His Technocrat inheritance was the key that would trigger its two states.

Zac couldn't be sure, but he guessed this was the first and the last core of this type that would ever exist under the Heavens. Not because it was the most complex one ever created, but because of its impossible requirements. A paradoxical core for a paradoxical person.

Zac was filled with a sense of release. Years of toiling had led to this, and the result was exactly what he'd hoped for. Even after looking over the schematic, he couldn't find a single mistake. Should Zac manage to create this thing, it would at least become a Middle-quality Cosmic Core.

It didn't sound like much, especially in the face of the claims that the Perennial Vastness could help cultivators form Peak-quality Cores that would remove most of the bottlenecks of Hegemony. Ultimately, that was only true for normal elites with simple and unimpressive paths.

The heavier one's foundations, the more difficult it was to form a High-quality core. The same was true for the complexity of your path. Even Iz only aimed for a High-quality Cosmic Core with her backing. For Zac to expect a Peak-quality Core right out of the gate was a fool's hope. Still, managing to form a Middle-quality core, Zac's short-term goals would be met.

Hegemony was similar to the E-grade in that it was divided into Early, Middle, Late, and Peak. But while the E-grade had 75 minor bottlenecks, D-grade had three major ones. After breaking through, you'd have an Early-stage Cosmic Core, which would last you until the first bottleneck at level 175. At that point, you would have to upgrade your core, which was risky and difficult.

A failed attempt would damage and lower the quality of your core, which could waste centuries of cultivation. If you really messed up, you could destroy your core altogether and cripple your cultivation. But if you succeeded, you would break through to Middle D-grade.

Upgrading your core from Early to Middle-stage came with all kinds of benefits. First of all, your level limit would increase by another 25 levels, where each level provided more attributes than the Early-stage. With a Middle-stage core, you'd also be able to store and transmit far more Cosmic Energy, giving a huge advantage in combat since it could both power stronger War Regalia and skills.

For many, the true prize of breaking through was something else. Longevity. Your lifespan was more related to your core than your race in the D-grade. There were no pills for a quick breakthrough. Your race would reach C-grade upon passing the final bottleneck, upgrading a Late-stage Cosmic Core to Peak.

Each breakthrough before then would also add roughly ten thousand years of lifespan, far more than any Longevity Treasures could provide. Even those with no hopes of Monarchy or even later stages of D-grade desperately wanted to upgrade their cores at least one stage for this reason. But it was easier said than done.

The fundamental requirement to pass each bottleneck was the quality of your core. If you managed to form a Middle-quality Cosmic Core from the get-go, you had the qualifications to assault the first bottleneck the moment you were level-capped. If not, you would have to slowly work on the quality of your Cosmic Core until you were ready.

Cultivators could use their manuals to accomplish this. A Middle-quality D-grade Cultivation Manual could gradually refine compatible cores to Middle-quality without any risk, though it took centuries to millennia of cultivation. Mortals such as himself didn't have that luxury. They needed to use treasures or risk everything by simultaneously upgrading the stage and quality.

Zac wasn't confident about reaching Late Hegemony before Ultom, even with the opportunities provided by the sanctioned war. Breaking through didn't only require your core to have reached the minimum quality, you also needed foundations and accumulations. For someone like him, he'd most likely need to upgrade his branches to Earthly Daos to act as the foundations for a Late-stage Cosmic Core. To reach that point in 3 years was simply too difficult.

But Zac felt the peak of Middle Hegemony doable, even if it would be incredibly difficult. The levels would be easy. Between pills and endless enemies during the war, he was confident in gaining levels quickly. There was no real bottleneck between levels either.

Normal Hegemons who entered D-grade with imperfect cores, either from relying on treasures or lacking understanding of their Daos, would find themselves unable to gain any levels before fixing the mistakes. But with a Cosmic Core perfectly aligned with his path and vetted by the wisdom of Ultom, Zac expected he'd be able to rush through the levels without any issues.

Of course, reaching that level didn't mean he would be invincible. Having spoken with Iz and Catheya, Zac was certain the top geniuses would be Late D-grade with at least one Earthly Dao. However, with his unique situation and various advantages, he wouldn't be like a fish on the chopping block.

Even if winning was hard to impossible, he should be able to make himself unpalatable enough to target that it wasn't worth the effort messing with him.

Zac shook his head, his abyssal gaze turning back to the two spheres. These matters were all problems for the future. The first step was to actually create this impossible core. In reality, the process would be far harder than chiseling two marble blocks. The real thing was a single core, meaning he had to craft both sides simultaneously.

In other words, he would have to keep swapping back and forth between each side while forming the core. Because if he added too much in one of the two states without the other side to balance it out, the core would collapse. He would walk the tightrope for who knew how long if he wanted to create something like this.

Zac wouldn't be surprised even if the process took years to complete. Years where a single slip of concentration would spell his doom. But if that was what it took, so be it. Zac was ready to meet the challenge to prove his path. A token with the rune for "Vast" appeared in his hand, and a smile spread across his face.

Not much longer now.

# RETURN

Zac spent another hour looking at the cores before stowing them away in two boxes. Even if the center of the museum were where they belonged, he didn't want to risk them being damaged or destroyed. He'd carry them with him, at least until he created the real thing. He left the inner sanctum and found Triv waiting just outside.

The ghost looked almost exactly like a posh Revenant butler by this point, though he was still translucent. His soul had benefited immensely over the past years thanks to the Eidolon Cultivation Manuals. As such, he gained better control over his previously slightly ill-defined form and had chosen an appearance more in line with Zac and the rest of the undead population.

"I'm sorry to interrupt your cultivation, lord," Triv said with a bow. "But I believe you would want to hear this."

"They're back?" Zac asked with excitement.

"Alas, Lady Vilari and the others have not yet returned, but another one has," Triv said. "Your little disciple."

"Emily?" Zac exclaimed, the matter of his core almost completely forgotten already. "Where is she?"

"She just arrived in your compound."

"Thank you, Triv," Zac nodded before disappearing.

A moment later, Zac stepped out from the teleporter to a both familiar and foreign scene. As his cultivation sessions intensified, he'd spent less and less time here. The few times he'd taken a break to clear his head, he mostly traveled off-world to satiate his boredom and somewhat quench his growing desire for adventure. But for a moment, Zac felt he was back in that first year of the Integration as he found Emily standing there, waiting for him.

It'd been so long. For him, it was over 15 years since he saw his disciple, and it had almost been as long for her. Zac had worried for her a lot over the past years since there was no news forthcoming from the Big Axe Coliseum. He'd even asked his new allies from the Allbright Clan to keep a lookout in the Million Gates Territory and put some pressure on the leaders of the coliseum to find out what was going on.

She was so young when she left, and almost half of her life had been spent off-world honing herself. Unsurprisingly, Emily had changed a lot since Zac saw her last. She no longer looked like a feral child decked in warpaint and animal furs. Instead, she'd grown into a young woman just a head shorter than him. Her build had filled out a bit, even if she would be considered skinny compared to someone like Zac or Qirai.

There was no sense of frailty to that thin frame. A palpable feeling of danger emanated from her, like there was a storm trapped within her body. Her gear looked quite odd, a patchwork of strips of bright leather armor. She was a splash of color to his compound's tranquil but slightly dull environment. Her hair was cut short in a practical pixie cut, and she was decked in all kinds of weird contraptions apart from her two tomahawks.

Emily grinned at Zac, but her smile turned crooked as tears pooled in her eyes. Zac didn't say anything as he enclosed her in a hug.

"You're finally home," Zac said as he lifted her from the ground. "I'm glad you're okay."

"You too," Emily said.

"Is your mission to the Million Gates Territory over?" Zac asked as he put her down.

"What mission?" Emily huffed. "We didn't even manage to find a single infiltrator before our ship was ripped apart."

"What?" Zac yelled, a pang of worry filling him as he thought of Ogras and the others.

No, they should be fine. Otherwise, the progression of his quest would have stalled out. Zac shook his head and led Emily over to her home. The old camper that nowadays hung twenty meters in the air from a carefully pruned tree, with a large sundeck around it.

"It's still here," Emily smiled as they jumped up and sat on a lounge sofa on the deck.

"Of course, always," Zac said. "What happened in the Million Gates Territory? Pirates?"

"No, a spatial storm swallowed the whole flagship. I managed to survive inside an escape pod. Floated around for over a year, cultivating and trying to rebuild it so I could get out."

"Holy crap," Zac muttered.

"That's nothing," Emily grinned. "When I was finally rescued, it turned out the ship belonged to a bunch of Kan'Tanu."

Zac frowned and leaned over, grasping Emily's hand before she had a chance to react.

He infused coruscating waves of Life-attuned Dao through her body while scanning every inch with Mental Energy. But there was nothing, allowing Zac to breathe out in relief as he stepped back.

"*As I said,*" Emily said as she lightly slapped Zac's hand with a roll of her eyes. "I had to take them all out before I snatched their vessel. You know, I'm pretty powerful nowadays. There were even five Hegemons among them. One was a bit too strong, so I had to use most of your talismans to blow up a section of the ship and fly away when he was launched into space."

"That's fine, I have more," Zac smiled. "Then what happened?"

"I sailed around for a few more months, but their ship wasn't much better than my old escape pod. It broke down after just three jumps, but I did manage to reach a more populated region of space. I traded the vessel for passage with a pirate crew, and they took me to a space station. From there, I joined a mercenary crew, and they flew me out of the Million Gates Territory so I could teleport home."

Zac looked at Emily with shock, and it almost felt like he saw her for the first time. The story was short and succinct, but he could tell a lot of hard work and hardships were hidden within those details. For example, trading a stalled Cosmic Vessel for passage? Most pirates would simply kill the lone survivor and take the ship. For her to walk out of it unscathed, she must have used both brains and brawn.

The same was true for the mercenaries, who were seldom much better than the pirates they usually hunted.

"The mercenaries sent you back, just like that?" Zac said with surprise.

"I was lucky to find one of the good crews. The captain was a former soldier of the Allbright Army. They mostly make a living hunting bounties and exploring the gates, but they have also started completing missions for the War Coalition lately. Besides, I presented them with a pretty good deal. You need to help me pick up a couple of people."

"Pick up?" Zac asked. "Who?"

"I poached a few of those guys," Emily grinned. "The captain was fine with it. He realized I had a decent background because of my items and talent. So, he sent me a few of the good ones, including his son. All are either talented Peak E-grade or Half-Step veterans. They're pretty good and have a lot of experience in the Million Gates Territory if you ever go there. The captain has trained them in warfare as well."

"No problem," Zac readily agreed. "We've already started recruiting some outsiders for the upcoming war. We have over 100 Half-Step Hegemons and four actual Hegemons in the Atwood Army, but we could definitely use more."

They spent the next couple of hours catching up, with Zac telling Emily of his experiences in the Twilight Ascent, Orom World, and Void Gate. She looked almost green with envy at the "fun" he'd had, even if she'd been through quite the ordeals herself. Hearing that Zac started on the path of techniques, her eyes lit up, and she dragged him to a nearby clearing.

"You're just back, and you want to fight?" Zac said with some helplessness.

"Show me that Evolutionary Stance of yours," Emily urged. "And I'll show you my Tempest Bop."

"Tempest Bop?" Zac smiled with a shake of his head as [Verun's Bite] appeared in his hand. "Fine, show me what the ogres back in the coliseum have taught you."

"Don't get too shocked," Emily grinned as over thirty small axes flew out from a small bag on her belt.

"An axe array?" Zac whistled, watching the array start a deadly dance around her while she gripped her two tomahawks.

"Vines?" Emily countered with surprise upon seeing Vivi make an appearance.

"I guess we're pretty similar, after all," Zac smiled, realizing Emily had moved in a similar path as himself. The only difference was that she chose a weapon array rather than an armament to supplement her combat style.

Zac wasted no time as he stepped into the whirlwind of axes, using Vivi and [Verun's Bite] to gently push the flying axes out of the way. He was immediately impressed by the speed and complexity of the array. Axes came at him from every direction, like a swarm of wasps trying to sting him to death.

Emily proved herself quite competent at controlling the axes as well. Zac was continuously hitting them in a way that was meant to disrupt the tempo of the storm, but she adapted and righted the ship every time. Suddenly, a larger, gleaming edge appeared among the blur. A tomahawk aiming for his throat.

It flew right past him, a small step enough to avoid the hit. A second strike followed the first, but a vine shot up from the ground, aiming for Emily's chin. She was forced to alter her swing, cutting off the vine. Doing so stole her momentum, though, and the axe array wasn't enough to slow down Zac as he launched a counter-offensive.

Emily wasn't so easily caught, even if she'd momentarily lost the advantage. A storm of blades forced Zac to slow and parry while Emily distanced herself. She was as elusive as the wind, flitting back and forth in the clearing. She worked in harmony with her array, only appearing when an opening presented itself, her strikes tempestuous and forceful.

Zac had his hands mostly full just dealing with the swirling axes, but he gradually started to regain control, forcing Emily to choose between a passive state or striking even when there were no openings. She chose the latter, trying to leverage her own attacks to regain control of the surroundings. But it was a losing battle.

Ultimately, Zac saw there was order to the chaos of the axes. The array was based on a set of cyclic patterns, something Zac was familiar with, thanks to his master. Their tempo rose and fell like the seasons. It still provided a surprising variance, like how no two summers were alike. But it wasn't perfect.

Zac could tell Emily hadn't reached the Integration Stage yet, and her cooperation with her array started to suffer when he pushed her. That created new openings, which ended with Emily being dragged to the ground by Vivi, [Verun's Bite] levied against her throat.

"What the hell, you only used 70% of my attributes," Emily panted, looking at Zac like he was a monster.

"Don't feel bad," Zac smiled, helping her up. "I started this path over a decade ago. The fact you've reached this far in just two years, especially while stuck in an escape pod, is amazing. With some proper training, you'll plug most of your weaknesses. It's just…"

"What?"

"Are you the axe, or are you the storm?" Zac asked.

"I am both."

"Then you need to work more on your actual axe-work," Zac said. "I felt like I was inside a storm when you fought me, and I felt the tempo of your Seasonal Dao. But I didn't really sense the deadly intent of the axe, the ferocity and indomitability. Let me guess, you haven't fully comprehended [Axe Mastery] yet?"

"I was busy working on other things," Emily coughed.

"You really are my disciple," Zac laughed.

"So you're saying my Tempest Bop was a mistake?" Emily looked a bit crestfallen.

"Not at all," Zac said with a shake of his head. "I did the same thing. A Monarch in the Orom World helped me fix my training method. Looking back at it, I don't feel like I wasted time with my first iteration of my Evolutionary Stance. I found something I liked, something that resonated with my path. Thanks to that, I had a goal to work toward as I shored up my foundations. It'll be the same for you."

"Shore up foundations," Emily muttered, her eyes lighting up.

"Right, and you'll help me spar. I haven't had any good sparring partners for years."

"Sure," Zac said. "I'm pretty free over the next month or two."

Zac wasn't exaggerating. It wasn't that he didn't need to cultivate, but rather that he couldn't. His [Void Vajra Constitution] was already at the very limit of the third layer. A single rotation and he would break through and reach Minor Vajra Sublimation. But why would he? He only managed to form the first three layers of the technique with the light of Ultom, and he still hadn't finished creating the fourth.

He'd hoped to use some leftover light from Ultom to finalize it, but his Void Core had used up his epiphany. Since he temporarily couldn't continue with his Body Tempering after breaking through, he would rather wait to break through inside the Perennial Vastness. Doing so might give him a leg up during his stay there, like during his previous experiences.

The Twilight Ascent and the Orom World had awarded you for progressing, though the reasoning differed. Zac leaned toward the Perennial Vastness being more like the Orom World. The owner of the Immemorial Realm had to have some reason to invite innumerable cultivators to their domain, teleporting them halfway across the Multiverse.

They probably got something from observing the process of cultivators forming their cores, possibly observing elites from across the Multiverse in general. It wouldn't be surprising if there were some kind of contribution system that awarded points for progress.

It was the same with his soul. Between the Moss Crystals and the attuned treasures from Iz and the elders of the Undead Empire, Zac had finished his third layer a century ahead of schedule. In fact, by the time he'd formed the nine sets of Outer-attuned Cores, the Inner Core was already halfway refined.

Since the Fourth Layer most likely was an undertaking measured in decades, even with a steady source of Moss Crystals, Zac opted not to break through a year ago and instead focused on his blueprint. As for his [Thousand Lights Avatar], it was gradually filling up on its own just by cycling the run-off energy of the Moss Crystal with the help of his Mental Energy. Cultivating the method would speed up the process, but it wasn't something pressing.

Obviously, there were always things to work on when it came to cultivation, though Zac believed he'd be better off relaxing and clearing his mind now that he had a plan for his core. The rest could be dealt with inside the time-dilated environment of the Perennial Vastness.

"Can't believe you're heading off to that Perennial Vastness just as I returned," Emily sighed. "Am I just supposed to sit around here after that?"

"You can help train the recruits," Zac said. "You should also start considering your role in the war. With your skill set, you would do well both as leader of a strike team or as a general of a large army."

"You're letting me go to the frontlines? Just like that?" Emily said, looking both pleased and surprised.

"You're not a kid anymore. Between your combat strength and support abilities, you are one of the most powerful people on Earth. I hope you can become someone our people can depend on."

"O-Of course," Emily quickly nodded. "I swear, I'll take this seriously. I'm done messing around like back then."

Zac slowly nodded as he thoughtfully looked at Emily. She was right. It was easy to forget since her cultivation had drastically slowed down her aging, but she was already an adult and an accomplished cultivator in her own right. Even if he didn't like the idea of Emily risking her life even further, he'd be doing her a disservice if he didn't give her the same option as Vilari and the others.

"There's something else going on too. Something beyond the war. It might present an enormous opportunity, but it might also spell death. There is even a chance that just knowing about it will impact your fate, so you will have to think long and hard before deciding if this is something for you."

"No need. I can take it," Emily said. "I don't want to stay on the sidelines anymore. This is what I've trained for."

Zac took a deep breath before telling Emily of Ultom, of the Left Imperial Palace and its subsidiary courts, and the upcoming trial. Emily first looked at Zac like he was crazy, but her brows slowly furrowed thoughtfully as he reached the part of forming a cycle.

"Sealbearers?" Emily slowly said. "What are they supposed to do?"

"I'm not sure yet," Zac said, not without some helplessness.

He'd visited and exchanged letters with Vai and Leyara over the past years. With Vai, he mostly discussed research, where she'd helped him approach some problems from a new direction. As for Leyara, he tried to get her and her master to give up some more information about Ultom. But even after years of trying, he hadn't managed to gain much.

"I only know the inheritance will start in just over three years. Since I have a quest to gather people from the nine Outer Courts, I think there will be a teamwork component, but I can't be sure. Either case, it will be incredibly dangerous with the powerful outsiders coming here."

"An ancient castle and Eternal Heritages," Emily said, a smile tugging at her mouth. "These sealbearers, they'd have to be pretty impressive to get chosen by such a place, huh?"

"I guess," Zac said, his eyes suddenly narrowing with suspicion. "Don't tell me?"

"Don't you know who you're talking to?" Emily laughed as a Quest Screen appeared. "I'm more than halfway there already."

# RECRUITMENT

Zac looked with blank incomprehension at the quest telling him Emily had two pieces of the Seal of the Radiant Court.

"I found the first piece while I still was part of the Big Axe Coliseum. I found the second one by chance soon after commandeering the Kan'Tanu ship. I was never able to find a third piece, though," Emily huffed.

"The System is keeping the final pieces as rewards during the war," Zac said distractedly as he stared at his protégé. "So, you're one of the four?"

"What?" Emily said with confusion.

"Nevermind," Zac said. "Can you tell me what you used the epiphanies for?"

"The first one was to create a skill and kind of understand my path in general. It helped me create my axe array later," Emily said. "The second one was to recreate a Cultivation Manual I got from my teacher at the coliseum and form a blueprint for my Cosmic Core. I was afraid I'd end up stuck in space, so I was planning on breaking through in case my ship blew up or something. That way, I wouldn't die from lack of oxygen, at least. I could just keep flying for a hundred years until I ran into someone."

"You're resilient, I'll give you that," Zac laughed. "You're getting ready to break through?"

"I think so. I'm not in as big a hurry now that I'm back on Earth, though. I'll probably spend a couple of months figuring things out, but I'll make the attempt before the war starts."

"Don't feel you need to rush it," Zac urged.

"No, it's fine," Emily said. "I feel it's better even. This way, there'll be a purpose to my breakthrough. I can protect the people around me. There's no point to cultivation if I hide in some cave for a hundred years before emerging as a slightly stronger Hegemon."

"I guess you're right." Zac smiled. "Who knows, you might break through before me."

"And the student becomes the master!" Emily grinned before her eyes suddenly widened. "Oh crap, my underlings."

"The mercenaries?" Zac asked.

"It's been longer than I planned. The idea was to come fetch you right away," Emily explained. "Can we go now?"

"Sure. I could use stretching my legs a bit."

The capital of Lua-lor wasn't much different from the other cities you'd find on low D-grade planets of the Allbright Empire. There were the Halls of Light in its heart, the administrative building with its appointed mayor, which doubled as an academy for cultivators. Academia and governance were tightly related in the whole Empire, which had proven an effective method to retain talents within the Imperial Faction.

Many who graduated switched to employment within the Halls of Light, never giving the clans, sects, and businesses a chance to headhunt promising elites. Here, right at the edge of the Empire, the Hall of Light wouldn't normally have as much prestige as in the central regions. In these chaotic parts, things were more fluid, and the power dynamics more complex.

With the war, the muddy waters had been cleared. Those who needed to be reminded which Empire they were part of had been reminded, and purges of problematic factions had taken place across the border. Zac didn't care about any of that, though, as he and Emily walked the streets, taking in the surroundings.

The architecture was more simplistic compared to the inner regions of the Allbright Empire, even if they still leaned toward structures made with large walls of spiritual glass and white stone. But here, the rounded and artistic styles had given way to squarish practicality, and the protective arrays were often engraved right on the outside of the buildings.

Doing so was far cheaper than embedding it into the wall, though it allowed anyone to observe the patterns for weaknesses. Zac, who had enjoyed hundreds of bouts of synthetic enlightenment over the past years, could easily spot numerous weaknesses in most of the arrays. A simple punch would easily topple many of these buildings, even if they were supposed to withstand much more.

His vast knowledge of patterns was something Zac hoped to utilize more in the future, though he hadn't decided how. He only knew it would be a waste not to benefit from all that knowledge after having finalized his blueprint. He even had a set of 72 artisan axes in his Spatial Ring that had proven useful on most materials.

He just lacked a crafting method that could allow someone with low Dao control to succeed. As it were, he could easily create F-grade or Early E-grade array disks simply thanks to his muscle control and skill with axes.

More powerful arrays required you also imprint continuous streams of patterns with Mental Energy and Dao, which was still beyond him. Zac had considered the possibility of creating Array Molds. He'd carve out a perfect mold, fill it with his Dao, and then imprint it on a clay disk or something similar. It was a bit like his method of forming Dao Braids.

Unfortunately, his few attempts at the idea proved unsuccessful, and the Volor Craftsmen weren't optimistic that the method was workable. They said crafting was an art where you put your heart and soul into the item you created. Literally. Using molds was more like mass production without heart.

Even if you managed to create workable molds, they probably wouldn't have the spirituality necessary for High-grade crafts. Zac even considered visiting the more brutish races of the Sector to see how they crafted, in case they had some ideas he could use. But when would he get the time for something like that? When he was dead, probably.

"So, where are your guys?" Zac asked as he looked around.

"I left them at a bar," Emily said. "They're either still drinking or sleeping it off in some alley outside. Although, with the current atmosphere, they might be in a drunk tank."

Zac glanced at a squad of disciplined soldiers patrolling the street. "I didn't expect the Dravorak Empire to have such a presence here."

"They apparently have one of their main bases in this neighborhood," Emily explained. "This planet has become an exchange spot for Dravorak and Allbright."

"I see," Zac said.

Luckily, they found the newest members where Emily had left them. The combination of adventurer poverty and Peak E-grade constitutions made it impossible to get overly drunk. There was almost an oppressive atmosphere at the table, but a few of them perked up upon seeing Emily.

"Little Chief!" one of them exclaimed before looking at Zac, who'd donned a new identity with [Million Faces], curiously.

"Only six of you? Where's Monkey and Elenka?" Emily frowned as she looked around.

"They… left," another grimaced. "Didn't think you were returning."

"I'll find them," Emily swore.

"Don't bother," Zac shrugged before paying for a VIP room in the establishment. "They've made their choice. Let's go somewhere more private."

Inside, he threw out a set of arrays, sealing them from the outside. The six cultivators looked warily at Zac with a mix of confusion and speculation.

"I want to begin by thanking you all for looking after Emily this past year," Zac said as six Cosmos Sacks appeared on the table. "A small token of appreciation from her teacher."

"What looking after?" Emily muttered. "I saved their hides more than once."

A few of the mercenaries picked up the sacks, and they immediately froze after scanning the contents.

"Holy crap," one muttered, looking up at Zac with awe.

For Zac, it was just a couple of crystals and natural treasures. The combined value of each sack was barely 1 D-grade Nexus Coin. Nothing for him, but a significant windfall for mercenaries eking out a living in this kind of environment.

"Now, you have the same choice as your other two companions. You can either go on and pave your own path or join us. I'll be clear, though. If you join us, it will be as part of our armies, and your freedoms will be restricted. The only reason we are recruiting people from the outside is for the upcoming war."

"What would our role be?" one of the men hesitantly asked.

"Pilots, warriors, technicians, navigators; wherever your talents lie. We don't need meat shields, we need competent veterans who can help nurture and lead the large number of recruits we've added to our ranks. You have lived in the Million Gates Territories for decades, which means you know how to survive. That's one of the most important skills of a soldier. Resources will be far richer than almost any faction in Zecia, and we are planning to hit the ground running with the upcoming war. There will be deaths, but I hope you can help us keep them to a minimum."

"Can you tell us which faction you belong to?" another man, who Zac suspected was the informal leader, asked. "Little Chie—ah, Miss Emily, never told us."

"No," Zac said as he took out a token. "It's complicated. But I can tell you that our leader is a close ally with both the Allbright Dynasty, the Peak family, and Zecian top factions like the Void Gate."

The token had the seal of the Allbright Empire and emitted a unique aura that was incredibly hard to fake. The token essentially gave Zac the same status as a nobleman within the Allbright Empire, which came with all kinds of benefits. It was also a clear indicator of status, and the eyes of the six mercenaries widened in shock.

The token and the Cosmos Sacks were more than enough to convince all but one to join immediately. The leader didn't move to accept the sack or join the Atwood Empire.

"Little Bolt!" Emily glared as a tomahawk appeared in her hand. "Your dad told me to beat some sense into you if you started making trouble."

"No, that's not it," Little Bolt said before turning to Zac. "Do you need more? People like us, that is."

"We might," Zac said. "But we don't need scum or unorthodox culti-vators. Even if they have some combat strength, they'll cause more trouble than it's worth."

"I have some contacts, but not here," Little Bolt said. "Mercenaries, adventurers. Various types of people who make a living at the edges of the Million Gates Territory. Some are fairly decent, and I think many want to join something bigger now that things are going south. Better to lose some of your freedoms than being caught between murderous invaders and those War Fortresses."

Zac thoughtfully looked at Little Bolt for a few seconds before nodding. He engraved a list of planets in the region he had access to, handing it over.

"Any of these planets work?"

"Kulga Soro," Little Bolt said without hesitation. "We've traded there before, and none of the large empires have a strong presence there yet. I can move unhindered there."

"We'll set up a base for you and provide a continuous source of resources," Zac said. "Each useful man you recruit will provide Contribution Points you can exchange for resources. But beware, this region is about to become volatile. Kulga Soro is close to the border. It might get caught up in the war before you have a chance to escape."

"I'm aware."

Ultimately, two mercenaries decided to follow Little Bolt to set up a recruitment station, and Zac sent them through the teleporter. He'd also send a squad of elites to help them get things started. Who knew, he might find some diamonds in the rough among the vagrants of the imperial border.

After that, Zac brought the remaining three back to Earth with Emily. Thankfully, sending people back home to his own planet didn't have as stringent restrictions, and all five returned in a flash. The problem was sending people to places he didn't control. Zac had already started nurturing a group of porters to lessen the pressure on him, but it wasn't easy for his followers to gain access to new teleportation arrays.

The quintet appeared in the fort which had been built around the Nexus Hub to protect against any surprises now that there was more traffic. The crystal itself had already been hidden within layers and layers of arrays, while they emerged on one of six connected teleportation arrays.

One manned by two Revenants and a Raun Spectral, while the room was flooded with Miasma.

"Y-You!" one of the mercenaries stuttered as he took three steps back. If not for Zac stealthily deactivating the array, he might have teleported back home. "What's going on?"

"Don't mind them," Zac said, his face turned back to normal because he didn't bother resisting the restrictive arrays. "They're just guarding the teleporter."

"Oh, that's fine then," a Peak E-grade cultivator called Shifty Ziv said, his voice dripping with sarcasm.

"My energy," Needle, a prospective pilot of the Atwood Navy, exclaimed.

"Sorry about that," Zac said as the guards walked over with three bracelets. "We have been forced to take a few precautionary measures with new arrivals."

The next moment, the three Revenants, their Miasma completely fine under the restrictive array, placed the bracers on the mercenaries.

"You—" the sole Half-Step Hegemon, Usko, said, his eyes thinning as he looked at Zac. "Why are you familiar?"

"Let me re-introduce myself," Zac said. "I am Zachary Atwood, the leader of the Atwood Empire, which you now are part of."

Emily grinned. "You might know him as the Deviant Asura."

"What! That lunatic?" Shifty Ziv swore, backing away to the edge of the room. "You're wanted all across Zecia. Send me back right now!"

"No turning back now," Zac said with a smile. "You should know those bracelets are designed to disintegrate you if you try to escape off-world through the teleporter. A safeguard to keep certain matters private."

"Like the Revenants?" Usko sighed, turning to Emily. "Ai, girl, what have you gotten us mixed up in?"

"Well, the Revenants are part of the 'complicated' part I mentioned," Zac said. "This is Earth, a Life-Death attuned planet. As such, we have both Revenant and spectral citizens in this faction. You'll be working with both in the armies, so I hope you'll put aside any preconceived notions you may have."

"All those rumors about Zac are exaggerated," Emily added with a roll of her eyes. "The bounties don't matter either. Only the Tsarun Clan dare hunt my teacher. And if even the big empires don't care about the Revenants here, why should you?"

"The Allbright know about the undead?" Usko said suspiciously.

"The news may not have reached you guys inside the Million Gates Territory yet, but the Undead Empire has stopped their war. They are now working with the ancient empires to fight the invaders," Zac

598 | JF BRINK & THE FIRSTDEFIER

explained. "Although, the undead here aren't part of the Undead Empire. They're citizens of the Atwood Empire."

"Teacher was the one who helped broker the peace," Emily added. "That's why he's got such a high standing everywhere."

"I can't believe this," Shifty Ziv muttered. "I can't believe I'm a prisoner of the Deviant Asura."

"I-I'll work hard," Needle stuttered as his hands moved toward his crotch. "I'll teach you all I know about flying Cosmic Vessels. Just don't—"

"Just stop," Zac groaned. "Like Emily said, the rumors are *false*. And even if I were a deviant, why would I go for three wretched-looking mercenaries?"

"Now that I can believe," Usko laughed.

Zac snorted before turning back to Shifty Ziv. "And you're not prisoners. Everything I said before was true. I'll send you over to some Wandering Cultivators who'll catch you up to speed. I think you'll soon find you made the right choice, even if it wasn't what you expected. If you still want to leave afterward, you'll be free to do so. But until I can trust you, the bracelets stay on for the safety of my citizens."

Emily stayed with the unwitting conscripts to mollify their shock while Zac sent out a few orders to accommodate the trio. He wasn't a fan of the prison bracelets he'd had all the outsiders wear after arriving at Earth, but it was hard to enforce System-generated contracts with people of equal or higher levels.

After becoming a proper Hegemon, his faction would automatically upgrade, and he'd be able to hire them all as outer elders with ironclad contracts. Until then, he'd have to be a bit heavy-handed. It wasn't even that he was afraid people would find out about his undead followers. The news had already started to spread through certain circles.

It was more about resources. Two thefts had already occurred, leading to one enterprising Half-Step Hegemon escaping Earth with a battalion's worth of cultivation resources. The second one who tried the same thing was killed during the pursuit. After that, Zac put the hammer down, forcing all recruits to wear the bracer for the time being.

In the following days, Zac spent most of his time either tutoring Emily or catching up on the various matters of Earth. He had all but sealed himself in his cultivation cave during the final years of his retreat, where he fully focused on his core. Thankfully, he'd always been a mostly hands-off boss, and his people had long since learned to manage themselves.

Emily was making incredible progress now that she had some proper guidance in technique. She reached the final level of her E-grade [Axe Mastery] in just two weeks, and Zac could feel her daily progress. She probably wouldn't reach the Integration Stage in the short run, but she definitely had a talent for techniques. It was just a matter of time and experience. She would get the latter in spades during the war.

Eventually, Zac received the update he'd be waiting for. The squad who set out into space three years ago were back in the Red Sector. Ogras had already returned and waited for him in his compound. Zac canceled his inspection of a military drill and made his way back to Port Atwood. He found Ogras lounging in his courtyard with a glass in hand like he'd never left.

The demon looked the same as before, though Zac could feel an increased pressure coming from his body. Zac guessed he'd either evolved a Dao or, more likely, broken through with his odd Body Tempering Method. However, Zac frowned when he saw the cursed flag fastened to his belt. It emitted a far-stronger aura than before, to the point Zac's hair stood on end.

Zac could almost hear distant wails when looking at the rolled-up flag. His [Immutability of Eoz] heated up a bit as well, nullifying some sort of weak curse-like effect it passively emitted. Zac put the matter aside, happier to see the demon alive than worried about him dabbling with the unorthodox.

"You're back," Zac smiled as he sat down. "Nice to see you."

"Nice to be back," Ogras grinned as he looked around. "You know, this place is really starting to feel like home, even if you've drowned half the city in death. Even the blue sky is starting to feel normal."

"Don't get too attached. We're leaving soon," Zac said, taking out a vat of wine himself.

# CHALLENGE

"Thought you'd want to stay to the very end, looting and pillaging," Zac commented.

"Things grew too dangerous. Had to sacrifice my sweet *Temptress* to get away," Ogras grunted as he threw over a docket. "That place is rough, and it seems like it will only get worse. By the end, even the pirates were running from the deeper regions. There are *a lot* of invaders in our waters already. Since we found more seals than expected, I decided to leave while we were ahead. Even then, we lost seven of our people."

Zac sighed as he read the report. This was the price of progress. Each step was paved with blood, and not just of your enemies. Two Revenants, one Valkyrie, one demon, a Zhix, the Mavai Shaman, and a non-combat pilot had lost their lives. Each one the best of the best among the Atwood Empire's elites.

"I'll make sure their dependents are provided for," Zac said.

The losses hurt, but the gains were astronomical. Zac knew they'd found a lot of seals because of his quest, but he hadn't expected there to be multiple sets of a few. If things continued like this, he might even be able to form two cycles. Perhaps even lend one to Iz if the price was right and she agreed to keep his followers safe. Then suddenly, a familiar name appeared on the docket.

"Wait, Jaol?" Zac blurted, barely able to believe his eyes. "Is that real? A Technocrat navigator named Jaol?"

"It's all too real," Ogras said, his mouth widening into a smile. "He's being kept at the compound back on Crimson Edge. Didn't dare bring a Technocrat here, even if he's an exile. I have no idea if it'd create problems for you, or the faction in general, for that matter."

"I can't believe it," Zac whispered. "It's really him."

"I knew it!" Ogras laughed as he slapped the table. "When I heard his story of how a shapeshifting lunatic appeared out of nowhere and blew up his ship, I knew it had to be you. How in the nine hells did that happen?"

"It was the second-to-last level in the Tower of Eternity," Zac said with a wry smile. "The System sent me out of the tower and onto a Technocrat ship that was leaving integrated space. I only realized midway it was real and not another trial."

"Sounds like the Ruthless Heavens, alright," Ogras snickered. "It really doesn't seem to like your ancestors."

"Looks that way," Zac said with a helpless shake of his head. "I can't believe that scaredy-cat became a sealbearer. Some of the other names are surprising as well. Carl Elrod, that's the archer, right?"

"That's him, alright," Ogras snickered. "Complained his way right into the Radiant Court. Either those things are more common than we thought, or your fate is even more useful. It's almost like every person you've shaken hands with ends up with a piece or two."

"Wait, this doesn't make sense," Zac said as he read the report. "My quest is lacking one seal."

"What?" Ogras said with confusion. "Some of our people were doubles. Shouldn't you be lacking three?"

"Janos is back. He has the seal of the Mercurial Court, making it seven. Emily also returned with a seal, but it was the Radiant Court, like Carl. I have no idea who the final person is, though."

"There's another one?" Ogras mused. "Your undead girl?"

"I think she'd automatically become part of the Undead Empire's team because of the commandments," Zac said, though he wasn't sure.

"Shouldn't be random assignments, either," Ogras said. "We've heard some rumors. People are starting to realize something is going on because of the Kan'Tanu. They're offering exorbitant bounties for sealbearers, except they don't call them that outright. I heard the pirates have already turned a few in. If everyone who got a seal automatically got assigned to a Flamebearer, you'd probably have completed your cycle already."

"Then who would I know on the outside that might have a seal?" Zac muttered.

"Someone in the Void Gate?" Ogras offered. "Some of them might have picked up seals, even if they're saying they'll stay out of it."

"Maybe," Zac said. "Probably best we'd try to get a spare, just in case."

"We still have some time," Ogras said before his smile widened. "So, Janos is alive, after all? That guy has nine lives. He keeps returning from the dead."

"You should swap pointers with him before we leave," Zac said. "He's lived inside an illusion for the past years. His skills have become quite terrifying. It might be useful with the direction your path has taken."

"I'll visit him later," Ogras nodded. "Are we still leaving in a month? I'm as ready as can be."

"You have a blueprint ready?" Zac asked.

"Most of us sealbearers do," Ogras said. "We knew the war and upcoming trial would become real slaughter-fests. We need to break through sooner rather than later, so we used some of the inspiration from the seals to pave the way."

Zac wasn't surprised. He'd done the same, as had Emily. For the people on Port Atwood, figuring out a top-quality design for a core blueprint was probably the best choice for the Ultom-provided epiphany. It wasn't as exciting as unique cultivation methods like the [Void Vajra Sublimation], but it was practical for both their long and short-term prospects.

The core was the focus of the D-grade, and a proper blueprint and a viable long-term plan was the difference between being stuck right at the start of Hegemony and having a shot at Monarchy.

"I'm pretty much done from my side. The only thing left is to check out the Limited Trial to see if I can gain a final burst of inspiration," Zac said. "I haven't heard back from Catheya, though. She might still be inside the Million Gates Territory."

"That's fine," Ogras said. "I'll visit the crazy Tool Spirit and get the second piece of my inheritance. I've improved my Body Tempering

Method, and I need more creatures. And if that bastard of a soul-whisp tries something this time, I'll add him to my flag."

"Just be careful with that thing," Zac said.

"Don't worry, I've finally found a path," Ogras smiled. "Fake is real, and real is fake. Unorthodoxy is Orthodoxy. I'll reform it before Ultom, though I'll need to head deeper into the night before I can welcome the daybreak."

"I trust you know what you're doing," Zac shrugged. "I guess I'll go deal with the Technocrat."

"I think you should check up on the spear lass first," Ogras said with a shake of his head. "She's not doing well."

"Joanna?" Zac said with a frown. "What's going on?"

———

The spear cut through the air in an indomitable arc, soon turning into a mirage as one stab turned into one hundred. Activating **[Glorious Advance]** moved her over two hundred meters in an instant. Her spear slammed into the hill, and it was like a bomb had erupted from its heart. A shockwave spread over a hundred meters in each direction as a cascade of weapons stormed out.

Left were broken trees and fragmented stone—a scene of utter destruction. Yet it didn't help. Joanna still felt suffocated. Drowning. She didn't know what else to do, so she continued swinging her spear, waging war on land to drown out the war raging in her head. Suddenly, an axe met her spear, locking it in place.

The collision pushed away the clouds of dust she'd kicked up in her desperate dance, showing Zachary Atwood standing opposite her. She couldn't believe she'd missed his advance, so enraptured with her own problems. The two stood in place for a moment, neither saying anything.

"I failed," Joanna said, trying but failing to keep her voice stable.

Shame, despair, and irreconciliation filled her heart as she looked at the man in front of her. He'd grown calmer, to the point he seemed like a non-combat class cultivator. Yet there was an unfathomable depth to him that Joanna had never been able to sense before. It was almost like she was being sucked in, her very existence swallowed by his mere presence.

Once more, he'd elevated himself, climbing further up the ladder of cultivation. More and more, he was becoming a towering tree that protected the whole world. Joanna was happy for him. He wasn't a genius when it came to cultivation, and neither did he have a backing like the scions of the more flourishing regions of the Multiverse.

Each step he'd taken, every morsel of strength seized, had been fought for. He'd walked down one perilous road after another, his life hanging by a thread. And it wasn't even for himself, but for those around him. For Earth. For her and the other Valkyries so that fewer would die under his command. She was happy for him. She really was.

Yet her stomach felt like a pit.

This should have been her chance. If not to catch up to him, at least be able to see the same sky he did. To help him in the upcoming trial while reforging her fate like the others on the trip had. But three years later, she returned the same Joanna Thompson as before. A bit stronger, sure, but she certainly hadn't spread her wings to fly.

"Continue," was all Zac said, and Joanna was happy to oblige.

There was one thing she'd realized over her journey over the past years. Zachary Atwood was fate incarnate. Fighting him was almost like fighting against the Heavens, which was exactly what Joanna needed. The sky filled with spears falling like rain while Joanna launched a ruthless offensive using everything she'd learned.

Each of Zac's movements was a work of art as he almost danced through the battlefield, bending it to his will. She couldn't touch the hem of his robes, even when she used skills while he didn't. Soon enough, the ugly feeling she'd felt over the past year rose to the surface, and she couldn't hold herself back anymore.

"Vilari got one," Joanna said as she furiously tried to at least land a hollow hit on her lord. "That's no wonder. She's the most talented one around. Rhubat, too, I can understand. But *Rhuger*? I'm just as talented as him, and his body is hundreds of years old, even if he is not."

Zac didn't answer. He only kept swinging his axe, his simple swings putting her under more pressure than the various deathmatches she'd survived in the Million Gates Territory. The whole area shuddered under a tremendous aura of war spread from his body, increasing the burden even further.

"Ibtep got one. The worm-merchant," Joanna continued with grit teeth. "Even a stinking Technocrat pirate we randomly ran into is a freaking sealbearer. *And I failed.*"

She wanted to shut up. She hated being so jealous and cynical, but the words that had stayed pent-up in her body just kept pouring out now that she'd started. No longer bothering with finesse or skills, she furiously beat at the iron wall of her opponent.

"Since the day you saved me, I've struggled without a break. I've fought, I've bled. I've pushed myself beyond anyone else, both during the second Incursion and the mission to the Million Gates Territory. Yet I'm the only one to come back empty-handed!"

More strength, more speed, more precision. Just once. She wanted to hit him just once. Why was it so hard?

"Is this it? Is this my fate? Was I deluding myself, thinking I could be something beyond a somewhat talented captain of a local faction? That I could soar into the sky with the rest of you?"

Her vision clouded, but her arms kept moving as she advanced with everything she had. If she could, she'd even burn her life force to give her a chance at this small, pitiful goal of hers. Because this was unbearable.

"Why? WHY!" Joanna screamed, tears pouring from her eyes. "What am I *missing*?"

Then it coalesced, and Joanna found her spear sneak beneath the axe, piercing right through a vine before punching a hole in his robes. It wasn't a real hit, but it was a hit. Joanna's strength suddenly left her body, making her stumble. She lay on the ground panting, too emotionally and physically spent to move.

She saw Zac sigh and sit beside her, looking up at the sky.

"Vilari gained the seal of the Anima Court, which makes sense considering her terrifying talent for Soul Cultivation," Zac said. "Rhubat became the sealholder of the Tethered court. He's the Chainbreaker, the one who ended thousands of years of suffering. He's also consumed with breaking the chains of the Zhix to pave a path for them in this new reality.

"Ibtep and Jaol both are sealholders of the Farsee Court. Both have inherent natures leaning toward exploration. Ibtep comes from an incredibly rigid race, yet he has the most insatiable curiosity of anyone I've met. Jaol has more to him than meets the eye as well.

"Did you know that he somehow managed to flee the equivalent distance of a whole Sector through the Endless Storm, until he reached the Million Gates Territory? All while having actual Monarchs looking for him? You've seen what that place is like. To survive that journey as an E-grade cultivator, the Farsee Court sounds fitting.

"Rhuger's body is old, but Cervantes was possibly the most talented cultivator to ever have appeared inside the Mystic Realm. A place where the Tsarun Clan brought the greatest talents they could find to further refine their bloodlines. Cervantes cultivated the Dao of Lunar Light, while Rhuger cultivates Darkness. A perfect match to the Starfall Court that chose him.

"To me, it doesn't seem that the courts choose people based on combat strength but compatibility," Zac concluded. "Fate, I guess."

"So I'm not fated, after all," Joanna sighed, blankly staring at the sky. "So much for hard work."

Zac looked down at Joanna, slightly smiling. "I've talked with some people who deeply understand the inheritance. I still don't know much, but I know the name of the two final Courts that none of my people have. The first is the Daedalian Court. I don't think it's for you. You're more like me, except you've focused even further on the path of War. That leaves one court."

Joanna's gaze shifted, seeing Zac take out a wooden seal, expertly carved and radiating a fierce aura. "This one, I think, might be more suited to you. Here."

"If things were this easy," Joanna lamented, but she still accepted the carving.

The rune was one she'd seen before. It was one of the nine that haunted her dreams since the Ensolus Ruins. Yet, for some reason, it looked different this time. Was it because Zac had infused his Dao into it, somehow giving it new meaning? It felt incredibly imposing, like a sea of soldiers bearing down on her.

"What's... this one called?" Joanna asked.

"The Indomitable Court," Zac said as he stood. "I refuse to believe you're not fated for more. I've seen you walk down your path with conviction and determination that would shame most scions of the Multiverse. I rather want to believe your stage has not yet been set. Seeing that seal, where do you think you'll find it?"

"The battlefield…" Joanna instinctively muttered as she looked at the oppressive rune.

"The battlefield," Zac nodded, looking down at her. "Not some old ruins in the middle of nowhere. On the battlefield, where you are the closest to your path. So don't lose hope, and don't give in. Don't bother with the path of others. We all have periods of rapid growth and periods where we slow down to digest what we've accumulated.

"Believe in yourself, that your time is still to come."

---

Zac's heart was heavy as he left Joanna to her thoughts. He'd sounded confident speaking to her, but he really didn't know if he was just making things up about the Indomitable Court. There was a real risk of her not being fated with the inheritance of the Left Imperial Palace. As to whether it was because of lacking affinity or lacking talent, it was hard to say.

This was the reality of cultivation. The Multiverse wasn't lacking for hard-working and dedicated cultivators. Yet few even reached Hegemony, let alone the higher grades. It was hard to say why some managed to continue climbing while others found themselves stuck, even though they outwardly seemed of similar backgrounds. Talent, dedication, opportunities, luck. Not a single piece could be missing or you'd get dragged under by the river of fate.

Cultivation was ultimately to go against the natural order, to steal from the Heavens. How could it be easy?

Zac could only hope that Joanna would keep going and not give up on herself and her path. Her situation was a tribulation of a sort, one of the heart. Either she'd emerge stronger or lose her direction, most likely killing her momentum. It wasn't something his wealth or treasures could solve, and he wasn't qualified to do more than give some words of encouragement.

He was supposed to teleport back to the border of the Million Gates Territory by this point, to deal with Jaol and the other recruits Ogras had picked up for his 'Shadewar Armada.' But he felt suffocated after seeing Joanna, like he was drowning. He felt a desperate need to push back against fate, so he set course for Ensolus.

To this day, not a single person had passed the final level of the Gates of Rebirth, no matter if it was through the Gate of Life or the Gate of Death. Even the fifth layer seemed out of reach, with less than five entries on each ladder. The final layer was regarded as an impossibility, a hoax to punish hubris.

That would change today.

73

# GATE OF LIFE

Soon enough, Zac appeared in Rebirth City. Today, it was a sprawling settlement only dwarfed by Port Atwood and a few other cities on Earth. It was the de-facto capital of Ensolus, even if Sandy, the second Stargazer recruited to administrate, and the Nexus Hub were still located at Fort Atwood.

It was a natural consequence of its proximity to the Gates of Rebirth and the result of a strategic decision to keep Fort Atwood separate from the trial and commercial ventures. Even Hegemons would require days to reach Fort Atwood from Rebirth City, giving his people ample time to prepare in case someone wanted to try something.

Not that some random Hegemon could take over Fort Atwood. Not even a Late Hegemon could break inside in short order with the immense resources put into its defenses. By the time the Assimilation came around, Zac wanted to have protective measures prepared even for Monarchs.

The streets were quite empty for what one could expect from a city of this size. There was certainly foot traffic, but few of the pedestrians had a powerful aura. It was mostly F-grade civilians heading to work or getting some tasks done, with E-grade auras being incredibly rare. It wasn't a unique scene for the City of Rebirth. The same thing could be observed across all of Ensolus and Earth.

The clock was ticking, and the Atwood Empire War Machine was running on all cylinders. Dozens of war games and exercises were happening throughout the two planets. In forests, in cities, the ocean, even the Underworld. The Flotilla of Atwood Empire ships had grown to over 100 vessels, an absolutely shocking number for what essentially was an Early D-grade force.

The bombardment of the Creator Vessels alone could blow up a planet or dismantle a Middle D-grade force in a matter of minutes. Even a Late Hegemon would be turned into mincemeat if he let himself get caught in the crossfire.

By now, those willing to fight for the empire had already joined the army, either as temporary or permanent fighters. Those with the means but lacked the will weren't allowed to slink away from the upcoming threat. After a year of waiting, they'd been conscripted whether they liked it or not, losing out on the best resources available at the training camps.

The forceful approach created some uproars, especially among the humans on Earth, but they'd been quashed. Some considered Zac a tyrant by this point, but he didn't care. His people needed to be whipped into shape. Still, it created an oppressive atmosphere in his empire, which only exacerbated his mood as he walked toward the huge half-circle in the distance.

"Lord Atwood," the guards outside the trial said with a bow.

"Are there any slots remaining?" Zac asked.

"Following procedure, there are ten remaining of today's allotment," the guard replied, clearly looking expectant.

"I'm going in. Keep one open on the other side as well, just in case," Zac said.

"Of course," the guard nodded, and Zac stepped into the Gate of Life.

Zac didn't know what he'd expected when entering the Gates of Rebirth, but it wasn't the dark and blisteringly cold tundra that stretched out in every direction. The ground was covered in a sheet of black ice, and Zac felt tendrils of death trying to burrow into his bare feet and steal his strength. This was just the first layer, though, and Zac's Void Vajra Constitution was more than enough to rebuff the effect.

The cold tendrils couldn't withstand the raging vortex of Life that always lived inside his cells, and Zac started down the sole path in the whole realm. He didn't know how he knew, but there was a gate at the end of the road. Passing through meant passing the first layer of the trial. Each step infused his feet with another burst of cold, but Zac kept speeding up.

He only had six hours for the whole trial, and Zac had no idea whether time worked differently inside. Besides, the quicker he passed the whole thing, the more time he would have in that state of epiphany the previous trial takers mentioned.

It soon became clear there was some dilation at play as there was no end in sight, even after rushing for over two hours while using [Earth-strider]. The endless tundra appeared the same, and there were no real markers that could confirm he was moving at all. The only thing that changed during the journey was that the cold grew more intense and deadlier.

Still, it was far from enough to hamper Zac's progress, and he made an impressive time by relying on Supreme Nexus Crystals to activate his movement skill continuously. Experiments had long since confirmed that people could use items inside, and Zac's Spatial Rings were stocked with enough supplies to keep fighting for decades if need be.

Eventually, there was a change as Zac started spotting figures in the distance. There were humans, beastkin, and all kinds of races, shuffling about. They were all stark naked, their bodies covered in cold sores and frozen blood. They were mindlessly stumbling in the same direction as Zac. But when approached, they turned their heads toward him, their arms reaching to grab him.

Zac hesitated only for a moment before taking out a club. He'd already realized where this place was. It was Naraka, one of the Hell Realms depicted in Buddhist mythology. It was essentially purgatory and the lowest of the six paths of reincarnation. Zac didn't know if the trial was actually Buddhist or if its challenges were just modeled after their beliefs.

Perhaps it was unavoidable for a trial of this nature. According to his conversations with the Undead Empire, the Dao of Samsara was one of the main branches of the Sangha. It was their method to harness the Daos of Life and Death, bringing them away from the Dao of Chaos and toward the Dao of Order. Imposing a cycle of reincarnation, making random chance predictable.

In fact, that was one of the reasons the Undead Empire chose to side with the Blood Clan all those years ago. The Primo already had reasons to target the Sangha because of their claim on the Dao of Death. Something was going on at the peak, where the cultivators asserted some control over the Grand Dao itself.

For example, if the Eveningtide Asura ever reached the very limits of cultivation, like the Apostates, he might actually impact Zac's Daos. According to Alvod, Life was not life, and Death was not death. How could that mesh with Zac's path of purity? And with Alvod reaching the limits of cultivation, the Dao would shift in his image.

That was what happened with the Elemental Daos and the Apostate of Mercy, and it was a source of constant conflict among the factions at the top.

In either case, the fact the first layer of the Gates of Rebirth was modeled after Naraka provided Zac with some clues about the trial. First, it meant these people were tormented sinners who were slowly moving toward a chance at rebirth. They would have to suffer for a nigh-eternity before expunging Karma and moving on to the upper realms.

Cutting them apart with [Verun's Bite] felt too ruthless, especially since they were weak. Any Peak E-grade cultivator could easily force his way through the gauntlet of ice-bitten damned. A light tap with a club was enough to throw them away. And Zac was moving far quicker than these people were, making it impossible for them to catch up.

The hours passed until there was finally a change in the scenery. Zac vaguely made out that the darkness deepened in the distance. And soon he realized it was a towering mountain of black ice. By the time he reached it, roughly seven hours had passed, and Zac suspected it wouldn't be much longer.

The whole mountain was covered in damned souls, their bodies completely disfigured from the cold. All climbed toward the peak, a scene reminding Zac of his [Pillar of Desolation]. Zac followed suit, each jump taking him dozens of meters farther up. Eventually, he passed through a thick cloud of extreme cold, which placed him on the peak.

A swirling gate filled with the warmth of Life waited for him there, and Zac passed through it after taking a final look at the world around him. Entering didn't immediately move him to the next trial. Instead, Zac found himself in a comforting world of gold. Hundreds of Lifegiving streams gently caressed him, and he was filled with a sense of warmth and tranquility.

It was the sensation most trial takers described after emerging. It was impossible to tell whether he was floating inside an ocean or in space. All was Life. Zac didn't get a chance to enjoy the environment for long before a screen appeared in front of him.

### [Gate of Hell passed. 5:38 remaining. Continue?]

Just over eight hours had passed in the first trial, yet only twenty-two minutes passed in real-time. Zac guessed each hour outside meant one day inside the trial, though there were no guarantees the subsequent trials would be the same. Not wanting to waste a second, Zac chose to continue.

If he'd chosen *no,* he would most likely have gotten to spend the rest of the time inside this golden womb. It wasn't bad, but the intensity of the environment simply wasn't at the level where it could allow him to make any significant gains to his Branch of the Kalpataru. Zac felt it more at the level of the threshold between a Dao Seed and a Dao Fragment.

Though that may sound extremely weak, it was worth remembering that most cultivators entered the E-grade with an Early Dao Seed rather than an Early Dao Fragment. By the time these cultivators reached Peak E-grade, if they ever did, this first layer may have been useful to push their Daos further.

The moment Zac made the decision, a powerful tug encircled him and he was dragged into a black vortex. The surroundings shifted, and Zac found himself standing on another road. He'd arrived in some sort of ancient ruins, with most buildings being so run-down that only the foundation remained.

A haze covered the surroundings, making it impossible to see farther than a hundred meters. Like last time, Zac instinctively knew where he needed to go. He started running down the sole path toward the next gate. Another road, another journey toward rebirth.

The hazy mist contained a bit of deathly drain, but Zac was surprised to find it wasn't even at the level of the ice of the previous realm. It didn't take much longer before Zac was met with the real challenge of the trial. A prickling pain flared up his left arm, and a noticeable drain of energy followed.

Looking down at the spot, Zac couldn't see a thing, yet something had latched onto him like a leech. His club would do him no good here, but circulating his Branch of the Kalpataru had an immediate effect. Zac vaguely heard a pained wail, and the drain disappeared. As expected, a hungry ghost of the second realm of reincarnation.

Only a minute passed before Zac felt another tug. This time, Zac used his Branch of the Pale Seal. The result was similar, but it took a bit more Dao to rebuff the invisible ghost. His Branch of the War Axe was just as effective as his Branch of the Kalpataru, but that was probably because it was a stage higher.

The hours passed as Zac ran through the ruins, where an increasing number of ghosts assaulted him. Eventually, he had to circulate his Dao Branch continuously, but it barely cost him any Mental Energy thanks to the [Thousand Lights Avatar]. Zac estimated most people would be fine in this kind of environment if they had a somewhat tempered mind and a Dao Fragment or two. Those with only Dao Seeds would likely find themselves under strain, and reaching the end would be challenging.

There was a second challenge to the trial as well. The second path of the cycle of reincarnation was the Preta, and it was filled with people who'd given in to desires. Occasionally, Zac would get a whiff of something alluring in the distance, like powerful natural treasures. It seemed as though he could get all kinds of benefits if he just took a small detour.

That wasn't enough to move Zac's heart, and he refused to step off the path. He had a strong feeling that while leaving the path was easy, stepping back onto it would be far more difficult. Even if he found the treasures, he would have wasted a bunch of time. And most likely, the treasures weren't even real.

The second layer took almost exactly as much time as the first. It was even a few minutes faster since it was easier to walk on gravel than the ice of the first layer. Zac wasn't exhausted, either. He'd used a good chunk of Mental Energy because he opted to simply rotate his Dao continuously rather than only when bitten. It was a bit wasteful, but he had mountains of Soul Crystals.

Thanks to that, he was fully topped off when passing through the gate. Zac found himself in the golden ocean of Life once more. It'd grown slightly more condensed, but it wasn't enough for his purposes, so he continued on.

The third layer placed him in a sweltering jungle, and he was beset by an almost deafening clamor of millions of different beasts. After the previous realms, Zac didn't expect such a lush environment, but he soon got an answer as a tiger came lumbering over. It seemed like a living creature but emitted a palpable aura of sinister rot. Getting hit by that thing would be noticeably worse compared to the draining ghosts.

With a thunderous roar, it lunged for Zac, its claws veritably oozing killing intent as though it were poison. A deep thud was followed by a pained yowl, and the beast was flung into the bushes by a lazy punch. Zac frowned as he looked at his hand, seeing a dark haze swirl around it. So even hitting these guys left sinister energy on your body.

Like before, Zac was easily overqualified for the level, and a bit of Dao was enough to cleanse his hand. The trusty club made its second appearance, and Zac set out, leaving a path of clobbered beasts in his wake. The tiger was just the first of many, and Zac made a few discoveries along the way.

The more you wounded the beasts, the more of their fell aura you had to deal with. But if you tapped them too lightly, they'd be back for more in no time. They weren't cowed by killing intent and a domineering aura either. They were as aggressive and stupid as beasts came.

Ultimately, it took Zac just over nine hours to reach the end, the few scrapes and bruises he'd accumulated mostly healed already. That was the benefit of having a Life-attuned Constitution at the peak of the second layer.

The breakthrough had only increased the base attributes by a factor of ten, which meant 50 Base Attributes, 100 points in Vitality, and 50 points in Endurance. That was barely noticeable for Zac, whose defensive attributes far eclipsed 10,000. But the recovery factor was a separate impressive boost.

The whirlpools in his cells were more than two-thirds gold by this point, and the flakes helped his body naturally heal almost 30% faster than before. He saw similar results when Healers of the Atwood Army used Life-attuned blessings or healing skills on him. They simply worked better on his constitution.

Zac really looked forward to reaching the Minor Sublimation of the

616 | JF BRINK & THEFIRSTDEFIER

**[Void Vajra Sublimation]**. He suspected it would give an even greater boost to these features since his body would officially become Life-attuned.

Having passed through the realm of animals, and thus the three lower realms of the sixth paths, the golden world had grown noticeably stronger. Yet it wasn't enough. Zac wasn't aiming for just the upper realm. Joanna's plight still echoed in his heart, and the first three layers had been far from enough to alleviate the stuffy feeling in his heart.

Be it the challenge of humans, Asuras, or Devas—they wouldn't be enough. Even the Devas were ultimately chained down by the bhava-cakra. Only by snapping the chains of fate and leaving the cycle would he get rid of this feeling.

He needed to break into Nirvana.

# BREAKING THE WHEEL

Zac continued through the Gate of Life like a bulldozer. As expected, the fourth trial was the realm of man. He was met with innumerable familiar faces. Friends who tried to slow him down, enemies who attempted to impede his path. A million voices clamored for his attention, each wanting to siphon some of his speed and Life.

An illusion and combat trial mixed into one, and Zac crushed anything in his path. His heart had been tempered by the Remnants and later his **[Void Vajra Sublimation]**. Even when he found himself standing in front of Thea and Kenzie by the end, he passed them by without a ripple in his heart.

The fifth layer, the layer of the furious Asuras, was more straightforward. Each step had to be taken over a corpse. The club was no longer enough, and Zac was forced to take out **[Verun's Bite]**. The axe keened with excitement upon finally tasting flesh, and roars of supremacy echoed through the endless battlefield of the fifth layer.

It was also a good opportunity for Zac to shake off some of his rust. The fifth layer was the final challenge of most elites of his faction, where they were forced to go all out to reach the end. For Zac, it wasn't that desperate, though he found himself forced to fight seriously.

The six-armed Asuras fought with both ferocity and skill, using all kinds of techniques aimed at killing or at least maiming. Zac, in turn, opted to counter with his Evolutionary Stance. It was good practice, and Zac came to understand that his combat style, which was partly based on the Dao of Life, was quite effective at dealing with these demonic beings. He became one with his path. Each swing was a birth that ended in the death of an opponent. He was unmatched, creating a path of carnage that echoed with Life and Conflict.

Zac hadn't specifically trained in techniques that much since secluding himself six years ago, but that didn't mean he hadn't improved. Simply filling his body with his soul made it easier to enter that illusory state of oneness that he first encountered when being pushed by Kaldor inside the Orom World. Now, he didn't even need to be in a desperate fight to become one with his path.

It came naturally as his Daos were allowed to circulate through his spiritual body. His study of patterns had also elevated his skill and refined his technique. Everything was connected. The patterns he'd drawn when trying to figure out his Cosmic Core were echoes of his path, just like his Evolutionary Stance.

As his patterns grew more exquisite while removing imperfections, it didn't only mean he was getting closer to a working blueprint. It meant gaining a deeper understanding of himself, of his Dao, and how it all fit together. Vivi's vines were a web of carnage, seemingly everywhere at once while [Verun's Bite] delivered death.

Zac could see it, the shadows of his core manifesting in his attacks. He somewhat sensed it while sparring with Emily and Joanna, but it wasn't as palpable then. Some things could only be figured out on an actual battlefield, and Zac was awash with inspiration as he progressed.

His speed of advancement gradually slowed, but Zac didn't care. There was a risk of him not remembering this when emerging, but he didn't care about that either. He was consumed by the feeling of rebirth through struggle, and his Evolutionary Stance shifted by the second, moving closer to the truth.

Even Vivi seemed to feel a change, and Zac sensed how she started to absorb more and more energy from the World Ring she and Haro resided in. Zac was shocked but delighted at the scene. The matter of Vivi's waning life force was always a matter of regret in the back of his mind. If possible, he really wanted to accomplish what Heda had thought impossible—to allow Vivi to break through.

At least once more would be enough. It would allow Vivi to live for tens of thousands of years longer. Allow her to see Haro, who had essentially become Vivi's daughter after years of nurturing, grow from a small sapling into a great Plant King. To that end, Zac tried all kinds of things, from providing Longevity Treasures to burying energy-dense Beast Cores and Natural Treasures in the ground around her.

But nothing had worked—until now.

For some reason, Vivi was gaining inspiration alongside him, from her vines following the true and perfected paths of Life and Conflict. He was like a guiding hand, leading Vivi toward the Grand Dao. And since she finally showed an appetite after a decade of barely eating, Zac was happy to oblige. The huge energy catchers around the moon provided him with an almost endless source of Divine Crystals, and mountains of them entered his World Ring while he continued with his carnage.

The hours passed as Zac's technique shed its weakness and was reborn stronger. Zac barely registered his surroundings, only vaguely ensuring he didn't step off the path as he advanced. Eventually, Zac realized there were no more enemies to fight. He already stood in front of the gate with an endless trail of corpses strewn in his wake.

Zac didn't immediately pass through, content to absorb what he'd experienced. Only a few hours later did he open his eyes. By that point, Vivi had stopped absorbing energy. Zac could tell she was still unable to evolve into Hegemony, but she felt more vibrant than when he got her from Heda.

As for himself, Zac knew he'd passed a threshold sometime during the journey. He'd entered the Middle Mastery of the Integration Stage, mostly thanks to Ultom's impartment. It perfected the patterns on his blueprints, which in turn elevated his technique. And it wasn't a case of barely breaking through either.

Zac could tell his foundations were still incredibly solid. He only lacked the fundamental understanding of his Daos required to push his techniques. As long as he upgraded his Branch of the Kalpataru and continued gaining experience, he had a decent chance of evolving his technique again before the trial for Ultom began.

That might also be the key to evolving Vivi, which would be a huge victory. Haro was still far from strong enough to be used as a weapon. Meanwhile, Vivi was a top-quality Spiritual Plant. If she evolved into D-grade, she should be able to match up to War Regalias in might.

Since the breakthrough was done with, Zac stepped through the gate for the fifth time.

**[Gate of Asura passed: 3:32 remaining. Continue?]**

The Path of Asura had taken over an hour of real-time, almost as much as the previous four trials combined. Still, Zac felt the reward was worth it. You could never be sure inspiration would strike so clearly again if he suppressed the feeling until he was outside the trial. And there was only a single trial remaining. As long as he could rush through it, he'd have over three hours of inspiration.

Zac entered the next trial, finding himself in a celestial realm of purple clouds, with the occasional mountain peak breaking through the rippling curtain. It was the highest realm of the six paths, the final obstacle of Nirvana. There was a golden road leading through the realm. Zac set out, **[Verun's Bite]** already held at the ready.

It didn't take long for him to encounter his first enemy. A humanoid decked in jewelry floated over, a halo behind its elephantine head radiating a strong aura of providence. In its hands, it held a partisan spear, and it stabbed it against Zac the moment it was close enough.

Zac dodged the somewhat simple strike effortlessly, but he was surprised to find himself nicked at his shoulders. The strike should have missed, yet something went wrong. Stepping aside to reorient himself, Zac almost stepped out off the edge of the road.

A strange drunkenness clouded his mind, even if he had full clarity. This was something far trickier. It was Karma. Not as palpable as the Karmic cultivator Zac fought inside the Tower of Eternity, but it was there. Almost like the humanoid Deva radiated an aura of luck, or misfortune, depending on whose perspective you looked at it from.

Zac had no way to rouse or target his own Luck, but just understanding the situation helped. A vicious strike and the Deva fell into the clouds, never to be seen again. New figures were already floating toward him, their auras seemingly superimposing to create an even stronger effect.

The Devas were the beings closest to attaining Nirvana, each carrying immense Karma. Zac guessed their will impacted the river of fate, bending it to their advantage. Unfortunately for them, Zac was an unmovable rock thanks to his huge amount of Luck. Their providence failed to contain him and keep them safe from his counter-attacks.

This effect seemed to be further augmented by his Branch of the Kalpataru since it siphoned some of the good fortunes of the realm for Zac's use. Zac sped up, a Life-attuned Dao Field covering his surroundings while he launched fractal leaves at any Deva who dared get close.

Zac felt the constant resistance of fate, but it only managed to deviate his blades slightly. Ultimately, it didn't matter if a three-meter fractal leaf was pushed a few hands to the side. The various demi-gods who got close were cut down all the same. For Zac, the sixth realm was actually easier than the fifth, where you could only fight fire with fire. And together with the fact he used his skills this time, Zac veritably flew through the paradisal world of clouds.

Twelve hours was all it took until Zac stood at the final checkpoint of the Gate of Life. Zac wasn't surprised none had reached this point, even if they'd dared attempt it after the gauntlet of Asuras. Fighting against the Devas was almost like fighting against fate. If you didn't have a huge amount of Luck like he did, you'd have to absolutely overpower the Devas to the point their luck couldn't save them.

The number of deities he'd left in his wake was shocking. If this were the real world, he would probably have accumulated enough fell Karma for ten lifetimes for killing so many creatures with such positive Karma. Luckily, this was just a trial ground, and there was no way these creatures were real.

Either case, it was over with, and Zac was ready to collect his reward. He passed through the gate, entering a supercharged swirl of pure Life. By this point, even Zac could feel there were noticeable benefits from staying inside the swirls of Life. It was akin to an impartment, much like the Life-Death Pearls of the Twilight Ocean. Using this kind of energy would allow Zac to quickly work toward the next stage of his Dao Branch.

Zac didn't even get the chance to enter a state of revelation before something changed.

**[Gate of Deva passed: 3:01 remaining. Continue?]**

Continue? Zac blankly stared at the line, wondering what was going on. The System clearly told him the Gates of Rebirth had six layers when he received it as a reward, and they perfectly matched the six realms of rebirth. Yet there was another one? Was it *actually* Nirvana? Or maybe a hidden level? Something awarded because he'd passed the trial with more than half of the time remaining?

The reasons didn't matter. What mattered was whether he should accept or not. Looking around at the vibrant swirls of Life, Zac made his decision.

It wasn't enough. Zac could tell that while he'd make improvements in the current environment, it wasn't enough to crystallize the insights he was lacking to form a Middle-stage Dao Branch of the Kalpataru. The fact that the energy was already useful made Zac hopeful for the next stage, and he chose to continue into the hidden trial.

This time, the environment was different. There was no world stretching to the horizons. He simply stood at the edge of the universe, gazing upon golden gates hundreds of meters tall. To its sides, a wall stretched toward infinity in either direction. Had he really been taken to paradise? Were these the pearly gates leading into Heaven?

There was nowhere to go but through the doorway, and staying wasn't an option either. The universe was draining him, stealing his Vigor faster than any of his Hidden Nodes ever had. After he ran out of that, he'd probably start losing life force. Zac ran toward the huge gates, but he stopped in place with shock just a moment later. The moment he'd started circulating his Branch of the Kalpataru as usual, the drain more than doubled.

Zac urgently changed Dao and was both relieved and confused to find that his Branch of the Pale Seal noticeably stemmed the loss. Meanwhile, the Branch of the War Axe neither helped nor hampered him. Why was it the opposite?

For each of the previous tiers, Life helped resist the challenges of the gates in various ways. But here, it became a liability while Death saved his bacon. Zac only hesitated a moment before swapping over to his Draugr form, and he breathed in relief upon feeling the loss lessening even further. Between his Death-attuned branch and his Death-attuned body, the drain was negligible.

As long as he kept eating to replenish his Vigor, he'd be able to last a good while in this environment before running into trouble. Of course, that was only so long as the drain didn't get too bad deeper into the trial.

Surviving to the end probably meant you'd get sent out with a title of the previous tier but no epiphany, but Zac couldn't be sure. Besides, his goal in this place was less about the Limited Title and more about the insight waiting at the end. There was no point loitering at the entrance after having solved the danger. Zac rushed into the enormous complex, and it almost felt like passing through the gates of Heaven.

The feeling didn't last long. There was no paradise on the other side. Instead, it was a long golden hallway with paths veering both to the left and right. Some pathways started a couple of meters into the air, proving the structure had at least two layers. The scene reminded Zac a bit of the research base Mystic Realm, though there was no ceiling.

A maze?

Just standing at the entrance left Zac a bit light-headed, and not just because of the dozen paths he'd already spotted. Every inch of the golden walls were covered in black scripts, forming a dizzying array of patterns stretching as far as Zac could see. Having worked on a blueprint for years, Zac recognized many of the overarching themes.

These were patterns related to the Dao of Death, there was no doubt about it. However, Zac only recognized snippets, where most patterns were mostly foreign to him. Zac could only tell they had the same 'flavor' as his own Dao, meaning they were probably different aspects of the Dao of Death. Just observing them filled him with some inspiration.

Zac took a few hesitant steps forward while chewing on a strip of dried meat of an undead Beast King, but he soon stopped again. Just how should he deal with this place? If this was a maze, there had to be some sort of clue on how to pass it. He'd seen just how massive this place was from the outside. He could run around for months without finding the exit if he didn't have a plan.

Zac took a calming breath, not letting the unexpected scene impact his heart as he sought solutions. It was a trial, not a trap. First things first. Zac turned into an abyssal wraith, shooting toward the sky a few hundred meters above. However, no matter how many thousands of meters he moved, the edge of the maze grew no closer.

There was an array that prevented cheating. Zac expected as much, but he had to make sure. He landed back on the ground, turning to the walls and paths around him. The key had to be the scripts and the Dao of Death. First, Zac tried to figure out if some paths were false or imperfect, but it didn't look like it.

All sixteen paths he could pick from the initial entrance seemed equally perfect. None had any obvious flaws Zac could discern. Although, his eyes gradually turned to the third path. There were hints of his Branch of the Pale Seal in every path except five, but runes that resonated with his path were denser in the third.

Was that it? Pick the one that fit you the best? Zac had no better option, so he entered the path. It continued for almost a mile, with a few paths veering to the sides. Each held a smaller concentration of his Dao, so he ignored them. Eventually, he found a path that looked a bit better and entered it.

Having to constantly observe and analyze the endless runes around him was taxing, but also illuminating. Most of the patterns weren't directly related to him, but they were related to the Dao he practiced. There were all kinds of connections and relationships he'd never seen before. And while he couldn't utilize any of it right now, he felt they might come in handy in the future.

Zac even suspected this wasn't the originally intended way to pass the trial. The runes emitted a weak energy, and Zac suspected a normal cultivator would be able to resonate with the runes that matched their affinity. Zac was essentially brute-forcing it with his brain filled with patterns thanks to Ultom and his inordinately powerful soul.

Thank the Heavens he hadn't given in to his curiosity back then and entered the Gates of Rebirth early, instead opting to save the opportunity for when he'd accumulated insights after his years of cultivation. Without a proper theoretical foundation, he wouldn't have been able to move nearly as fast as he was.

Zac continued this way, running through the winding maze, constantly feasting on meat to keep his Vigor topped up. The hours passed, and Zac started to realize it wasn't just the inscriptions on the walls that formed complex patterns. The paths themselves formed enormous runes, creating a shockingly vast array.

He was running inside the Tapestry of Death.

# DEATH FROM LIFE

Zac remembered some of his breakthroughs, where he'd seen the endless tapestries of the Grand Dao and tried to grasp some corners that resonated with him. This was essentially the same, with the only difference being he'd been physically placed in the middle of the vast emblem. The realization didn't change much, but it filled Zac with greater confidence that he was on the right path, even if the drain kept increasing.

At first, he could only see a few percent of his path being reflected on the walls. After an hour, more than 10% contained pieces of his Dao. By the time Zac ran five hours, more than half of the patterns reflected his own. This was reminiscent of when he walked through the spiral after returning from absorbing Ultom's light. The only difference was that he was now retracing the steps of Dao comprehension instead.

Except the drain was becoming a problem. He was losing energy fast, and no amount of food was enough to stem the loss. Zac suspected he had at most four hours before running out of Vigor entirely. Yet he continued without looking back. As the drain grew more palpable, so did the aura of Death from the runes.

He felt he had entered a semi-enlightened state where the repeating patterns engraved themselves in his heart.

Eventually, his constitution failed him. He was a hollow husk, with not an ounce of Life left in it. He only wanted to lie down and sleep, to shut out the unbearable hunger that threatened to consume him. Only he

626 | JF BRINK & THEFIRSTDEFIER

couldn't stop. Not now. Not when the walls were 90% filled in with his path. He was so close he could taste it.

Zac continued on pure willpower, forcing his legs to keep moving and the turbid ichor in his veins to keep flowing. His life was slipping out from his body, but a Longevity Treasure allowed him to mostly spend an external source. But the drain grew stronger, and external treasures soon weren't enough to stem the loss.

Days turned to weeks and soon months. Zac didn't care. He was walking in a perfect representation of his Branch of the Pale Seal. Until he suddenly wasn't. The pathway he'd stumbled through ended in a small room no larger than ten meters across. There was a simple well in the middle, and the sloshing of water resounded from within.

A golden radiance spread out from the reservoir, proving it wasn't normal water, drowning out the intense darkness of the runes. Zac walked inside filled with wonder, barely noticing the drain had reached a fever pitch. In the heart of Death, there was Life. Zac's mind was fuzzy, but he understood clearly what he needed to do.

He stumbled over to the well and simply tipped over. Staying any longer in the maze environment would be his end. Besides, there was a powerful calling coming from the depths. The well was surprisingly deep, giving him time to send an exhausted nudge into his Specialty Core, prompting it to transform him back into his human form.

Death receded, both within his body and in his surroundings. A storm of Life jolted Zac's drained mind wide awake a few seconds later, and he felt how torrential amounts of energy were entering his body while the truths of Life were laid bare all around him. No matter if it was the density or depth, it was on a whole other level compared to the sixth checkpoint.

His utterly drained Vigor was rapidly being replenished, the bone-piercing exhaustion replaced with exuberance. The Dao of Life was so clear and intimate, like a long-lost friend caressing you in an embrace. Was it because he'd walked down the corridors of Death for half a day, like how you were blinded by even the weakest of lights after having stayed in darkness for a while?

This was it. This was the one. Death from Life, and Life from Death.

No screen was forthcoming, though Zac wasn't sure he'd notice it even if one appeared. He was fully consumed by the Branch of the

Kalpataru, swept away by his path. It had been years since he felt his Dao so close and palpable. Ultimately, the lake water of the Lost Plane, or even the divine light of Ultom, was bereft of Dao.

Their inspiration could break anything apart and show you the mechanical underpinnings of the Dao and its absence, but it could not elevate Zac's understanding of Life. But now, practical understanding and spiritual comprehension became entwined as Zac gazed at the fundamental nature of Life.

There was nothing that Zac needed to change with his understanding of the Kalpataru. He just needed to stay the path, just like he had through the Tapestry of Death. Life was the motor of change, the breaker of fate. It was progress manifest through the evolutionary dance of his technique.

The truths he'd grasped onto while inside the Orom World grew more condensed and robust, and Zac lost any sense of anything else but the warmth of Life. But suddenly, Zac felt something amiss, and his eyes shot open as he warily looked around. It took him a moment to realize what was happening, and he scoffed before closing his eyes again.

There were no threats, at least not in the corporeal sense. The trouble Zac sensed was a few insights that tried to sneak into his Dao, hinting at the fusion between Life and Death by adding a set of concepts to create a working microcosm. The first steps toward Samsara. As expected from a Trial of a Buddhist nature.

Luckily, Zac had tempered his heart in the Void for years already, and he effortlessly rejected those thoughts while greedily taking what he needed from the storm around him. Due to Zac rejecting a chunk of the truths, the energy entering his body also decreased. That could barely be considered a problem. A white box appeared in his hand, and Zac swallowed the golden peach before stowing the container.

It was a top-tier Life-attuned Dao Treasure that helped Zac make up the loss and speed up his breakthrough. It joined the external streams of truth, flowing into the floating tree in his Soul Aperture. The Kalpataru didn't grow any larger, but the branches grasping for the Heavens did. The golden leaves also became more radiant, while the movements of the dancing vines turned more capricious.

The tree shone like a small sun inside his aperture, annealing the golden Outer Cores with Life of a higher order. And just like that, it was done. Another Dao Branch pushed to Middle Mastery. Zac warily

628 | JF BRINK & THEFIRSTDEFIER

opened his eyes and peered around, both relieved and disappointed that no angry clouds gathered above him.

Ultimately, the Old Heavens didn't care about minor breakthroughs like evolving Dao Branches, and it wouldn't come down at him with Tribulation Lightning until he formed an Earthly Dao. However, from that point, each step would draw a tribulation as long as he stayed on the Boundless Path. That was a worry for later, and Zac opened his Dao Screen to see the results.

[**Branch of the Kalpataru (Middle):** All attributes +50, Dexterity +750, Endurance +1500, Vitality +4750, Intelligence +50, Wisdom +450, Effectiveness of Vitality +25%]

Having accomplished what he set out for, Zac blocked out the golden light. He'd taken what he needed. Any more and he might find his path deviate. This place really was a Buddhist heritage, trying to sneak in some insights to move his Dao toward Samsara. Looking back, it seemed like a deliberate action with the maze of Death leading to a well of Life.

Instead, Zac turned his attention to his upgraded Dao Branch. He hadn't been certain he'd be able to upgrade the Dao with the help of this trial, even if he made huge strides since the Orom World, both in the Void Gate and during his years of study of the Dao of Life. His worry had been warranted. If not for the secret seventh layer, he wouldn't have reached all the way.

A Middle-stage Dao Branch wasn't required for him to form his Cosmic Core—it would only be a prerequisite for upgrading his Cosmic Core to Middle-stage. But even if it weren't a must-have for the Perennial Vastness, it would certainly help. The better the balance between Conflict and Life, the easier it would be to forcibly form and contain the sections of his core.

Besides, the upgrade provided him with over 8,500 attribute points—more than a 10% boost to his attribute pool. If he could do the same with his Branch of the Pale Seal, he'd be far better prepared for any conflict inside the Perennial Vastness. Because one thing was for sure, no matter where you went in the Multiverse, there'd be a struggle for resources and to get ahead.

As for the attributes, there weren't any real surprises. Zac was happy to see Dexterity had gone from +300 to +750, an increase of 150% rather than a simple doubling. That came at the cost of no extra Intelligence and a reduced gain in Wisdom and Endurance. As far as Zac was concerned, it was a worthy trade.

His Wisdom was starting to fall behind a bit, though, so he might have to put some points into it after reaching Hegemony. His soul was incredibly powerful, but it could not be fully utilized without the Wisdom to run it.

Zac closed the screen, looking around. There was no timer, but he could somewhat sense time was almost up. The golden streams had grown dim, having been robbed of a chunk of their truths. Actually, the theft was still happening, and Zac was happy to see a steady stream enter his World Ring. He'd been too swept up in his own breakthrough to notice before.

Being a product of Heda, Vivi was obviously Life-attuned. Haro was not. However, between Zac's nurturing and Haro's closeness to Vivi, Haro started to absorb more and more Life-attuned Energy. Zac hoped he could have it diverge from the norm and become a Life-attuned Heaven-render Vine, just like Ogras accidentally diverged into a Shadow-aspected demon.

The minutes passed as Zac waited for the trial to conclude and to see what kind of title the seventh layer of the Gate of Life awarded. The normal trials provided 1% of your main attribute and either Vitality or Endurance, depending on which trial you chose, per layer. Would the seventh layer push the attributes to 7%, or would the title change as it did with the Havenfort Chasm?

Finally, the trial ended, but Zac felt no pull or any sensation that he was about to be placed inside one of those flowers outside. Instead, another prompt appeared.

**[Trial Ended. Continue into the Gate of Death?]**

Zac didn't give it a second thought as he accepted. This was exactly what he'd hoped for. The chance to enjoy the other half of his trial. Hopefully, there would be a second hidden level waiting for him on the other side, giving him the inspiration needed to evolve his final Dao Branch.

But as Zac accepted, he felt an uncomfortable pull. Like part of him was being held back in this sea of Life. He tried to hold on as best as he could, but it still slipped between his fingers. It was his memories being purged of his experiences in this place. Zac held onto a small hope he'd be able to retain his memories, either through his powerful soul or because he conquered the whole thing.

He was wrong, but that didn't mean Zac was willing to give up without a fight. Ultimately, Zac only managed to hold onto a few key pieces by furiously rotating his Soul Cores. The maze, the timer, and his technique. A familiar gate appeared beneath him, and Zac had a final thought before it was whisked away.

*What happened with the title?*

A moment later, Zac found himself standing on a path of molten ground, filled with a conflicting sense of loss and gain. He looked around, trying to make sense of a confusing hole in his mind. He'd been purged just like the others, though he remembered what he was doing here. He'd fully passed the Gate of Life and evolved his Dao Branch, and it was time to climb the second half.

The hellscape of fiery Life filled Zac with an odd sense of déjà vu. He guessed the previous trial was the same, except there had been Death within the flames rather than Life. The same odd burning sensation came up through his soles, but he soon realized the Branch of the Pale Seal was effective at stemming the invasion.

As expected. Going by his current form, Zac had clearly completed the previous trial as a human, and this one was best dealt with in his Draugr form. Between the hazy memories and instinctual knowledge of what he needed to do, the level was completed in less than six hours thanks to [Abyssal Phase]. He passed through the gate and found himself in a sea of endless black.

If not for the visions of the Abyssal Lake, Zac would have thought this was how a real lake of Death felt like. Now, it seemed like a cheap mimicry of the real thing, almost like the Towers of Myriad Dao in the face of the Tower of Eternity. Of course, this was still just the first level. As the days passed and Zac knocked out one layer after another, the sea became increasingly filled with meaning.

Each level passed also unlocked a bit more of his memory. He was walking in his own footsteps, his experiences mirroring each other. By the time he reached the Fourth Layer, he could almost see himself running in step. Zac sensed it wasn't a case of finding meaning where there was none. This felt intentional, like the trial showed him two sides of the same coin.

Unfortunately for the creator of this place, it wasn't for Zac. This kind of fusion the Gates of Rebirth were trying to nudge him toward was probably an expression of the Dao of Samsara. He had his own path to tread, and his heart was stable enough to ignore the pull. He would take what he needed and discard the rest.

Soon enough, Zac reached the fifth layer, and a smile spread across his face as **[Black Death]** appeared in his hand.

'*It's been a while,*' *a content hum echoed in his mind.* '*Are we going out again?*'

"We're heading to the Perennial Vastness soon," Zac smiled. "Hopefully, we can find a way to upgrade you there. For now, I'm going to evolve my technique. See if you can feel anything from my control."

'*I'll follow your lead,*' Alea answered before her consciousness receded into the depths of the coffin.

It was a shame that short conversations were all Alea could manage, even after being fully healed and stabilized from her series of breakthroughs. It took a lot of effort to condense her consciousness to the point it worked like a person's. Its natural form was more of a passive state spread through the coffin, much like Mossy's normal conscious state.

Alea didn't have the monstrous reserves of Mental Energy that Mossy did, either. So while the moon could speak how much it wanted, Alea could not. Zac hoped that would change by the time she became a D-grade Spirit tool, and her soul evolved along with it. And perhaps, this would be the first step in that regard.

Death and Conflict filled Zac's body, propelling him down the road of carnage. The Asuras teemed with seemingly unquenchable Life, each of their attacks trying to leave part of it in Zac's body behind. Though it was more accurate to call it a virus the way it acted. If Zac had been in his living form, it would have sought out his Life and poisoned it.

The effect was stifled by his Draugr heritage and his Dao, allowing Zac to fully focus on his technique. The echoes of himself were even more poignant as he advanced, his chains and axe weaving an inescapable net of Death. The hours blurred until he found himself standing in front of the swirling gate leading toward the sixth and final realm.

Or wait, was it really the final level? Something felt off.

Half a day later, Zac stood in front of a black gate with a tremendous wall stretching toward infinity. It looked like the entrance to the Underworld, yet a smile spread across Zac's face as he swapped over to his human form. It had finally come back to him, all the memories of his previous trial.

One final journey into the Tapestry of Life to find the answers to Death.

# FULL CYCLE

"Why are we here?" Carl asked, warily looking at Ogras.

"You're the one who said you had to speak with the Lord *immediately*," Ogras said with a roll of his eyes. "That your happiness depended on it. And this is where he went, apparently, leaving the boring stuff to me."

"But this place is trouble," Carl muttered. "I can sense it."

"What trouble," Ogras scoffed. "The Ruthless Heavens shrouds us, and we're stronger than any warriors on this planet."

"But how will that protect us against the boss?" Carl countered.

Ogras studied the cowardly archer for a moment, a smile forming. "I guess you have a point there."

"See, over there," Carl sighed. "I told you. Trouble."

Ogras glanced over, frowning upon seeing hundreds of people gathered in front of the trial.

"What's going on?" Ogras asked after flashing over.

"You are…?" the guard asked with some confusion before spotting Carl next to him. "Ah! Captain Elrod! Thank God you're here."

"At least one of us feels that way," Carl muttered. "What's happening?"

"It's Lord Atwood… He…" the guard hesitated, glancing at the huge half-disk behind him.

Ogras ignored Carl's pointed look, snapping his finger to regain the guard's attention. "The lord *what*?"

"He entered eleven hours ago and still hasn't come out. We even tried cutting open a bunch of flowers in case he was trapped, but we couldn't find him. Ultimately, the vines started releasing dangerous energies, forcing us out of the graveyard."

"He's eleven hours in," Ogras muttered. "Well, let's just wait for another hour. He probably passed the first one and somehow entered the next."

"You know what, my matter is silly," Carl said. "It can wait."

"You sure?" Ogras grinned. "It's hard to know with you. You were so adamant about not joining our mission just an hour ago."

"That's because you told Lissa," Carl said with grit teeth. "Forcing me to choose between hell with the boss or hell in my home."

"That's my mistake," Ogras sighed. "I simply felt I hadn't talked with my former subordinates enough, and it somehow slipped out when she was listening."

"I'm sure," Carl spat.

"Now, don't be like that," Ogras laughed. "Whether you like it or not, you have one of the most powerful fates of any earthlings. Excluding that guy, of course. Are you going to keep resisting it, or will you seize the opportunity? Aren't you a man? Shouldn't you have the power to protect Lissa?"

Carl's face scrunched up like a dried Palo Fruit, but he still sat down when Ogras took out a table and some chairs. The minutes passed until people started to stir, their gazes turned toward the huge disk.

"It's about time," Ogras muttered, a sense of anticipation filling him.

Who knew? There might be some benefits to be had if that guy really caused a scene. The ground started to shake, and Ogras looked on with shock as the whole half-disk started to spin. Was the thing really a coin? The somewhat simple half-moon with the ladders and the two entrances entered the ground as a completely different scene emerged.

Paradise.

An exquisite diptych engraving in black and gold was hidden on the other half of the Gates of Rebirth, depicting with excruciating detail a Buddhist paradise. Arhats were guarding the mountains, and Buddhas spread their boundless love from the peaks. Enlightened beasts, celestial lotus flowers, bodhi trees, and temples.

A huge silhouette of a Buddha appeared in the sky, its two hands clasped in a Dhyani mudra. Inside its palm, a wheel of gold and black turned, and Ogras' soul shuddered. Almost as though he were looking at both his future and his past.

"What in the…" Ogras muttered, but the avatar was gone the next moment.

Suddenly, two doors opened in the middle of the scene, and a familiar figure stepped out. Ogras hadn't even spotted the gate—they perfectly blended into the mural. Zac took a few steps before turning back, looking at the huge coin as it gradually spun back to its original position. Ogras glanced at the ladder, not too surprised to see no name had been added to the tally.

That bastard had obviously enjoyed some sort of special opportunity.

"That's the boss, alright," Carl sighed as he got to his feet.

---

Zac turned away from the Gates of Rebirth and immediately spotted Ogras and Carl walking over. Ogras wasn't too unexpected, considering he'd been stuck in that place for twelve hours. But why was Carl here?

"Hey," Zac said. "Sorry, I got a bit derailed."

"That's fine," Ogras said. "Some scene. At least nothing exploded this time."

"I know, right?" Zac laughed before turning to Carl. "Welcome back to Earth. Good job out there."

"Thank you, lord," Carl said with a small bow, glancing at Ogras, who shrugged and summoned a swirl of shadows around them.

"As you've heard. I have attained the first piece of a Seal of the Radiant Court. I was hoping you'd allow me to join the command group and the excursion in the future. As such, I'd appreciate any clues as to where I can get the missing pieces of my seal."

"Uh, of course," Zac said. "I don't have any solutions right now, but you might want to check the Ensolus Ruins, just in case. The seals are connected to the war. We'll all have to fill out our seals there."

Carl nodded. "I understand. Then I shall start preparing. Have a good day."

With that, he walked toward the teleporter with a straight back, slightly nodding at a few soldiers who came up to greet him.

"I thought I'd have to bribe that guy to join," Zac muttered. "Guess he grew a lot during your outing."

"Something like that," Ogras laughed.

"I'm sorry about the commotion," Zac said to the guards waiting in the distance.

He was about to head back to Earth, but suddenly turned back toward the public.

"Add a new warning to the trial. No one should attempt the Sixth Layer without having 500 Effective Luck. Less than five people in the Atwood Empire have the strength to break through without providence on their side, and they should know who they are."

"We will immediately add it to the missives," the guard assured.

Zac nodded, and he and Ogras walked away.

"You remember the situation inside?" Ogras said curiously.

"I do," Zac said. "For a moment, I thought I'd lose it, but after passing both trials, I got it back."

"So? What's with the Luck?" Ogras asked.

Zac thought about it for a while before simply explaining. He hadn't decided whether to also divulge the details yet to the wider population. Zac wasn't sure if doing so would do more harm than good. Some people would overestimate themselves after reading about the challenges, pushing farther than they should.

At the same time, the first five layers didn't have any special traps or pathbreaking elements. They provided a comprehensive challenge, testing everything from your Dao to intangible things like determination and Dao Heart. Furthermore, all of the trials could be overcome with raw strength if need be.

"Providence, huh? Well, like you say. Should be possible to force it," Ogras muttered before looking at Zac suspiciously. "That's not the whole story, though, is it? Don't tell me you just passed the normal way."

"Well, turned out there's a secret seventh layer." Zac smiled as Ogras groaned with disgust. "But that one has *extremely* specific requirements to survive. They require the Daos of Life and Death, but they're inverted from the rest of the trials."

"Inverted?" Ogras frowned. "So, you'd need a Dao of Death in the Gate of Life?"

"Exactly," Zac nodded.

"Sounds like a death trap. Any Revenant who even had a shadow of a chance of reaching the last layers would obviously pick the Gate of Death because it seems more suitable from all the experiments," Ogras said before looking at Zac with a scrunched-up face.

"What?" Zac said.

"I just felt it's nice to see some things stay the same with all the crazy things going on," Ogras said with a shake of his head. "It sounds like the Ruthless Heaven created that trial just for you, huh?"

"I don't know about that," Zac said. "As you saw, I think the trial was made to train monks. An extremely powerful cultivator might also pass it, provided they have the right Daos."

"What about me?" Ogras asked. "You think I could brute force the hidden layer?"

"Impossible," Zac said without hesitation. "It's a trial requiring Life or Death. Anything else is useless."

"That's just great," Ogras muttered. "Well, I guess the Sixth Layer title is better than nothing."

"Better than nothing?" Zac scoffed. "6% to two attributes for a total of 12% boost is right up there with any of the top titles available in Zecia."

"Then what did you get?" Ogras asked curiously, and his face collapsed upon seeing a smile appear on Zac's face. "No, never mind. Don't tell me."

Zac laughed. "You sure? It's a good one."

"Spare me, great lord," Ogras said with a roll of his eyes.

Zac grinned, but he still opened his Status Screen to marvel at his latest gains.

**Name:** Zachary Atwood
**Level 150**
**Class:** [E-Epic] Edge of Arcadia
**Race:** [D] Human - Void Emperor (Corrupted)
**Alignment:** [Zecia] Atwood Empire – Baron of Conquest

**Titles:** [...] Blooddrenched Baron, Connate Conqueror, The Second Step, Singular Specialist, Apex Attainment

**Limited Titles:** Tower of Eternity Sector All-Star – 14th, The
Final Twilight, Equanimity, Big Axe Gladiator, Gates of Rebirth
**Dao:** Branch of the War Axe – Middle, Branch of the Kalpataru –
Middle, Branch of the Pale Seal – Middle
**Core:** [E] Duplicity

**Strength:** 29,272 [Increase: 149%. Efficiency: 319%]
**Dexterity:** 13,005 [Increase: 106%. Efficiency: 222%]
**Endurance:** 24,578 [Increase: 140%. Efficiency: 319%]
**Vitality:** 22,853 [Increase: 138%. Efficiency: 319%]
**Intelligence:** 3,920 [Increase: 100%. Efficiency: 222%]
**Wisdom:** 8,646 [Increase: 107%. Efficiency: 234%]
**Luck:** 721 [Increase: 124%. Efficiency: 248%]

**Free Points 0**
**Nexus Coins:** [D] 9,491,406

For so long, his attributes had barely moved, except for the small
amount of flat attributes his Body Tempering provided. But the years of
accumulation set the foundation for a massive leap forward. As
expected, a well of Death awaited him in the heart of the maze engraved
with the truths of Life, which led to a chain reaction of benefits.

**[Branch of the Pale Seal (Middle):** All attributes +50, Strength +750,
Endurance +4750, Vitality +1500, Intelligence +50, Wisdom +450.
Effectiveness of Endurance +25%.]

The attributes of his Branch of the Pale Seal perfectly matched those
of Kalpataru, just like when the Dao Branches were at Early Mastery.
Together, the two provided another huge boost to his survivability. Of
course, that wasn't the end of it. It was, after all, a trial.

**[Gates of Rebirth:** Conquer the Gates of Rebirth. **Reward:** All
Attributes +3%, Strength, Vitality, Endurance +7%. Effect of Strength,
Vitality, Endurance +3%.]

Passing both sides of the Gates of Rebirth resulted in a similar situation to his experience in the Havenfort Chasm. But since the difficulty and requirements were far greater in the Gates of Rebirth, the gains were noticeably better. First, the two titles had been fused into one, giving +7% to three attributes instead of two. On top of that, it both added a boost to all attributes and a small push to Attribute Effectiveness.

The title was more than twice as strong as his other 'normal' Limited Titles, such as Heart of Fire and Big Axe Gladiator. Unfortunately, the challenge wasn't enough for the System to provide him with Title Permanence, which forced him to give up his Heart of Fire title.

Having to give up a title to retain the new one made the boost a bit smaller than a real title. However, it still pushed him just past 100,000 attribute points without relying on [Forester's Constitution], which gave him a title he'd lacked before.

[Apex Attainment: Reach 100,000 Attribute Points before reaching D-grade. **Reward:** Effect of Attributes +8%]

It was the third Apex title he'd received, after Apex Hunter and Apex Progenitor. Unfortunately, the title only provided 8% instead of 10% like the others, most likely because he didn't get the equivalent title while still in the F-grade. Zac could probably get a redo token and fix the title in the future, but it wasn't a high-priority matter.

Looking at his attributes, Zac couldn't help but marvel at his progress. Half a day and his attribute pool increased by almost 25% while his effective combat strength had improved even further. If he met Uona today, he was confident he'd be able to defeat her without relying on the Remnants or his bloodline.

The attribute limits of having a D-grade race were between 40,000 and 50,000, depending on your body's potential. When Zac broke through to E-grade, he'd thought it crazy high and unattainable. Clearly, he underestimated the compounding gains of elite E-grade cultivators. Had he followed a simpler path with three Strength-based Dao Branches, he'd probably have hit the limit already.

Zac closed the screen, turning to Ogras. "Talked with Vikram yet?"

"I could kiss that man," Ogras laughed, his scrunched-up face blooming into a radiant smile. "I'm richer than the whole Azh'Rezak Clan."

Everything was either on or ahead of schedule, mostly thanks to the shocking amount of wealth his shipwright business brought in. Between his trade agreements and Calrin gradually selling off the excess resources he gathered before returning to Earth, Zac's private fortune had already ballooned to almost 10 C-grade Nexus Coins.

If you included his remaining resources, treasures, and Cosmic Vessels, his actual net worth was almost triple that number. And he was still making money hand and foot, even if he spent exorbitantly to shore up the foundations of his soldiers. Every week, thousands of D-grade Nexus Coins poured into his coffer thanks to Calrin's agreement with the Allbright Dynasty.

"Speaking of, you're still not heading home?" Zac asked. "Even if you've lost your teleportation access, I can still teleport you to the border towns. Shouldn't be difficult for you to find a porter to send you over."

"No. Not yet, at least," Ogras said after some thought. "Still don't know whether I want to kill or help my cousins."

"Alright." Zac nodded. "But it's fine if you want to bring your grandpa over."

"The only way I'd get the old coot to come here would be if I stuffed him in a burlap sack," Ogras guffawed. "But I still want to see the old man. Hopefully, he didn't get too much flak for the failed Incursion. After all, we were pitted against the crazy Deviant Asura."

"I was no asura back then," Zac snorted. "You guys were just disorganized."

"I had to keep up pretenses, you know," Ogras winked. "So, Million Gates Territory?"

"Not sure what I should do about Jaol," Zac sighed. "He's seen both my identities. I never expected to see him again, even after realizing the trial was happening in the real world. Even if I go with a disguise, he'll eventually find out about me one way or another as long as we bring him back."

"How about this?" Ogras said. "The guy isn't even Peak E-grade yet. There's some sort of issue with his metallic body parts. You can sign a contract with him and keep him contained on Ensolus. In return, you'll figure out how to fix his issue."

"Easier said than done," Zac muttered. "Not like my ancestry gives me any inborn knowledge of Technocrat parts."

"Seemed to have for your sister," Ogras said pointedly but lifted his hands in surrender upon receiving a glare. "Whatever, guess she got the smarts in the family. But you don't need the know-how to help him. You just need wealth."

"How so?"

"The more levels he gains, the worse his components work. According to him, he either needs to upgrade his components or swap back to a fleshy body. The former is definitely impossible now that he's been hauled deep into Zecia, but the latter should work. Either find a Transcender heritage for him or cut out the metal parts and provide some body-restoring treasures and skilled healers."

"That could work," Zac said.

If that was all, Zac only needed to knock the guy out and infuse him with some Creation Energy. It was faster than any Healing Treasure, and he still had enough Longevity Treasures on hand to not waste any more lifespan than the spark needed to start the process. Someone like Jaol shouldn't require too much energy, either.

Someone like him, with a physical class, high attributes, and now an attunement, would require far more to recover his organs. According to the small experiments he'd performed over the past years when forced to exhaust some of his pent-up energy, it would take about three times as much energy today compared to when he was stuck at the bottom of the Twilight Chasm.

"Let's go get the guy."

"Go get him yourself. Since I'm here, I'll snatch a title myself before dealing with the inheritance," Ogras said.

"Enjoy yourself," Zac waved. "Remember, don't enter the seventh even if the trial presents you with the opportunity. It'll get you killed."

"I know, I know," Ogras muttered, and the two split up.

An hour later, Zac stepped into the guarded compound on Crimson Edge, immediately spotting a few familiar faces. He smiled and waved, though he had to admit his mind was elsewhere. Everything was finally dealt with. The blueprint, his Daos, his foundations. His followers knew what they were doing, and the war preparations were all-but-complete. Nothing was holding him back.

The moment he got word from Catheya, he'd activate the token and leave for the Perennial Vastness.

# REUNIONS AND DEPARTURES

A spiritual nudge dragged Zac out of his thoughts, and he looked up to see Vilari walk over.

"It's nice to see you again," Zac said, and he felt an odd yet comforting sensation as a consciousness wrapped itself around him in a spiritual embrace.

"Likewise," Vilari smiled, stopping in front of him. "I've missed home."

"Things have changed a lot since you left," Zac said. "The undead population has quintupled. Pika and her husband are working in the Atwood Academy, overseeing the undead students."

"It's really happening," Vilari hummed, looking up at Zac. "Thank you."

"Of course," Zac said. "You had the right idea from the beginning."

Vilari nodded before looking Zac up and down. "Your current aura is shocking."

"It's just a bit unstable after a couple of breakthroughs," Zac explained. "I had planned on bragging about my Soul Improvements when you returned. But it looks like you've made even greater improvements somehow."

"I've encountered a few opportunities of my own," Vilari said.

"I heard you found your piece early?"

"I was lucky," Vilari said, her smile widening. "It allowed me to finally resolve the matter of my bloodline. My cultivation speed will drastically increase going forward."

Zac whistled. "That's amazing."

Vilari's bloodline was one of the most powerful he'd seen, but the previous owner of her body likely came from the central regions of the Multiverse. Like his own bloodline, it proved incredibly hard to rekindle no matter which method they'd procured over the years. That, in turn, led to Vilari being unable to awaken and utilize her soul-based bloodline.

No wonder her soul felt so powerful. If he could get another Moss Crystal from Mossy, Vilari would be ready to evolve into Hegemony sooner. Zac almost shuddered at the thought of an elite Mentalist with an incredibly refined soul and a Soul-related bloodline in a place like Zecia. She'd be a one-woman army.

"Let's catch up more later," Zac said. "For now, let's deal with the Technocrat."

"Of course, this way."

Zac stepped into a guarded building, and a wry smile spread across his face as he saw the familiar figure toiling over a workbench. It didn't look like a blueprint or a schematic for some machine but rather a genealogical study. Jaol looked up when Zac entered, their eyes locking.

"Long time no see," Zac said, not finding any better words after meeting the person whose fate he'd so utterly derailed.

"Wh—" Jaol froze, his mechanical eyes slowly widening in alarm and rage. "YOU—BASTARD!"

Zac didn't have a chance to say anything else before the navigator flung himself at him, seemingly trying to claw his eyes out. Of course, it was fool's hope, and Vivi bound him before he even got close.

"I heard you've had a bit of a rough go at it the past years," Zac sighed. "I'm sorry about that."

"A bit of a rough go!" Jaol screamed while desperately trying to break free from Vivi's entanglement. "You blew up my place of work, which was also my *home*! You then framed me and pushed some of the blame on me, even though I was a hostage. I've been hounded and hunted for over a decade. The moment I go back, I'll get executed!"

"That framing bit was to get you off the ship," Zac said as he sat down. "If I didn't, you'd be dead now."

"I would have flown right back into the explosion if I knew I'd end up in your hands after all these years of suffering."

"Don't say that. We worked quite well together the last time," Zac said. "Either case, things have reached this point. You have to admit, the odds of us running into each other again are essentially zero. Fate's at play here. So let's talk about your future in Zecia and the Left Imperial Palace."

Zac stepped out of the compound an hour later, a hooded Jaol by his side. A contract had been signed, and he'd gained another follower for his journey into Ultom. Jaol was surprisingly agreeable upon hearing that more than ten people of his faction would go. Then again, it made sense. Jaol wasn't even a Hegemon and had a non-combat profession at that.

Even if he wanted the opportunities inside, he neither had the means to get the other pieces of the seal nor the confidence to enter alone. He was probably planning on using Zac and his people as meat shields while looking for treasure or more bursts of insight. For now, Zac could live with that kind of attitude. He did ultimately owe Jaol one.

Perhaps even more important than getting a second Plainswalker of Ultom, Zac gained a navigator who knew more about the Endless Storm than anyone in Zecia—something that might prove vital for his distant goal of reaching the Six Profundity Empire. The most promising method was finding a gateway, possibly the same as the one Leandra used, that would take him to that section of the Multiverse. Going blindly would be incredibly dangerous and akin to finding a needle in a haystack.

Of course, Zac would wait a bit before informing Jaol they would be setting out on that kind of adventure in the future.

Jaol wasn't surprised by Zac's ability to use Creation when he explained his offer. In contrast, Jaol was quite pleased, though he didn't want to be reformed just yet. Turns out the navigator was working on a Transcender path on his own, researching various eyes and bloodlines to incorporate into his body.

Since Zac couldn't create something he couldn't understand or imagine, Jaol wanted to first gather samples for Zac to analyze. That was fine by Zac, though it meant Jaol would have to wait until he returned from Perennial Vastness to get his new body parts. That was a good safety measure since Jaol was now bound by the System's contract.

Zac wasn't worried about Jaol causing any troubles with the Neural Network either. Because of Kenzie, he'd already invested heavily in

DEFIANCE OF THE FALL ELEVEN | 645

blocking out any Technocrat Signals. It was more than enough to deal with a low-grade navigator from a weak corporation like the *Little Bean*'s owners. More to the point, Jaol had a terrifying bounty on his head because of him.

It was no doubt the result of him flashing Leandra's command token. The exact details of his and Jeeves' birth were a bit blurry, but it seemed like many powerful Technocrat factions had betrayed the Kayar-Elu after the System weakened them. Now, they were looking for Jeeves, hoping to use it to create the Machine God.

Of course, Jaol didn't know all that. He'd just thought some bigshot had sent Zac onboard *Little Bean*, and the Technocrats wanted to find this person. In a sense, it was half-correct, except Leandra had nothing to do with his heist of the Shard of Creation.

After learning it was part of a mission of the Tower of Eternity rather than some conspiracy, Jaol's anger mollified somewhat. The Technocrat's inborn disdain for the System allowed Zac to place all the blame on it, hopefully making their cooperation easier going forward.

Zac shuttled Jaol back to Earth while the rest of the elites of Ogras' mission resumed their roles in the Atwood Empire. There was still a year left before the war officially started, according to the Void Priestess. But there were no guarantees. The main thing that held the Kan'Tanu back was that the Space Gate wasn't stable enough to shuttle through Monarchs.

The moment they could send a real Vanguard, they'd likely start trying to conquer planets to create beachheads. By that point, the System might just go ahead and erect the War Platforms across the two sectors.

With all the elites returned and the situation clearer, Zac spent the next two weeks in a series of meetings to make final decisions. Some meetings were with the core members of his faction, while others were large war councils joined by both the experts he'd hired and visiting consultants of the Allbright Empire.

The consensus was unanimous—the number of resources spent on low-grade warriors was far beyond what any D-grade force in Zecia could stomach. Unfortunately, there were limits to how far Nexus Coins could take a faction. Money didn't breed elites, and killing random beasts on his planets or their moons wasn't enough of a challenge to temper an army.

True warriors could only be forged on the battlefield. Zac prayed his preparations would keep the initial losses at a minimum.

Ogras didn't participate in the meetings, instead opting to enter the heritage of the Umbra, riding on the success of becoming the first official name on the Sixth Layer of the Gates of Rebirth. The demon emerged five days later, some nasty wounds filled with the Dao of Shadows covering his body. However, by his happy look, he'd accomplished what he set out for.

Zac also spent some time every morning teaching Emily. He mainly focused on helping her find a direction and stabilize the fundamentals of her technique. That way, she could continue progressing after he left for the Perennial Vastness.

After a few days, Joanna also joined. Zac was relieved to see that some time to stabilize her heart had borne fruit. The franticness was gone, replaced by a steady calm. Her aura made Zac think of a veteran army—steadfast and precise like a well-oiled machine. It was very different from Zac's chaotic path for the Dao of Conflict, and most likely better suited to lead armies. Hopefully, that temperance would be the key to cinching a seal of her own.

Two more weeks passed like this until the day Zac had waited for arrived. A report from Vikram confirmed a Communication Crystal and a Spatial Ring had been sent over from the Undead Empire, and Zac soon had the delivery on his table. Zac called Ogras over before sinking his consciousness into the crystal.

He'd hoped for a confirmation from Catheya that it was time to go. Instead, he heard the voice of Laz Tem'Zul. And the more he heard, the deeper his brows furrowed. The shadows congealed a few minutes later, and a grinning Ogras appeared in front of him.

"It's finally time?"

Zac only shook his head with exhaustion.

"What is it?" Ogras asked. "What happened?"

"Listen to this," Zac muttered as he activated the Communication Crystal again.

'*Young master Umbri'Zi, we hope this message finds you well. With the date of your ascension coming close, we wanted to send a short message of well-wishes and a few items that may prove useful inside the Perennial Vastness,*' Laz began.

What followed was a long, detailed list of the ways their agreements and preparations had progressed, proving the Undead Empire had gone above and beyond keeping their end of the bargain. It almost sounded like the Draugr Monarch was gearing up to complain about something, but the topic changed to another direction.

'*As you head into the Perennial Vastness, I hope you will remember that there are as many truths as there are viewpoints. Nothing is black or white or necessarily what it seems, and you'll see more if keeping an open mind. The Undead Empire is sincere in their desire for cooperation and welcomes you with the highest honors to the Abyssal Shores in the future.*'

A few more cryptic lines about misunderstandings and friendship followed, along with the customary invitation to meet in person to discuss further.

"Well, that's not great," Ogras grunted.

"What do you think?"

"Something must have gone wrong," the demon said.

"Why would they frame it like I shouldn't believe any rumors that come my way? What should I keep an open mind over?" Zac muttered.

"Still haven't heard from Catheya?" Ogras asked.

"You think it's about her as well, huh?" Zac frowned. "You don't think she's…?"

"Unlikely," Ogras said after some thought. "I feel it's more likely she'll be the source of whatever new information they don't want you to listen to. This *reeks* of internal politics."

"You think they'd put such things aside when it comes to a matter as important as the pillar," Zac muttered.

"It's during these kinds of times, in particular, they *can't* give up on the internal struggle. Something like a Pillar of the System will completely upend the power dynamic of whatever faction ends up with the prize. If the clans don't position themselves properly ahead of time, they might find their achievements and struggle result in their doom."

"So, what should I do?" Zac asked. "This is outside my wheelhouse."

"Depends on what your goal is," Ogras said.

"First of all, I want to ensure Catheya's safety. And unless necessary, I don't want to rock the boat with our agreements," Zac said. "The Undead Empire is the guarantor for the long-term plans of the Atwood

Empire. Without their support, we might not have even managed to sell our Cosmic Vessels."

It wasn't an exaggeration. Calrin had almost been thrown into the brig because of scheming from certain Mercantile Clans. At first, Zac planned to use Alvod Jondir's name to slap away any such conspiracies. The Allbright Empire was an external subsidiary force of the Radiant Temple, so Zac figured they'd know a bit about the situation and back down.

At the same time, Alvod would likely stay in seclusion for centuries, perhaps millennia. He barely managed to break through while simultaneously fighting off multiple factions, including an actual Autarch. It was a miracle he managed to survive, let alone break through. By the time he emerged, the matter would be long forgotten, and it wasn't like a subsidiary force like the Radiant Temple would dare inquire with him even if they remembered.

But it turned out his gambit was unnecessary. The Undead Empire had already made some moves on his behalf. Casses Allbright, the third Prince of the Empire, had been sent into the Million Gates Territory to investigate a huge and sudden presence of undead cultivators. It was there he'd met, or rather had been captured by, the Imperial Monarchs.

Instead of a forceful conversion, it had turned into the first diplomatic meeting between the Zecian forces and the Undead Empire. And Casses had flown right back from that meeting to quickly accept a most generous agreement with the Thayer Consortia.

In fact, Zac could have increased his earnings tenfold if not for the production limit. After getting a chance to prove their wares, the Creator series had become quite popular on their own merit, and each War Fortress wanted at least a hundred. The ship's unique technology was an incredibly useful tool that could turn the tide of war. What were some C-grade Nexus Coins in the face of that?

The factions on the frontier obviously couldn't compare to the real behemoths of the Multiverse Heartlands, but they were still established dynasties with millions of years of history, powerful backing, and trillions of citizens. Even the innumerable F-grade cultivators could help fill the war coffers by killing beasts, getting money from the System, and selling anything worth Nexus Coins at the System-run stores.

"If you want to retain the status quo, send an equally vague letter back," Ogras said. "Something along the lines that you're happy with how things progressed through Catheya's hard efforts. That you're looking forward to seeing her in the Perennial Vastness or something."

Zac agreed, and they spent the next hour crafting an ambiguous message to send back to the Undead Empire. As for the items in the Spatial Ring, they were top-quality core formation treasures. Zac wasn't sure if he'd dare use them after how they tampered with the [Essence of the Abyss], but he could perhaps sell them to a cultivator in the Perennial Vastness.

"What do you want to do?" Ogras asked after things were dealt with. "If you ask me, I think the Draugr lass has already entered. That's why they were forced to send that message rather than just catch her."

"I think so, too," Zac said. "Which means she might already have been inside for weeks, with the time dilation. Are you ready to go?"

"Been ready for a while now," Ogras grinned.

"Give me one hour," Zac said, then he sent out a series of messages through his communication device.

The core of his faction already knew he was leaving to form his core, so a flood of well-wishes entered his Communication Crystal over the next hour. Joanna, Vilari, and Emily visited as well.

"Good luck," Emily said. "Come back sooner, this time, alright?"

"I'll try." Zac smiled, and turned to Joanna and Vilari. "In case the war starts without me…"

"We'll hold the fort," Joanna confirmed. "Don't worry about Earth and its people. You have done more than enough already. It's time for us to prove ourselves worthy of your nurturing."

"Just remember, survival comes first. I don't need some small-scale victories if it means mountains of dead."

Finally, he turned to Ogras, both of them holding their tokens. "You ready?"

The demon's grin widened. "Time for the Deviant Asura to create another scene. May the Heavens have mercy on the Perennial Vastness."

---

**Defiance of the Fall will continue in** BOOK TWELVE!

# THANK YOU FOR READING
# DEFIANCE OF THE FALL 11

We hope you enjoyed it as much as we enjoyed bringing it to you. We just wanted to take a moment to encourage you to review the book. Follow this link: Defiance of the Fall 11 to be directed to the book's Amazon product page to leave your review.

Every review helps further the author's reach and, ultimately, helps them continue writing fantastic books for us all to enjoy.

---

**ALSO IN SERIES:**
**DEFIANCE OF THE FALL**
BOOK ONE
BOOK TWO
BOOK THREE
BOOK FOUR
BOOK FIVE
BOOK SIX
BOOK SEVEN
BOOK EIGHT
BOOK NINE
BOOK TEN
BOOK ELEVEN
BOOK TWELVE

*Check out the series here! (tap or scan)*

Want to discuss our books with other readers and even the authors? Join our Discord server today and be a part of the Aethon community.

Facebook | Instagram | Twitter | Website

You can also join our non-spam mailing list by visiting www. subscribepage.com/AethonReadersGroup and never miss out on future releases. You'll also receive three full books completely Free as our thanks to you.

**Looking for more great LitRPG?**

*Ashlock wakes in the courtyard of a demonic sect... as a tree. A tree that eats people. An odd start to a new life. Almost as strange as the humans flying through the skies on flaming swords and challenging the heavens. After all, this is a world where one could chase the goal of immortality through the art of cultivation. But Ashlock is merely a sapling in a desolate courtyard, left alone with his thoughts and unable to speak to those passing him by. Unless he does something about it... Every day that passes he grows continuously stronger as he cultivates and uses a suspicious daily sign-in system that grants him powerful skills, mutations, summons, and items, all in exchange for credits earned from devouring flesh and watching the seasons pass. But his peaceful life and man-eating ways can only go unnoticed for so long and those around will soon grow suspicious. If that isn't bad enough, his Qi-rich bark makes him a target for many young masters, and tensions in the demonic sect are at an all-time high, with the cataclysmic Beast Tide festering on the horizon. Ashlock's only chance of survival is to grow faster and stronger than any tree has ever done in the history of the nine realms—all while trying to avoid being turned into firewood. **Don't miss the start to this unique reincarntion isekai LitRPG set in a Cultivator world. With millions of views and tens of thousands of followers, this was one of the most popular web serials of 2023. Now, experience the definitive version of the hit story on Kindle, Print, & Audible!***

## Get Reborn as a Demonic Tree Now!

Made in the USA
Las Vegas, NV
14 September 2024

95252816R00385